24 PAGES. SPLENDIDLY ILLUSTRATED. ONE PENNY.

CAPTAIN MACHEATH

THE PRINCE OF THE HIGHWAY

Nos. 1 & 2.   London: CHAS. FOX, 4, Shoe Lane, Fleet St., E.C

CAPTAIN MACHEATH,

The Prince of the Highway.

CHAPTER I.

THE UNBIDDEN GUEST.

"WINE—more wine!" cried a splendily-attired gallant. "Here's a health to the bright-eyed bride!"

A wedding-feast was proceeding, and a joyous company was assembled.

A burst of melody from the bells of Old Hampton Church filled the air with gleeful and musical sounds.

Behind the speaker, and he was one of about twenty persons of both sexes, who stood upon a raised terrace, was a grand old mansion.

The turrets, pinnacles, deep embayed windows, and general aspect of one portion of the building, bespoke the Gothic style.

The apartment immediately behind the speaker, the windows of which all opened wide on to the terrace we have mentioned, was one of a size and appointments rarely to be met with.

A feast—a marriage feast—was spread in this hall, for a hall it was, rich in all the emblazonry of Gothic taste,

The mirrors were nearly hidden by the rich floral gifts of a glorious autumn.

Richly embossed covers yet kept the curious eye from the secrets of the rare and dainty dishes that were beneath them.

Wine! nothing as yet but wine had begun to flow freely at that festive board upon the occasion of the marriage of the owner of all the taste and of all the wealth that met the eye on every hand.

But if at the back of that terrace, with its slim marble balustrades, and its statues, and its vases, and its flowers, there was much of art to attract attention and to fill the imagination with agreeable associations, in what language shall we paint the glorious space of hill and vale that nature had spread out in front of it?

By successions of marble steps you might descend from the terrace to the gardens, and from the gardens you might wander into the meadows —from the meadows to the pleasant hills, and to the little village of Hampton.

"Truly," cried another of the throng upon the balcony, which consisted for the most part of young men—"truly, the old bells make a merry din. Upon my faith, I did not think there was so much life in them."

"A toast—a toast!" cried another.

"Yes, a toast," cried the whole party. "And let it be a bumper, whatever it is."

"Aye! a bumper—a bumper. Now, friends all; let us drink to many a jovial meeting beneath this roof, even though Sir Charles Engall be going to give it a young mistress."

"A young mistress is better than an old one," cried another of the somewhat disorderly assemblage. "She will make a good wife, I'll be bound, and so that we keep the flavour of our cigars from the drawing-room there will be no fault found."

"Ha! ha! ha!"

"The toast—the toast! Let us have the toast! Every glass is charged."

"Then, 'Here's health, long life, and every blessing to Lady Lily Engall.'"

"Hold!" cried a voice.

There was something in the tone of the voice that uttered the one simple but significant word that suspended every man's uplifted glass, and all eyes were directed to one of the open windows, in the centre of which stood a tall figure, in the dim and dusky twilight.

During the stillness that prevailed for some seconds the church bells rang clearly and distinctly; then there came a sudden jarring sound, and the gay strains abruptly ceased.

"Lights—lights!" cried one.

The sound of that one voice seemed to have a magic in its tones, for it at once awakened to animation every person, and the cry for lights came from every throat.

The stranger who had cried "Hold!" still preserved the same attitude in the window, where he looked like some dim portrait set in a frame.

"Lights—lights!"

The cry was raised again, and in the course of a few moments a pair of folding doors opened at the farther extremity of the room, and several servants appeared, bearing silver candelabra, in which there were wax lights.

"The bells have stopped," said a voice.

"Aye!" cried another, "one of them has broken down, and spoiled the whole set. I thought the old belfry would not stand such a peal."

"It's ominous!" said a third. "Indeed, it bodes not well for the bride and bridegroom. It is a bad omen."

"Very!" said the stranger at the window, who, now that the lights, having recovered from the flaring occasioned by their passage to the room, began to cast a steady glare around them, advanced into the centre of the apartment.

All eyes were naturally bent upon him.

The stranger could well bear that scrutiny.

Tall, and slim of figure, with remarkably small feet, and hands, and he stood in an attitude that a sculptor might have sighed in vain to animate his marble with—so fine, so airy, and so graceful was it.

His eyes were of the dark and sparkling hazel which is so rarely to be met with, and his long silken lashes might have been a proud appendage for a court beauty.

His coal black hair, instead of being, according to the barbarous fashion of the time, confined in a peruke, flowed down his back and shoulders in massive folds rather than curls.

His dress was a rich one, and might well have graced a wedding guest. At his side hung a sword, with a jewelled hilt but the sparkle of its gems was nothing to be compared to the brilliancy of the rings that adorned his fingers, and the diamond that held together the folds of a long laced cravat.

The age of this apparition of manly grace, for such to the bewildered guests he almost seemed to be, did not appear to be above twenty-two.

"Gentlemen," he said, slightly bowing, "accept my apologies for being rather late at these festivities."

No one could help returning the salute.

"The fact is," said the stranger, in the most fascinating manner possible, "a little affair on the road detained me."

He took from his pocket a richly-chased gold repeater, and made it strike the hour.

"Seven! Really, gentlemen, you will hardly forgive me for being a whole hour behind my time. But business must be attended to."

The idea of the elegant and sumptuously-dressed personage before them having anything to do with business, was too out-of-the-way, and caused some of the party to smile.

One only had the boldness to say—

"Sir, I regret I have not the pleasure of knowing you."

"And so do I, sir, from my soul," said the stranger.

This was a sort of answer, coming from such a personage, too, that it was by no means an easy matter to make a rejoinder to.

The young man who had spoken only bit his lip and was silent.

"A fragrant and delightful evening," said the stranger, taking from his pocket a snuff-box set with brilliants and slightly smelling it.

"That may be sir," said he whose toast and sentiment had been so singularly interrupted. "That may be, sir; but perhaps you will allow me for my own private satisfaction, to ask you who you are?"

"Certainly, sir—certainly," replied the stranger with a merry twinkle in his eye. "Of course. Why not, indeed?"

"Well, sir?"

"Extremely well, I thank you. I never felt better in all my life."

The stranger, with an easy grace, reclined upon one of the gorgeous couches with which the apartment was amply provided.

A general titter ran through the room at the expense of the discomfited toast-proposer, who had evidently met with one by far his superior in badinage and in the science of repartee.

"Sir," he said, "this shall not suffice; I am as fond of a joke as any man; but you interrupted my toast, and for that I insist upon a reason."

"Insist!" exclaimed the handsome stranger. "My dear sir, you shall have one without the necessity of insisting at all upon it. What was your toast now?"

"The health of Lady Lily Engall."

"Indeed! There is no Lady Engall. Allow me to put a question or two to you, sir in a courtesy?"

"Say on, sir."

"Well, is it not true that Sir Charles Engall is a Catholic?"

"Quite true, sir."

"Then, sir, is not Lily Lambert, whom he is about to do the high honour of calling his wife, a Protestant?"

"It is so."

"Very well. If my information respecting these espousals be correct, the parties, in order to satisfy the scruples upon both sides, are to be married according to the forms of both churches. At the little church yonder, by the Protestant minister, and at the Catholic chapel attached to this house by the Catholic priest."

"You are right, sir."

"'Tis well. I hope, then, before we talk of Lady Lily Engall, we can afford to wait till both the ceremonies are performed which appear to be thought necessary to make her such."

"Oh! a mere quibble."

"Indeed, sir!" remarked the stranger, tapping the jewelled hilt of his sword. "There's many a slip between the cup and the lip."

"Well, sir, we will not quarrel about such a trifle. Let the toast be deferred until the ceremony is over. Then will you pledge it?"

"With all my heart, sir."

"Agreed."

"And as you wished to know how I came here," said the mysterious and somewhat unwelcome guest, "I can only inform you that I am here upon the urgent request of him who has most right to be present at the nuptials of Lily Lambert."

"That is sufficient, sir. Of course, you mean the bridegroom?"

"Of course I do, sir."

A loud hurrah now proclaimed the arrival of the wedding-party within the gates of the Oaks, as the little estate was called, which could boast of a mansion of such beauty and character.

"They come!" cried every voice. "They come!"

At this moment an individual made his appearance up the steps from the garden to the terrace, and thence into the room.

This was none other than the parish beadle of Hampton, who, in full official costume, had run on before, and the moment he reached one of the windows, he cried—

"Gentlemen and ladies—leastways, ladies and gentlemen—Sir Charles has giv'd me a guinea to run and denounce to you all—Oh—oh—only wait till I catches my breath, and I'll denounce it."

"What's the matter—what's the matter?" cried everybody.

"Ladies and gentlemen, Sir Charles Engall has giv'd me a guinea."

"You said that before, stupid," said one.

The beadle's cheeks inflated, and he looked from one to the other in surprise and wrath, as he cried—

"Stupid—stupid! Me stupid! Oh—oh! and after what's here."

He tapped his head significantly to intimate that the quantity of brains therein contained ought at once to refute the allegation.

"Stupid! Well, after that, gentlemen, I can only say, I wonder all the candles don't burn blue."

"Never mind," said another, "you tell us what you came to announce."

"Denounce, if you please, sir. Mind your purnunciwation. What I come to say is, that the Rev. Peter Pickles didn't come to the church, and that the wedding ain't a wedding."

"Not a wedding? Why, we heard the bells!"

"Very true," gasped the beadle, faintly endeavouring to catch his breath, "but the ringers ringed 'em without being told—then one on 'em breaks down; but as to the wedding not being a wedding, that ain't neither here nor there, for the ceremony in the Catholic sort of way is to be done first, and then, when the Rev. Peter Pickles does come, they will go back to the church and finish off, you see, gentlemen; but what Sir Charles wanted me for to say to you all was, not to make no remarks to the wirgin bride about it."

"Oh! certainly not—certainly not."

This communication, with its caution, was not made a moment too soon, if it were intended to be effective, for the bridal party was seen approaching the terrace at the moment that the beadle ceased to speak.

The first couple that put in an appearance in the room, and came within the full blaze of its numerous wax-lights, consisted of a superannuated old beau, whose attire was a ludicrous burlesque upon the fashion of the day, and a female of the most awful dimensions.

The lady was one blaze of satins and jewels, and the turban upon her head was a most triumphant structure indeed.

This was no other than Mrs. Lambert, fair Lily's mother.

The elderly beau, upon whose arm she leant, was a Major Crumby.

Mrs. Lambert was speaking loudly and rapidly, partly addressing her discourse to those who followed her, and who consisted of some ladies and gentlemen of no particular mark or likelihood, and partly to the occupants of the large room, towards which the whole of the party seemed to be making its way as quickly as possible.

"It's not the least consequence!" cried Mrs. Lambert. "There's no harm done."

All this was intended to polish over the flaw in the proceedings contingent upon the non-arrival of the Protestant divine at the little church, and everybody understood it as such.

Almost immediately, now, all eyes were fixed upon the bride and bridegroom as they entered the room together.

A more remarkable contrast than they presented could not have been found.

Sir Charles Engall was a man about fifty years of age, but a long life of dissipation had left its traces upon his form and face.

He was attired in a splendid suit of blue velvet, and upon his shrivelled fingers he wore jewels that would have bought a principality.

And now let us glance upon the fair young creature by his side, whose arm hung, rather than clasped his.

This was Lily Lambert.

Her age was seventeen only, and yet, by the intrigues of one who should have been her best friend under Heaven she was brought to the sacrifice—to be the victim of such a man as Sir Charles.

The beauty of Lily was of that character which can scarcely be described; it was rather the beauty of expression than of features, and yet a more fascinating creature was never fashioned.

Her hair was a glossy auburn, her eyes blue, her complexion purity itself.

She shuddered as she entered the room, in which now about forty people were collected.

"All is well," said Mrs. Lambert. "The first marriage can take place here, and by then, no doubt, the Rev. Peter Pickles will have arrived. How are you, my darling?"

"Sir Charles," said a servant, "the priest, Father Claire, has not come yet."

Sir Charles Engall dropped the fair hand that he had been holding in his own, and drew himself bolt upright, and cried—

"What is the meaning of all this? Can we get no clergyman, Catholic or Protestant, to do his duty?"

There was a slight inclination to laugh upon the part of the younger portion of the company.

The released Lily sunk upon a chair, the deep arms and high back of which shielded her from most of the company, and wept alone.

"One would think," added Sir Charles, speaking with bitterness—"one would think, if one was not aware that that Captain Macheath had been shot through the head by a gentleman last night, that he had stopped both the reverend gentlemen."

Captain Macheath shot!" cried a voice, "Is that indeed possible?"

"Yes," added Sir Charles Engall. "He has kept the neighbourhood in terror for some time, but I have been credibly informed to-day that last night he was shot by one whom he tried to stop."

"Did he die easy, sir?" said the stranger, who had before excited the curiosity of Sir Charles' guests.

"Sir?" said Sir Charles, grandly.

"I repeat, did he die easy?" said the stranger, crossing one foot over the other, and posing himself in an attitude of ease."

"Sir," replied Sir Charles Engall, loftily, "I neither know nor I neither care whether highwaymen die easy or uneasy. I only know that I have been uncommonly uneasy since he robbed me of my gold repeater and my snuff-box set with brilliants, only last week, in my own park. Yes, in my own park, sir!"

"Uncommonly impudent that," said the stranger, laughing lightly.

"Yes, sir," said Sir Charles: "but I see nothing to laugh about. I can truly say that I have not been so vexed since by anything as by the non-appearance of the two clergymen, whose good offices were required to unite me to the lovliest and most amiable of her sex."

The old rake cast an amorous glance at Lily, and then he muttered to himself—

"I suppose this puppy has been invited by Mrs. Lambert, my troublesome mother-in-law that is to be."

Mrs. Lambert looked at the stranger through her eye-glass, and muttered—

I wonder at Sir Charles asking so young and good-looking a man here to-day."

Mrs. Lambert then took Sir Charles Engall aside, and, laying her hand upon his arm she said—

"My dear Sir Charles, be assured that all will be well, and that the less you show any sign of disappointment the better. Only recollect the trouble I have had in breaking down the spirit of that girl."

She pointed to her daughter, shrugged her shoulders, and sighed.

"Never mind, madam," said Sir Charles: "you shall have the money I arranged to pay you."

Mrs. Lambert bit her lip, and then said—

"Well—well, make as much bustle as you can, and get the dinner over. The wedding ceremony can be performed after that, as you are to be married by special licence, and both the parsons will, I daresay, be in the way."

During this brief dialogue, the mysterious stranger sauntered up to the chair in which Lily sat, and, as he passed it, he dropped a small ring in her lap.

The moment her eyes fell upon it she uttered a piercing shriek; and then she cried—

"Not dead—not dead!"

There was a general scene of confusion in the banqueting-room, and in an instant Mrs. Lambert made her way to Lily, and with angry gestures, cried—

"What is this—what is the meaning of this childishness?"

"Not dead—not dead!" was all that Lily replied, as she clutched the ring tightly. "Not dead—not dead!"

"What does she mean?" said Sir Charles Engall.

"Seize the man!" said one of the guests. "Seize that man! I saw him make some communication to the bride."

"Did you, sir?" said the stranger, retreating a step, and shaking his long hair from his brow.

"Aye! did I. Do you know him, Sir Charles Engall?"

"Not I."

"Nor you, Mrs. Lambert?"

"Gracious Heaven, no!"

"Then he is an intruder here. Perhaps a—"

"Beware!" said the stranger, as he stepped nearer to the window at which he had entered. "Beware, sir, how you finish a sentence with a word you may find it hard to swallow again. I know I am an unbidden guest. I never avowed myself aught else."

"Speak to me!" cried Lily rising. "Speak to me, be you whom you may, and tell me he is not dead!"

"He lives."

"Oh! joy—joy!" ejaculated the lovely girl. "Then I say to all here that I am sold to this man, whom I abhor, and to whom, although presented by my mother, and assured of the death of one I truly loved, I believe I never should have found strength in the presence of Heaven to pledge my troth to."

"This is madness!" cried Sir Charles Engall, in a towering rage.

"It is villainy!" said the mother; and then, pointing to the stranger, she added, "Look, girl, if you have eyes. Yon man is a head taller than the drowned sailor you fancied loved you."

"Yes—yes," added Lily, hysterically, as though answering her own thoughts rather than anything another said to her. "Yes, I am strong now. They told me he was dead—that the ring and he to whom I gave it as a token of my love had gone together to the depths of the ocean; but it is not so."

"It is not so!" cried the stranger with a voice that sounded through the apartment like the sound of a trumpet. "As Heaven is my witness, it is not so!"

"My heart told me it was not," Lily said; "but my mother wrung from me a slow consent to give my life—for my life it would have been—that she might pass her remaing years in luxury. It was a cheat! He lives—he lives!"

"Yes," said the stranger; "he lives, and loves as he ever loved. I know him, and a better, truer heart never yet beat in human bosom than in that of Jack Jeffery."

"Yes," shrieked Lily, sobbing with joy; "that is his name!" And then, as if to deprecate any scorn at the mention of it in such a place, she drew herself up proudly, and added—"I love him!"

By this time several of Sir Charles Engall's dissolute guests, finding that the stranger was the cause of the breaking up of the feast to which they had looked forward with so much satisfaction, drew their swords, and made a rush in a body towards him, to make him prisoner.

The handsome stranger, however, was not to be as easily thrown off his guard.

The bright blade he wore by his side performed a circle round him like a flash of light, and two of his foes shrank back with wounds that brought cries of pain to their lips.

"Down with him—down with him!" cried those who were in the background.

Ladies fainted.

Mrs. Lambert screamed and clung to Sir Charles, as though her security were compromised in the grasp by which she held him.

Some of the rich ornaments of the room were upset and broken; and by the din of voices it would seem as if every one had something to say.

It was in the midst of this tumult that Lily rushed between the swords of the combatants, and clung to the stranger's left arm.

"Take me to him!" she exclaimed. "You tell me that he lives, and I will trust to you. Take me to him. Let us go—oh! let us go at once. What arm will dare to stay us? He lives, you say, my love?"

"I swear it, lady, by the stars above us!"

"Now for it!" cried one of the stranger's opponents.

And, as he spoke, he made a rush forward.

At the same instant Lily cried—

"They attack you from the terrace. Turn and save yourself?"

The stranger plunged his hand into his breast, and drew forth a pistol and handed it to Lily.

"Dare you frighten them with this?" he demanded.

"Oh! yes—yes!"

Still upon her knees and grasping the arm of her defender, she presented the weapon to two lackeys, who had been ordered to go round and seize the stranger from behind.

They shrank back aghast.

The swordsman who had sought to profit by the opportunity of the attack from the rear had dashed forward, and the blades of the weapons borne by him and the stranger clashed together.

"Beware!" said the latter. "Tamper with me another moment and your death be on your own head!"

"Yield, robber! For I take you to be no better!"

At this moment he made a furious thrust at the breast of the stranger, who easily parried it; but by doing so, the sword's point touched Lily on the arm, inflicting a slight wound.

She uttered a cry, and, before the echo of it could die away, there leaped through the open window a young man in a slight undress naval uniform.

He had a cutlass in his hand, and with one blow he sent the aggressor senseless and bleeding to the floor.

"Well done, Jack!" said the stranger. "Are the horses quite ready?"

"Quite."

"Jack—my dear Jack!" screamed Lily.

And in another moment she was in his arms.

"Flee!" said the stranger. "I will follow."

"No—no," said Lily. "Come with us—they will kill you! Come with us, now."

"Fear nothing," he replied, in a voice that sounded like a strain of music; "fear not, all will be well. I will follow directly. Flee, Jack, flee! for well I know there are those here who would take your life."

The young sailor caught Lily in his arms, and as though her weight were nothing, he dashed down the steps of the terrace into the garden.

In his right hand he still waved his cutlass, crying—

"Let any one who may be weary of his life stop he and mine!"

"Who are you? Fiend! monster! speak! Give me a name that I may append my maledictions to!" cried Sir Charles, still writhing in the grasp of Mrs. Lambert. "I will have you prosecuted—transported—hanged! I will spend thousands upon you, but I will have my revenge upon you! Speak! Who are you? Will none seize him?"

No one seemed exactly disposed to risk a personal encounter with a man who possessed such prowess.

A pistol was fired at him.

All looked to see the effect; but there he stood as before, one foot on the terrace, and one upon the window-sill.

"A bad shot!" he said. "I shall not forget who fired it. And now, Sir Charles Engall, you want to know who I am?"

"I do—I do, villain!"

"Hold, Sir Charles!" the stranger said, smiling. "I am no friend of yours, so do not call me villain. First let me explain to you the unavoidable absence of your two clergymen. You know the little wood called Bluebell Hollow, close at hand? In that wood are two gigantic elms. The Protestant clergyman is tied to one and the Catholic to the other."

"Irreverent man!"

"Ha—ha! 'tis well for the hoary reprobate, who would sacrifice youth, and innocence, and beauty, such as Lily Lambert's, to talk of irreverence. Sir Charles Engall, I wish you and all your goodly company Good-night!"

"Who are you?" cried a dozen voices.

"Who am I? Who should I be but Captain Macheath, the Prince of the Highway? Ha! ha! ha! A prize for him who can catch me. Ladies, I am your humble servant. I admire and salute all, and would marry you all if there was not an absurd law against bigamy. Adieu!—off and away!"

A rush was made in the direction of the terrace, but the only effect it had was to upset the table on which all the lights were placed, and the consequence was that in the darkness most of the guests sprawled amid the fragments of the marriage feast.

In the confusion nothing could be easier than the escape of the renowned Captain Macheath.

The two lackeys appeared again, and this time on the top of the terrace.

One carried an enormous blunderbuss, which he discharged in the air, and the other flourished a poker about most majestically.

"Back, you varlets, back!" Macheath cried. "Back, or I will make dead meat of you!"

The lackeys took the hint, and retired.

Hastily descending the terrace steps he looked anxiously about him by the light of the harvest moon for his young friends, but he could not see them, and he was constrained to call upon them aloud—

"Jack—Jack!"

"It is our friend," he heard a voice say, and he knew the voice to belong to the fair Lily.

"Yes," said Jack Jeffery. "This way—this way!"

Both Jack and Lily emerged from the shelter of a little copse of laurels, leading three horses, and they testified the greatest pleasure at the sight of Captain Macheath.

"Oh! how shall I thank you?" said Lily.

"By mounting and fleeing from this spot at once. Remember, at your age, that your mother has legal power over you, which she will not fail to exert, if once she can find an opportunity. A panic just now possesses those who would pursue you, but that will soon pass away."

"It will," said Jack Jeffery; "and the pirates are too many for us. Come, my Lily, let us be off."

They all three mounted, and Captain Macheath, casting only one glance behind him, took the lead, and, at a canter, went through the gardens.

So sudden—so full of daring and dash had been the whole of the proceeding, that the guests in the large hall were too thunderstricken to take the advantage one would have supposed they might and ought to have taken of their numbers; and when they did recover their senses of what avail was a pursuit of three persons mounted upon three of the fleetest steeds England could produce?

We may leave Sir Charles Engall to settle his own affairs with Mrs. Lambert, and to make such excuses as he may think.

Rage, mortification, revenge, disappointment—all were struggling in his heart for mastery, and finally, unable to control his feelings, he fell into a partial swoon upon the gorgeous carpet of that banqueting-room, which exhibited now such a scene of confusion.

This was probably the only circumstance that could very well have freed him from the importunities of Mrs. Lambert, who stuck to him with a pertinacity that could only belong to the delicate nerves of a fat old lady who would sell her child for a thousand a-year.

Some of the domestics had hastily taken horses from the stables, and with a great show of zeal, if not with much inclination in reality for the job, they professed their readiness to pursue the fugitives.

It was not until Mrs. Lambert said—

"I will give fifty pounds to whoever brings back my daughter!" that any of them really started upon the errand.

That was a stimulant to exertion that for a time led them on in the hazardous and uncertain chase.

CHAPTER II.

CAPTAIN MACHEATH AND THE FUGITIVES.

WE return to the fugitives.

The whole scene that had taken place was, to Lily's apprehension, so like a dream that she had ridden some miles before she could really venture to tell herself that it must be real.

The road skirted some meadows—or rather, we ought to say, that this was the road which the bold and adventurous Captain Macheath chose to make for the occasion, for road it was not in reality.

The fact was that he had carefully considered the spot and all its capabilities for advance and retreat before he had conceived the enterprise, and he had taken care that no great impediment should be in the way.

A large, ornamental gate at the end of the garden opened upon a little paddock.

Captain Macheath led the way, every now and then looking back to see that all was well, and speaking a few words of encouragement to his companions in the rear.

There was another gate, but that was open.

Captain Macheath had propped it into that condition with a large stone some hours previously, and after they had passed through, and were fairly in the open meadows, Macheath paused for a moment.

"Let us listen," he said. "If there be no pursuit now we need not harass Lily by a more hasty ride than is necessary. Do you hear anything, Jack?"

The young sailor listened, but no sound came upon his ears.

"No," he said, "all is still."

"I think so, likewise. Of course, pursuit there will be, but they have not yet sufficiently recovered from their panic to set about it, and now tell me which way you wish to go."

"To London, where Lily and I can be united in those bonds that no one can tear asunder."

"Then to London be it," said Captain Macheath.

"You consent, my own darling?" whispered the young sailor to the still half-insensible girl.

All she understood was that he who was her heart's treasure asked her something, and she replied to him at once—

"Save me, Jack—save me! Anything, so that I am with you. I will meet any danger, only save me from the horrors of calling that man by the name of husband."

"Enough!" said Jack Jeffrey. "Let us push on."

"This way," cried Captain Macheath—"this way."

The Prince of the Highway, who so well became and justified his name, led them along two meadows, keeping close to the hedge, but upon emerging into a third, he rode completely across it, and, pointing a little before him, he said—

"That is the high-road to London."

In another moment, the horses having cleared a trifling obstruction in the shape of a newly-planted privet hedge, they stood in the high-road.

It was planted upon each side by tall elms, through which the beams of the moon came straggling with great beauty.

"There, my friend—my true friend," said the young sailor. "I need not trespass longer on your kindness."

"Nay, I will see you safer than you are now," Captain Macheath replied. "You know not the power in these little country places of such men as Sir Charles Engall. Partly because they dread his vengeance, and partly from the fact that they expect his charity, most of the country people are willing and ready to commit any sort of iniquity that he or his agents may choose to dictate to them. Believe me, that the old principle of serfdom exists to a large extent yet in the rural districts of free England.'

By this time Lily had sufficiently recovered to be able to view her situation in a more calm and rational light, and when the first joy of having

escaped the obnoxious nuptials to which her tardy consent had been given was over, she burst into a flood of tears.

"My Lily," said Jack Jeffery, "do not weep now that you have escaped."

"No—no!"

"Well, then, dear one—"

"Pardon me," said Captain Macheath, as he laid his hand upon the arm of the young sailor—"pardon me, if I ask you to let those tears flow awhile without check or question. Lily will recover from this natural burst of feeling quickly and be more herself."

"Thank you," said Jack. "You seem to understand the ways of women-folk."

"I ought to do so " said Captain Macheath, with a smile.

In a few moments Lily's tears ceased and she turned to Jack.

"Indeed—indeed! Jack," she said, "I thought that you were dead. The tale of the loss of your ship was proved, and all seemed so exact and circumstantial."

"Pshaw! Lily. Never say another word about that. They made you believe I was at the bottom of the sea, and then, in your despair, you did not care what became of yourself, but yielded to your mother."

"I did—I did!"

"Come—come, my darling, don't speak in that desponding way," said Jack Jeffery, cheerily; "all will yet be well. You see, the old ship that I went out in did go down off the coast of Africa, dragging all hands into the deep with its old timbers; but I had had the luck to change out of her before that, you see."

"I ought not to have consented, Jack."

"To what?"

"To the unnatural marriage proposed by my mother."

"I don't know that, dear," the young sailor replied. "When once you thought I was gone it was rather a natural thing for you not to care much what became of you, and so you got tortured into saying Yes to anything you detested with all your heart."

"Yes, Jack—yes. Oh! how good you are to orgive me."

"Forgive you! May I sink the first craft I put my foot into if I don't love you more than ever."

"Hark!" cried Captain Macheath, holding up his hand.

"What do you hear?" demanded the young sailor, placing his hand upon his trusty cutlass. "Are there breakers ahead? What! are there pirates on our lee?"

"We are pursued, I am afraid," Captain Macheath said. "Listen! Do you hear nothing now?"

"I am rather slow at distinguishing sounds on land," Jack Jeffery replied. "But I think I hear something like the sound of horses' hoofs upon the hard road. Let them come. I think I am equal to quite a dozen of such cowardly rascals!"

"That may be so," said Captain Macheath; "but since we have a lady with us we don't want to get into a hot corner unless we can help it."

"No; you are right," Jack Jeffery returned, with a glance at Lily Lambert.

"This way," said Captain Macheath. "Ride under the shadow of these old elms. This way. Perchance, those we take for pursuers may be only harmless travellers, and if so they will pass us."

It was not difficult to hide among the deep shadows close to the bank.

In a few moments a horseman came on at a good round trot.

"They will make their way to London," said a voice. "We must get ahead of them and rouse the police. It will be better than running the risk of getting our brains blown out; besides, the reward is worth having."

"Yes," said another voice, "and then the fifty pounds will be ours."

It was evident now that the horse carried double, and just as it was passing Captain Macheath called out in a loud voice—

"Help—help!"

The man who sat foremost on the horse pulled up as he heard the cry.

"What is it? Who calls for help?" he shouted back.

"I," said Captain Macheath. "Only stop a moment, I want to get rid of two rogues! I'll make it worth your while, gentlemen, to stop a moment."

He dashed out from among the deep shadows and laid his hand upon the bridle of their horse, and then he added—

"I have them."

"Hands off!" said the foremost rider—"hands off! Do not delay us. We have nothing about us, if you be a highwayman."

Captain Macheath clapped the muzzle of a pistol to the forehead of the speaker.

"Dismount!" he said, in a calm, quiet tone of voice.

The man rolled to the ground in a moment, crying "Murder!" which so alarmed the other, that he followed his example.

A slash with a small riding-whip carried by Captain Macheath, given with all the force he was master of, sent the horse off at full gallop, to the astonishment of the two men.

"Now, my lads," said Macheath, "I'm only hammering the flints of my pistol a little; so, if you like, while I am about that little job, you can run, for whether you do or not, I intend to shoot you. I'm bound to practise upon everybody I meet riding double after sunset, you see; so—"

With a roar of fright the two men scampered off.

Captain Macheath fired one shot after them; but he took care it should fly above their heads, and then, laughing, he returned to Jack and Lily.

"The pursuit is stopped, I think," he said. "Those two fellows would have put the constables on our track; but it's all over now. Let us come at once, my friends. It is but a sharp hour's ride to London, after all."

They all started forward at a rapid pace until they came to a rather steep hill, when Captain Macheath, who was in advance, set the example of walking his horse up the hill.

Lily and Jack were a little in the rear.

"Who is this good and valiant friend who has done you such good service, Jack?" whispered Lily.

"Humph!" said the young sailor, "if I were to run up to the yard-arm for it, Lily, I could not tell you."

"Not tell me! And why not, Jack?"

"For the best of all possible reasons, my darling, and that is—I don't know."

It will be recollected that before Captain Mac-

heath made the astounding declaration from the steps of the terrace of who he was, Jack and Lily Lambert had reached the garden, and although they heard him say something in a loud voice they were not sufficiently near to catch what it was.

No doubt, too, they were too intensely interested in each other to pay much attention to extraneous words.

"But you don't really mean to say, Jack, that this gentleman is a stranger to you?"

"Indeed, I do; although I only hope I shall know such a noble fellow as long as I live. I'll tell you how I became acquainted with him."

"Do, Jack—do!"

"I only landed at Sheerness yesterday, and upon making inquiry about you, I, of course, found out you were living with your mother about this place. It took me the whole day, though, to get the news, and then this morning off I started to you, for, you see, then I knew not a word of this marriage affair, or that you had been imposed upon with any notion of my death."

"Yes, Jack, yes—go on."

"Well, when I got about a couple of miles from here, I went into an inn to rest myself, and there, for the first time, I learnt that Lily Lambert was to be the bride of Sir Charles Engall."

"Oh! horror—horror. Do not remind me of that again."

"It was horror to me, Lily," Jack continued. "For a time it almost took away my senses; and I sat in a little arbour in the garden of the old inn with my head upon my hands, as nearly mad as any man could very well be."

"My poor Jack!"

"I thought over all our old affections, Lily," the young sailor resumed, "and how I had loved you since you were a wild little girl, running about the lanes and culling wild flowers to put in your hair; and how it cost me an hour's chase to catch you and get a kiss of those pretty lips. By-the-bye—Lily!"

"What, Jack?"

"I should like one now."

"Hush! Jack—hush! Go on with your story."

"Well—well, there I sat thinking of past times till the night came upon me. Ah! how well I recollected when I used to call at your mother's cottage before I went to sea. Even then, Lily, there was a look of craft and subdued ambition upon the old woman's face, though she was pretending to be humble, and to live in a cottage, and all that sort of thing."

"My mother had fallen from wealth to poverty, Jack," Lily said. "She was once in the midst of all the gaieties of London, as she tells me."

"Ah! there it is—'What's bred in the bone you can't get out of the flesh.' The old lady thought that by this marriage she would get back again, no doubt, to the old haunts. Well, as I was saying, I sat till dark, and then the thought came over me of going to see you, and asking yourself if this wedding were a thing of your own choice or not."

"But, Jack, you ought to have known—"

"Well—well, perhaps I ought; but only suppose now that you had heard all of a sudden that I was going to marry some girl with plenty of money, what would you have thought, Lily?"

"It would have been too dreadful for thought, as it is now too dreadful to be dwelt upon, even as a supposition."

"Very good. Then don't you wonder at my doing and thinking all sorts of odd things."

"I will not, Jack. And so you came here?"

"I started to come. They told me of a near cut across the fields, and I took it, and, of course, as folks always do when they try near cuts that they know nothing at all about, I lost my way. I got into such a collection of fields, and lanes, and trees, and hay-stacks, that it would have puzzled a conjuror to find out his latitude. I completely lost mine."

"And what did you do?"

"Why, I stood still in a little green lane that did not seem to have been trodden since the flood, and I shouted. That brought two men to me, and while I was civilly asking them the way to Hampton, one of the rascals struck me unawares a blow on the head."

"The villain!"

"Yes, I felt partially stunned; and then they robbed me of all the money I had, as well as the ring that you had given me, Lily, and which I held as more precious than my life."

"But you recovered it? I have it."

"Yes; I will tell you. Just as I was recovering a little, and as they were going I fancy to give me a finishing touch with the bludgeon they had first struck me with, a man on horseback leapt the hedge and attacked them both."

"That man was our friend yonder?"

"It was," Jack Jeffery replied. "He routed them and took one a prisoner. It was the man who had the ring, luckily; the other got away with my money. From the rascal we took we got all the news about your projected marriage, for it appears, by some means or another, that he knew all about it. Then it was that after I had told my new friend the story, he said, with a smile—

"'Come, this will be a little adventure; I will help you in it.'

"It was he who waylaid both the parsons, and tied them to two trees—and such a bawling as they made I shall never forget—and it is to him that I owe the joy of once more calling you my own, Lily."

CHAPTER III.

"OFF WITH YOUR BOOTS, SIR!"

THE explanation of the young sailor, rapid as it was, was quite sufficient to make Lily fully acquainted with all that had passed, save and except the one important item, concerning which she may be well pardoned for feeling a deep curiosity—namely, the position in society and the name of the stranger who had done her and Jack such good services.

There was all the air and manners of the chivalry of old about him, and the way he had conquered the difficulties of the position in which she had been placed, combined with his strikingly handsome appearance and his amusing manners made an impression upon Lily that, if her heart had not been previously occupied by Jack Jeffery, might easily have ripened into a more tender sentiment.

As it was, she could admire without loving.

By this time the brow of the hill had been reached, and a varied scene, illumined by the moon's refulgent rays, was presented to the gaze of the travellers.

Jack and Lily found their unknown friend gazing around him with evident pleasure.

"Behold," he said, "what is to be seen here. It is an every-day sight, but yet palls not upon the senses."

"It is beautiful!" said Lily.

"You should see the ocean by it," said Jack.

"Ah!" said the stranger, "that is what I should like to see."

"Yes," said Lily. "And then, Mr.—a—a—"

Captain Macheath smiled as he placed his hand lightly upon hers.

"You shall know who I am before I leave you," he said. "After giving that information to your enemies I ought not to withhold it from you; but not yet—not yet."

Lily looked all the vexation she felt at the innocent little ruse for the discovery of the name of her unknown champion being so very easily seen through, and Jack only whistled slightly, as though he would have said—

"That had better have been left alone."

And so, indeed, it had, so far as regarded the effect it had produced.

There was nothing, however, in the behaviour of their unknown friend that could in the smallest degree lead them to suppose that they had given him any offence, and this was no piece of acting on the part of Captain Macheath, for he was not in the smallest degree hurt at the natural curiosity Lily Lambert displayed.

After gazing for a short time at the sweet landscape laid out before him, he said—

"We must not linger here. Do you not see, Jack, the dark cloud that hangs over London, even from here?"

"I do."

"And you too, Miss Lambert?"

"Yes. It makes one shudder to look at it."

"It disappears when you once get fairly beneath it. Your path now is all before you, and—and—"

He paused.

"You have something to say," remarked Jack, "which you hesitate to give utterance to. Is that necessary with us, whom you have placed under such heavy obligations?"

"Perhaps not; but yet I do not feel that I ought to be prying into your affairs. The fact is, I was going to ask you frankly, what you intended to do."

"And," said Jack, "with the permission of Lily, I will as frankly tell you. May I not?"

"Oh! yes—yes," Lily Lambert replied.

"Then I intend to take Lily to my old Aunt Jeffery, who lives at Mortlake, and there let her remain, until in calm and cool judgment she makes up her mind what to do."

"My mind," said Lily, "is made up."

Jack Jeffery looked at her with fond affection.

"Lily," he said, "if I were not so sure of your faith, I should not propose the measure."

"And in the meantime," said Lily, "what a joy it is to have broken off that dreadful marriage!"

"One question more," said Captain Macheath.

"Speak it."

"Is your aunt at Mortlake in such circumstances that she can well afford not only to keep Lily comfortable, but to protect her, in the event of her retreat being discovered?"

"Circumstances!" said Jack Jeffery, with rather a confused look. "We sailors have so little to do while at sea with the affairs of life on shore, that we hardly ever think of how folks live.

"I honestly think that she is about as poor a gentlewoman as can be."

"That is bad," said Captain Macheath.

"It is. The fact is, it was no small trouble to her, poor soul, to fit me out for sea, after I had got my berth as a midshipman on board a line-of-battle ship. I hold the rank of lieutenant now, but have no ship."

"Then the long and short of it is," said Captain Macheath, "that you ought not to place Lily with your aunt unless you can place some gold along with her. What is your opinion?"

"Just that."

"Well, we shall see. Now, ride on. Hark! I hear the sound of wheels in the valley below."

"And I, likewise," said Jack; "but I don't see how the sound of wheels can much interest us, or make our position better than it is. It is doubly provoking, too, that the scoundrels who attacked me in the lane took away what money I had with me. By-the-bye, my good friend, how did you in such a magical way procure these horses for our use?"

"In a magical way, if you like to think so," said Captain Macheath, coughing; "all you will have to do when you reach London will be to oblige me by leaving them at a certain stable to which I will direct you, and there will be no further trouble upon that score."

"It shall be done."

During the progress of the last portion of this little dialogue the party had gone on, and were now descending the hill at an easy pace.

When they reached the foot of the declivity Captain Macheath paused, and turned to Jack Jeffrey.

"Will you do me the favour to ride on, until you come to an inn on the right-hand side of the road, called the Red Rose?" he said. "There I will request of you to bait the horses, and await my coming."

"Certainly," said Jack. "You have but to direct us, and we will comply with your wishes in any way."

Captain Macheath waved his hand in adieu, and they both trotted briskly on the road.

Not knowing what might be the motive of their friend for this manœuvre they made it a point of honour not to turn a glance in the direction where they had left him.

Captain Macheath watched them till a turn of the road hid them from his sight, then in a deep-toned voice, that had something of dejection in it, he said—

"And they are innocent as I once was!"

This thought for the space of some few moments seemed to produce such a degree of dejection as completely to unman him, but it was only for a few moments, after all.

Suddenly, as though he had been touched by the wand of the enchanter, he looked up.

Fire flashed in his eyes, his mouth lost its downcast expression, and raising himself in his stirrups, he shouted, rather than cried—

"Hurrah for the road!"

The sound of his voice seemed to have an equally inspiring effect upon his horse as upon himself, for the animal gave a bound that would have unseated a less practised rider, and then darted forward at full speed.

For about a minute and a-half the highwayman suffered his gallant steed to dictate the pace at which they should go, and then he gradually drew the rein and patted the arched neck of the noble creature.

"So ho! my boy," he said—"so ho! You, too, if you had the power, would cry hurrah for the road, and in truth, in your own fashion, you do cry it. Well, we have now a little bit of work to do. Ha! ha! how the blood dances in my veins, when I hear the sound that assures me a traveller comes. Listen—listen, my steed, listen! Do you not hear the grating of wheels! Ha! ha! 'Tis well—'tis well! Now to work."

No doubt at that moment everything was forgotten by Captain Macheath save the wild and adventurous calling in which he had made himself so celebrated.

He rode to the top of a small hillock, and then holding his hand to the side of his face, so as to shut out surrounding and distracting objects, he took a long and steady look in the direction whence the sounds of the approaching carriage proceeded.

"'Tis well," he said, at length—"'Tis well. Here comes one of the right sort."

Without another remark he dashed down the hillock, and at an easy canter went along the road to meet the vehicle.

The moon had by this time climbed high in the sky.

It shed a clear, silvery light upon the scene below.

The highwayman glanced up at it as though he would have wished that some light cloud might cover the fair face of the queen of the night for a short time; but if he had any such feeling, it very quickly passed away.

He trotted forward with the same joyous look as before, as though he were going upon some ordinary pleasurable errand, and not by any means upon one that perilled life and limb.

As he was approaching towards the carriage, and that vehicle itself was going at a fair speed, they soon came tolerably close to each other, and then, to the astonishment of the postillion, Captain Macheath stopped and said in a loud, clear voice—

"Hold! the blood of those who resist be upon their own heads!"

"Murder!" cried the postillion; "it's—it's Captain Macheath!"

With the rapidity of magic, Macheath cut the traces of the horses, and then, as he passed the postillion, he said—

"Stir, on your life. I have a long arm, and will reach you, if you afterwards hide yourself in the bowels of the earth."

"Murder, sir! no, sir! Bless you, sir—I won't stir for a month, sir, if so be, sir, as you says don't, sir. Oh! murder—spare my life and take my goods. I have got a large family, sir, and nothing a-year."

A pistol was fired unsuccessfully at Captain Macheath as he approached the door of the carriage by one of the inmates.

"Fool," said Captain Macheath, "will you force me to do a deed that I shrink from? See here," he added smiling, "you have put a bullet through my hat."

"Who are you?" said a soft voice.

"Madam," said the gallant captain, "I am a gentleman, and that you may ever hold me in remembrance I will trouble you for your purses, rings, and watches. Indeed, I do not turn up my nose at any kind of valuables; I assure you that the smallest contributions are always thankfully received by your humble servant."

A faint scream came from another corner of the carriage, and then another lady said—

"Mr. Highwayman, go away—go away, and let the carriage proceed at once. We don't intend be robbed."

"Robbed, madam!" said Captain Macheath gaily; "no, neither you nor any other lady shall be robbed while I am on the road; I flatter myself I keep this road very clear of robbers, indeed. But by your voice I know you are beautiful, so I feel that you will at once comply with my request to have some little remembrance of you, as well as you may have one of myself."

"Well, I cannot say but that you are very polite."

"Very," said the lady who had first spoken to the captain. Before he could make any reply to these speeches the first lady cried suddenly—"Mr. Pounce, am I to be pinched black and blue because a highway gentleman happens to be polite?"

"Mr. who?" demand Captain Macheath. "Who dares pinch you, madam, of any colour but the delightful and natural one you possess while I am here? He must be a singularly bold man."

"It's my husband, Mr. Pounce, up in the corner here."

"Is this possible?"

"No—no," cried a man's voice. "I—no—no."

"Pray, sir," said Captain Macheath, "step out."

"I have got no money, not a farthing, and no jewellery but a mourning-ring upon my finger, and you would hardly take that."

"Come out, sir."

"But—but—"

"Ladies," said the captain, in his softest accents, "allow me the pleasure of handing you out of this bear's den, and then I can ferret out the odious animal himself."

"It's all your own fault, Mr. Pounce," said the lady—"it's all your own fault, and I hope it will teach you not to be so handy in pinching one, as you usually are, you mean-spirited, ugly—"

Captain Macheath had taken the hand of a young lady—he felt it tremble in his—and assisted her from the carriage.

"Be under no apprehension," he said. "Not the smallest hurt shall be done to you, or to any whom you may wish to protect."

"Spare all," she said.

"I will."

Captain Macheath next handed out the other lady, who, although double the age of the young one, who could not be above eighteen at the most, was still a comely woman.

They were both very elegantly dressed, and when they stood upon the road Macheath glanced around him and saw a pretty green spot among some trees, where the short grass was a much more inviting place to stand upon than the road.

"Yon grass plot," he said, "will be more befitting the tenderness of your feet than this rough road."

Upon the instant, and before the slightest opposition could be made to him, he lifted up the young lady, and with all the tenderness in the world he carried her to the grass plot.

"The devil, sir!" cried an angry voice now from the carriage, while a fist was flourished in the air—"the devil sir! What do you mean by carrying my niece?"

"Your niece, is she?" said Captain Macheath. "She has the disadvantage of a very ugly and disagreeable uncle. Lie down, sir!"

Neither of the ladies could help laughing to hear the uncle of the one and the husband of the other addressed as though he were some vicious dog, merely, and when Captain Macheath now took up the elder of the ladies, and likewise carried her to the grass-plot, the conquest of her affections appeared to be quite complete.

"Oblige me, ladies," he said, "by remaining where you are for the present, if you please."

"Have mercy, sir!"

"Mercy? Oh! it is not needed. There will be no harm done. This is a mere farce."

He walked to the carriage, and holding open the door, which had a tendency to swing to, he said to the gentleman within—

"Now, Mr. Pounce, I will trouble you to alight, or, if it be more convenient or pleasant to you, from where you are to surrender to me your money and valuables. I am perfectly ready to take them."

"There is my purse, and the deuce comfort you with it," gasped Mr. Pounce.

"Thank you," said Captain Macheath, doffing his hat.

"The idea of carrying my wife!" spluttered the irate Mr. Pounce. "I—I could—I don't know what I could not do."

"Therefore," added Captain Macheath in his blandest tone, "it is much better to leave it undone, you see, sir; and now I warn you, if you attempt to act inimical to my safety, I will scatter your brains in this carriage with as little remorse as I would those of a mad dog."

Mr. Pounce sank to the bottom of the carriage as though he were half-dead already, and Captain Macheath slammed to the door. In another moment he was with the ladies, to whom he said—

"Who is the young man who fired at me?"

"My step-son," said the elder lady. "I hope you will forgive him for so foolishly firing at you?"

"It is done. But now tell me what is your husband?"

"A stockbroker."

"He has given me this purse," said the gallant captain. "Is it all he has? I ask you, ladies, to tell me the truth in this matter, as I have, I trust, behaved to you with gentleness."

"I can say nothing," said the young lady.

"Nor I," said Mrs. Pounce. "My husband is rich, and his boots may be worth something; but you cannot expect me to tell you where he has hidden his pocket-book and his watch and seals."

"I owe you many thanks," said Captain Macheath, "and now my time presses, or what a pleasure it would be to me to enjoy a dance upon the green lawn by the light of the moon. It cannot be, though, and now permit me to hand you back to the carriage. The postillion, when I am gone, will soon find a means of repairing the traces, and you can pursue your journey in absolute safety then."

"We have not forgotten," said the young lady, "that you asked us for our money and jewels. There are mine, but I must ask you to make one exception."

"Make what exception you please," said Captain Macheath, "I am quite agreeable. It may appear rather strange that with my feelings towards you and all of your sex that are admirable I should lay this species of contribution upon you all, but if I were not upon the road, believe me,

CAPTAIN MACHEATH

THE
PRINCE OF THE HIGHWAY.

THE TRAP OPENED AND DOWN WENT THE OFFICER.

you would have some vulgar species of ruffian who would add insult to injury and perhaps use violence. I pray you, therefore, to pardon me."

"We do—we do."

"I am much beholden to you."

"Let me tell you that the only thing I wish to retain is a small purse of beads, with a few valueless coins it. You can inspect them."

"Certainly not."

The ladies handed to him their purses, which he found by the weight to be tolerably well filled, and then they would have given him their rings from off their fingers, but it was a sacrifice that he would not permit.

"No" he said, "I am quite content."

So saying, he handed them back to the carriage, within which the stockbroker was fuming and fretting, but quite at ease in his mind regarding the treasure hidden in his boots.

Captain Macheath was determined to possess himself of those articles, let their value be what it might, but he wished to do so without, in the smallest degree, compromising her who had given him the information concerning them.

"Sir," said Captain Macheath as he reached the carriage door, "what you have handed to me is a sum not at all consistent with your station. Will you amend it?"

"I have no more. '

"Well," observed the captain, "I never leave a gentleman the means of following me quickly, and so as I would not be so barbarous as to cripple you, I will content myself by taking your boots."

"My boots?" growned Mr. Pounce gathering up his knees.

"Yes, sir, only your boots."

"Then you must be the devil himself," said Mr. Pounce. "Permit me to take them quietly off, and you shall have them."

"I will assist you, sir. The least I can do when I am about to take your boots from you, is to help you off with them."

Captain Macheath duly handed out the stock-broker, who, with a groan, found his cunning artifice detected.

"It is all in vain!" he said; "I can give you what you want without at all disturbing my boots. My pocket-book is in one, and my watch and seals in the other."

The captain smiled as the articles were handed to him, and opening the pocket book he took from it a thousand pounds in bank notes, and then handed it back with all its papers untouched.

"This is generous of you," said the stock-broker, "for, to tell the truth, the papers in that pocket-book are worth more to me than a thousand pounds."

"Then," said Captain Macheath, "perhaps you will tell me if the numbers of these notes be known to you?"

Before an answer could be returned to this question, the young man who had fired at Captain Macheath called out—

"Help—help! thieves!"

The captain turned in a moment.

"Is this right?" he said.

A pistol was in his hand, and presented at the young man, who cowered down, expecting to be shot; but the young lady in the carriage leant from the window, and clasped her hands.

"For my sake spare him," she cried. "I implore you to spare him, sir."

"'Tis done," said Captain Macheath, "and when you tell this story, do not say you had to ask twice for me to spare one who shot at me once, and then broke his faith, by which I risked my life."

Macheath felt that the call for "Help" from the young man was not a mere impulsive thing, but that there was some special reason for it, and he glanced around him to note if he could observe any signs of approaching succour at hand.

He gave a low and peculiar whistle, which had the effect of bringing his horse immediately to his side.

On the instant he mounted, but still he was reluctant to leave the spot until he was sure from what direction the danger was coming, for that there was danger he did not for a moment entertain a shadow of a doubt.

It was soon made apparent to him.

From the road whence the carriage had proceeded he heard the sound of horses' feet, and he felt convinced that the number was considerable from the great accumulation of the sounds.

He turned to the young man who was still by the tree.

"Another word for help, and it is your last," Captain Macheath said in a terrible voice; "no more intercessions shall save your life, and I will not allow my own existence to be trifled with."

The young man was still.

Sweeping up the road, and talking and laughing as they came, there appeared a party of about twelve horsemen; Macheath could plainly hear one of them saying, as they came within sight—

"Yes; it's an odd termination to a wedding. They say Sir Charles has broken a blood-vessel with vexation."

Captain Macheath bit his lips.

He knew now that the approaching party consisted of some of the guests from the residence of Sir Charles Engall, where he had made himself anything but popular.

His determination was taken in a moment.

He dismounted at once, and, in all appearance, strange as it may seem, he said something to the horse, who immediately trotted a short distance upon the road, and then vaulted over a hedge into a meadow close at hand.

In another moment Captain Macheath got into the carriage, and then, before he closed the door, he said to the young lady—

"What is his name?"

He pointed to the young man by the tree.

"George Pounce."

"Very well. I thank you. George Pounce, if you don't come here and quietly sit down in the carriage, I will shoot you."

Master George thought that it was good policy to come at once, rather than throw away his life for the foolish bravado of not coming just because he was ordered to do so.

He stepped into the carriage, which quite easily and conveniently held them all.

Captain Macheath made him a place by his side.

"Now," he said, "if either of you two gentlemen contradict me by a word, I will not only blow his brains out who does so, but the other's likewise. As for the ladies, I only rely upon their gentleness. What they may choose to do they will be unharmed by me."

Not one said a word.

Macheath then let down the front window and looked out to the postillion—

"Silence," he said, "on your life!"

"Oh! murder—yes, sir."

"That is well. The weather has been decidedly pleasant to-day, ladies."

Any one would have thought by the tone that Captain Macheath was quite at his ease, and that nothing of a very particular character was going on, so wonderful a command had he of his nerves and his voice.

But now the horsemen, whose approach had been detected by the quick, listening ear of George Pounce, before Captain Macheath was at all aware of their approach, made their appearance upon the spot.

The affair began to get quite critical.

By the light of the moon the ladies looked at Captain Macheath to see if his firmness in any way failed him, but they could n ot perceive such to be the case.

His countenance was perfectly calm and un-ruffled.

CHAPTER IV.

CAPTAIN MACHEATH PLAYS A BOLD GAME.

"HULLO there!" cried one of the horsemen, riding up in hot haste; "did any of you call for help, or was I mistaken?"

"You were not," replied Captain Macheath pretending to be in a great fluster. "We cried for help, and not without reason. We have been robbed."

"Eh! What? Robbed did you say?"

"Yes. By a highwayman," Macheath returned. "Confound the fellow! I wish a rope was round his neck. I only wish you may catch him, that is all!"

"Confusion seize me," George Pounce groaned under his breath, "but I can't stand this."

"Perhaps you understand this?" Captain Macheath whispered.

The indiscreet George Pounce felt something touch his forehead.

He put up his hand, and discovered to his horror that it was the muzzle of a pistol pressing against his brow.

The effect was instantaneous.

He shrank back with a shudder.

"Who has robbed you?" cried several of the horsemen, crowding to the carriage window. "Who is it the villain?"

"Why no other than the well-known audacious scoundrel, Captain Macheath."

"Captain Macheath!"

"Yes; that's his name. Do you know anything of him?"

"Too much. He has left such a scene of confusion at the house of Sir Charles Engall that I don't know how it will end."

"Can such things be?"

"They not only can be, but they actually are, I can assure you, and if you will tell us which way he went we will take a ride after him, desperate fellow as he is."

"You must have passed him," said Macheath, "for he went the very way you came, only just now."

"Did he?" said the man. "Confound him! I'd ride to Old Harry after him. Come back, my friends. Let us make a hue and cry after this scamp. It will be some sort of satisfaction to our friend Sir Charles as well as to ourselves if we only can succeed in catching him to night."

"And a great surprise to me, too," said Captain Macheath.

"A surprise, sir?"

"Yes; don't you know that the fellow has as many lives as a cat, and that it is actually thought by some folks that he never will be taken at all, but will go off some day like a will o' the wisp, and no one know what has at all become of him."

"There may be people superstitious enough to believe such nonsense, but we are not of the number. Come, my friends, come, let us ride back, and try our fortunes against this wonderful Captain Macheath."

The horsemen all turned, and with one accord, spreading themselves along the road, they went off at full gallop.

"Ladies and gentlemen," said Macheath, "I thank you. I rather think by your very discreet conduct you have saved my life. Be assured that to those who preserved silence without threats, I am deeply grateful. To the others I think I may cry quits and be off."

Macheath had opened the coach door, and then before any one could be aware of what he was about he had gallantly kissed both the ladies, and sprang from the vehicle into the road.

"This is unpardonable!" said Mr. Pounce, furiously.

"No one asked your pardon," said Captain Macheath, "so it is easily withheld."

"Confound it!" muttered George Pounce, "I have known my cousin Emily now for eight years, and never kissed her yet.'

"And never will," said the young lady.

"Bravo!" cried Captain Macheath. "Ladies and gentlemen, I look forward to the pleasure of our meeting again, some day or night. Gentlemen, good night. Perhaps we shall meet again."

"Yes, at Tyburn!" said Mr. Pounce. "I shall be most happy to make one to see you dance upon nothing, with a halter round your neck."

"Well," said Captain Macheath, "it may be so—you know best; but if we do meet at Tyburn, perhaps I may be in the crowd and you in a cart. Postillion, mount your horse and push on."

"Yes, sir. Oh! dear, master, what a night this is."

"Remarkably fine, I think," said Captain Macheath. "A little dew failing, that's all."

He walked up the road, in the direction that his horse had gone, and in a very few moments disappeared from their sight, although they all looked after him from the carriage windows.

Then they heard a whistle, similar to the one which had before summoned his horse to his side, and in a moment or two after that the hard beating of a horse's hoofs upon the road.

He was gone.

"Now for it," said George. "I'll do something."

"What—what?" said his cousin.

"Why, I will take one of the coach horses and ride back after those gentlemen on horseback and let them know the truth."

"Beware!"

"I don't care for your cautions, Emily. I shall call you the highwayman's bride after this, for you know he kissed you."

"And spared you," said Emily.

The young man sprang from the carriage, and ran up to the horses to get one out of the harness, and put his threat into instant execution.

The postillion shook his head.

"No—no, Master George; don't you do that."

"Don't do what, fellow?"

"Don't you be putting your not overwise head into the fire, Master George. I have known you and your family some time, and give you advice gratis, sir, and that is, to let Captain Macheath alone so long as he does not interfere with you."

"But, confound him, he don't!"

"Yes, sir, he does now."

"I do not care one straw; if all the world stood between me and him, I'd have some try for revenge. Get out the off-horse for me, Peter."

"Very good, sir. Wilful people must have their way, but sooner or later they are sure to run their heads against something."

With this wise remark, Peter no longer hesitated to make the effort that was necessary to get out the off horse, and in a few moments George was duly mounted, although the mission he was going upon was neither a very safe, nor, under all circumstances, a very proper one.

As he passed the carriage windows he said to his father—

"Don't go from here, sir, till you see me again. If you do, and should happen to meet the highwayman, Emily, here, will tell him that I have gone to get help to apprehend him."

"Yes," said Emily, "and I could tell him that George Pounce thought it required twelve men, besides himself to take one highwayman."

With this taunt—which was tolerably well-deserved—ringing in his ear, off set Master George at a tolerably smart pace, for the coach-horse had had some rest during the proceedings of the last quarter of an hour.

We may now leave the party in the carriage, in order to follow the more immediate fortunes of Captain Macheath.

It will be recollected that they had distinctly heard him whistle for his steed, and then, by the rapidly succeeding sound of footsteps, they could entertain no doubt of the fact that he had ridden off.

They were right.

. . . . .

The secret by which Captain Macheath had contrived to hold communication with his horse is easily explained.

There was a particular phrase which he, Macheath always used when he wished the creature to go and take what pasture it could in the open country, whilst he himself perchance passed some portion of his time in sleep beneath a tree, and the sagacious creature of its own accord knew what direction to go in.

Hence was it that the horse had so instantly leaped the hedge into the meadows upon Macheath speaking to it.

Upon hearing his well-known whistle, as it was close at hand, it at once returned to him.

The great object of Captain Macheath now was to reach the inn where he had told Jack Jeffery and Lily Lambert to stop at, in order that he might hand to them sufficient of the money he had taken from the Pounce family to make Lily's presence at the abode of Jack's aunt anything but a burden to her.

With this he determined upon handing to them all the gold and silver, let the amount be what it might, and keep back the notes for a time.

For all he knew, the stockbroker might be well acquainted with the numbers of the notes, and if such were the case, his gift of any of them to the innocent young lovers might be the means of bringing them into the greatest possible danger.

More than once he paused and listened intently to feel assured that pursuers were not upon his track.

No sound of such a nature met his ears, and after proceeding thus about two miles with caution, he banished all such apprehensions, and setting off at a good gallop, the hedges and trees appeared to fly past him with great rapidity.

Nothing of any moment occurred to Captain Macheath now until he saw the old sign of the inn of which he was in search swinging by the road side, and strongly illumined by the moon-beams which fell full upon it.

The landlord of the house was at the door, straining his eyes down the road, and the moment he saw Captain Macheath, he came towards him.

"Anything amiss, my friend?" said Macheath.

"I don't know; but here's a lady and gentleman waiting for some one, and by the description, it must be you."

"It's all right," said Captain Macheath, "I sent them. Many thanks to you for your caution, though. It might have been all wrong."

"Of course it might, and what seemed so odd to me was, that though they both described you exactly, they did not seem to know who you were."

"True. They do not know who I am. I hope you did not enlighten them on that score, landlord."

Not I, captain. I never give folks more news than they can give me, unless I know them well. But I'm glad all's right. Come in."

Captain Macheath at once entered the inn, and here, we may say, that he owed much of his safety to his trusting disposition.

He put so much confidence in people, that, as he was accustomed himself to say, he shamed many a man out of betraying him.

The landlord had taken the precaution to place Jack and Lily in a room free from the usual interruptions incidental to a small country inn. Captain Macheath looked at them both gravely.

"You have no refreshments," he observed.

"We did not think of it," said Lily.

"Ah! that's my fault," said Jack Jeffery. "I will ring."

"Never mind. The landlord will in a moment bring us a bottle of his best wine, and then I have something to say to you both, which I hope you will take in good part as it is intended."

"How is it possible that we can take ill anything from you," said Lily, "to whom we owe so much?"

Captain Macheath smiled.

"Lily," he said, "you will really make me believe at last that I have done something deserving thanks; but here is the wine, and now, Jack, pledge me a bumper to Lily's health and happiness."

"Right willingly," said Jack; "and now—"

"Hush," said Macheath, sadly. "My heart tells me what you are going to say—you would now ask who I am?"

"You are right."

"I grieve, then, to say that there are circumstances that compel me to keep that a secret for the present."

Both Jack and Lily looked disappointed.

"I say only for the present," said Macheath; "but I have a question to ask of you both, which is—have you seen enough of me to give me the privilege of a friend?"

"Oh yes—yes," cried Lily.

"Quite enough," said Jack, as he grasped Captain Macheath's hand—"quite enough. Ah! what is this?"

"Money," said Captain Macheath, as he left in the hand of the young sailor a purse—"it is money. You want some, and I can and do lend you some, as I am sure you are in need of it."

"Lily, we ought not to accept this," said Jack Jeffery.

"Nay, I say you ought, or else shame upon the feeling of friendship which you have only just now said existed between us," Captain Macheath remarked.

"Take it, Jack," said Lily Lambert. "It comes from a friend."

"Well," said Jack, "I will repay this as soon as I can draw a bill for my pay in advance upon a navy agent in London. How much is this, sir?"

Captain Macheath looked a little puzzled.

"I really don't exactly know," he said.

Jack Jeffery elevated his eyebrows, and looked, as he might well look, rather surprised at a man offering another the loan of a purse of money, without knowing the amount it contained.

He counted the gold, and found there was more than a hundred pounds.

"This is too much," he said. "I don't want half of it."

A bell at that moment rang violently, and the landlord appeared.

"Your horse," he said, "is ready—quite ready."

"I understand," said Captain Macheath.

CHAPTER V.

MORE PERILS.

CAPTAIN MACHEATH was gone before either Lily or Jack could utter a word of thanks.

Both rose as if to go after him, but the landlord stood at the open door and blocked the way.

An instant later there came from the road the sound of a hand-to-hand conflict.

"By heavens!" cried Jack Jeffery. "I never allowed myself to be cooped up when a friend is in danger. Get out of my way or I will fling you down the staircase!"

He spoke in such a way that he evidently meant what he said, and the landlord moved hastily aside.

Jack dashed past mine host, and down the staircase.

He found Captain Macheath surrounded by several men who were aiming furious blows at him to prevent him from mounting.

Jack Jeffery rushed into the middle of the throng knocking down all before him.

"Bravo! well done!" shouted Captain Macheath.

In another moment he was firmly seated on the saddle.

By a slight movement of his knees, he made his horse fully understand what was wanted of him.

There was a bound and then a rush, and Captain Macheath was off like the wind.

"Forward!" cried one of the discomfited horsemen—"forward! follow him. Never mind his companion here; we will come back for him."

Jack Jeffery stood the picture of amazement with a pitchfork in his hands, while Lily who had flung open one of the front windows of the inn, stood with terror in her looks regarding the scene below.

Fortunately, although every one of the horsemen knew her, not one looked up, so intent were they on the capture of Captain Macheath.

Being in her wedding dress, with only a loose cloak over her that Macheath had lent her, she must, if she had uttered the least cry to attract any attention have been at once recognised; but, fortunately, she did not.

Surprise and terror kept her silent.

The whole of the mounted men dashed off in good style in the track of Captain Macheath.

"Gracious Heaven!" said Jack, "what is the meaning of all this?"

The landlord tapped him on the shoulder.

"My friend," he said, "did you hear what they said?"

"Who?"

"The horsemen."

"Confound their sayings! what are they to me? How dare they attack my friend in that dastardly way, and why should he be pursued as though he were some notorious malefactor, that the hands of all men are raised against? I repeat, what is the meaning of all this?"

The landlord shook his head.

"My dear sir," he said, "you and the young lady have two good horses. As you value your safety and hers, mount and be off."

The young sailor passed his hands over his eyes as he muttered to himself—

"Is it all a dream?"

Then suddenly he looked up and saw Lily at the window, and his eyes brightened.

"No—no!" he said. "At least that joy is real."

He threw down the pitchfork, which, up to this moment, he had held in his hand, and dashed into the house again.

"Lily are you ready?" he cried.

"Yes—yes."

"Come on then. We will mount and take the road to London, which is the same that our friend and his pursuers have taken, and we may find at least some clue to the mystery. The horses—the horses!"

"All ready," said the landlord.

"What's to pay?"

"Nothing."

"Nothing! How's that? It is something odd to stop at an inn and have nothing to pay, is it not?"

"No, not here; I never charge any friends of his anything."

"Ah! and who may he be?"

"Oh! that's neither here nor there. I wish you a good and prosperous journey, sir."

The landlord turned upon his heel and walked into the house.

"Well," said Jack as he helped Lily to mount, "of all the inexplicable inns that ever I heard of this is the most inexplicable; and of all the odd friends I ever met with, our late one is the oddest."

"I am bewildered, Jack."

"And so am I."

"But—but surely there must be some mode of arriving at the truth, and at an explanation regarding all these things?"

"There may be, Lily, but as yet, at all events, it is far beyond my limited comprehension. Let us be off, for if ever there was an enchanted inn, where all the people are bewitched, this is the one."

"Go—go—go, at once," cried the landlord, looking from one of the upper windows of the inn.

"Go, while you can, young man, with a whole skin."

Jack shook his head at this, and then having ascertained that Lily was quite ready, they both set off from the inn door at a rapid canter on the London road.

We may now safely leave Lily and her lover, the gallant young lieutenant, to pursue their journey, while we scamper upon the road with the reader some few miles in advance of them, and keep company with Captain Macheath.

The importance, after what had happened, of making good his retreat, stared Macheath sufficiently in the face, and he gave his good steed the rein, a thing he seldom did, for he was always much more intent upon saving the good qualities of his horse, than upon using them.

But the present was an emergency which banished all scruples, and, accordingly, he flew along the road with the swiftness of the wind.

"They must have indeed rare cattle," he said. "if they beat me at this sort of thing; and after a mile or two more, I think this speed may be with safety slackened. Ah! that must be the toll-house light. Why, I am further on my road than I thought by a good mile."

"That's him!" cried a voice from behind a hedge, to the right hand side of the road. "That's him! He has escaped them!"

"Stand!" said another voice.

Two men, well mounted, came into the middle of the road.

"Ha! ha! George Pounce," cried Captain Macheath, "is that you?"

He had recognised the voice behind the hedge, and without paying at the moment any attention to the two men in the road, he fired a pistol in the direction of George Pounce's voice.

Macheath considered that, after all that had passed, this young man deserved a taste of lead.

"Help! he has hit me!" cried George.

"Serve you right!" said Captain Macheath.

"Stand, or we fire!" said one of the two men. "You are our prisoner. We know you, Macheath, villain and highwayman that you are."

"Then, gentlemen, you have the advantage of me," said Macheath, "for I neither know you nor do I wish for such very doubtful acquaintance."

As he spoke, he dashed forward without giving them a moment's time for further consideration.

The pistol was in his hand which he had just discharged at George Pounce, and although two shots were fired at him, one of which slightly touched his right cheek, he knocked down one of the men with the barrel of the weapon.

The other made a vain attempt to impede him, and on he darted.

He then replaced the discharged pistol in his pocket, and took out one that was loaded, and presented it over his arm at his enemies; but he did not pull the trigger.

"Pooh!" he said. "I will not waste powder and shot upon one man."

Macheath put up the pistol and rode on; but scarcely had he got a hundred yards off, when he heard the man behind him calling—

"Shut the gate—shut the gate!"

"Ah!" said Captain Macheath, "he means the toll gate, and there are two high garden walls on each side for a leap."

"Open!" shouted the captain, when he came nearly to the gate.

"Ha! ha! no," cried the toll man. "You are caught, Macheath, my beauty; your time has come, and I've got five pounds for shutting the gate on you."

"Surrender!" said the man from behind.

Captain Macheath turned his horse's head so rapidly, that he threw down both the horse and rider who were behind him. Then turning back again, after a gallop down the road of about fifty yards, he came on clear at the gate.

"Catch who may—catch who can!" he cried. "That's the game we play at on this road."

By a prodigious effort, his horse not only cleared the prostrate steed and its rider which lay in the way, but the gate likewise, coming clear upon the head of the toll-man, who, not at all expecting such a feat lay within human power, was exactly on the other side.

"Hip! hip! hurrah!" cried Captain Macheath. "A cheer for the girls whom we love."

Like a flash of light he went down the road.

The toll-keeper never spoke again, and when the horse and his rider gathered themselves up, the one was lame, and the other half stupefied by his fall upon the hard road, where his head had come in contact with a stone. His eyes seemed to strike fire, and fifty Captain Macheaths, and as many turnpike-gates appeared to be flashing before his vision.

When in about ten minutes more the whole of the party that had been so signally defeated at the inn by Jack Jeffery arrived at the toll bar at full gallop, they found the gate fast and no one to open it.

This was a serious delay, for after calling several times upon that man who would never again hear the voice of mortal, one of the party had to dismount and clamber over the gate to find the means of opening it.

The first thing he did in the semi-darkness of the place was to stumble over the dead body of the gatekeeper.

"Help!" he said. "There has been murder done here."

"Murder?"

"Yes. Here is a dead man."

"Open the gate—open the gate!" was now the cry. "How can we come to you if you don't open the gate?"

After some fumbling, all of which delayed time, and so far was eminently in the favour of Captain Macheath, the man found the fastening of the gate, and swung it open, when the whole party passed through. They looked for a few moments in silence at the dead body, and then one, in a loud voice, said—

"Friends all, our duty now is to hunt this highwayman to the death. Do you not see that confusion and murder are upon his footsteps? Let us not waste another moment's time. Keep on after him."

"Aye—Aye! Hunt him down!" said another.

They now dragged the dead body into the toll-house, and without waiting for the man who had been thrown down to recover sufficiently to go with them, they pushed on after Captain Macheath.

He was three good miles ahead of them now, and the lights of London were gleaming upon his eyes, as he made his way towards that city in which he certainly knew there was much danger for him, but likewise security as well.

Macheath had travelled far enough. His clothing and general appearance were calculated to draw upon him the attention of pedestrians in the quaint old streets.

But then the hour at which he arrived in London was one at which but few people were stirring.

It was nearly one o'clock in the morning, and the good folks of that time were not so fond of turning night into day as they are now.

Even the watchmen confessed to being mortal, and shut themselves comfortably in their boxes and slept.

Occasionally from the corner of some small thoroughfare the cry of drunkenness and riot would come, and all would be still again, and for the space of a few minutes London would seem like a city of the dead.

Captain Macheath pursued his way at a fast walk until he reached Finsbury-square, then by no means the aristocratic-looking place that it is now, but infinitely more rural, inasmuch as it was backed by the Finsbury Fields, in which wild flowers grew in profusion.

Captain Macheath and his horse both sniffed the grateful perfume from a second crop of new-mown hay in the fields, but although they both would willingly have taken that direction, it did not suit his mind at that time, and turning off to his left, he at once plunged into a labyrinth of streets.

He had not to proceed far before he reached his destination. He drew up at an old-fashioned looking inn that seemed to occupy one half of a street with its numerous suites of rooms. An emblazoned sign proclaimed it to be The Blue Boar.

CHAPTER VI.

CAPTAIN MACHEATH'S QUARTERS IN LONDON, AND WHAT HAPPENED THERE.

THE Blue Boar had but a dubious reputation with the magistracy of the good City of London, and yet they found it hard to fix anything of a very particular character upon the old inn.

How could the landlord pretend to know when a gentleman well mounted stopped at his door if he were a lord or a highwayman?

It would be going rather too far upon the part of the keeper of an hostelry, who professed to find good entertainment for man and beast, to be very urgent in his inquiries respecting the private history of his customers.

But yet folks, sailing close to the law—personages that Newgate might be said to pant for—had been known to walk in at the open door of the Blue Boar, and when the authorities walked in after them, lo! they were not to be found.

This was mysterious, to say the least of it.

Then, the landlord, one Henry Luck, was also so ready to oblige the police.

All the keys were so immediately at their service, and he never made the least secret of any part of his house—then what could they say?

Indeed, he would himself, not unfrequently, quite assist them in eking out a description of some gentleman, who was by them 'wanted,' and assert how he had seen—"The very image of such a man" in his coffee room, and be himself quite lost in wonder, as to where he could have got to out of the way!

All this, then we say, had given the Blue Boar equivocal reputation; and, by the conduct of Captain Macheath, when he stopped at it, we should say it deserved such a repute. He paused for a moment or two, and looked up and down the street to see if any one of an obnoxious character

were at hand, and then, with a silver whistle which he took from his pocket, he blew two peculiar calls.

The patience with which Macheath waited after this, was in its way something quite exemplary.

The delay lasted about five minutes, but he was not tempted to repeat his challenge to the inn; nevertheless, he kept his eyes fixed with some anxiety upon the exterior of the building, until a small window was suddenly thrown open upon the first floor, and a night-capped head appeared.

"Who is there?" said the voice appertaining to the head.

"The moon is on the wane," said Captain Macheath."

The manner in which he repeated these words, evidently showed that they constituted a kind of pass, and the landlord, for it was no other than Mr. Luck himself who looked from the window, suddenly shut it, saying as he did so—

"It is the captain. Who would have thought it?"

Captain Macheath had not now to wait many moments before one of the very numerous doors of the old inn was opened for him, and the landlord appeared, partially dressed.

"Come in," he said—"come in!"

"Is all right?" demanded the captain.

"Stop!"

"Stop for what, Luck? What's amiss?"

"Look there. Who's that?"

Captain Macheath glanced in the direction to which the landlord pointed, and he saw a man scamper at headlong speed round the corner of the street.

"Who was that?" said Captain Macheath.

"A spy. Do you know, captain, I have had my own thoughts and ideas about some fellows that have been lurking about the old inn lately."

"Indeed!"

"Yes; they can't get the upper hand of old Harry Luck by fair means, so they want to do so by foul, which is a mean thing, to say the best of it; but I'll show them a trick or two yet."

"Not a doubt of it."

"Come in."

"With the horse?"

"Yes; it will do all the same. You must get the creature to stoop—but if a highwayman's horse won't do all that a man can, he ain't fit for the trade of his master."

"I believe," said Captain Macheath, as he fondly patted the animal and dismounted, "that I have as true a friend here as any man need wish to have."

"Now for it."

The landlord held the door open, and Macheath led in his steed by the bridle. The creature trod as carefully as though it felt the necessity of secrecy in its movements, and when the door was closed again, barred and locked, and a total darkness ensued—a darkness that really seemed as if it might be felt—the breathing of the creature could be scarcely heard so still did it keep itself.

"I'll bring a light in a minute," said the landlord.

Captain Macheath heard him walking swiftly away, but in less time than he had said, he reappeared with the lantern.

"Now follow me," he said, "and I'll show you a new way to the stables. This way, there's no stairs and nothing to run against. By all that's good, I hope that fellow saw you come in."

"You hope he saw me, Luck?"

"Yes, I do; for so sure as he lives his occupation is gone."

"How can that be?"

"Just this way. He will be off the first thing in the morning to the Mansion House, and tell them all that he saw Captain Macheath come in here on horseback by the little door near the front entrance, and if that don't make him a liar I don't know what will. Who do you suppose would believe such a tale? If they come down to me about it, I shall say the fellow must have dreamt it, and tell them to look at the door and fancy how a man on horseback could come through its entrance. Then they may search the place and find neither horse nor man answering the description, and the fellow will get his discharge for romancing. Ten to one but they send him to a prison for a week for trying to impose upon the authorities. Ha! ha! ha! That would be good."

"I hope it may be as you say."

"It will be—it must be. Stop one moment."

They had passed along a narrow passage and through two rooms, when the landlord desired Macheath to stop.

It was only that he might unlock a door, and then, when it was thrown open, there appeared a sloping sort of wooden pathway with pieces railed across as a foothold for horses.

"This is what I call rather an ingenious mode going to rack and manger," said the landlord.

"It is, indeed." said Macheath.

"Now, look sharp. Just hold the horse half a moment, and you shall see how the affair is managed."

The landlord suddenly exerted all his strength upon a portion of the wall, and it gradually gave way before him, revolving upon a centre. A dim light shone through the opening and Luck said in a suppressed tone—

"Joe—Joe!"

"Here you are!" replied some one.

"Lend a hand here to the horse. Give him a good feed, and mind, above all things, that you attend to the bell."

"I sleeps under the manger," said Joe, "and it's close to my ear. Lor' bless you, master, if so much as a mouse's tail was only to touch it, I could not be off hearing of it."

"Very well, Joe. There will be no inquiry without occasion, and when there is, there will be no hurry."

"All right, master. Woa! so ho! you are a nice'un. Ah! you are one o' the right sort, you are—sleek and slim as a young lady."

The revolving portion of the wall was just by a manger in the stable, and was so well contrived that it might defy all ordinary examination.

Of course, if any one came prepared to make such a discovery there it was to be made; but the secret was in few hands, and those few all interested in it's preservation.

"I must confess," said Captain Macheath, "that the more I think of the mode of entrance to the stable, the more I am of your opinion, Luck, that no one will believe it. And now I may tell you that I have had a narrow escape."

"I thought as much, or you wouldn't be here at such a time, captain."

"No—I should hardly have disturbed you."

"The disturbance is nothing. I am always glad to see you, by night or by day, for the sake of those that you have been a good friend to. And now, if you like, I can show you where to stow yourself, that, if they find you out, they must be greater conjurers than ever I took a police-officer to be."

"I shall be beholden to you, for, to tell you the truth, I am somewhat tired, and have done a day and night's work without much rest, Luck. But I don't think that any one is upon my track now."

"Don't make too sure of that, Captain Macheath. However, we will take good care of you. Safe bind, you know, safe find, and—

Luck stopped abruptly, for a tremendous hammering at the front door of the inn came upon his ears.

"That's my friends," said the captain, laughing, "I'll be bound; but I did not expect them so soon."

Luck shook his head.

"That's the game is it?" he said. "Why didn't you say you were closely pursued, captain? I wouldn't have wasted so much time. But come along. All's well. I give 'em leave to do their worst. We'll have a good laugh at them yet at breakfast time."

"I hope so."

"Now look you here, captain. Upon the road, and well in your saddle, you are everything; but here, in a house, you are rather out of your element, you know," continued the landlord.

"I confess it," assented Captain Macheath.

"Well, it's no odds; I know what I am about; so follow me, and all will be right. This way—keep close, and don't go much to the left. That will do—here we are."

They had ascended a small flight of twelve stairs, and the landlord entered a room, comfortably furnished, into which he showed Captain Macheath.

He placed the lamp on the table, and took a key from his pocket.

"You see that door in the corner?" he said. "It looks like a cupboard, and it is a cupboard, too, and yet not only a cupboard. The back of it slides up, mind, like a window-sash, and it takes you into a narrow space between the walls to many of the rooms of this house. But, mark me, I don't wish you to stay there, for, after all it is dangerous, and some of these days will be found out. But I do wish you to make use of that passage and this key as a means of getting from one room to another without the trouble of doing so by the common entrance. Do you understand me?"

"I do."

"Well, you will find many a cupboard opening by a sliding back from that passage. I will place lights in some of the rooms, and in every one that is looked at; and as they send their rays through the crevices of the cupboard you will find that a sufficient guide to know what rooms to venture into."

Bang! bang! bang! went some one at the door and a loud voice cried—

"House! house! house!"

"Be careful," said the landlord. "I now leave you to yourself, for it won't do to keep them at the door any longer. The moon will be all the light you want just now."

The landlord abruptly left the room, conveying the lantern with him.

Macheath found that the room was well lighted by the moon's rays; but it was far from an agreeable thing to know that there were some twelve or fourteen men at the door of the inn thirsting for his life.

"I have chosen my course in life," he said in a low tone, "and I must abide its chances."

The key was in his grasp; but before he made any use of it he was anxious to catch a glimpse, if that were possible, of his enemies in the street.

The house, however, had so many windings and turnings about it, that he found, when he came to look from the window of the room in which he was, that it did not command a view of the front of the old building, but looked into a much narrower thoroughfare, full of mean, squalid habitations, that, though under the magic influence of the bright moonbeams, could hardly be made into beauty, or to produce a picturesque effect.

Under these circumstances he at once made use of his key.

He unlocked the door of the cupboard, and found, as the landlord had told him, that the back of it easily slid up like a window-sash.

This was likewise the back of another cupboard in another room, so that for a few moments Macheath was puzzled to know where the passage was that Luck had mentioned to him.

A slight touch, however, on one side of the walls of the first closet showed him that it was of the same construction as the back pannelling.

He raised it, and at once saw a dark and dreary-looking passage about four feet wide.

Before he plunged down it, he thought he would try and obtain a view of the street from the adjoining room, for he heard that Henry Luck had not yet let in his foes.

The captain was so far gratified that the room into which he stepped did give him the prospect into the street that he wanted.

He felt that the danger of his being seen was too small to take it into account, and, accordingly without hesitation, placed himself close to the window to watch the proceedings without.

From the general appearance of the party, he saw that it was the same that had followed him up with so much pertinacity from the house of Sir Charles Engall, but how they had contrived to discover that he had come to the Blue Boar was beyond his comprehension.

It certainly was just possible that accident brought them there; but it was very improbable that such was the case, when to reach that part of London they would have to pass many more unexceptionable places of entertainment.

They were parleying with the landlord at the door, and Captain Macheath heard one say suddenly—

"It's no use beating about the bush. I am an officer, and I am also fully satisfied that the man we are in search of is here."

"A man, sir," said Henry Luck. "What sort of a man? Your description is rather a vague one."

"Perhaps so," growled the first speaker; "but you may as well save yourself from being prosecuted by giving him up. Your house is surrounded, and nobody can leave it without being observed."

"Well," said the landlord of the Blue Boar, "perhaps you will tell me who it is you want? I have several gentlemen staying in the house, so if you will tell me the name of the right one, I'll rouse him up."

"You know who it is very well," the officer remarked, sneeringly; "we want Captain Macheath, the famous highwayman, and what is more, we know he is here."

"Dear me," he said "is that a fact?"

"Yes," the officer replied.

Mr. Luck put on one of the most incredulous looks in the world.

"Bless you! gentlemen," he said, "I should go right down crazy if I thought any such a person as a highwayman was in the house."

"We shall see."

"Certainly. Come in, gentlemen; come and search where you like; I can only say that we have a lady and gentleman, sleeping in the best bed-room, and I hope you will not disturb them."

"We shall do our duty."

The party entered the house, with the exception of two, who were left to guard the door with pistols in their hands.

Captain Macheath thought it then high time to leave the window and betake himself to the more secure retreat of the narrow passage.

He felt that his head was continually encountering huge cobwebs, but the exigency of the moment enabled him to think nothing of the crawling of the spiders about his neck, which would otherwise have been anything but bearable.

Holding out both his hands to feel his way—for although he did not expect any obstacle, yet he could not help, in the intense darkness, fancying there might be one—he stepped on for the distance of about thirty feet, and then he found there was an abrupt turning.

Suddenly a faint glimmer of light streamed into the passage, and then by applying his ear to the wall he heard Luck say—

"Well, gentlemen, I hope you will soon be done! You have begun at the top of the house, and intend, you say, to search it thoroughly?"

"Jukes," said a voice, "come here."

"What is it now?" said some one, with a voice like a Polar bear.

"Why, I don't like the look of this panelling at the back of the cupboard. When I was here last, I recollect it looked suspicious, but now I am quite resolved to satisfy myself about it."

"As you please, gentlemen," said the landlord. "The house is old, and may have odd places in it that I know nothing of. They say that in old times, many a long year ago, it was part of an old convent."

Captain Macheath did not wait to hear more.

He felt that the passage between the walls was discovered, and that, consequently, it was no longer a tenable place of refuge for him.

He hastened on, blundering against many things in the dark, against many turnings and projections, until he saw again a faint light through some crevices.

He cautiously slid up the panel that hid the room from whence the light proceeded, and at once—for the door of the cupboard was open—he saw into a chamber with a large four-post bedstead.

From the appearance of the clothing that lay about upon chairs, Captain Macheath could at once see that a lady was in the room, and it at once struck him that he had pitched upon the bedroom of the married folks of whom the landlord had spoken.

He was considering what to do when he heard the sounds of feet in the passage behind him, and voices came upon his ears.

To close the sliding-panel was the work of a moment, and then he stood in the cupboard, the door of which was open, gazing into the Blue Boar's best bed room.

Truly, the position of Captain Macheath was now a fearful and complicated one, and nothing but some extraordinary movement, combined both of skill and courage, could save him.

He did not hesitate, but dashing into the room of the married couple by means of one of the secret modes of entrance at the back of the cupboard, he stood before their bewildered eyes, covered with dirt, and a miserable spectacle to behold.

A death-like silence was in the room.

To tell the truth Captain Macheath felt all the disinclination 'n the world to disturb the good people in the bed-chamber; but desperate emergencies require desperate remedies, and he had no other resource.

The lady sat up in bed, and uttered a cry of alarm, when she sufficiently recovered from her first fright to do so; but the husband—yes, the husband, who certainly, if anybody ought to have done so, should have been the man to take the initiative upon the occasion, shrank under the bed-clothes, and shook like an aspen leaf.

"What do you want?" said the lady.

"My life," said Captain Macheath.

"Your life! And who is your life?"

Probably she took it as some sort of declaration of attachment uttered in the high-flown language of a melo-drama.

"You mistake me," said Macheath. "I am pursued by those who would take my life. That is what I mean."

"But—but—"

"You would say, how can you assist me?"

"Yes—I—"

"Your husband shall be my preserver, but I will repay to you the service. Sir—sir!"

"Mercy—help!" cried the smothered voice of the man under the bed-clothes, "murder! I am not here."

"Oh! Albert," said the wife, "how can you be such a coward! and you an officer, too! I am surprised at you—I am indeed. Albert! Albert!"

CHAPTER VII.

DEATH OF THE SPY.

CAPTAIN MACHEATH'S position was one of the greatest danger, but he did wait with as much patience as he could command for the lady's indignations to have their proper effect upon Albert, and they certainly had some, for a head, enveloped in rather a remarkable looking blue silk night-cap popped out from among the bed-clothes.

The face beneath the night-cap presented quite a picture of serious alarm, and the eyes glared upon Captain Macheath with such agony, that at any other time he could not have restrained from laughing at such an apparition of fright.

"Can it be possible that you are an officer?" said Macheath.

"In the militia," said the lady.

"Oh!" said Captain Macheath, "that is it. Now listen to me, sir. My life is in danger. It hangs upon the events of the next five minutes. I dare say there are plenty of unoccupied beds in this house. I will trouble you to go and find me one."

"I find you a bed, sir?"

"Yes, you; and that upon the instant, too I will not be trifled with. Rise, sir, at once, and leave the room. By-the-by, I will borrow your nightcap."

"Good Heaven!" said the lady, "what's the meaning of this?"

"Simply, madam, that to save the life of a fellow creature, who, whatever may be his errors, has never failed in his devotion to your charming sex, I am sure you will permit me to remain in the room a few minutes."

The lady gave a faint scream.

"Good gracious, sir!" she said; "you don't talk of remaining here."

"Precisely so, madam."

At this, even Mr. Albert plucked up something of a spirit, and shaking his head, he said—

"No—no, that won't do. You have come into my bedroom, sir. You have seen my wife in her night-cap, and I warn you to mind what you are about, or you will rouse the British Lion, sir."

"If you consider yourself that individual," said Captain Macheath, "I may as well tell you what in the event of your refusal I mean to do."

"What, sir—what?"

"Why, I shall be under the disagreeable necessity of throwing you out of the window. I will not blow out your brains first, because that would make a noise, but running you through is an easy and quiet process, and that I may do; so, as there is no time to lose, pray make up your mind, sir."

"Maria!" gasped Albert, "Maria!"

"Well?"

"I think I'll go. Life is—is—"

"Oh! you mean-spirited wretch."

"Sweet, you know, and—and—I'm a-going. Oh! have mercy upon me, sir. Who are you?"

"It cannot matter to you who I am," said Captain Macheath. "But I warn you if you say one word about what has happened, and so be the means of my capture, although I may not be able to reach you myself from the prison to which I should be consigned, I have associates who will hunt you from one end of the world to the other."

Macheath caught the night-cap from his head, as he stepped out of bed, and put it on himself.

Albert made a bolt at the door of the room, and was gone in a moment.

"Madam," said Captain Macheath as he sat down on the edge of the bed—"madam, trust me."

"Oh! I shall never survive this night," said the lady.

"Yes, you will, madam. I am only sorry you are yoked to a husband who would rather leave you in the way yours has done than be thrown out of window. I would have suffered death twenty times and been thrown out of one hundred windows, before I would have stirred from the side of so much loveliness."

"Don't speak to me!"

"But, my dear madam—"

"Don't move or I'll scream. Indeed, I will, and then you will be taken, and serve you right."

"No—no. Do not say so."

"Oh! I shall never forget this night. Go away, monster!"

A loud crash at this moment came from somewhere in the house, and Macheath listened eagerly for the sound of approaching footsteps. He had been most careful to fasten up the sliding panel at the back of the cupboard, so that there should be no suspicion excited by finding that open that all was not right in the chamber.

The fact was, that the officers, although they had found out the secret passage by dint of tapping upon the wainscot, and ascertaining by the sound that there was a circuitous hollow space behind it, had not found out any of the regular modes of entrance, but had reached it by knocking a hole in one of the panels in a room which they selected for the purpose of a careful examination.

Thus, then, was it that Captain Macheath heard a great crash, which was occasioned by their breaking out the passage again into another room, not far from the bed-chamber in which he was.

"They come," he said.

"Mercy!—oh, mercy! what will become of me, to be found in such a situation as this?" said the lady. "Oh! sir, be you whom you may, this is most ungracious and unmanly conduct of you."

"Nay, do not say that," replied Captain Macheath. "The secret of the whole occurrence rests with yourself and your husband. He, surely, for his own sake, will keep the tale to himself, and you know that you have been compelled merely to endure my presence for a few minutes."

"Yet, sir, it is ungracious to compel me."

"Very well," said Captain Macheath. "It shall never be said that I owed my safety to such an act. I will defend myself against my foes as best I may."

He made a movement as if to go to the door.

"Stop a moment," she said. "How am I to know that this is not all a fiction? If you were indeed in such danger as you say the whole affair would assume a widely different aspect. But how can I be assured of that?"

"By my telling you, madam, who I am, and so placing my life in your hands."

"Tell me, then?"

"I am Captain Macheath."

The lady gave a start and a slight scream.

"What! Can I believe my eyes? Are you Captain Macheath, the—the highwayman, and the man who is always so kind and so gallant to the ladies that they never regret even being robbed by you?"

"I am that individual, madam, whatever may be my merits or demerits. You have but to say when the officers who are searching about this house for me, come into this room, which assuredly they will—'Here is Captain Macheath,' they will at once attack me. I will not be taken, and they will kill me, so that you will have the satisfaction, if you please, of being my destruction."

"No—no, I cannot."

"You will not?"

"You have conquered. I cannot betray you, much as I condemn your life, and your presence here. No, I cannot say to any one—die!"

"Then I owe you my life; that is clear and distinct. I owe you my life, for it would, without your generous aid, have inevitably been sacrificed this night. I will not speak of my gratitude, but—"

"Hush! speak not at all. They come."

A confusion of voices outside the door of the room now came upon Macheath's ears, and he heard the landlord say—

"Stuff! You know as well as I do that the house is part of an old convent, and no doubt there are all sorts of odd hiding places and corners in it. I am by far too much occupied in my bar to ferret them out. You may come as often as you please and do so; only if you break the walls, I shall fully expect that you will make them good again."

"That may or may not be," replied some one. "What do you say is in this room?"

"A gentleman and his wife, who came to town from Guildford only to-day. You will be the ruin of my inn if you go into folk's bedrooms disturbing them in this sort of way."

"We must do our duty, Mr. Luck."

"Confound your duty, it will spoil my business; of course, I can't help it—but I have no doubt the lady and gentlemen won't sleep another night in a house where they liable to such visits."

"Oh! they won't mind us, when we tell them what we came about."

"Won't they?"

The principal officer tapped at the chamber-door; and then, after a short pause, Captain Macheath in a capitally assumed voice, called out—

"Who's there?"

"Police officers, sir, in search of a highwayman," was the reply. "We are very sorry to disturb you, sir, but we are bound to search every room in the house."

Without waiting for any further parley, the officers opened the door, and with lights in their hands, walked into the room. Captain Macheath who had divested himself of his coat, vest, and boots, and looked as if he had just got out of bed, pulled the silk night-cap right down to his eyes, as still in the assumed voice he said—

"Bless me, Maria, this is very unpleasant indeed."

"Very," said the lady, faintly.

"Come—come," added Captain Macheath. "Landlord, do you call this a quiet house, where people are woke up in the middle of the night with a cock and bull story about a highwayman? You may be all housebreakers yourselves, for all I know."

"It's all right, sir," said the principal officer, exhibiting a small staff with a little gilt crown at top of it. "It's all right, sir. We shall not disturb you longer than just the time it will take us to be quite sure he has not slipped into this room and hidden, which he might do without your hearing, sir."

"I should say not," said Macheath.

"Oh! dear, yes, sir. He's as cunning as a fox, and has as many tricks as one, but he won't get the better of me very easily. No, no.; I know a trick or two—and, though I say it myself, it is very difficult to deceive me."

"So I should think. Maria, my dear, we will leave here in the morning."

"Yes, said the lady; "yes, Albert."

"Confound you all," said Captain Macheath, "have you done? I can tell by my wife's voice that she is as near fainting as possible."

"We are going, sir. He ain't here, Snooks."

"No that's clear enough."

At this moment the door of the room, which had only swung shut, was flung violently open, and the husband—the veritable Albert—made his appearance.

"I can't stand it," he cried, "I can't stand it any longer—I'm a desperate man. My brains are like a flame—I can't and won't put up with it—I'm really mad. Where is my wife?"

"Why, landlord," said Captain Macheath, "you told us you would shut up that poor lunatic; and you know when we saw him last night we would have left the house if you had not strictly promised he should be taken care of."

"My wife—my wife!" roared Albert. "Death and the devil—my wife!"

"I did promise to shut him up," said the landlord, "and forgot. Come along, Tommy, come along—no violence, Tommy."

"Who the devil do you call Tommy, sir?" cried Albert. "Don't stand between me and my wife."

CAPTAIN MACHEATH

THE
PRINCE OF THE HIGHWAY.

UNDISMAYED BY THE FEARFUL ODDS AGAINST HIM, CAPTAIN MACHEATH FOUGHT BRAVELY.

NO. 3.

"Come, come, Tommy," said Captain Macheath, "go away."

"What is the meaning of all this?" said the principal officer.

"It's my poor brother Tom, sir," said Luck; "the family cannot keep him among them. He ain't very dangerous; but he will have it that every woman he sees is his wife, and if we ever neglect locking him in his own room he is sure to alarm the whole house."

"I ain't Tommy—I have no brother. That's my wife."

"You hear, gentlemen?"

"Poor fellow!" said the officer, "he ought to be in Bedlam."

"I think he is happier out," said the landlord.

"That may be all very well," said Captain Macheath; "but I don't see why I and my lady are to be disturbed, because your mad brother is happier out of Bedlam. Upon my word this is too bad. Don't faint, Maria—don't; I am here, you know, your own Albert."

"The lion is roused!" cried the husband. "He calls himself Albert, and my Maria his Maria! Death and the devil! Murder! Curse all the world!"

"Take him away," said Captain Macheath.

"Do I smell a rat, or do I not?" said one of the officers.

"You had better call the cat, for fear," Captain Macheath remarked quietly.

"Come on," cried the principal officer. "Lay hold of your brother, landlord, and keep him under lock and key. We have wasted time enough with his folly. Push him along. We will lend you a helping hand if he be obstropulous at all. Be off, Tommy—be off. What, you won't—won't you?"

"I ain't Tommy! I never was Tommy. I am Albert and that's my Maria. I ain't mad now; but I am going fast—fast, I shall be quite so in a little while if this goes on. Maria—Maria! I ask you if you don't know me, and acknowledge as your husband. If you say no, I shall be satisfied that I am nothing but a madman."

"Answer him, my dear, to satisfy him," said Captain Macheath.

"Poor fellow! Take him away," said the lady.

Albert, upon this, made a dash towards the bed, and Heaven only knows what might have resulted if the officers had not rushed upon him in a body and laid hold of him tightly.

"Open the door," said one, "and we will take him out. Why, he is as mad as a March hare. It's too bad to let such a dangerous lunatic about, it is, indeed. You are to blame, landlord."

"I fear I am," said Luck; "but if you knew all, gentlemen, you would alter your opinions; and so I will only take him up in his room till morning, poor fellow. Ah! gentlemen, once he had a fine mind, had Tommy. But now you see what a wreck it is. He reminds me when he talks of the old harp in the drawing room, with one half of the strings broken. Once it was all sweetness and melody, and now what a humdrum it is."

Albert was forcibly removed from the room, and the door was closed again upon Captain Macheath and the lady who had so delicately acted her part in the drama of his preservation.

She had not said a word too much upon the occasion, and scarcely one too little.

Of course, the search through the remainder of the inn for Captain Macheath was perfectly fruit-

less, and the officers were compelled to leave the house at length, with but a half conviction that they were mistaken, and yet with a complete one that, let the facts be how they might, they were baffled.

"Now," said the lady to Captain Macheath, after the room door had been closed for some few minutes. "Now, sir, you can with safety to yourself leave me."

"I will do so."

"I have but one request to make to you, and I think I am, after what I have done for you, entitled to have it granted."

"You have but to name it, and it is granted."

"It simply is, that the transactions of this night may be buried in oblivion, and that you name them to no one either in jest or earnest. Do you promise me that much?"

"I do, upon my life and honour."

"I am satisfied. Now go."

Before Captain Macheath could put on his coat, the door was opened again, and the landlord made his appearance.

Captain Macheath was taken completely by surprise at the manner in which Luck spoke, but he soon found that there was good and substantial reason for it; and in a moment the conviction crossed him that the perils of that night were far from over.

"Sir," said Luck "I have come to apologise for the manner in which you have been disturbed."

"Don't mention it," said Captain Macheath; "I understand it all now. I don't think anything of it."

"Thank you, sir—you are very kind."

Luck threw a small piece of paper on the floor and at once left the room.

There was light enough to read anything by, and Captain Macheath felt confident that upon the piece of paper he should find the reason of the mysterious conduct of the landlord.

He looked at it earnestly.

It contained the following words—

"Be cautious. Eight officers came into the house—seven only left. Is the eighth hiding in your room?"

Macheath crushed up the little piece of paper in his hand, and sat down upon the edge of the bed again.

There were several considerations of moment connected with this alarming fact.

Of course Macheath was not really afraid of the one officer; but he did not wish to commit the landlord in any way.

The one man who had stayed behind might or might not have an understanding with his companions who had gone.

If he had, they might yet be lingering close at hand in waiting for some signal.

If he had not, cupidity alone could have prompted him to remain, for there was a reward offered for his, Macheath's, apprehension.

How was he to be baffled without killing him, or compromising the house and its landlord? That was the question.

"Are you going?" said the lady.

"In a moment."

"Is this your good faith, your lingering here after all I have done for you, when you may safely go? Is this generous—is it just?"

"I go," said Captain Macheath "I go. Bless you, madam; I owe you much."

Captain Macheath was not sure that he should

be permitted even to leave the room without some interruption.

He thought it most probable that the officer who had remained was the one who had said he smelt a rat, and who had been advised by the captain to call the cat.

If it were that man, the Captain felt certain he should know him again, for he had regarded him particularly.

Upon the landing he paused a moment.

He heard a stir in the room he had just quitted, and then he knew that the officer was there.

That was an important piece of intelligence, and he ran down the stairs as fast as he could.

At the foot of the stairs he met the landlord of the Blue Boar with a light.

"Have you seen him, captain?"

"Yes, above."

"I thought as much. There is only one way now—only one way. Come on after me as quick as foot can fall. This way—this way. Don't mind what noise you make—come on quickly."

The landlord ran along the passage of some twenty feet in length, and then unbarred a door at its extremity.

He still kept saying "Come on—come on!" and Macheath followed him with a light and rapid step. The door, when opened, only showed a continuation of the passage; but soon the landlord stopped at a door to the left, which he flung wide open, and then when Captain Macheath was about to pass its threshold, he called out—

"No—no—no!"

"Not there?"

"No. Not unless you wish—but no matter. There is but one way. I don't like it—I shake at it—but there is but one way."

"What do you mean?" demanded the hunted highwayman. "Explain yourself, Luck. Why are you trembling in that way for, man? What do you purpose that it has such an effect upon you?"

"Only one way—only one way!"

"I insist upon knowing what you mean."

"Yes, captain, you shall know—of course you shall know, and you only. The secret must be kept locked up in your breast and in mine. This way—this way."

"What secret—what secret?"

"Patience, captain. Only a little patience. Follow me, and you will soon know. Trust to old Harry Luck. There's only one way. If there were another you should take it. On—on through this room. You are sure he is up stairs?"

"Quite, but—"

"Hush! I know who it is. It's Bilkins. He shot poor Joe Gunn—don't you recollect hearing of it, captain—poor Joe Gunn, who was as kind a soul as ever lived. He shot him last year, and did it wantonly, too. Oh! he's a regular brute is Bilkins."

"Confound him! Is that the fellow?"

"Yes, captain. He came in, but he did not go out."

The landlord had now opened another door, which led into a large room, with a smaller one beyond.

"Wait here," said Luck.

He drew a table as he spoke, so that it was visible through the two open doors, and then placing a chair by it, he added—

"You have nothing to do, captain, but to sit down here."

"This is mysterious, indeed," said Captain Macheath. "I know that whatever you do is for my benefit; but still, Luck, I should like to know what it all means, and what in the end it is all to come to. I should have thought the closed door would have suited us better than all these open ones."

"Don't ask."

"But why not?" demanded Captain Macheath. "Am I a child that I am to be told to do this, or to do the other, and not know a why or a wherefore?"

"You will thank me for not telling you," said the landlord of the Blue Boar. "Sit down, my friend, and, if you have any faith in me at all, ask nothing. Ah! I hear something."

Rapid footsteps approached.

"It is the officer," said Captain Macheath, as he took a pistol from his pocket. "He surely will not be so foolish as to encounter me."

"What would you do?"

"If he will rush upon his own destruction let him."

"Captain, put up your pistol. There's no occasion for it in the world. Put it up, I say, and sit still. When he comes to yon open door and asks you, which he will, to surrender quietly, all you have to do is to pay no attention to him."

"But the doors are all open. He will come."

"Let him."

Henry Luck went into the room adjoining the passage, and Captain Macheath, with a perfect faith in the good feeling of Luck towards him, and knowing that the existence of his house depended upon the police having nothing actually against him, he felt that he ought to submit to the plans dictated by him.

He accordingly sat down by the table, and looked through the outer room into the passage beyond, where he momentarily expected to see the officer.

He was not for many minutes kept in a state of suspense.

Guided by the light which the landlord had placed upon the table at which Captain Macheath sat, and which sent some beams right through the outer room into the passage beyond, Bilkins, the officer, for it was he, soon reached the spot.

He had in his hand one of those short, stunted-looking pistols, so much patronised by the police in days gone by, and that he presented full at Captain Macheath through the open doors.

"Captain Macheath," he said, "I know you. I suspected from the first the whole trick. You are my prisoner!"

Macheath only looked at him.

"Your time has come, Captain Macheath," the officer said, in a determined tone of voice. "You are wanted. You know that sooner or later this hour would be sure to arrive, so it is quite useless to resist your fate. I tell you you are wanted."

"By whom?" demanded the captain, with all the coolness in the world.

"By me. I am not a man to be trifled with, and I will have you, dead or alive. I have made up my mind to it, and set my life upon this task."

Captain Macheath still looked at him.

"Come out," added the officer. "None of your deep-laid tricks. Come out, or I will shoot you dead as you there sit. I have shot as determined a man as you before to-day. Come out, I say."

"That is reasonable."

"What is reasonable? Come—come, this sort of thing won't do. Do you yield yourself up, Captain Macheath? If so you may depend upon the best treatment from me, and it may do you good at your trial that you did not resist."

"If you want me," said Captain Macheath, "take me. It is worth while coming across a room to do so. I am here, and you are there; you talk a great deal, but you do little, Mr. Bilkins."

"Very well, I will come and take you, and, mark me, Captain Macheath, I have taken a solemn oath—may I be smothered if I don't shoot you through the head if you make the least movement that I think looks like opposition !"

As the officer said this he advanced.

On—on across the threshold of the room that opened to the passage, he made his way step by step.

His eyes were fixed upon Macheath, and the pistol was presented.

"Surrender—surrender !" he cried. "Now, Macheath, resistance is of no use, I tell you. If his were the last moment you had to live, you—"

"It's your last," said Luck, suddenly emerging from the gloom of the room and standing close to the door of connection between the two apartments. "It's your last, Bilkins, the murderer !"

The floor opened, and down went the officer.

One wild shriek came up from the deep abyss, and then all was still.

"Good Heaven !" cried Captain Macheath.

"Hush," said Luck—"hush !"

He leaned over the aperture and looked keenly down.

"Hush—hush ! It's all over."

Captain Macheath heard the rush of water.

He sank back into the chair again and said—

"This is horrible !"

"Humph ! I don't see it," said Luck. "You must have died by his hand or he by yours. Now neither has happened. He has been, as it were, his own executioner, and if the spirit of the poor fellow he murdered was not there to receive him it's an odd thing to me. He's gone for ever."

Captain Macheath shuddered.

"Luck," he said, "I don't know that I can blame you. It was a case of life and death, and that man has perished. I had no idea you had any such contrivances as this in the house."

"It's no contrivance of mine," said Luck— "it's no contrivance of mine. I found it out by accident only myself, captain, and an awkward accident it was. I only saved myself by holding on to the edge of this deep hole."

"Hark ! what's that ?"

"What ?"

"I hear a cry," said Captain Macheath—"an awful cry. It comes from below. Do you not hear it ? It is horrible ! The wretch is not dead. He has found some resting-place."

"No—no ; impossible !"

A convulsive shriek came from below.

It was the last cry of the man who had said he had set his life upon a cast, and who had so awfully—

"*Stood the hazard of the die.*"

The trap-door, which was composed of two portions, slowly closed of itself.

It looked like the grave yawning over its victim.

Luck went back for the candle, but he trembled so that the light got loosened in the stick.

At the moment that the double-doored trap closed it fell from the stick and all was darkness.

"What's that for ?" cried Captain Macheath.

"An accident—only an accident," said Luck. "Don't stir, for your life's sake. The slightest step upon this trap and down it goes."

"Be careful yourself."

"I will—I will. I must come your way, and by keeping close to the wall I am safe enough. Remember, captain, that this is one of the secrets of the old Blue Boar that only you and I know."

"And Bilkins ?"

"Why do you mention him ? He has gone to his account. All's right. This is your arm I am touching ?"

"My arm ? No !"

"Heaven ! what is it, then ? Something soft and warm."

The landlord made a leap into the room where Macheath was, and upset the table, crying—

"Off—off ! Keep off, Bilkins. You—you brought your death upon yourself. It was your own doings. You know it was your own doings. Off—off—off !"

Macheath heard a heavy fall.

"Luck—Luck !" he called.

There was no answer.

The landlord had fallen upon the floor of that inner room in a swoon.

CHAPTER VIII.

CAPTAIN MACHEATH IN DANGER.

THE situation of Captain Macheath was anything but a pleasant one.

He had seen quite enough of the inn to feel abundant faith in what the landlord had stated regarding the odd and secret passages in it, and there he was in the very focus, as it were, of such mysteries, with the only person who could guide him clear of them in a state of insensibility.

Call for assistance he could not think of, and he was fearful of moving much lest he should fall down some other trap-door that might be as conveniently placed for his reception like the one that had already received its victim.

All he could do was to wait with what amount of patience he could command for Luck's revival.

At length that happy event seemed to take place.

The landlord uttered a deep groan that seemed to come from the bottom of his heart.

"Luck," said Macheath—"Luck !"

"Ah ! yes," replied the landlord, in a vacant sort of way.

"Rouse yourself, man."

"Ah ! yes."

"Come, Luck," said the captain, "bethink you of where you are, and don't be foolish, man. Get up and show me the way out of this abominable place."

"I begin to comprehend a little," said Luck. "Ah ! it's all coming back to me now, I recollect. What on earth made me faint, I wonder ? I am not in the habit of doing that sort of thing."

"I should suppose not. But never mind the cause of it. Let it suffice now that you are recovered, and that, consequently, you can lead me out of this place, for which, I assure you, I have no sort of affection."

"I should wonder if you had."

"Get up, then."

"All right. Only tell me, did Bilkins call out again after the trap closed, or was it after all only my fancy that made me think so ?"

"He did."

"It's a very dreadful thing, then. But still, he brought his fate upon himself."

"To some degree, that is true," said Captain Macheath. "But let us forget the past. It is irremediable, and we may only embarrass ourselves by recurring to it."

Captain Macheath was glad to find that Luck had no recollection of the immediate cause of his swoon, namely, his supposition that he had encountered some one in the dark.

Of course, it could only be a matter of imagination, and it was quite as well that the landlord should not be unmanned by a recollection of it.

"Do you know the way," said Captain Macheath, "in the dark?"

"Yes, pretty well; but I would rather have a light for all that. It was stupid enough of me to drop the candle."

"Don't say any more about it, but lead on. There, I have got hold of your coat, and will follow closely in your footsteps."

"Are you sure it is you that have hold of my coat?"

"Don't be a fool, man. Of course I am sure. Why, you are quite wandering in your intellect to-night, Luck. I can't think what has come over you, man."

"Nor I neither."

Captain Macheath had really no great faith in Luck's guidance, considering the state of mind he was in.

But there was no other resource.

He knew nothing of the route he had to take himself, with the exception of a steady determination not to pass through the open door leading to the room where the yielding trap was, and that he felt confident he knew the direction pretty well.

Luck avoided the door.

"Well you are right enough now," said Captain Macheath.

"How do you mean, captain, by right enough?"

"You know your way, I mean."

"Yes—yes, for the matter of that I know my way; but I would give something if I could tell what was that I touched in the dark. The idea of it comes over me with a cold shudder now; and when you said it was not you, my heart seemed to leap into my mouth, and then I seemed to step down a trap myself, and I knew no more till I was speaking to you about my recovery. Answer me one question, captain, if you please, and answer it candidly."

"What is it?"

"Do you believe in ghosts?"

"No."

"Are you only saying that to encourage me, or do you really think what you say?"

"I really think what I say," Captain Macheath replied. "If there were any such things as ghosts, Luck, the world would not have wagged so many hundred years without the fact being established, which you know is a long way off from being the case."

"There is something in that," said Luck.

During the continuance of this little dialogue, the landlord had been leading Captain Macheath from those strange chambers, which had echoed with the death shriek of the officer; and suddenly, upon opening the door, there came a sudden blaze of light.

This effect, though, was only comparative, for all the light only came from a little oil lamp standing upon the first step of a small flight of stairs.

"Thank Heaven!" said Luck, as he put up a bar against the door they had to pass through, "we are out of that part of the house."

"I am glad we are out of it," said Captain Macheath.

"So am I. I don't think, captain, I shall ever venture there again. It don't rightly belong to the inn, you know, but is part of the old original convent, they say."

"And the water?"

"What water?"

"The water that I heard splashing down the trap?"

"I know just as much about that as you do, captain, surmising that you know nothing at all. Where it comes from, or where it goes to, is a mystery. I only hope neither you nor I will ever have occasion to go near it again."

"Amen!" said Captain Macheath.

A very few moments now sufficed to carry them to the habitable part of the inn; and then Macheath, taking from his pocket-book the notes he had relieved the stock-broker of, he showed them to Luck, saying—

"I think the numbers are known of these, for they came from a man of business. What shall I do with them?"

"I know some one who will deal with you for them. They will go famously on the Continent. But you must want rest now. It is nearly three o'clock in the morning, and the best thing you can do is to go to bed till the dawn."

"But my horse?"

"Trust me, that's all right; I rang the bell, and that's quite sufficient for my stable-man. Your horse was put in a secure place, you may depend."

"Then, Luck, I will lie down for an hour or two."

"Good."

"But, remember, I must be off before the daylight has fairly opened its eyes."

"I shall be up and stirring. There is the disposal of the notes to look to. But that can easily be done. It is only in Finsbury that we have to go. Come this way, captain, and I'll show you to your room."

Captain Macheath followed him to a bed-room, and soon cast himself upon a bed, having only taken off his coat and boots.

Bidding the landlord, then, a brief Good-night, although he might more properly have said Good-morning, Macheath was in a few moments fast asleep.

"Lucky fellow!" said the landlord, musingly. "He can sleep, but I'm afraid I can't. What could it have been that I touched in that room—what could it have been? I shall not forget to-night in a hurry."

*   *   *   *   *

To Captain Macheath the few hours' rest he got seemed merely like so many minutes.

He was quite astonished when he felt some one shaking him, and heard Luck crying to him—

"Up—up, captain! The sun is rising and you must follow the example."

"Agreed!" said Captain Macheath.

He sprang from his couch, and stretched himself.

"Cold water, Luck, and in plenty, if you please. It is the only thing that will thoroughly wake me up. Ah! what's that?"

A confused noise, and then some moans, came upon his ears.

"It's the couple in the next chamber," said the landlord, ' When the officers were gone I unlocked the door of the room in which I had confined the husband, and told him I was very sorry, but couldn't help it. He is taking his revenge upon his wife, I suppose."

"Which he shall not do," cried Captain Macheath, "while my name is—"

At this moment the cries became so loud, that the landlord ran out of the room to ascertain what was going on, and scarcely had he left it a moment, when there rushed into it the lady fully dressed, crying us she did so—

"Help—help! He is really mad!"

Captain Macheath caught her in his arms.

"You are safe—quite safe," he cried, "with me."

"Ah! you here?" she said, and then shuddering, she closed her eyes, and fell into a swoon.

There came into the room through the casement sufficient of the rays of the young day to fall upon the face of the lady and clearly render it observable by Macheath.

He was surprised at her youth and beauty; and as she lay helpless in his arms, he could not help feeling how blessed he should be if he could call such a creature his own.

"Where am I?" she said.

"With one who will protect you."

"Where is she—where is she?" cried a voice in the passage. "Where is she? I will have her life, I will be hung for her! Only let me find her and kill her, and then they may hang me. I am really mad now! Where is she?"

"It is my husband!"

"Fear nothing," whispered Captain Macheath, as, still holding her in his arms, he set his back against the door of the chamber. "Fear nothing, lady, I will protect you. He shall not enter here."

"I will kill her—I will kill her!" cried the husband again. "Get out of my way. She came into this room. Death and the devil! I will kill her and be hanged for Maria!"

"Don't be a fool," said Luck, in the passage.

"I will—I will!"

"Come, come, Mr. Spinks, your good lady has gone downstairs, I think, and if you must go after her, that's the way."

"Ten thousand devils! I will have her life—I insist upon being hung for Maria—I will be hung for Maria!"

They heard him go down the stairs, at least, by the voice they felt certain that he had; and then Captain Macheath spoke—

"So your name is Spinks?" he said.

"Yes—yes. Let us now part, sir, once and for ever."

"No Ma—"

"Yes; it must be so."

"What! to await the ire of an infuriated husband?"

"By the time he returns his passion will be gone. He is only this way by fits and starts, and his threats mean nothing, although I admit at the time they alarm me much, and to-night they were worse than usual."

The door opened.

"Mrs. Spinks, go to your room at once," said Luck. "Your husband has hurt his foot over something, and is coming limping upstairs."

She darted from Captain Macheath and was gone in a moment.

"Confound you!" said Captain Macheath; "I could knock your head off."

"My head off?"

"Yes. But no matter; I was only enjoying a mild flirtation."

Luck shook his head at Captain Macheath.

"Well," said the latter, "what now, stupid?"

"Ah! captain—captain. But it's no business of mine. Look out. Is it early enough still for you to go to Finsbury about the notes?"

"Excuse me," said Captain Macheath: looking rather confused. "I have been rather, in a manner of speaking, forgetful, Luck; but if I have said anything harsh, pray forget it."

"Don't mention it. She is a nice-looking creature."

"Don't say another word about her to me just now, Luck. I am sorry for her, poor thing! for she is united with one who cannot make her happy. Come, if you are ready to go out, I am. I suppose my horse is all right?"

"At the side door."

"Good! I thought once last night it was a doubtful chance whether I ever bestrode my good steed again."

"Things looked queer; but come on. You may make up your mind now that Bilkins was quite alone, and had stayed thinking to outwit his comrades; and a pretty piece of business he has made of it."

Captain Macheath found a boy holding his horse at the side door of the inn.

He gave him a guinea—Captain Macheath always paid his way manfully—and then mounting, he said to Luck—

"How will you get on?"

"I will walk upon the pavement, captain, and seem to take no sort of notice of you; but when you see me stop at a door, you can stop likewise, for it will be the one you want."

"Very well. I will ride slowly so you will have no trouble in the matter."

"That will do. How clear the streets are! We seem to have London to ourselves."

"It looks like it. Hark! what is that?"

"St. Paul's striking four."

They crossed Finsbury-square, and Luck took his way down a street called Green-street, at the north-east corner of it.

It led them somehow to the back of Bishopsgate.

Suddenly he stopped at what, to all external appearance, looked like an empty house.

Stooping close to the ground, he found an obscure bell handle, which he gave a hearty pull at.

The street-door then opened as if by magic.

"Go in," said Luck.

"Whose shop is it?" said Captain Macheath, as he dismounted. "I know some of the folks in this line, What's his name?"

"Lake."

"Lake—Lake! No; I don't know him by that name. Will you hold the horse a minute or two, Luck? Is the fellow rapacious?"

"Of course"

"Humph!"

Luck held the horse while Captain Macheath crossed the threshold of the house.

He was hardly two paces in the passage when a harsh voice cried—

"Who is it?"

"What's that to you?" said Captain Macheath. "It's a customer; that's enough."

"Turn to the right"

He found a door a few paces to the right, which conducted him into a squalid parlour. It was half

A WATCHMAN RUSHED UP AND AIMED A FURIOUS BLOW AT CAPTAIN MACHEATH'S HEAD.

of miserable worn-out furniture, and in one corner was a wretched pallet bed, on which lay an old man.

He glared at Macheath from amidst a mass of filthy bed-clothes, and then said—

"It is Captain Macheath!"

"You know me?"

"Yes," said the old man with a cunning leer. "It is my business. What have you got, my boy? I am glad to see you here. You will come again. I often thought I ought to have you for a customer, but you used to go to Joel's."

"I did."

"Well, you will come to me again. What have you got for the old man, my boy?"

Somewhat amused at the singular mode of address on the part of the old man, Captain Macheath handed him the notes, saying—

"I'm afraid of getting anybody into trouble about the numbers. They may be known; but I am not at all certain."

"And you don't mind me getting into trouble?"

"Not a bit."

"Ha, ha! my boy, I like you. A thousand pounds in notes! Ha!—Humph! Dear, dear me! Worth nothing. I shall have to send them to Germany, and then have them all sent back, for they won't now even pass at the roulette tables of foreign princes, who support themselves by keeping gaming-houses. And yet, my boy, I will give you something for them. You shall have—you shall have two hundred pounds in good notes, that you shall."

"Be quick."

"You will take it—you are satisfied?"

"Oh! yes."

The old man fell back among the pestiferous bed-clothes with a deep groan. Captain Macheath thought he was taken suddenly ill, or was perhaps dying.

"What the deuce is the matter now?" he demanded. "Is the devil going to have his own at last?"

"No—no! Oh! dear—oh! dear. Oh! he says he's satisfied, and I might have offered him less. He says he is satisfied!"

"Ha!—ha!" laughed Macheath. "That's it, is it? Comfort yourself. I would not have taken less, you old rascal; so hand out the notes. Quick! Be quick about it, for I am in a hurry."

"Yes my boy, yes; and so you would not have taken less?"

"Not a farthing."

"What a comfort."

The old man dived his hand among his bed-clothes and produced a pocket-book, from which he took two hundred pound notes, and handed them to Captain Macheath.

"There, my boy," he wheezed. "There, you are a rich man I shall never see my money back again, I know; but then you are my gallant captain, and that makes all the difference."

"For all I know to the contrary," said Captain Macheath, "these two notes may be in the same predicament as mine. If such should be the case, and I find you have played me a trick, you may depend upon me coming back and smothering you."

"My boy—ha! ha! what a noble boy you are."

Macheath made no further remark, but rose and left the house.

"You have made short work of it," said Luck, impatiently.

"Yes. I have got two hundred pounds in notes

of him. I suppose I may depend that they are all right, Luck, and not stolen ones?"

"Oh! yes; but it is too little by at least half. It is scandalous."

"Never mind, I can afford it. Here's one of them for you, and the other will provide me with a little pocket-money."

"I do not require so much as a hundred pounds, captain. It's too much, indeed it is."

"Pooh! pooh! not a whit. Put it in your pocket, man; I'm glad I have the opportunity of handing it to you. Don't have any scruples about it."

"Well, all I can say is, that as long as my house stands there's a home for you, captain, and confusion to all your enemies. If you are hard pressed, and should be a hundred miles off, make for the old inn; and the moment you cross its threshold I'll answer for your safety."

"Thank you, I know that, and it's no slight thing."

They had now reached Finsbury-square again, and Captain Macheath had just turned his horse's head westward when three men appeared.

"That's him!" cried one, pointing at Captain Macheath with a sword. "That's him. Down with him!"

"Indeed!" said the highwayman.

In a body the men made a rush at Macheath, and the one with the sword struck at him, which, if it had hit him on the head as it was intended, would have finished his career.

But such was not to be.

Macheath swerved a little, and the blow fell almost harmless upon his shoulder.

He then drew one of his holster pistols, and fired it clean in the face of the man with the sword, who fell across the horse's neck with a deep sigh.

At this moment Macheath was dismounted, and this was rather cleverly effected.

Two of the men dismounted, and allowing their horses to gallop away, attacked Macheath vigorously.

A couple of pistols were fired at him the same moment by the mounted officers, who kept their steeds and were unhurt; but the shots missed him, and in a moment he played one of them the same trick as regarded the unhorsing as had been played himself.

The only man who was now mounted tried to cut Macheath down with a police-cutlass; but Macheath, who had remounted parried the blow with the butt end of his whip, disabling the man's arm with a terrible blow.

One of the dismounted men made a rush to lay hold of Macheath by the legs to dismount him again; but he met with such a kick from the heavy boots that Macheath wore that he lay upon the road insensible.

The affair was now merely a struggle between Macheath and the only one of his assailants who was in a condition to follow him.

He could have shot the remaining man for for he had his other holster pistol ready at his hand.

He half drew it out, but then, thrusting it back again with the words, "Blood enough already!" he started at a gallop towards the City Road.

The man, who did not want for courage, was after him in a moment.

"A highwayman! Stop him!—stop him!— a highwayman!" he shouted.

The cry was of little use at that time in the morning in the streets, for they were nearly deserted; and at the busiest part of the day that was no very great thoroughfare, bustling as it is now-a-days.

The man fired at him once, and Macheath heard the bullet whistle past his head.

He took no notice of it, however, but rode on, for he was quite satisfied that the other's horse was no match for his steed. Macheath's only danger was in the event of meeting with horsemen, who, in consequence of the hue-and-cry kept up by his opponent, might try to capture him. But this was not likely at such an hour.

For a mile, all he met was a market-cart, the driver of which drew up as near to the kerb as he could to get out of the way.

The man, whoever he was, fired again, and then Macheath turned in his saddle rather angrily, and looked back.

He saw sufficient to put him quite at his ease regarding his enemy.

His horse was terrified at the discharge of the pistol, and was rearing in rather an uncomfortable manner; then it suddenly dashed into a gallop and fell, throwing its rider some yards over its head.

"That will do," said Captain Macheath.

A ten minutes' swift canter brought him to a turning to the left, which upon pursuing, conducted him to the back of the Strand.

Then he let his horse subside into a walk.

"This won't do," he said. "I must not show in my true character for some time, or London, and perchance its environs, too, will get too hot to hold me?"

He paused at a livery-stables near Charing Cross, and rang a bell that, without dismounting, he could reach. It was answered by a man in stable costume, who respectfully touched his cap.

"Is William here?" asked Macheath.

"No, count," said the man.

"Very well. Take the horse, and when you see him, say that I am in town again."

"Yes, my lord."

Macheath dismounted, and abandoning his horse—which showed not the least sign of having had a gallop—to the man, he walked very briskly in the direction of Spring Gardens.

"I will do the gentleman awhile," he said to himself, "and mix in some of the gaieties and the frivolities of this great city, to which my title of count gives me admittance; thanks to the folly of the young Lord Glasse. Ha! ha! if he only knew who it really was now that he introduced as the Count Lintledale!"

He laughed as he walked on, and soon reaching the quiet aristocratic thoroughfare called Spring Gardens, he knocked and rang at a large house, a plate on the door of which announced that it was No. 5.

* * * * * ¶

It will have been observed that during the late affray in Finsbury-square, Luck had been remarkably quiet, taking no part in it at all.

This was sound judgment, for, completely unarmed as he was, he could have done nothing effectual, and would have only brought suspicion upon himself, and hindered him from being of the remotest benefit another time.

Besides, he had great faith in Captain Macheath's power to cope in the open air with three adversaries.

The result was favourable to Luck's powers of judgment, and when he saw Macheath, to all appearance uninjured, fairly ride away, he ran home alone, telling himself as he went that he

believed Captain Macheath had both the devil's luck and his own.

The fact was, that in the contest that had taken place in Finsbury Square, the great difference between Captain Macheath and his opponents consisted in that he was fighting for his life, and they only for a reward.

He knew that if he were worsted in the contest his death upon the gallows-tree was certain, and he felt that it was best to die in the midst of a manly struggle to keep his life and liberty than be made the holiday show of a crowd that would have gaped at his dying agonies, and made food for after gossip of his last convulsions.

Hence arose, then, that daring recklessness which actually made such a man an equal and more than equal match for three others, who were not actuated by any such motives.

The pistol shots were all that he had to dread, and any one who knows anything of fire arms knows how very little, in a struggle, such a weapon is to be at all depended on.

CHAPTER IX.
DOINGS AT THE SALOON.

THE hour is six, and the scene we would present to the reader is a very different one to what we have had occasion to bring under his notice.

Just rid the mind entirely of all that is poor, squalid, or ungraceful, amid the numerous images that the fancy will suggest, and step into an atmosphere of so different a complexion, that while inhaling it, and feasting the eye upon the many charms of art that meet it, one may well, for a time, forget that there is such a thing as misery in the world.

In an apartment of most luxurious proportions and appointments sits one who, by the negligent attitude he assumes upon the silken couch, and his dress of in-door ease, is evidently the temporary or the permanent master of the place.

Rich draperies hang from the windows, shutting out the noisy world and the too glaring light of the day; for although it is long past noon the sun has not yet got below the house tops.

A chandelier, looking as though it were composed of millions of sparkling jewels, depends from the ceiling.

The floor is covered with carpeting, and strewed here and there in apparent confusion, but real taste, are many articles of furniture, contributing to ease and artistic effect.

And all this reflected by mirrors, placed upon every wall, so that to the unpractised eye that apartment might seem of immense extent. He who sat, or rather lolled, upon one of the couches, however, did not cast one glance around him upon the beauty of his house.

A small table, richly inlaid with pearl, was drawn close to him, and upon it was one of those tall-necked bottles that proclaim the vintage of southern Europe.

Occasionally he raised a glass of the sparkling liquid to his lips, and then he would sink back among the luxurious cushions of the couch, and appear to be half asleep.

This was only in appearance, though—the brain of that individual was sufficiently active. Our readers will not believe we are introducing them to any one remarkable for indolence, either mentally or physically, when we announce that the personage surrounded with all this splendour is no other than Captain Macheath! Yes; vulgar robbers retire into caverns and fastnesses deep in the earth when they require repose, or they make a home along with the owl in some dim old ruin.

But Captain Macheath did no such thing.

When he for a short time—sometimes it was for days, and sometimes for weeks—retired from the road, he at once plunged into an elegant line of life that presented for him many opportunities.

Fascinating in his manners—distinguished in his appearance—and with a delightful air of majesty about him, he was just the sort of person to make his way in good society.

The acquaintance of a young nobleman of un-doubted rank, a Lord Glasse, had stood him in good stead as an introduction, and few personages at that time were more popular than the mysteri-ous, handsome, dashing Count Lintledale.

Where he derived his countship from—where were his domains, and what were his resources, were all profound mysteries; but that he had the habits of a gentleman, and that he had resources in abundance, were facts totally evident to all who in any way came in contact with him.

He gambled, intrigued, and rioted with the best of the set, among whom he found a ready-enough welcome; and when in town he was always to be found at Spring Gardens.

He kept but one personal attendant, and that was a young man named William, to whom he, Macheath, had behaved with singular kindness.

William knew who and what his master was, and kept the secret faithfully; attending upon him with all the zeal and devotion as though he had been a veritable count, and his good will was of the greatest importance to him.

The room in which Macheath sat was one of three on the same floor.

One was a reception room, one a bed-room, and one a kind of private apartment—half drawing-room, half boudoir, in which he commonly sat.

That is the room in which we find him.

Macheath touched a small hand-bell of richly wrought silver that lay upon the table, and William in a few moments appeared.

"Well, William," said Macheath, "how goes it with you?"

"Quite well, sir, thank you."

"I'm glad to hear it. Is your mother well?"

"Oh! yes, sir. Thanks to you, the old dame looks younger and more hearty every day. She loves so the little cottage you bought for her; and her prayer each day is that you—"

"There—there—enough, William—enough. If she be happy, and you are pleased, I am quite satisfied."

"But our gratitude—"

"Say no more about it William. How much worse use have I made of many a few hundred pounds than those that gave your mother in her old age a home?"

"Instead of the workhouse, sir," added William, as he wiped a tear from his eye. "And I, too, was quite destitute and could do nothing for her."

"Anybody been, William?"

"A few cards left, sir. Lord Glasse has called here, and offered me a guinea the last time to tell him who you were."

"Ha—ha!"

"And the little marchioness, sir."

"Ah!"

"She came once and told me that she had heard that you were a married man, and had a wife in Hungary—I think she said it was in Hungary."

"That is good," said Captain Macheath. "Who could have imposed upon the marchioness with such a story, I wonder? So those are all the calls, William, that I have been honoured with?"

"All, sir—here is a letter that came to-day."

Captain Macheath opened it and read as follows—

"MY DEAR COUNT,— One of those general enter-tainments at St. James's, at which it is possible to introduce a friend, takes place to night. If you should chance to be in town, I will call at twelve for you.—Yours truly,   "GLASSE."

"To night!" said Macheath. "To-night! Humph! I may be busy. By the-by, William, how are you off for money? You should always speak to me upon that score, as I am apt to forget you.

"You seldom forget me, sir. The last supply was considerable, and I have some of it left, and I have paid up everything, sir. Yet, if I am not to have the pleasure of seeing you for another month, it may be necessary to meet some trades-men's bills; and I know it is your wish that every-thing should be paid the moment the demand is made."

"It is, William. Get change for this hundred pound note, and take of it what you think you will want. Give me back the remainder."

"Yes, sir."

"You feel quite sure, William, that there has been no suspicious inquiries, and that I am by no means in any way confounded with a certain des-perate character called Captain Macheath?"

He smiled as he said this.

"Oh! yes, sir, quite. Who would fancy for a moment that the good Count was anybody but just what he says he is? You may trust to me, sir, to let you know as soon as the least shadow of suspicion arises. We servants are in a position to hear much more than our masters."

"I believe it—I believe it. Go for the change, William; and when you come back, it will be time to light up; I shall remain in to-night until Lord Glasse comes, and then I don't know but I may go to this palace ball."

"I would not, sir."

"Why so, William?"

"Because, sir—it is generally understood that your title is a Hungarian one, and you may meet with some real nobleman of that country, who may, by the officious zeal of some of your friends, be brought to speak to you."

"Well, that would be a little awkward. I will consider of it."

William left the room, and Captain Macheath threw himself back upon the cushions of the couch, and taking from his pocket a small morocco case, he opened it where there were some memoranda.

"Let me see," he said. "What have I in the shape of amusement, now that I am in London for a few days?"

He commenced reading the memoranda.

A French clock upon the chimney piece began to strike.

Macheath counted the silvery sounds.

"Seven o'clock," Macheath said. "So late! Ah! William, so you have returned."

"Sir, as I turned the corner—"

"Yes—yes?"

"The marchioness—"

"Oh! only her? I will see the marchioness."

"Very well, sir."

"Ah! there is a summons at the door. It is, no doubt, the marchioness. I wonder what her servants think of her coming here?"

"They fancy she calls upon the celebrated Court milliner, who occupies a part of the ground floor."

"Grand—grand! If it be her, show her up at once."

"Yes, sir."

William left the room, and as he went down the stairs he muttered to himself—

"I wonder how much of this money he wants back, or if he will forget it altogether? I have known him do such a thing as that before now. How I am grappling money! I shall be rich some day—quite rich, and what care I how it is got? He thinks me quite a pattern of gratitude. Gratitude—ha—ha! I will stick to him as long as he has got plenty of money, but not a minute longer."

Captain Macheath had no suspicion of William. He believed him to be the simple-minded, honest fellow that he appeared.

This was a mistake, indeed!

Macheath should have asked himself what right he had, as a general thing, to find common decency of feeling, common honesty or faith, in human nature more than any one else?

He waited somewhat impatiently for the appearance of the marchioness.

The door of Captain Macheath's room was thrown open, and the well-instructed William merely bowed as he ushered in the lady without announcing her at all by name.

Macheath rose to receive her with a fascinating smile upon his really handsome features.

"It is impossible!" cried the marchioness. "The count in London?"

"To his happiness—yes," replied Macheath. "What could keep him long away from the atmosphere of your presence, lovely marchioness?"

"Ha—ha! Well, that is something new, count. You have managed to survive a month in some totally different atmosphere."

"But I am overjoyed, now that my hour of exile is over, to find I have, while absent, filled so important a place in your ladyship's recollection."

"In my recollection?"

"Yes; else the period would not have been computed so exactly. I have been from London one month to-day, and it has appeared to me an age. You are more beautiful than ever, if that be possible. More fascinating you cannot be!"

"Indeed!"

"Yes. Permit me upon those lips to—"

"Count—count!"

"Marchioness!"

"Well, you certainly are the most impudent, ugly fellow that I have known for a long time past. If I had had the least idea of such rudeness, I should certainly not have come myself with an invitation to a little supper at two this night."

"Two this night? To-night, or rather to-morrow morning, I'm afraid I have to go with Lord Glasse to the palace."

"Well," said the Marchioness, "if you must, and I suppose you must if you have promised poor stupid Glasse, you need only walk through the rooms, and then you can come to my house."

"That I will do, and now that you have honoured me with this visit permit me upon those vermilion twin cherries you have by way of lips to—"

"Count—count! are you quite sure—"

"Of what?"

"That the door may not suddenly open?"

"Quite certain. You are positively radiant with beauty this evening, my charming marchioness. Ah! who is like you? Who, of all the fair beings who flit about the realms of fashion, are to be compared with you? You stand alone, the queen of love—"

"Count—count!"

"Of beauty, of my affections. I seem to you—"

"I have delivered the letter," said William, just popping his head in at the door sufficient to make himself heard.

"Hang you!" said Captain Macheath.

"I said so," screamed the marchioness. "The door was open, and I am ruined."

"Stuff, my dear madam! I—I, upon my word it is very awkward, but someone has come upon business of the very first importance, and I am under the painful and cruel—oh! how cruel!—necessity of seeing him directly."

"Her, you mean."

"No, on my honour. What her in all the world is to be compared with you? No, marchioness; you, and you only, are my heart's idol! Do not fancy you share the throne of my affection with anyone. I have not words to tell you how I love you!"

"Very well. How long will your business occupy you with him?"

"I hardly know."

"Well, be it a long or a short time, I will wait here for you. This is your private room, and I know you will not bring anyone in here who comes upon business, so I will take a glass of wine and look at a book or a newspaper or anything, until you are quite at leisure again, dear count."

"Ah! how good of you, dear marchioness. But it is impossible."

"What is impossible?"

"For you to stay here!"

"Not at all; I have only to will it, and here I am, you see. The impossibility vanishes."

"It seems to do so, and yet remains. I am going to bring my man of business into this room, and where we shall be some time settling our affairs, and you will be so good as to recollect your carriage waits."

The marchioness rose with sparkling eyes and flushed cheeks.

"Very well, you ought to make your lawyer—I suppose it is your lawyer?—"

"Yes—yes."

"You ought to make him come at more reasonable times, count. Since my presence here is such an affliction I will leave you, and I don't think I shall be at home to-night at all, at any hour."

"Very good."

The marchioness bit her lips, and walked to the door.

Then, making a rapid step or two, she opened the door of the reception-room, and, standing in the very centre of it, she saw a female, closely veiled.

"Ha! ha! A female lawyer," she exclaimed. "Count, I have done with you."

"Pooh!"

"Sir, dare you laugh?"

"Aye! dear marchioness, I can't help it," said Captain Macheath. "Have done with me? Impossible! You and I are made for each other, and what fate has done you cannot undo. I will be with you at two, you may depend."

"The doors will be closed against you."

"I will break them open."

"The other guests in my house shall by force, remove you, impertinent villain !"

"I will fight them, and kiss you, my dear marchioness, so don't say another word about it. Good evening. William, see my sister, the marchioness, to her carriage."

"Sister !" screamed the marchioness.

"This way, madam," said William. "This way, if you please."

.   .   .   .   .   .

At that period there was a degree of laxity about the minds of the nobility of this country which, although it may now be as much the case, is certainly more concealed.

People of decent connections, and moving in the first circles of society, do not now boast of their vices and make ornaments of them as they used to do.

It was thought to be so important that monarchy should rally round it as many friends as possible, that some very exceptional characters were at times to be met with in the saloons of St. James's.

Hence, perhaps, it was that Lord Glasse found no difficulty in procuring a card for his friend, the count—a count whom no one knew, and who certainly ought to have been introduced by the ambassador in *charge d'affaires* of the Court from which his countship was derived ; but, as we have remarked, there were circumstances then happening upon the continent of Europe which had given a heavy blow and a great discouragement to courtly etiquette.

Lord Glasse's carriage had some difficulty in wading its way through the crowd of vehicles in St. James's-street ; but at length the old gate of the palace was opened.

A string of yeomen of the guard filled up the entrance, and in the open street was a company of the foot guards.

The martial music of a military band could plainly be heard from the court-yard of the palace now called the colour-court, just within a great gate to the left.

The admission cards of Lord Glasse and Captain Macheath were slightly inspected by a couple of officials from the Lord Chamberlain's office, and they were returned to them to facilitate their re-entrance, should they, in the course of the night, leave the entertainment and wish to return to it again.

After this brief ceremony, they had nothing to do but to pass in through a double row of yeomen of the guard, until they reached the gateway that had been appropriated for the entertainment.

"Now, count," said Glasse, "I shall, of course, be at the marchioness's to night. I suppose if chance should separate us in this throng, as it may very well do, we shall for certain meet there at some hour before daylight ?"

"You may depend upon me," said Macheath. "The marchioness has taken a tiff at me, and let me know that her doors will be closed against me ; so, you see, I am bound in honour under such circumstances to go."

"Indeed? Why, what have you done to her vivacious ladyship ?"

"Nothing particular ; but I shall be at her soiree, and I am very much mistaken if she does not expect me."

"But if she really carries out her sentence of exclusion, and has her saloons denied to you ?"

"Ha ! ha ! that will be rich. I don't intend to take a denial, Glasse ; a pretty woman cannot offend me, so I feel as easy about it as possible. I do not for one moment believe that she wants me to leave her ; but if she did, she would find it about as easy and as complete as shaking off her features."

"You are an odd fellow, count. Do you dance to-night ?"

"Perhaps a little."

"Well, then, I fancy you would just as soon be left to your own resources in the saloons of royalty, as to be clogged with a companion ; so don't mind me. Find what fun you can."

"All of which means," said Captain Macheath, with a smile, "that you have some intrigue or adventure on hand in which you think a companion would be rather troublesome."

"No ; I really protest—"

"Nay ! don't begin protesting, or you will quite convince me of my correctness, my lord. What's the odds, man ? Such things will happen, of course ; so commence yourself, but recollect that some time before the dawn makes the ladies' cheeks look queer you and I meet at the marchioness's ?"

"Be it so."

Captain Macheath's suspicions regarding the wish of Lord Glasse to get rid of him were strictly correct ; but our business is not with the faults or frivolities of Glasse, and we will permit him to go where his pleasure leads him, while we remain by the side of our hero, Captain Macheath.

"I suppose," he said to himself, "as I am here, I may as well dance as not, if I can see any one that my fancy can hit upon. It is always a hard case, in such assemblies as these, to find a natural face. There is always so much frigid artificiality !"

In this humour, Macheath was probably disposed to be over and above critical in his choice of a partner, and, indeed, he took the round of the principal saloon twice without being able to see any one to whom he would take the trouble of offering his hand for the dance.

He knew that some small recesses were set apart for refreshments close to the saloon, and he sought for one of them, feeling a desire for a glass of wine.

He found more trouble—so well concealed were these little alcoves by the heavy and gorgeous hangings of the room—in finding one than he anticipated ; but at length he was successful.

He saw a slight movement of a piece of tapestry, to which a gold cord and a heavy bullion tassel was appended ; and by pulling the tassel he found that the tapestry could be drawn aside sufficiently to allow him to pass from the saloon into a small but exquisitely-furnished room, in the centre of which was a table spread with every luxury that could be procured in the way of fruits, confectionery, and wines.

The room was lighted by several wax lights.

This was the very place Macheath wanted, and pouring himself out a bumper of pure Rhenish wine, he raised it to his lips, and was upon the point of tossing it off, when he was astonished by a long slip of the wainscoat opposite to him suddenly opening like a door.

Some one put one foot into the refreshment-room, and then, apparently seeing him, cried— "Oh !" and immediately disappeared.

The panel was closed again in a moment.

CAPTAIN MACHEATH

THE
PRINCE OF THE HIGHWAY.

"YOU SHALL DIE IF YOU DO NOT FIND ME MEANS OF QUITTING THIS PLACE!"

Captain Macheath's curiosity was very much excited.

But it did not prevent him from drinking the wine that he had at his lips.

Perhaps he drained the goblet a little hastier than he otherwise would have done; but that was all, and then he sprang to the panel and made an effort to open it.

That effort was a vain one.

"Who on earth now could that have been?" he said to himself. "I saw a foot, and it was a man's by the costume. Confound the panel! There must be some means of opening it from this side."

The door—for door it undoubtedly was—was so well-contrived in the wall, that no casual observation could possibly have detected it; it fitted so admirably into the rich mouldings of the highly-wrought wainscoting.

Macheath was not the sort of man to be deterred by difficulties.

He knew that a door was there, and he knew that some mystery was connected with it; so, quite heedless of the danger it might lead him into, or, indeed, which he ought to have thought of, the unjustifiable nature of the intrusion, he used all his endeavours to find out the means of opening it.

Perseverance will do wonders, and Macheath at last found that what fastened the door was a long thin spring piece of steel, painted so exactly like the moulding, and lying so flat upon it, as to utterly defy ordinary detection.

Upon pressing one end of this spring with his thumb, the long panel opened and remained open.

Macheath took one of the candles out of a silver stand, and held it at the opening while he looked carefully through that doorway, the discovery of which had come so unexpectedly upon him.

What he saw beyond was a passage, that did not at the first look very inviting, it was so very black; but as the candle gave a better light he saw that the apparent blackness arose from the walls the floor of the passage being lined with thick, dark-coloured velvet.

He only hesitated a moment, and then, after ascertaining that he could easily open the panel from the passage side he closed it, and heard the spring hold it with a snap.

He kept the light with him, and, let that secret passage in the palace lead to where it might, Macheath's love of adventure made him determined to explore it.

It was well as regarded the secrecy of the proceedings that he did close the panel as quickly as he had, for some parties the moment after came into the refreshment-room, and he could hear them talking.

"Good," he said, "I have got the discovery, such as it is, all to myself, that is quite clear, and all I have to do is to follow my nose and make the most of it."

He held the wax-light so as to diffuse the rays that came from it as much as possible, and at a slow pace he proceeded along the passage, which was not wide enough to allow more than one person traversing it at a time, except they chose to go in Indian file, one treading in another's footsteps.

He took the precaution to count his steps as he went, and he fancied he had gone the length of twenty-two, when something amazingly like the shutting or the opening of a door close at hand struck upon his ears.

Macheath immediately grew apprehensive that the light he carried might, by being seen, materially interfere with his adventure, and without any ceremony he gave it a dab against the velvet wall that immediately extinguished it. He then threw it on the floor.

The moment he had deprived himself of his light, he saw a faint glimmer proceeding from some few paces in front of him, and, guided by it, he cautiously advanced.

If that passage had been laid down and covered with velvet for the purpose of preventing the sound of any footsteps traversing it being heard, certainly the greatest success attended the plan, for Macheath, although he did not take any exceeding pains to produce such an effect, was quite struck by the noiseless character of his own progress.

When he reached the spot from which the light proceeded, he found that it came through the partial opening of a door; but it was so very faint that Macheath could not imagine what species of lamp or candle could send forth so very poor and and sickly a ray.

He soon, however, found from what cause this effect proceeded.

The light that he saw issued from an inner room beyond the one the door of which he found partially open, and from that inner room came the sound of voices.

Impelled by the most irresistible curiosity, the captain glided into the first room.

It was not sufficiently illuminated for him to see accurately what it contained; but from the sparkle of the light from the other apartment upon gildings and rich mirrors, he had no difficulty in persuading himself that it was luxuriously appointed.

Creeping close to the door of the inner room, he was able to hear with tolerable distinctness the conversation that was taking place there.

A female voice broke upon his ear.

"No—no!" she said, "I must and will go. I do not know what spirit of infatuation brought me here to-night."

The tone of agony in which these words were uttered was really so intense that Macheath was painfully affected by them, and he crept close to the door with the hope of seeing through the narrow opening of it who the parties were that consulted in secret converse together.

He found that by pushing the door a little, which he was able to do without the least noise, he could readily open a space wide enough to enable him to see into the room.

It was in more ways than one worth looking into, for it was most splendidly appointed, so much so, that it seemed quite a show; but Captain Macheath was much more interested by the persons in the room than by the room.

One of those persons was a female in man's attire.

An elegant court suit, complete in every appointment, to smart ruffles, wigs, *et cætera*, so metamorphosed her that but for the voice, Macheath himself would have been puzzled to say that she was not what she appeared to be.

This person was leaning upon a table with her face buried in her hands, so that Macheath could not see if she were beautiful.

That this was the person who, by his presence, had been checked in escaping through the refreshment room, was, after what he had heard, sufficiently evident to him.

The figure, in its graceful proportions, looked

promising, and like that of some young girl, rather taller than the ordinary ones of her sex.

After uttering the last few words, which Macheath had overheard she seemed to have completely given herself up to a species of despair, and the very agony of remorse.

The other person in the room was a fat, fair, thick-lipped, sensual-looking lad, for he could not be called a man, and he was little—but only a little —beyond a boy.

He was dressed in full court costume.

"Come—come!" he said. "What's the use of all this? I'm sure, Harriet, I am willing to make you comfortable, if you will make me comfortable, and I don't see why you should not stay in London somewhere, where I can come to see you."

"Peace—peace!"

"Only," continued the fat youth, "I am so watched that I can hardly move but someone is at my elbow, with a 'Can I assist you to anything?' Plague take them all if they would only leave me alone. All I want is to be quite comfortable, and I'm sure if I had as much to eat as I wanted, and as much to drink, and you to see me when I liked, I should be quite comfortable."

"And this," said the female, looking up suddenly with vehemence, so that Captain Macheath saw her face, "and this is the animal for which I have sacrificed fame and friends, and made myself the thing I am? This is the man— no, no, not man!—for whom I have been disgraced and discarded from the Court, which I can only enter in such a disguise as I now wear! Oh! Death, now is the time to come to me, and to be sure that I shall smile upon you and cry welcome."

The fat youth glared at her in dismay.

"Let this farce have an end, sir," she said. "Let this farce have an end. I have done with you, and you with me. I know that at Hesse-Darmstadt I shall still be welcome; but you know as well as I that it is of no use going there without money. I demand the means from you of providing for myself."

The corpulent youth's eyes glared horribly, and his fingers nervously twitched the table-cover.

"I—I haven't got above a hundred pounds in the world," he said.

"A hundred pounds! What, sir, is the use of a paltry hundred pounds to me? I want at least a hundred times that amount, and then you will never hear of me again."

"What! A hundred times that? Why, that comes to—a—hundred—a hundred times is—I don't know how much exactly, but it's a large sum, and where am I to get it, Harriet? I wish you would not make me so uncomfortable. If you will stay now somewhere quite close at hand I could often get you money, and that would be much more comfortable. How hungry I am getting to be sure. Really, I could almost eat anything."

"Hungry?"

"Yes. Surely one can't help feeling hungry, you know. I am almost always hungry. Dr. Blott says that if he could only push half the learning into me as they can get me to eat things, I should be the finest scholar of the age, and the most polished gent in Europe."

"You will always be just what you are," said the lady. "A glutton! stuffed up with unmanly pride and bloated stupidity. Of course, you will find your flatterers—you will find your sycophants, who will fawn upon you, because you are what accident made you; but if ever you come near me

again I will put this sword into your heart, if you have one, which I doubt."

She drew the delicate-looking court sword that she wore from its sheath, and, while her eyes flashed with the fury of a woman who feels all the bitterness of having cast herself away upon a worthless wretch, she advanced a step towards him. He plumped down upon his knees before her, and cried—

"Murder—oh! murder! Harriet, spare my life —oh! spare my life! It is so uncomfortable to die while there is plenty to eat and drink in the world —it is, indeed. Oh! have mercy upon me."

"It would be a mercy to society to make an end of you—but speak! how am I to leave the palace?"

"I—I don't know, Harriet. Can't you try the refreshment-room again? Oh! dear, the thought of a refreshment-room makes me feel worse and worse, and I know there is no end of cheese cakes there, of course. Well, well, don't begin again, and I will get you an order to pass the gentlemen-at-arms, and you can go out by the private staircase, and so on through the main court. I'll go at once. Dear me, how uncomfortable I feel—I haven't felt so decidedly uncomfortable for a long time."

"Go," she said. "Get the order at once or I will kill you. I will wait for you here. You ought to be able to write one."

"Ah! they won't let me do that," said the corpulent youth; "of course, it would be more comfortable for both of us if I could. And so you will go, Harriet? Come, now—"

"The order!" cried the girl stamping her foot passionately. "Obey me at once, or beware of me."

"Well, well," said he, "there's no need to fly into a passion, I'll get the order. Dear me! what a strange creature you are. Why, you used to be so good tempered, but now there is no pleasing you anyhow."

"I was mad," the girl said, bitterly—"I was mad, I tell you"

"Mad! eh? what, mad," cried he; "oh! if I had only known that before—if I had suspected such a thing, I would have kept my distance from you. Why I might have had my eyes scratched out, or —no, Harriet, you are only joking. You can't mean what you say you know."

"By Heaven! you shall die if you do not find me the means of quitting this place"

She advanced sword in hand, and so threateningly that her companion fell back step by step, and finally vanished through a doorway, which Captain Macheath had not observed.

The moment that the corpulent youth was safe out of the room, and the door bolted on the outside he put his mouth to the key hole.

"You don't catch me back again," he said with a chuckle, "and as for getting out of the palace that is your own business. Ha! ha! my lady, you are caught in your own trap."

She flew to the door, but finding that it was fast locked and resisted all her efforts, she sank upon a couch and burst into tears.

Captain Macheath had watched the scene with great curiosity, but while he despised the youth he could not feel much admiration for the lady. And yet he pitied her, so young, so lonely, so helpless, and, yes, because she was so pretty and graceful of figure.

It was not in Macheath's nature to leave a woman in distress, and as soon as the sound of hurried footsteps proclaimed that the personage had taken his departure, the captain walked boldly into the room.

The lady uttered a cry of terror as she beheld him.

"Fear nothing, madam," Captain Macheath said, with a courteous bow. "You require a friend ; and I beg to offer myself in that capacity."

"A friend !" the lady repeated as if she could not believe the evidence of her own ears.

"Yes, madam," Captain Macheath replied smiling. "It appears to me that you wish to leave the palace, and as you seem to be in a strange predicament, I am here to offer you my services."

"Who are you, sir ?" she demanded, hesitatingly.

"What does it matter who I am so long as I protect you ?" said Captain Macheath.

"Ah ! me," the girl cried, pressing her hand to her brow. "I almost fear to trust myself to any one. This place seems to be the abode of villains ?"

"Madam," said Captain Macheath "you use harsh words, and wrong me ; I am no villain. He who has so recently left you might merit the title."

"Forgive me," the lady returned. "I scarcely know what I say or do. If you can aid me to leave this place, I shall ask still one more favour of you."

"Name it," said Captain Macheath.

"That you will forget me and keep the occurrences of the night a secret."

"The secret is safe enough," Macheath replied ; "but when you ask me to forget you, I fear that you ask an impossibility."

The lady bowed to this compliment.

"Lead on, sir," she said. "I will follow you."

Captain Macheath intimated that the outer room was the route which they would have to take, for the only way of getting out was by the secret panel in the refreshment room.

"Let us hasten !" she said, when they entered the outer room, which happened to be clear— "Oh ! let us hasten."

"Certainly," Captain Macheath replied. "I assure you that, save your presence, I have no particular wish to linger here."

Macheath proceeded with caution. He first ascertained that the room into which the secret passage opened was empty, and then turning to the lady he bade her follow him quickly.

"Are you quite sure that there is nobody about ?" she asked, shrinking back.

"As sure as can be," Captain Macheath replied ; "but it would be madness to turn back now, even if there be some trifling risk to run."

He opened the panel as he spoke, and found to his great satisfaction that he was right.

The room was quite vacant.

Both were out of the secret passage in a moment, and the panel swinging back closed with a sharp clicking sound.

"Now," said Captain Macheath, "I will see you safely through the saloon, and then bid you adieu."

"There is not the remotest occasion for that," she replied ; "let us part here, sir."

"If it must be so I bow to your wishes," Captain Macheath replied.

They reached the door of the refreshment room, or rather the velvet curtains which served in lieu of a door, and the full blaze of the magnificently lighted saloon fell upon them.

It was now crowded with numbers of splendidly attired people who were gathered together in little knots as though some more than usually interesting subject was being discussed among them.

The disguised lady slipped from his side in a moment, and he was alone, although in the midst of such a glittering throng.

Presently he saw Lord Glasse approaching with all the haste consistent with his dignity, and that of the place in which he was an honoured guest.

"Why, count," said his lordship, "where have you been hiding yourself for the last hour ? I have been looking for you everywhere. There is quite a commotion in the saloons."

"I am not aware that I need plead guilty to hiding anywhere," Captain Macheath replied ; "but tell me, pray, what all this commotion is about ?"

"Oh ! the most absurd thing in life," Lord Glasse said, laughing ; "a rumour has got about to the effect that the notorious Captain Macheath is in the palace."

Captain Macheath opened a jewelled snuff-box and took a pinch very deliberately.

"Dear me !" he observed, drawling out his words, "you don't say so. How absurd !"

"That is just my idea," said Lord Glasse, speaking in a louder tone as his excitement rose. "Absurd, indeed ! how is it possible. Even with all the fellow's well-known stock of impudence brought into play, how on earth could he find his way into the palace ?"

"Well," said Captain Macheath passing his hand before his mouth to hide a smile, "all I can say is that if he has really gained admittance it must have been through the instrumentality of some fool who did not know his real character."

"Precisely !" Lord Glasse replied, twisting his cravat uneasily. "To think of the rascal gives me a feeling as if I had a rope round my neck. But enough of him. Have you found any amusement, count ?"

"Not the least," Captain Macheath replied ; "the mantle of dullness seems to have fallen upon me to-night, and I care not how soon I leave to go to the marchioness ; but don't let me drag you away, my dear Glasse, for what may appear melancholy to me may have some charms for you."

"Oh ! not at all—not at all," said his lordship." "Ah ! my Lord Stiffleman how are you ? Allow me to introduce my friend Count Lintendale to you."

Captain Macheath and Lord Stiffleman exchanged bows.

"Oh ! by the way," said his lordship, "I suppose you have heard the idiotic report ?"

"What report ?" Macheath demanded.

"Oh ! about Captain Macheath being here," replied Lord Stiffleman. "It seems that in one of the ante-rooms an officer from Bow street was so placed that he could see everybody who passed without being seen himself, and he declares that Captain Macheath, disguised in a magnificent court dress, passed into the saloon."

"Why on earth did he not arrest the fellow ?" Captain Macheath demanded, as he took another pinch of snuff, and then handed the box to Lord Stiffleman.

"Upon my life ! that idea never occurred to me," said Lord Stiffleman, "I'll be off and see about it at once. That is a magnificent snuff box of yours, Count Lintendale."

"A mere trifle !" Captain Macheath returned ; "I picked it up cheap one day."

Lord Stiffleman made his bow, and went off to enquire why the suspected party was not arrested, or at least challenged.

"Well," said Captain Macheath, "I think I will go, my dear Glasse. This is a very slow affair indeed, and the absurd report only adds to the stupidity of the scene. Ah! here comes Lord Stiffleman again and brimming over with news. My lord I guess by your countenance that the fellow is taken—is it not so?"

"No—no," Lord Stiffleman replied, "my countenance is very deceiving. I regret to say that I do not bring the news you desire to hear."

His lordship's countenance had about as much expression as might be found in an apple dumpling.

He went on chattering, presently adding that half-a-dozen of the yeoman of the guard, together with the Bow-street officers were keeping watch behind a screen in one of the ante-rooms.

This was news indeed to Captain Macheath, and important in more ways than one.

It assured him that he was comparatively safe in the saloon, and secondly it warned him against departing by the ordinary route.

Naturally enough he thought of the secret passage again.

Let it lead where it might it could not take him into greater danger than awaited him between the saloon gate and the palace gate.

"Well," said Lord Glasse, "shall we be going. I am entirely in your hands."

"Ah!" Macheath exclaimed suddenly, "who is that lady?"

"Who—who?"

"There—there. The charming creature with the ringlets. Ah! she has disappeared in the throng."

Captain Macheath had wisely indicated a crowded part of the saloon, but as for the charming creature Lord Glasse might well look puzzled, inasmuch as there was no such person.

"I should like to see her," his lordship said, "as I dare say that I could have gained you an introduction. But let us go."

"Nay!" said Captain Macheath, "my heart is enslaved. Bear with me a little longer, for I must catch a sight of that fair face again."

"Ha! ha!" laughed Lord Glasse. "You amuse me. Come then, let us find your beauty in ringlets. Which way did she go, count?"

Lord Glasse slid his arm within Captain Macheath's and they walked together in the direction where the latter had called attention to the visionary charmer.

It was Macheath's intention to part company with his two obliging companions as quickly as possible.

"Do you see her?" Lord Glasse demanded.

"Really, no," the captain replied; "I think she went this way."

He continued to get as near as possible to the refreshment room, and then pausing, he cried—

"She is on the other side. Will you do me the favour of going to look at her, I should like your candid opinion with regard to her beauty."

"Certainly."

Off went Lord Glasse, and Macheath entered the refreshment room.

To his horror Lord Stiffleman was there.

"My lord—my lord!" cried Captain Macheath. "They have caught the rascal, and are calling for you in the ante-room."

"For me? Good gracious! For me? You don't say so."

Away flew Lord Stiffleman, and Captain Macheath, touching a spring in the wall, passed into the secret passage.

CHAPTER X.

OUT OF THE FRYING PAN INTO THE FIRE

THE panel closed with a snap. Captain Macheath drew a long breath,

"Safe at last!" he cried. "Safe from the worst danger of being beleaguered in a crowd. Confound the fellow! What officer can it be who is sufficiently familiar with my features to recognise them in even such an unlikely place as the palace? Well, well, it don't much matter. It will only make him a little more particular in identity another time; for when he finds I don't pass his post again, he will get nothing but derision and incredulity for his pains."

There was nothing to interest Macheath connected with the refreshment room, and he accordingly did not pause for one moment upon the other side the panel; but on he boldly traversed the secret passage until he reached the room through which he had so recently conducted the disguised lady.

The light which had at first attracted him to that apartment was still burning in the inner room; and after listening for a moment or two, Macheath felt convinced it had remained quite vacant as he had left it.

He hoped to get through the door-way by which the corpulent youth had made his escape; and, upon touching it, he was agreeably surprised to find it open; for although there might be other modes of emerging from the other room, yet he, Macheath, could not see any regular door.

He made no doubt but that he was rapidly approaching the private and domestic portions of the old palace.

What might be the difficulties or facilities in the way of his leaving the building by the route he had chosen, was entirely a matter of conjecture.

He was supremely ignorant of the place, and had nothing but chance for his guide.

He only felt he had escaped one danger, even if he fell into another.

But then he was armed, and the stake at issue with him was his life.

If taken, he knew that an ignominious death awaited him; and he felt that he would by far rather die with a good sword in his grasp, than by the rather revolting formalities of law, not one of which would, in his case, be abated.

He loosened the court sword he wore in its sheath, and keeping his pistols ready to his hand, he passed on.

The room in which he found himself was handsome and spacious—if we may except the roof, which was much too low to give anything like dignity to the apartment.

The captain's head only just cleared a chandelier that hung from the ceiling, the glitter of the cut glass of which made it look like a collection of brilliants.

He took the light from the other room with him.

He found he had quite a choice of modes of leaving this room, for there were no less than four doors opening from it.

To hesitate would have answered no purpose at all, so he opened the first that come to hand, and found that it led him to a picture gallery of considerable length, but still low in the roof.

He shaded his lamp with his hand, and glanced around him.

Not a soul was there to impede him or ask him questions, and he strode on, holding the light above his head in such a way as to shed he most diffused rays around it.

He soon came to a staircase, the balustrades of which were richly carved and gilt.

After descending about twelve steps down this staircase, he came upon a landing place where there was a brilliant light and some exquisite statues.

This landing was about twelve feet square; and as there was not much light there, Macheath placed his lamp upon the stairs to relieve himself of it.

From this landing, which, by-the-by, was richly carpeted, several rooms seemed to open, and one of them was ajar.

From that room there came the subdued murmur of conversation; and Macheath with great daring, stepped up to the crevice and peeped in.

A glance showed him the king sitting upon a very low chair or stool, while opposite to him stood a man whose stately bearing proclaimed him as one of the ministers of the state.

"Very well," said the king, rising, "let it be so."

This was all that Macheath heard the king say, and then fully expecting, by the backward movement of the stately individual that the interview was over, and that in another moment he would come out, Macheath recoiled slowly and noiselessly.

At the same time, however, he felt that escape was out of the question, for whether he went upstairs or down it was palpable that he must be seen.

Macheath's quick brain told him all this, and instead of retreating he halted, and assumed an attitude of ease.

The minister of state backed himself out of the royal presence, and on turning round found himself face to face with Captain Macheath, who made him a profound bow.

The bow was returned and the minister in a soft oily voice said—

"Your lordship is in waiting, I suppose?"

"Exactly so," Captain Macheath returned.

They exchanged bows again in the most affable manner.

The minister of state moved away towards the staircase, and Captain Macheath thought he could not do better than keep him company.

At this moment a gentleman usher made his appearance, and regarded Captain Macheath in a dazed and bewildered manner.

"His lordship will leave now," Macheath said, returning the usher's stupid gaze coolly. "The carriage is close at hand, I presume?"

"In the courtyard," replied the bewildered usher. "May I ask who—"

"Pray do not ask any questions," Macheath interposed. "His lordship is in a hurry to depart, and so am I. Lead the way."

The usher, fearing that he had made some terrible mistake in daring to address the handsomely dressed, and evidently illustrious stranger, bowed almost to the ground.

'His majesty seems remarkably well," said Macheath to the minister of state.

"Very," was the reply. "I am glad to say that he is in the best of health."

"Oh! it's all right," thought the usher; "but how he came here without my observing him, and who he is, is a perfect mystery to me Your lordship's carriage waits."

He added these last words aloud as the courtyard was reached, and it was then that Macheath determined upon a bold course of action.

"My lord," he said, "my carriage will not arrive for some hours. If you are going towards Westminster, may I beg the favour of—

"Certainly," said the minister of state; "pray do not name it."

The two footmen touched their hats, and in less than another minute the carriage was speeding rapidly along

"And now," said the minister of state, "I shall be pleased to know you better. Pray introduce yourself."

"Certainly. I am Captain Macheath."

The minister of state slipped off the seat to the floor of the carriage.

"You Captain Macheath?" he gasped. "You the—the notorious—I mean— Good gracious! is it possible that you are the man so much talked about?"

"I am indeed that man," Captain Macheath replied; "and if you give the least alarm I shall be reluctantly compelled to make a vacancy in the ministry. My lord, you perceive that I fully mean what I say?"

Captain Macheath displayed the burnished barrel of one of his silver mounted pistols, and his terrified victim was taken with such a fit of trembling, that Macheath became a little alarmed.

"I must trouble your lordship to take things with a little more fortitude," he said. "You have really nothing to fear from me, providing you consent to make a little sacrifice. Come, my lord, sit up in your proper place."

The minister of state gathered himself up with an effort, and resumed his seat.

"I - I took you for some lord in waiting," he stammered. "Oh! that I had known—"

"Tush!" Captain Macheath interposed. "I was in waiting. I am always waiting for something to turn up. And now, my lord, I will trouble you to make me a present of the few valuables such as I am assured you are possessed of at this moment."

The minister of state groaned as he parted with his watch, money, and jewels.

"Now," said Captain Macheath, smiling, "I will trouble you to put me down."

His lordship pulled the check-string, and as the horses came to a standstill Macheath leaped from the carriage; but before he got twenty paces away, he heard a shout.

"Stop thief—stop thief! A highwayman!"

Turning back, Macheath saw that the minister of state was leaning out of the carriage window and shouting at the top of his voice, and that the two footmen were already in pursuit.

"That's all you get," said Captain Macheath, "for trusting to the generosity or gratitude of one of the aristocracy. If I had only put a couple of bullets through him all would be well enough."

"Stop him!" shouted the foremost of the footmen. "Stop thief—stop thief!"

This footman had in his hand one of those long wands which the fraternity hold in so martial a manner over the roof of a carriage, and Captain Macheath, turning suddenly upon him, caught it from him and with one blow smashed it over his head.

He continued labouring him with it until the other footman came up, who had the fool-hardiness to lay hold of Macheath by the collar, a step which he soon found abundance of reason to repent, for dropping the remainder of the stick with which he had been belabouring the first footman.

AS THE OFFICER FIRED THE LANDLORD—ACCIDENTALLY, OF COURSE—STUMBLED AGAINST HIM.

the captain only paused to be quite certain he had got a good hold of the second one, and then he canted him over his shoulder on to his head, and he lay upon the pavement without sense or motion.

The sudden stoppage of the carriage, however, and the vociferations of the minister of state and his flunkeys had some effect, and the few watchmen who were in the street had taken the alarm, and were hurrying after Macheath as fast as their infirmities would permit them.

"A hundred pounds reward for that fellow!" shouted the minister of state. "It's the notorious Captain Macheath. A hundred pounds reward for the man in the court suit—a hundred pounds!"

The captain's danger was more increased by these words than by anything else.

In the course of five minutes he had about twelve men upon his track.

"Confound the rascals!" he muttered to himself; "if I can but get round some corner, and baffle them for the space of half a minute, all will be right enough."

A corner of a street was close at hand; but just as Captain Macheath got up to it a watchman appeared, and made an attempt to hit him on the head with his bludgeon.

Captain Macheath caught the stick in its descent in the hollow of his hand and wrenched it from the guardian of the night in an instant, and then, before a word could be spoken, it came down upon the watchman's cranium with a loud-sounding crack.

A novel idea flashed into Captain Macheath's brain.

Stooping down, he removed the watchman's coat, and put it on himself, and then thrust the insensible man close against the wall, and in such a position, that he would escape observation.

He then bolted into the watch-box which stood a little way off, rumpled his hair, distorted his features, and was so disguised that his most intimate acquaintance would have failed to recognise him.

Macheath had scarcely time to complete these arrangements.

His pursuers, out of breath and panting, and tumbling over each other, dashed round the corner.

"Has anybody passed this way?" the footman demanded.

"Anybody," growled Captain Macheath. huskily. "What do you mean by anybody?"

"We are looking for a highwayman, and there's a hundred pounds reward for him," cried another.

Macheath shook his head and grinned idiotically.

"He must have passed this way," the footman cried. "He came all the way along here."

"Let me think," said Captain Macheath, scratching his head. "The only person that has been past here was a gentleman in a mighty fine suit of clothes, and a sword by his side. He seemed to be in a great hurry, and ran down Rochester-street."

"That's the man!" they all cried.

And off they went, leaving Captain Macheath to laugh in his sleeve.

The moment they were out of sight Macheath emerged from the box, and approached the watchman, who by this time was returning to consciousness.

Macheath saw that the man was wearing a pair of grey worsted stockings in the form of over-alls, reaching above his knees, and the captain determined not only to borrow them, but the watchman's hat as well.

"My friend," said Macheath, "I will trouble you for those over-alls, and the sooner you take them off the better it will be for you."

"Murder!" yelled the watchman—"Murder! Oh! lor', he is here again."

"Another such cry, and it will be your last!" Macheath hissed, as he presented a pistol at the head of the terrified man.

This kind of argument was irresistible, and the captain was enabled to complete his disguise without delay.

"And now, my friend," said Macheath, "I will trouble you to walk in that box."

The man did not dream of making the slightest resistance, so in he walked.

No sooner had he done this than Macheath whipped the box round, so that the door pressed close to the wall, and then walked away composedly, crying the hour in an assumed tone of voice.

"Past twelve o'clock, and a cloudy morning!" he bellowed out, and then smiled at the ridiculous part he was now acting.

His object now was to change his disguise as quickly as possible, and then to go to the marchioness's assembly.

This he effected in a dark, unfrequented street, and then strode along, humming a merry tune.

CHAPTER XI.

STILL IN A FIX.

"LADIES," the marchioness was saying to her guests, "of course, you have all had lovers; but a young friend of mine lately spoke about a lover that quite surprised me."

"Indeed!" cried several of the beauties.

"Yes, my dear friends," said the marchioness. "It appears that this lady had done her lover the honour of inviting him to an entertainment, but she discovered something that induced her to forbid him the house."

"And very proper, too," said a lady.

"No doubt of that," said another.

"But," continued the marchioness to the admiring throng which pressed closer around her in the hope of hearing some bit of scandal of the most delightful character, "that was not the difficulty, ladies; and what perplexed this young lady was that the wretch said that having an invitation to the entertainment, he would not take a denial, but attend in spite of her."

"In spite of her?" cried several of the ladies, holding up their hands.

"Yes. He said, come he would whether she forbade him or not; and that she had no power to keep him out. Now, ladies, as this young friend of mine is in great distress upon this account; I would fain seek your advice by asking you what she had better do under such ordinary circumstances?"

"Keep him out by all means," said the whole lot.

"Yes, ladies, that is quite agreed; but the means of doing so? That is the question. What would you do, and how far would you go in strong resources, provided he should have come to the door, and made an effort to force his way past the servants?"

"Really, my dear marchioness," said the ugliest

of the party, " I should call upon some gentleman friend to protect me."

" I should give him to the watch," said another.

" And I," said a third, " should stand myself in my hall, with a drawn sword, and run him through, if he persisted in entering the house without my permission."

" But the lady," resumed the marchioness, " has plenty of servants to keep the fellow out, and surely they ought to do it !"

" But what," said Captain Macheath, suddenly making his way into the circle of ladies—" but what, my dear marchioness, if he came down the chimney ?"

The marchioness gave a shriek, and then cried—

" There he is !"

" Ladies," said Macheath, " I hope you are well. Ah ! I need not ask of you such a question ; your blooming cheeks and love charming eyes sufficiently assure me of the fact."

" You monster !" cried the marchioness.

" Monster !" cried all the ladies. " Call the handsome Count Lintendale a monster ? Why, we have been looking for him all the evening. Surely, marchioness, the case was not your own, and you really could not wish to exclude the count ?"

Her ladyship bit her lips with rage, and her eyes flashed as though fire were in them.

" Audacious man !" she said, " how dare you intrude here ? You have suborned my servants ; but not one of them shall remain here another day with me."

" My dear marchioness," said Macheath, " do not blame your servants, and, above all, I beg of you not to make a scene. If you must say something angry to me, let it be elsewhere than here."

" Where, sir ?"

" Oh ! anywhere."

The ladies tittered, and the marchionesss seemed upon the point of fainting.

" Madame," said Captain Macheath, " I said that, in spite of all the impediments you could possibly throw in my way, I would be here to-night, and I have kept my word. Having done so, I am satisfied ; and, if you wish it, I will I will now leave this house at once, and in that case with an equal obstinate adherence to my word, I promise you that its threshold shall never again be crossed by me."

At these words the marchioness turned rather pale. She had wanted to triumph over Captain Macheath, not to lose his society.

" Say the word, madam, and I am gone."

" You deserve that I should say so," the marchioness observed in a low tone of voice. " Your audacity deserves as much."

" I acknowledge it, madam," returned Macheath, bowing.

" Then," said the marchioness, smiling sweetly, " since you confess your faults, I will pardon them."

It was now getting time for the party to be over, and, indeed, a number of the guests of the marchioness had already left.

Macheath was rather surprised at not finding his friend, Glasse, there, and as he thought it would be anything but prudent for him to go home to Spring-gardens, he had no wish to leave the marchioness's house just then.

The guests, however, were going so quickly that it was really a very difficult thing to stay.

After some consideration with himself, he hit upon a mode of proceeding which no one but himself, would for one moment have had the audacity to dream of.

What it was will be speedily seen in its action.

He approached the marchioness, and with much grace of manner, announced that he had come to bid her adieu.

" Allow me to hope," he said, " that I have a full pardon for the past, and that all that I have done may be attributed to its right motive— namely, intense admiration of yourself, without the countenance and acquaintance of whom, believe me, I could not and would not, exist in the world of fashion in London. May I hope for the happiness of seeing you soon ?"

" You may hope."

He then bade adieu to some others of the guests with whom he was personally acquainted, and who were all upon the point of leaving, and then with all the coolness in the world, when he reached the landing, instead of walking downstairs he walked up.

No one noticed this remarkable deviation from the ordinary route upon the part of the Count Lintendale, or if they did they were much too well-bred to take the smallest apparent heed of it.

It was no business of theirs, and in the course of another quarter of an hour the last carriage rolled away from the door of the witty, elegant, beautiful, but not very particular marchioness.

Macheath did not stop till he got to the top of the staircase he was ascending, and then he paused to hear that last guest depart, and to listen to the fastening up of the outer door.

" All is well," he said. " I shall be safer here to-night than at home, and the marchioness will be none the wiser."

Macheath entered a room kept in order for visitors, and it was there he meant to conceal himself and trust to luck to slip out in the morning.

He had not been in the room and closed the door ten minutes, when a maid-servant, carrying a small silver lamp, made her appearance.

She gave a scream and dropped the hand-lamp, and the cry was sufficiently loud to be heard all over the house

Macheath felt that further concealment would be impossible now.

" Jane," he said, " don't you know me—I am Count Lintendale."

" What business have you here ?" demanded Jane, her face flaming with indignation.

" No business at all," Macheath said, abashed, and taken aback. " Your foolish squalling has placed me in a disagreeable fix, so off I must go. Now mind, Jane—and here are a couple of guineas for you—you have seen nobody."

" But—but—"

Captain Macheath did not wait to hear what objections the girl had to keeping his secret, but dashed out of the room without delay and placed himself in an obscure corner of the landing.

In a moment the marchioness came up the stairs. She passed him, and went into the room.

" Jane," she said, " was that you ? What is the matter ?"

" Oh ! madam, I thought I saw—"

" What—what ?"

" A ghost, madam !"

" You are a silly girl. I thought that you were above such folly as that. Really, Jane, I shall have to part with you if anything of this sort happens again."

"I am sorry, madam, but I did think at the moment that I saw something in the room, and I screamed; but if I have frightened your ladyship I am very sorry."

"You have not frightened me, girl; but folly of any kind or description always annoys me. You can go now; I shall not want you any more to-night."

Jane left the room, and as she passed Captain Macheath upon the staircase, she placed her finger upon her lips to intimate that she had said nothing of his presence in the house.

He comprehended in a moment what she meant, and nodded and smiled his thanks.

When she had got down the staircase some distance she beckoned to him, and he crept softly towards her.

"Follow me," she said. "I will let you out."

"Nay Jane, I am decidedly too late to go anywhere else to-night, I must needs stay here."

"But you cannot; it is impossible, I tell you. There is a reason."

"What is it?"

"I beg of you to go. Besides, you will compromise me now by staying, for I told my mistress that I had seen a ghost, and if she should see you now, she will guess that it was you whom I saw, and that I only mentioned a ghost to screen you."

"There may be something in what you say," replied Captain Macheath, "and if anything could induce me to leave at once, it would be that by staying I did any mischief to you. But cannot you conveniently hide me somewhere? I tell you in confidence that I have a particular reason for not going home to-night."

"No—no, I cannot." Come this way at once.

Macheath said no more, but, holding by the balustrade of the staircase, he crept after the waiting-maid into the hall, where a lamp upon a marble slab was still burning, by the light of which he saw the street-door was formidably barred and bolted.

"Now," said the girl, gently, "you must permit me to let you out my own way."

"Pray, what is that?"

"I must not betray to you the secrets of other people," she replied; "and in order that I may not do so you must permit me to blindfold you. And you must give me your word of honour that you will not peep or make any effort to find out the secret?"

"Humph! Cannot you unbolt and unbar a door, Jane, without making all this fuss about it?" queried Captain Macheath.

"The door is securely locked, and the key with my mistress, and no one can get in or out of the house by it without her express permission; but there is a mode of letting you out, if you will agree to the terms."

"Very good; be it so. Only I think you might trust me."

"I dare not."

Captain Macheath was quite curious concerning this mysterious mode of exit from the marchioness's house, and he the more willingly consented to be blindfolded, inasmuch as, whatever it was, he had very little doubt that it would not escape his perception.

Jane placed a handkerchief securely over his eyes, and then turned him round several times, so as to confuse him a little.

Macheath then suddenly found cold air blowing upon his face.

"Lift your feet," she said. "There is a step."

He did so.

"Go on, now—go on."

He half stumbled over some obstruction, and then felt quite confident he was in the open air; but Jane spoke to him again, saying—

"Go on—go on."

He did as he was told, and the result was he rolled down the four stone steps leading up to the door of the marchioness's house.

Fortunately for him, he did not hurt himself to a great extent.

And then, tearing the handkerchief from before his eyes, he found himself in the street.

The door of the house was closed.

Captain Macheath was determined to find out the secret.

But he thought it highly probable that Jane might be on the watch.

So he played her a trick by walking off noisily; after which he tripped back again on his toes, as gently as he could.

All was still in the hall, for he placed his ear quite close to one of the panels of the door, and if anything had been stirring within he must have heard it.

He then set about examining the door.

"Ah! I have it," he said, suddenly. "Of course, one of these long panels is movable, and if I could only find out how it works, I could at any time enter this house."

As he spoke, he tried and pressed the panel in all directions, and suddenly it slipped aside, passing into a recess made for it in the thicker portion of the door.

"That will do," he said, as he closed it carefully again. "Who knows of what use this may be to me?"

"Halloa!" said a watchman, suddenly coming up. "What are you doing there? Cracking a crib, I'll be bound! You must come along o' me, young fellow."

"Hush!" said Captain Macheath- "hush!"

"Eh?"

"Hush! Don't speak so loud. There's something very odd going on in the passage now."

"Is there? In the passage?"

"Very curious indeed! It's in the passage,' said Macheath. "I would not lose it for I don't know how much."

"You don't say so?"

"Hush! Come softly, or else it may leave off. Come very softly, and listen. Hush—hush!"

The watchman crept up the steps as though he were treading upon eggs, and when he got to the door, inclined his head towards it.

Captain Macheath, at the moment that it was about six inches from the panel, gave it such a rap that the skull of the watchman nearly cracked the door.

"There, do you hear it?" said Captain Macheath.

In another moment he was off like a shot, leaving the half-stunned watchman sitting upon the top step, with such a singing in his ears as he had never heard in his whole life before.

Whether he should go home or not was still with Captain Macheath a most doubtful question.

If he could by any possible means have got rid of the Court suit he wore he would not have cared.

But there it was at once as a proof that he was the person who had upset the minister of state, and the captain had no doubt but that there were persons lingering about Charing-cross ready to pounce upon him the moment he should make his appearance.

Still, it was an awkward thing to be kept out all night, and at length he stepped out quickly towards Spring-gardens.

The distance was by no means great, and he was soon at that entrance to the street of his abode which is nearest to Pall-mall.

He was rather surprised to see no one peeping or prying about, and he almost began to think that the affair had been given up as a bad job.

With this idea he went on, step by step, to his own door.

He was, perhaps, not so much upon his guard as he ought to have been, for he was rather taken by surprise when a man rushed out from a deep and dark doorway, crying—

"I have you !" and clutched him by the collar.

"What's the matter?" demanded Captain Macheath.

"Not much ; only you are my prisoner," replied the man.

Macheath gathered all his strength into one effort, and fairly lifting his opponent from the ground, he held him for a moment in the air.

"Murder ! Let me go !" said the man. "Help —murder !"

"Once—twice—thrice," cried Captain Macheath.

And then away went the man over the rails of a neighbouring house, and down the area with a crash.

Captain Macheath did not wait one moment then to see what was the result of this affair ; but dashing on to his own house, he took a key from his pocket, and opened the street door.

He had it still in his hand when he saw four men coming from some hiding-place over the way at full speed, crying as they ran—

"That's our man—that's our man ! We have him now ! That's the fellow !"

"You don't say so," said Captain Macheath, as he slammed the door shut in time to exclude them.

It was a massive door, and although they all four made a rush at it with the hope that it would give way, it remained firm as a rock, and they only got some bruises for their pains.

To bar the door, and to secure it with a chain was but the work of a moment, and Captain Macheath leaving the officers to batter at the panels with their feet and fists made his way upstairs.

"Is that you, sir?" demanded his servant William, meeting him on the top stair with a light in his hand.

"Yes, William."

"What a dreadful knocking, sir ?"

"Yes," Captain Macheath replied, "there are some unfortunate friends of mine at the door, that's all. You may admit them in a few minutes, but mind that Count Lintendale has not come home yet. Give me the blue bag, that is hanging behind my bed-room door."

William did as he was told, and Captain Macheath continued his ascent upstairs without the slightest appearance of hurry, though the noise at the door continued.

The blue bag contained a complete change of clothes, and Macheath soon changed his Court dress for one suitable for riding.

Opening a trunk, he produced a rope ladder, and securing it to the window-sill went down hand over hand, and was soon standing in the back yard.

Climbing a wall he dropped into a narrow lane, and then with the din at the door still ringing in his ears walked leisurely along until he entered St. James's Park.

Here he was comparatively safe, for the night was very dark, and Macheath knew full well that even if there should be a few homeless wretches about they would not care to interfere with him, armed with sword and pistols as he was.

Captain Macheath had made up his mind what to do.

Reaching Whitehall he walked up the Strand until he came to Wych-street, and, striking up a narrow turning, entered Clare-market, and turned into a public-house known as the Black Jack.

This hostelrie was squeezed into a corner of a street, and seemed as if it shrank from the rest of the buildings, as if fully aware of its doubtful reputation.

Captain Macheath was well known at the Black Jack.

The landlord grinned and pulled a lock of his hair, and his plump, good-looking wife smiled and courtesied graciously.

Captain Macheath took a glass of wine from the landlord's hand and quaffed it at a draught.

"Has Peacham been here?" he demanded.

"Not only been here, but you will find him in the kitchen now," the landlord replied.

"Good," said Captain Macheath. "I want to speak to him."

Passing out of the bar and down a long passage illuminated by a single candle stuck into an iron socket, the captain came to a door.

As he pushed it open he was confronted by a strange-looking young man, with closely-cropped hair, hungry-looking eyes, a small turned-up nose, and a straight, artful-looking mouth.

"What, is it you, Mat o' the Mint ?" demanded Captain Macheath.

"It's as much of me as the traps have left," Mat o' the Mint returned, with a leer ; "and I thought they had come for me again."

"They won't venture here, I think" said Captain Macheath, as he peered through the clouds of tobacco smoke, and at the faces of a number of men seated round a table. "Oh ! there's Peacham. Peacham, old fellow, you are the very man I am in quest of."

Peacham, a middle-aged man, dressed in a snuff-coloured suit with wig to match, rose to his feet, and without taking the pipe from his mouth, slouched solemnly across the room until he stood face to face with Captain Macheath.

"Hullo, boy !" said Peachum, as his hard, rugged features relapsed into a smile. "Glad to see you again. I am at your service. What ca— I do for you ?"

"Look here, Peachum," Captain Macheath said, "I am in a bit of a fix. I have often done you a good turn, and I want you to do me one."

"What is it ?" Peachum demanded, thrusting his hand into a capacious pocket.

"No—no !" said Macheath. "It is not money I require, but shelter for a little time. Take me home with you. How is your wife, and how fares the lovely Polly ?"

"One thing at a time," Peachum observed. "Home you shall come with me, and welcome. I'll not charge you much for the accommodation, lad ; but you see I am a man of business, and my game is to make money."

"Of course it is," Captain Macheath assented. "We shall not fall out on that score."

"Well then, I am at your service. We will start at once if you like,"

"But you forgot to tell me about Polly," said Captain Macheath. "It seems an age since I saw her."

"Polly is very well," Peachum replied, rubbing his stubbly chin thoughtfully; "she has more lovers than I can count on my fingers, but I'll not have her marry one of the fellows who comes to my place. She is too good for that—much too good for that."

"There I agree with you," said Captain Macheath, as something like a sigh escaped his lips. "Let us go, Peachum; I have had a hard day's work, and am weary of it all. Sometimes I think I am weary of my life."

"Bah!" sneered Peachum. "That is the way with you all, when hot pressed or down on your luck. Come," he added fixing a three cornered hat on his head, "I am ready."

Peachum's house was not far away from the Black Jack, and Captain Macheath soon found himself before a well spread table.

Of Polly he saw nothing, but thought it better to make no further enquiries for her.

At last he expressed a wish to retire, and Peachum, taking up a lamp, led the way to an oddly shaped little room at the top of the house.

"You will be safe here, my boy," he said. "No one will interfere with you. Good-night, or, rather, Good-morning."

When Captain Macheath was left alone he sat down and fell into a reverie. It was almost daylight when he cast himself on the bed without removing his attire, but he did not sleep long.

It appeared to him that people were continually entering and leaving the house, and at last he rose, dashed some cold water over his face, and walked out upon a landing.

He had scarcely done so when a door opened, and Polly Peachum, a charming girl of about eighteen years of age, very neatly and prettily dressed, appeared.

She uttered a faint scream and started back as she saw Captain Macheath standing there.

"What is the matter, Polly?" he asked. "Do you not know me?"

"Captain Macheath!"

"Yes, Polly; the man who has sworn to love you, and who does love you with his whole heart."

"No—oh! no," Polly almost moaned, as she covered her face with her hands. "It must not be—it cannot be! You do not know the danger you are in. Away to your own quarters, and never come back. Forget me. Nay, do not reproach me. I command you to leave this house."

"Polly," Captain Macheath returned, reproachfully, "I do not know what to understand by this great change in you. But I will obey you, and in an hour I shall either be a dead man, or lodged in Newgate. What danger am I in—what danger have I to fear?"

"Danger from my father," Polly replied. "He is eager for your capture; he thirsts for the reward offered for you. His is a horrible baseness. He uses men for his own profit, and when tired of them hands them over to justice."

"But he has not grown tired of me," said Macheath; "for I am not one of his very particular friends."

"I don't know—I cannot tell," sobbed Polly. "For all I know he may be on his way at this moment to inform the officers that you are here."

"The miserable fence—the traitor!" muttered Macheath, under his breath.

His countenance grew dark; but it soon cleared again.

"The house is quiet," he said, "and at least I can get away."

"Stay," Polly said; "you must leave all to me now."

She ran downstairs and Captain Macheath presently heard a sound convincing him that Polly Peachum was locking and bolting up the doors.

In a few minutes she returned to him, and with a face so white and scared that Macheath felt quite alarmed.

"It is as I thought," Polly said. "There is nobody in the house except you and I, and my mother. My father—"

She ceased speaking, for at that moment a sharp knocking come at the street door.

"Again!" Captain Macheath said, smiling grimly. "My enemies have scarcely done knocking at my own door, than they come to this. Polly, I must go, let the risk be what it may. Here I am, like a rat in a trap."

"Hold!" Polly cried. "Come in here."

She dragged him into her room, and closing the door spread her hands across it as if that frail defence would avail against Macheath's enemies.

"Oh! what shall I do!" she cried. "When you first came here I did not believe you to be like the rest, and I will not believe it now. Speak again. Are you guiltless of bloodshed?"

"No!" Captain Macheath replied; "I have killed men, but only when fully aware that it was a question of my life or theirs. For the value of what could be got by my destruction, I have been attacked and I have defended myself."

"And that is all?"

"It is all, Polly," Captain Macheath replied, earnestly. "I have many a time spared those who would not have spared me, and when I saw a road to safety open without a deed of violence, I always took it."

"And yet you are Captain Macheath, a highwayman?"

She clasped her hands and uttered a low, wailing cry.

Then, bending upon him a look of inexpressible tenderness, mingled with woe, she said—

"I have heard much of you, and the worst I have heard of you is that you have a hollow heart—that you glory in lighting up the flame of affection in some pure and gentle bosom, which you afterwards leave to disappointment and despair."

"No—no—no."

"You—you love me, then? Oh! no—no. You are what you are, and there is a gulf between us which I will not, or dare not, cross. Oh! go, sir—go, sir," Polly entreated.

"To my death? Yes."

"No—no. I had forgotten; but what can I do—a poor, weak, and helpless girl? Tell me what I can do to save you? Alas—alas! I am bitterly helpless!"

"Hark! The knocking ceases. The outer door is opened, Polly, and those who have come in will not be content unless they search the whole house. It is here, and here only that I must hide. Run down and open the door now."

As he spoke he approached the bed, which was a very large and well-filled one, and to the amazement of Polly, he got fairly under it, between

CAPTAIN MACHEATH

THE
PRINCE OF THE HIGHWAY.

THE MAN WITH THE PITCHFORK MADE A SAVAGE THRUST AT THE HORSE.

the feather bed and the mattress, and by dint of pushing the feathers about he left the surface very little disturbed, notwithstanding he was quite beneath it.

"Polly," he said, peeping out of the little breathing place he had left near the bolster, "remember that everything depends upon your calmness."

Polly Peachum made no reply but ran downstairs, and admitted her father and three men.

"How now, wench?" Peachum cried. "Who locked this door?"

"I did."

"Why?"

"Because when I came down and found the house deserted, I grew frightened for fear that thieves might get in," Polly replied.

"Humph!" Peachum growled. "I suppose you did not let anybody out before you locked up?"

"Yes, father. A gentleman who said he came last night, and finding you out now, was going to look for you."

"Fool!" hissed Peachum. "Well—well! Away with you, Polly. Gentlemen," he added, turning to the constables, "I regret to inform you that the bird has flown."

"Flown?"

"Yes; my innocent daughter let him out."

"In that case he cannot be far away?"

"No," Peachum replied; "I will go with you and point him out, but—but I don't want to appear as a witness."

"No need for that," said a constable; "all we want to do is to get hold of him, and we will supply plenty of evidence. Now, then, if we expect to catch him it's time we started."

Away they all went, and Polly, who had been listening at the top of the landing, uttered a cry of delight.

Captain Macheath knew what that cry meant and crawled out of his hiding-place.

"I was nearly suffocated," he said, laughing, "which way did they go, Polly?"

"Towards the City."

"Ha! What is that?"

"My mother is getting up. I can hear her moving about."

"Then it is time that I was off," said Macheath. "Give me a kiss, Polly; you shall hear from me soon. I am going back to my old lodgings for a few minutes, as the officers have evidently lost scent there. I can plainly see that there is no rest for me just yet."

Polly Peachum did not object to be kissed, but it was a great relief to her in one sense when she saw Macheath speeding away.

Captain Macheath reached his lodgings unmolested, and at once summoned his servant.

"I am tired of London, William," Macheath said, "and shall be off for a week or two to the country. You will keep everything in order while I am away?"

"Yes, sir."

"And you will write to me to the post-office at Hounslow as usual, letting me know what is taking place here?"

"Certainly, sir."

Captain Macheath by this time had put on a pair of white pantaloons, horseman's boots, a waistcoat of plum-coloured satin, and a scarlet coat.

"Now, William," he said, as he went to the door. "I shall, as usual, leave you in full charge and authority here, depending entirely upon your vigilance and sagacity."

"You shall not be disappointed, sir. At what time may I hope to have the pleasure of seeing you return here?"

"When I am least expected," said Captain Macheath, and in another moment he was gone.

"So," said William, when he was alone—"so, he will come back when he is least expected? I could have told him that. He always does. Well, I am of course faithful to him. Why, I gain more by being faithful to him in one month than I could sell him for, out and out. No—no! I don't kill my goose that lays me the golden eggs; but when I take it in my head to retire, I may as well do so with a few hundred guineas as not; and then, Captain Macheath, look out."

The look of diabolical hatred upon the man's face would have been amply sufficient to warn Captain Macheath of his danger in that quarter, if he had chanced to see it.

But he did not.

He was on his route to the stable, where he had left his trusty steed, which was now ripe and ready for the road.

Upon reaching the street, Macheath, of course, kept his eyes open; but only one old man, skulking about the corner of Spring Gardens, met his gaze.

Although Captain Macheath's costume, as we have cursorily described it, would soon have got a mob about him in these days, it was then nothing more than a smart style of dress affected by young men of fashion.

Macheath, therefore, neither expected nor met with any interruption on the score of his costume.

He walked rapidly on until he reached the stables, where he had put up his horse, and, although the hour was a very early one indeed, his summons at the ostler's bell was quickly enough replied to.

A boy with a profusion of red hair opened a small wicket in the gate.

"All right, Mike!" said Macheath. "I see you are determined to earn a guinea this morning by bringing me out my horse."

The boy's eyes brightened at these words.

Without wasting time by a word off he went, and in an incredibly short space of time Captain Macheath's gallant steed made its appearance.

At the sound of his voice, as he addressed some kind words to it, the creature rubbed its head upon his breast, and showed the most marked signs of attachment to him.

"He knows his master," said the boy, "as well as I shall know a guinea when I see one."

Captain Macheath smiled as he tossed the boy the coin.

"I should not have forgotten my promise," he said. "Good-bye, Mike."

The boy touched the front portion of his hair, and in another moment Macheath was off.

CHAPTER XII.

THE SCRIMMAGE ON HOUNSLOW HEATH.

"To Hounslow Heath," said Captain Macheath, as he turned his horse's head westward. "A sharp canter in the cool morning air will not do me or you any harm."

He patted the horse's neck as he spoke, and then putting the creature to the pace he wished, away they went at a good ten miles an hour from the city of smoke and disorder. It was not long ere the fresh pure air of the open country had its effect upon the senses of both horse and rider.

After a ride of six miles Macheath found himself upon an eminence, commanding an extensive view around him.

To his right lay Hounslow Heath, with its dark patches of verdure; and to his left was a village, the faint blue smoke from the cottage chimneys tinting the fresh morning air.

The distant bark of a watch-dog and now and then a faint tinkling of a sheep-bell were the only sounds that disturbed the blissful calm.

Macheath allowed the horse to crop the sweet, soft herbage at his feet, and, in good truth, the captain could have lingered there for hours, watching the beautiful scene, had he not felt that it was not in his vocation to be such an idler, and that safety for him could only lie now in deeds of daring, and activity of spirit.

His path in life was chosen; and being so, he felt that pursue it he must, let it lead where it might.

With a start he awoke from a kind of reverie into which he had fallen, and that start aroused his horse, too.

"Hurrah for the road !" he cried. "Hurrah for the road, and no skulking ! What I am thinking of ?—Of turning hermit, and forswearing the world ? Ha! ha! No—no, Captain Macheath, your time has not yet come for any such fancies."

He cantered down the further side of the little hill, and made direct for the village of Hounslow, which was close at hand.

He only paused as he rode through to say something to the keeper of the little post-office; and from the manner of the woman whom he addressed as she looked out of the window, it was tolerably clear that she knew who it was.

She called him captain, and promised to attend to his letters.

"Good-bye !" he said, as he waved his hand. "I shall not forget you when good things are going."

The post-mistress nodded, and shut the window.

"She must have the first pretty-looking trinket," said Macheath to himself, "that falls in my way; for I am really much indebted to her for her care of my letters, and I suppose for not, when I come for them, screaming out, this is Captain Macheath."

Another mile of road brought him to a very old dilapidated-looking road-side inn, called the Crown.

The roof of this ancient inn contained a world of red tiles.

The door was a study for an antiquary, and a huge chestnut-tree growing against one corner of the house seemed to be, as in all likelihood it really was, its principal support.

Macheath dismounted at the door of this place with all the ease as though it were his own house.

"Turn the horse into the paddock, Jack," he said to a man who made his appearance in a lounging manner from the stables; "I shall stay three or four hours."

"Yes, captain," was the reply. "Nothing amiss, I hope, captain ?"

"No, thank you. All is well ; but I am sleepy, that's all. Is Thompson about ? I want a bit of breakfast."

"All ready, sir; you'll find master in the bar parlour. Ah! here he is."

At this moment a jolly-looking personage made his appearance at the door of the hostel, munching a new roll—

"Ah! captain; who'd ha'thought of seeing you this morning ?" he cried.

"Is there anything extraordinary in a man coming to a place where he knows he will get a good breakfast ?" said Captain Macheath ; "have you got room for one ?"

"To be sure, captain—of course we have," Thompson replied. "Come in. But I thought you were down west a long way ?"

"Not I. I have been in London a few days, and got heartily tired of it, as usual. No news stirring, I suppose, in this neighbourhood ?"

"Not a word, captain ; except that Captain Macheath has found Hounslow Heath too dangerous a spot now, and has gone far abroad.

"You don't say so ?"

Both Macheath and the landlord indulged in a hearty laugh as they together crossed the threshold of the Crown.

In the bar-parlour of the house there was about as ample and substantial a country breakfast laid as any man—or a dozen of men— could well have desired.

A huge round of beef made the table groan at one corner. At another there was a ham ; and a basket of fresh boiled eggs. There was tea, and coffee ; but the host of the Crown had a large silver tankard of ale by his side.

The milder infusions and decoctions were for his wife and three buxom daughters. Some perfectly astounding loaves of brown bread and a large platter of cream-cheese completed the table arrangements.

"Are they all well ?" said Macheath.

"Oh ! yes, all but Netty. She's rather off her feed, I think."

"That's your eldest ?"

"Yes, and here she comes. Well, my lass. Here's the captain. How are you this morning ?"

"Better, father," said Netty. "How are you, captain ? Have you brought me the earrings you promised me some time ago ? You can't think how delicate I've got lately ; father, cut us a round off the beef, I don't think I can take much more than that this morning."

"You will be able, perhaps," said Captain Macheath, "to subsist until your appetite comes back to you ?"

"Yes," said Netty, quite gravely, and not seeing in the least that Macheath was having a laugh to himself at her expense.

Louise and Sue, the other daughters, and the landlady presently made their appearance.

"Come, my loves," said the mother, "attend to the captain—you know what a little eater he is, and what a deal of encouragement he wants to get him to take anything."

"I am really so afflicted," said Captain Macheath, "to see Netty not taking anything ; I am certain she has not had yet above a pound of beef and half a loaf."

"I have had a trifle," said Netty, in rather a languid tone.

"You are in a very poor way, Netty, and, really, if you don't eat, you will fall ill," observed the captain, gravely.

Captain Macheath breakfasted well and heartily with this amiable family, and at the conclusion of the repast presented the delicate Netty with a pair of earrings, much to the girl's delight.

Macheath then informed the landlord that he would be glad of a couple of hours' rest.

He was shown to a room, the windows of which be darkened by closing the shutters, and then, pulling off his coat and boots, he lay down and dropped off into a sound repose.

It was one o'clock in the day when Captain Macheath felt some one shaking him by the shoulder, and upon looking up found it was Thompson the landlord.

"Anything amiss?" he said.

"No. Not that I know of," replied Thompson. "There are two men below that seem rather inclined to stay. They came well-mounted, and their horses are in the stable. I thought they looked curiously at your horse, for he was having a rub down after being tired of the paddock. Will you get up and have a look at them?"

"I will at once."

Captain Macheath's toilette was soon made.

A sluice of cold water over his face and head, and his boots and coat put on, was all that he required, and then he followed the landlord downstairs.

Thompson told him as they went that the two men were in the coffee-room, and Captain Macheath, without any ceremony, walked in.

The two strangers started at his appearance, and exchanged significant glances with each other.

"A nice day, gentlemen!" said Macheath.

"Very, sir," said one.

Macheath bowed slightly.

"I shall perhaps have the pleasure of seeing you again!" he said, as he left the room.

The moment he reached the bar-parlour again Thompson eagerly asked him if he knew them.

"Not personally," replied Captain Macheath; "but that they are after me I don't entertain a doubt for a moment. I will go now, not upon their account, but because I intended to go at any rate. Let me have my horse."

At this moment the coffee-room bell rang smartly, and when Thompson returned from answering it, he said—

"They have ordered their horses."

"Good," said Captain Macheath. "You can let me have mine first, and then you can serve them as soon as you like."

"Won't I," said the landlord, "and if they find their girths all right after a gallop across the heath my name is not Thompson, and I have not got one of the loveliest young families in the country. Ah! captain, what a wife Netty would make."

"Yes," said Captain Macheath, "especially if you happened to run short of provisions. I should expect her to eat me by dinner-time, if the breakfast was not a tolerably ample meal. But the horse, Thompson, the horse, if you please."

"All right," said Thompson.

The landlord left the bar-parlour to expedite the getting ready of the captain's horse, and he had hardly been gone a moment, when both the strange men came out of the coffee-room.

They glanced around them, and seeing Macheath, the taller of the two came up to him.

"Are the roads safe, my friend?" he demanded.

"No," replied Captain Macheath.

"No? Indeed, you don't say so. Why, are there any highwaymen about these parts?"

"Oh!" said Macheath, "you need not be particular as to any highwaymen being about. There are plenty of thieves of all sorts to be met with as well as those on the road."

As he spoke he made a dart out of the house, for he heard the tramp of his horse in front of the old inn.

"Stop—stop!" said the man who had spoken to him; "I only want to speak to you a moment."

"I am busy, and can't wait," said Captain Macheath.

"Then you shall; for if you don't stop, I'll send a bullet through your skull."

The man, followed closely by his companion, rushed to the door after Macheath as he uttered this threat; but the captain had reached his horse, and placing his left hand upon the pummel, he was in the saddle in a moment, and the bridle firmly in his hand.

"Blaze away!" he said.

Bang went the pistol; but at the moment it was fired, the landlord had—quite accidentally, of course—ran up violently against the man who fired it, and away went a pair of bullets about twelve feet above Captain Macheath's head.

"Hark ye," said Macheath, "I don't want to make a disturbance outside an honest man's door, so as to bring disrepute upon him; but if you have the pluck to do it, follow me. I will wait for you a couple of miles or so down the road."

With these words he gave his horse a touch with his right heel, and away he went like the wind.

"Our horses!" cried the two men—"our horses! Get us out our horses directly! Confound you! landlord, for a fool or a rogue. Don't you know that that is Captain Macheath, the great highwayman, and he will escape us yet if we are not upon his track in a moment?"

"Lor'!" exclaimed Thompson, "you don't say so, gentlemen? Oh! it's enough to one feel ill to think that the notorious Captain Macheath has been in one's house, and one has not nabbed him. Cut away after him as quick as you can. Didn't you hear him say he'd wait for you?"

"He wait for us?" said one of the officers. "I think I see him doing it! A highwayman wait for a couple of officers—I think I see him doing such a thing! No—no. We may catch him yet by raising the country after him; but with all his bounce he knows a trick worth two of waiting for us. Why the deuce don't you get us our horses?"

"They are here, gentlemen—they are here. It's all right; I only wish you may catch him, that's all."

"I strongly suspect you," said the officer, who had not yet spoken, "of being his accomplice."

"Me—me?"

"You—you! He has been here for some time, and was evidently on capital terms with you and your family."

"Of course; but how was I to know he was Captain Macheath, the highwayman? I always thought he was a traveller in the hardware line," Thompson gasped. "I can't tell who's who when they come to my house. You may be the greatest rogue in the world, for all I know; and though you are both so bold-looking, you may be all of a shiver of fear in case Captain Macheath should be waiting for you a couple of miles away, as he said he would. I know I should. Why, I wouldn't be in your shoes for all the money in the world!"

The two officers cut Thompson's speech short by mounting their horses and taking to the road after Captain Macheath, who, by this time, at the rate he travelled at, must have been considerably in advance of them, and in a condition completely to give them the slip if he felt so inclined.

After the captain had ridden about a mile, he stopped to have a laugh at his adventure at the inn, and to give his horse a rest after the sharp gallop.

"It was absurd enough," he said, "Thompson running against that fellow just as he was on the point of firing at me. Well, it may have saved me, though these fellows are generously slovenly shots."

The manner in which Macheath examined his pistols showed, however, that if the two officers did venture after him, he did not wish to be trifled with, and that it would be at the risk of their lives.

He never for one moment thought of breaking his word, although he had from his experience of similar adventures, the greatest doubts as to whether they would follow him at all.

He was aware that the next mile would bring him to a barren bit of country, where there were very few houses; but he knew that in more than one of those houses he could find not only a shelter but a welcome.

With a wise forethought he had made earnest friends with the poor occupiers of many a lone cottage around the suburbs of London.

They had felt what it was to have a generous friend in the hour of distress, and Macheath had, as regarded his money, often verified the old proverb of "Lightly come, lightly go."

As he had mentioned a couple of miles or so, he rattled on until he came to the barren spot where, amid the heath, only now and then the gable-end of a cottage was to be seen.

There he waited for whatever adventure it might please fate to send him.

He kept a wary eye upon the road to London, for there was just a possibility of the officers coming, and that was all.

He had waited many minutes in this place, so full of beauty, barren as it was, before he heard the sound of a horse's hoofs upon the heath; but it came from the opposite direction to that in which he expected the officers.

As he looked anxiously to see who was approaching, he was rather surprised to observe a young girl of about fifteen or sixteen years of age, attired in a handsome riding-habit, and mounted upon a small chestnut pony, emerge from a lane.

The flush of youth and beauty was upon her face; but a glance at the pony was sufficient to show Captain Macheath that it had had a hard gallop.

The creature was panting, and the foam was hanging to the bit, while its reeking sides testified likewise to the violent character of the exercise it had taken.

When he looked again, Macheath could not but see that there was an appearance of alarm upon the countenance of the young lady; and he at once came to a correct conclusion upon the subject—namely, that the pony had run away with her.

With all that easy grace of manner that he found rarely failed to be for him a sufficient introduction to any one, Captain Macheath approached the fair stranger.

"Can I be of any service to you?" he asked, bowing.

"I know not, sir," she replied; "but I have certainly lost my friends. Something came over my usually quiet little pony, and at a headlong speed I have been brought here."

"I guessed as much," said Captain Macheath. "Permit me to escort you back. The roads are not particularly safe just now. If you will tell me in which direction your home lies, I will do myself the pleasure of acting the part of an escort to you."

"I am truly obliged, sir," she said. "I am the daughter of Sir Henry Hollebrook, and my home is at Hollebrook Lodge, which should not be very far from here."

"I know it well," replied Macheath. "It is only a sharp trot of some few minutes."

"Indeed! I am truly much beholden to you, sir; but my father will be able to thank you better than I can."

While this conversation was going on, Captain Macheath had quite forgotten the fact that the two officers might be coming after him, and that a rather disagreeable encounter might possibly take place in the presence of the young lady.

That all this was really to be expected was soon rendered sufficiently manifest by the appearance some distance off of the two officers and a farmer-looking man on horseback, whom they had met upon the road, and tempted to accompany them by the promise of a handsome reward for so doing, provided the whole three should succeed in capturing the renowned Captain Macheath.

They all three evidently hung back, and as the captain saw that such was the case, he resolved to make an attempt to free himself from the encumbrance of their presence.

"I am truly glad," he said to the young lady, "that I am with you; for to the best of my belief those fellows are no better than highwaymen."

"Highwaymen!" exclaimed the young lady. "I was told that the well-known Captain Macheath kept this road all to himself."

"And I, too, have heard the same; but there will be interlopers and trespassers upon everybody's manor house. Have you anything of importance that you would regret to lose?"

"I have a watch that was my mother's, and I would not willingly part with it. It is of considerable value, too."

"Then you shall not part with it," said Captain Macheath. "I will soon disperse those fellows for you. Do not stir from where you are, and you will see what real cowards these kind of men are."

As he spoke he turned his horse's head in the direction of his foes, and approached them at a gallop.

Of course, such a proceeding, of all others, was calculated to astonish the officers, who fully expected that, if he galloped at all, it would naturally be in the opposite direction. The farmer-looking individual was seized with a panic, and at once rode off as hard as he could make his nag set foot to the ground, so that the two officers were alone.

CHAPTER XIII.

CAPTAIN MACHEATH IN GOOD SOCIETY.

MACHEATH did not pause in his career until he got close up to the officers, and then, drawing a pistol from one of the holsters of his saddle, he cried—

"I will soon rid the world of you two. You shall have my life, or I shall have yours."

Bang went the pistol; but he purposely missed the man he fired at.

The words he spoke, and the daring of the whole affair, combined with the discharge of a pistol, had such an effect upon the spirits of the officers, that they turned, and, setting spurs to their horses, galloped off down the road.

Macheath pursued them for some short distance, and fired another pistol at them, which had the effect of adding wings to their flight; and then the captain quietly trotted back to the young lady.

If she had not seen the whole affair with her own eyes, she might well have doubted that one man, be he ever so bold and resolute, could strike terror into three stalwart men.

But such things are of much more frequent occurrence than generally supposed.

The courage of a man depends almost solely upon what he is fighting for.

He who engages in a contest merely for money, does so with a widely different feeling to him who feels that his life is dependent upon the issue.

Such a man as Captain Macheath had everything to fight for; while those who, in most cases, sought his capture, had only the prospect of the acquiring of a few pounds to urge them on.

"This is an exploit, indeed," said the young lady, when the captain returned to her. "You are as redoubtable as any knight of old in romance."

The paleness of her face, and the slight quiver of her lip, showed that, notwithstanding the light manner she spoke of the affair, she had been very much frightened at the encounter.

"It would have been the delight as well as the duty of any knight to have protected you," the captain replied.

"You did not kill either of them?"

"No, nor wound them either. I have the greatest repugnance to shedding even bad blood. I fired twice at them, but I purposely missed them."

"You are in the army, I presume, sir?"

"Yes, in the King's Guards; but this is not my uniform exactly. This is my fancy merely to dress in such a way when I am on the road; and now, if you will trust yourself to my guidance, I will take you in safety to Hollebrook Lodge."

"With pleasure," replied the young lady. "I shall at least feel I am safe from highwaymen."

"That you shall be truly; and yet, it is a strange thing, but I was actually robbed yesterday upon this very heath."

"You robbed?"

"Yes; strange as you may think it. I was taken unawares, and actually robbed by a man in a gig—a fat man—"

"Why, sir, look there. There is a fat man in a gig."

Captain Macheath affected for the first time to glance in the direction of one of the roads that traversed the common, and there, sure enough, was a gig coming slowly along.

Within it was a man who was not only fat, but of such a size that it was quite a wonder how he got into the vehicle, or having once got in, he ever got out again.

"That man," said Captain Macheath, "who looks like a highly respectable man, took me at unawares, when half-asleep beneath a tree, and robbed me and then drove off."

"You astonish me."

"Look at him, if you please, and as you are a resident of the neighbourhood, perhaps you may know him by sight?"

The young lady shook her head.

No; she knew nothing of the fat man.

She had never seen him before, and what was more, she considered it quite incredible that he could be a highwayman at all.

"The rascal!" said Macheath; "I fully believe that his fat is all a sham; but if you will do me the favour to pause for a few moments only, I will make him restore what he took from me."

"Certainly—I will wait by this tree."

"I thank you. I will make short work with him."

"Would it not be proper to apprehend him?"

"Yes, highly proper; but then I should be kept in England to prosecute, and a beloved mother and sister expect me by a certain time on the continent, so I cannot encumber myself with a prisoner, or the trouble of a prosecution. Ah! how often such fellows escape from such reasons."

"They do, indeed," said the young lady, "and it is a sad pity that they should. I will wait for you, sir. I shall never forget the singular adventures of this day."

Macheath rode up to the gig; and addressing the driver, he said—

"Come, I am glad I have met with you; I now insist upon restitution."

"You insist upon what?" said the corpulent gentleman, suddenly drawing up and fixing his staring eyes upon Captain Macheath; "you insist upon what?"

"Restitution. Your money, watch, and valuables are mine, or as good as mine. You may give them up without having a bullet in your head previously or not, as you like; but give them up you shall, some way or another."

"Murder!" cried the old gentleman. "It's a highwayman, and in broad daylight, too!"

"Quick," said Captain Macheath. "That young lady is waiting for me, and nothing can be more unpolite than to keep her long. Be quick, I say, or I shall be under the necessity of shooting you, and she and I will bury you on the heath."

From the appearance of the old gentleman and the blue colour that appeared about his nose, Macheath really thought he was going off in a fit of apoplexy from fright, so he hastened to say—

"You will have no harm done you if you comply with my request, and then you can pursue your journey with perfect safety, and you will be a little lighter than you were before, which will be a great consolation to the horse," the captain said. "Do you hear?"

The old gentleman only glared at Captain Macheath, but he said nothing; and as his watch-seals, together with nearly a foot of gold chain, were hanging out of his fob, Macheath laid hold of them, and by one vigorous pull possessed himself of a valuable gold repeater.

"Have you much money about you?" he said.

The old gentleman only stared a little more wildly than before, and Macheath was so amused at his manner, and the effect which the robbery had upon him, that he forbore to trouble him further, contenting himself with the really valuable watch-chain and seals.

He gave the horse, which was a strong but sluggish beast, a smart cut with his own riding whip, and the lazy animal, astonished at being so wakened up, started off at a hard canter, and soon carried the old gentleman far away over the common.

"I have got my watch back again," said Macheath, as he rejoined the young lady.

"I am glad of that. Did he resist?"

"He threatened a little, that was all; but upon finding I was resolute he told me to take it, and I did. I am afraid he will soon make it up by some other robbery; but the career of such a man must be cut short some day. It is quite melancholy to think how people can give their minds to such a life."

"It is indeed, sir. Honest industry surely ought to have charms that would more than compensate for all the robber's gains, even if the end of his career was not certain to be disgrace and death."

"Very true," cried Captain Macheath. "But, my dear miss, did you ever hear of honest industry getting its reward in this world? Did you ever hear of it getting ordinary comforts?"

"Often."

"Indeed!"

"You seem to doubt it, sir; but I feel assured that a honestly-earned crust and a draught of spring-water is a banquet far more delicious than an Apician feast which is corrupted by injustice and stolen from the resources of others," pursued the young lady, earnestly.

"Humph!" cried Captain Macheath. "This is our way. By a trot of half a mile down this shady lane we shall come to the hall, or close to it. Ah! who have we here?"

From the lane to which Macheath alluded there came four persons on horseback.

One was an old gentleman with white hair and without his hat, another was a young man about nineteen or twenty years of age, and the two others were ladies.

The moment the young lady who was with Captain Macheath saw them, she exclaimed, in eager delight—

"That is my dear father!—that is my dear father!" and springing forward, she, in a moment, was by the side of the old gentleman.

The others crowded around her, each expressing the greatest joy at beholding her again; but upon her saying something, suddenly they all turned towards Captain Macheath.

"Sir, I am extremely obliged to you," said the father.

"Sir," said Macheath, "you are welcome."

"My daughter, Lena, tells me that she had the good fortune to meet you on the common; and that you have since that time protected her from some dangers."

"From three highwaymen, father," said the young lady.

"Yes," added the father, "as I hear, from three highwaymen; but I really was not before aware that our neighbourhood was so infested."

"Ah, sir," said Captain Macheath, "you don't know what troublesome and bad characters you may have near you, when you least expect them to be near at hand."

"That is very true, sir," said the old gentleman. "Allow me to introduce you to my son, and to my other two daughters Norah and Louise."

When they reached Hollebrook Hall, and were fairly seated in one of its handsome reception-rooms, Macheath at once cast off any shyness of manner that might at first have beset him, though not having made up his mind as to what course of conduct to pursue in the present adventure.

He turned with a smile to the baronet.

"I greatly regret that I am compelled to appear in riding costume," he said; "but if you will permit me to seek it, I can find in my valise a more suitable coat, at all events."

"Now I am glad to hear you say that," cried the baronet, "because that shows, my young friend, that you have gracefully yielded to the request that we have all made you to stay a few hours

with us. I will give the necessary orders to have your valise, which I see is strapped to your saddle, taken to a room at once. Now, pray do not disturb yourself, I beg."

"I am much obliged to you," said Captain Macheath, "but the fact is, sir, that my horse, from long association and much petting upon my part, would not rest or eat unless I paid him a short visit in his stable to assure him that all was right. It's a singular whim of the animal's, but a fact that I cannot get over, so I indulge him in it."

"Well, sir, in that case, then, of course you must. Simpkins, show this gentleman the way to the stables directly."

"Yes, sir," said Simpkins, bowing low, and preparing to lead the way.

Of course, Macheath's great object was to know where his horse could be found at a few moments' notice.

He followed Simpkins with all the gravity in the world, and that individual, upon reaching a lawn at the back of the house, called upon Robert to do the rest of the honours of that portion of the premises.

Robert was rather a rough-looking specimen of the groom genus, and when Simpkins was gone Macheath took from his waistcoat-pocket a guinea, and handed it to Robert.

"It's a fancy of mine," said the captain, "always to take a look at my horse in his stall, and it's a fancy of his to expect me."

"Certainly," said Robert, as he gave the guinea a twirl with his finger and thumb. "And a very good fancy it is, too. This way, sir, if you please —this way."

Macheath soon had all the information he wanted of the whereabouts of his steed, and then he returned to the drawing-room in which the baronet and his family were seated.

A servant had charge of the valise which Macheath usually had at the back of his saddle, and only waited the baronet's orders where to take it.

"Ah! my friend," said Sir Henry Hollebrook, "you will be put upon your mettle shortly if you leave us to-night."

"Indeed, sir?"

"Yes; I have just had information that the famous highwayman, Captain Macheath, is in this neighbourhood, and, as a magistrate, I am asked by a couple of officers who will be here directly, to back a warrant for his apprehension."

"Really," said the captain. "May I now proceed at once to change my coat?"

"Oh! yes, certainly; Simpkins, take that gentleman into my room."

Captain Macheath vanished after Simpkins, and was conducted into a sumptuous dressing-room adjoining a bed-chamber.

There he rapidly made the alteration that was so desirable in his costume; and then, without waiting one moment longer than was absolutely necessary, he repaired again to the drawing-room.

"Oh, my dear sir," said Sir Henry, "you dress with military expedition. The two officers who are seeking for that notorious rascal, Macheath, are anxious to see you to ask you, as you have been riding in neighbourhood, if you have seen anything of such a man as the highwayman."

"Indeed, no. The only highwaymen that I have seen consisted of two fellows that I had the honour of preventing from interfering with your daughter on the common. Perhaps one of those was the man these officers seek."

"Oh ! no, sir—oh ! no. Captain Macheath does all his robbing alone. As a magistrate, I have heard of some of his tricks, and I am quite sure that he would never admit a companion to share with him either in his dangers or his plunder. He is, I assure you, a very desperate character."

"And a most impertinent fellow, too, I should think," said the captain.

"As you say, a most impertinent fellow. Well, Simpkins, you can tell the officers that this gentleman is here, and will cheerfully answer any inquiries they may have to make."

"Yes, Sir Henry. They are both here on the door mat, and will come in directly."

"Let them come by all means," said Captain Macheath. "I am sure that any information I can give concerning that notorious rascal they will be most welcome to."

Upon this the two officers, one of them looking very rueful from the hurt he had got in a fall from his horse, made their appearance in the room.

All the precaution that Macheath took was to place himself with his back to the window, so that his face was rather obscured.

To that, and to the slight alteration he had made in the costume he wore, he entirely trusted.

"We are sorry, sir, to trouble you," said one of the officers, "but understanding you had been upon the road, we make bold, sir, to ask you if you had seen Captain Macheath."

"No," said the captain. "I saw nobody at all answering the description of the fellow ; and as I am well acquainted with his person, I can satisfactorily assure you that he did not pass me."

"Thank you, sir. Sir Henry has been kind enough to back our warrant against him, and to say that he will lend us what help he can to take him to-night on the heath, if so be he should be bold enough to show himself there."

"I wish you success," said Captain Macheath.

The officers then bowed themselves out, and the captain fully believed that he had succeeded in deceiving them.

Whether such was or was not the case we shall speedily see.

The baronet began to speak very freely to Captain Macheath about his family, and he particularly praised Lena's sweet disposition.

Probably the baronet thought that if the new acquaintance should turn out to be a young man of good family, it would be no great harm to make a favourable impression upon him.

Of course, Macheath, who was quite sufficiently wide awake to perceive this little scheme, made suitable replies, and in the midst of the conversation, Simpkins made his appearance, saying in a respectful voice—

"Dinner is laid, Sir Henry."

"Dinner !" said Captain Macheath. "I am afraid I am inducing you to sit down to that meal at a very early hour, Sir Henry !"

"Oh ! no, no—not at all, my dear sir—not at all. We are primitive in our uabits here. I live, as you see, the quiet life of a country gentleman among my girls, who will make the most excellent wives, though I say it But it will be a sad blow to me, my young friend—a very sad blow to lose any one of them, particularly Lena."

As he spoke, the baronet affected to dash a tear from his eyes.

"She is like a mother," he added ; "but never mind—never mind. I am content to suffer any privation so that I only see my children comfortably settled in life."

"A most praiseworthy object," said Captain Macheath. "My uncle, the duke, often says— a—a—hem !—I mean my uncle merely—often says that it is only in the sweet calm of domestic life that true happiness is to be found in this world, whatever stage of things we must look for in the next. That is his opinion, Sir Henry."

"How very true, my dear young friend—how very true. After you. Nay, I could not think of taking precedence. His uncle the duke," said Sir Henry Hollebrook to himself, as he followed Captain Macheath into the diining-room—"his uncle the duke ! That slipped out completely unawares. His uncle the duke ! I saw from the first he was a most distinguished young man. His uncle the duke ! What a chance for Lena.

The dinner was laid with a profusion of old plate, and the meal promised to be a sumptuous one.

"You do indeed keep primitive hours," said Captain Macheath. "Why, it cannot be very much past mid-day ?"

"Only two, about two," said Sir Henry, taking out a very handsome gold watch from his pocket.

"That's a repeater, I presume ?" Captain Macheath observed.

"Yes, and considered a capital one," replied Sir Henry, as he handed it to the captain. "Those brilliants round it are considered of the very first water, and match the ring on my finger."

"Do they match it ?" said Captain Macheath, dubiously. "At this short distance, and by this light, I really don't see that they are exactly of the same lustre. Nay, my dear Sir Henry, don't trouble yourself—don't indeed ; it's only imagination, I daresay."

"It's not a bit of trouble, my dear sir," said the baronet, as he worked the ring from off his finger, and handed it to Macheath ; "it's not the smallest trouble, I assure you. Pray compare the ring-gem with those round the watch."

"Ah !" said the captain. "I now see that I was wrong. They are precisely similar ; and they both put me in mind of a singular adventure I met with one day in Oxfordshire."

"In Oxfordshire ?" cried Sir Henry. "In Oxfordshire—an adventure in Oxfordshire, girls— do you hear that ? How very singular and how very delightful."

"Oh ! very," said all the young ladies together.

"But I am afraid," said Captain Macheath, "that I shall bore you by telling it to you."

"Oh ! no—no !" cried everyone.

"Well, then," said Captain Macheath, "since you are kind enough to say that it will not bore you to hear the anecdote, I will relate it to you."

"Fill the gentleman's glass, Simpkins," said Sir Henry.

Macheath sipped his wine ; and then, with an engaging smile, he commenced speaking.

"I was taking a quiet canter through Oxfordshire some few years ago," he said, "when I found, as the day darkened, that a raw and gusty air got up, accompanied by rain, so that it became highly desirable to find shelter somewhere.

"I rode on at a rapid pace, the gloom still gathering around me, until in the distance I saw lights, and urging my tired steed still more quickly forward, I, to my great satisfaction, soon reached a large old-fashioned-looking inn by the roadside.

"The sign of this inn I cannot just at this moment call to mind, but whatever it was, the indication of it made a terrible creaking, as it hung by some iron-work to an old tree before the door of the hostel.

"I drew up in a moment, and the ostler taking my horse, I strode into the house, and asked for a private room, and specified that there was to be a good fire in it.

"Well, they did show me into a private room, but I found that the fire had only just been lit, and that the chimney did not draw well, for the room was full of smoke.

"In answer to my remonstrances, the landlord said—

"'I would have accommodated you, sir, with a better room, but the fact is, a gentleman is now in occupation of our best room, and he has got such a beautiful fire, that it would do your heart good to look at it.'

"'Is he really a gentleman?' I demanded.

"'Oh, dear, yes, sir,' replied the landlord; 'he is a real gentleman; spends his money like a prince, sir; and won't drink any but the very best of wine.'

"'Give him the compliments, then, of a stranger,' I said, 'and ask him if it will be agreeable to him for me to sit by his fire and share his society for the evening.'

"Well, the landlord took my message, I presume; for in a few moments he came back, to say that the gentleman sent his compliments, and begged to say that nothing would give him more pleasure than my joining him.

"Upon this polite invitation I went to the stranger's apartment, and found him by the side of a roaring fire, and a very tempting-looking bottle of claret at his elbow. We were mutually polite, and soon got to be quite at home with each other."

CHAPTER XIV.

"SURRENDER, CAPTAIN MACHEATH!"

"SIMPKINS," said Sir Henry, "attend to the gentleman's glass."

"Thank you," said Macheath—"thank you."

"Pray go on with the very entertaining story, sir," said Lena.

"With great pleasure," replied Macheath. "Well, then, as I was saying, I and the stranger got quite intimate and delighted with each other; and at last, as the discourse turned on the beauties of the country, he suddenly said—

"'I received rather a check one day in my admiration of the picturesque, for not far from this house I was robbed by Captain Macheath, the celebrated highwayman.'

"'Indeed!' I replied. 'I was not aware that he practised in this part of the country at all.'

"'Yes,' replied my new friend, 'he robbed me in a most ingenious way: he took advantage of my having dismounted to tighten my horse's girths, and gave the creature such a slash with a riding-whip that sent it off at a gallop, and, as I was on foot and defenceless, he took from me my watch and money.'

"We then had another bottle of claret, and were getting on capitally with each other, although neither party had mentioned who or what he was, when he suddenly said to me—

"'That seems a remarkably pure brilliant in the ring you have upon your little finger, sir.'

"I thought this, at the time, only one of those common-place remarks that are made over a glass of wine, and I drew the ring from my finger and handed it to him, saying, 'Yes; it is considered pure, and matches with the jewels round my watch;' for it was a most singular coincidence, Sir Henry, that, like you, I had then a watch surrounded with brilliants of the same lustre as my ring."

"Very remarkable," said Sir Henry Hollebrook. "You hear that, girls. How very curious, to be sure, things do come about."

"Very, oh! very," said all the young ladies. "Pray go on, sir."

"I took out my watch," added the captain, "to show him that the brilliants resembled that one in the ring; and he took about five minutes comparing them, and then, with all the coolness in the world, he took up my ring—as I might this of yours, Sir Henry—"

"Yes—yes."

"And put it on his little finger—as I put this on mine."

"Exactly. How very droll."

"Well, Sir Henry, he then took up my watch—as I do yours now—and with all the assurance in the world, he put it in his pocket in this way—just as I put yours in my pocket now."

"Precisely," said Sir Henry. "Upon my word and honour, it was a very cool proceeding on the part of a stranger."

"Very. A most impudent thing, I call it."

"Uncommonly so."

"Well, then, up he got in this way, while I stared at him in utter amazement, and as you might stare at me and leaving the table as I do now, just in this way, he made towards the door.

"'Sir,' he said, 'I have made perhaps more free than welcome with your watch and your ring, but when I tell you that I am no other than Captain Macheath, you will scarcely feel any amount of surprise at my doing so; and I have the honour of bidding you good day, and more wit.'

"That was just what he said; and then, Sir Henry and ladies, out he went from the room as I do now, and shut and locked the door behind him."

As Macheath uttered these words, he walked out of the dining-room with Sir Henry's watch in his pocket, and his ring on his finger, and finding the key in the lock of the door outside, he rapidly turned it so that the worthy baronet and his family, together with Simpkins, who was officiating at the sideboard, were made prisoners in a moment.

Before he left the door, Macheath heard Sir Henry roaring out—

"Capital—capital! Excellent! Upon my word this is capital. Ha—ha—ha! Really this is good. Ha—ha—ha!"

It was now that the captain felt all the importance of knowing his way direct to the stable, and he flew rather than walked in that direction.

He felt confident that not for many minutes could the delusion last, and that there was no time to lose.

The moment he got within sight of the stable, he saw the man to whom he had given the guinea.

"Robert," he said, "earn another guinea by showing me how quickly you can saddle my horse, and bringing him out to me here."

"Yes, sir," said Robert, and he vanished into the stable like a shot.

Macheath felt certain he should be in the saddle in the course of a few moments.

He knew how very precious every moment was, and he had the greatest difficulty to keep himself from entering into the stable and helping Robert to bring out the horse.

Suddenly he heard the violent ringing of a bell.

in the house, and he said to himself, "They are now beginning to suspect that all is not right. Oh! for my horse."

Robert made his appearance at that moment with the steed already harnessed for the road.

"That's right," said Macheath; "there's nothing so delightful to me as a scamper by night. Where does that little door in the wall lead to, Robert?"

"Into the meadow, sir."

"Open it then. That will be my way. Here is your guinea, my man."

Tingle, tingle, tingle, went the bell again.

"There's two gentlemen in front of the house, sir," said Robert, "who offered me five shillings for letting 'em know when you went to bed, if so be as you slept here, and the same money for letting of 'em know if you ordered your horse."

"Five shillings, Robert," said the captain laughing. "I have outbid them, then. Open the door, and then be busy in the stable; and say nothing and hear nothing until you are forced, and I'll turn their silver bribe into a golden one. Here are five guineas, Robert, and remember that I trust you."

"You may, sir."

Robert flung open the gate, Macheath, waving his hand to him, darted on horseback into the meadows.

The bells in the house were now ringing with a fury that threatened the absolute destruction of every wire in it.

But Captain Macheath was off and away.

Close to the small gate-like door, at which Robert had let him out, was a remarkably beautiful row of poplars, and Macheath crept close under them, walking his horse, until he should come to some gap in the hedge that would enable him to get into a lane which he saw was close at hand, and which, no doubt, joined the highroad.

He did not court a collision with the officers any more than he took pains to avoid one, although of the two he would certainly have preferred avoiding them, because he did not wish to take a life or lives, which, in the event of their attacking him, he might be obliged to do.

It would appear, however, that in their measures for the apprehension of Macheath—they did not wholly trust to Robert, for suddenly, as Captain Macheath emerged from the trees and was thinking of dismounting for the purpose of clearing a sufficient gap in the hedge for his horse to pass through, he heard a whistle sound.

"Hilloa!" he said, "the enemy is nearer than I thought. Well, the lane will be as good a place, and perhaps better, than the meadow in which to meet them."

With this he cantered back about a hundred yards, then putting the horse to a gallop, he gave him his head and over he went, clearing the hedge in a beautiful style, and alighting in the lane.

Bang went a pistol, and the bullet whizzed past Macheath's head.

"Oh!" he said, "that was a coward's shot, let it come from whom it may."

Glancing in the direction from whence it proceeded, he saw a man crouching down, and creeping along, close to the hedge, with the recently discharged pistol in his hand.

Macheath always kept one of his large holster pistols loaded with good-sized shot, and drawing that weapon from his saddle, he took good aim at the man and fired it.

"That won't kill you," said Captain Macheath, as the man uttered a yell and rolled over and over

at the foot of the hedge. "That won't kill you, but it will make you rather uncomfortable, my friend, for some time, I think."

"Surrender, Captain Macheath!" cried a man, springing out of the hedge, and then another followed him, and then a third appeared armed with a pitchfork.

The two first who appeared presented pistols at the captain, and from their general aspect he could see that they were officers.

"The game is up, Macheath," said one. "You are wanted. Your time has come, and we must have you; sooner or later, you know, it was sure to come to this, so it is of no use shirking it. You are wanted. Resistance is useless. We have lots of help, and you can't escape this time. I warn you not to shed blood uselessly, but to give in at once, for you have not the ghost of a chance of getting away from us now."

"You are very kind," said the captain; "and I daresay that your advice is excellent. That my time to die will come some day, I don't doubt; but I have a sort of faith that it has not come yet, so blaze away."

"Don't be a fool," said the officer. "Don't be a fool. I have made up my mind to have you, dead or alive. I have a dozen men, armed, at all parts of the lane, and you may throw away your life if you like, but that is all you can do."

"Hark you," said Macheath. "I have never any faith in those who talk much of what they are going to do. If you were serious you would do it, but I have an opinion of my own to the effect that you dare not. I'll trouble you to get out of my way."

Captain Macheath whilst speaking had prepared himself for a bold dash.

Touching his horse on the flank with that peculiar movement that the creature had been taught to understand, he bounded forward with a tremendous leap that cleared one half the distance between him and the officers.

They both fired their pistols, but in that moment of surprise and hurry it is not to be wondered at that they missed him, Captain Macheath.

The man with the pitchfork made a savage thrust at the horse, which would have killed the noble creature had not the flap of the saddle partly saved it.

As it was, it inflicted a long graze on the skin, ripping it up completely for the space of about a foot.

If anything more than another was calculated to thoroughly infuriate Macheath, it was an injury wantonly inflicted upon his horse.

His eyes flashed fire, and swerving in the saddle, he caught the pitchfork by the prongs and tore it from the hands of the man who had made so cowardly a use of it.

He tried to escape, but the captain was too quick for him, and with a crashing blow that had quite a horrible sound upon his head, he struck him to the earth with the handle of the fork.

One of the officers sprang forward, and caught the bridle close to the bit, calling out—

"I have him—I have him!"

"Hold him tight then!" cried Macheath, as he again urged the horse on.

The officer was galloped over in a moment, and away went Macheath down the lane with his blood thoroughly heated now by the little battle that had taken place.

The officer's assertion that there were others in the lane to oppose him was pretty well borne out, for a man suddenly started up and pointed a gun at him.

He pulled the trigger.

The gun missed fire and Macheath cried as he passed on—

"Thank your stars for that. It has saved your life."

Taking the bridle between his teeth, the captain, with a loaded pistol in each hand, galloped down the lane.

Another shot was fired at him and struck his hat.

He immediately discharged one of his pistols in the direction whence the shot came, but with what effect at the speed he was going at he could not tell.

In one minute more he was out of the lane and on the highroad to Hounslow.

"Hurrah !" he cried. Hurrah for the road ! Hurrah !"

Then like the wind, he and his horse sped away, leaving behind them a barren triumph for the officers and the people they had summoned to assist them in attempting his capture.

The man who had wielded the pitchfork was dead ; and the officer who had spoken so grandly about Macheath's time having come, and his determination to have him, sat in the middle of the lane examining the contusions he had received from the horse galloping over him.

At a short distance off a great lubberly-looking fellow was blubbering at the pain he suffered from the charge of shot Captain Macheath had favoured him with ; and upon the whole a more lugubrious-looking party than that which made its way back to the house of Sir Henry Hallebrook after the battle could not very well have been conceived.

"I ought to know the time of day," said Macheath, as he drew rein at about three miles from the lane where the fight had taken place— "I ought to know the time of day, for I have watches enough."

By the road-side was a pleasant-looking little copse, only protected by a swinging-gate.

Macheath opened it and led in his horse, in order that it might crop the sweet herbage.

He carefully examined the wound the faithful creature had received ; and, although it was only a superficial one, he felt the necessity of having it attended to ; and observing a finger-post at some short distance off, he went to it, and saw that it pointed to Guildford.

"I will go there," he said. "It can't be many miles ; I will go there and get a farrier to sew up the wound, or it will grow serious if neglected."

Could he have had any hope of getting in sufficient time to Guildford to do his horse any service, Captain Macheath would willingly have gone on foot, and led the faithful creature.

But that was out of the question ; so he at once mounted and rode sharply, convinced that the delay was of far more importance to his wounded steed than anything else.

He met with no adventure on the road, and with but very few passengers indeed.

The few whom he passed he paid no attention to, nor did they trouble him with any notice, so that he reached Guildford in the quietest manner possible.

His first inquiry was for the best farrier in the town to whom he could apply to for the hurt his horse had received.

There was no difficulty in such a place as Guildford in finding not merely a farrier but a skilful one ; this man was possessed by the very demons of loquacity and curiosity, and he nearly drove Macheath distracted by the questions he asked and the questions he implied.

"Perhaps, sir," he said, "your horse was where he ought not to have been when he met with this accident ?"

"Of course he was," Macheath returned, tapping his foot impatiently upon the ground.

"Was it an accident, or was it wilfully inflicted ?" the farrier demanded.

Captain Macheath pretended not to hear these questions and hummed a tune.

"Ah !" continued the irrepressible farrier, "of course—er—I daresay you think me a great bore. Do you come from London—of course—er—it is no business of mine. Beg pardon for asking so many questions. A fine horse, sir ; indeed, I may say a very fine horse. Got him a bargain, I hope ?"

"I forget," said Captain Macheath.

"Forget, sir ?" cried the farrier. "Dear me ! how odd."

"Very !" Captain Macheath replied, dryly. "I was always afflicted with a bad memory. The affliction runs in the family. I am forgetful and absent-minded, and yet, he added, significantly, "I think I should know you anywhere after this interview. How is my horse ?"

"Oh !—er—just so," said the farrier. "It won't be a bit the worse for this little scratch. It's after all only a skin wound. Going to London, I suppose, at once, sir ? Don't happen to know anybody, I suppose, sir, who wants a good horse ? Much rain on the roads, sir, the way you came ? Didn't happen to hear if anything in shape of a highwayman was about this common ?"

"I heard nothing, and know nothing," cried Macheath. "I am not at all inquisitive, and never pester strangers with impertinent questions."

"And very right, sir, on your part. I only wish all the world was of your opinion. Folks come here and go on talk, talk, talk, and asking so many questions, that one can't get in a word even edgeways. Did you say it was accidental, this cut on the horse, sir, or done purposely ? In a hurry, sir, or travelling only for pleasure ? Going to see a friend in this part of the country perhaps, or on business of importance ? Got a beautiful bay horse to sell, sir. Tim—Tim—Tim !"

"Yes, master."

"Tie this bandage carefully while I show this gentleman Trip Away," said the farrier. "That's what we call the bay, sir, and a finer creature you never clapped eyes on This way, sir—won't take you half a minute. Don't want a new set of harness, perhaps, and don't know anybody that does ? Name ain't Jones, is it, sir ?"

Captain Macheath saw that the loquacity of the farrier was a kind of insanity which it would be no use to combat with.

While Tim, the man, was putting a bandage over the skin wound on the horse, which, to do the talkative farrier justice, he had sewn up with great skill, Macheath accompanied him to the stable to look at the fine horse, Trip Away.

The farrier opened the stable-door, and Captain Macheath followed him ; but the moment he got about half-a-dozen paces in, the farrier turned round, and placing his back against the door, said—

"Captain Macheath, I know you !"

The captain started at the moment.

But he did not lose his presence of mind, and with admirable coolness he turned his eyes upon the man

CAPTAIN MACHEATH
THE
PRINCE OF THE HIGHWAY.

"OH! LOR', I AM A DEAD MAN," CRIED THE COACHMAN AS MACHEATH PRESENTED THE PISTOL.

"Well?" said the captain. "What then, my friend?"

"I tell you what it is," added the farrier, "I'm the best boxer and the best wrestler in the county. How far have you come? Did you meet anybody worth robbing on the road? What did you really give for the horse now? I intend to arrest you. The money I shall get for your apprehension will be very useful. It's of no use your looking big, for I mean to do it."

"I have not the slightest desire," said Captain Macheath, coolly, "to look bigger than I am. But since you are the best boxer and the best wrestler in the county, perhaps you have no objection to a fall?"

As he spoke the captain flew upon him with a vehemence that the farrier did not expect, but he nevertheless maintained his ground.

"Easy—easy," he said. "Now for it. You talked of a fall and you shall have one. To prison you go, and it's odds but you carry with you a broken bone or two. Now, my man, I'll show you a trick."

"Is it anything like that?" asked Captain Macheath, as he suddenly let go his hold of the farrier's waist and dropped him to his feet.

Seizing his legs about a couple of inches above the ankles, he tossed him over his head in a moment.

The farrier lay stunned, for the stable was paved with rather large round stones, and his head, thick though it might be, was not exactly calculated to resist a hard knock against one of them.

"Fool!" said Macheath, "I hope I have not killed him; but he forced it on me. The fellow surely must be a little insane to go on in such a way; and yet how in the name of evil fortune came he to know me? If he can so surely recognise me, others may. It is time that I left Guildford behind me as far as possible."

Macheath left the stable and the farrier.

When he returned to the yard again, he found that his horse was all ready.

Tim was putting the head-gear to rights.

"I wouldn't ride him no further than I could help to-day, sir," said Tim.

"I will not," Captain Macheath replied. "He shall have rest enough. This crown-piece is for yourself. I have already settled with your master."

The captain mounted and at a quiet canter left the stable.

He would have been well enough pleased to have galloped from Guildford, but his consideration for his horse prevented him.

Notwithstanding all the danger that might beset him—for the farrier, in all probability, would give an alarm and raise a hue-and-cry when he recovered—Macheath went at an easy pace.

He took care, however, to look to his pistols, and to see that they were all ready for active service, in case any extraordinary occasion for their use should arise.

More than once Macheath thought that he heard sounds indicating that he was being followed and looked around him long and carefully.

There was an expression of anxiety upon his face.

His horse—his beautiful horse—was really the only friend he could trust upon earth, and Macheath's first thought was of the noble creature.

At last the captain made up his mind that he had been mistaken.

Nobody seemed to be on his track, and he rode gently along until he had put three miles between himself and Guildford.

Checking his horse into a walking pace, as the roads were rough, Macheath reached the top of a high hill.

Here he took another survey of the surroundings, and the captain bit his underlip as he saw no less than half-a-dozen well mounted men coming towards him at a hard gallop.

They were however half a mile distant, and to reach the object of their haste and fury they would have to climb the long, steep, and toilsome hill.

"Well!" muttered Captain Macheath, "I suppose I ought to have expected this, and therefore it is a comfort not to be taken altogether by surprise, and yet—"

The captain ceased speaking for a moment, and leaning forward, patted his horse's neck affectionately.

"And yet," he continued, "I am afraid it would go as hard with you, my friend, as with me if yonder bloodhounds contrive to overtake us. If things were as they ought to be, I should have no more objection to a sharp gallop of half-a-dozen miles than eating a good dinner, but I dare not venture upon it now. We must get under cover, my brave steed. Yes, we must house ourselves somehow or other."

After a little consideration he waited until, by the gestures of the approaching horsemen, he felt quite satisfied that they saw him.

Waving his hat, he made as though he had started off at a tearing gallop; but he pulled up before he had got twenty yards, and being then quite satisfied that the brow of the hill was between him and his foes, he looked anxiously about him for some place of shelter.

"They will assuredly pass on if we can but get under cover," he said, as he patted his horse affectionately.

After trotting a little way, he saw among the trees the top part of a mansion.

Feeling that it was only for a short time that he required a place of concealment, he made up his mind to ride up to it and get within its gates, if possible, by adopting a plan which he had found successful in more than one instance.

This plan was to boldly ask to see the owner of the house, and when favoured with an interview, to regret to find that he was not the gentleman whom Captain Macheath had thought resided there, and so comfortably put off the time until the outside danger had passed away.

In some cases when he had done so, the people had been so favourably impressed by his gentlemanly and engaging manners that they had pressed him to remain and take rest and refreshment both for himself and his horse.

There was a small hedge by the road-side, and then a small meadow, and beyond that appeared the small garden wall, but Captain Macheath could not find any entrance.

Probably it was on the other side, so as time with Macheath was by far too important an object just then for him to tamper with, he pushed his way through the hedge, and dismounting, he led his horse close along under the wall, which was of unusual height, with the hope of discovering some door.

He fancied he could hear the thundering sound of the horses' hoofs of his pursuers as they came up the hill. His situation was now, in truth, a most critical one.

Had there been sufficient wood about the spot for him to trust to concealment, he would have done so.

But there was not, and Macheath felt quite certain that upon reaching the top of the hill his pursuers would pause and look carefully about them.

Macheath was just bracing up his nerves for a life and death encounter with his foes, when he came to a small door in the wall.

To try it, and find it fast, was the work of a moment.

It was of no strength, however, and that was no time to stand upon any ceremony, so Macheath, placing his shoulder against it, with one push sent it in, nearly falling after it himself.

He had destroyed one hinge and the whole of the lock.

There was not a moment to lose.

Propping the door open, he led his horse through it; the creature, after a glance at the height of the opening, stooping with great precision just sufficiently low to go comfortably through it.

Then Macheath replaced the door in its proper situation as well as he could, so that it showed no signs of having been broken through to the casual observer.

He found himself in a spacious garden, well laid out in gravelled walks, and abounding in fine shrubbery.

It was evidently a well kept place; and as he was looking about him for the most eligible path to pursue, he heard a light footstep upon the gravel path close to him, and in a moment there appeared round some bushes a young lady of the most fascinating beauty, attired with great elegance, and carrying in her hand a small bouquet of flowers.

At the sight of Captain Macheath she smiled, and advanced more rapidly.

"Ah! what joy is this?" she cried. "So, my own one, you have come at last? How long I have expected you! Have you no smiles for your own Minna?"

The captain was, to tell the simple truth, so utterly astonished at this address from one who was a perfect stranger to him, that, for once in the way, even he, with all his admirable tact and self-command, found himself perfectly at fault.

"You do not know," added the young lady, as she came quite close to Captain Macheath, and looked confidingly and affectionately in his face— "you do not know how long and weary the hours have been to me without you. How I have wept and sighed for you to come! But now that you are here, all is joy again—yes, all is joy again."

She fell upon his breast, and burst into tears; and while she sobbed bitterly, he was compelled to place his arm around her waist to support her, or she would have fallen.

He was compelled to let go his horse, for he could not very well attend to it and a young lady as well, so that the animal sought out a comfortable grass plot, and began to crop the sweet herbage at its leisure, leaving its master to look after the young lady.

"I beg you will compose yourself," said Macheath. "These tears will be injurious to you. Pray be calm."

She only wept the more.

"What, in the name of fate," thought Captain Macheath, "is the meaning of all this? If it be some crafty mode of apprehending me, I am done, and I shall be taken, for I cannot be such a brute as to shake off this young creature."

As he spoke, he felt rather inclined to press her closer to his heart, and he was pleased to find that her sobs were not so very frequent, and that she was becoming each moment more composed and rational.

Suddenly, with an alarmed look, she gazed in his face, and then a blush overspread her face, and extricating herself from his arm, she said—
"Where am I? Oh! where am I?"

"That," said Captain Macheath, "is a question which I am sorry to say I have the greatest difficulty in answering. I can only offer you all the service in my power."

"But—but— Oh! what has happened?— Where am I? What place is this! Uncle— uncle! where are you now? Oh! save me—save me."

A pretty garden seat was close at hand, upon which she threw herself; and then, wringing her hands, she gave herself up again to the most hopeless sorrow, and sobbed as though her heart would break.

Captain Macheath was more and more puzzled to know what to say or do.

He gazed upon her, though he almost doubted if she were a being of this world.

"Is this all a dream, or am I really wide awake? Let me see," he said to himself. "There is my steed, and here am I. Everything is too clear for a dream. It is, it must be, a reality. But what it all means passes conjecture. I am fairly bewildered."

He thought he would wait until this fresh burst of emotion upon the part of the mysterious young lady had passed away before he said anything more.

After a time the young lady's tears gradually subsided, and then Captain Macheath, burning with curiosity to know who and what she was, and what was the occasion of her very strange conduct, approached her, and spoke kindly to her.

"If there be anything," he said, "that I can do for the purpose of alleviating the great distress under which you evidently labour, I beg that you will command me fairly; for in some sense I look upon myself as a sort of knight-errant of old, and feel bound to redress what grievances I can in my progress through life."

"Thank Heaven!" said the young lady— "thank Heaven that I am able to speak rationally to you now!"

"Rationally!" thought Captain Macheath; but he said nothing, and the young lady continued—

"Yes, I am now able to implore your protection, if you are a gentleman, and not leagued with those who will destroy me if I am not rescued from their dreadful hands."

"I assure you," said Captain Macheath, "that I am leagued with no such persons. I am here alone, knowing no one in this place, and I have seen no one but yourself. Pray tell me what it is you would have me do."

"But you are true? Oh! pardon me, sir, for suspecting all whom I see in this place. You are true?"

"Yes. But when I tell you how I came here, I think you will acquit me of being in any way connected with your enemies. I broke into the garden, I assure you, and know not whose house it is that I see yonder among the trees. So, if you have any grievance, pray speak it freely to me."

"I will—I will!" the lady replied. "Your words speak to me a language of sincerity, and I will not doubt you. My uncle, Mr. Briarley, has placed me here that he may keep all my poor father left to me. He lives at Oxford, and will be in this house to-night to threaten me further. Oh! if you can take me from hence, I pray you do so. If you would have the blessing of an orphan, aid me in escaping, for I shall die if I remain here?"

"But what house is it? Who keeps it?"

"It is a madhouse."

"A madhouse!"

"Yes. This is an asylum. It is a lunatic asylum; but, alas! how it belies that word asylum. I am not mad, I assure you, sir—indeed, I am not!"

"Mad!" exclaimed Captain Macheath. "Certainly not. That is to say, I—I don't think you are, and hope you are not."

The singular reception that the young lady had given him at that moment flashed across his mind, and made him doubt very much how far he was really called upon and justified in interfering in her case.

She could not but observe his indecision, and, with a look of the most poignant grief, she said—

"Ah! sir, you think because you find me here that I am indeed one of those who are deprived of reason. Oh! do not fancy because you find me in such a place as this that I am mad, but please to assist me."

"I repeat that I shall be delighted to render you any assistance," he said. "Do you know me?"

"No—no."

"Are you quite sure that you have no sort of knowledge of me?"

"Ah!" she cried, "now I understand you. When first I saw you I was suffering under the effects of some drug which they give me here, and which, for the time, is potent enough to unsettle my mind completely. The effect of it, however, does not last long. I know not what I may have said to you while under the influence of that drug, but, believe me, whatever it was, I am not truly accountable for it."

"If that be so," replied Captain Macheath, "it is one of the most atrocious affairs that ever I heard of!"

"Hush—hush! Oh! save me."

"What is it—what do you dread?"

"The man who keeps this place is approaching—I know his footstep!" the terrified girl replied. "It is too late to save me now, but promise that you will come here to-night at half-past twelve, and take me away. I will be upon this spot, for they do not always lock me up, and I think I can get away at that time. It is my uncle who pays the people here to keep me and to say that I am mad, and this is his day for visiting me. He will come from Oxford, and his name is Briarley. Say, oh! say, then, you will come."

"At half-past twelve?"

"Yes—yes. You will promise me? Oh! he will not promise!"

"I will," said Macheath.

Joy beamed in the face of the young creature.

She bounded away from the spot, and was in a moment lost to sight amid the intricacies of the path that wound among the thickets and the flowering shrubs of the garden.

Almost at the same moment a man of vulgar and coarse aspect made his appearance, and stopped short when he saw Captain Macheath, gazing upon him with the utmost surprise.

The captain was determined to let him speak first.

He pretended not to see him.

In the course of a few moments the individual strutted up to him.

"Hilloa!" he said. "Who are you?"

"A gentleman," Macheath replied.

"And pray, sir, how the deuce did you get here, I should like to know? Will you oblige me by answering me that question?"

"Oh! yes, of course. You see that part of the wall over there, where the fig tree is trained?"

"Yes. Well, sir—well?"

"My horse is passionately fond of green figs," Macheath replied, "and although he was coming along the road outside in the quietest manner imaginable, no sooner did he see a branch of your fig tree projecting over the wall, than he made one leap and over he brought me. I fancy he thought it would not be safe to try such a leap again, for he obstinately refused to take me back again. So, if you will show me the way to the regular entrance, I shall be very much obliged to you indeed, sir."

"And, sir," said the asylum-keeper, "do you think to gammon me into a belief that there is any horse in the world who can jump a wall eighteen feet in height? No, sir, I am not a idiot."

"Very good," said Captain Macheath; "I did not ask you to believe it. Here we are, that's all I have got to say. There is the horse and here am I."

"But—but—the deuce, sir!"

"Ah! I don't know where the deuce is. You ought to know better about your own acquaintances than I can by any possibility expect to."

"But I don't believe it, sir; I don't understand it."

"Sir," said the captain, "I am not bound to furnish you with belief or understanding. It is quite sufficient if I supply you with an extraordinary fact. Whether you believe it or understand it is to me a matter of supreme indifference."

"Very good, sir—very good. We shall soon see, sir, who will have the laugh. I flatter myself that I am not quite alone in this place, and that those who are in my employment here will not be very scrupulous in executing my orders. I will have you taken up, sir, for being found upon my premises—no doubt with a highly felonious intent. My name is Wiggles, and I put up with nothing."

With this the madhouse-keeper started off as hard as he could to the house, no doubt to give the alarm to his myrmidons, and in all likelihood he thought that Macheath was safe enough until he returned, for the door in the wall had never occurred to him.

Macheath considered now that all danger from his Guildford pursuers must have passed away, and, accordingly, his impulse was to leave the lunatic asylum garden as soon as possible.

A sharp whistle brought his horse to his side, and Captain Macheath and his steed passed out of the garden as easily as they had entered it.

He took some pains to replace the door, and then, mounting his steed, he rode off at the same easy pace at which he had come from Guildford.

He could see nothing whatever of his pursuers.

"This will not do," said Macheath to himself. "I am really doing no business of any importance. I must take to the road in earnest now, or I shall find my supplies run rather short when I reach London again, where I have several affairs on hand that may cost me something. Polly—Polly! I feel that I love you better than any one now, and that I cannot keep for very long absent from you."

Finding that his horse was rather inclined for a sharp canter, Captain Macheath would not baulk the creature, but let it take its own pace down one of the beautiful green lanes that lie between Guildford and Hounslow-heath.

They had not proceeded far, when Macheath heard quite distinctly the sound of horses' feet and the grinding noise of carriage wheels.

He got to the side of the road and waited until he saw a very strong vehicle make its appearance.

A coachman with an immense powdered wig was upon the box and two footmen were behind.

"Come," said Macheath, "here ought to be some sport. It will keep my hand in, at all events."

Darting suddenly out into the centre of the road he called out—

"Stop—stop! A toll here!"

The coachman pulled up so rapidly that the pair of horses were thrown upon their haunches and the vehicle gave a tremendous lurch.

"Hark you, my fine fellow," said Captain Macheath, as he presented a pistol at the coachman; "move another inch, and I'll knock that powdered wig about your ears with a couple of bullets in a manner that you won't like."

"Who are you?" gasped the coachman, as he rolled off the coach. "Oh! lor', I am a dead man."

"The lord of the manor," Captain Macheath replied.

And then, feeling satisfied that the coachman was past doing harm, he cantered to the door of the carriage and confronted a fiery-faced individual.

"Coachman, drive on!" the gentleman shouted. "What is it? The deuce seize you, what do you mean by stopping? Drive on—drive on, I say! Am I, the under-sheriff of the county, to be kept one moment? Drive on, I say—drive on!"

"He cannot," said Macheath. "It is of no use, sir, your bullying the poor man. I have ordered him to stop, and he has stopped on his back in the middle of the road."

"You—you ordered him to stop?"

"Yes, I."

"And who, in the name of all that's horrible, are you?"

"It is of little consequence who I am," said Macheath, smiling. "Let it suffice that I have taken it into my head to establish a toll in this lane, and here I am to enforce it. Ah! you are not alone—a lady, I perceive. Madam, I beg you will not be alarmed in the least. The under-sheriff, madam, seems rather a hot-headed kind of man; but you should be firm with him."

"A highwayman!" said the gentleman, "by all that's dreadful."

"Now, sir, your money, watch, and jewellery."

"Gracious heavens!" cried the lady, "are we to be robbed?"

"No, madam," said Captain Macheath; "you may give me what you like, but I will take nothing from you without your consent. As for the under-sheriff, he will see the force of this little argument, as my time is rather precious."

Macheath rested a pistol-barrel upon the edge of the coach window as he spoke and the sheriff changed colour.

It was at this moment that Macheath fancied some shadow crossed his face, and looking up, he saw the two footmen with their staves uplifted ready to bring them down upon his head.

"That's right, my fine fellows," said the captain. "Defend your master and hang the consequences. I'll find you work enough."

He raised the pistol and fired it at the two footmen.

But he took care that the bullets should go over their heads.

They both fell off the back-board of the carriage, and lay in the road as bereft of all movement as though the pistol had divided its contents between them.

"Are you a murderer?" said the lady.

"No, madam. They are both unhurt."

"For Heaven's sake, Mr. Gilson, give him what he asks for and let him go at once. Do, I implore you!"

"You rascal!" said the sheriff, "you shall swing for this. I will have the whole country raised about you. It will be the very worst day's work you ever did. I should like to know who you are?"

"I'm not an under-sheriff," said Captain Macheath, as he pocketed a magnificent gold watch and seals that were handed to him and then a purse tolerably well-filled.

The lady, too, handed a small purse.

"Is it your own money, madam," said Captain Macheath, "or this man's?"

"My own."

"Then keep it."

"You are Captain Macheath," said the lady. "You have convinced me by that one act. I have never heard of any other—other—"

"Highwayman," put in Macheath, as he saw that the lady hesitated about the word, no doubt, for fear of offending him. "I am not at all nice, madam, about a word or so. You would say that I am the only highwayman who knows how to behave himself to a lady, and I really believe it is a melancholy fact in these degenerate days."

Macheath deliberately took a pinch of snuff.

"So you are Captain Macheath, are you?" said the sheriff. "By Jove! I'll have you hung, you rascal. Just let me get a good look at you, that I may know you again, you thieving vagabond!"

"Perhaps that will clear your eyes," said Macheath, as he flung the whole contents of his snuff-box right into the sheriff's face.

Then, turning his horse's head from the carriage, off he went a hand-gallop.

CHAPTER XV.

THE OXFORD COACH DOES NOT REACH ITS DESTINATION.

"WELL," said Macheath, as he rode off, "this is doing business, at all events. I wonder, now, if I shall have the luck to come across the Oxford coach?"

Macheath knew right well the route that the Oxford coach would take, so he hovered about a gloomy part of the road.

The road at this spot was only just wide enough for two vehicles to pass each other, and in the centre of the hollow, during the rainy seasons, the vehicles had to pass right through a sheet of water stretching across the road.

It was here that Macheath purposed waiting for the coach.

The twilight was coming on, and by the time the coach might be fairly expected at that spot no doubt it would then be sufficiently dark for any daring deed to be perpetrated.

Macheath backed his horse between two lofty fir trees, and there he waited with all the patience of a sentinel for the approach of the vehicle.

Occasionally he whiled away the time by humming the air of some ditty then popular in London, and at times his thoughts wandered to the fashionable lodgings in Spring-gardens and to the fair Polly Peachum.

"Yes," he said, after rather a long pause, "I do begin to think really that I am in love at last, and that Cupid has sent into my heart one of his most fiery darts, with Polly's name upon its point. She is without doubt a beautiful young creature; and there is such an exquisite charm about her youth and innocence, that it is quite out of the question to look upon her and to hear her speak and not to love her. I—'

Macheath stopped short, for he felt certain he heard the sound of coach-wheels traversing the road from the direction whence he fully expected the Oxford coach to come.

"Ah!" he said, as he patted the neck of his steed. "The time for action is coming. It comes—it comes, and tolerably rapid, too; but they will decrease speed upon reaching the hollow, and then will be my time. Ah! this is life. This is what I enjoy, now. I will stop that coach, and all its passengers, when they have got over their fright, shall have a story to tell of how one man said 'Hold!' and how then they all obeyed him. Ha, ha! It has been so, and it will be so again and again."

The coach appeared in sight—a misty, bulky-looking object in the gathering twilight.

The lamps would not be lighted until at the place where they next changed horses, so that the vehicle looked dark and shapeless as it came carefully guided down into the deep hollow, where Captain Macheath was waiting for it with all the impatience of some ardent sportsman for his game.

One touch of his horse's flank and, like a flash of light, out he bounded into the centre of the road.

"Stand and deliver!" he cried.

The coachman impulsively pulled up with a suddenness that brought the leaders to a standstill.

"Who is that?" the man demanded.

"Drive on!" shouted a voice. "Drive on! Over him—over him, coachman! I will stand all the consequences!"

The coachman in another moment might have recovered from his first state of stupefaction and obeyed this order, but Macheath, making for the horses' heads, at once cut the reins close to the bits with a small but exquisitely sharp knife.

"We shall be overturned," said the coachman. "The leaders will start off."

"Let them go, then," said Captain Macheath, as he severed the traces, and unhooking the guide-chain, the leaders were free, a circumstance they did not omit to avail themselves of in a moment, for they started off as if a thousand fiends were pursuing them.

"Stoop, coachman!" cried the same voice that had urged the desperate measure of riding over Macheath. "Stoop while I have a pop at him."

"Why don't you stoop, coachman?" cried Macheath. "The gentleman behind you wants a pop at me, and I am quite willing to let him have first fire, because I feel that my turn will come."

The coachman did stoop, and so low, too, that he fell off the box on to the wheel-horses and then to the ground, where he lay upon his back roaring.

Murder!" he yelled.

"If you don't cease that noise," cried Captain Macheath, "I'll request my horse to stop it by putting his near fore-foot in your mouth. Now, sir, where's this pop you were so anxious to have at me?"

The passenger who had been so violent stood up upon his seat behind the coachman and presented a large horse pistol at the captain's head.

"Blaze away!" cried Macheath, as he carelessly handled one of his own long, thin, bright-barrelled holster-pistols. "Blaze away, sir; but, remember, I have second fire, and in that case it's a pity if you have anyone dependent upon you."

The passenger slowly let his arm drop and the pistol hung by his side.

He muttered something that was unintelligible to Macheath and then sank back into his seat.

"You are wise," said Macheath. "What's the use of a man throwing his life away in the defence of a few guineas a the utmost? Pooh—pooh! sir, you know better."

The coachman was now still, being, in fact, petrified with terror.

The extraordinary threat of Macheath that he would speak to his horse to silence him with his foot had had its due effect.

The wheel-horses of the coach were, however, evidently getting uneasy at finding there was no controlling hand over them, and Captain Macheath thought the best plan was to save accidents and give them their liberty at once; so when he cut their traces, off they went after the leaders.

It has taken some time to tell all this, but the real space occupied in its transaction was short indeed.

The inside passengers had hardly become thoroughly alive to what was going on before Captain Macheath made his appearance at the coach-door, and projected the barrel of one of his pistols in through the window.

"If there are any ladies here," he said, "or a nervous gentleman, he need not be at all alarmed. Only I warn people not to hide their watches in their boots, or to stuff their purses under the seats of the coach, for I know as well what anyone has as he or she do themselves. I want your watches, rings, and purses, ladies and gentlemen, if you please. One lady only, I think."

"A poor w—w—widow, sir!" stammered a voice, in the last extremity of fear.

"Fat and old?"

"Fat and old!" screamed the lady; "certainly not. How dare you, you ugly, impudent fellow, say such words of me? I declare, if I were a man, I would never cease following you up till I got you hanged."

"Ah! my dear madam, what a release from his earthly troubles it must have been to your poor husband when he died. Now, gentlemen, I will trouble you, if you please, to be quick."

"I am very poor," said one.

"And I never travel with anything of value about me," said another. "I am not such a fool!"

"A guinea and some silver is all I have," said a third. "You will find this anything but a good night's work, Mr. Highwayman."

"I always take my chance," said Captain Macheath. "Of course, I cannot expect more than you have; but if I don't get two watches out of four people inside a coach, and some well-filled purses, I have a very troublesome habit."

"And what may that be, pray?" asked one of the insides, in a very soft tone of voice.

"I generally blow out somebody's brains," the captain replied, coolly. "But upon this occasion, gentlemen, for fear I should be mistaken, I will be content with one watch."

Macheath paused, and then he heard one of the passengers say –

"Give him yours."

"Not I," said another ; "give him yours."

"Nay ; why should I be the victim ?"

"Now," said Captain Macheath, "I increase my demand to three watches, and if I don't have them by the time I count three I will fire into the coach and you may take your chances of what may ensue. One—two—thank you, gentlemen."

Three watches were duly handed out to Macheath.

"Now, madam," he said, "I can, even by this light, see that you have a watch by your side."

"But you would not rob a lady ?"

"Nonsense," said the captain, laughing. "I am quite convinced you are a man in petticoats, or you never would have talked of taking any pleasure in seeing anyone hanged."

The widow, with a groan, handed Macheath a watch of considerable value.

"I wonder at three sticks," she said, sneeringly, "calling themselves men, allowing themselves to be robbed by only one highwayman."

"Oh !" said one of the passengers, "the pleasure of seeing you disgorge something out of your unhallowed gains quite reconciles me to my loss, I assure you, madam."

"Who is the animal ?" said Macheath.

"Mother Bonus, they call her at Oxford. She keeps a pawnshop, and lends money at the trifling rate of two hundred per cent. to the improvident gownsmen. I am a poor man."

Macheath laughed as he said—

"Is your watch a silver one ?"

"Yes, and I value it, for it was my father's."

"Take it back then, sir, by all means. Come, gentlemen, your money—your money, if you please. Be quick, Mr. Briarley."

"Good gracious !" cried one of the insides, "he knows my name. Who are you, and where do you come from, you infamous rascal ?"

Macheath had been most anxious all along to find out which was Briarley, the uncle of Minna, the young lady at the madhouse, and now that he had made that discovery he at once dismounted, and opening the door of the coach, out he handed him on to the road.

He did not ask him to give up his papers, but by giving his pockets a flap or two, Macheath found out a large leathern pocket-book, which he at once appropriated and placed in the breast of his own apparel.

Briarley dropped down upon his knees in the road.

"Take everything but my papers," he cried. "Spare my papers and take all my money. I will send you one hundred pounds where you like, but give up my pocket-book. You had better kill me than take that, and there's not a thing in it that will fetch you a penny piece. Oh ! good sir, do give me back my pocket-book."

Captain Macheath mounted again, and his principal object being now accomplished, which was to get hold of Briarley's papers, which he felt convinced by the outcry the fellow made about them were in the black pocket-book, he prepared to leave the spot.

"Gentlemen on the outside," he cried, "I shall not trouble you, with the exception of my friend who wanted to pop at me, and I will take his pistol from him as a present."

"There's one of them, then," said the outside passenger, who now thought he had Macheath at a disadvantage and fired right at his face.

It was not a bad shot, for the bullet tore a slight furrow in Captain Macheath's cheek, which, however, at the moment he did not feel at all.

He pointed his own pistol at the man, who roared for mercy, and rolled himself about the coach top in the most horrible and extraordinary manner.

"Take the reward of treachery," said Captain Macheath, as he pulled the trigger of one of his long, bright-looking holster-pistols.

The pistol which Captain Macheath fired was only loaded with small shot, and he watched an opportunity of discharging it when none of the little leaden pellets would hit the man's face.

Mingled with the report of the pistol came such a yell from the outside passenger that the place rang with it again.

"Now we are even again," said Macheath. "You can try your luck a second time, if you like."

"Oh ! good gracious, no ! I'm all in pieces ! I'm a dead man ! I'm done—done—done !"

"Farewell to you all !" said Captain Macheath. "I'm afraid the Oxford coach will be very much behind its time to night ; but these things will happen sometimes, you know, and you must take the world as you find it, and don't give way to grumbling."

With these words he put his horse to a gallop, and did not pull up until he had put four miles between himself and the disabled coach.

A light gleamed a little way ahead, and Macheath, shading his eyes with his hand for a few moments, regarded it attentively.

"It's all right," he said. "That's the Roebuck, and I'll stay there for the night. In the morning it will be time to get in the saddle again, and to make my way to the madhouse. I feel more tired than usual after to-day's work."

At a gentle trot he made his way to the little roadside inn.

"Frank—Frank !" he cried.

A poor, miserable-looking man made his appearance.

"Is that the captain?" he demanded. "Has he come to do good to our eyes at last ? Ha—ha ! Is that the captain, let me ask ? He ! he ! he ! I hope it is the captain."

"Well, old Screw-'em-all," cried Macheath, as he dismounted, "how does the world use you now, eh ?"

"He—he ! it is the captain. I said it was the captain. But don't call me Screw-'em-all, captain. My name is Jowles, you know. Why, good heart alive ! anyone to hear you talk would take me for a miser."

"And how far from being right should I be ?" said Macheath, with a smile. "I never met with or heard of such a miser as you are. Confess, now. Do you ever cook anything for yourself or your wife, or do you really still depend for you own eating solely upon what any chance guest at this dog-hole of an inn may happen to leave upon his plate ?"

"We—we must be economical," said the old man. "In these times we must be economical, good captain. We don't know what we may come to. He—he ! don't fancy that I'm a miser, good captain, for misers have chests of gold, but what have I? Not a penny—not a penny. I am miserably poor, as all the world knows—most miserably poor. He—he!"

"Poor!" exclaimed Captain Macheath, as he followed the old man into the inn, after a half-starved-looking boy had taken his horse. "Poor, do you call yourself? Why, if I wanted a thousand pounds I should be down upon your strong box in a moment, with a certainty of getting it, too. Poor, indeed! No, that won't do by any means —no, no."

"My strong box!—my strong box!" cried the old man. "Oh! dear—oh! dear. Wife—wife— Lucy! The captain fancies we have got a strong box with a thousand pounds in it! Oh! dear— oh! dear. I shouldn't believe my eyes if I saw a thousand pounds!"

"Oh! dear, how can the captain say that?" cried a little shrewish-looking woman, with a red nose, as she made her appearance in the room into which Jowles had conducted Captain Macheath. "But the captain is always at his jokes, he is."

"Well," said Macheath, "it is no joke that I am desperately hungry, so let me have something to eat as soon as possible; and as I am tolerably sure you have neither of you had anything to eat for the last fortnight but cheese-parings and crumbs of bread you had better sup with me."

The old man's eyes glistened, and he rubbed his hands together.

"Sup with the captain!" he cried— "sup with the captain! Do you hear that, Lucy, my dear? —sup with the captain. It's the honour of the thing I look at, not the eating and drinking. Oh! dear, no—it's the honour of the thing, Lucy, that we look at."

"To be sure," croaked the old woman— "to be sure it is, Joe. But the captain is like me—he has a free heart, and gives away with an open hand—just like me is the captain, ain't he, Joe?"

"Yes, Lucy, and like me, too. There's nobody in all this world, or the other either, who knows what I give away. He! he! he!"

"And never will, I'll be bound," said Macheath. "What you both give away anyone might paste on to his spectacle glasses without dimming them in the least. But be quick with the supper. I know you can put a supper upon the table if you like, and you know that I shall not look twice at the bill."

The old couple, half-starved as they were, bustled about, and it was astonishing how, in the course of half an hour, they had managed to kill, pluck, and dress a couple of fine fowls, which, with some fine crisp rashers of ham, made truly a very delectable kind of supper.

"Fowls are very dear," said the old man, "just now, but we thought you'd like them, so we killed them. He! he! he! It's not an economical supper at all, and I'm afraid we shall have to charge you a good price."

"Bother you!" said Macheath. "Don't talk to me about your prices. Charge a guinea a couple for your fouls, if you like, and another for cooking them."

"Lucy, do you hear that?" said the old man. "What a man the captain is, to be sure. Do you mean it, captain?"

"Yes, I do."

Jowles rubbed his hands together, and looked as delighted as possible.

Macheath cut one of the fowls into three portions, and handed the old couple one each, and then he said, as if a sudden thought had struck him—

"The deuce take it! my horse has a bandage on him. I ought to have spoken to your boy about it. Can you ring for him?"

"Bells," said the old man, "are not economical. The wires will wear out; but I can tell him in a minute. Don't you stir, captain, the young rascal shall come in here to you, he shall."

After screaming out "Joe!" for about five minutes the boy came shuffling into the room, with a lank, half starved look.

"Joe," said Macheath, "don't touch the bandage on the horse's side, and mind you give him a first-rate feed."

"Yes, sir," said the boy; "this here's the place for first-rate feeds, above a bit. Oh! my eye, how my inside is a-rumbling!"

"You wretch!" exclaimed Lucy. "You ungrateful, greedy wretch! You think of nothing from morning till night but of eating and drinking."

"I'm forced to think on it, missus," said Joe. "When a chap is always hungry it makes him think on it, whether he will or not, and there ain't much chance of being anything else in this crib."

"It's a disease," said old Jowles, lifting up his hands—"it's a disease that the poor boy has got that makes him feel always hungry. Don't scold him, Lucy. He can't help it. Go to the cupboard, Joe, and help yourself."

"Yes, with the deal shelves," said Joe, "for there's nothing else there that a half-starved mouse wouldn't turn up his nose at."

Macheath was much amused at this scene.

But he had sent for Joe for a purpose, and beckoning to him, he put into his hands a whole loaf and the third of a fowl.

"There, Joe," he said, "don't say you have not had a supper to-night."

"Oh! murder," cried Jowles, springing up and throwing Lucy over, chair and all—"oh! murder. I can't sit and see this. Oh! dear—oh! dear. Put it in the cupboard, Joe, and we will warm it up to-morrow."

"Doesn't you wish you may get it?" said Joe. "Thank you, captain; and if ever you wants a boy to go through fire and water for you, only come to me, and I'll do it pretty quick."

With this Joe vanished from the room, but not before Captain Macheath had given him a pantomimic hint to draw himself a pot of beer from the bar.

Both Lucy and the miserly Jowles groaned over the loss of the third of the fowl; but they found by Captain Macheath's manner that to say anything would be utterly useless, and as for making any attempt to get the eatables away from Joe again, there was not a shadow of a chance.

Macheath carved the other fowl for himself, and he was much amused at the manner in which the old miserly couple pretended to eat, but in reality took very little, and pocketed at sly moments when they thought he was not looking many pieces of both ham and fowl, with the hope that they would be able to dish them up to someone and get paid for them again the next day.

They could not bring their minds to enjoy the supper, although they were actually treated with it by their liberal guest, whose pursuit in life they both knew very well, but never betrayed on account of the liberal manner he spent his money with them at their old inn.

Captain Macheath knew that when he chose he might stop in perfect safety at the Roebuck, provided he was sufficiently cautious not to permit of his being tracked to the old place.

In the present instance he felt quite confident that such was not the case, and he was well enough pleased to find some six or eight hours of calm and quiet rest, both for himself and for his horse.

Some old wine was produced by Jowles, for well he knew that Captain Macheath would not drink any of an inferior quality, and so about an hour after Macheath was shown to his chamber.

"What's the reward for him, Lucy?" said Jowles to his wife, as they were clearing away the remnants of the supper. "What's the amount of the reward that's out for the captain now?"

"Two hundred pounds, I think," said Lucy.

Jowles shook his head.

"Two hundred. No—no; it would not pay—it would not pay. You can't invest two hundred pounds to bring you in anything like one-fourth of what Macheath spends with us in a year. He! he! So you see, Lucy, the best way is to take the greatest care of him. He's worth much more than two hundred down to us—oh! yes, much more. But what a shocking thing it was to see him give Joe the third of a fowl and a whole loaf! I sha'n't forget that for weeks—weeks. Couldn't we deduct it from what Joe gets in some way?"

"It would be very difficult," said Lucy, "as he gets nothing at all from us but liberty to sleep in the stable. I don't see very well how it is to be done."

"Well, well, I must think of it—I must think of it. I shall never forget it, I'm sure, while I live. Dear—dear! it's enough to break one's heart to say nothing of the whole loaf—yes, to say nothing of the whole loaf. It is a dreadful circumstance. But shut up for the night, Lucy. It's quite clear that we must take every care of Captain Macheath."

Perhaps the captain would not have been quite so comfortable at the old inn had he known upon what calculation he owed his safety.

The morning dawned in beauty, and Macheath, after paying his host and hostess even beyond their expectations, mounted his horse, and was on the road again before eight o'clock.

He trotted gently to the neighbourhood of the madhouse, and then riding into a road-side meadow he turned his horse loose to graze, while he himself sat down under a tree, fully intending to occupy the next half-hour in a careful view of the pocket-book he had taken from Mr. Briarley.

The book was one of those usually carried by business men, having no encumbrance in the way of fastenings.

"There should be something here," said Macheath, as he opened it, "to account for the state of anxiety that Briarley was in to get it back; and we shall soon see upon what particular documents he fixes his affections."

The contents of the leathern case were in truth most voluminous and multifarious.

There were notes of all kinds and descriptions, relating to legal and parochial business in Oxford.

But what surprised Macheath more than anything, especially when he thought of the anxiety of Briarley to get the case back, was the absence of money.

Neither note, cheque, nor order for money were to be found, although Macheath looked with care at the papers.

Finally, however, in a compartment of the case he discovered a document, and the one which Briarley was so afraid of parting with.

CHAPTER XVI.
THE RESCUE.

THE document was tied up with red tape and endorsed—

"Deed of assignment from Minna Briarley to William Briarley, of the Thistledown Estate, Oxon."

"This must be the matter of importance," the captain said. "Humph! let me see. 'In consideration of four thousand pounds received.'—Ah! I understand it all now. The price of Minna's liberty would have been her signature to this document, and then in all probability they would not have kept faith with her, but she would have died in that miscalled asylum. I am glad to be able to foil this villainy."

There was nothing else of any importance in the pocket-book, and Macheath, after carefully placing the prepared deed of assignment in a side pocket, carelessly enough bestowed the book with the remainder of its contents into one of the ample pockets of his over-coat.

He had scarcely completed the arrangements when a loud voice aroused his attention.

"Hilloa—hilloa! you fellow!" cried the voice. "What do you do there? Don't you know you are trespassing? How dare you come into my meadow, and turn your horse loose in it, eh?"

Captain Macheath's steed gently cantered towards its master, and a rough, farmer-like-looking man followed it.

He had a thick stick, with a large knob at the end of it, in his hand.

"My friend," said Captain Macheath, "don't fly into a temper. I shall not steal your land."

"What do you mean by that? Don't you think you are going to gammon me, young fellow. I'll have you in the cage and your horse in the pound, or else my name ain't Giles Gobblings."

"What for, Giles Gobblings?"

"Why, for trampling down my grass here, besides letting the horse eat some of it up. Do you think I rent meadows to turn your horse into?"

"Certainly not," said Macheath. "I will pay over and above for what my horse has eaten or destroyed. Will that satisfy you?"

"No, it won't. I'll have the horse in the pound, dang my buttons if I don't. I have said it, and my name is Giles Gobblings."

"Come and take him, if you dare," said Captain Macheath. "And now I warn you if you so much as lay a finger on him I'll give you such a thrashing as you never had in all your life!"

"I don't care for such a whipper-snapper as you," cried Giles Gobblings. "If I fell upon you I should crush you. Your horse goes to the pound, and you to the cage, or else my name ain't Giles Gobblings."

With this Giles made an attempt to seize the horse by the bridle, but Captain Macheath gave him such a cut across the knuckles with his riding-whip that he howled with pain.

"Pinem—Pinem—Pinem!" he roared.

Macheath could not, for the life of him, make out what he meant by Pinem.

But he soon found that it was the pet-name of a ferocious-looking, blear-eyed bull-dog, who made his appearance in answer to the summons, with his tongue lolling out of his mouth, and seemingly as intent upon acquiring a pound of somebody's flesh as ever Shylock was.

Macheath drew out a pistol from his pocket and shot Pinem dead.

"You and I," said the captain, "can settle this matter without any dogs as witnesses."

The farmer was infuriated at the death of his dog, and grasping the stout stick, he advanced upon Macheath.

At the moment he was about to commence an attack with it Macheath rushed at him, and grappled him so closely that their faces were not six inches apart.

Under such circumstances the stick was completely useless.

A brief struggle ensued, and the farmer began to call out lustily for help, for he found that, with all his brute strength, he was no match for his young and agile antagonist.

Down he went to the ground, and Captain Macheath above him, with a concussion that seemed to shake the earth, and which did for a few moments deprive him of breath.

"Now," said Macheath, "you will be a little more civil another time."

"Murder!"

"Say that again and I'll make it one. Do you see this?"

Macheath pushed the barrel of a pistol into his mouth.

"Oh! yes—yes. Spare my life! I'm a miserable man! Spare me, good sir, do! Master Briarley—Master Briarley, where are you now?"

"Of whom do you speak?" said Macheath. "Did you mention the name of Briarley?"

"Yes, sir, I did. I've got to go with him to the 'sylum, to witness a deed as his niece, Miss Minna, is to sign, if you please, sir, to let me go."

"And when are you to meet him there?"

"Soon, sir, if you please. Your horse may take what he likes, only let me go, for I'm to have twenty pounds for the job."

"Now, mark you, Giles Gobblings, if you set any value upon your life, you will be pleased to tell me at once why it is you are to get this twenty pounds you speak of. Can't be for witnessing a signature, you know."

Giles Gobblings wriggled about on the ground.

"Why, no, sir," he said. "But if the young lady were to say anything afterwards about the matter I'm to swear she did it with free will, you see, and owned she had had the money, and all that sort of thing, and kissed her uncle, and—and—dear me, I've got it all set down on a bit of paper somewhere."

"And did it never strike you, Master Giles, that you were to play the part of a great rogue in this transaction? I say, did that not strike you?"

"Folks must live, and crops is bad."

"Very good," said Macheath. "Now I will trouble you to get up. Is that your farmhouse yonder among the trees?"

"Yes, it is, and if you'll only come there, I'll give you the best jug of ale you ever had in all your life, dang my buttons if I don't!"

Macheath began rummaging in his pockets, and having found some pieces of strong cord, he tied Giles Gobblings' ankles together and his wrists behind his back, despite his protestations and prayers for mercy.

He was afraid to cry out loudly for help, since the pistol barrel had rattled in so very ominous a manner against his teeth.

He began to shed tears in great abundance, for he had an awful misgiving about the fate that was intended for him.

"You will come to no harm if you will only be quiet," said Captain Macheath. "That paper you mention I should like to have, although, perhaps, after all, an easy death now is preferable to being laid upon a bed of sickness, as one day you might be."

"Oh! dear, no—no. It's in my waistcoat-pocket—it's in my waistcoat-pocket."

"Oh!" cried Macheath, "is it? Ah! sure enough, here it is. And this is the hand-writing of Mr. Briarley, is it, Master Giles Gobblings?"

"Yes, it is. Won't you let me go now?"

"I cannot let you go just yet; but you shall come to no harm," Captain Macheath replied. "I will promise you that much, although you may be rather uncomfortable for an hour or two."

Mr. Gobblings glared at Captain Macheath with both wonder and fear depicted upon his countenance; but he was not for a long time kept in a state of ignorance as to what was to be done with him.

Macheath cut a stout branch of an alder tree, and providing himself with a piece about six inches long, he made Gobblings take it in his mouth like a bit, and then he twisted some cord round each end of it, and tied it firmly at the back of his head.

"How do you feel now?" Macheath demanded.

Gobblings made an ineffectual attempt to answer him, and from that Macheath was satisfied that the gag was effectual.

He then laid Gobblings close under the hedge-row, saying—

"Someone will see you, I daresay, in the course of the day; but until they do, I am inclined to think that you are harmless. You can fume and fret as much as you like to yourself. Perhaps it will do you good to do so, and if you feel an inclination, pray don't baulk it at all upon my account. I now bid you good-morning."

Mr. Gobblings made a vain attempt to return what, no doubt, would have been some very furious answer; but the gag prevented him, and the cords that held his wrists and ankles stopped him from rising.

He could only roll about a little, and as Macheath had placed him in a kind of rut or drain close to the hedge, he could not fairly get out of it.

"Now then," said Captain Macheath, as he sprang upon the back of his steed—"now then for Minna and the asylum."

The hour had arrived when he had promised the imprisoned girl that he would make an attempt to rescue her, and at a sharp trot he made towards the lunatic asylum.

All was quiet, and dismounting close to the door, he led his horse right up to the wall.

He felt certain that the creature would wait for him, and he hoped that the time would not be many minutes that he would have to be in the garden.

The grand thing was to ascertain if the door had been re-secured or not.

A touch convinced him that it was in the same state as he had left it the preceding day.

He did not enter the garden with any degree of precipitation; but after listening for a few moments to be quite certain that no one was at hand, he cautiously pushed the door open sufficiently wide to enable him to enter the garden and then he stepped lightly in.

A glance was sufficient to show him that he was alone, and then, gently closing the door, he began to hope that Minna would not be long in coming to him, as the time was past.

In the course of a few moments he heard the

sound of voices, and feeling confident that the speakers were approaching, he concealed himself behind a sycamore-tree and awaited their arrival.

Presently, round the same angle of the shady walk which Minna had turned when he first saw her, two females appeared.

One of them he saw was Minna—the other was a female of large proportion and most inconceivably ugly.

She was dressed in a style of flaming vulgarity, and from the manner in which she walked and talked to Minna, it was quite evident that she considered herself as exercising some sort of authority over her.

"May I rest here, madam?" Minna asked, when they reached the garden-seat that was close to the spot.

"Very well, you may," said her companion, or keeper, whichever she was. "I only hope that you see your own interest in what I have said to you."

"Oh! yes, I hope so."

"Of course, your uncle's affection for you will always procure you a comfortable home, and it's much better for a man to have an estate than a young girl. You would only have a parcel of fellows running after you for the sake of it; whereas, if you have nothing in the world but what depends upon the will of your uncle, Mr. Briarley, you will, when you do marry, be able to say that you were chosen for yourself alone."

"Certainly, madam. I am very glad that in some way the usual dose that confused my faculties has been omitted from my food last night. I do not feel this morning confused at all, as, since my residence here, I have been in the habit of feeling."

"Oh! nonsense, child, that is all your fancy," said the old woman; "you have had no doses. You have made up your mind to do what's the right thing by making over your property to your uncle, and that makes you feel better this morning."

"Do you really think so, madam?"

"I do, of course. I hope you will never forget your duty, and I can assure you, that when you have signed the deed that your uncle ought to have brought with him before now, you will thank us all for our kindness to you, and, of course, you will never be mad enough to say you were ever in a lunatic asylum, for if you do, you will never get a husband as long as you live, I can tell you; so I hope you will not be so foolish. I expect your uncle here every minute, and he is going to bring a very respectable man with him, a Mr. Gobblings, to witness the transaction."

"Oh! Heaven," cried Minna, "is there no hope for me? What if I don't sign, after all?"

"Your life, wretch, shall be sacrificed if you falter in the least," the woman hissed. "We are above all law here. You are within these walls, and if you do not do as you are advised, there are cells here that will be good coffins and that keep secrets quite as well as graves."

"I am lost—I am lost!"

"What do you mean, hussy?"

"He does not come! Oh! Heaven he does not come! He forsakes me—"

"Do you mean your uncle?"

"No—no—no!" Minna cried, frantically. "I tell you, madam, I will not sign the document that will make me a beggar—I will not do it! Kill me, if you will, but I say again I will not do it."

"That's right," said Captain Macheath, as he sprang forward. "I am a witness to that."

With a cry of joy Minna fell upon her knees.

"Heaven be thanked! He is here, and I am saved!" she cried.

The large female's huge face became of a purple colour with rage.

She rose and made an attempt to fly from the spot, no doubt to seek assistance; but Macheath caught her by the head-dress.

"Stop a moment, madam," he said.

And then all the head-dress, including an immense wig with a forest of black ringlets, came off in his hand.

The large female, who was no other than the wife of the keeper of the lunatic asylum, tried to take advantage of this accident to escape; but Captain Macheath was too quick for her and held her tight by the back of the neck.

"No, my dear madam," he said. "We cannot spare you just yet, I assure you. You are too good company to be easily parted with, and without your wig you really do look particularly fascinating, I assure you."

The woman uttered a shriek. Macheath faced her about in a moment, and looked at her sternly.

"Hark you, madam," said he, "I don't wish to say anything uncivil to a lady, especially one so very delicate and lady-like looking as yourself; but if you don't be quiet I shall be under the disagreeable necessity of digging a hole in the ground and putting your head into it."

"Monster, who are you?"

"Minna," said Captain Macheath, "open that door at once, and we will be off. It will be necessary to take this sweet creature along with us a little way."

"Then I won't go," said the lady, resolutely. "I will raise an alarm. Help—help—mur—"

Macheath still had the interesting creature's wig in his hand, and he at once put a stop to any further vociferations by cramming it into her mouth.

She kicked and plunged, and turned very red in the face.

Minna was alarmed, and said—

"Oh! do not smother her. You have stopped her mouth completely. She cannot breathe."

"Oh! yes," said Macheath. "Rather than choke she will make her nose do duty. Open the door. That's right. Ah! what bell is that?"

"It is the great gate-bell. We are at the back of the house," said Minna. "Oh! we shall be stopped. Let us hasten—let us hasten! It is my uncle arrived."

"Don't be alarmed. All will be well. We have plenty of time," Captain Macheath returned. "My horse is outside, and if they have anything on four legs that can beat him, I will make them a present of my steed."

Macheath caught up the wigless lady and handed her through the door in the garden-wall.

The horse stood in precisely the same spot in which he had been left by his master.

But he testified by his movements how well pleased he was to see him again.

Minna, in obedience to Macheath's directions, carefully closed the door again.

"Now, Minna," said Macheath, "have you the courage to wait here for me two minutes quite alone? I give you my word that I shall not be gone longer."

"Yes—yes; anything you wish."

"Very good."

To the astonishment of the lady of the asylum, Macheath lifted her on the horse and then sprang up beside her.

CAPTAIN MACHEATH

THE
PRINCE OF THE HIGHWAY.

THE GARDEN DOOR OPENED AND SOME MEN RUSHED FORTH.

"Madam," he said, "you and I will take a little ride. If you don't hold me tolerably fast I'm rather afraid you will fall off. So ho! boy—off and away!"

One touch to the flank of the gallant steed, and away they flew in a direction towards the open country like the wind.

The female shrieked with dismay, but she held Macheath with the clutch of a tigress.

A gallop of a few minutes' duration took them out of sight of the lunatic asylum, and then the captain drew rein close to a heap of mud by the road side.

"Now, madam," he said—"now, madam."

"You wretch, what do you mean? What do you want, you odious monster?"

"I want you to dismount, madam, if you please."

"Then I certainly will not, you murdering vagabond. I'll cling to you until I see someone who will take you into custody. Oh! you will find that I am not a woman to be so easily frightened as you seem to fancy, you highwayman."

"Then you decline dismounting?"

"I do; and you can take that in the meantime. You find that I have got rid of what you stuffed into my mouth, and I can speak now."

With this the lady dealt Macheath such a cuff on the side of the head that made his ear sing again.

By a peculiar movement of the rein Macheath made the horse buck, and being quite unprepared for such an undulation the lady found herself fairly landed in the midst of the mud heap.

"Good-day, madam," said Macheath.

He turned at once, and at the same speed he had used in riding away from the asylum with its mistress he rode back to where he had left Minna.

As he approached near to her he saw her beckoning to him to be quick, and by her manners she was evidently in a perfect agony of fears.

"Oh! let us fly at once," she cried, as he came up. "They seek me now in the garden."

"Do they?" exclaimed Captain Macheath.

"Yes. I have heard their voices and I nearly fainted with dread, lest you should be too late to aid me," Minna answered, excitedly.

"All right," said Captain Macheath. "I only went a little way to dispose of your friend. Place your foot upon mine and give me your hand. That is right. You will find a comfortable seat enough behind me here. Are you all right?"

"Yes—yes."

"Hold me by the belt and you need fear nothing," the captain said. "We shall go a few miles, perhaps, rather fast; but do not fancy there is any danger. Fix your mind upon the pleasant idea that you are leaving the odious house behind you."

"Yes—I will. Oh! how shall I thank you?"

"Don't think of that."

The garden door opened at this moment, and three or four men made their appearance.

With one voice they all cried—

"There she is!"

"Ha!" cried Macheath. "Yes; here is she who is rescued from you, and who will yet live to call you to account."

"Villain! who are you?" cried the proprietor.

"Why, the Lord Chancellor, of course," said Macheath. "Who else should I be, I should like to know? If you've a mind for a race, and have very good nags, come out. The roads are good, and you'll find me a few miles ahead."

"Fetch the blunderbuss! Fetch the pistols! Call the dogs!"

"Ha! ha! ha!" shouted Captain Macheath. "Off and away! Hurrah for the road—hurrah!"

He gave rein to his horse. The creature lowered its head, and for a moment was still.

Then, shaking its mane and giving a loud snort, off it flew at a pace that made Minna close her eyes to shut out the terrifying effect of the flying objects that seemed to dash past her.

"So—ho! Gently—gently!" said Macheath.

The pace became steadier, but not a jot slower, notwithstanding the double burden the creature had upon its back.

A small market cart appeared suddenly from a cross-lane, and dawdled out into the very middle of the road in order to cross it and continue its progress still in the lane.

Macheath waved his arm, but the driver of the market cart did not, or would not, understand.

He stopped his vehicle exactly in the centre of the road, and with a half-stupid, half-malicious kind of grin, waited the issue.

Macheath did not relax his speed for one moment, and over went the horse, making a most magnificent leap of the market cart and its contents.

There was a bunch of turnips on the top of all the other things, and that the horse struck with his hind feet.

It did not look more than a touch, but away flew the bunch of turnips, as though it had been discharged from a cannon, and taking the driver of the cart on the side of the head, it sent him sprawling and howling into a ditch.

"Bravely done!" cried Captain Macheath, as he patted the neck of the gallant and high-spirited creature. "Truly, when I love thee not chaos has come again! Away—away! Look up, Minna. Is not this delightful?"

Minna opened her eyes for a moment, but she closed them again.

"I am terrified!" she said. "We fly—we fly!"

Another minute and Captain Macheath thought that they had placed a sufficient distance between them and the lunatic asylum to justify him in relaxing his speed.

He was the more inclined to do this as a hill was in front of them.

By a gradual tightening of the bridle he soon reduced the gallop to an easy canter, and then he spoke to Minna.

"Open your eyes now," he said. "They are too bright and beautiful to keep closed. We are not now going at a speed that will alarm you, and the asylum is five miles behind us."

"Five miles!" said Minna, as she gazed around her. "Is it possible, my friend, that we have come that distance in so short a space of time?"

"It seems incredible, but it is so, for all that, and you see the horse is not at all distressed, notwithstanding. But now you must tell me where you wish to go? Have you any friend upon whom you could rely for protection?"

"Alas! no—yes."

"No and yes? I don't quite comprehend that."

"I meant that I had no relation to whom I could apply; but there is a friend with whom I should be quite safe if—if—"

"If what, Minna? If you have any doubt of him you had better not trust in him."

"Oh! no—no. I have no doubts. I only asked myself if it would be proper for me to go with him at all."

"Oh! then, he is your lover?" queried Captain Macheath.

The bright flush that instantly spread itself over the face of the fair girl, and which Macheath caught a glimpse of, was quite a sufficiently conclusive answer without any words passing upon the subject.

"No one but yourself can be a competent judge upon that point," he said. "If there be an honest, honourable man who loves you, and you find yourself deserted—and more than deserted by your relatives—go to him at once, and laugh at what the world will say."

"Do you think so?"

"Upon my honour I do,' said the captain. "The opinion of people never has any effect on me. No doubt, whoever this lover is, he will be quite delighted to see you, and the very best thing you and he can do is to get married as fast as possible."

"You are a true friend," said Minna, "and I will follow your advice."

"Very good. Only tell me where he lives, and I will take you to him. Who and what is he?"

"He is a young artist, and his name is Raymond Atherley; I can take you to his abode. It is in the north of London, and he is, I am afraid, very—very poor."

"But you are not?"

"I hardly know," said Minna, sighing. "I am, I suppose, possessed of something, or else my bad uncle would not have taken such measures to get it from me; but he always said it was some mere trifle that had been left me by my father's will, and that he really had in a great measure to pay for my education out of his own pocket."

"Indeed!"

"Yes, that was the language he always held to me; but his conduct of late, of course, gave me reason to think I was differently situated."

"You may well think so. And now, tell me, did you ever hear of a place called the Thistledown Estate?"

"Oh! yes; that is where my uncle lives."

"Do you know what it is worth?" Macheath asked.

"I once, by accident, overheard that it was worth twelve hundred pounds per annum; but I always understood that it was my uncle's property, although I may have some slight claim upon its revenue, which he wished me to give me to him."

"Well, listen to me. I stopped the Oxford coach last night, and took from it your uncle's pocket-book."

"You?"

"Yes, and in that pocket-book was the deed you were to be compelled to sign this morning, if you had not escaped from the asylum. In that deed the whole of the Thistledown Estate is mentioned, together with the furniture, plate, carriages, and everything belonging to the house known as Thistledown Manor House. That is what you were to have been desired to surrender, and the deed is a proof that it is all yours."

"You do astonish me."

"Very likely, but it is an agreeable surprise, I hope?"

"Yes—yes. Oh! how happy I can now make poor Raymond."

"I hope he deserves it," said Captain Macheath. "Does he so?"

"He does, indeed. You don't know him as I know him, sir, or you would not find it necessary to ask that question of me.'

"I only asked it for one simple reason."

"May I know what that is, sir?" Minna demanded.

"Certainly you may," said Macheath. "I only thought at the moment that if he loved you as you ought to be loved, it ought not to have been left to the chance arrival of a stranger to rescue you from the perilous and extraordinary position you were in at the lunatic asylum; but he may have some good and sufficient reason for not having achieved that adventure very likely?"

"Yes, he has—I feel assured that he has," said Minna. "Oh! sir, you do not know him, or you would not doubt him for a moment. He is all goodness — all nobleness — all courage and generosity."

"There is London," Macheath observed, as they reached the summit of the little hill they had been ascending.

"Indeed!" Minna said. "Have we made such rapid progress in so very short a space of time? I really thought that we must be far off yet."

"No. We have travelled quicker than you could imagine; but we will not go through the streets in this fashion, as it might subject both of us to remarks. I will put up my horse, and we will get a coach at the end of Oxford-street."

"I am a great trouble to you."

"Oh! no," said Macheath. "I am so rejoiced at rescuing you from that dreadful house, where you must have seen and heard enough to drive you mad in reality. Only tell me that you do really wish to place yourself under the protection of the young artist you have named, and I will take you to him forthwith."

"Indeed, I do," Minna replied. "Such is my wish, I assure you. It is the true wish of my heart. You do not know him, sir, but I do. But I know his truth and the loyalty of his love for me."

"That is quite sufficient," Macheath returned. "Five minutes more will take us to the top of Oxford-street. We will then get a coach and drive on to the address of your lover, who is one of the happiest of men to have inspired a tender sentiment in such a bosom as yours."

To this Minna made no reply.

It sounded like a common place compliment, that she did not like to come from the lips of one to whom she owed so much as she did to Captain Macheath.

He could not but feel that she shrank a little from him, and their conversation was rather restrained than otherwise for the next few miles.

The end of Oxford-street was gained at last, and Captain Macheath, seeing a lumbering hackney-coach disengaged, handed Minna into it, telling her to wait for him a moment, while he went to put up his horse, which he did at a first-class livery stable in the immediate neighbourhood.

Macheath often put up his horse at strange places without exciting the least suspicion of who he was.

"Now, Miss Briarley," he said, "have you given the coachman his instructions where to take you to?"

"I have. He knows the way well."

"That will do," said Macheath, as he threw himself back in the coach; "that will do. And now, my dear girl, tell me how long you have loved this young man whom you speak of?"

"He has loved me," Minna replied, "for more than two years now."

"Indeed," said Macheath, as he took hold of her hand in a careless manner and held it in his own.

She tried gently to withdraw it.

"Why, Minna," he said, "is this not rather prudish to me?"

As he spoke he placed his arm round her waist, and drawing her towards him, kissed her cheek.

Minna burst into tears.

"Tears!" cried Macheath. "Have I produced them, my fair one?"

"You have—you have," she said. "Oh! sir, how ungracious it is of any man, under any circumstances, to force his attentions upon a young girl; but how doubly ungracious—how base it is of him to do so, when her natural feelings of gratitude have allowed her to give him the opportunity."

The colour rose up to Macheath's face.

No man living was more likely than he to feel keenly such a rebuke as this.

It sank deeply into his heart, and for some few moments he was silent.

But he withdrew his arm from around Minna, and suffered her to escape, sobbing, to the other corner of the coach.

"Well," said Macheath at last, with a feeling of desperation. "Well, I am a most unlucky fellow. Of course, now, the sooner you get rid of me the better, Miss Briarley. I know you can't and won't forgive me, so I will not ask you."

"No—no," said Minna. "Do not say that, my friend. Let this little affair pass over. It is enough that you regret it; and now I feel that we know each other and understand each other far better than we did before. Is it not so, my kind friend?"

"You certainly know me better," said Macheath, as he took the fair hand that was presented to him in reconciliation. "I don't think I shall commit myself again in such a way with you; so if you can forgive it and forget it, do so."

"With all my heart; and you will not pay me any more compliments upon what you are pleased to call my—my—"

"Beauty, which transcends the—"

"Ah! Stop—stop."

"There I go again," said the captain. "It is a bad habit, I am afraid, I have got, and sometimes it will at unawares show itself; so if it does so—Why, what is the coachman stopping for, I wonder?"

"Because," said Minna, clasping her hands, "we are at Raymond's door. Oh! sir, will you go in and see him first, and prepare him for my presence? I wish to do so that you may satisfy any doubts of his honour that may still cling to you, despite all I have said."

"I will go to him, if you please, Miss Briarley, but not from any doubt that I now have. I only go, if it be your wish that I should do so. Shall it be so?"

"Oh, yes—yes."

Macheath then left Minna in the coach, and having ascertained from a woman who opened the door of the house in answer to his knock that the young artist was in his own rooms, the first floor, Captain Macheath ascended, and tapped at the door of the front room.

A voice from within cried him to enter, and opening the door, he found himself in the artist's studio.

The walls were adorned by some excellent copies of the great masters, and some unfinished pictures were in the room.

Raymond was a young man of engaging address; and, as he advanced towards his visitor, Captain Macheath thought he had scarcely ever seen any one with so engaging and gentlemanly an exterior.

"Sir," said the captain, "I hope my visit will not be considered as an intrusion; but I have come to say a few words to you concerning a Miss Minna Briarley."

Raymond's face turned as pale as death, and he was compelled to lean upon the back of a chair for support.

"Good Heaven!" he said, faintly. "You do not bring me ill news of her?"

"Before I answer you any questions, sir, will you allow me to ask you one?"

"Certainly. What is it?"

"When did you last see the young lady?"

"Before her uncle took her to Bath, sir."

"Bath—Bath!" Captain Macheath exclaimed. "Fiddlesticks, sir! She has no more been to Bath than you or I have. What put Bath into your head?"

"This letter, sir, from Mr. Briarley, her uncle," Raymond replied. "I own that its contents rather surprised me, but they held out a hope that I dared not trifle with. You are at liberty to read it, sir. I have no secrets that concern Mr. Briarley, or my love for Minna, his niece."

Macheath took the letter, and read the following lines—

"Sir,—My niece, Minna, has candidly made confession to me of her esteem for you. She is going with me to Bath for a short time; but the moment we return I will do myself the pleasure of calling upon you. In the meantime, believe me to be—Yours, very truly, "W. Briarley."

"What a piece of villainy!" said Macheath.

"Villainy! sir!—how?—in what way? How is this letter a piece of villainy? Pray, sir, explain yourself. You put me on the rack."

"Believing this letter to be written in good faith," said Macheath, "of course, you waited patiently for the return of Minna, with her uncle, from Bath?"

"Not very patiently; but I did wait, of course. Under such circumstances it was no use my going to look after her; and yet, the time has seemed to me very, very long indeed. I endure much suspense."

"No doubt of it. I can tell you that that letter was written to keep you quiet—to prevent you from making any troublesome enquiries about Minna, and it has succeeded. Her uncle placed her in a private lunatic asylum for the purpose of terrifying her into signing a deed that shall convey to him all she possessed."

"Oh! Heaven."

"Yes, sir," said Macheath; "and there she languished until chance brought one to her aid, who rescued her."

"Heaven bless him!"

"You knew that she had property?"

"Yes, I did," Raymond replied. "I knew that her father left her something, and that her uncle was her guardian; but I could not believe in such villainy as you have detailed to me. Oh! Minna—Minna! Tell me where she is, sir? Let me fly to her. She resisted her uncle?"

"She is free from him, but she is penniless," Macheath said. "She now, at this present moment, is literally possessed of nothing but the clothes she actually wears."

"Then she is mine!" cried Raymond, with animation in his tones, and throwing off his dressing-gown preparatory to putting on his coat.

"She is mine, and no one can say to me that I loved her but for herself alone. She is mine, and mine only. I will toil for her; if needs were I would beg for her. Heaven bless her! she is mine. The most welcome words I have heard for many a long day are these which tell me she is poor, for now I can offer her a heart and a home. Take me to her, sir. Where is she? Oh! where is she?"

"You deserve her," said Macheath, as he strode to the door. "You deserve her, sir, and I have only to ask your pardon."

"My pardon? For what?"

"For submitting you to a little trial of affection, sir. Pray forgive me for being a little suspicious. There are so many rogues in the world—highwaymen and all sorts of iniquitous characters—that I feel quite refreshed in meeting with an honest man. Will you do me one favour?"

"Name it, sir. If within my power, I—"

"Oh! it is very simple. All I ask of you is to stand where you are for three minutes and then I will bring you the address of Miss Briarley; I promise you that, sir, upon my honour."

"I do not know you sir, I—"

"Then know that it was I who rescued her from her uncle and his good friends and rascally accomplices at the lunatic asylum."

"I will refuse you nothing. How can I thank you, sir?"

"Just by waiting three minutes where you are," said Macheath. "I do not ask you anything else. You may watch the time if you please."

"I will not be impatient."

Captain Macheath immediately left the room and walked quickly down the stairs and out of the street door to the coach that was still waiting close to the kerb-stone, and which the young artist could not see on account of the lower half of the shutters in his room being closed in order to give him a top-light for his studies.

"Will you permit me to take your place in the coach while you go up-stairs?" said Macheath to Minna. "You will find your lover in the first floor; and if it will give you any satisfaction to hear me say so, I assure you that he is in every way worthy of you. Now don't say that that is a compliment to you. It is one to him only, and a very high one indeed."

Minna Briarley looked her thanks, but she did not say anything.

Macheath helped her descend from the coach, and then he saw her mount the staircase. He flung himself into the vehicle and closed the door.

"Well!" he said, as he threw himself back on one of the seats; "let her be happy with him, who is a thousand times more deserving of her than I. What could I bring her to? A happy home?—No. A contented fireside, and an honest position in life?—No. Sorrow and shame are all that I have to offer to anyone."

Macheath was aroused from his reverie by someone looking into the coach with a full stare at him.

CHAPTER XVII.

MACHEATH MEETS POLLY PEACHUM AGAIN.

"WELL," said Macheath; "who are you?"

The face of the person who glared into the carriage was about as ugly a one as Dame Nature had ever thought of producing to astonish the world with.

"Well, who are you?" cried Captain Macheath.

"Humph! said the man.

"What do you mean by humph?"

"Only that you are my prisoner, Captain Macheath—that's all."

With one blow of his clenched fist, Macheath hit the ugly man right upon the nose, and he flew backward right up the steps of the house and into the passage.

"Coachman!" cried Macheath; "drive on."

"But, but—" said the coachman.

To tear down the front window, and project his hand through the opening with a pistol that he clapped against the back of the head of the coachman, was the work of a moment, while in a voice that to the affrighted ears of the man sounded like his death knell, Captain Macheath cried—

"Drive off, or I'll blow your brains out this moment!"

The coachman hesitated no longer but plied his whip to the horses.

They started off with the old crazy vehicle at full gallop.

"Stop him—stop him!" the captain heard voices shout. "A highwayman! Stop him! Stop the highwayman!"

What a pang such cries shot even to the bold heart of Captain Macheath!

For a moment—but only for a moment—he quailed before them, and fell back in the old coach.

And then, ashamed of his own temporary weakness, he sprang forward again, and shouted to the coachman.

"Quick—quick!" he cried. "Quicker still, or your life will answer for it."

There was a little square window at the back of the coach, and by kneeling on the seat, Captain Macheath could just look through it; and then he saw his danger.

By the rapidity with which the coach had started from the young artist's door, a party of six men, who had been in the company of the fellow whom Captain Macheath had knocked down so unceremoniously, had just been eluded.

That party had been foolish enough to hide in a doorway a little behind the coach.

Had they hidden in advance of it, nothing could have been easier to them than to have rushed out and stopped it; but nobody can be wise at all times, and even constables are mere mortals.

Immediately following these men was a rabble rout of people, who had joined the chase on the cry of "Stop him!—stop the highwayman!" being raised by the officers.

It was evident that the present state of things could not last many minutes in the streets of London.

The coach rattled on; but Macheath undid one of the doors, and held it so that he could fling it open in a moment.

"Round the next corner," he shouted to the coachman—"round the next corner with you. You will find ample payment upon the seat of the carriage."

As he spoke, Macheath threw a couple of guineas upon the box-seat, and in another moment the vehicle, at the great risk of turning over, twisted round a corner.

For a few moments Macheath knew he was out of sight of his foes.

He sprang from the coach, and calling out—"Drive on—drive on!" Macheath rushed up the steps of a house, and knocked sharply at the door, without caring whom it belonged, or thinking for a moment upon what excuse he had to make.

Before the door was opened, however, a brass

plate upon it caught his eye, upon which was the announcement of "Doctor Clitheroe."

"Ah! that will do capitally," said Macheath.

The door opened, and he entered the hall.

It was closed again, just as his pursuers turned the corner of the street, and went on full tear after the hackney-coach.

"Is Doctor Clitheroe at home?" asked Macheath of the powdered footman who opened the door.

"Yes, sir. Walk this way, if you please."

Macheath was shown into a handsome room, and as he thought it would be highly imprudent to go forth until the chase and the excitement contingent had died away, he thought that he might as well give the learned doctor a fee, and keep him in talk as long as he possibly could.

In the course of a few minutes a little primly-dressed elderly man, with his white hair violently drawn back from his forehead and the sides of his head and tied behind, entered the room.

Macheath bowed, and the doctor was at once convinced that he had a gentleman in his consulting-room.

"Doctor Clitheroe, I presume?" said Captain Macheath.

"Yes, sir—yes, sir—certainly," said the little doctor. "Pray be seated, sir, if you please—a-hem! Pray be seated."

"I have come to consult you professionally," said Captain Macheath, as he took a guinea from his waistcoat pocket and placed it upon the table. "I expect that mine is a most singular case. Have you had much experience, sir, in affections of the brain?"

"Oh! yes—yes. I am now attending a lady who fancies she is a post-office, and will swallow any letter she can get hold of, seal and all."

"Really! Well, doctor, my case is, if anything, more singular than that. I will detail it to you."

"Do so, sir—I shall be most happy to pay any attention to it, I assure you, sir."

"Well, sir," said Macheath, "I have one of the most strange and curious propensities in the world. I am at times seized with a desire to order my horse, and to gallop to one of the roads, a little way out of town—the western road usually; and then, with a pair of pistols, all ready primed and loaded, I stop folks, and cry—'Stand and deliver!' and take possession of their purses, watches, and rings, whether they like it or not. At times, too, I stop a coach, and actually, in my frenzy, rob all the passengers, and then I gallop up to town again, and for a little while the fit goes off. Now, sir, is not this a most distressing case?"

"Bless me! yes, it is," said Doctor Clitheroe. "A most distressing case, indeed. Dear me! yes. Well, I really do not think that in the whole course of my practice I have met with anything so truly singular as your symptoms."

"They are positively distressing, sir, I assure you."

"So I should say—so I should say. But what do the people whom you, in your partial aberration, stop on the road say to it?"

"Oh! they take me for a highwayman."

"I don't wonder at it, my dear sir. Let me feel your pulse. Ah—oh—hem! Rather feverish. It is a most remarkable case. Pray, sir, what do you do with the things that in your mania you take from the people?"

"I sell them, and eat and drink up the proceeds."

"You don't say so?"

"Indeed, I do. Of course, it's a very distressing thing, but I am afraid if I go on in this sort of way,

that people will give me the character of a professed highwayman, and instead of according to me their pity for my slight hallucination, will be hunting me up some day, and actually put me in Newgate."

"I should not wonder, my dear sir. What do you eat and drink usually? Diet is a great thing in these cases. Are you abstemious?"

"Remarkably so," said the captain. "A roast duck and a pound of ham will, with the assistance of a couple of bottles of wine, always make me a snack before dinner."

The doctor opened his eyes to an unusual width, and then he said—

"My dear sir, I'm very much afraid that you eat a little too much—just a little, you understand; and that that circumstance has much to do with your truly distressing case. Of course, I shall be happy to prescribe for you. When did you last feel the paroxysm come on?"

Macheath suddenly put his hand to his head, and in a startling voice, cried—

"'Tis coming now—'tis coming now!"

The little doctor sprang to his feet.

"No—no," he cried. "Stop it—stop it; don't go mad here, my dear sir, whatever you do; I beg that you won't."

"But I can't help it," cried Captain Macheath; "I'm off now. Hurrah for the road! Your money, watches, and rings, gentlemen. Hurrah—hurrah! for a dark night and a lonely road. Fire away! What ho! my gallant steed. Hilloa!"

"Murder—murder!"

Macheath rushed past the doctor, and in a moment left the house, and took his way down Charlotte-street, Fitzroy-square, at a rapid pace. None of his pursuers were in sight, and as soon as he turned the corner, he lounged along at his ease.

He kept, however, a sharp eye upon any passengers whom he might chance to see eyeing him rather curiously.

His first idea was to go to the stables at the top of Oxford-street where he had left his horse, and gallop into the country again.

But when he came to consider that he must have been recognised by someone who might yet be about the streets, he thought it would be more prudent to go to his lodgings, in Spring-gardens, for a short time.

At all events, he could stay there until night, and then, if he chose, be off to the road again.

Besides, he could send his man, William, for his horse, which would be better than running the risk of fetching it himself.

There seemed to Macheath so many more reasons for going to Spring-gardens than for taking the road again at once, that he bent his steps in the direction to his fashionable lodgings at once.

He was as well acquainted with the bye-ways as with the highways of London, and he went by a circuitous route to Charing-cross, as he was attired in rather a suspicious-looking costume.

He could not help thinking as he went along how anxious Minna Briarley and her lover, the young artist, would be about him when they heard —which they must have done—that hue and cry raised after him; but he knew they would soon be able to conclude he had escaped, for if he were captured, the news of such an event would soon enough be patent to the whole town.

It took Macheath about half an hour to reach Charing-cross; and then he rapidly went over the oad, and was upon the point of going down Spring-gardens, when he saw a small throng of persons coming up towards him upon the pavement.

"Why don't you let the girl go?" cried a voice.

"I let her go?" screamed a woman, whom Macheath at once recognised as Mrs. Peachum. "I let her go? Not I, indeed! I'm a respectable woman; and I'll see if a month at Bridewell won't bring down her pride a little. I'll teach her to run wild after a highwayman. She shall know what it is to defy her parents!"

To Captain Macheath's amazement, he saw that Polly Peachum was in the hands of a rough-looking fellow, and that several people were trying to persuade Mrs. Peachum to allow her to be let go.

"Oh! save me—save me," Polly cried.

"None o' that bawling," said the ruffian who held her. "I don't see nothing to make a rout about. Come home with me and your mother."

"Drag her along!" cried Mrs. Peachum. "I'll bring down her nasty pride, I'll be bound. Drag her along!"

"Mercy—mercy!" cried Polly. "Is there no one who will help me now? Have I no friend?"

"Stop!" cried Captain Macheath, as he strode up to the group. "What is all this about? Hold, I say!"

Polly Peachum knew his voice, and with a cry of joy, she broke away from the ruffian.

"Ah! Heaven has at length sent me a friend. He will protect me now!" she cried.

"I will," said Captain Macheath. "Fear nothing, Polly—fear nothing."

"And pray who are you, you rapscallion?" shouted Mrs. Peachum. "Who are you, that dare say you will protect my daughter, you ill-looking vagabond? Ah! I know you now. You are—"

Before the irate lady could say another word, Macheath floored the ruffian, who in turn upset Mrs. Peachum.

"Off with you!" cried a man in the crowd that was now rapidly collecting: "off with you before the man gets up. Do you want a coach?"

"Yes," said Captain Macheath.

"Follow me, then."

The crowd cheered Captain Macheath, as, with the half-fainting Polly upon his arm, he made his way towards Charing-cross.

No one made the least attempt to stop him; and a coach being procured from a stand that was close at hand, Macheath handed Polly into it, and they drove off, saluted by a loud cheer from the assembled people.

Macheath had merely told the coachman to drive on up the Strand, without giving him any more precise direction, but it was necessary to tell him where to go to directly.

"Polly," said Macheath, "dear Polly, you are safe now—you are quite safe now."

"Ah! yes; I knew that you, count, would save me."

"Do not call me count. Recollect that you know really who and what I am. Have you any other friends in London?"

"Alas! I have no other friend now in all the wide world."

"But me?"

"Yes, I ought to have said but you," said Polly. "You are a friend to me, and you will tell me what I ought to do. You will be my guide and my protector? I rely wholly upon you."

"Then, my dear Polly," said Captain Macheath, "I must find a home for you. Hilloa! coachman, drive to Kentish Town."

"All right, sir."

"And now, my own charming Polly," added Macheath, "you may dismiss all your fears. I will find you a lodging in a quiet suburb of London. You may depend upon me for supplying you with ample resources, and you may be much happier, if you will, than you have ever been yet."

"You are very good to me. But I can work—indeed, I can."

"But you shall not, Polly," Macheath said. "Do you think I would let you work while I can with ease provide most amply for your wants? No—no. You must not think of working, Polly."

"But—but, indeed, I would rather, and you can come and see me sometimes, you know, for me to thank you for your great kindness to me."

"Oh! yes, you may depend upon my coming to see you, for you know I love you, Polly—you know how truly and fondly I love you. Ah! my dear girl, can you be insensible to how very happy we may be in each other's society? Beautiful Polly!"

He clasped her to his heart and for a few moments she permitted him to hold her in his arms.

"You will not fail to find what I say is true," the captain continued, "and in a short time you will smile with pure joy to find what a happy change has taken place in your condition."

"Shall I, indeed?"

"Yes, dearest and best—my own charming Polly."

Again he clasped her to his heart, for Macheath really loved this young and innocent girl as much as he could love anyone.

The coach rattled on, and reached what was then the quiet little village of Kentish Town.

It became necessary that they should seek for some lodging, and having dismissed the coach, they strolled through the village, until, at a pretty vine-covered cottage, they found a lodging to let.

"Would you like this place?" said Macheath.

"It is humble but very pretty."

"Is it far better and prettier than I thought I should ever be able to call home?" said Polly. "It is charming."

They entered the cottage and found that they might be well accommodated.

An old woman kept the place, and she said—

"Is this young lady your sister, sir?"

"No," said Macheath. "My wife."

Polly turned pale and trembled.

She was not prepared for this.

But the words had been spoken, and she had not at the moment the courage to contradict them, and when the moment was passed, she felt how very awkward it would be to do so.

When, however, the lodging was taken and she was alone with Macheath, she clasped her hands and fell upon her knees, saying—

"Oh! spare me—spare me."

"Spare you, Polly! What do you mean?"

"You will not—you cannot wish to bring me to lead a life of hollow deception. You have said that I am your wife when you know that I am not. Why did you say so?"

"Polly, you have no confidence in me!"

"Yes—yes."

"You shall be my wife if you will not despise an alliance with me," Macheath said. "I make you a solemn promise to that effect. Have you ever found me deceive you in any promise that I made you? No, Polly. Do you think that I could have said to this woman here that you were my wife, unless I intended to make you such? If you refuse me, it is another matter."

"Refuse you? Oh! no—no."

"Rise, then, dearest Polly, and feel assured that in saying you were my wife already, I could but have one object in view, and that was to spare you the fuss, and the observation, and the inquiries, that in a little place like this you would have been directly subjected to if I had announced you as only going to be married. I will leave you now, and when I return it will be to lead you to the altar and make you my own darling wife."

Polly Peachum flung herself upon his breast and wept aloud in the fulness of her heart.

CHAPTER XVIII.

MACHEATH SETTLES ACCOUNTS WITH HIS SERVANT.

DAY was just dawning upon London when Macheath, after staying at a roadside inn, made his way back to Spring-gardens.

By the aid of his latch-key he easily let himself in, and he crept very slowly upstairs, for he did not want to disturb anyone, as he knew he could get into his rooms by the master-key he had to the doors of every one of them; and he would have had no objection to take a nap of an hour's duration upon one of his couches before he saw William.

By the time he got to his own rooms he was rather surprised to see a faint gleam from a candle or a lamp coming from under one of the doors.

This was the more astonishing to him, as he knew that William had no reason to expect his return, and why he should sit up, Macheath could not conceive.

After making this discovery, Macheath with the utmost caution proceeded the rest of the distance up the stairs, and when he got to the door from under which the light came faintly streaming, he laid his ear quite close to its panels and listened attentively.

All he could hear was a confused murmur of voices; but that was amply sufficient to let him know that someone besides William was there; and now it required no small amount of boldness to do what Macheath did, which was to open the outer door gently and listen to what was going on in his apartments.

The inner door was so thin, and light, and ornamental, that it afforded very little obstruction to sound.

William was speaking in a steady, business-like tone to someone.

"I have thought the affair over," he said, "in every shape and way; and for a very long time I felt that it was to my interest to be faithful to him, but as I think that his career is nearly over, for I know that the greatest exertions will soon be made to take him, I fancy I may as well get what I can by the transaction."

"Assuredly," said another voice, "most assuredly. You take an exceedingly sensible view of the affair; and as you have sent for me to advise with you, quite confidentially, of course, I have no hesitation in saying that I can get you a hundred pounds at least."

"Are you sure of that?"

"I am. The fact is, that the old king and the state minister are so dreadfully wroth at the visit of Captain Macheath to the palace, that they will pay almost anything to be certain of his destruction."

"Do you think his capture alive is a great object?"

"It may be."

"Well then, I tell you it can't be done; and if you and I are to do the job between us, we must kill him."

"Kill him! Won't that be attended with no small amount of risk? I, somehow, from all you have told me of Captain Macheath, don't like the idea of having anything to do with him in a scuffle, although we may be two to one."

"A scuffle! Do you think, knowing him as I do, that I would go into a scuffle with him if we were six to one? No—not I. But I have a plan—aye! such a plan."

"Indeed!"

"Yes; it's one that can't fail."

"Well, that is the strongest recommendation to any plan that I ever heard of in all my life. What is it?"

"I will tell you," said the traitor William. "When he comes here again, you, from your lodging opposite—for you must take one forthwith, and be in it to-morrow morning—will be able to communicate with me. I will, when he is here, place a wafer on the middle pane of glass in the left-hand window of this room. By that you will know that he is here. Then, the first bottle of wine he takes, I will so drug that he will fall fast asleep in his chair. You understand?"

"Yes, perfectly."

"When that is accomplished I will remove the wafer," William continued. "You will know he is asleep and helpless, and you can come over, and from the open doorway shoot him dead, and we can easily say he resisted, and we were forced to take his life to save our own. After having once tried to effect his arrest—"

"Oh! yes, it's easy enough, but why don't you shoot him? What is to hinder you from shooting him?"

"Because I don't see," William replied, "why I should do all the work, and you have half the money. If I hocus him and get him all ready for death, and open the door, and betray him to you, you may as well, I think, pull the trigger that will finish the whole affair. If you will not, our bargain is off."

"Well, well. I will do it."

"Agreed then. Our bargain is made, and whatever we get we divide fairly, guinea for guinea."

"Certainly, that is well understood; and I take it, it will be the best day's work you or I ever did, William."

"Will it?" muttered Captain Macheath to himself, as he carefully closed the outer door again and slipped down the stair case. "Will it really? We shall see about that. This is one of my luckiest escapes, after all. We shall see, Master William, if diamond cannot cut diamond."

Macheath did not pause, but without making the least noise he left the house, and repairing to an hotel in Covent-garden, he easily obtained admittance, notwithstanding the early hour, at which, if any, one had seen him, they would scarcely have suspected he was cognisant of a well-laid plan against his life.

But Macheath was celebrated for his remarkable sang froid.

While at his breakfast, Captain Macheath matured the plan he intended to adopt in this emergency, the only part of which that touched him at all being the treachery of William, whom he had loaded with benefits and favours of all kinds and descriptions.

At about ten o'clock in the day, Macheath started to Spring-gardens as if nothing at all were the matter, and letting himself in as usual, he walked up stairs, treading as he went sufficiently heavy to give to William ample notice of his coming.

The fawning traitor met him on the stairs, within a few paces of the top.

"Well, William, any news?" Captain Macheath asked.

"No, sir, none."

"Well, I did not particularly expect any. Help me off with my coat, William. I will dine here to-day."

"I am glad to hear you say so," said William, as he closed the door of the splendid room. "I am very glad to hear it indeed."

"Why so?"

"It's so much more cheerful to have you here."

"Ah! I daresay it is," Captain Macheath remarked; "and now, my man, you must get me a nice little dinner to-day, for I have no appetite for anything that is not more than tempting."

"I will do my best, sir."

"That will do. We ought all to be abundantly satisfied with anyone who does his best. I am."

The captain strolled into the adjoining bed-room, and made some slight alteration in his dress.

When he came out again a glance showed him that a small red wafer was fastened on the centre of one of the window panes.

If the smallest doubt had remained in Macheath's mind with regard to William's treachery and perseverance in the diabolical plan that he had heard hatched, the observation of the wafer would have removed it effectually.

Captain Macheath sat down with a bland smile upon his face.

"William," he said, "I think it is time that I set you up in a snug little inn, although, of course, I should not like to lose you, William. Good and faithful servants like you are so scarce."

"And good masters, too, sir. You have been a kind friend to me, sir, always."

William wiped his eyes with the corner of a table napkin, and Macheath was so disgusted at the rank hypocrisy of the rascal that he was compelled to rise and pretend to look out at the window in order to conquer the propensity he had to catch William by the throat and hold him until he breathed his last.

As he stood at the window, he saw that one of the casements on the second-floor of the house immediately opposite was opened just far enough to permit the end of a telescope to be projected out of it, and he did not doubt but that William's accomplice was gloating over the presence of the wafer on the window pane.

William was more than usually attentive to his master that day, and particularly fawning and obsequious in his address and manner towards him.

He was just the man to be so under the circumstances.

When the time came near for William to lay the table for the dinner of that master whom he was about to betray, Macheath looked continually at the wafer to assure himself that there could be no mistake.

Perhaps even William could not help noticing that his master was ill at ease.

"Are you quite well, sir?" he said, in a tone of voice that had guilt in every accent of it.

"Oh! yes, quite well. I never was better, William."

"How glad I am to hear that, sir. It is so—so very pleasant and satisfactory to me. It is, indeed."

Macheath felt as though he could really have forgiven his man William anything but this rank hypocrisy; but still he did not betray himself, but sat down to his dinner as if nothing were the matter.

"Are we well stocked with wine?" he asked.

"Pretty well, sir."

"That's right," said the captain. "Always keep up our stock, William, for we don't know what may happen."

"No, sir. We don't know what may happen, as you very truly say, sir."

Captain Macheath caught sight of William's face in the glass, and he saw come across it a most diabolical smile.

That was sufficient, and Macheath from that moment got rid of all compunction regarding the traitor's fate.

"Well, William," he said, "I think we will have some of the old Madeira to-day."

"Very good, sir. I happen to have a couple of bottles in the wine-cooler all ready, for I thought you would probably drink it to-day, sir."

"That is well, William," Captain Macheath remarked; "and now that we are quite alone, we will take a glass together."

"Thank you, sir."

Of course, as William knew perfectly well who Captain Macheath was, there was not upon all occasions much ceremony between them, and at odd times, when the humour took him, it was not at all unusual for the captain to say—"Here, William, take a glass of wine with me," so that his doing so upon the present occasion did not seem to the traitor to be anything extraordinary or out of the way.

Indeed, if it had at all upon his mind any special effect, it was only to convince him more and more of Macheath's total want of any suspicion of what was going on.

The wine was duly produced, and glancing at the bottle Captain Macheath felt convinced that it had not been at all tampered with, and, consequently, he felt rather curious with regard to the mode in which William purposed giving to him the dose that was to put his resistance out of all question.

He was not long kept in a state of suspense.

In the glass that William placed before him, Captain Macheath's watchful eye at once detected about a couple of drops of some perfectly limpid-looking fluid.

So slight was the effect produced upon the richly-cut crystal, that had not the captain been looking for some such thing it must have quite escaped him.

"Fill, William," he said.

William filled both glasses.

In Macheath's there was a slightly tinged appearance about the wine for a moment and then it passed off, leaving the pure-looking Madeira clear.

Captain Macheath took hold of the glass, and was in the act of raising it to his lips, when he suddenly paused and put himself into a listening attitude.

"What is it, sir?" said William.

"That is what I should like to know," Macheath replied. "I really thought I heard something on the stairs."

William cast a hasty look at the wafer on the pane of glass. He thought that perhaps it had come off accidentally, and that his accomplice, conceiving that the signal was given to him, had, perchance, come over to do the deed of blood.

But, no, the wafer was all right as before.

"I don't hear anything, sir," said William.

"Nor I, now. Perhaps it was imagination after all," Macheath replied. "Fill your glass, William. I know this is prime wine, and I will for once in a way give you a toast."

"Thank you, sir. I shall drink it with peculiar pleasure, I'm sure, and I am truly obliged for all favours, past and present, sir."

"Oh! don't mention them. Fill, William!"

William filled his glass, and Captain Macheath, raising his voice, said—

"I give you, William, the— Ah! what is that I hear again—an odd noise on the staircase?"

"Confound it!" said William, springing up half wild at the delay. "Confound it! I will soon see what it is, sir, if it be anything at all. Perhaps it is only some cat or dog. I will be back in one moment, sir, if you please."

"Do so."

William passed through the outer room and opened the door leading to the staircase.

He was not gone for half a minute; but Captain Macheath changed the glasses.

The moment he had made this exchange he went rapidly after William, so that the perfidious valet thought he had been followed instanter.

Of course, nothing was seen upon the stairs, and William said—

"What was the sound like, sir?"

"It sounded to me like some person trying to come very softly up the stairs with creaking boots on than anything else, William," the captain replied.

"It's very odd, sir; for not only did I hear nothing of it, but I am quite certain that there is no one on the staircase."

"Well—well, it is no matter," Macheath returned. "I don't see why I should all of a sudden be so nervous and fidgety. Let us take our wine, William, and dismiss the circumstance from our minds."

"Yes, sir; that is indeed the best way," said the traitor. "I am quite anxious, sir, to hear that toast you were kind enough to propose giving. Will you be so kind, sir, as to let me know it?"

"Certainly," said Macheath; "but let me remark that it is a toast that must be drank with a full bumper, and without reservation. You must drain your glass."

"Trust me, sir."

They both sat down to the table, and Captain Macheath raised his glass—the one that he felt quite sure now it was safe to drink out of—to his lips, while William took the drugged portion to himself, and looked, or affected to look, as pleased as possible.

"May we all meet with our deserts!" cried Captain Macheath, laughing, and then he tossed off his glass of Madeira.

William did the same.

"It's rather an odd toast, sir," said William, his eyes sparkling with triumph; for now, in his own mind, he felt certain that his master had taken the drugged wine. "It's rather an odd toast, sir, don't you think?"

"Why?"

"Why? Because really if we all had our deserts we should some of us be poorly enough off."

"Do you think so?" demanded Captain Macheath.

"I am sure of it, sir," said William, giggling. "Now you, sir, might be hanged some of these odd fine mornings, you know."

William was getting bold and impertinent, for well he knew that in the course of five minutes or so the powerful narcotic must begin its drowsy work.

"You really think so?"

"In faith I do, sir."

"And yet how much worse than I there are in this world, William," said the captain. "Just fancy now, some cringing hound, who has been feasted, petted, and made much of by a generous master, suddenly turning upon him and betraying him, merely for filthy lucre. Oh! William, are you such a hound?"

"I, sir?"

"Yes; if you are, down upon your knees and confess at once," said Captain Macheath, sternly. "Confess that you had some abominable plan against my very life. Nay, move your hands towards your breast an inch, and I will blow your brains out as you sit there. I make no doubt but that you have a weapon concealed about you. Stir an inch, I say, and you are a dead man."

William sat and trembled.

"I say confess!" cried Captain Macheath—"Confess."

"I have—nothing—to confess," the wretched traitor groaned. "You are mad or dreaming, sir. What have I done? Nothing — absolutely nothing."

"Granted, William," said Macheath; "but by this time you would have done something if I had not taken the opportunity of changing the glasses, while you went to see what it was made the imaginary noise upon the stairs."

It was quite a sight to see the expression of William's face as Captain Macheath made this, to him, terrible revelation.

Horror was depicted on every line of his features.

He made an attempt to rise from his chair, but the time had arrived for the powerful narcotic to begin its work, and his enfeebled limbs refused him support.

He fell back again with a deep groan.

Feebly, very feebly only, he gasped—

"Mercy—mercy!"

"Yes," said Captain Macheath; "such mercy as you intended for me, William, will I show to you. No man can complain of having anything meted out to him in his own measure."

William's head sunk upon his breast.

He was fast merging into a state of insensibility, and if Macheath had not risen and clutched him by the throat he would have fallen to the ground.

"Vile traitor!" Captain Macheath hissed; "I will not take your life; but into the snare you and your associate have laid for my destruction, shall you and he both fall."

Macheath hastily stripped off the embroidered dressing-gown he wore, and wrapped it about the now insensible man, whom he then placed upon the couch where he had himself been sitting.

He propped the arch traitor up, so that he might be fairly seen from the door of the room, and then he crept to the window, and taking care that nothing but his hand was visible during the operation, he removed the wafer.

That done, he left the rooms, and leaving all the doors open behind him, he ascended a few of the steps leading to the second floor, until he got to a dark corner, and then he waited the result of his arrangements.

Macheath was not kept long in suspense.

In a very few minutes he heard the street-door open and shut, and then the footstep of a man upon the stairs came plainly on his ears.

He had the advantage of looking down from the dark corner in which he was on the much lighter staircase below, and he saw William's associate coming stealthily on.

The fellow seemed as though at every step he expected to meet the traitor.

" Hist—hist !   Where are you ?" he whispered.

" Here," replied Macheath, in an assumed voice. " It's all right.   Shoot him—shoot him ! He sleeps, and all the doors are open."

" I'll do it !"

" Quick—quick !"

The man drew from his pocket a pistol with a long bright barrel, and then boldly entered Captain Macheath's apartments, with the full belief that he had it in his power to take the life of the man for whom so handsome a reward was offered.

Owing to Macheath having spoken in a whisper, the fellow had been completely taken in, and had thought that to be sure it could be none other than his vile associate William who had addressed him.

Macheath waited the result.

Bang went a pistol, and in another moment, with a face as pale as death itself, William's associate came out of Macheath's rooms.

" I have done it—I have done it !" he said.

" What have you done ?" Macheath demanded, clearing the half-dozen stairs beetween him and the villain, and alighting close to his feet. " What have you done ?"

The fellow's hair stiffened on his head, for he knew Captain Macheath by sight.

" What have you done ?" repeated Macheath, as he took a firm clutch of the assassin by the collar.

The man could not speak.

He only glared at Captain Macheath, and went back until the balustrades of the staircase prevented him going any further.

Macheath hurled him over, and he fell a depth of twenty feet to the marble-paved hall beneath.

Macheath glanced below, and saw the man without sense or motion.

He went into his own room again, closing the door after him as he proceeded.

Upon the couch was William's dead body.

The bullet from the pistol had struck him in the face, and had gone right through his head.

His death must have been instantaneous.

" An easier exit than you deserved," said Macheath.   " But, no matter, you have met the fate you deserved, poor fool !   And now these rooms are no more for me."

In the course of the next quarter of an hour Macheath had got about him all his papers and little things, chiefly arms and trinkets, which he had any regard for, and throwing a large cloak over his shoulders, he cast one more glance around him.

" Farewell !" he said.   " I have passed some pleasant hours here, and in good truth I did not think that my leaving would be such a one as this. Farewell !"

He closed all the doors after him and locked them up, and walked downstairs composedly.

In the hall there was a crowd of people round the dead body of William's friend, whose skull had been fractured against the marble pavement.

Macheath, as he was passing out, was stopped by a man, who said—

" There's been a murder here, sir."

" Well, my friend, what then ?"

" Oh ! I beg your pardon, sir.   I only thought you might like to know about it, sir, as you came from upstairs—that's all, sir."

" Not at all," said Macheath ; " it's no affair of mine."

He left the house quite composedly, and was soon in the busy bustle of the Strand.

It so happened that about a year before this time, Macheath, having been very successful on the road, had had a sum of five hundred pounds to spare, which, with the idea that some day it might be most peculiarly useful for him, he had deposited in the hands of a banker in Clement's-lane, in the City, giving the name of Smith as he did so.

And now, as he neared Temple Bar, he thought that if he were to give that sum into the hands of Polly Peachum, it would be something for them, for they were married now, should anything happen to necessitate his leaving the country, to fall back upon.

Macheath was, as the reader has found, very much a creature of impulse, and all this had scarcely flitted through his mind when it was decided upon, and at a rapid pace he was making his way towards the banking-house in Clement's-lane.

The streets of London were not then near so much crowded as they are now.

Macheath passed up Ludgate-hill, through St. Paul's Church-yard, and so on by Cheapside and the Poultry, to the place of his destination without much hindrance or difficulty, and at length dived into the dingy banking-house, where, summer and winter, candles had always to be kept burning.

The clerks looked dim and faded by the spectral light, and the few people who stood by the counter looked like anything but beings of flesh and blood.

" Oblige me with a blank cheque," said Macheath to a bald-headed old man who had glared at him for some seconds without speaking.

" Have you an account with our house, sir ?" said the old man.

" Yes, my name is Julius Smith, and I have an account with your house."

" Oh ! very good—very good, sir ; Julius—Smith —hum—ah. Oh ! yes—I see. We have not had the pleasure of seeing you for some time, Mr. Julius Smith, I think, if I may presume to say as much. Hum—ah !"

" You had better take a good look at me now then," said Macheath, " for it may be as long again before you have the pleasure of seeing me here."

" Hum ! Ah ! I will bring you the blank cheque in a moment, sir, if you please. Mr. Julius —Smith. Hum ! Ah ! In a moment."

Macheath thought that this reception at a banking-house was rather a strange one ; but he waited patiently for the return of the old clerk, who, in a few moments came hobbling back.

" Will you be so good, Mr. Smith, as to step this way ?" he said in a soft oily voice.

" Certainly," Captain Macheath replied. " Any way you like, so that you transact my business for

CAPTAIN MACHEATH

THE
PRINCE OF THE HIGHWAY.

"YOUR REWARD IS LEAD INSTEAD OF GOLD," SAID CAPTAIN MACHEATH.

me as quickly as possible, for I have no time to lose."

"Oh! sir, there will be no delay, only Mr. Stubbs, our principal partner, wishes to speak to you for a few moments—that is all, Mr. Smith."

Macheath followed the old bald-headed clerk through the intricacies of a number of desks, through a half-glass door, and then through one covered with green baize, and so into a dingy-looking room, where, with a multitude of books before him, sat Mr. Stubbs, the senior partner of the banking-house.

"Mr. Julius Smith!" announced the old clerk.

He left Macheath with Mr. Stubbs, who was a florid, insolent-looking man, of about fifty years of age, with a very odd crop of wiry-looking hair, standing up quite on end, like the bristles on the back-bone of a pig.

"Well, Mr. Smith?" said the banker, putting his pen behind his ear.

"Well, Mr. Stubbs?" said Captain Macheath, reaching himself a chair and sitting upon it.

"I believe, Mr. Smith, you left with our firm a considerable time since the sum of five hundred pounds sterling? That is correct, I presume, Mr. Smith?"

"It is correct," the captain replied; "and no one ought to know that better than you, sir. I have now come to take it away again, and will give you a cheque for the amount."

"Not so fast, sir—not so fast," said the banker. "I am a man of business, Mr. Smith, and I strongly suspect that that five hundred pounds was not honestly come by; and until you give us a reference or two as regards your respectability we shall not pay it again."

"Indeed?" queried Macheath, smiling.

"Yes, sir—indeed," said Mr Stubbs. "So you can do your worst or your best, Mr. Smith. I am not a man to be trifled with or bullied. Oh! no—no! How do I know but there may be some very peculiar circumstances connected with—Hilloa! what are you about, sir—what are you about? I will call a constable, sir."

Captain Macheath had risen, and very calmly locked the door of the room.

Then, advancing to Mr. Stubbs, he took a pistol from his pocket.

"Sir," said Captain Macheath, "if you make the slightest disturbance I will blow out your brains with more satisfaction than I would those of a mad dog!"

The bristly hair of the banker actually moved upon his head.

His face turned blue, as he shrank back in his chair in a perfect paroxysm of fright—so much so, that he could not speak a word.

"Now, sir," said Captain Macheath, "understand me. I am this day going to commit suicide. Do you hear me, sir? Su-i-cide!"

"Ye—s."

"Very well, sir; since you refuse me my money, I will go into the other world arm-in-arm with you."

"With me? Oh! don't!" the banker gasped.

"Yes, sir, with you," continued Captain Macheath. "I will blow your brains out with one barrel of this pistol, and my own with the other. It can, you see, make no difference to me, although it may possibly make just a little to you."

"A little?" groaned the banker. "Oh! it makes a great deal—it does, indeed, my dear sir."

"Well, you may save yourself," said Captain Macheath.

"May I—oh! may I, indeed, sir?"

"Yes, easily," the captain replied. "Before I take leave of this world, I want to hand some money to a friend, and that was why I came for my five hundred pounds. Now, as you have given me some trouble, I will have interest for my money. Give me a blank cheque, and I will draw for a thousand pounds; come with me to the counter and tell them to pay it; and then you shall only walk with me a little way, after which I will let you go."

"A thousand pounds!" Mr. Stubbs ejaculated. "Oh! dear—oh, dear! Cent per cent!"

"Exactly. Do you refuse? Because—'

"Oh! no—no! There is the blank cheque—there it is!"

"Very good," said Captain Macheath, as the terrified banker gave him a blank cheque from his drawer; "very good, sir."

He then filled it up for the sum of one thousand pounds.

"Now, Mr. Stubbs," he said, "you and I will go out together; and if you attempt to leave my side, or by word, or look, or gesture to give any alarm or indication that you are in a coerced condition, that moment shall be your last I am a man to keep my word. My name is not Smith. Take your hat, sir; we shall have to go out-of-doors together."

"Will you tell me who you really are?" said the terrified banker.

"Oh! yes; I have no objection. They call me Captain Macheath!"

"Then my money is gone," said Stubbs wringing his hands; "then I feel now that my money is gone. I shall never see it again."

"You are right," said the captain; "you never will; and take this to your heart, if you have got one, that you pay this five hundred pounds for your own insolence and folly. Of course, you thought me some one who upon the least hint of anything wrong would be glad to get away and leave you the money; but you have mistaken your man."

If the banker had such an idea, and there can be very little doubt but that he had, he certainly mistook his man, for Captain Macheath was just the very last person in all the world to be so intimidated.

The banker's face assumed a most lugubrious expression.

"You—you—will take," he said, "your own five hundred pounds, and let this be an end of the transaction."

"Certainly not," said Captain Macheath. "Not one penny piece less than a thousand pounds now. You will pay the extra five hundred pounds for the little pleasantry of the last quarter of an hour; so now you had better come out with me and put as good a face on the matter as possible. I know if I am taken that death is my lot, and before I go to the other world, I am quite resolved to send you there."

The banker groaned and followed, or rather went ahead of Captain Macheath into the open part of the premises.

The clerks bowed and smiled as their principal passed them.

"Tell them to pay the cheque," said Captain Macheath, in a whisper.

"Thompson," said the banker, "pay this cheque at once, if you please."

"Yes, sir," said Thompson, with a smirking alacrity that made the banker mentally resolve upon his discharge. "Yes, sir. How would you like it Mr. Smith—notes or gold, sir?"

"Notes will do."

"Thank you, sir. One thousand. That is right, Mr. Smith, I believe. A very nice day, sir."

"Mr. Smith and I will soon be back, if any one asks for me," said the banker.

Captain Macheath airily put the notes in his pocket, and taking the arm of the banker, out they sallied into the open street.

Captain Macheath stuck to him like a leech.

"Beware," he said. "The least attempt to escape, or to give the slightest alarm, and you are a dead man."

The banker groaned.

"I will not take you far from your business," added Macheath. "Indeed, I will not take you one step farther than is consistent with my own safety. Why do you tremble in that way?"

"My money. My five hundred pounds! All at one swoop. In a morning. Oh! my money. It will kill me."

"Oh! nonsense," said Macheath, laughing. "Don't you believe it. It will do no such thing. You can very well afford it, and it will be a useful lesson to you not to attempt to cheat anyone again, unless you thoroughly know your man. There's no saying how much the experience of to-day may really and truly be the means of saving you."

"You are only joking! You will give me back my own?"

"You may as well ask me for my eyes," the captain replied. "This way, sir, if you please—this way. How mild the weather is to be sure. Is it not mild, sir? Come, sir, is it not mild?"

"Oh! very—curse it!"

"Sir, I am surprised at you," said Macheath. "I really wonder that a man of business cannot keep his temper."

"But who in the name of all that's abominable could keep his temper when he was being robbed of five hundred pounds?"

"Robbed, my good sir? Robbed? Really I never in all my life heard a term so misapplied. You embarked in a speculation—in the speculation of frightening me—by which you hoped to get a sum of of five hundred pounds; but luck was against you, and you lost that amount."

The banker groaned, and while he was so groaning, Macheath looked about him for some mode of disposing of himself.

He had no wish to be encumbered by his company for a longer time than was necessary under the circumstances.

A rather gloomy-looking private house was close at hand, and Macheath, with his characteristic decision, at once pitched upon it as he wanted to get rid of the banker.

He approached the house, still taking care that the banker did not give him the slip, for a race through the city after him would have been anything but an agreeable thing; and then he knocked smartly at the door.

"Are you going in here?" said the wretched man of money.

"No, I am only going to make a call and leave something."

"Then you will let me go now?"

"In a moment or two I will."

The door of the house was opened by an extremely corpulent red-faced girl, upon whose head was some prodigious head-dress that, like Joseph's coat, was "of many colours."

There was a look upon her face of wild indignation at the startling knock that Captain Macheath had given at the door, and the moment she got it open she likewise opened her mouth to commence a volley of expletives, but Macheath was too prompt for her."

"Here he is, my dear madam," cried Captain Macheath. "Make much of him, I beg of you."

With these words Captain Macheath gave the banker such a tremendous push into the passage, that encountering the female, over she went, and the unhappy man above her, and they both rolled and kicked and scratched, and fought in the passage, while Captain Macheath deliberately slammed the street-door, and at a rapid pace sped from the spot.

He was far enough away before anything in the shape of explanation could be entered into between the banker and the lady.

"This is not a bad day's work," said Macheath, "and—"

He stopped suddenly for standing in the doorway of a house was Mrs. Maria Finch, whose acquaintance he had so oddly made at Luck's inn known by the sign of the Blue Boar.

"Why how do you do, Mrs. Finch?" said the captain.

"I am in great distress," the lady replied. "My husband has left me through a fit of jealousy, and I am most unhappy. Will you walk in and partake of some refreshment?"

"Your husband is a foolish man," said Captain Macheath as he followed Mrs. Finch into a cosy sitting room.

He was drinking to the lady's good health and the speedy return of her husband when the servant came flying into the room.

"Oh! mum—mum," she cried. "Here's Mr. Finch at the door, mum!"

"Oh! hide yourself—hide yourself," cried Maria to Captain Macheath.

"But where?" Macheath demanded. "Confound it! where am I to hide? I'd much rather, if you will allow me, kick him downstairs, or throw him out of the window. Pray do not disturb yourself, I will do either in a moment."

"Oh! no—no," cried Mrs. Finch. "If you have the shadow of regard for me, I pray you not to let him see you. I implore you, sir, to hide yourself."

"As you please," said Macheath. "I will do your bidding. Where shall I hide? Only tell me where and I will do so. I pray you dispose of me as you like."

"Here—here. This way. Come, I pray you."

Macheath followed her into an inner room, and frantically opening a large cupboard, Mrs. Finch pushed him in, and closed and locked the door upon him, leaving him so cramped up that it was with the greatest difficulty he could breathe, for the space between a shelf and the door was about an inch or two too narrow to hold him.

He, however, succeeded in turning his arms round, and then he knocked the shelf down pretty easily, and had plenty of room in the cupboard, so that without any sensation of bodily pain, he could listen to what was going forward in the room adjoining.

For a time all was quiet enough, for the servant took good care not to let Mr. Finch in until she was sure her mistress had disposed of Macheath, and then Mr. Finch was permitted to ascend the stairs.

He walked into the room adjoining that in

which Macheath was in the cupboard, and in a low, constrained tone of voice, he said—

"Maria, I have come to say that I have no more suspicion of you, and that while we both live, I hope that we shall live quietly and comfortably together."

Mrs. Finch seemed pleased at her husband's return and placed wine before him.

He drank heavily.

"More wine," he said—"more wine, Maria. Why don't you drink?"

"I have taken one glass."

"One glass! What is one glass? "Nothing at all. Take another," he returned hoarsely. "Who knows how long we may live? The term of life is short at the longest, and while we do live we ought to enjoy ourselves the best way in our power. Drink, I say—drink!"

She tremblingly took another glass, and then laying her hand on his arm, she said, rather to hear what he would say, than with any hope of gathering safety from his words—

"And you have banished all your suspicions, then?"

"All—all. Every one of them," Finch replied. "Every one of them, I say. What have I to do with suspicions now?"

"What do you mean by now?"

"I mean the present time, Maria. I repeat that suspicions are odious, and that I have done with them. They are all gone. I have forgotten them. But drink. Why don't you drink? Don't you recollect that I used to say I should be hanged for you?"

"You did," his wife murmured, shudderingly.

"Ha—ha!" laughed Albert Finch. "It was a droll thought, was it not? Very strange things happen. The idea of my being hanged for you! Why, that could only happen in the case of my murdering you. That is the only way it could happen."

"What the deuce has this stupid fellow got in his muddled brains now?" thought Captain Macheath.

"But you have no such thoughts?" said Mrs. Finch.

"Certainly not," her husband replied. "How truly absurd it would be of me to say I had any such thoughts. I am weary! We will retire early to-night. I have not had a long night's sleep for many a night. I say, we will retire early, Maria."

"As you please," said she. "I will just see if the bed-room is right, and then, when I return, I will have another glass of wine—"

"No—no—I say no."

"What, must I have no more wine? Do you think I have had enough then, or too much perhaps? Well—well."

Mrs Finch tried to speak in a jocular tone, but she very much belied her heart in doing so, and Finch sternly replied to her—

"You may have what wine you please, Maria, and as much as you please; but you do not leave this room until you and I go together to our chamber. Do you understand that?"

"I hear, sir," Mrs. Finch replied; "I will not be dictated to in such a manner; I will not be made to drink or not to drink, to stay or to go, like a child."

"You will not?"

"I will not. It is time that this farce should end," she cried, stamping her foot. "If you are out of your mind, which I thoroughly believe you

are, I will for your own sake, as well as for mine, summon the people of the house. I will go and come at my pleasure, Mr. Finch."

"Bravo!" thought Captain Macheath.

Finch was staggered, and for a few moments he did not speak.

Then, suddenly, with a strange wild hilarity of manner he cried—

"Go—go. Ha! ha! Go at once, Mrs. Finch —go at once. I will sit here. There is no other outlet from the rooms, I know. Go, Mrs. Finch, go; but do not deprive me long of your admirable company. Ha! ha! I have no suspicions now—no suspicions; I am happy. Ha! ha! ha! Go, Mrs. Finch, go."

This conduct upon the part of Finch was still more perplexing than before; but Mrs. Finch availed herself of the opportunity to go into the next room where Captain Macheath was in the cupboard, and she took good care to close the door of communication between the two apartments.

She approached the cupboard.

"Hist—hist! It is I—it is I!" she whispered. "Do you not hear me?"

"Yes; but I can't get out," answered Captain Macheath.

"Oh! I had forgotten," Mrs. Finch replied. "Here is the key. Oh! what will become of me? Have you heard anything?"

She unlocked the cupboard-door, and Captain Macheath stepped into the room.

"I have heard it all," he said.

"All—all?"

"Yes, every word that Finch has said," replied Macheath; "and do you know I think him in the most dangerous mood he has ever been in yet? I will not leave you while he is in the house. When such a man alters so completely you may depend upon it that he means mischief."

"You make me tremble."

"Be under no alarm. I will remain here," said the captain. "Give me the key of the cupboard. I will lock it on the inside, and so if he should take it into his head to come to it, I shall be safe, at the same time that I can get out at any time I please. Give me the key. Quick!"

"Oh! Heaven, what will happen?"

"Maria, are you coming?" roared Finch, from the next room. "Where are you, Maria? Are you coming?"

"Yes—yes; instantly."

"Go to him," said Macheath. "Go to him, and depend upon my continued presence here to protect you; and I am but an indifferent judge of human nature and a bad prophet if you will not need my protection. How dark it gets!"

"It is late."

"Maria, I say!" cried Finch. "Where the deuce are you, Maria?"

"I come—I come!"

"Fear nothing," whispered Macheath, "I will be near to you. Fear nothing now, Maria. Go to him at once. Go—go."

Macheath kept the cupboard ready open so that he could pop into it in a moment, and lock it on the inside; but he was by far too anxious to listen to what might pass in the front room to get into the cupboard before there was any obvious necessity for it.

"What were you about?" cried Finch. "But no matter—no matter; life is so very short. Drink—drink, I say."

"Only one glass more."

"As you please—as you please, Maria. What

do you think there is beyond the grave? Have you any serious belief that way?"

"Surely—yes, there is another world, and the wicked are punished."

Finch's head sunk upon his breast for a few moments, and he was silent.

"Murder!" he muttered in a low strange voice.

"What say you?" cried his wife. "What do you mean?"

"Say—mean? I said nothing."

"You did, indeed. You said murder!"

"I say murder?" said Albert Finch, starting. "No—no. That is all imagination. Only a day-dream Why should I say murder? Oh! no—no. We will go to bed early and have a long night's sleep. Oh! how I want a long night's sleep. My eyes have not closed for a long time. My heart and soul are weary. More wine—let us have some more wine. Ring for more, Maria—ring."

More wine was brought by the servant, and still Finch drank of it, and still it had no effect upon him.

He was dead to all such ordinary impulses.

Possibly it might have added something to the insane feeling that had thoroughly taken possession of him, for if ever any man was mad, Finch was at that time.

Lights were brought with the second bottle of wine, and then Finch got rather gloomy.

At times he would sit with his head resting upon his hands, and then he would start up and pace the room with disordered strides, muttering to himself, and once he caught up his hat.

"Oh! if I could only leave you?" he said.

"And why not? You can do so, if you wish," she said. "I am growing tired of this nonsense."

"Let it only suffice that I cannot, that is all," he said. "I cannot, no—no, I must stay. It is my fate and it is your fate. I must stay."

"I do not understand you," his wife observed. "If you will stay, you will stay; but if you choose to go there is nothing to prevent you that I can see, and I am sure any explanation that you think we ought to have will be much better made in the morning than now."

"Explanations in the morning!" gasped Finch. "Oh! yes, there will surely be some explanations in the morning."

"You are full of riddles. You seem to have something on your mind to say and you never say it. Why is that?"

"I know not. Drink more wine—oh! if I could only induce you to drink more wine. Come, another glass—only another."

As his face began to assume a threatening aspect again, Mrs. Finch did not think it quite prudent to refuse the proffered glass, and she sipped its contents.

All that we have related had taken a much longer time in passing than it has taken us to tell.

There are some actions of the human mind occupying hours that can be told in a few words, so that the reader will not be surprised that a clock in the hall of the house suddenly struck the hour of eleven.

Finch sprang to his feet.

"To bed—to bed!" he cried. "It is more than time."

"So soon?"

"Soon? It is not soon. No—no, it is late—very late," said Finch. "What is there in all the world worth keeping awake for, that anyone should care to keep from sleep? Let us drink

some more wine, and then to bed—to bed. You look as though you had a dread of something horrible upon your mind, Maria!"

"What should I dread?" his wife demanded.

"Ay! what indeed?" said Finch. "And we will go to bed dreading nothing. Come—come, I wonder what the matter will be to-morrow?"

"Why do you say that?"

"But it won't matter one jot to— But come—come; I am in good truth very weary. What a fool I was to say I should be ever hanged for you, Maria. But that was when I only suspected."

He suddenly sprang to the only door of egress from the small suite of rooms and locked it.

In another moment he caught up both the candles, and still kept crying—

"To bed—to bed!"

Mrs. Finch humoured him.

She followed him through the back room up the little corkscrew of a staircase that led into the bed-room above.

Captain Macheath heard them go, and as the light disappeared, he opened the cupboard door and stepped out on to the soft carpeting of the room.

"What on earth," he said to himself, "does that idiot of a Finch mean? I never saw a man so altered in all my life. He must be thoroughly and completely mad! I have a dread of something, I know not what, tugging at my heart. What can be the meaning of it?"

Captain Macheath trod very lightly.

He went into the next room and helped himself to the wine left upon the table.

On the sideboard, too, in the room he found some fruit and some biscuits, so that, after all, he found a very tolerable supper, if it were not exactly the one he would have chosen.

All this took up some time, and when he had finished off the wine the clock on the staircase struck twelve.

Captain Macheath counted the strokes, and as the last two or three sounded in the silence of the house he thought he heard a strange noise.

He listened very attentively, and then fancied it must be rain upon the window-panes, for the night had set in very wet.

But after a few moments' more listening he felt satisfied that that did not sufficiently account for the noise, which was like some one moaning from afar off. The door between the room that he was in and the back one had closed, but now he hastened and threw it open.

One of those strange presentiments of evil which have at times, when probably least expected, attacked the bravest and strongest of us now came over Captain Macheath.

The moment Macheath got there the odd noise could no longer be mistaken for the moaning of someone in great mental and bodily pain.

The sound, too, localised itself, more than it had done before, and he was able to tell himself that, without a doubt, it came from the room above.

The reader has seen and heard enough of Captain Macheath to feel assured that he was not a man to shrink back when he was required, and now with a bound he reached the staircase that led up to the sleeping chamber of Mr. and Mrs. Finch, and ascended it at a pace that soon brought him to the door of the room.

It was fast.

He knocked sharply.

"Oh! mercy," he heard a voice say from

within, and then something sounded like a heavy fall.

He knocked again.

"Who is there?" said a voice.

"Open the door, or I will kick it in," said Captain Macheath.

"Wait—wait!" said the voice again.

Macheath did wait while it would have been just possible for anyone to approach the door and open it, but no longer.

When that brief period had elapsed, he felt pretty sure that there was no intention to let him in, so placing his knee against the door and his shoulder to the upper part of it, he, by one vigorous exertion, smashed it in.

The sight presented to Captain Macheath was one that he had little calculated upon, and one that almost for the moment unnerved even him.

CHAPTER XIX.

THE MURDERER'S FATE—MACHEATH'S RUSE.

UPON the floor, just at the foot of the bed, lay the dead body of Mrs. Finch weltering in her blood. A knife, with which the fatal and unmanly deed had been committed, lay by the side of the poor victim.

"Where is the murderer?" cried Captain Macheath, loudly.

That Mrs. Finch had perished by the hand of her husband, and that jealousy had been the cause of the commission of the appalling act, there could not be a doubt.

But where was he?

That was the mystery.

A candle was burning upon the dressing-table and shedding its shadowy ray upon the scene of blood.

But no Finch was to be seen.

Macheath hastily looked into every possible hiding-place in the room, and satisfied himself thoroughly that he was not there.

It was then only by the merest accident in the world that Captain Macheath happened to look up to the ceiling, and he there perceived a little trap-door, which communicated with the roof of the house, wide open.

Of course, this was the route by which the murderer had escaped, and this, equally, of course, was the route by which Macheath was determined to follow him.

A chair was in such a position upon the floor that by standing upon it anyone could reach the trap-door edges with both hands, and so, in a shorter space of time than we could possibly take to tell how it was done, Captain Macheath had raised himself bodily through the trap.

There was a vacancy between the trap-door and the outer roof, so that Macheath paused a moment to try to pierce the obscurity, lest the murderer should there have hidden himself.

The outer trap in the actual roof being open, though, was sufficiently convincing that such was not the case, and that the wretched man had sought to get away by that means from the house.

In a moment Captain Macheath was on the roof of the house.

It was quite a relief to be there in the cool night air after being in the heated atmosphere of the bedroom, and he paused a moment to draw a long breath or two of the cool, damp atmosphere.

He did not lose any time by so pausing, for he did so, his eyes were getting accustomed to the night air and the dim light that it carried with it.

He found he could see clearer.

Many objects appeared to come out of the darkness and to make themselves visible to him.

Chimney-stacks, gable ends of old houses, quaint old water spouts, all came out of the darkness and presented themselves to him, and then at some distance off, close to a parapet, beyond which was the deep chasm between two houses, separated from each other by a space which upon level ground anyone could jump easily, Captain Macheath thought he saw something crouching.

A dark object!

Yes.

He was certain something was lying in the gutter close to the parapet.

He kept his eyes upon the object, and in the course of a moment or two it slowly moved.

Suspicion was now converted into certainty.

"Nothing would be easier," said Macheath, "than to shoot him from where I am; but I must have the rascal alive if possible, and give him up to justice for the foul and dreadful deed that he has done."

Captain Macheath did not at the moment reflect how very ticklish a thing it would be for him, circumstanced as he was, to appear in evidence against Mr. Finch.

No.

At the moment he forgot everything but that a very foul murder had been committed and that he was cognisant of the facts.

Slowly and circumspectly indeed he crept along the roof towards the spot where the murderer lay crouched.

Macheath wanted to seize him before he could make an attempt to spring across the chasm from one house to the other, for in that neighbourhood he knew that if once he did so, he might find some means of escape, as there were houses about it where any criminal would find secrecy and comfort if he had money.

Macheath did not make the least noise; but the murderer was glaring about him in order to debate upon the best means of escape, and just as Macheath was within half-a-dozen yards of him, he saw the crawling figure coming over the house top towards him.

On the instant, with a cry of terror, the murderer sprang to his feet in the drain close to the parapet of the house.

"Hold!" cried Captain Macheath. "Resistance is quite useless."

Another moment and he would have had him in his grasp; but Finch made a spring to clear the chasm between the two houses, and leaping short, he fell right down into the street beneath, disappearing from before Captain Macheath's eyes as though he had suddenly sprung down some deep well.

"Gone!" said Macheath.

He heard a loud crash far below, and then all was still.

Crawling close to the parapet, he looked over, and strained his eyes to see into the depth.

But all was as dark as any dungeon for a few moments.

Then, however, a light flashed upon the scene from a doorway, and he saw a man appear shading a light with his hand.

"What was that?" said the man.

"I'm sure I heard something," said a female voice. "I'm quite certain I heard something."

"GIVE MY RESPECTS TO THE GENTLEMEN WHO ARE FOLLOWING ME!" SAID CAPTAIN MACHEATH.

Then a woman made her appearance in the street.

At that moment the rain, which was falling heavily, put out the light, and all was pitch darkness again.

The gloom appeared to be much more profound than before, in consequence of its temporary dissipation by the light that for a few short moments had glanced upon surrounding objects.

"He must be dead," thought Macheath.

The man who had had the light began to call—"Watch—watch!"

Captain Macheath lingered to see what would ensue, and in the course of a few minutes, as the man kept up his cry for the watch, the dubious gleam of a watchman's lantern came upon the scene.

"Watch—watch!" continued the man.

Macheath could hear with perfect distinctness every word that was uttered.

"Coming!" cried the watchman. "What is it now?"

"I don't know," said the man; "but something has happened."

"Ah!" said the woman, "that it has, watchman. Bring your lantern this way. We don't mind giving you a glass of something nice and warm, Mr. Watchman, if you will find out what it is."

"Thank you, ma'am. It's a dirty, cold sort of night, ma'am. Nobody knows what we goes through."

"My light went out," said the man; "but something seemed to come from the top of that house, and I never heard such a crash on the pavement in all my life."

"We'll soon see what it is," said the watchman.

The guardian of the night then walked slowly along, with his lantern close to the ground, moving it along in circles, so as to illuminate every portion of the pavement.

The man and woman followed him notwithstanding the rain, and at last they came upon the dead body of the wretched husband.

"Hilloa!" cried the watchman. "It's murder!"

"Murder!" echoed the man and the woman.

"Yes, it's murder, and I shall have to take everybody up. He's a dead man, as sure as a gun," cried the watchman.

Finding that the matter was one of sufficient importance to warrant him in so doing, he dropped his lantern and began springing his rattle.

Macheath thought that he had seen enough, and that it was time for him to provide for his own safety.

Nothing would now have been easier than for him to have gone back through the trap-door in the roof of the house into the chamber of death again, and so have made his way out of the house.

But he had insurmountable repugnance to passing through the room in which was the dead body of Mrs. Finch.

He preferred running any risks and falling into any danger rather than do so, and he made up his mind to jump across the chasm which Mr. Finch had lost his life in attempting.

To Captain Macheath it was one of the most ordinary feats in the world, and he was over in a moment, alighting fairly upon the parapet of the house opposite, which was the one from which the man and the woman who were so busy with the watchman had come.

The rattle was going still vigorously, and from far off it was being answered, and presently, like so many Will o'-the-wisps, watchmen, with their lanterns swinging to and fro, hurried to the scene.

"Enough!" said Macheath. "I have seen enough of all this, and I am sickened at the night's adventures."

With this he began to turn his whole attention to providing for his own safety, and, creeping along the parapet of the house, he looked about for some window by which he might get into one of the rooms.

He was not long in finding an attic window; but, do what he would, he could not see sufficiently through it into the room to be at all able to say if this apartment was inhabited or not, so he was forced to chance it.

The rain beat in that direction, so the slight noise he made in opening the window was completely smothered, and presently he got one of the little doors of the frame-work open.

It was no easy thing to get into the room through such a small opening; but Macheath made a spring through the casement, and fell upon the floor.

"Murder—murder!" screamed a voice.

The voice was that of a woman, and Macheath felt how utterly in vain it would be to say anything deprecatory of the uproar she had made.

He made a hasty search for the door.

Suddenly the voice of the female ceased, and Macheath concluded that she had fainted from excess of terror.

He snatched a sheet from the bed, and hastily wrapping it completely round him, he made his way to the door of the room, which, he conjectured, was opposite to the window.

The door was only fastened by the latch, so that it yielded to his touch in a moment, and he stepped out on to the landing.

Captain Macheath was above the middle height, and now that he was from head to foot enveloped in a white sheet he looked quite gigantic and awful.

An attic door was opened next to that from which he had emerged, and an old woman appeared with a candlestick in her hand.

"Dear me!" she said, "what is the matter? Is it fire? Eh? Is it fire? Oh! gracious. A ghost!"

She had caught sight of Captain Macheath, and she immediately fell backwards into her attic, candle and all, and rolled out of sight.

"That will do," said Macheath.

He had by the aid of the candle seen the situation of the staircase, and now he began to descend, hoping that his ghostly appearance would have the same terrifying effect upon anybody else whom he might chance to meet as it had had upon the old woman.

When he reached the second-floor landing a door opened, and a man rushed out on to it with a lamp in his hand.

"What in the name of all that's horrible is this disturbance?" he cried. "Are we never to have a quiet night's rest in this house? Am I and Mrs. Jenkins to be night after night continually—the devil!"

"Repent!" said Captain Macheath, in a deep, sepulchral voice.

Down went the lamp, and with a shout of terror the man flew into his own room again.

"This will do capitally," thought Captain Macheath. "I do believe I shall work my way to the street by the assistance of this sheet."

He descended the next flight of stairs without any opposition, and gained the landing of the first floor.

But he had not had time to cross it, when the flash of a light came up from below, and a voice cried—

"Hilloa—hilloa! Who calls murder?"

Captain Macheath made no answer.

Then a female voice spoke.

"I insist, Mr. Watchman," said the voice, "that you go up and see what's going on. I heard murder called by somebody upstairs."

"Well—well, I'm going," said the watchman.

Captain Macheath heard him stamping up the stairs, and in a moment or two the faint reflection from the light of his lantern was plainly visible.

The captain took his station exactly at the top of the stairs, and if he looked tall to anyone who was on the same level with him, he must have indeed appeared prodigious to anybody ascending, and looking up to him.

He did not utter a word as the watchman was approaching; but he trusted entirely to his appearance.

"Come, Mr. Watchman," said the woman's voice, "get on, will you? How do we know but there may be murder doing in the attics while you are creeping up the stairs like a snail?"

"I creeping, mum?"

"Yes, you know you are," said the female; "and if I don't complain to the parish, I am not a woman, that's all. It's my honest belief that you are afraid to go up."

"Me afraid?"

"Yes, you. And for all your thick stick and your great white coat, I believe you are as great a coward as ever lived—that I do; so you had better go on, or you will run a good chance of losing your situation if I make any complaints against you."

"Good gracious!" said the watchman; "protect me from female women, when once they do begin to talk."

"What's that you say?"

"Nothing, mum, nothing; I was only a-saying that I like to protect women, mum, that's all."

"Oh! very well."

Up went the watchman, and when he was within three stairs of the top he saw the lower part of the sheet in which Captain Macheath was enveloped, and he came to a full stop.

Then slowly raising his eyes, he looked up—up —up to the tall figure in white, until it appeared to him as if in height it were endless.

Human nature—at least, watchman's nature— could not stand this, and backwards he went, lantern and all, on the woman, who was following him closely.

The consequence was that they both rolled into the passage together, and Captain Macheath thought that he could not do better than embrace that opportunity of leaving the house.

Gathering up the sheet, so that it should not impede his progress, he darted down the stairs.

Scrambling over the watchman and the lady, who lay roaring in the passage, he made for the street-door, which was open.

The first obstacle he met was a man who was running in, and as Captain Macheath had by this time nearly got rid of the sheet, so that he did not present so ghost-like an appearance, the man was not a bit confused, and made an attempt to seize him.

"Who are you?" he cried.

"Don't ask ridiculous questions!" said Captain Macheath, and with one blow he sent the man sprawling on the top of the watchman.

In another instant Captain Macheath was in the street.

He did not run, but walked very swiftly, and he very soon left the neighbourhood behind him.

His first care was then to procure his horse, and then, when he was fairly mounted and upon the road to Kentish Town, he began to breathe a little freely, and to think over the events of that most extraordinary night.

He let his horse lapse into a walk, and the most serious thoughts that had ever touched him crept over him.

"To-day," he said, "within the space only of a few short hours, four people have come by their deaths through me directly and indirectly. Am I to become a destroyer? Are my footsteps henceforward to be tracked by blood?"

He shuddered from head to foot.

The rain was still coming down, and the night was intensely dark, so that, although he held his hands close to his face to see if there were any blood upon them, he could not tell.

The mere idea, however, that such might be the case at once turned the current of his thoughts from any idea of proceeding to the cottage where he had left his wife, Polly.

"No—no," he said, "I dare not go to her with probably the evidence of murder clinging to me, although I did not do the deed. I must wait until the morning's light shows me if I have such marks upon my hands or clothing."

With this idea, instead of going to the right to get to Kentish Town, he galloped up the Hampstead-road, and drew bridle at the Load of Hay, nearly opposite to a cottage which had been built by Sir Richard Steele. A dim light came from a room over the stables of the inn.

"Hilloa!" cried Macheath. "House—house!"

"Hilloa! yourself," answered a voice; "what's the row?"

"I want shelter till morning for myself and my horse. Can I get it here to-night?"

"Oh! yes," replied the voice, now much more respectfully. "I burn a light in my room over the stables on purpose to be ready for customers. I'll be down to you directly, sir."

Captain Macheath had not to wait many moments before the ostler and a boy made their appearance.

The boy was rubbing his eyes with his knuckles very hard.

"Come, bustle—bustle, Dick," cried the ostler; "take the gentleman's horse into the stable. This way, sir, if you please. You won't mind sleeping in a double-bedded room, I suppose, sir?"

"Not at all, if the other bed is vacant."

"Why, sir, it ain't quite vacant, in a manner of speaking. I rather think—"

"Which means that someone is there. Who is it?"

"Oh! a very respectable man, sir. It's Mr. Fleetfoot, the Bow-street runner, sir. We ought to be safe enough while he's in the house—oughtn't we, sir?"

"Oh! very," assented Captain Macheath.

"Then you don't mind, sir?"

"Not a bit," Captain Macheath replied, "now that I know what a very unexceptional man is in the other bed. It is quite a pleasure to feel so sure a protection against thieves and highwaymen, as one must do in his company."

'Oh ! dear, yes, sir ; in course—in course. This way, sir, if you please. Mind the step, sir."

"Thank you, I see it."

Captain Macheath followed the man up a crazy flight of steps, and through a door opening into the first floor of the old inn, and then cautiously opening another door, upon which in quaint letters was painted "32," he said—

"This is the room, sir. At what hour would you like your horse in the morning ?"

"As soon as you are up and about," Captain Macheath replied.

"That's as soon as we can see, sir."

"Then that will do for me very well. Good night, my friend."

"Good night, sir, and a good night's rest ; you will find it a very nice bed, sir, and well aired."

The ostler put a rush-light into Captain Macheath's hands, and then left him on the threshold of the double-bedded room.

Captain Macheath closed the door very gently, for as the officer had said nothing he considered that he was asleep, and as yet Macheath had no wish to disturb him.

He knew that Fleetfoot had been several times especially upon the hunt for him, and for all the captain knew to the contrary, the officer might be then only resting a little before proceeding in the morning upon the same errand.

Macheath advanced into the room, shading the little light with his hand, so as to keep its rays out of the eyes of the officer as much as possible.

After noticing that the curtains of the bed were all drawn close, he tripped up very lightly to the dressing-table, upon which the officer had laid a variety of articles.

There were a pair of hand-cuffs, a pair of pistols, a stout cord, a knife, and a pocket-book, which was lying open at a part that had evidently been recently looked at, for the book had a marked inclination to remain open at that point, and some writing was upon the page thus exposed.

Captain Macheath read as follows—

"Memorandum.—To devote my whole time to the apprehension of Captain Macheath, by which I shall get enough to take a farm in the country, and retire from the profession."

"Memorandum.—Captain Macheath is not quite six feet high, and his real hair is a very dark brown. He has a slight scar upon one hand, they say."

"Memorandum. —To take him alive, if possible, but at all events, to take him any way, and by no means to let anyone else have a share in the transaction, as what is quite enough for one is by no means enough for two."

"Well !" whispered Captain Macheath to himself, "this is pleasant, I must confess."

He tried the pistols and found them both loaded and very carefully primed.

The first thing he did was carefully to shake out the priming of both of them, and to wipe the pans quite clean, so that there should be no chance of an explosion.

He then considered what it would be best for him to do.

No doubt the most prudent thing would have been to have retreated at once, and got clear away ; but Captain Macheath was by no means the sort of man to do the most prudent thing, so that although that course occurred to him naturally enough, he quickly dismissed it from his consideration.

"No," he said. "I will not let this man disturb me from a few hours' repose. I will lie down ; and as I generally awaken at whatever time I determine to do before closing my eyes in sleep, I will take my chances. He seems sound asleep enough at all events to be harmless for some hours to come."

CHAPTER XX.

CAPTAIN MACHEATH'S ADVENTURE WITH THE OFFICER.

FEW indeed could have been found to lie down to sleep in the manner that Macheath did with that officer, who was so intent upon his capture, in the other bed ; but it happened to be just one of the things in which the captain took a kind of reckless delight.

Indeed, of the two it is doubtful if he would not rather that the officer should awaken and have some talk with him, than continue to give him the security of his sleeping.

But probably the officer had fatigued himself very much during the day, for certainly he slept as calmly and as soundly as any man well could.

"Never mind," said Macheath—"never mind. He will perhaps awaken in the morning, and then I shall be able to say something to him ; and as it is, until then I shall indulge myself with a quiet nap."

With this Macheath drew the curtains of the bed so as only to leave him a little crevice through which he could take a peep.

Macheath knew very well that at the slightest noise he would be sure to awake, for it was a peculiarity of his to do so.

"Good night !" he said.

It might be that Macheath pronounced these words rather loudly, but certain it is that the officer moved very uneasily in his bed, and murmured something ; but as Captain Macheath made no further remark, and as all was still, he soon subsided into the deep sleep that he had been in during the whole of the proceedings that we have detailed.

In five minutes Captain Macheath was asleep.

How long a time he had slumbered he had no means of knowing. but he was aroused while it was still quite dark, by hearing some sounds from the road-way and the clatter of the hoofs of horses.

He rose in his bed and listened, and then he heard a voice say in clear tones—

"Hilloa ! ostler. Have you had anybody pass here lately well mounted ?"

"No," said the ostler. "I haven't."

"Well, there's been a murder in London, and people are going all over the country roads to pick up a man who is suspected A servant at the house has described him well, and if he be the man he'll swing for it yet, 'for murder will out.'"

"To be sure it will," said the other. "What sort of man is he ?"

"Tall and well-looking. It's a woman he has killed. He is well-dressed, and has taken the road by one of the avenues from London."

"Murdered a woman, has he ?" said the other. "Well, that's a good bit worse than murdering a man, to my mind, at any rate. Surely a man may keep his hands off a woman. But no such a one has passed here. If he should, and you or any of your people can come by him, I will soon mention it."

"Thank you. Are we right for the heath ?"

The clatter of the horses' feet now sounded upon the hard road, and then all was profoundly still.

Macheath was not a little puzzled to account for the reason the ostler did not mention him when the men described him, even so slightly as they had done.

There was not light enough for him to see his watch, so he could not find out what the time was, but as he lay awake he thought the dawn was coming, as the chamber grew lighter, or he got more accustomed to its darkness, and could faintly distinguish the dim outline of objects better.

"I won't sleep any more," he said to himself, "for I feel sufficiently rested by the repose I have had."

In the course of another quarter of an hour he could have no sort of doubt but that it was the daylight that was close at hand, and he was thinking of getting up, when he heard the ostler whistling and hissing under the window as if cleaning a horse.

"He is mindful of my orders," said Captain Macheath, "and no doubt is now getting my horse ready for me. I will get up, and perhaps it will be as well if I get out of the room, after all, before my friend in the other bed wakes up."

With this idea Macheath rose, and as he had not taken the trouble to remove anything but his boots, one may reasonably suppose that his toilette was tolerably quickly performed.

But he was disappointed in his idea of getting so quietly away, for in putting on his second boot he quite forgot the officer in the bed at the other end of the room for a moment, and stamped the heel of it upon the floor to get his foot right into it with a force that was enough to have awakened the soundest sleeper the world ever saw.

"Hilloa!" cried the officer. "What's that?"

"The deuce!" cried Captain Macheath.

The officer sprang up to a sitting posture in his bed and glared at Captain Macheath as though he thought him a spectre.

"Who are you?" he demanded.

"Don't trouble yourself," said Captain Macheath. "Don't put yourself out of the way. I have got it on now."

"What on?"

"Why, my boot, to be sure. Didn't I wake you up by knocking it down at the heel?"

"But how the deuce came you here?"

"That's self-evident enough, I think. It's a double-bedded room, and you didn't want both the beds, did you? Be a reasonable man. Good morning."

"But I must know who you are."

"Oh! nonsense," Captain Macheath retorted. "Why, I should like to ask? I don't see the smallest necessity in my life for your knowing who I am, my good sir. You don't find me asking all sorts of impertinent and ridiculous questions about who you are. Come—come, you had better take another nap."

"Now by all that's impertinent, I never was treated in such a way in all my life," cried Fleetfoot, spluttering with rage. "I'll pretty soon convince you that I am one who will be answered. I don't find a man in my bedroom, and part with him again in this free and easy sort of style, I can tell you."

"Don't you?" said Captain Macheath, as he put on his hat and adjusted it by the glass; "I don't see myself how you are to hinder it. Everybody has his peculiar way with him, and I must say you have described mine very nicely indeed by the words free and easy; so I leave you to the benefit of your definition, my friend. I am all ready.

Good morning. Don't put yourself in a rage; now I can see you are doing so."

"Not put myself in a rage?" roared the officer.

"No; it's the very worst thing you can do. I see by your complexion that you are a bilious man, and if you put yourself in a passion you will be ill."

"Ill? The deuce!"

"I speak to you as a friend," said Macheath, soothingly. "Good morning."

Captain Macheath opened the door of the room and walked out, but the officer was not to be so coolly baffled.

He sprang from his bed, undressed as he was, and running to the table where he had laid his pistols, he caught one up.

"Stir another step and I fire!" he cried, in a loud tone of voice.

"Fire away," said Captain Macheath, coolly; "only remember that it will be my turn after you have had yours."

"I do not wish to take your life," Fleetfoot remarked. "Why will you force me to use a weapon against you?"

"Upon my word you are considerate," said Captain Macheath; "you do not want to take my life? How very kind, to be sure you are, my dear sir. I came to an inn—a public place of entertainment, and am shown to a bed, and then because I don't happen with all the submissiveness in the world to answer your questions, not put in the most civil manner, you take credit for not upon the instant blowing my brains out."

"I am an officer in search of a criminal."

"Very well."

"And therefore I have a peculiar duty in speaking to anyone whom I may meet."

"Very good."

"Under these circumstances I feel justified in asking you who you are, sir?" said Fleetfoot.

"Well, I am Smith, cousin four times removed to Jones, who is distantly related to Thomson; so now again I have the honour—of course, feeling deeply grateful for your kindness in sparing my life —to bid you good morning, sir."

The officer was evidently puzzled and staggered by Captain Macheath, but he offered no further opposition to his leaving the room, only laying his pistol upon the bed, and began dressing himself with as much speed as he could put into the operation.

Macheath went downstairs, and upon issuing into the open air, he found that his horse was at the door nearly ready for the road.

"That will do," he said. "What do I owe you?"

"Whatever you please, Captain Macheath," said the ostler.

"Ah! you know me?"

"Yes, I do," the man replied, grinning; "but I shouldn't if you had not left in the pocket of your saddle a letter addressed to you by someone. It's never wise for gentlemen of your profession to do that sort of thing."

"No," said Macheath; "you are right. But, my friend, I heard you questioned by some mounted man about a murderer. How came you not to suspect that I was the person they were in search of?"

"I did suspect it, but I knew you didn't do it."

"You know I didn't do it?"

"To be sure I did. The man who after receiving a pistol-shot almost in his face, and only missed being killed by it by next thing to a miracle, and then didn't reply to it, though he had a pistol in his hand, because the man who had fired at him begged for his life on account of his children, is not the man to kill a woman."

"And who did that ?"

"Why, you did, Macheath, and my brother was the man. He was guard of the Oxford Mail at the time and an outside passenger lent him the pistol. He has often told me the story."

Captain Macheath nodded his head again.

"I recollect it now," he said. "It was more than two years ago."

"It was."

"Well, I thank you," said Macheath. "You are quite right. I had no more to do actually with the killing of the poor creature they spoke of than you have. The real murderer is dead, and I think it was in trying to get out of my way that he came to his death. I will be off now, as your friend upstairs is dressing himself not a bit faster than he can't possibly help to come after me."

"He does not know you?" the ostler demanded.

"No," Captain Macheath replied; "but he has his suspicions that I may be someone whom he would like to get hold of, and I don't want to be troubled with him. Impede him as much as you can."

"Leave that to me."

"There is a guinea for you."

"No, Captain Macheath," said the ostler. "Not a farthing from you. My poor brother owes his life to your forbearance, and his poor children would have been orphans if it hadn't been that you had a kind, a noble heart, in your bosom. Any service that I can do for you I would run a hundred miles to do, but I won't take any payment for it. Oh! no; I am paid enough."

"Ostler—Ostler !" cried the officer, from the window.

"Yes, sir."

"My horse directly, ostler. I shall be down in a minute. Get my horse out, for I want to be off.

After giving this order, the officer pulled his his head in again, and Captain Macheath, with a nod to the ostler, gave his horse the start up the hill beyond the Load of Hay.

The animal had been well fed and well groomed, so that it was in every respect well fitted for the road, and Captain Macheath felt the greatest confidence in his being able to beat the officer at a race on the heath, if such a thing should be a matter of necessity.

"I might have asked the old ostler," he said to himself, "how the fellow was mounted, as that would have been some sort of guide to me how to act. But it is better to suppose that he is well mounted than ill, so here goes for a sharp trot to the heath."

Captain Macheath avoided the village of Hampstead by leaving it upon his right, and cutting through the fields to the lower heath.

To be sure, he had to leap a hedge or two, but that to him and his horse was nothing but sport; so that in an incredibly short space of time they were both upon the heath close to the high road that cuts it into two portions, and from the left hand of which, looking westward, you have so fine a view of that picturesque space of ground, while to the right you can see the dark cloud of smoke that hangs over London.

Captain Macheath was always pleased with the view from Hampstead-heath, and he paused to look at it, as he always did, and not unfrequently when other people would have thought, and with some reason too, that he had little enough time to spare for such matters.

"Yes," he said, as if pursuing a train of reflection that he had not given utterance to until then ; "I have had many a good gallop on these roads and meadows and on this heath, and I hope to have many more yet. But I must not altogether forget my friend of the double-bedded room, nor must I forget that I have one waiting for me at Kentish Town who will think my absence strange. Yes, Polly, I must not forget you."

Raising himself in his stirrups, he cast an anxious eye on every part of the heath, and after a few moments he was convinced he saw someone on the lower heath trying to make a horse leap a hedge while the animal evidently did not like the effort.

By shading his eyes with his hands, and by looking very carefully at the person, he felt quite convinced that it was no other than Fleetfoot, the Bow-street runner.

"So, so; he is following on my track as nearly as he can," said Macheath. "Well, we shall see what will be the result. No doubt, by this time, he is beginning to have a suspicion that I am the man whom he seeks, and if so he will risk something to catch me. Well, it is his business, and if he will run into danger, he must."

After a few moments' reflection Macheath now determined upon riding along the public road right on into the country, for of all things he did not wish to bring any danger into the immediate neighbourhood of Kentish Town.

He only paused until he saw that the officer had succeeded in making his horse leap the hedge, and by the style in which the animal eventually did the leap Captain Macheath saw that it was a good one.

Patting his steed affectionately on the neck he said—

"Well, my friend, perhaps you will be put to your mettle to-day after all, so let us keep the start that we have got."

With this off went the captain at a slashing canter that soon left the heath far behind him.

But he had not got on above two miles when he saw a stage-coach approaching him rapidly from the other direction, and as they neared each other the coachman slackened his speed, and cried—

"Shall I give you a lift, sir, horse and all ?"

Upon this several of the outside passengers laughed, for that coachman was considered to be rather a wag, and his jokes were sure to be greeted by uproarious laughter, whether they happened to be good ones or not.

It so happened, however, that in picking up Captain Macheath for a butt he certainly made a very serious mistake.

In an instant Captain Macheath drew a pistol from his pocket, and presented it at the facetious coachman's head.

"If you don't pull up sharp I'll blow your brains out," said the captain.

The coachman turned as pale as death as he said, in a faltering voice—

"Who—who are you ?"

"A highwayman, to be sure. Who else should I be ?" said Captain Macheath. "Now, Mr. Coachman, as I know you took your money at your last stage I will trouble you to refund it to me, for I look upon myself as proprietor of this road."

"Gentlemen," said the coachman, with a rueful look to those who had laughed so loudly at his

CAPTAIN MACHEATH

THE
PRINCE OF THE HIGHWAY.

"THAT SHOT WILL SETTLE YOU. HOW DO YOU LIKE THAT, CAPTAIN MACHEATH?"

NO. 9.

joke, "are you going to see a poor fellow robbed in this way ? It's my own coach, too, and my own money."

No one laughed now, but everybody looked the picture of dismay.

"You brought it on yourself," cried the one who had laughed most. "Give up your money, and don't lead us all into danger by your obstinacy."

"Don't trouble yourself, sir," said Captain Macheath. "I shall come to you presently. If you don't produce your money, Master Coachman, you have not another moment to live."

The coachman, with a groan, handed to Captain Macheath a small leathern bag of money.

"Very good," said Captain Macheath. "Now be off with you."

As he spoke he clapped spurs to his horse and went on his road at full gallop, for he had already in this little affair which had come upon him at unawares put off much more time than he wished, considering that he had such an enemy in the immediate vicinity as the officer who had made it the object of his life to take him, alive or dead.

Captain Macheath always went upon the good principle that it was foolish to despise any enemy ; but if he had not gone upon such a principle the officer would not have been one who could be thought lightly of as a foe, for not only was he naturally a very determined man, but Macheath, by the accidental inspection of his pocket-book, had been made aware of how important a point his capture was.

It was, therefore, with a kind of conviction that he or the officer would not live much longer, that he now spurred along the road again after relieving the coachman of the bag of money.

He did not trouble himself even to look at the amount of booty he had secured by his encounter with the coach, but making his way right on through Hendon he soon got into the beautiful green lanes near Mill-hill.

More than once he paused as he got upon high parts of the roads and looked in the direction from which he came, but he could see nothing of the officer, and he began to fancy that he must be some three or four miles the start of him, when through a hedge about half-a-mile only in his rear he saw Fleetfoot suddenly emerge into the high road.

Captain Macheath was so astonished at this sudden appearance of the officer, who must have crossed the meadows with a rare knowledge of the locality, that for a moment or two he stood stock-still, not attempting even to preserve the distance between them.

The officer raised a shout of satisfaction when he saw Captain Macheath.

"He is resolved upon his own death or mine," said the captain, "but I will baulk him while I can. Nay, this looks so like fairly running away that I cannot do it. I will meet the fool, and if he will throw away his life, why he must, and there's an end of it."

With this feeling uppermost in his mind Captain Macheath checked the impulse to speed that he had given to his horse, and being in the centre of the roadway, he calmly awaited the arrival of the officer.

When Fleetfoot saw that this was the case he gradually slackened his speed, and came on at a gentle trot.

"Surrender yourself !" he cried. "I know you now. You are Captain Macheath ! Surrender yourself. I have made an oath to take you, and I will keep it or kill you !"

"And does it not strike you," said Captain Macheath, in a clear, loud voice, "that there is another alternative—namely, that I may kill you, and then ride off in safety ?"

"I know that I run many risks," Fleetfoot replied.

"Come on, then. I am waiting for you."

They both put their hands to their holsters and produced pistols.

But Captain Macheath was willing enough, for more reasons than one, to let the officer have the first shot.

"Blaze away, my friend," he said. "It will not be the first time I have given one of your fraternity a chance shot at me."

"You are a bold rascal, at all events," said the officer, "and it is a pity you did not take to something else than this trade, which you now see brings you to so lamentable an end."

As he uttered these words he fired at Captain Macheath.

When the smoke cleared away he saw his opponent still sitting as before upon his horse.

"That is the first shot I have missed for one while, but I shall not miss another," Fleetfoot shouted, in a rage.

Before Captain Macheath could say a word Fleetfoot discharged the other pistol at the captain, but as they chanced to be the weapons from which Macheath had drawn the bullets, of course, no damage was done.

"Confusion !" cried the officer. "Some more than human influence mars my aim."

"You are a dead man !" cried Captain Macheath, galloping up to him and placing the muzzle of a pistol against his cheek. "You are a dead man !"

"I know it."

"Will you yet save yourself by making me a promise that you will cease this pursuit of me ?"

"No—no !" said Fleetfoot, bravely. "Take my life if you will, but the pursuit of you I must continue, if I live."

"Why, this must be sheer insanity," Captain Macheath remarked. "Are you really in your senses or not ?"

"I am as sane as you are, Macheath, to the full, and I still say that I must and will have your life or your person to hand over to the law."

"Then take that," said Captain Macheath. "You are a greater fool than I thought you. But I should not feel myself justified in shooting you in cool blood in this way. I believe you are a madman."

With one blow of the pistol-barrel Captain Macheath knocked him off his horse, and then, without pausing to see how he fell or what became of him, he turned his own horse's head towards Hampstead again.

He had not proceeded far before he saw approaching him a complete cavalcade of horsemen. Instead of making the least attempt to get out of the way, Macheath rode into the very midst of them.

"Help, gentlemen, help !" he called out. "I am an officer, and was in pursuit of the notorious Captain Macheath. We have had a tussle together, and he lies on the road a little hurt, I think, and I ask you all to help me to take h'm."

"Won't we !" cried the horsemen, with one voice.

And off they went in the direction Macheath intimated, leaving him to pursue what route he liked at his leisure.

He galloped through Hampstead, when the few shops of that then very rural village were only just opening, and never drew rein until he reached the cottage where Polly was most anxiously waiting for him.

Perhaps of all the adventures that Captain Macheath had been engaged in, this one, which had terminated in the tragical end of Mrs. Finch, was to him the most unsatisfactory and the most full of painful recollections.

"Good Heavens!" he said to himself, as he reined in his steed opposite to the little cottage where Polly resided. "Who would have dreamt that even the utmost jealousy of such a man as Finch would have carried him to such a length!"

Macheath was right enough so far.

No one would have thought that Finch was the sort of person to do the deed which we have seen he did do; but then no one can properly estimate how far human nature may be completely transformed by passion.

Macheath dismounted, and tying his horse to the little gate of the garden of the cottage, he strode along the gravel path towards the humble but pretty abode.

The hour was still so early that the shutters of the lower room were not unbarred; but the ear of affection is watchful, and Polly heard the footstep of her husband upon the path.

She opened the little casement from which she had last bidden him adieu, and with a fresh morning face full of beauty she welcomed him.

"Are you quite well, my little wife?" he cried.

"Oh! yes. I will come down and let you in."

The door opened, and Polly, taking him by the hand, led him in, saying as she did so—

"How long and weary the hours are without you!"

"Are they really, Polly?"

"Can you doubt it?"

"No, no. I will doubt nothing that you say, Polly—nothing; and you shall be my only joy, dear girl. Time was when I thought I loved you; but until you became my wife, I never, in truth, knew how I really loved you."

"You flatter."

"Indeed, I do not," said Macheath. "Come, Polly, we must make a bargain with each other, that we are to have implicit faith in what each may say; and so, as we will always be complimentary, never will there be a happier couple in the world."

Polly smiled, and she would fain have induced her husband to remain and to pass the whole day with her.

But he was in too feverish a state of mind concerning what had taken place in the City to do that.

He felt nervously anxious to know what complexion the dreadful murder of Mrs. Finch had to the public; so, in about two hours after, taking some things from the valise that he always had strapped to the back of his saddle, and with these disguising himself, he put up his horse at an inn in Kentish Town, and taking advantage of a stage-coach that passed the door of the cottage, he went right into the City.

Macheath was not kept long in suspense regarding the light in which the murder of Mrs. Finch was viewed, for upon a lamp-post he saw a placard which stated that—

"An unmanly and dreadful murder had been committed by a man unknown upon Mrs. Maria Finch; and that it was supposed that the murderer, upon being pursued by Mr. Finch along the tops of some houses, had thrown down that gentleman to the pavement below, by which he was killed at once."

The placard then went on to state that—

"A reward of one hundred pounds would be paid to anyone who would give information as to who the party was who called upon Mrs. Finch on the evening of the murder, and a reward of another hundred pounds upon his being lodged in any of his majesty's gaols."

"Pleasant!" said Macheath, as he finished reading the placard.

"By your leave, sir!" said a voice behind him.

Captain Macheath stepped aside, and found that he had been impeding a bill-sticker in his work.

This man in a few moments appended a smaller bill to the foot of the other one, which contained a full description of Captain Macheath, given by the servant of the house where the Finches had lodged.

"A bad job, sir, that 'ere murder," said the bill-sticker.

"Very."

"They'll nab him, sir, don't you think?"

"It is very likely."

Macheath walked slowly away.

He had certainly all the information he wanted, and much more than was at all agreeable to him.

Galling as it was to be supposed to be the guilty party, he did not see the smallest chance of being able to prove the contrary, for Finch was dead; he might have owned to his share in the dreadful deed.

"Well," said Captain Macheath, "all I have to do is to take care of number one. I did not kill either of them, although I may have been the indirect cause of the dead of both. I will take to the road again, and try to banish these uncomfortable thoughts, or I shall know no peace in my life. This affair will blow over in a little time, and the secret must remain in my own bosom."

There was no conveyance from the City to Kentish Town, where Macheath had left his horse, so he resolved to walk the distance, and by getting across the fields by Finsbury, and then making his way to Islington, he knew that an hour's sharp walking would take him as nearly as possible to his place of destination.

With this intention, Captain Macheath struck off as nearly as he could for Finsbury-fields, which at that time were quite clear and open.

Macheath did not expect to be molested, but, however, Fate had decreed it to be otherwise.

He had got clear of the houses pretty well, and was in the neighbourhood of some citizens' villas not far from Finsbury, when he heard a voice cry—

"Stop—stop—stop!"

This was not a species of invocation which Captain Macheath was likely to let go quite unheeded, especially as he was upon foot.

Had he been well-mounted, probably, he would have treated it in a much more supercilious manner.

He turned on the instant, and saw a mounted man coming at a smart trot towards him up a lane in the immediate vicinity.

"Hilloa!" cried the horseman again. "Stop, my friend."

"What for?" queried Macheath.

"Only to answer me a question. Have you seen a man on a very dark bay horse in this neighbourhood?"

"No."

The mounted man came close up to Macheath, and they both looked in each other's faces for a few moments in silence.

To the intense astonishment of Captain Macheath this man was no other than the officer with whom he had had the encounter near Goldengreen, and whom he had succeeded in playing the trick of giving him into custody.

No sooner had Macheath made this discovery, by an attentive perusal of the officer's face, than the officer found out, by the same process, who he was speaking to.

"By Jove !" he cried, "it is Captain Macheath."

"Right !" said Captain Macheath. "You never spoke a truer word in all your life, my friend."

"You are my prisoner now. Scoundrel, your career is now at last at an end."

"My dear sir, you flatter yourself," said Captain Macheath.

Quick as thought, then, and before the officer could possibly divine his intention, Captain Macheath stooped, and seizing him by his foot, fairly canted him off his horse into the roadway.

The officer made two or three plunging attempts to rise ; but the large riding-boots he wore impeded him, and Captain Macheath had time to spring into the vacant saddle.

"Now, my friend," he shouted, "my career is not quite over yet. If you want your horse again, you must look for him some miles from London, and for fear you should be disappointed by taking the wrong direction, I am going north. Good day !"

The officer, without troubling himself to get up, pulled a pistol from his breast-pocket and fired it at Captain Macheath.

The bullet slightly touched his left arm.

"All right !" cried the captain.

No one knew better how to start a horse at a moment's notice to a full gallop than Macheath, and before the officer could get at another pistol he was off like the wind.

"Stop him ! It's Captain Macheath !" roared the officer. "Stop him ! Help—help ! It's Macheath, the highwayman ! A hundred pounds to anybody who will stop him. Help—murder—help—watch !"

As Captain Macheath galloped on, the sounds died away, and by the time the old houses of Upper Islington appeared, he was in complete solitude and silence, and the officer's voice had faded away in the dim distance.

"A narrow escape, that," said Macheath, as he slackened his speed a little and looked around him.

Not a soul was visible, and from the high ground upon which he was now, if anyone had been in his proximity, he must have seen them easily.

The horse was a good one, and far from being in the least distressed, seemed very much to have enjoyed the gallop.

What was to be done now might have puzzled some folks ; but Macheath was a man of rapid resolves.

After a very few minutes' consideration he made up his mind to ride to Kentish Town, and then, when he got very near to where his own horse was put up, he would be able to get rid of the one he rode by dismounting and letting it go loose.

He did not think it at all prudent to ride it to the door of the inn where he had left his own steed, for in Kentish Town he was as yet unknown, and that would have been, in all probability, a means of causing suspicion.

He was not, however, forgetful of the probability that he should be followed by some person on whom the discomfited officer might call for assistance, and he knew that where he had left that very unlucky individual a fresh horse could easily be procured.

Captain Macheath paused now and then to take a look around him.

Upon one of these occasions he saw three men on horseback coming on as rapidly as the nature of the ground would permit them in his direction.

"Humph !" said Captain Macheath, "people don't cross a ploughed field if they can help it. They must think it a near cut or they would have found some better path. No doubt they congratulate themselves upon the likelihood of coming up with me and taking me very comfortably. We shall see."

Captain Macheath had gone so much to the right that in the course, even of a very few moments, he arrived at Newington-green ; but still, if he could strike across the country, he was not so far from Kentish Town as anyone would have supposed, and it must be recollected that at that time there was by no means the amount of obstruction in the shape of buildings and enclosures that all that part of the suburbs of London now present.

Crossing the green, he dived down a narrow lane and soon came to a low hedge, beyond which stretched the open fields, and at some distance off, he could plainly see the cottages in Kentish Town, and mark the whole of the straggling road right up to Highgate.

It was now that he put the capabilities of the officer's horse to the proof.

He did not think it wise to give the creature a great leap to do in the first instance, for well he knew that such a course of proceeding will sometimes shake a horse at the outset of his career, and make him lose speed for a mile or two.

Macheath sought for a gap in the hedge, through which he charged the horse, and then walking him for a few moments on the turf, he gradually urged him on, and in the course of a few minutes was flying over the meadows at a tremendous rate.

Two magnificent leaps of enclosures were now taken with ease by the horse, and without relaxing in his speed in the least degree.

Captain Macheath seemed to be approaching the houses in Kentish Town with magical rapidity.

The captain did not pull up to look about him ; but when nothing but a level meadow was before him, he at times turned in the saddle and took a keen glance along the fields.

He saw his pursuers about half-a-mile behind him.

They seemed, however, to feel that their cattle were unequal to the leaps necessary in the cross-country ride, and they were making for the high road.

"That will do," said Captain Macheath.

He now felt quite certain that he should be able to reach the inn at Kentish Town, and to get his horse out and be off before they could reach him by the road.

His great object was that they should have no knowledge of where he had put up his horse, for of all places in the world, he did not wish any inquiry to be made concerning him in Kentish Town, and that was on account of his wife, Polly.

On he went at the same slashing rate, and now, before you could well have counted twelve, he was at the back of Kentish Town.

An unlucky obstacle presented itself to him in the shape of the long, straggling grounds belonging to a market gardener and florist.

To have gone round this place would have put off more time than Captain Macheath felt at all inclined to waste, so in the first instance he jumped the hedge, and let his horse alight in the middle of a bed of asparagus.

Then on he went right through a whole rotation of crops, until he reached the gravel path that led out into the village; but there he met the gardener himself, who flung a long rake at his head.

Captain Macheath had no wish to ride into the village, and as it was quite immaterial to him whether he dismounted where he was or elsewhere, he flung himself hastily from his horse, and catching up the rake, he felled the gardener with one blow of its handle.

"I can't stand upon trifles," said Captain Macheath.

In another moment he ran out into Kentish town, and found himself exactly opposite to the inn where he had left his horse.

The officer's steed, which had done him such good service, he left in the nursery-garden to amuse himself with such dainties as he might find suited to his palate.

Without the least appearance then of hot haste Captain Macheath went into the inn yard, and asked for his horse.

He held up half-a-guinea between his finger and thumb to the ostler, as he merely uttered the two words—

"Be quick!"

The sight of the glittering coin was quite a magical stimulus, and the horse was out and saddled in an incredibly short space of time.

The half-guinea was transformed from Macheath's finger to the hand of the well-pleased ostler, and in another moment the captain was in the high road, and firmly on his saddle.

"Now," he said, as he patted his steed. "Now those gentlemen behind us if they are inclined for a little excursion of some twenty miles or so into the country, can have it."

He trotted on until he got to the rise of the hill, and then he took a look at his pursuers.

The three horsemen had got quite clear of the village, and were pointing him out to each other.

"Very good," said Captain Macheath. "Half-a-mile is a long pull up; and if you catch me you will have me, my friends, but not before."

The whole of that neighbourhood was well known to Captain Macheath, and he fancied that Swain's-lane was not quite so bad an ascent as the high road to Highgate.

When he got to that turning he at once took it; and at a long gallop, which his horse in ascending hills had not his equal at, away they went up the lane, and in a few minutes were in Highgate.

Upon the level through the town Macheath went leisurely, for he was determined that his horse should have every chance, and although he did not believe that the ascent of Swain's-lane had winded him in the least, he was resolved to give him all the advantage in his power.

Highgate, so far as regarded the level upon which the village is actually situated, was cleared at a rapid walk; but after getting to the descent on the other side, just past the Wrestler's Inn, Macheath gave his horse the rein, and away they went towards Finchley at a tremendous pace.

"Bravely done!" cried Macheath—"bravely done, my gallant steed! Why, we must already

have made the half-mile that was between us and our foes a whole one."

He kept his ear on the stretch to catch the sound of the horses' feet of his pursuers, but no such indication of their approach reached him, and he concluded rightly enough that they were toiling up the steep bit of hill, and so going leisurely enough.

In a few moments Captain Macheath was right down in the valley by Finchley, but he did not pause.

He left East Finchley well to his left, and keeping still the high road, he ascended to a rising bit of country again, from which he could at intervals command extensive views for many miles round him on all sides.

CHAPTER XXII.
THE CHASE CONTINUED.

THE only thing that Macheath felt at all anxious about was that he should to a certain extent keep his enemies in view.

He did not like the idea of their leaving the high road, perhaps, and lulling him into a feeling of false security, and then pouncing upon him at some moment when he did not expect them.

Therefore he paused now upon the high ground in the immediate neighbourhood of Finchley to reconnoitre the surrounding country.

He took care to get so far to the roadside that the identity of himself and his horse would be very much lost against the trees and the bushes, if his enemies should happen to be looking for him.

Not for the space of about half-a-minute had Macheath been waiting, when he saw coming from Finchley a poor-looking boy, rather sadly mounted upon a miserable-looking nag, and as he neared the spot Macheath saw that he was one of the postboys belonging to the post-office, who for a few shillings a-week and a red jacket risked their necks twenty times a-week at the very least.

Captain Macheath waved his hand to stop him and the boy pulled up with an uncomfortable jerk.

"Any of my friends down the road?" cried Macheath. "We are after a highwayman, my lad."

"Oh! is you," said the boy; "I'm glad to hear you say that, for I was half afraid you were him, and you'd rob my letter-bag."

"Oh! dear no."

"Well, they are all a-coming," said the boy; "they have got a couple of young chaps from the village to come with them. They say they will be sure to have him. I suppose you do not like to try it alone?"

"Certainly not."

"Well, I must push on whether I meets him or not. A postboy mustn't wait for nothing no how."

"I suppose not," said Macheath.

"Oh! dear me, no. Good day. Kim up, will you!"

After a short wrangle with his horse, off went the boy again at the same rattling kind of half-trot, half-gallop which only such horses ever think of perpetrating.

"So," said Captain Macheath, "they are getting reinforcements, are they? Well, be it so. The more the merrier. Now I dare say I might manage to play them the old fox's trick of doubling upon them; but I am inclined for a gallop, so I will lead them by the nose some twenty miles or so further yet; and if they are not pretty well knocked up by that time, they are better mounted and better horsemen than I like them to be."

Macheath, however, was resolved not to start until he actually saw his enemies, for it was only by keeping them constantly in sight from any high portion of the road that he might encounter that he could gather any amusement in the chase.

But in a moment or two his attention was directed to the sound of wheels in the direction of which he was galloping, and a man in a cart appeared round a turn of the road.

"Hilloa!" said Macheath. "If you meet some men on horseback, just say that Captain Macheath is only a little way ahead, and they may get pretty close to him at dinner time, as he means to put up at a respectable house on the road."

The man in the cart stared, but Captain Macheath did not want to give him the opportunity of making any remark, but dashed on at his old pace.

He knew that his message would be delivered, for his pursuers would stop everybody they met now for a certainty to ask news of him, since they must have lost sight of him when he turned into Swain's-lane, and he did not wish that they should go straggling about the country searching for him, and so raise a great alarm on his account.

For the next three miles Macheath did not in the least slacken his pace, and it was a tremendous thing to take a horse for that distance at such a speed.

Gradually, however, he drew up, and stopped at the door of a roadside inn.

The landlord came out in a moment and, with a profusion of bows, wanted to know if his honour would bait there.

"No," said Captain Macheath. "I only want a pot and a pint of your best old ale, landlord, if you please."

"A pot and a pint, sir?"

"Yes, the pint is for me, and the pot is for my friend."

The innkeeper stood in the middle of the road, and shading his eyes with his hand, he gazed all round him to see the friend, but finding no one but Captain Macheath, he shook his head, saying—

"I don't see him, sir, if you please."

"Never mind," said Captain Macheath, "only be quick with the ale, or else I shall have to ride on to the next house."

This was a threat to the landlord of a roadside inn which was not at all to be despised, and accordingly the pot of ale and the pint were produced in two foaming tankards.

Macheath drank the pint himself, and then taking the pot in his right hand, he leant over his horse's neck and held it to the creature's mouth.

It was gone in two or three seconds, and the horse gave a snort of satisfaction.

"Well, I never!" said the landlord; "that's the finest old ale as was ever brewed, and almost too good for men, and the idea of a horse whipping up a whole pot of it is—is—"

"What is it?" said Captain Macheath.

"Oh! nothing at all, sir, if you thinks proper—nothing in all the world, sir, in course."

"Very good—there's your money."

Macheath threw half-a-crown on the ground, and then with a slight touch to the horse, a hint that the creature well understood, they cleared the horse-trough standing outside the inn, and were off again at full speed.

"Give my compliments to the gentlemen who are following me," shouted Captain Macheath.

"Stop that man—stop that man!" roared a person without his hat, rushing out of the house.

"What—him, sir?" said the landlord.

"Yes; stop him—stop him!"

"Bless you! sir, he's a mile off by this time," said the landlord. "He's had a pint of the old ale himself, and the horse has had a pot. Do you know him, sir?"

"Do I know him? To be sure I do. He took a hundred pounds from me all in gold one day on Finchley-common. It's Captain Macheath, the highwayman."

"Captain Macheath?"

"Yes; I should know him again, if it were a hundred years hence. All I got for my money was a good look at him, and I have dreamt of him ever since, and now I shall dream of him still more, for here I have missed him by a hair's breadth only."

"Missed him, sir?" gasped the landlord. "Why, you don't mean for to go to say as you'd a' interfered with him?"

"Wouldn't I?" said the man. "I was taken by surprise when he robbed me, and was not very well, but if I only had a chance of meeting him again face to face, I'd soon rid society at large of such a vagabond—that I would. I shall always regret that I did not notice him till he was going away—that I shall."

The landlord put his hand up to his eyes and took a long look down the road.

"What are you looking at, landlord?" said the bold guest.

"Well, I—no—yes—to be sure."

"What is it, landlord?"

"Why, if he isn't a-coming back for his change, as I'm a sinner. Yes, he is."

"Murder! Help! Hide me somewhere, landlord!" roared the valiant individual. "Put me in the cellar—in a cask—under a bed—anywhere, and don't say I mentioned him. Murder—murder!"

The bold guest rushed into the inn in a frantic state, and the landlord laughed so—for Captain Macheath was not coming back at all—that he was forced to hold by the horse-trough to keep himself up.

While this farce was going on at the inn door, Captain Macheath had made great progress on the road, and began to get into a very beautiful and finely wooded bit of country.

The ale that the horse had taken seemed to stimulate him to every exertion, and if it had been at all necessary, Captain Macheath could have made an amazing ride of the splendid animal.

As it was, he pulled up, and finding that he was quite alone, and that not even a house was near him, he dismounted, and climbing a high tree, had a splendid view for miles around.

CHAPTER XXIII.
THE CAPTURE.

FAR off he saw a cluster of horsemen coming on at what his practised eye told him was a good pace.

"So," he said, "they think to run me down at last. But they will be mistaken. If I am ever taken it will be by treachery, and not by a race across the country. Let them come. I am right glad to see that they place such value upon my word as to believe that I am to be sought in the north only because I said as much."

He came down from the tree and again

" WHY, YOU—YOU ARE NOT MY OLD FRIEND MUFFER!" GASPED ALDERMAN SMUGGS.

mounted his faithful horse, and he took the road again.

"Let me think," he said. "If I were to pause, it would take them now half an hour to come up to me. That is not time enough for me to dine in; I must have three-quarters of an hour at the least; so I must find some means of detaining them upon the road."

What those means were to be Captain Macheath did not know at the moment.

All he had made up his mind to was that he would stop and dine somewhere, notwithstanding the pursuit that was so steadily kept up after him.

But he was turning the matter over in his mind, and there was but little doubt that his fertile genius in such matters would hit upon some scheme to accomplish what he desired.

He was not galloping now, so that he had an opportunity of looking about him a little, and in the course of a few moments he was rather startled to see the head of a man, as it appeared, just peeping over a hedge at him.

"Hilloa!" cried Captain Macheath. "Who are you?"

No answer was returned, and upon riding up to the hedge he found that it was a scarecrow in the field beyond it.

A coat, breeches, and an old three-cornered hat stuffed out with straw and supported upon a stout stake, made up the illusion.

Macheath could not but laugh at the idea of his saying, "Who are you?" to the scarecrow; but he had not ridden half-a-dozen paces from it when the idea struck him that it might be the means of procuring him the delay necessary to stop and refresh both himself and his horse.

Macheath was quick in action, and with him the conception of every plan was quickly enough followed by its execution.

He glanced round him, until he saw a tall chesnut-tree which would just suit his purpose, and then dismounting, he proceeded to carry it out.

He made his way through the hedge, and got possession of the scarecrow, which he threw over into the road.

Following it there, he lifted it up, and by a happy jerk he cast it right into the middle of the chesnut-tree, where it lodged securely enough, presenting as nearly as possible the appearance of someone hiding in the tree.

"I think that will do," he said; "and if it does not, it is not a bad joke, and I will keep a good look-out notwithstanding."

He immediately mounted again and rode on, when to his great satisfaction he met a groom upon horseback.

Macheath on the instant rode up to him.

"I have been robbed on this road," he said.

"Robbed, sir?"

"Yes, and by the notorious Captain Macheath. I have had my watch, a diamond ring, and sixty pounds taken from me only half an hour ago, and I hid in a hedge after he had left me, and saw him turn his horse adrift and climb up a large chesnut-tree and hide in it."

"The deuce he did, sir!" exclaimed the groom. "Then we will have him—I will go back with you, sir."

"No, I cannot. I am on a very particular business indeed, which must be transacted quickly —my dinner," added Macheath to himself—"or I would go back with you at once. If you can get any assistance on the road, take him, and as I come back I will join you. I am Sir Robert Marmaduke."

The groom touched his hat.

"Which tree is he in, sir?"

"It's a large chesnut on the right-hand side of the road as you go to it from here, and it's near a gate with a lot of brambles stuck in it to shut up the field."

"I know it, sir—I know it. It's just a little way on, sir—a big tree with a large branch coming right over the road?"

"The same."

"Thank you, sir; I know it, sir."

"Very good. I believe there is a large reward offered for the apprehension of this Captain Macheath. Of course, in my position of life, the money is of no sort of consequence to me, so you can share it with any persons who may assist you in apprehending him; and when you have him safe, I will take care that justice is done, and that you are not cheated out of it."

"Oh! sir, you are very good," said the groom.

"Not at all, my friend—not at all. I am sorry, indeed, that my pressing engagement prevents me from having the pleasure of going back with you."

The groom, who was only out to give a horse an airing, was not at all sorry that the sham Sir Robert Marmaduke could not go back, for he hoped to have most of the reward to himself by the knowledge that he thought he now possessed of the whereabouts of the notorious highwayman, Captain Macheath.

He rode on until he came to the tree, and one glance was sufficient, by showing him a portion of the scarecrow hidden among the branches, to convince him that the information that had been given him was quite correct.

"Oh! it's all right," he said. "There he is. Of course he has got fire-arms, and will have a pop at anybody who pretends to look at him. Dear me, what shall I do? I have heard a good deal about this Captain Macheath, and they say he's a most desperate fellow, and no more minds blowing a fellow's brains out than smoking a cigar. I must be very careful, for what's the use of the reward to me if I am a dead man before I get any of it?"

Having arrived at this highly philosophical conclusion, the groom was half afraid to look up into the tree for fear of encountering the much dreaded glance of the highwayman's eye, and he began to think that after all it would be better to share the danger and the reward with someone else.

In this state of mind he waited quietly enough, keeping only now and then an eye on the tree, for fear the highwayman should suddenly slide down its trunk and escape.

In due time, up came the mounted party in pursuit of Captain Macheath, and with a groan the groom noticed their number. He made up his mind, however, to make the best of a bad job, and to pocket with perfect security what he could; so, riding forward so as to meet the party at some distance before they reached the tree, he said—

"Gentlemen, I can tell you of a good thing, if you will let me have some of the advantage coming from it."

"What is it?" cried one. "Be quick, for we are busy."

"But you can't be after anything that will pay you as this will," said the groom.

"You don't know that, young fellow. We are

after Captain Macheath, the notorious highwayman, and there are sufficient rewards offered for him to make us all, and you, too, if you could find him; so if you have anything to say, say it quickly and at once, for you find we are not upon any trifling business."

"Captain Macheath, did you say?"

"Yes, to be sure. Are you deaf?"

"No—no. But speak low or I don't know what may happen. I beg, gentlemen, that you will speak low."

"What for?"

"Listen to me. There are five of you and one of me. Now if you will promise me upon your words, all of you, a sixth part of what you get by aking Captain Macheath, I will put you in the way of getting him without much trouble."

"You will?"

"If I don't you have nothing at all to pay me, so you are quite safe enough."

"True—true, we are!" said the officer, who was the chief person of the party.

"Upon my word you shall have the sixth of whatever we get if you carry out what you say. I make you that promise with all these four persons as witnesses to it."

"You all hear him?" said the groom.

"Yes—yes. Of course we do."

"Then, after robbing Sir Robert Marmaduke of sixty pounds, and his watch, and a diamond ring only half an hour ago, he turned his horse adrift and got up into that chestnut-tree, where he is now hiding."

The five pursuers of Captain Macheath started at this most unexpected and extraordinary information.

"In that tree?" cried the officer—"in that tree?"

"In—that—tree," said the groom, solemnly.

"Come on, then. We shall soon see that. Come on!" cried the officer, excitedly.

They all trotted up to the tree, followed by the groom, and then the first thing the officer said was—

"There he is, sure enough."

"And I can see his eye," said one of the others.

"Look out," cried a third. "I can see the barrel of a pistol. He has got up there to shoot us as we pass."

There was a general scattering of the party all over the road, each one being anxious that if any one were shot it should not be him.

"Oh! don't—don't. Murder!" cried the groom, shielding his head with his arm.

When it was found that no pistol was fired from the tree, the panic gradually subsided, and the officer, gathering courage, cried out, in a loud voice—

"Captain Macheath—the game is up now. You are wanted, and you cannot escape. We see you, and that is sufficient. You had better come down from that tree a live man, for if you don't you may be quite sure that you will have to come down a dead one, or so badly wounded that you will wish yourself dead."

"Bless us!" said the groom, "what does he say?"

"Nothing at all."

"Ah!" said one of the men, "he is all the more dangerous on that account, I know."

"He's only plotting and planning something," said one of the young men from Highgate, "and I'll go home."

"And so will I," said the other hero from the same place.

"What!" cried the officer. "Go home now, will you, my lads, while we are on the point of catching our man? You must be mad. My idea is that he has hurt himself in some way, and has crawled up the tree to hide."

"But why don't he speak?"

"Oh! he is too much chagrined to do that."

Upon this the two young men who would have taken flight home again plucked up a little courage and remained; and the other officer again spoke in a loud tone of voice—

"Captain Macheath," he said, "do not be foolish. Who knows but there may be some flaw in the indictment against you even at the Old Bailey, and then you may get off this time; but if I am compelled to shoot you, you have no chance."

"What does he say?" cried the other.

"Oh! he's as obstinate as the very deuce. He won't speak."

When they found that they could not get a word from the figure in the tree, they grew more and more cautious, for to their imaginations there was something extremely exciting in the fact of the highwayman being in a tree, and keeping that contemptuous silence.

"I really would not fire into the tree," said one. "Who knows but it may explode some mine and blow us all up!"

"Eh?" cried the officer as he started back. "What do you say?"

The man repeated his view of the case.

"Oh! stuff," said the officer; "I can't think that at all possible. How can he blow us up?"

"I don't know. He's an outrageous kind of chap, and has as many doubles and twists as an old fox."

The others laughed at this illustration, and that put the officer on his mettle.

"Nonsense!" he said. "No doubt he thinks by preserving this silence and mystery, that he will frighten me, as he has already frightened you; but I am not exactly that sort of man; so if he don't come down and give himself up I shall fire at him. I feel that it is my duty so to do."

Upon this the officer walked under the tree again.

"Captain Macheath," he said in a solemn voice, "you may fancy this is a very fine joke, but I can assure you that it is not; I am determined that I will take you; I have made up my mind to it, I can tell you, and set my life upon it. Eh? Did you speak?"

"He didn't say anything," said one of the others.

"But he moved," said one.

"Did he move?" cried the officer, turning round sharply to the man who had spoken last. "Are you quite sure you saw him move, my man?"

"Oh! yes, sir."

At this moment a very large chestnut suddenly fell right on the crown of the officer's hat, and as it came from rather a considerable height it dealt his hat a smart rap, and splitting open, rattled about his ears.

For the moment this event took him by surprise.

"Murder! What was] that? Stop him! Murder!" he cried.

A roar of laughter from the men, who had seen exactly what it was, at once awakened him to the fact, that at all events there could be no danger where there was so much hilarity.

"It was only a chestnut, that fell on your head," said one.

"A chestnut?"

"Yes, that was all. He is pelting you with chestnuts, that's all, sir. It's just his way to be always up to some joke or another."

"Joke, does he call it—eh? Joke—I'll joke him. There! I think that will settle you, Macheath."

Full of anger, the officer at once presented his pistol at the scarecrow in the tree, and pulled the trigger.

Bang! went the well-loaded weapon, and a shower of leaves and two more chestnuts came down upon the officer. But to the great surprise of the whole party there was the figure in the tree, sitting on a branch to all appearance as calm and as composed as though nothing at all out of the common way was taking place.

"Confound him!" said the officer. "I must have hit him."

"He don't move, sir."

"But I could not miss him," said the puzzled officer. "Captain Macheath, you are wounded. Are you intent upon self-destruction that you remain in that tree so perversely? Come down, and no further harm will be done to you; but if you remain there you will be destroyed, and your dead body will hang as a scarecrow amid those branches."

The figure maintained its position.

"Did he move?" said the officer.

"I think I saw him move a little," said one.

"I saw him wink his left eye," said another.

"His eye? Can you see his eye?"

"Yes. If you come here, sir, and look right along where I'm pointing to, you'll see his eye just above a little branch of the tree that bends round in this way, just as I'm a-bending my finger. Do you see it, sir?"

"I—think—I—"

"Don't you see it a-glistening?"

"Well, I wouldn't like to swear to it," the officer said, "but I do think that I really, now you mention it, see a something like a human eye. Yes, surely—upon my word, though it is difficult to say. One is rather apt to imagine the eye, but I feel quite sure I can see his nose and a part of his chin."

"That's very near it, sir."

"Yes; we may safely conclude, under such circumstances, I think, that the eye is there likewise."

"Quite safe, sir."

"Well, my friends," the officer said, "you know that this affair has already cost me a good deal of money, and that when I have paid each of you what I have promised you, and that groom what I promised him, I shall not be very much the gainer by apprehending Captain Macheath; but if any one of you will climb up the tree and fairly make him come down, I'll stand a five-pound note down on the spot."

The men looked at each other rather dubiously.

"Recollect," added the officer, as he took out his pocket-book, and produced a five-pound note from its capacious enclosure, "recollect that five pounds are not easily earned every day in the week by climbing a tree."

"It's an awkward job, sir," said one.

"Oh! very," said another.

"Five pounds," added the officer, holding the note at arm's length. "Five pounds."

"Hang it all!" said one, "I'll do it."

"Will you, my friend? Then the five pounds are yours, and what is more, I will remain with a loaded pistol pointed at the tree, so that if needs be I can render you effectual assistance. My opinion is that when he sees we don't intend to stand any of his nonsense, he will give in with a good grace at last."

"I'll try it, sir. I should think he'd have shot some of us already if he had had any pistols, don't you think so?"

"Of course he would," the officer returned. "It is as clear as possible. There is no danger whatever in going into the tree! I would do so myself, only I think I can be of more use here where I am. Take the note, my friend, and I hope it may do you a deal of good."

"Thank you, sir," said the man, cramming the note into his pocket. "Thank you, sir, I hopes as it may. Bill, will you give me a leg-up to that first branch?"

"All right," said Bill. "I'll do it."

"Very good."

The man slipped off his coat, and Bill gave him a leg-up to a low branch of the tree.

When he once got a fair hold of it, it rendered the rest of his progress easy enough.

The others all watched his proceedings with intense eagerness, and the officer, with one eye shut, and a pistol pointed to the figure in the tree, kept on the watch.

The adventurous man went cautiously from branch to branch until he came near the scarecrow, and then the interest of those below became painfully intense.

They saw him kick it with his foot, and then they heard him shout out—

"Oh! my eye."

"Is he dead?" said the officer.

"As mutton!" said the man.

"Then, my friends, that first shot of mine must have done the business. Is he shot right through the head? I aimed at his head."

"Everywhere," said the man from the tree. "Catch him, some of you, I'm going to throw him down."

At this intimation, far from coming forward to catch the supposed dead body, they all retreated, officer included, some paces further off.

They saw their comrade lay hands on the dead body.

They saw it fall from branch to branch, and at length down it came to the ground and lay huddled up at the foot of the tree.

"How light the poor fellow fell!" said one.

"Very," said another.

"I take you all to witness now," cried the officer, "that before I shot Captain Macheath I said all I could to him to get him to come down from the tree and give himself up quietly, but he was so obstinate that he would not. You will all, I am quite sure, be able to depose to that much, my friends?"

"Oh! yes—yes."

"Very good," said the officer. "Then now we will get a hurdle and take the body to the watch-house at Hampstead. Come on, my friends. He is quite dead."

Curiosity, joined to a thorough conviction that Captain Macheath was quite dead, induced them all to come forward, and at the same moment he who had ascended the tree dropped to the ground.

"We are all done," he said, "except me."

"What do you mean?"

"Why you may have Captain Macheath among you."

So saying, he picked up the scarecrow, which was as light as possible, and flung it right among the advancing group.

The scene that ensued beggars all description. Some fell flat down upon the road.

Others fought madly with their comrades to get away, fancying that they were obstructing them in some way, and one and all raised such a chorus of shouts and yells that the one who had produced all the confusion thought his safest plan would be to take to flight with what he had got; so off he went with his five-pound note in his pocket, and catching his horse and his coat he quickly disappeared from the scene.

The unfortunate officer was knocked down and trodden over by the whole party, and as the scarecrow likewise had come right against him, he was more bruised and bewildered than any of them.

It was not until one suddenly cried out—"Why, it's Farmer Stubbins' scarecrow!" that anything like order was restored, and then they regarded the cause of their terror with careful looks and glared at each other like men in a dream.

The officer sat on the ground looking half-stunned, and there we shall leave him and his companions while we follow the fortunes of Captain Macheath, who had been so succesful in playing off such a ruse upon the enemy.

A quarter of an hour more saw him quietly trotting down the hill of Hampstead.

"I wonder," he said, "how long they will continue staring at the scarecrow in the tree? But it does not matter. The north road for about a week will be too hot to hold me; so, perforce, I must go west for a little time, whether I like it or not. I can easily ride into town of an evening and see my wife."

With this intention, when Captain Macheath got quite to the foot of the hill where Chalk Farm Tavern stood, he turned up a shady lane to his left, and soon got across a few meadows to where Regent's-park now rears its aristocratic abodes.

Then it was only a large tract of not very inviting fields, damp and muddy in bad weather.

Striking across these fields, he easily made his way to the west end of the town, and came out into the western road about half-a-mile below Tyburn-gate.

"Good," he said. "I have made a tolerably short cut of that, at any rate. Something seems to tell me that I shall have some luck on this road. I am glad I relinquished my original intention of going on northward to dine, for I should soon have had the whole country about my ears. I will make a stop at the Old Hats at Ealing."

Having made this determination Captain Macheath went down the road at an easy canter.

He passed the old wall of Kensington-gardens, and rapidly leaving Bayswater behind him, was soon at Shepherd's-bush, then a little straggling collection of about twenty houses only.

He took the right-hand road and soon reached Acton.

A very short ride then brought him to the Old Hats, which then stood quite alone by the road-side, and was an old-fashioned, one-storied house.

This hostel was well known at that time to the knights of the road as being kept by a man who never asked any questions of anyone who made no demur at the bill.

Captain Macheath drew up at the door, and the ostler at once made his appearance and took charge of his horse, while he strolled deliberately into the house as though no price were on his head.

———

CHAPTER XXIV.

THE OLD INN AT ACTON AND WHAT HAPPENED THERE.

"THAT'S Macheath, the highwayman," said the landlord of the Old Hats, as the captain descended from his horse at his door.

"You don't say so?" cried the landlady.

"Yes, I do, my dear."

"What! the famous Captain Macheath who is so gallant to the ladies, and such a very nice man?"

"Humph!"

"The good, handsome Captain Macheath—the—"

"My dear, he won't thank you to be bawling out his name in that sort of way, I am sure. It is enough that you and I know him, without letting everybody in the house into the secret of who he is; and you know, likewise, perfectly well that young Mr. Muffer is here now on his way to dine with the Lord Mayor; and his father, you know as well as I can tell you, is Alderman Muffer, so, of course, he would feel bound to try to apprehend Macheath, and then only think what a pretty disturbance there would be in the house."

"He apprehend Captain Macheath!" cried the landlady. "Why, Macheath would eat him up."

"Very likely, my dear; but would it do any good to our house to have the son of Alderman Muffer eaten up in it by Macheath?"

"Well, who said it would?"

"Nobody, my love; only don't be bawling Macheath's name out so loud, for we don't know what may come of it. You know our mode of carrying on business is to charge well and ask no questions, and you know that no class of customers pay us better than the—"

"Knights of the road," said the landlady.

"Precisely, my dear."

"I know all that quite as well as you do, and I am quite as little likely to do any mischief to any guest. As for Mr. Muffer, as I say, Macheath, from what I have seen of him, would eat him up with half a grain of salt."

"Very likely; but—"

Tingle—tingle—tingle!

"Ah! there's the bell, I declare—it's the coffee-room bell, and Mr. Muffer is there. I only wish, wife, you had not kept me talking here; I could have met Macheath and got him to go into the bar-parlour, or some other room; but now—"

Tingle—tingle—tingle!

"Are you going to answer the bell, Peter, or is Mr. M. to pull it down, I ask you?"

"Coming, coming, coming!" cried the landlord as he made a rush now to a long, low-ceilinged, dingy apartment called the coffee-room.

There he found Captain Macheath taking off his riding gloves, and Mr. Muffer, the alderman's son, looking at him with amazement, for that young gentleman had been to school in Holland, and had very little experience of life.

He probably thought no one would venture into the coffee-room at the Old Hats while so very important a personage as himself was there.

"Well, landlord," said Captain Macheath, "have you anything very tempting in the house that one can have to eat?"

"Oh! yes, sir."

"What is it?" demanded the captain.

"Why, sir, we have something of all sorts. There is a roast haunch of as fine mutton as you would wish to see."

" Uncut ?"

" Oh ! yes, sir," the landlord replied. " Nobody but the cook has so much as looked at it ; and then there is a—"

" Stop ; don't let me hear any more," Captain Macheath interposed. " Bring me the haunch at once, one of your home-made loaves, and a bottle of your best claret. I only want a slight snack, and that will do very well for me—only pray be quick !"

" Certainly, sir."

Mr. Muffer by this time began to think that the newcomer must be some important personage from the deference with which he was treated by the landlord.

The young man was sufficiently new in the world to be completely taken in by dashing manners, whether in man or woman, so he thought he would do the civil thing by the newcomer, with the hope of finding out who he was.

" A remarkably nice day, sir," he said.

" Very," replied Captain Macheath.

" Perhaps, sir, you would like to sit here, as it is more in the light ? I will give you this seat, sir, if you prefer it."

" You are very kind," said Captain Macheath ; " but where I am will do very well indeed. I would not incommode you on any account. What a time this tiresome landlord is, to be sure ! Here have I been waiting for dinner no less than three minutes and a-half !"

As he spoke, Captain Macheath took from his pocket a superb watch, set in a circle of brilliants, and glanced at it.

" He must be some nobleman," thought young Muffer. " I'll get into talk with him, and show him that I, too, have a watch."

With this he took out his watch, which, by comparison with Macheath's, was but a very shabby affair, and by way of letting the supposed nobleman know that he was somebody, he said—

" How slow the time goes, to be sure ! My father, the alderman, told me to be at the Mansion House by five, and it is now only half-past three. I am going to dine with the Lord Mayor, sir, you must know."

" Oh ! indeed."

" Yes, sir," said Mr. Muffer, proudly. " The old gentleman has got the gout, and can't go, so he gave me his invite, and I am to go, you see, sir, and he has written to the Lord Mayor to say as much, and his lordship sent back a very flattering reply indeed, saying he should be happy to see me."

" You don't say so, sir ?"

" Oh ! yes, sir ; it's true, upon my life. My father is Alderman Muffer—a well-known man in the City, sir."

" Very likely, sir, indeed," said Captain Macheath.

" Humph !" thought young Muffer, " I did think he'd be forced to tell me who he was after I had said that. How close he is, to be sure ! I'll try him again, though."

Then turning to Captain Macheath, he added—

" My phaeton, sir, is in the inn yard, and I am going to drive myself to town, you see, sir."

" Very probable," said Macheath.

" I have managed very nicely," Mr. Muffer continued, " I think, for I have put the card of invite in the box under the seat, besides my white gloves and a charming bouquet. I rather think I am a bit of a manager—don't you think so, sir."

" Your forethought," said Macheath, " is only equalled by your subsequent discretion, my good sir."

" No—you really don't say so, sir ?"

" Indeed I do," the captain declared ; " and your experience of the world will let you see at a glance that I am not the sort of man, my dear sir, to say what I do not think."

This compliment to Mr. Muffer's experience of the world quite won his heart.

" Sir," he said, " you don't know how happy I should be to take a glass of wine with you !"

" With great pleasure, sir," Captain Macheath replied. " I will just finish the little snack that I am taking, and then we will manage a couple of bottles of our host's claret here."

" Certainly, sir—certainly."

" I presume you have been in the army ?"

" Not exactly, sir."

What not exactly in the army could mean, Captain Macheath did not stop to enquire.

It was quite sufficient for him that the young gentleman was highly flattered at the supposition.

When Macheath had finished his repast by making a rather considerable inroad into the haunch of mutton, they both sat down by each other as comfortably as possible.

After a few glasses of the really excellent claret had been despatched Captain Macheath said—

" I have been riding so much to-day that I feel really fatigued with that kind of exercise, and yet I must get to London."

" My dear sir," cried Mr. Muffer, upsetting his glass of claret on his breeches in his eagerness— " my dear sir, if you will condescend to accept of a seat in my phaeton, I shall be proud of the honour of driving you to town."

" Really, sir, I fear that it would be too much of an intrusion upon your kindness."

" Not at all—not at all, sir. Only say that you'll do it, that's all, my dear sir."

" Well," said Captain Macheath, " since you are so very kind as to make me such an offer, and in so gentlemanly a way, too, I feel that I ought not to think of refusing it."

" Of course not, sir—of course not, and I hope you will not think of such a thing for a moment. You cannot think, sir, how very comfortable two can ride in my phaeton. I have no servant with me because I can always put up the horse and vehicle at father's old shop—I—I mean in the City —dear me."

" Exactly, sir. Shall we have another bottle ? Claret is not a very insidious wine."

" Why, really, sir," said Mr. Muffer, " I'm almost afraid to venture, as I shall have to drink a good deal of wine at the Mansion House, for the Lord Mayor is sure to keep his eye on me, and to cry out—' Come—come, Mr. Muffer, don't shirk your glass.' "

" Very likely."

" Yes, sir. Our present Lord Mayor actually began life by dealing in rags and bottles."

" You don't say so," cried Captain Macheath in a voice of astonishment.

" Yes," replied Mr. Muffer ; " and so he got on by degrees until he became the great man he is now ; and they do say that in a box under his bed he still preserves the original black dolly that used to swing outside his door in the Minories, where he first set up in business."

" It shows a proper and profound humility," Captain Macheath said, smiling. " How did he get on in his business then ?"

" Oh ! very well indeed," replied Mr. Muffer.

CAPTAIN MACHEATH

THE

PRINCE OF THE HIGHWAY.

MACHEATH AND THE WATCHMAN HAD A REGULAR SET-TO, BUT THE STRUGGLE DID NOT LAST LONG.

"They say he swindled—no—I mean he got the better in business, and, you know, sir, in business that nothing that keeps to the windward of the law is swindling."

"Certainly not," Captain Macheath rejoined.

"Well, sir, he got the better of everybody, and from one thing to another, he forsook the bottle business and took contracts for the army."

"That, I should think, was profitable," said Captain Macheath, insinuatingly.

"Oh! yes, sir; there was not a pair of breeches worn by our army in Flanders but were made by the Lord Mayor of London and my father.

"Really, I quite congratulate you upon the useful and ornamental position in which your house stood with the military character of the nation."

"Thank you, sir, you are very good."

"Not at all; modest minds like yours should always be properly appreciated, in my opinion. Permit me to hand you the decanter."

"Thank you," said Mr. Muffer.

The young scion of the City house had not a head-piece that was either proof against Captain Macheath's flattery or the claret which was so liberally administered to him, and he soon showed signs of having had quite enough.

It was no part of Macheath's scheme to render him quite helpless.

"Bless me!" said the captain, suddenly looking at his watch. "It is time to start for London."

"Is it?" cried Mr. Muffer, starting to his feet. "Let's be off then. My phaeton! Hilloa! there, my phaeton."

"All right," said the landlord. "It is at the door."

In the course of five minutes Captain Macheath and his new friend were seated in the phaeton together.

The young man took the reins—nobody is so tenacious of driving as your half-tipsy man—and away they went at a good pace from the Old Hats.

The open air, however, soon began to have a very curious effect upon Mr. Muffer's head, and from the manner in which he swayed from side to side, it was quite evident to Captain Macheath that in the event of their meeting any other vehicle upon the road the chances of a collision were great.

"Well," he said, suddenly, "I have had a good lesson. That is beautiful."

"A lesson?" said Mr. Muffer, speaking thickly. "A lesson, my dear friend, did you say? What's beautiful?"

"Your driving; and as I have had the advantage of seeing it, of course, I have had a lesson in the art."

"Oh—ah! yes—to be sure," said Mr. Muffer. "Come up, will you? I rather think there are not many who can come near me in this sort of thing."

"Not one," Captain Macheath remarked.

"No; really, though, you ain't joking?"

"Joking, sir? Perish the thought of it!" said Captain Macheath, solemnly.

"Then you do think I drive rather uncommon well?"

"I am certain of it," Macheath replied; "and I have, contingent upon that conviction, a very great favour to ask of you, my friend."

"Name it. What—is—is—it?"

"It is that you would let me try to put in practice the admirable lesson in driving that you have given me, by allowing me to take the reins for a minute or two only now that we are still in the country. I own that with you by my side I should feel very diffident about driving in London, but here nobody sees us."

The young dupe smiled blandly.

"Well—well," he hiccuped, "nobody sees us here; I don't mind for once in a way. There, my ir—friend. Take the whip and reins and I will see that you do not go—go wrong."

"A thousand thanks for that kindness," said Captain Macheath, as he took the whip and reins. "There now, how stupid I am!"

"What's the row?" demanded Mr. Muffer.

"I have dropped the whip, and owing to sitting in an awkward position I have got the cramp in the calf of my right leg and can't move. Oh—oh!"

"I have had the cramp in my calf sometimes," said Muffer.

"Then you must have been in dreadful pain," Captain Macheath returned. "My dear friend, will you get the whip?"

"To be sure I will," said Muffer. "Don't you move. I'll get it. Don't you trouble yourself, my dear friend, I'll get it in a moment. All's well. Some people couldn't have taken as much claret as I have and been so decidedly so—sober—very sober."

He rolled, rather than stepped out of the phaeton, and the moment he gained the road, Captain Macheath made a slight noise with his lips, and at the same instant gently jerked the reins, and off went the horses at a sharp trot, leaving the unfortunate owner of the vehicle in the middle of the road with the whip in his hand, glaring after it in such a state of bewilderment that he was unable even to cry out about it.

Captain Macheath never even troubled himself to look back.

He was quite satisfied that pursuit was out of the question, and he knew that Muffer was not so tipsy as not to be able to take care of himself so far as regarded any danger to life or limb, so that he looked upon the whole affair as quite a professional thing.

Tyburn Gate was very soon gained, and then Captain Macheath thought it was time to think upon what he was to do to carry out the plan he had determined upon in his own mind of going to dine with the Lord Mayor in the character of Mr. Muffer.

He recollected that in the plenitude of his foolish confidence the young owner of the phaeton had mentioned that under one of the seats were his gloves and his card of admission to the banquet at the Mansion House; and now Macheath drew up at an Inn, near the Edgeware-road, and pausing at the door, he made the examination of the seat and found the articles named.

Fortunately Macheath, by merely getting rid of his riding-boots, was in a fit dress to go to the City feast.

To be sure, he wanted a pair of shoes and another cravat, and gave his order for a bottle of wine and for a hair-dresser to be sent for.

The style of the "turn out" at once insured him every attention, and the best hair-dresser in the whole neighbourhood was speedily in attendance.

"My good fellow," said Captain Macheath, "I want you to dress and powder my hair for an evening assembly, and I want you to take a couple of guineas and get me a pair of dress shoes and a lace cravat."

"Oh! yes, sir; certainly, sir."

"The change, if any, I desire that you will be good enough to keep for your trouble."

This was quite sufficient to induce the hair-dresser to obey the orders of so munificent a customer with the greatest possible alacrity, and in the course of twenty minutes Macheath was fully accommodated with all that he required.

The phaeton was at the door, the horses having been refreshed with a little hay and water, and off went our hero at a slashing pace to the City.

At that time the Mansion House was easier to get at than it is now, when you have to thrust your way through an army of omnibusses and cabs.

The streets of the City were bustling and animated, but that was all.

There was none of the wild rushing of vehicles which characterise the present day.

Without being forced naturally to relax his speed Captain Macheath got to the Poultry.

There he found a collection of carriages conveying persons to the banquet.

A constable stepped up to him, and exhibiting a little gilt staff he said to him respectfully—

"Sir, you cannot pass this way. You must go down King-street unless you are going to the Mansion House."

"But I am," said Captain Macheath.

"Beg pardon, sir. Will you be so good as to show me your card?"

"Oh ! yes ; certainly."

The constable looked at the card.

"Make way for Mr. Muffer—way for Mr. Muffer !" he cried in a loud voice. "Make way ! Move on !"

This was a common form observed there to all the guests, and was for the purpose of keeping the route as clear as possible, as well as informing the servants who were drawn up at the door of the Mansion House who it was that had arrived.

"I want someone to take charge of my carriage," said Captain Macheath, "and take it to a livery stable."

"I'll see to that, sir," said a man in the Lord Mayor's livery.

"Very good."

"Mr. Muffer !" cried a tall footman, as Macheath entered the Mansion House.

"Mr. Muffer !" shouted another as he went upstairs.

"Mr. Muffer !" bawled a third, and he entered a brilliantly-lighted room, where there was an assemblage of at least a hundred persons waiting for the welcome and momentarily expected announcement of dinner being on the table.

"Ah ! Mr Muffer," said a little fat man advancing, "glad to see you in the City again. Hilloa !"

Captain Macheath bowed.

"Why, you—you are not my old friend Muffer— You—you—"

"I am his son, sir," said Captain Macheath.

"Bless my heart and life, my dear boy, I am very glad to see you, indeed—very glad. And how is it that your father has not come to-night ?" said the little fat man, who was an alderman and one of the sheriffs, and rejoiced in the name of Smuggs.

"I am here to represent him. He is incapacitated with a sharp attack of gout."

"Dear me ! I shall be pleased to hear of his speedy recovery."

"And so shall I, sir."

"Look—look—look !"

"At what, sir—where ?"

"The Lord Mayor is consulting his watch. We shall soon have the dinner announced now. That watch, sir, cost three hundred pounds. It is studded with diamonds and inside the outer-case is the Lord Mayor's arms, two donkeys on a field azure, and an owl for a crest, with the motto of ' Business is business.' "

"Hem !" said the Lord Mayor.

A buzz of approbation at this remark ran through the assembly, under cover of which Captain Macheath said to himself—

"I will have that watch, and if possible the gold chain that his mightiness the Lord Mayor has round his neck."

Macheath was not without hopes of getting something from the worthy sheriff likewise, and some of the other guests looked promising in the way of watches and pocket-books ; so that, upon the whole, Macheath was not without a hope of paying himself very well for his trouble in coming to the Mansion House.

"Dinner waits !" cried a loud voice at the door of the drawing room, in which the guests were assembled.

If etiquette and the customary form of English gentry would have permitted such a thing, what a rush there would have been ! But they were a little too civilised for that.

The guests, according to rank, proceeded in a long, gay, sparkling procession to the feast.

Macheath took care to keep very close to his friend Mr. Smuggs, by which means he secured a capital place at the principal table close to the Lord Mayor.

"I beg pardon, sir," said a footman to Macheath, "but that seat was reserved for the Recorder."

"Eh ?" said Captain Macheath.

"That seat, sir, was reserved for the Recorder."

"Oh ! thank you," said the captain. "I am very comfortable ; I don't prefer the corner."

"Deaf as a badger," said the flunkey, and he moved away to state the difficulties of the case to the learned personage whom it concerned, and who, it appeared, laughed it off and left Captain Macheath in his seat, for he was not interrupted again.

The feast now began, and Captain Macheath was truly astonished to see the great execution which the guests did upon the rich viands that were placed at their disposal.

He ate but very little himself, for his mind was intent upon some plan of operation by which he could contrive to possess himself of the Lord Mayor's watch, the chain and seals of which hung temptingly out of his fob.

He did not sit absolutely next to his lordship, so it was by no means easy.

A cabinet minister occupied the post of honour, but luckily for Captain Macheath that personage all the time he was there was in a perfect agony to get away, and left as soon as with any decency he could.

Captain Macheath popped into the vacant chair in a moment, and the sheriff joined up close.

"Hem !" remarked the Lord Mayor again.

CHAPTER XXV.

A DISTURBANCE IN THE CITY.

IT was quite evident to Captain Macheath that his worship the Lord Mayor considered that a great breach of etiquette had been committed by Captain Macheath taking possession of the vacant

chair of the minister of state, and that the "Hem!
was the mode in which he so expressed himself.

Under any other circumstances Macheath would
not have troubled himself upon the occasion; but
now he had an object in view, and leaning towards
the Lord Mayor, he said—

"My lord, I was stopped on Ealing-common as
I came here by the celebrated Captain Macheath."

"Ah!" said the Lord Mayor.

"I should not trouble your lordship with so very
trivial a circumstance were it not that after
robbing me, Macheath said—'I know, Mr.
Muffer, where you are going, and you can tell the
Lord Mayor that I fully intend to dine with him
to-day.'"

The Lord Mayor upon this gathered in all the
breath his lungs would hold and puffed out his
cheeks, looking unutterable things the while.

He stared at Captain Macheath as though he
would eat him up, and then in a low mumbling
voice like distant thunder, he said—

"Captain Macheath, the highwayman, dine
with me?"

"He said so, my lord."

"Bah!"

"Exactly, my lord," said the captain. "I consider that last remark of yours as highly intelligent
and satisfactory; but for all that Captain Macheath, who they do say would keep his word in
such a particular if he died for it, declared his
intention of dining with you to-day."

The colour slightly faded from the face of the
civic king, and he ran his eye along the line of
familiar faces on each side of the table, almost expecting to find some strange physiognomy among
them that should seem like what he could picture
to himself Macheath's would be.

But no; all were known.

He never thought for a moment of suspecting
his informant; besides, had not Sheriff Smuggs
introduced him as young Mr. Muffer, and was
not that conclusive?

"He not only, my lord, swore he would be here,
but that he would rob you of your diamond ring."

"My ring—my ring!"

"Yes, my lord; that one on your finger which
becomes you so well, and which upon no other
finger would look as it does; and if Macheath—"

"Hush! don't speak so loud, young man. I
don't want all the world to know that it is possible
any highwayman could have the impudence to
come here."

"Impudence indeed, your lordship. It shall go
no farther."

"I would not lose this ring for a thousand
pounds—no."

As he spoke he drew it from his finger and
handed it to Captain Macheath to look at.

The guests at the table, in the midst of the
clatter of the knives and forks and the constant
changing of plates, paid no attention to the
whispered conference between the Lord Mayor and
his neighbour.

It was not then that the attention of his worship
was required to the general company.

After dinner it would have been quite another
thing.

"It is a handsome ring," said Macheath, "a
very handsome ring indeed."

As he said this he dropped it on the floor at the
feet of the Lord Mayor.

"My ring—my ring!" said his lordship as he
stooped to pick it up.

Macheath stooped at the same time and adroitly

drew the gorgeous watch from the Lord Mayor's
fob, who was so intent upon picking up his ring
that he never missed it or felt the slightest movement of it escaping.

"I am so sorry your lordship troubled yourself
to stoop," said Macheath; "I would have got it in
a moment for you."

"Don't mention it," said his lordship, looking
almost purple with the exertion of stooping. "I
would not lose it for a thousand pounds, that I
would not—eugh!"

"It was very awkward of me to be seen to drop
it."

"Don't mention that, sir—don't mention that,
sir. Do you think you should know this Captain
Macheath if you were to see him again?"

"Oh! yes."

"Ha! that is a very good thing indeed," said
the Lord Mayor. "Just look around you and
tell me if you observe him."

Macheath affected to look very carefully all
along the tables, and then he shook his head
dubiously.

"I should hardly think, my lord, that he has
ventured to come. I don't see anything of him."

"Hem! I'm very glad of it indeed."

"The probability, my lord, is that he will hide
somewhere and pounce upon you when you least
expect it," said Macheath.

"Gracious! in my private room perhaps."

"Nothing more likely," acquiesced Captain
Macheath. "I hope you will permit me to accompany you there to look for him. If you could
take him into custody it would be very much
talked of. There could be no danger here, I
should say."

"Let me think," said the Lord Mayor. "Ah—
hem! Mr. Sheriff, will you have the goodness to
take my chair for a few moments?"

"Certainly, my lord. I am much honoured."

"Come," added the Lord Mayor to Macheath,
"follow me. We will, at all events, give such
directions as shall prevent the possibility of his
escape if he is now in the Mansion House, or of
his entrance into it if he is not—hem!"

Macheath followed the Lord Mayor through a
little door in the end of the dining-hall, and after
traversing a short passage they reached a small
room, which was lighted by an elegant lamp upon
the table.

"Now, my young friend," said the Lord
Mayor, closing the door, "what do you advise?"

"Are we quite alone, my lord?"

"Oh! quite—quite."

"And can no one overhear us?"

"This, sir, is my private room, and no one pre-
sumes to overhear anything that takes place
within it—hem!"

"Then, sir, I would advise you not to make
the smallest resistance; but to take things perfectly easy."

"Er—what do you mean, sir?"

"That I am Captain Macheath!"

"Ah!" cried the Lord Mayor, and staggering
back, he fell into the recesses of a great arm-
chair.

For a moment Macheath thought he would
have fainted away.

But he did not.

His face only assumed a purple hue, and his
eyes opened particularly wide, and he glared at
Captain Macheath as though he would devour him.

"Yes, my lord," added the captain, in a low,
cautious tone, "I am Captain Macheath. I said

I would dine with you, and I have dined with you. I said I would have your diamond ring, and —I have it."

As he spoke he slipped the magnificent ring from the finger of the bewildered Lord Mayor.

"I said I would have your gold chain, and, lo! I have that likewise; and now, my Lord Mayor, upon your making the least out-cry for the next half-hour or so, I shall be under the disagreeable necessity of throttling you."

His lordship only groaned slightly.

"I have the honour to bid you Good evening, my lord," said Captain Macheath. "Your dinner was excellent, your wines first-rate, and I must say that I have enjoyed myself very much indeed."

"He—has—enjoyed himself!" gasped the Lord Mayor. "Hem! Oh—oh—ah!"

Captain Macheath suddenly started, for a confused clamour of many voices came upon his ears.

The more he listened, the louder the sounds grew, and then stepping to the door of the private room he opened it a little way and listened.

He could hear that it was from the dining-hall that the confusion of voices proceeded, and feeling confident that, with amazement and terror combined, the Lord Mayor was incapable of making any resistance, or giving any alarm, he walked hastily down the narrow passage connecting the private room with the banquetting-hall, and listened at the door that led into it.

"Yes, gentlemen," he heard a voice say, "he left me in the road and drove off with my phaeton, and I do believe he is a highwayman. I am Mr. Muffer. I can prove it. He is a highwayman. I have walked all the way till I got a hackney-coach at the top of Oxford-street. Oh! gentlemen, I am an injured individual."

Captain Macheath easily recognised the voice of young Muffer, and for the moment he felt rather undecided what to do.

"Justice!" shouted Muffer. "My phaeton—my horse—my card of admission—my gloves—my everything. I had to bawl out thieves at the top of my voice before I could get into this place at all, and now I bawl out murder!"

About thirty voices said something all at once, and Captain Macheath felt all over the door for some mode of fastening it.

"Where is the Lord Mayor?" shouted some half-dozen people at once. "Where is the Lord Mayor?"

"I only hope," thought Captain Macheath, as he shot a small bolt into the socket, "that you won't find the Lord Mayor yet awhile."

With a conviction that there must be some other mode of outlet from the Mayor's private room than through the banquetting-hall Macheath returned thither, and found his lordship still seated on the large chair and looking about him as before.

A glance showed Captain Macheath a small door opposite to the one at which he had entered, but he had hardly time to reach it before he heard a crash, and felt certain that the little door leading from the banquetting-hall to the narrow passage was broken open.

There was no time to lose.

"All are not lost that are in danger," said Macheath, as he pulled open the little door and darted through it.

He closed it after him, and finding a key in the lock upon the outer side he rapidly turned it, and then hurried along totally in the dark.

He knew that he was not likely to fall down any trap-doors or secret places, so he darted on heedless of the total darkness until he came bump against a wall.

"Where there is a wall," he said, "there is a door somewhere, so I have but to go on feeling for it. I must take care, though, that I do not make a precipitate tumble down some staircase."

As Captain Macheath was on the first floor of the building, this was by far the greatest risk that he ran.

But he came to the handle of a door, which he tried to turn but found it fast.

As he stood for a few moments quite still he heard a rattle sprung fiercely.

"What the deuce are they at?" he said. "Do they want to summon all the watchmen of the City?"

He made another attempt at the door and shook it.

From the manner in which it shook he felt confident it was only slightly fastened, so placing his shoulder against it he forced it open at once with a crash.

The room beyond it was quite dark, and the first thing Captain Macheath did was to tumble over a chair.

"Confound the chair!" he cried.

Almost as he spoke a door nearly opposite to him suddenly flashed open, and he saw right into the banquetting-hall.

How he had got round to it again he could not conceive; but there was really no time for reflection.

The danger was imminent, for a number of persons armed in different ways were about to come through the doorway.

As Macheath was in the dark they could not see him, and he had time and presence of mind enough to shrink back before any flash of light could fall upon him.

He had now no resource but to go on following the wall, and as he did so he reached the head of a flight of stairs and slipped down several of them.

He heard the trampling of feet behind him, and once he heard quite distinctly a loud voice say—

"No doubt it is Captain Macheath, as the Mayor says."

"Ah!" thought the captain, "they know me then, do they? Well, they will not get me quite so easily for all that now, I take it."

He flew rather than walked down the flight of stairs now, and was in a moment or two at the foot of them.

A faint light, as if reflected from some apartment, flashed upon him, and a man came towards him with a branch candlestick carrying three lights in his hand.

"Who's that?" said the man.

"I!" cried Macheath.

And rushing forward he knocked him down, candlestick and all, before he could say another word.

"Stop him!" shouted another voice.

Captain Macheath drew the dress sword he wore and dashed on.

He came to another flight of steps, but they ascended instead of descended, and then he bounced into a room in which were some dozen of lacqueys.

One of the windows was open, and a glance told the captain that it looked out on to the landing of the stone steps in front of the Mansion House.

Turning to the lacqueys for a moment, he cried—

"If anyone is in love with death, let him follow me !"

And then he sprang out into the open air.

"There he is—there he is !" cried a hundred voices.

CHAPTER XXVI.

PERIL IN THE CITY.

CAPTAIN MACHEATH felt a little staggered at the danger of his position ; but he felt that if anything was to be done for his safety it must be done at once.

Each moment brought with it many dangers.

Without more hesitation, then, than was sufficient to let him see his way down, he rushed from the elevated portion of the Mansion House and reached the street.

One man made a plunge at him, crying—

" I have him !"

"Not yet," said Macheath, as he run him through the breast with the sword he still had possession of.

The man fell back with a groan, and his fate seemed rather to stagger those who were pressing on with speed, and a lane was made for Captain Macheath, through which he made his way, brandishing his sword.

In this way he darted down Mansion House-street and gained Bucklersbury before anyone could muster courage enough to lay hold of him.

There was one thing added to his safety, and that was that he kept the drawn sword still in his hand.

A watchman in Bucklersbury threw himself in his way.

" Just stop a bit !" he shouted.

"Out of my path, idiot !" cried Captain Macheath.

" Not quite so foolish !" said the watchman, and he aimed a blow at Captain Macheath with his bludgeon.

Captain Macheath did not want to kill him, but he caught the bludgeon in its descent, and twisting it out of the hands of the watchman he dealt him a blow on the head with it that sent him reeling into the roadway.

A loud shout behind him now warned him that the mob and the officers were close upon his heels.

He paused for a moment at the corner of a court to take breath.

" Whither shall I fly ?" he said. " Of a truth I did not exactly calculate upon being thus hunted through the streets of London. This is something more than a perilous adventure, and how it will end yet has to be seen."

" Stop him !—stop him ! Stop thief !" cried many voices.

" Indeed ! Well, be it so. I will run, and let the peril be his who is fool enough to overtake me."

Macheath dashed down the court.

He had not the remotest idea where the court led to, but he took it at a venture.

It was only when some distance down it that he thought that the place might have no outlet.

Suddenly he came to what appeared the end of it, and he paused irresolutely.

A boy was standing upon a doorstep.

"Can't I get out of this court but by going back ?" said Captain Macheath to the lad.

" Oh ! yes, sir," said the boy, pointing to what looked like a doorway. "There is the way out. It leads into Cannon-street."

" Stop him—stop him ! A highwayman !" chorussed a crowd of voices.

Captain Macheath had just time to dart off in the direction the boy had pointed out to him, when his foes rushed down the court in a dense throng.

The alley into which he had plunged was so dark that for a moment he thought the boy had deceived him, but as he ran on he found such was not the case.

The passage widened, and he got into another court somewhat similar in size to the one he had at such a venture darted down.

In a moment or two he reached Cannon-street, along which he went at a great rate.

The mob kept close upon his heels, and the worst of the affair was that it was a time of night when so very few passengers were in the streets that the captain became an object for observation, and his dress sufficed to attract the notice of the few people he did chance to meet.

If he had seen an open door he would not have hesitated to take such shelter as it afforded ; but none such presented itself, and he was compelled to rush on, a fugitive hunted through the streets of the City.

And now he heard behind him a hard and rapid tread upon the pavement, and upon looking round he saw a man who had outran all the others and was gaining fast upon him.

The man did not speak, for well he knew that by doing so he should only lose his wind, and so incapacitate himself for continuing the chase.

"He runs well," thought Captain Macheath. " Perhaps he would like to be a little in advance."

With these muttered words Macheath slackened his pace a little, as though he were quite exhausted, upon which the man, with a short cry of satisfaction, made superhuman efforts to come up with him.

Captain Macheath let him get nearer and nearer.

" The reward will be mine !" the man said.

Suddenly, with the rapidity of lightning, Captain Macheath dropped upon his hands and knees on the pavement, and in an instant the fast runner, who was unable to check his headlong speed, flew over him, and went rolling and scudding along the pavement.

" How do you feel now, my friend ?" demanded Captain Macheath, as he walked leisurely past him.

The man was incapable of answering a word, for he was effectually stunned by the fall, and there Macheath left him lying without seeking to inflict any further injury upon him.

Macheath now hoped that he had distanced his foes and thrown them off the scent.

He looked about him to see where he was, but he was not sufficiently conversant with the City to feel quite certain upon that point, so, at a venture, he took the first turning that he came to.

He found that it brought him out close to St. Paul's Church-yard, and he had hardly had time to assure himself that it was the cathedral he was close to when out of Cheapside about twenty people suddenly turned.

" There he is—there he is ! Hold him, somebody ! Stop thief—stop him !" they bellowed.

Captain Macheath had sufficiently recovered his breath, so off he started round St. Paul's, hoping to get into Newgate-market, and amidst its intricacies find some mode of baffling his pursuers.

He reached Paternoster-row ; but some of his enemies kept close upon his heels, and as he fled

MACHEATH DEALT THE WOULD-BE ASSASSIN A TREMENDOUS BLOW WITH HIS FIST.

down Ave Maria-lane he was compelled to turn and face two men who pressed him closely.

Here it was that Macheath gave evidence of his great strength, which he only put forth when very much pressed or very much angered.

He seized the foremost of the two men, and fairly lifting him off his feet, he flung him with such force against the other that they both fell, bellowing for assistance.

By that action Macheath got a start of nearly the whole length of Ave Maria-lane, and he came out into Newgate-street.

He ran round the corner of the Old Bailey, and when there he paused to listen which route his pursuers had taken. He soon found that some were coming after him down Newgate-street, while from Ludgate-hill another party of some thirty or forty persons advanced with furious cries.

Macheath now showed that remarkable presence of mind and daring which had preserved him in many dangers.

He hit upon a scheme, the daring insolence of which was almost certain to make it succeed.

He knew that day and night warders were in the lobby of Newgate.

A light was gleaming there, and he boldly ascended the stone steps and knocked authoritatively at the wicket.

"Who's there?" growled a voice from within.

"A gentleman from the sheriff," replied Captain Macheath, in a clear voice. In a moment the door was opened.

"Pray, sir, walk in. Anything amiss, sir?" said the turnkey.

"Not much," Captain Macheath replied. "I suppose the governor is asleep by this time, is he not?"

"Why, no, sir!" said the turnkey. "He is at my Lord Mayor's entertainment at the Mansion House; but Mr. Mithers, who acts for him, is only lying down, sir, in his room."

"Take me to him at once, then," said Captain Macheath. "I have a message to him from the sheriff."

"Yes, sir. Hilloa, Bodkins!"

"Here you are!" said the half-drowsy man, getting up from a bench upon which he had been indulging in a nap. "Here you are. What's the row now, old fellow—eh?"

"Show this gentleman to Mr. Mithers' room, Bodkins. He comes from the sheriff with a message."

Upon this intimation Mr. Bodkins shown signs of great activity.

The appearance of Captain Macheath in his apparel was quite sufficient colour to what he said, so Mr. Bodkins went before him with a light, and after conducting him through some windings and runings, paused at the door of a room and tapped at it.

"Come in," said a voice.

Bodkins opened the door and said in a humble tone—

"A gentleman from the sheriff, sir, if you pleases."

"Oh! ask him to walk in. Pray be seated, sir. I hope nothing is amiss in the City."

"Nothing of material consequence, I believe, sir," said the captain; "but it has been proved that by some means the notorious and impertinent Captain Macheath has found his way to-night into the Mansion House; and some say he has left, and some say he remains, and that it is a companion of his who has left; so my Lord Mayor and the sheriff have requested me to ask you if you have anyone here who knows him by sight, and if so that you will be good enough to send such a person at once to the Mansion House."

"Certainly—certainly, sir. I think we have several officers in the prison who can recognise him. Will you excuse me a moment, sir, and I will give the necessary orders?"

"Oh! of course," said Captain Macheath. "Pray do not hurry yourself upon my account, for I have made such speed from the Mansion House here on foot, not being able to find my carriage in the Poultry, that I am really glad of a little rest."

"Pray draw near to the fire, sir, and make yourself at home," Mr. Mithers returned. "I shall be back in a few moments."

"Humph!" muttered Captain Macheath, when he found himself alone; "I am to make myself at home, am I? I think that by this rather hazardous adventure I have distanced and outwitted my pursuers. Egad! I'll make myself at home, too."

Macheath drew a chair near the fire, but he took good care to keep an eye upon the door and an ear open to any sound that might appraise him of danger.

Such precautions were, however, quite unnecessary, for Mr. Mithers had not the remotest suspicion regarding the genuiness of the mission upon which Captain Macheath said he had come.

In about five minutes he returned.

"I have sent three of our officers, sir," he said, "who know Captain Macheath by sight very well indeed; and if he be still in the Mansion House among the guests, you may depend they will find him out."

"His lordship will be very much obliged to you indeed for this promptitude," the captain said, "and I only hope that they may be as successful as their zeal deserves."

"It seems," said Mr Mithers, "to be the general idea that he has escaped and is somewhere in the street; for a mob of people has just passed Newgate, no doubt eager to catch him on account of the large reward that has been offered for his apprehension."

"That is their motive, no doubt, sir," Captain Macheath said, passing his hand before his face to conceal a smile; "but the Lord Mayor is decidedly of opinion that he is still in the Mansion House."

"If so, sir, you may depend my officers will have him."

"I am rejoiced to hear it."

Captain Macheath now intimated that he must leave; but he kept protracting the time by thanking Mr. Mithers in the most engaging manner for the kind alacrity with which he had acted upon the occasion; and Mithers fancying by the style and appearance of Captain Macheath that he must be some person of consequence, was all urbanity and suavity.

At length Captain Macheath thought that all danger from the mob must have ceased and he gave a slight shiver.

"I shall feel cold, I daresay, in the night air going back," he said.

"My dear sir," said Mithers, "will you do me the favour to accept the loan of a cloak? I have one quite at your service."

Captain Macheath could scarcely refrain from laughing at the great alacrity of the Deputy-Governor of Newgate to assist him in his escape by lending him a cloak to cover up his evening dress.

"My good sir," he said, "you are very kind,

and if I thought it would not be putting you to any inconvenience—

"Oh! none in the least."

"Then, sir," said Captain Macheath, "I accept your kind offer with pleasure, and perhaps you will add to your kindness by letting somebody fetch a hackney-coach for me?"

"Of course, sir. I was just going to propose it. I will fetch the cloak in a moment, if you please."

"Mighty complacent," thought Macheath, when he was once more alone. "Now this fellow will be ready to eat his own head off when he finds what a mistake he has made. In good truth it was a lucky thought this of coming to Newgate. By-the-bye, it will look bad not to give him some name. Ah! here he comes."

Mr. Mithers made his appearance with a large and handsome cloak upon his arm.

It was made of blue cloth and lined with rich crimson velvet.

"This, sir," he said, "will at all events keep the cold out, and a coach will be ready in a few moments."

"I do not know how to thank you for this kindness," said Captain Macheath, as he put on the cloak. "You shall have this back in the course of to-morrow. My name is Cranks—Sir Slily Cranks."

Mr. Mithers bowed.

"It don't look exactly the thing for a baronet to be running about the streets of the City at night," the captain continued; "but you must know this Macheath actually stopped Lady Cranks one night upon Ealing-common, and the Lord Mayor, knowing that I felt rather sore upon that matter, said to me, 'Sir Slily, I am quite sure you will do anything to capture this rascal.' 'Indeed, my lord,' I said, 'I will.' 'Then,' he added, 'if you don't mind taking your carriage and going as far as Newgate I think you will do us good service.' So you see I came."

"Yes, Sir Slily. It was very good of you to come, indeed."

"The coach is ready, sir," said a man at the door.

"And so am I," said Captain Macheath; "Mr. Mithers, good night. Lady Cranks and myself will be very glad to see you at our little park close by Watford at any time that may suit your convenience. Nay, my dear sir, I beg that you will not leave your room to see me off. Now, really!"

"But allow me, sir—the honour."

"My good sir."

Mr. Mithers would insist upon it, and accordingly, with all due ceremony, Captain Macheath was seen to the door of Newgate, where a hackney-coach, the driver of which had been awakened from a comfortable snooze on his stand by Fleet-market, was in waiting.

In got Captain Macheath, and then waving his hand to Mithers, he said in a loud voice to the coachman—

"Drive to the Mansion House as quickly as you can, my friend. Good night, Mr. Mithers. Good night."

"Good night, Sir Slily."

Off went the coach, and the wicket was shut to keep out the cold air.

The moment the coach got half way up Newgate-street Macheath pulled the check-string, and the driver pulled up.

"Did you go for to want anythink, sir?" the driver asked.

"Yes, my friend. I have altered my mind; I won't go to the Mansion House, but if you will drive me to the corner of Oxford-street I will give you a guinea for the job."

"Won't I, your honour," replied the man, grinning. "All right. Lor', if this isn't the Governor o' Newgate, I'm smothered. He's arter some cove now, I'll be bound, as has been and gone and done somethink in the robbery line, or the murdering, for all I knows on."

The horses' heads were turned in the direction of Holborn, and Macheath was carried away from the scene of his dangers in the City.

He wrapped the cloak well around him, for the night was very chilly, and as the vehicle rumbled up Holborn-hill he could hardly keep from laughing aloud, to think how easily he had duped the Deputy-Governor of Newgate.

The coach made good progress, and they reached the corner of Oxford-street in perfect safety; but as they turned into that thoroughfare Macheath heard the sound of horses' feet in the direction of Holborn.

He had kept both the windows of the coach down in order that nothing might impede him in hearing if any pursuit were attempted, and he now placed his ear outside one of them and listened intently.

He became convinced that some three or four horsemen were on the road, but whether they were after him or not, of course, he had no possible means of judging.

Suspicion haunts the guilty mind, and Captain Macheath could not help fancying that he was pursued.

"It is possible," he thought, "that some suspicion may have arisen; and if so, I will die game, at all events."

The thought then struck him that he might make a friend of the coachman, and accordingly he leaned out of one of the windows, and, without stopping the coachman, touched him on the arm.

"My friend, a word with you," said Macheath.

"Oh! lor'," gasped the man. "How you did frighten me to be sure, sir. I was in what you calls a brown study, and didn't expect nobody to say nothink."

"Listen to me," said the captain. "If anyone should stop you and ask you if you took up a fare at Newgate, it will be a five-pound note in your way to say 'No!'"

"Will it, sir?"

"Yes, and here it is," said Captain Macheath. "You can keep it whether you are asked the question or not; but mind, no shuffling."

"Bless you, sir!" the driver replied. "No, indeed! Haven't I got a matter o' nine babbies at home, and did I ever so much as see a five-pound note in all my life? Oh! no, sir; only you say what I am to do and I'll do it."

"Then in plain language," Captain Macheath said, "I suspect that you may be stopped and questioned, and I don't want anybody to know that I am here or where I came from. I will leave the mangement of the affair to you."

"All right, sir! I supposes as you are the governor of the stone jug, and arter some desperate rum 'un?"

"Exactly."

Captain Macheath resumed his seat, but he carefully felt the priming of his pistols, for he had a sort of presentiment that danger was at hand; and with all his usual strength of mind, his very mode of life had tended to make him rather superstitious.

"I hold the lives of two men in my hands at all events," he said, "and woe be to those who may tempt me too far. I will not be hunted like a wild beast to death without turning upon my pursuers."

The horsemen had turned into Oxford-street, and in a few moments Macheath was convinced that his suspicions that they were after him were correct.

"Coach—coach! Stop! Coach, there!" one of the horse men cried.

The coachman paid no attention to the cry, nor did he urge his horses a bit the faster.

He treated the matter with cool indifference.

But the horsemen were tolerably well mounted, and were not to be baulked in this way, and as of course any attempt to escape with a couple of hackney-coach horses would have been truly ridiculous, the mounted men soon reached the vehicle, and one, riding to the head of the horses, stopped them.

Another spoke angrily to the coachman.

"Why did you not stop when I called 'Coach?'"

"'Cos I was hired. I couldn't take you."

"Did you take up a fare at Newgate?"

"Newgate?"

"Yes. Answer me directly. Were you fetched from the stand at High Holborn Bars to take up a person at Newgate?"

"N—o! Why you are out o' your mind. My fare comed out o' Gray's Inn, and my stand was opposite the old pump. Ask the gemman hisself as is my fare. I knows what you is—you is highwaymen, and wants to rob a poor fellow. Watch—watch—watch!"

"Hold your row. will you, and drive up to the next lamp? We want to speak to your fare."

"Werry good."

"Danger," said Captain Macheath to himself; "three men well mounted and well armed. I must be off. Oh! if I only had my horse now with me I would desire nothing better than to give them a run; but on foot they are just one too many for me."

As he spoke, and as the coachman drove very leisurely to the nearest lamp, which was on the near side, Macheath opened the door of the coach on the off side, and merely held it from flapping wide open by one hand, while with the other he had one of his pistols ready for immediate action.

"Here you are!" said the coachman as he drew up, so that although he was pretty close to a lamp, not much of the light of it could fall into the coach.

At the same moment, too, a watchman crossed the road from the other side of the way, calling out—

"What's the row? I'll take you all into custody. Who was it called out 'Watch?' Here I am."

The mounted man who had given his orders in so very peremptory a manner now leant from his saddle to look into the coach.

When he saw Captain Macheath he said—

"All resistance is useless. You are a prisoner. If you stir hand or foot I will put a bullet through your brain. I am not a man to be trifled with, I assure you."

"Very likely," said the captain. "For whom do you take me."

"For Captain Macheath!"

"Then you ought to be more careful."

Bang went Macheath's pistol, and the man fell back in the saddle.

"He has killed me! Help—help! He has killed me!" he exclaimed.

Macheath had kept his hand still upon the handle of the opposite door of the coach, and the moment he had pulled the trigger of his pistol, he opened it and dashed out, upsetting the watchman in the mud and rolling over him, and a short struggle took place, but it was scarcely of a moment's duration.

"Let go your hold," cried Macheath as he clutched the watchman by the throat, "or I will kill you!"

The terrified watchman relaxed his hold and Macheath leaped to his feet.

Only waiting to deal the prostrate watchman one hearty kick, he darted over the road, and dashed down what is now Wells-street.

All this was done with such rapidity, that the horseman who was close to the horses' heads of the hackney-coach, and another who was just behind it, hardly knew what had happened, except that a pistol shot had been fired by someone, before Macheath had vanished from before their eyes like a phantom.

Perhaps, too, there was some little fear mingling with their own feelings when they saw their comrade fall.

"After him," cried one of them, recovering from the momentary confusion into which he had been thrown. "Come on. He went this way. Shoot him down if you see him!"

They both started off in the direction that Macheath had taken, and when the hackney coachman found himself alone, he placed his finger by the side of his nose and said—

"Five pounds for that 'ere job," he said, tapping the side of his nose. "Good! Off I goes, and not never a one on 'em knows my number, I'm sure."

With these words he turned his horses round, and in a few moments was going at an easy pace down Wardour-street, quite satisfied with his night's work.

Macheath did not go far up Wells-street, but turning off to the left, he at a slashing pace made his way to the upper part of Oxford-street.

Fortunately for him, the officers did not turn in that direction, but rode on stopping to ask every passenger if they had caught sight of the fugitive.

But no one could give them any information, and they rode right out into the fields where the Regent's-park now stands before they began to to think that they might as well give up so fruitless a chase.

They then made the best of their way back to Oxford-street, where they found about half-a-score of watchmen round the body of their comrade, who had received his death wound, and had only lived long enough to utter the few words that we have recorded before he fell from his horse to the ground.

In the mean time, Captain Macheath pursued his way on foot at a good round pace towards the Old Hats Inn, which he reached as the Acton church clock struck the hour of five in the morning.

If the young City gent, instead of making the best of his way to the Mansion House when Captain Macheath so unceremoniously ousted him from his phaeton, had gone back to the Old Hats, he might have done Captain Macheath a much greater amount of injury than he did, for he might have laid hands upon his horse.

As it was, however, we have seen that he did not adopt that course, but rather chose to make the attempt at the Mansion House, which, although it had certainly placed Captain Macheath in no small peril, we have seen signally failed in making him a prisoner or in killing him, either of which objects would have been not at all displeasing to the authorities.

But still Captain Macheath knew that there had been time enough ever since his escape to send an officer to the Old Hats to detain his horse; for he had, it will be recollected, lost considerable time in Newgate.

It was, therefore, with some slight amount of anxiety that he now approached the ancient inn.

All was still, and from that the captain drew a favourable omen, and he boldly rung the ostler's bell.

In a few minutes a voice from within called out to know who was there.

"My horse!" said Captain Macheath; "I want my horse, and here's half-a-guinea waiting for you if you bring him out quick."

"Oh! you are the gentleman who went away in the phaeton?"

"Yes—I am he."

"Very good, sir. I will be with you directly."

"All's well!" thought Captain Macheath. "Only let me get into the saddle, and I care for nothing. Ah! what sound is that I hear upon the road? Surely I am not pursued? That would, indeed, be too provoking. By all that's unlucky! yes, I feel assured of it. Some half-dozen horsemen are on the road, and I don't know anything more likely to hurry their movements than the chance of catching me."

With this conviction on his mind, Macheath hammered at the stable-gate, and called in a loud voice—

"Quick! ostler—quick!"

"Coming, sir!"

The stable-gate was opened, and the ostler appeared with Captain Macheath's horse, all ready for the road.

"Hilloa!" he said, "are they friends of yours, sir, who is coming from town at such a slashing pace? My eye! ain't they going it?"

Captain Macheath did not waste time by replying, but vaulting at once into his saddle he faced round on the road, with his face to his pursuers.

"That half-guinea, sir!" said the ostler.

"There is a whole one. Halt!"

That word "halt" was pronounced by Captain Macheath with such a sudden and startling distinctness that the horsemen, one and all, on the instant drew up. Then one who seemed to be the leader of the party, cried out—

"Who says halt? Are you anybody in authority?"

"Of course," said the captain.

"Who are you, sir? We are officers, and after a notorious highwayman. Perhaps you are a magistrate, sir?"

"Oh! my eye," said the ostler.

The officer who had last spoken trotted up to Captain Macheath, and the moment he turned his eyes upon him he turned pale with passion.

"Confound your impudence!" he said in a voice hoarse with excitement; "you are Captain Macheath! But your race is run at last. Surrender, or I will have your life—you vagabond!"

"Keep off," said Captain Macheath, "if you

are a wise man. I am not used to be called names, my friend."

"You ain't, ain't you? We will soon see what you are used to. Come on, my men, here's our customer; come on, here's Macheath, and we must have him dead or alive. Here he is on his horse; we are just in time. He is afraid to run away; we are sure of him now."

"Well," said Captain Macheath, "you are the greatest fool in your business I ever met with yet. Come on, my men."

The captain uttered these last words so ironically that the officer's rage very much increased; and but that he felt very sure indeed that any movement on his part would be the signal probably for a pistol bullet in his brains, he would have made a dash at Macheath and tried to capture him alone.

The others here rode up, but they trotted back again about twenty paces from the audacious highwayman.

That was a quite sufficient indication that they considered the service they were on to be one of no small danger, and Captain Macheath took advantage of their momentary hesitation to increase their too evident fears.

"Hark you!" he said, "there are six of you altogether, and I think that you are in force enough to get the better of me; but in so doing it strikes me very forcibly that you will run some risks, and some of you I should not be at all surprised to find stretched in death upon the road. I feel that I am to take the lives of three of you, and if you think that my capture is worth the risk of finding out which three it shall be, why, you may set about it at your earliest convenience."

The officers looked very shy.

"What!" cried the chief of them, "do you mean to say that you shrink from seizing this fellow now that you are face to face with him?"

"Of course they do," said Captain Macheath. "They are wise enough to prefer enjoying life a little longer to dying now, and you will do well to imitate them; for I warn you that the first among you who makes a hostile demonstration against me will perish. Now, take your own course. I am not going to wait here while you consider whether you can screw up your courage or not."

Captain Macheath turned away very slowly, and the officer, who may be said from courtesy to have command of the party, immediately took a pistol from his pocket and fired it at him

"All right," said Macheath. "You will find it more difficult to hit with a pistol bullet than it looks, my friend. It was not a bad shot, but what do you think of this?"

As he spoke he produced one of his pistols; but the officer, with a cry of alarm, got behind his men.

They, however, were by no means anxious to act as a shield to him, and they dispersed right and left immediately, leaving him fully exposed to Captain Macheath's fire.

But the inclination to shoot him had passed away, and Captain Macheath no longer thought it worth his while to take such a life.

However, to his great alarm, Macheath kept him covered with the pistol, until unable any longer to stand such a state of mortal apprehension, the officer turned and galloped away.

This served quite as a sufficient impulse to his men to follow his example, so that for the time being Captain Macheath got rid of them without firing a shot.

"This is a panic," he said to himself, "and won't last long. I must take advantage of it at once."

He gave the word to his horse, and off from the Old Hats he went at a speed which defied pursuit.

He thought it would be much better to get out of the high road as soon as possible.

Observing a green lane on his right, he at once turned down it, and went half-a-mile at a good pace without a pause.

The lane had taken several turns, principally to the right, so that Macheath did not know very well where it led to, as he had never to his knowledge been in its intricacies before.

Of course, it could not take him out of his way, as his course just then was any way that promised him temporary safety until the ardour of the pursuit subsided.

A dog suddenly bounded to his side, and then a lad came lounging along the lane.

"Hilloa! my boy," said Captain Macheath, "where does this lane lead to?"

"To East Acton, sir. It's only round those alder trees to the right there, sir."

"Thank you. Humph! East Acton," Macheath replied. "I must have described almost a circle to get here; but it is a quiet place enough among the trees, and perhaps after all it will be no bad plan upon my part to pass the day there. I will look about me first though when I get fairly into the village."

He only walked his horse now that the boy had told him it was so very near at hand, and then he found that he had been correctly informed, for upon turning the alders, he found himself in the village.

But a sight met Captain Macheath's eyes which induced him to come to an abrupt standstill.

In the centre of the road was a man holding a couple of horses, and from the accoutrements of the steeds it was quite evident to the captain's practised eye that they belonged to the new mounted officers, which had during the last six months been organised as a body of men ready to take the road against any highwayman who might become notorious in the district.

It was from this small body of mounted men that the horse-patrol eventually sprang, and which gave the first severe blow to highway robberies.

Macheath was not afraid of two men, but then it was his policy invariably to avoid an encounter with anyone if he could, and accordingly he drew back under the cover of the alder trees again.

Upon glancing around him then, he saw that he was close to a park paling, immediately above which was a board announcing "This Mansion to be Let."

Rising in his saddle a little, Captain Macheath got a fair view of the mansion, and seeing all the shutters closed, he concluded that it was empty.

"This may be as good a chance as any," he said, musingly, "for all I know. I may find this a capital place to retire to."

He gave his horse as good a run as he could, and leaped him over the park paling with ease.

"That will do," he said, as he dismounted, finding that he was now free from observation from the village or the lane.

A little in advance of him he found a shrubbery, and having made his way into it, he tied his horse to a tree.

With a light step, and keeping all his senses on the alert, Macheath went up a long shaded avenue towards the mansion.

Once he paused, for something amazingly like a a cry of terror came upon his ears.

"What can that be?" he said. "Surely it was a scream, and yet it is possible it might have been the sharp sudden cry of some startled bird; and yet it did sound strangely. However, I will walk slower and listen."

As he went on, no other sound met his ears until he came to the termination of the shady walk which terminated in a flower garden that had been for some time suffered to go to decay.

The moment he stepped into it he heard the cry again precisely as before, and it seemed to him evidently to come from the house.

"This is more than strange," he said.

He crossed the garden hastily, and keeping the shrubs between him and the mansion, he reached an angle of it where there was a window rather close to the ground.

Putting his ear close to this window, Captain Macheath heard a loud voice saying something, but what were the precise words he could not distinguish.

It was sufficiently evident, however, by their tone that they were words of violence and menace.

This was enough for Captain Macheath, and he immediately sought the means of gaining admittance to the house.

This was by no means a very easy matter, for the window by which he had listened was defended by some ornamental iron-work, and although it could not have offered any protracted resistance, yet Captain Macheath's object was to get into the mansion quietly.

CHAPTER XXVIII.

MACHEATH SAVES A LIFE.

ANOTHER cry, similar in tone to the two that he had before heard, acted as a powerful impulse upon Macheath, and he ran round the house in order to seek for some mode of entrance.

He tried three doors, but they were all fast.

A fourth, however, yielded to his touch.

He found himself at once in the house.

The moment he got in he listened attentively, but for a few moments he could hear nothing.

Then came the sound of the man's voice again —for a man's it undoubtedly was—and it sounded to him harsher than it had done before.

Yet Captain Macheath could not hear what he said.

"The sound, however, will guide me," he said. "Surely I shall soon find out what is going on?"

There were sufficient windows open in the place for him to be able to see well about him; and as he proceeded through a number of rooms and corridors he could hear the loud, angry voice at intervals.

Macheath was most anxious to ascertain from what room it came, and he, after traversing at least a dozen, and ascending one staircase and descending another, at last paused, for he knew not which way to go.

He had not long to wait, however, for a renewal of the sounds, and then he started to find that he was so near at hand to the room in which they were uttered. The cries evidently proceeded from a room a little way from him on his right hand.

He dashed towards it at once; and opening the first door that presented itself, he found himself impeded by a curtain of some thick substance

CAPTAIN MACHEATH

THE
PRINCE OF THE HIGHWAY.

"LEND A HAND HERE," SAID CAPTAIN MACHEATH. "THERE IS NOT A MOMENT TO LOSE."

NO. 11.

that hung in front of it facing the room.

Behind that curtain he felt convinced were the persons whom he sought.

He now paused and listened, for he was anxious to ascertain the state of affairs in the room before he hazarded anything by a hasty, and, perhaps, ill-timed interference.

The stern, harsh, high voice of a man came upon his ears, and it was quite evident that the man spoke without the smallest suspicion that it was possible for his words to be overheard.

"I tell you, girl," said the villain, "that you are here beyond all human aid. If you prefer death to signing this paper, you shall die, and then, knowing your handwriting so well as I do, I will sign it for you, and all will be as I wish it."

"Oh! no—no; spare me! A dreadful thought comes across my brain. Tell me, did you kill my mother?"

Perhaps Macheath had heard as sweet voices, but he never had heard one that was more full of soft, natural music than that which sounded in his ears.

"The knowledge of such a fact may perhaps influence your determination," the man said. "Listen to me, Annette. When I courted your mother, who had been then a widow two years, and who I found was most warmly attached to you—her only child, it was by pretending affection for you that I succeeded in winning her. Now I tell you that I always hated you!"

"Hated me?"

"Yes, I detested you, and your mother likewise; but I knew that she had considerable property, which was to descend to you at her death, and I married her solely with the view of getting that property."

"But you do not tell me if you took her life."

"I did."

"Oh! horror—horror."

"Ha—ha!" laughed the ruffian. "And so you had so slight an appreciation of my character as to fancy that I would let a human life or two stand between me and my objects! No! Not twenty lives should warp me from a purpose once fully entertained and resolved upon."

"Monster!"

"Rail on. It matters not. This old mansion is deserted. No human ears but mine will give heed to what you say. You are here shut up from all the world. You have no chance—no hope of succour, so I will freely tell you all. I prepared a deed, the effect of which, provided both you and your mother signed it, would be to vest the entire property in me. If you had both signed it freely she might have lived; she refused, and she died."

"You did not get her signature, then?"

"I wrote it myself after her death. I am an adept at such matters. It is now your time. Sign and live, or refuse and die, and I will sign for you. Choose!"

"You cannot be so base?"

"Can I not? You will see."

"You asked me to call you father," the girl said, sobbing. "Can you look upon me and talk of killing?"

"Yes, I can talk of killing; but upon your own head be the death you prefer to the mere parting with certain gold or gold's worth. You are more fond of possessions than I am, for you hesitate about even saving your life at the expense of this, which I would not do; for, much as I love the riches of the earth, I yet hold my life as my chief

possession. With you, however, the case seems to be different."

"No—no."

"But I say yes, girl; and every moment that you delay signing this document convinces me of that fact."

"No—no; it does not," the girl said. "You have made with me a fearful confidence. You have told me secrets which the grave alone can hide; and if I sign that deed, who shall assure me then that you will not kill me? You are too great a villain to permit me to live. I am lost!"

"All is not lost yet!" shouted Captain Macheath, as he dashed aside the curtain and made his way at once into the room; "not quite. We will have something of a fight for you yet, unless this man is such an abject coward that he dare not raise a hand in his own defence."

With a shriek of joy the young girl flung herself at Macheath's feet, and the father-in-law was so absolutely staggered and confounded at the sudden appearance of the captain that he stood like a statue for several moments, and all his faculties appeared to be in abeyance.

"Villain!" Macheath cried.

The man recovered his senses, and drawing a knife from the breast of his apparel, he made a rush at Macheath; but the latter had fully expected that some effort at violence would be made, and he was prepared for it.

He met the would-be assassin by so tremendous a blow in the face that it stretched him on the floor at the farther end of the room in a state of insensibility.

"Saved—saved! I am saved!" the girl shrieked.

"Yes, you are safe now," said Macheath. "But calm yourself, and tell me who you are, and how you came here?"

She could not reply to him; but, bursting into tears, she wept bitterly.

"Do not try to check those tears," said Macheath, tenderly. "Your feelings must have vent. Your heart has been surcharged with grief and horror. Weep freely; you will be better."

She did weep freely.

But at length she subsided into sobs.

"Take me from here! Oh! take me from here, I pray you. I feel as if I should die if I remained longer in this dreadful place."

"But your worthy father-in-law must be handed over to the watch. I think you must be desirous that such should be the case—are you not?" said Macheath.

"Oh! no—no. I only wish to leave here. Let him be. Heaven, in its own way, and in its own good time, will punish him."

"Well," said Captain Macheath, "if such be your wish I, of course, can have no other. Where would you like me to take you to?"

"Anywhere but home," the girl replied.

"You forget that I don't know where your home is, nor have I the smallest knowledge of who you are, except that you are that man's daughter-in-law," the captain said. "I am a complete stranger here, and my coming was one of the most accidental things that could possibly take place."

"Ah! no. Heaven sent you," the girl returned. "But I will tell you all as we leave this house. I have a friend in London—an old friend of my own father's. He is an attorney and lives in the Temple. Oh! sir, if you can but take me to him all will be well. He disapproved so much of my mother's second marriage that ever since that event we have seen nothing of him; but I know he will protect me."

"In the Temple?" the captain repeated.

"Yes. It is not so very far. We can go to the village of Acton, and get a coach easily, or we will walk. Anything, so that I soon leave this dreadful place."

It was not one of the most safe or practicable things for Captain Macheath to go to the Temple, inasmuch as to do so would be to march into the very locality from which he had only recently escaped with no small difficulty.

These considerations crowded upon his mind, but he banished them for the sake of the lovely girl.

He gave one glance at the prostrate form of the wicked father-in-law, and then he supported her from the place.

Macheath took her by the same way that he had come.

"This is my horse," he said, when they reached the garden; "and whatever mode of conveyance we may hit upon to the Temple, I must first place him in safety."

"Oh! my friend, there will be no difficulty in that," Annette replied. "I know people in the village who will be kind to your steed if I ask them, and then we can easily find some means of getting to the City. There is no sort of difficulty, my dear friend; but it would vex me much if you were to leave me until I am in safety. I seem to feel when I am by your side a sensation of security that I should be loth indeed to lose. You will stay with me?"

"I will," said Captain Macheath; "and having made you that promise, you may rely upon my carrying it out. Allow me, however, to take my own course in placing you in a position of safety, as I have very important reasons for doing so."

"Oh! yes—yes."

"Then, I decline going into East Acton; and if you will allow me to place you on the saddle of my horse I will likewise mount, and he will carry us both well to Hammersmith, where, if you have no particular objection to that course, I would like to go to the Temple by water."

"Your way, my friend, shall be my way," Annette replied. "Have you not saved me from death? I will go with you anywhere."

"Then let us lose no time."

With this Captain Macheath assisted Annette to the saddle, and, springing upon it behind her, he held the reins in his right hand, while with his left he supported her.

Off they went down the lane at an easy but brisk canter.

Macheath knew the way across the country to Hammersmith very well indeed, so he did not find it at all necessary to relax his speed in the least; and as the total distance was something under two miles it was soon performed.

"How could anyone," Captain Macheath said, "be so barbarously wicked as to think of injuring you?"

"Ah! my friend, all the world is not so good as you are."

This was rather a home-thrust to the captain.

It was taking his goodness by far too much upon credit, in consequence of this one good act he had done in rescuing her from her evil father-in-law.

Macheath was still silent.

By this time they had reached Hammersmith,

where he dismounted, and determined to put up his horse, while they went by water to the Temple.

This having been accomplished he went down to the river-side, and engaged a boat with two good rowers to carry him and his young and beautiful companion to the Temple.

As the boatmen, aided by the tide which happened to be running down, and so was perfectly favourable to their progress, made rapid way, Captain Macheath and the girl sat in the stern of the boat, conversing in low tones.

"And so you are quite sure," he said, "that the person you are going to will prove a kind friend to you?"

"Oh! quite—quite. He is very old, but he can and will protect me, and he will get others to do so likewise. He will, too, being in the law, know exactly what to do as regards my mother's husband."

"You do not like to call that man father?" said Captain Macheath.

"Oh! no—no," Annette replied. "That is too sacred a name. I would have all children call their mother's second husband by merely his name, and never by that of father."

"Indeed!"

"Yes; I think that that ought to be the children's prerogative, and the only sort of reproach that the mother ought to hear for marrying again with the children of a former union about her."

"You have thought, then, upon this subject?" asked Macheath.

"Not much, but I have heard such a sentiment, and I so fully agreed with it that I at once adopted it. Oh! how very beautiful this progress through the water is."

"It is Miss—Miss—"

"Call me Annette, if you please."

"Well, Annette, I will call you by that name since you wish it," said Macheath. "But now, are you not curious to know who I am?"

"Oh! you are kind and good."

"Humph! But do you not feel that you would like to know my name and condition?"

"I might, but I ought not to ask you. You will tell me at your own time, and until you do so I can admire and respect you for the service that you have done so opportunely for me."

By this time the Temple stairs were in sight, and one of the rowers paused a moment, as he said—

"The tide is high enough to land your honour on the terrace of the garden."

"Will that do?" said Captain Macheath to his fair companion.

"Oh! yes—yes. Anywhere so that we get into the Temple at all; and from one of the gardens, now I bethink me, there was an entrance to the chamber of my mother's old friend."

"That will do, then," said Macheath. "Let it be the garden."

Upon this the two watermen pulled lustily, and in the course of seven or eight minutes more they had the boat just on the level of the stone coping to the long gravel-walk of the Temple Gardens.

Macheath sprang on shore, and then assisted Annette to do so, after which he gave the two rowers a half-guinea.

"Keep where you are until I return," he said, "and you shall have as much again for taking me back."

The payment was so much more than they could have thought of demanding, that they were profuse in their thanks.

"We shall be here, your honour," said one.

"There's no danger of our forgetting a customer that pays so well."

"Very good," Captain Macheath returned. "I will be back as soon as possible, and if I detain you an unreasonable time, that shall be likewise remembered and well paid for."

With this he placed Annette's arm beneath his, and as they paced along the garden path, he said—

"Now, how will you find out your friend? Had you not better make an inquiry of the gardener, who is rolling the grass? He doubtless knows every resident in the Temple."

"Oh! yes—yes. That is a happy thought," the girl said. "I will ask him at once for the precise house."

Annette did this, and was at once directed to one of the houses which could be got to from the garden.

She pointed out the house to Captain Macheath.

"Come, my friend," she said, "we will go and see my mother's old friend."

"You would prefer, perhaps, going alone?" said Macheath.

"Oh! no—no. You will come with me—you would not deprive me of the pleasure of showing to him my preserver? Do come—do come!"

Captain Macheath did not much relish the idea of going into a lawyer's chambers in the Temple; but, as he was then pressed by Annette to do so, he yielded, thinking that, after all, if by any accident he was recognised, surely, after what he had done in saving the girl from death, even her legal friend would hardly think of denouncing him.

They ascended a small flight of stone steps, and went into a sort of vestibule, where they met a woman who had been cleaning the chambers.

"Is Mr. Arrowsmith within?" Annette asked.

"Oh! yes—you will be sure to find him," said the woman. "He is sure to be in while the sun shines."

Neither Annette nor Captain Macheath could understand this very enigmatical answer of the woman.

Why he should be always in while the sun shone was rather extraordinary.

"What do you mean?" Captain Macheath demanded.

"Mean? Why, I mean what I say—that such as he don't often go out in the daylight. It don't suit his goings on."

"What goings on?"

"Oh! don't ask me," said the woman. "The least said is soonest mended, of course, and it ain't no business of mine."

With this she made a hasty retreat, and left Annette and Captain Macheath on the threshold of the chambers, both of them wondering at the oddness of her speech and manner.

"The woman must be out of her wits," said Captain Macheath.

"Indeed, it seems like it," said Annette.

"What will you do?" Captain Macheath asked.

"Oh! I will go in at once to my mother's old friend; and then, when I introduce you to him, you will find how kind and good he is."

"I hope so."

They both went into the chambers.

"I will wait here, Annette," said Captain Macheath when they had reached an outer room, "while you explain to your friend the circumstances that bring you here; and when you have done that, you can call to me, and I will come in at once and speak to him; but I will not intrude at the first part of your interview."

"As you will, my friend; but why not come in now at once? Mr. Arrowsmith will be well pleased to see you."

"Why, I feel a little diffident," said Captain Macheath.

This excuse went down very well with Annette, who did not happen to know that diffidence was not exactly one of Captain Macheath's failings, and she accordingly opened a door that led into another apartment, and went in.

The door swung shut after her; but Captain Macheath had noticed there was in the wall a window, with a curtain to be seen on the other side of it.

He did not fancy exactly that that curtain was so good a fit as to prevent him from peeping into the adjoining apartment; and he meant to form his own conclusion regarding Annette's legal friend before he made his appearance before him, if he made it at all.

"Now that she is in safety," he said to himself, "I can leave her so, and my disappearance will do her no harm, if I don't happen to like the look of this Mr. Arrowsmith; and it is not very many lawyers that I do like the look of."

With this, Captain Macheath tripped across the outer-room very cautiously, and placed himself at the window in the wall, which commanded a view into the inner one.

He found that the curtain by no means fitted so well as to exclude any observation, while from the window being the only obstruction, everything that passed could be seen and heard by Captain Macheath.

He saw and heard enough to invite all his attention, and to alter his intentions of going away alone.

CHAPTER XXIX.

THE DUEL IN THE LAWYER'S CHAMBERS.

THE room into which Captain Macheath looked was a large and handsome one.

In the centre of it was a table laid out with all the materials for a very luxurious breakfast, and the whole place was very well furnished indeed.

At the table sat quite a young man, whose dissipated countenance bore sufficient testimony to his habits.

He was attired in a splendid morning-gown, and the untasted breakfast before him had given place to a liquor-stand that had greater attractions.

The room was strewn with whips, sticks, swords, boxing-gloves, and apparel of all kinds and descriptions, such as what was then considered a fashionable man might be supposed to indulge in and find his enjoyments.

When Annette entered it was with a quick step and a sparkle of the eye, for she expected to find the grey-headed friend of her mother in that room instead of the dissolute young spark who sat in it.

"What the deuce now, Mother Simpkins?" he said, as the door was opened. "I thought you had done with all your mopping and brooming for to-day, surely. Ah! who are you, my dear?"

The sight of a young and charming girl like Annette filled the libertine with astonishment, and he rose with his eyes wider open than they had been for many a long day.

Annette paused, and looked embarrassed.

Then, in her low, sweet tones, she said.

"I am afraid, sir, that I have made some mistake."

"I hope not," said the young rake.

"I come, sir, to see Mr. Arrowsmith.

"By Jove! then it is no mistake, for that is my name."

"But Mr. Arrowsmith is an elderly gentleman," said Annette.

"You mean the governor?"

"The who, sir?"

"The old man, my governor. I am young Mr. Arrowsmith, as you see, my dear. The old gentleman is ill at his house at Islington, but I am quite at your service, my dear."

"Oh! sir, is he very ill?"

"Why, they do say that he won't get up again. If I thought he would, I would not have made quite so free with the crib here. But come, my dear, you are only gammoning! I suppose Mother Phillips sent you here? Come, own it now, and sit down and make yourself comfortable. Upon my life! you are the nicest little girl I have seen for many a long day."

"Sir," said Annette, who only felt disgusted at the coarse manner of the young man, without understanding his allusions—"sir, as the friend I expected to find here is not here, I will leave you now, and trouble you no further."

"No, by Jove! you won't, though."

As he spoke he darted past Annette, and, turning the key in the lock of the door, he put it in his pocket.

"No, you don't go quite so easily as all that comes to!" he said, laughing. "You have come here, and here you shall stay for some time, at all events."

"Help!" cried Annette.

"Oh! it is of no use your crying out. No one will pay the least attention here."

"But I have a friend without!"

"Then he has gone, or he would hear you and knock at the door, in which case I should have to go out and start him, which would not take me much trouble to do."

"Let me go, sir!"

"Not a bit of it. Come! a kiss, my charmer. A kiss at once, and no nonsense about it."

"Sir, hear me for a moment, I beseech you," said Annette. "It seems to be my unhappy fate to-day to fall into the company of ruffians. My mother was your father's friend; my father, too, knew him well. I came to see him, sir, and not to be insulted by his son."

"Oh! stuff," sneered the rascal. "Don't I tell you that the old boy is on his last legs? You won't see him any more, and I am master here now; so the best thing you can do is to make a friend of me, and you will not find me a very bad one."

"I despise you and your friendship, sir," Annette replied. "Unlock that door and let me go at once. I command you, sir!"

"What! Are you an actress? By Jove! you must be. I never saw anything so prettily done. Bravo! But all this nonsense won't do, so a kiss I will have."

Annette darted round the breakfast table as he approached her and snatched up a knife.

"I will die first, sir, before you shall approach me," she cried. "I am but a poor, weak girl, but at such a time as this Heaven will lend me strength to cope with you. Look to your own safety, coward that you are!"

The countenance of the libertine flushed with anger.

"What! will you defy me?" he hissed.

"I do defy you."

"Then you shall suffer for it, you little idiot," he replied. "What the deuce did you come here for to play these heroics? Put that knife down!"

"Then let me leave this place, sir!"

"Oh! you won't?" said young Arrowsmith. "Well, we shall soon see how you will like to carry on the war. I will let you into the secrets of a little fencing. I am the best swordsman in London; and mind, now, I don't intend to get a scratch from you, but I will disarm you pretty quickly, and if you get hurt, mind, it is your own fault, and you can't blame me."

With this he took a sword from a corner close to the door, and drawing it he cast the sheath to the ground.

"Do you surrender?" he demanded.

"Help!" cried Annette.

"Do you surrender, I say?"

"Coward! You would not dare to brag thus to a man, if one were only within my call."

"Would I not? I am always ready and willing to fight the best man in all England. I am a first-rate fencer, as I tell you, and my courage is true as steel."

"I am delighted to hear it!" shouted Captain Macheath, in a voice that rang through the rooms again.

With one rush against the locked door he dashed it open, and appeared, with a face glaring with passion, in the room.

Arrowsmith rushed to the farther end of the apartment, and stood upon his guard, and Annette, passing him, threw herself before Captain Macheath.

"Save me—oh! save me from him!" she cried. "Save me, my friend—my preserver!—a second time!"

"Fear nothing!" said Captain Macheath—"fear nothing!"

"And who are you," cried Arrowsmith, "that dares to break my doors open, and intrude upon my privacy?"

"Your superior!" said Captain Macheath.

"My superior? Insolence!"

"Beware, sir," said Captain Macheath. "You have already quite a sufficiently long account to settle with me as it is. You had better not add another item to it. Annette, will you wait for me in the outer room?"

"Oh! come away—come away at once," cried Annette. "You need not pursue this any further. You have come in time to save me from this man, and that is enough. I beg of you to come away now at once. He is far beneath your further notice."

"So far, Annette, you are right; but I cannot go without punishing him for his dastardly conduct," said Captain Macheath. "Hark you, sir! You call yourself the best swordsman in England. I have no such extravagant pretensions, but with one of your own weapons I will try your skill."

As he spoke Macheath drew his sword and stood upon the defensive.

"Be off with you," said Arrowsmith, "and take your girl with you. I don't want to have anything more to say to either of you."

"Not so easily," said Macheath. "You must apologise to this young lady, and humbly, too, for your conduct towards her; or else I will force you, in self-defence, to exert some of your much-boasted skill in swordmanship, unless it all deserts you when you face a man."

Young Arrowsmith was close to the door of a cupboard, and before anyone could be at all aware of his intention, he darted his hand into it, and drawing it out again armed with a pistol, he levelled it at the head of Captain Macheath and pulled the trigger.

The aim was good, but the weapon missed fire.

"Well, sir," said Captain Macheath, "you must confess you have all the chances. Now defend yourself. Annette, you will be only my destruction if you call for any help, or interfere in any way."

The girl dropped upon her knees close to the shattered door, and covered her face with her hands to shut out the sight of the conflict which immediately began upon both sides with fury.

When the libertine saw that fight he must, he made up his mind to defend himself with desperation, and in every way to do his adversary all the mischief he could, whether in fair fight or not ; but Macheath was prepared, and a more consummate master of the sword than he was could not be found.

From the moment that the two weapons crossed each other the rake had no chance, and he seemed to feel that himself, by the desperate mad way in which he fought with his powerful antagonist.

Captain Macheath let him exhaust himself, merely acting for his own part on the defensive, and parrying all the furious assaults which the other made against him.

This he did with an ease and coolness that drove Arrowsmith quite frantic.

"Coward—coward!" he cried, through his clenched teeth; "you know you are a coward. You are fighting the safe game ; you dare not attack me."

"Do you wish it ?" said Captain Macheath.

"You dare not—you dare not ! Coward—coward !"

"Very good. Now, look to your guard !"

Macheath immediately commenced a rapid assault.

His sword flew from point to point like a flash of light, and then, before three minutes had passed, he suddenly took his opportunity and ran the libertine right through the body.

With such tremendous force was the thrust given that the sword, with a crash, went right through the cupboard-door against which Arrowsmith stood, and the hilt struck against his chest before it stopped.

The wretched man uttered one cry, and then there he remained pinned to the cupboard-door.

Macheath let go the sword, and turning round he caught Annette up in his arms and dashed out of the chambers in which a horrid scene had been enacted.

He knew that the wound he had given to his antagonist was mortal, or he would not have left even such a man as that without some sort of help.

Annette had fainted, but her light weight was nothing at all to Macheath.

He rushed across the Temple Gardens with her as easily as he would have carried a little child, and in a very few seconds he reached the water side.

The tide had sunk a little, but the boat was there with its two rowers.

"Lend a hand here !" cried Captain Macheath. "There is not a moment to lose."

And then one of the men stood up and received the insensible form of the young girl and laid her carefully in the boat.

Captain Macheath sprang in after her.

"Push off—push off !" he cried.

The boatmen looked rather astounded at these proceedings ; but they did not every day get a customer who paid so magnificently as Captain Macheath, and they did not feel called upon to take any steps in the matter, but such as might seem pleasing to their customer.

"Pull away again !" cried Captain Macheath. "Pull away. You will find it pay you well."

"All right, master !" said one. "We have no doubt of that when we have you for a fare."

"The young lady ain't hurt ?" said the other.

"Not a bit !" said Captain Macheath. "The only mischief that has been done has ensued in protecting her from a rascal."

"All right, then. Pull away, Bill."

They bent to their oars with right good will, and the boat, not being by any means heavily laden, shot through the water swiftly.

Captain Macheath had been rather glad at the moment to find that Annette had fainted, and so had escaped the sight of that final and really dreadful and sickening catastrophe in the chambers ; but now he wished that she would look up again.

"Annette," he said—"Annette, you are quite safe now."

"Safe as a coffin," said one of the watermen.

"Will you be quiet ?" said the other. "Haven't I told you not to mention such things in wherries, and yet you always will. Do you want this to be the unluckiest boat on the river ?"

"I didn't give it a thought at the moment, mate," said the other, "and I won't say it not never no more, no how."

"Mind you don't, or else you and I will have to go out o' partnership together, I can tell you. I don't like it."

Annette made no answer to Macheath, so finding that she was still in a state of stupor he dashed some water on her face.

She gave a slight shudder and opened her eyes.

"All is well," said Captain Macheath, "you are saved from that bad man."

"Saved !" It was evident by the tone in which she uttered the word that she was not yet sufficiently recovered to be quite conscious of the meaning of the word even when she uttered it.

"Yes," said Macheath ; "look at me. Do you not know me ?"

Both the watermen seemed to lend rather attentive ears to the conversation.

Probably, in their minds, there might be yet some lingering doubt regarding the work they were doing.

But if they had any idea that Macheath was an enemy of the young girl's it would have been quickly enough dispelled by the trustful manner in which, now that reason and recollection had both come back to her, she looked up into his face and spoke to him.

"Oh ! yes," she said. "You are my preserver. I owe you my life, and more than my life. You will not desert me now ? Oh ! tell me that you will not, for I feel that I have no friend else in all the world but you."

"Depend upon me," said Captain Macheath. "I will not fail to protect you against all enemies, whether secret or open. Do not weep. You have no cause now for tears. All is well."

"Where is he ?"

"Whom mean you ?"

"That man in the Old Temple who is so unlike his father, and yet bears his name," Annette replied. "Oh ! sir, was it not most villainous to

MACHEATH POINTED TO THE PROSTRATE FORM AS THEY PASSED BY.

speak to me as he spoke, and to threaten me as be threatened, when my sole object of visiting that place was to ask protection. I did not—I could not think that in the world there could be any one so base as he."

"Do not agitate yourself," Macheath said. "Believe me that you are quite safe now, and that all will be well. I am with you, and you already know that I have both the will and the power to protect you."

"Oh ! yes—yes ; both will and power ; and I am so poor in thanks."

"I desire none," said Captain Macheath.

"Sir," said one of the watermen, "just look in our wake half a minute, will you, and tell us what you think of that ?"

"Of what ?" demanded the captain, turning his head, hastily.

He saw two boats evidently chasing them as hard as four rowers in each could do so.

Had Captain Macheath changed colour or shown anything like trepidation, the watermen would likely enough have lost confidence in him.

"Do you know what stairs they come from ?" he coolly asked.

"The Temple," said one of the watermen. "I saw them push off in no end of hurry and bustle."

"And you think they are after us ?"

"Sure of it."

"Then, my friends," said Captain Macheath, "I tell you that they are after me from no good cause why they should be so after me. This lady has enemies. Only this morning she would have been murdered by one of those enemies but for my active interference. I say this much to you to convince you that if you exert yourselves it is not in a bad cause, and, in addition, here are twenty guineas in this purse. Follow my directions, and I will give them to you. You will run no risk, for come what may of it, all you have to say is that I told you I was escaping from the bailiffs. Such things, you know, are quite common and of every-day occurrence, both on the river and on land."

The watermen looked at each other for a moment in silence, and then one said—

"It's all as true as if fate had spoke it."

"It is true," said Captain Macheath.

"All right," said the other. "All I have got to say is—'Pull away, Bill.'"

"Here you are, then."

They bent to their oars, and scarcely had they done so when a loud, clear voice came across the water.

"Boat a-hoy—boat a-hoy !"

"Don't heed them," said Captain Macheath, as he flung the purse with the gold in it to the bottom of the boat, as a proof that he meant to be as good as his word. "Don't heed them, but pull away."

"They near us !" cried Annette.

"Yes, they will near us," said one of the men ; "and in the long run they will overhaul us ; but a stern chase is a long chase, and we may put you ashore somehow yet before they make way enough to get within boat's length of us."

"Yes," said Captain Macheath, "that will be it. Oh ! that another pair of oars were in the boat. Put us on shore as near Hammersmith as you can, and we will then shift for ourselves. Pull away. Look how they are bending at their oars !"

"Aye—aye ! sir. It's quite a kind of race be-

tween the two of 'em and us, and then between one of 'em against the other, but easy will do it yet. They go three feet to our two, but it takes a deuce of a while at that rate to get over a quarter of a mile."

"You are right," said Macheath. "Annette, there is no cause for apprehension ; I pray you to be tranquil. It will be better for you not to look at these pursuing boats. You but vex yourself to watch them."

Annette could not keep her eyes off them, however ; and now for the space of about ten minutes not a word was spoken in the boat, but the two men rowed as though it were for life and death.

The boat shot through the water with amazing speed.

"Hurrah !" cried one of the watermen, suddenly. "They have run one into the other. There's beauties !"

It was a fact that, in the anxiety of the watermen in the two pursuing boats to get a-head of each other, they had run so close alongside that they each had for a moment to stop their oars.

Perhaps you could not have counted eight before they were in full pursuit again, but still that was a great gain to the fugitives.

"If they come that sort of game again," said one of the watermen, "we can take you easy up to the bridge and land you comfortably where we took you from."

"I hope they may," said Macheath. "But don't trust to that. It is not very likely. Only see in what a mad sort of manner they make the boats spring out of the water to make up for lost time. Ah ! we shall beat them yet."

Annette held one of Macheath's hands in both hers and wept freely.

She knew that he had fought with the young spark in the Temple, who had treated her in so villainous a manner, and although, if she had been put upon her oath, she could not positively have taken upon herself to say what had been the issue of the combat, yet the fact that her preserver was then with her, and unhurt, was to her mind good proof that something serious had happened to the other party.

"They will drag you to a prison," she whispered, "and it will be all upon my account."

"No. We shall beat them," said Macheath. "Be under no apprehension."

At this moment a sharp crack, that could not be mistaken for anything else but the report of a pistol, sounded across the water, and the watermen involuntarily paused a moment upon their oars as a bullet plunged into the water about twenty feet to the stern of the boat.

"On—on !" cried Captain Macheath ; "it's no matter. We are out of pistol-shot. Pull away now !"

"All right, sir," said the waterman. "But they do seem rather bent upon it, don't they now ? Pull away, Bill."

Bang went another pistol-shot, and that was echoed by a shriek from Annette.

In all this she could read nothing but the total destruction of the man who had done so much for her, and who, she felt, was incurring all this danger on her sake and service alone.

As before the shot fell short.

"They will soon get tired of that sort of thing," said Captain Macheath. "We are completely out of range of their pistols, and at every shot they retard their own boat by confusing their rowers. We gain upon them now, and there is

Hammersmith. Pull on—the twenty guineas are nearly earned already, my friends."

"They shall be quite, sir," said one of the men. "Don't you cry, lady. It will be all right soon now. Let them blaze away as much as they like."

Captain Macheath now became aware of a new danger, which neither the watermen nor Annette had an opportunity of noticing.

They merely looked in the wake of their boat, and her whole attention was fixed upon the pursuers.

It was Macheath only who looked out ahead, and as he did so he saw a long narrow wager boat with six rowers in it, coming right towards his wherry.

It was evident from the manner of the rowers in the long boat that they intended to make an effort to stop him, for two of them stopped their oars, and got out a couple of boat-hooks as they neared.

"Do you know those people?" said Macheath, pointing to them.

The watermen both looked.

"They belong to the club," the waterman replied. "What business have such fellows with us?"

"They are going to try to stop us."

"Are they?"

"Don't you see?" said Macheath. "They are sidling up so as to get alongside us. Let them take the consequences."

"You be still, sir," the waterman returned. "Leave Bill and me to manage them. We know how to do that sort of thing best. You keep quite quiet, sir, and depend upon us that they shall not stop you.

"That will do," said Captain Macheath.

He shrank back in the stern of the boat with Annette, but he kept himself for all that ready for action at a moment's notice if there should arise any occasion for his interference in the matter.

The affair now assumed a very exciting aspect indeed.

The two watermen in Macheath's boat felt that they dare not relax in their speed lest they should bring themselves within pistol shot of the men who seemed well enough disposed to use such weapons against them, from the pursuing wherries.

On the other hand, they were called upon to navigate their boat with very great skill, so as to avoid getting into such a position with the six-oared wherry which was coming down upon them in the opposite direction, as would give that craft any advantage over them.

But they were experienced men.

It was easy to perceive that their blood was up; and that now, quite irrespective of the money that Macheath offered to them, they were far from being disposed to give in to their pursuers.

CHAPTER XXX.

YET ANOTHER DANGER.

ANNETTE's fear would have been excessive had it not been that courage and confidence are really as contagious as fear.

One glance at Macheath's calm face gave her wonderful nerve; and as he saw that she was glancing at him for strength to bear what was about to take place, he smiled gently.

"You are confident?" she said.

"Very," he replied.

"Then I will trust all, and look at nothing."

She lay down by his feet and covered her face with a portion of her cloak.

"That is a wise determination," said Macheath. "Do not stir until I call upon you by name to do so. Hear what you may, and fancy what you may, remain as you are, and you will be quite safe."

"I will," she said.

Macheath hardly thought that it was possible she could have constancy of purpose enough to remain so hidden.

He only hoped that she would; but his attention was soon drawn from both hopes and fears as regarded that minor subject, by the rapidity of the occurring events around him.

It was quite clear that the two pursuing wherries had in some way managed to let the parties in the wager-boat know that they wished the wherry with Captain Macheath and the girl to be stopped.

It was equally clear that owing to the lightness of the craft, the party of six rowers resolved to do the work as carefully as possible.

They no doubt considered themselves to be more than a match for three men and a young girl, and so they wished to get alongside and grapple with the stouter boat.

The watermen were not slow to perceive all that could be done by the enemy.

He who was on the river side of the boat said to his companion who was nearer shoreward—

"It will be your job, Bill."

"Yes, I know it," said the other. "You ship your oar in time, and I'll do it."

"Very good. Now pull away, and here we have 'em."

"Hilloa!" cried the steersman of the six-oared boat. "Ship your oars, will you? There's something wrong about your cargo."

"Where did you buy them whiskers?" demanded one of the watermen.

"Come—come, no insolence. Pull alongside. Out with the boat-hooks."

"Can you swim?" cried Bill. "'Cos if you can't you'd better give us a berth longer than a boat-hook, that's all."

This language from the watermen served to enrage the six men in the wager-boat, and with some amount of skill they pulled so as to come broadside down upon Macheath's wherry.

But the two old hands who had charge of the latter were more than a match for the amateurs in handling the oars.

In a moment whisk went the boat's head round crossways to the river, and then with two vigorous sweeps of their oars, the watermen shot the head of their boat right over the shallow side of the other.

It began to fill with water directly, and there was such a scrambling among the six rowers and the coxswain as never was seen.

The state of consternation they got into was excessive, and all idea of interfering with Macheath's boat was lost in the fear of a grand upset of their own.

"Back—back!" they all shouted. "You will sink us. Murder! Help!"

"Back it is," said Bill.

Another sweep of the oars in the contrary direction disengaged the two boats, but the six-oared wherry was neary full of water, and upon the point of sinking.

"Now, gentlemen, I tell you what it is," said Bill. "If you sit uncommon steady, and bale it out, you won't go down; but if you don't, you will, and let me give you an old waterman's advice: Don't poke your nose into another man's affairs. We have a proverb on the river that says—'Nobody sees anything but his own wherry,' and it would be a good thing for you to mind it."

Not the ghost of an answer was attempted to be returned to this speach, for the six rowers felt that indeed their only chance of safety lay in slowly and cautiously baling out the water from the boat, as otherwise the slightest thing would have upset it.

"Give way now," cried Captain Macheath. "Pull hard, and we shall soon be to land. The others have gained upon us now."

"Aye—aye! sir. But not enough for mischief, and they won't fire at us now for fear of killing those pretty fellows with the white jackets, who we can manage to keep in our wake now pretty well. I consider that that job was done in a business-like way now."

"It could not have been better!" cried Macheath. "I owe you a world of thanks for it. Annette, look up. The danger is now over."

Annette uncovered her face.

It was very pale.

"Don't you take on, miss," said Bill. "All is right now."

"Are we indeed saved?"

"Yes," said Macheath. "We shall land directly now."

"They are giving it up," said Bill. "Look, the other two are putting-in at the nearest stairs. They think now that as they don't know exactly what sort of a dance we may lead them up the river, it will be best for them to land and get up a riot along shore."

"Not a doubt of it," said Captain Macheath. "But if we do get to Hammersmith and have but five minutes the start of them, I will give them leave to do what they like and can. Can you ride, Annette?"

"Oh! yes. They say I ride well."

"That is everything."

In about five minutes the keel of the boat grated on the Hammersmith shore, and Macheath, taking Annette in his arms, sprang on shore with her.

"The money is in the boat!" he cried. "Take it, and my best thanks with it. If ever we meet again, which I hope we may, I will thank you again; and if we don't, I shall not forget the good and gallant service you have done me to-day."

"Nor I!" said Annette, as she waved her hand to the two men.

"It wasn't done for the money," said Bill; "but my heart, after a little while, was in the work. So bless you, my pretty lass, and good luck to both of you!"

Macheath waved his hand, and then placing Annette on her feet he put his arm in hers, and walked up to the inn where he had left his horse.

"There is not nor can there be any occasion for your joining your better and more innocent fortunes to mine," Captain Macheath said. "I must perforce escape the best way I am able; but you need not be under any fear. You are far more sinned against than sinning. Can you bethink you of any home to which you could go?"

"Alas—alas! not one."

"Is that possible?" the captain exclaimed.

"It is too true," Annette replied. "We had never many connections, and no relations in this quarter of the world. I believe there are some people in Canada with whom I may claim kindred, but—but none in England. He to whom I thought that I was going in the Temple is the only one I know who would afford me shelter, and now that that hope has fled I am desolate indeed."

"Not so; but—but—"

"You mean to cast me off—I am a trouble to you."

"Ah! Annette, how much you misconstrue my motives. I did not, and I do not, think you a trouble," Captain Macheath said. "Far—very far from it, indeed. But what I was so anxious about, was not to compromise you in any way by taking you about with me."

"Compromise me?"

The tone in which these words were uttered made it quite clear to Macheath that in her own innocence of heart Annette did not know what he really meant.

"Listen to me," he said. "If I continue to protect you, the world will think and speak ill of you. I was in hopes that you knew some family where you could go; for as you tell me, your wicked step-father wished you to sign a deed transferring property that belonged to you to him—that is a sufficient proof that you need not be a burden to anyone. I would have bought you a horse, as you say you can ride, and I would have seen you to anyone's door who would have received you."

"Alas! there is no one—not one."

"That is very awkward," said the captain, musingly.

"I can feel, though, how much I may be a burden, and perhaps a disgrace to you, and I will leave you."

"No, Annette, no; that you must not do. But I have no time to explain my circumstances just now; I am on the brink of a precipice. If I am taken by those who are my pursuers, all is lost with me. Let us place some miles of cross-country between us and this place, and then I can talk more freely to you, but for the present we must remain together. Be of good cheer."

"With you I am sure to be happy."

By this time they had reached the door of the inn where he had left his horse.

They entered the house, and Macheath gave Annette into the charge of the landlady, while he sallied out to a livery-stables in the vicinity.

There he quickly enough found a horse for forty guineas that would suit Annette, and he rode it back to the inn door himself, where by that time, as he had previously ordered that it should be, his own steed was waiting ready saddled.

Annette had no riding-dress, but Captain Macheath bought a large and handsome shawl, and completely wrapped up her feet in it, tying it round her waist, so that she was completely protected from the cold.

He then lifted her on the horse, and he saw in a moment, by her management of the rein, that she was an accomplished horsewoman.

"Are you comfortable?" Macheath asked.

"Quite."

He paid trebly for the slight accommodation they had had at the inn, and then off they went.

The horse that Annette rode turned out to be a capital one; and as Macheath's steed had had a good two hours' rest, it was in good condition, so they both made good speed, and in the course of an hour had placed no less than eight miles of cross-country between them and Hammersmith.

About half an hour after they had quitted the inn, a party of twelve mounted officers of the police rode up to its door.

"Ostler—ostler!" cried the man in command.

"Yes, sir. Here you are!"

"Did a man put up a dark bay horse here about an hour or two ago?"

"Without any spots?"

"Yes."

"Uncommonly full and bright in the eye, and thoroughbred?"

"The same."

"Then he did, in course; and a better bit of blood I never came near. As quiet as a lamb, too, in the stable, so long as you were kind to it and patted it a bit. Why, it was as playful and gentle as a kitten, it was."

"Had he a young girl with him?" the officer demanded.

"To be sure he had, and as pretty a little creature she was as ever you laid eyes on," the ostler replied. "They both went off a goodish time ago. She had a clever little nag he gave a matter of forty pounds for to Mr. Snaggs, as keeps the stables up above here."

"Confound it, then, we are too late!" the chief officer exclaimed. "I'd give another forty pounds to see them both. Which way did they go?"

"Well, it's lucky I can tell you. A man came here to have half-a-pint of something, and said he saw them both go over Fulham-bridge; so that's the way you will find them."

"Thank you—thank you," said the officer. "Come on; they are on the other side of the water, it appears, comrades. This is the way over Fulham-bridge."

"Is it?" said the ostler, when they were gone. "If they went over Fulham-bridge, I'll eat it, all the old wooden piles and all. No—no, I ain't going to peach upon a man as gives me a guinea for myself!"

CHAPTER XXXI.

MACHEATH DECLARES WHO HE IS TO ANNETTE.

"I THINK," said Captain Macheath, as he and Annette paused upon some high ground in the neighbourhood of where Kensal-green Cemetery now stands—"I think we may give ourselves joy that we are past all pursuit now."

"Do you think so?"

"Yes, Annette," said the captain. "Take a long look around you—your eyes are rather younger than mine—and tell me if upon the roads you see anyone in haste."

Annette looked anxiously in the direction from whence they had come; but she could see no one.

All was calm and still, and the only objects that met their gaze were a few labouring men in the fields, and in the lanes now and then a farmer's cart rumbling along lazily.

"We have distanced them," added Captain Macheath; "and I should feel happy and comfortable enough, but for one thing."

"What is that, my friend?"

"It is that, frankly speaking, I don't know what to do with you. Nay, do not weep, my dear girl, I pray you. It is because I have known you

now long enough to feel a great respect for you, and seen enough of your courage and gentle disposition to feel that you ought to adorn some happy home, and I feel sad, and wonder what to do with you."

"Alas!" said Annette, "you do not know what grief it is to me to hear you speak in such accents as that. Only let me be ever near you, and you will find me a dear friend, and one who for ever will share any dangers that the world can present!"

"Ah! Annette, you know not what you say—indeed, you do not! The time might come when you would learn to detest and shun me."

"Oh! no—no—never!"

"Do not be too sure. But yet—"

"Why do you pause? Ah! I am all confidence with you, and have no secrets; but you pause in speaking to me. Why is it that you fear to trust me as I trust you? Speak to me freely, my friend."

"What condition of life, now, do you suppose I fill?" the captain demanded.

"By your dress then," said Annette, "you are in the army."

"No."

"Then—then I know not what to say, or what to think. You will tell me at once. It cannot be anything very bad, or you would not smile."

"Indeed; but it is something very bad. Did you ever hear of Captain Macheath?"

Annette turned very pale and started.

She looked fixedly at Macheath.

"Is that your name?" she asked.

"It is," he replied. "And now, perhaps, you know worse of me than I deserve, for I have heard enough of myself to know that my character is coloured one way or the other by the feelings and the prejudices of those who converse of me."

"Captain Macheath!" said Annette, as if talking to herself. "He is Captain Macheath of whom I have heard so much. He is Captain Macheath. Oh! I might have made a guess at this, surely. Surely I might have thought that no one but such a man could do as he has done."

"Indeed!" said Macheath. "Then you have heard of me. Well, Annette, now that I have made this revelation to you, listen to me. I will take you to my wife and she will treat you as if you were her own sister."

Tears were in Annette's eyes as she looked up to him.

"I am very thankful," Annette said; "my heart is full, I cannot say any more now."

They now rode on.

The little time they had paused to have so very important a conversation had sufficed to give the horses a rest, and in less time than Macheath had mentioned they were in the winding lane that leads to the village of Willesden.

They soon emerged opposite to the Old Cage, with its picturesque window and its projecting direction-post.

Captain Macheath pointed to it with a smile.

"The good folks of this place once thought that they would place me in there," he said; "but they reckoned entirely without my consent."

"Is it not then dangerous for you to come to this place?"

"Oh! no," Macheath replied; "it was some time ago, and it is very unlikely that they will again recognise me. Besides, there is an inn where we shall be perfectly safe for a time, and where we can take some refreshment."

Turning to the left from the Old Cage, instead

of going right on towards it, Captain Macheath paused at the door of an old, straggling, long, low-roofed public-house, and taking a whistle from his pocket he blew a long, shrill note upon it.

In a moment an elderly man came to the door, and looking at Macheath for a moment or two his face then lit up with a smile, as he said—

"Oh ! it's 'ee—it's 'ee. What ! art in this part of the world now? No good to be done here. The high road is the place."

"I know it," said Macheath, as he dismounted and assisted Annette to do the same. "We only halt here a short time to rest."

"Aye—aye ! Well, come in—come in. I hardly knew you. Why, it is a matter of I don't know how many long months since you have been this way. Come in—come in."

"All is well, I presume?" said Macheath, as he stooped to cross the threshold of the old place. "You have no suspicious characters here, I hope?"

"Not one," said the old man, then sidling up to the captain, he whispered—"Who is the young lady?"

"My wife, man," Captain Macheath replied, after a pause, and a glance at Annette, which warned her not to contradict him. "Did you not hear of my marriage?"

"No, surely."

"Why you must indeed then be out of the world. Pooh—pooh ! I got tired of a single life so I married. Don't you approve of my choice, landlord?"

"To be sure, captain. As far as beauty goes you could not have done better, and I noticed how she sat her horse—it was first-rate; only it does seem an odd thing for a gentleman in your profession to marry—a very odd thing, I may say."

"It does," Captain Macheath assented. "But if you knew more of me you would find that that's nothing at all to the many odd things that I think of doing at times. So now get ready the best you have in your house, and as quickly as you can, too, for our stay is never very long in one place."

"I know it—it I know it. All right. A couple of chickens and a knuckle of ham. We have got, too, some of the old Madeira left."

"Yes," said Macheath. "That will be all right."

Giving his arm then to Annette Captain Macheath led her into a room above stairs, which, for a little old country place, was rather prettily furnished.

The chickens and the ham, together with the old bottle of Madeira, were no fiction, but in a very short space of time indeed were laid before Captain Macheath and Annette.

When the repast was over Macheath, after paying liberally for what he had had, ordered the two horses to be brought after him by a lad, while he and Annette took a short walk.

They had scarcely returned and mounted their horses when a rabble of people appeared, shouting and gesticulating wildly.

"Seize him !—seize him !" cried the people. "Lay hold of the highwayman !—seize him ! To gaol with him ! Shoot him !"

"Try it," said Macheath. "Are you sure you know me? I am Captain Machenth, with a thousand pounds reward on my head ! Why, it would make anyone of you for life. Why don't you come on? It is but the chance of a bullet through your head, you know."

At this intimation the mob of people, which was each moment increasing, hung back a little.

"As the constable of this village," cried one, "I take you into custody, you most horrid and notorious malefactor."

"Very good," said Captain Macheath. "I am quite at your service. Pray come on—come on. Surely there are enough of you?"

Someone fired a gun at him, and the bullet whistled past his head.

In a moment he clapped spurs to his horse, and dashed forward towards the throng, saying—

"Who did that ? Show me the man !"

Horsemen and those on foot alike turned upon this sudden and unexpected movement, and one over the other they tumbled in an effectual attempt to get out of the captain's reach.

The man with the gun was thrown down and trampled on by his neighbours, and Macheath, seeing the state of confusion into which they were all thrown, thought that he could not have a better opportunity of being off, which, after all, was his only policy.

He turned his horse's head abruptly, and made for a little gate that led into a lane.

Annette was close to the gate.

"Over !" cried Captain Macheath.

And in an instant she made the horse leap the obstacle.

Macheath followed her.

There was a loud shout from the rustics, who, when they found that Macheath did not absolutely ride over them, had recovered from their first fright.

Captain Macheath and Annette darted up the lane at a great pace.

But before they reached the top of it which joined the high road, they were encountered by two horsemen, who blocked up the narrow roadway, and one of them said—

"Captain Macheath, I arrest you in the king's name !"

"Indeed ! How do you mean to do it ?" queried the captain.

"I say I arrest you in the king's name. I am the sheriff of the county—the high sheriff."

"Are you ?" said Captain Macheath, as he dashed against him and overthrew him, horse and all, by the suddenness of the shock. "Are you? There, now ! I have converted you into the low sheriff, and down you go, in my name or your own, just which you like."

"Help !" cried Annette. "Oh ! help !"

Captain Macheath turned rapidly, and found that the other horseman had seized her by the arm.

If anything was more calculated than another to make Captain Macheath thoroughly angry it was to see anybody attempt any violence to a young girl.

He spurred forward, and seizing the man by the collar dashed him from his horse.

The man, as he half-scrambled to his feet, drew a pistol and snapped it at Macheath.

Luckily for the latter it only flashed without discharging.

The man immediately rose, and ran back as fast as his legs could carry him.

"It's my turn," cried Macheath.

Taking from his breast one of the pistols he always kept loaded with a good charge of shot instead of a bullet, he took good aim and pulled the trigger.

A yell from the man, and his rolling over and

CAPTAIN MACHEATH

THE
PRINCE OF THE HIGHWAY.

"BACK, YOU BLOODHOUNDS," CRIED CAPTAIN MACHEATH. "I AM A MATCH FOR YOU."

over in the lane were sufficient evidences that he had been hit.

"On—on!" said Captain Macheath to Annette. "We shall have the others upon us if we don't make speed. "Come on, Annette.

It was well not only that Annette was so capitally mounted, but that she was so well able to manage her steed, as was the case, or she would have hardly been able to keep up with Captain Macheath, notwithstanding he did not by any means put his horse to its utmost stretch of speed. As it was, however, they both at a very rapid pace went down the road that led towards Harlesden-green, but Macheath did not pursue that for long.

He turned to the right and made towards Neasden as quickly as he could, for he thought that by going that way he would easier get across the country to some other district.

There were no signs or sounds of pursuit, and still taking advantage of every turning to the right that they came to, they at length emerged in the Edgware-road, very nearly as high up as Crickle-wood.

"Safe enough now, I think, Annette?" said Captain Macheath.

"Oh! yes—yes. But what a fearful risk for you to run!"

"Nay!" said the captain, smiling. "I confess that you have chanced to be in the midst of my adventures on the road; but I have been in many a worse strait than I was a little while ago. I hope you will never—never again be in the midst of such a scene!"

"Did you kill that man in the lane?" Annette asked, shuddering.

"Certainly not," he replied, laughing. "I only left with him a few grains of shot as a remembrance of me, and as a verification of his story when he tells it."

CHAPTER XXXII.

MACHEATH PLACES ANNETTE UNDER POLLY'S PROTECTION, AND MEETS WITH SOME STIRRING ADVENTURES.

CAPTAIN MACHEATH did not think it at all prudent to continue so near to Willesden or the Edgware-road after all that had happened.

He knew that a hue and cry would certainly be made after him, and taking advantage of a lane to the right near the Brent River, he led the way down it, and contemplated crossing Hampstead-heath, and getting right away by Highgate.

"My poor Annette!" said Captain Macheath, "you have but little rest indeed now that you have joined your fortunes in a manner of speaking to mine."

"Your dangers," she said, "shall be my dangers."

"Nay—indeed, I hope not. My first endeavour will be now to place you somewhere in safety. You are most unfit to battle with the world as I am forced to battle with it; and my duty is to save you from its rude shocks. We need not ride so fast now. There is an inn not far from Highgate where we may rest in safety, and after that I will take you to my home, and my wife Polly shall look after you."

By this time they had got right across Hampstead-heath, and up the long lane or road that leads to Highgate.

Just as they reached the high road they heard the sound of horses' feet rapidly approaching from the direction of London.

Captain Macheath did not wish for any useless contest, and as it was just possible they who were approaching might be enemies, he rode through the old churchyard, which, although it took him some little way out of his route, yet got him clear of the approaching horsemen.

The evening star was twinkling faintly in the twilight, when, having rested at the inn, they made their way to Kentish-town.

The door was opened and Polly rushed out to meet her husband.

"It is you!" she cried. "Ah! yes, my dream is prophetic. I thought you would come soon. What a truant and a wanderer you have been; and but that I know well no other could hold my place in your heart, I should be so jealous—oh! so jealous. Ah! who is the young lady?"

"She is a young lady who needs your friendship and protection," Macheath replied.

He then told Annette's story, and Polly took her in her arms and kissed her affectionately.

"You are quite safe here," she said; "and I will be a sister to you—indeed, I shall be pleased to have your company, as my husband is so often absent."

In less than five minutes Annette was quite at home, and a few merry hours were spent.

About noon the next day Captain Macheath said Good-bye to his wife and Annette, and took to the saddle again.

"Once again," he said—"once again I am on the road! I already feel lighter in spirit and more like myself, and if I do not have some adventure before midnight, it shall go strangely with me. Let me see. I will pick up some money and then dine at an inn, and wait until sunset, which will give my horse a capital rest, and then at midnight my life will begin. Hilloa! what have we here? The St. Alban's waggon, I declare!"

Slowly creeping along the road, with its team of eight horses, came the waggon of St. Alban's.

It only took eight hours to do the distance in, and as it had started at a very early hour indeed in the morning, it had actually neared Highgate by the time that the captain was upon the road.

Captain Macheath would hardly have thought it worth his while to interfere with a waggon and the the sort of company that was usually to be found in such vehicles, had it not been that he saw the driver leading by the bridle a very handsome saddle-horse, and the idea struck him that the rider might be inside the waggon.

Captain Macheath rode up to the man who was driving, and said, with all the calmness in the world—

"My friend, whose horse is that?"

"Not yours," replied the waggoner. "You go your way and I'll go mine."

"Have you made your will?" demanded Captain Macheath.

"My will—what do you mean by my will?"

"Just what I say," Macheath replied. "If you have got anything to lose it will be a good thing if you have made your will, for I am going to blow your brains out for being insolent on the highway."

"Oh! murder," cried the waggoner, dropping on his knees as Captain Macheath levelled a pistol at him. "It's a highwayman, as sure as a gun. Oh! dear sir, spare me. I'm a poor man with a large family."

"Are you?" said the captain. "Why the

greatest favour I could do you would be to put you out of the world under such circumstances. But stop your team, and keep quiet, or you will never see your large family again."

"Oh! dear, yes, sir—oh! yes. Woa—woa! Oh! yes; I'll stop 'em, sir, if you please."

Macheath left the waggoner holding fast the leading horses of his team, and then, the waggon having stopped, he went to the back of it, and drew aside the canvas.

"Your money or your lives!" he cried

A chorus of screams came from some half-dozen females who were in the waggon.

"Oh! good sir, spare us all," cried one shrill voice. "We are helpless women, and the only gentleman here is the tax-gatherer."

"Murder—I'm a dead man!" cried another voice.

"The tax-gatherer?" said Captain Macheath. "Where is he?"

"Scrambling under the seat, sir, to hide himself!"

"Oh! is he?" cried Macheath, laughing. "I'll soon have him out. Come out, you rascal—come out, will you?"

"Pull him out, sir—the ugly wretch!" cried all the women. "You are quite a gentleman, sir!"

"And such a very nice-spoken man!" said another.

"And such eyes!" said a third.

"Come out and be killed, Mr. Tax-gatherer," said a fourth, "and don't make the gentleman angry."

Macheath leant as far off his horse as he could, and after routing about a little among the straw near the back of the waggon with his left hand, he got hold of the tax-gatherer's foot, and out he pulled him.

"Oh! murder—murder! Spare my life and take the assessed taxes!" gasped the wretched man.

"Come," said Macheath, "your money—quick!"

"Oh! dear—oh! dear, I shall lose my situation."

The captain placed the muzzle of a pistol against the tax-gatherer's head.

"If you detain me much longer, I shall have to shoot you first and take your money afterwards," Macheath added. "I call all the pretty girls in this waggon to notice what a deal of trouble you give me."

"Oh! yes—yes," said the females; "it is abominable;" and then one added—"It's a wretched thing that a tax-gatherer should be so troublesome. Anybody but so very polite and handsome a gentleman would have shot him at once."

The poor tax-gatherer, who was by no means good-looking, saw that everybody was against him, so with a great many groans he produced a little yellow bag half full of money, which he handed to Captain Macheath.

"I take you all to witness that I am robbed of the assessed taxes!" he said. "I call upon you all to witness that. I'm a ruined man!"

"Pooh—pooh!" said Captain Macheath, "you know you will make a good thing of this, for you will pocket as much again, and say that I took it."

"So he will!" said all the ladies.

"Oh! murder," cried the tax-gatherer; "I only wish the waggon would break down with you

all. Indeed, I wonder it don't with such an ugly lot."

"Ugly!" shrieked all the females at once—"ugly!"

They sprang upon the unfortunate tax-gatherer, and Captain Macheath, putting his horse to speed, left them in the midst of a desperate fight with that unhappy individual.

He galloped on until he had placed two or three miles between him and the waggon, and was not very far off from Barnet.

He then looked at the tax-gatherer's bag, and found there were in it one hundred and seventy pounds in gold.

"Not a bad morning's work," said Captain Macheath. "I will try another adventure this morning, and then I will turn in somewhere to dinner, for I won't go home until midnight."

Captain Macheath, when he made up his mind to an adventure, had seldom to look far before finding one; and almost us he spoke he heard the sound of horses' feet upon the road, and in the course of a few moments a lady and gentleman on horseback appeared.

"Shall I stop them, or shall I not?" said Captain Macheath, musingly. "I won't alarm the lady, if she is young and pretty, especially if I like the looks of her companion, too; but we shall see—we shall see."

As the parties rode up the young lady appeared to be in great dejection, and the gentleman turned out in appearance to be anything but a pleasant-looking personage.

There was a disagreeable foxy look of low cunning and malice about his face, and Captain Macheath heard him distinctly say to the young lady—

"If you were to cry for a month, Jane, you you should not get it from me. I don't care what are the consequences to you, I will show it to father and have my revenge on the fellow. He threatened me once and I have not forgotten it."

"But, George," said the lady, "how mean and dastardly it is of you to take such a revenge as to steal and then show my letter."

The words had come so plainly upon the ears of Captain Macheath that he could not help being struck by them.

No doubt the beauty of the young lady, too, had a great deal to do with the sympathy which he felt upon the occasion.

"Who is that?" he heard the man say. "Who is that, I wonder? I don't like the look of that man, Jane."

The young lady was weeping, and did not look up.

The sight of her tears at once determined Macheath to interfere in the matter.

He considered himself as a sort of knight-errant, called upon to succour in particular distressed damsels.

Riding up, to the gentleman he said, in a very solemn tone—

"George, my boy, how are you this morning?"

Upon this the gentleman stared and drew back his horse's head, while surprise seemed to choke his utterance.

"As usual, I suppose," added Macheath. "Answer me, sir, for I have many souls to see to-day."

"Souls!" gasped George.

"Souls!" said the young lady, looked rather alarmed.

But Macheath, still preserving the utmost gravity

of countenance, and speaking in the same mysterious deep tone, pointed to the young lady, as he said—

"With you I dare not converse. Purer spirits than I am only have power to do so. Your presence nearly blinds me, and causes me the most excruciating pain; but such is my inheritance. It is George, your brother—he only that I dare speak to, for he is mine."

"What—what do you mean?" cried George, his face turning very pale, and the hair almost bristling upon his head with fright.

"I mean that which I say. I dare not speak that which is not. I ask you again if you feel well?"

"Yes—yes; pretty well. Oh! dear, Jane, speak to him. It's the—the—I'm sure it is the—"

"Devil!" said Captain Macheath. "That is what you were going to say; but it's better not said, young man. I have travelled some distance to meet you this morning. We have not met for some time."

"Oh! dear—oh! dear. Help! Murder!"

"Your outcries are of no avail. I want a letter that you have about you, and which is addressed to Jane."

"Yes, good Mr. D—no, don't mean that—anything you like, only let me off, do, this time. Only say you have not come for me, and you may have everything else."

"Give me the letter," said Macheath.

"Yes—oh! dear, yes. I didn't indeed think of meeting with you, sir, this morning—indeed, I didn't. Here's the letter, sir. It's from young Lieutenant Hill, sir, to my sister Jane, and—"

"Hush! Do you think that anything has been hidden from me? I yet retain sufficient of my celestial gift to dive into the secret thoughts of men. You would tell me nothing. You were about, from mere revengeful motives to show this letter to your father."

"Oh! dear, yes. Have mercy upon me, good Mr.—oh! dear."

Macheath took the latter and handed it to the young lady.

"It is yours," he said. "If ever again this brother of yours—this fool, whom I know well—crosses your fair purposes take a small roll of brimstone and, wrapping it up in a piece of paper, upon which the name 'Satan' is written in blood, cast it into any flame, and I will come and take note of what is doing. Farewell—farewell—farewell!"

With these words Macheath uttered a mournful groan, and struck his chest as though he were in great agony, and then giving his horse the rein, off he galloped, leaving the young lady and her brother as thoroughly terrified and bewildered by what had passed as any two persons could possibly be.

Macheath was so mightily amused at this adventure that when he got about half-a-mile off from where he he had left the young lady and her brother he fairly stopped to laugh aloud.

"I would wager anything now," he said, "that that fellow passes some sleepless nights, and will be afraid to venture out in the dark for the next six months to come. I never saw in all my life such a picture of absolute fright as he presented. I only hope Miss Jane, who, I think, shrewdly suspected the trick, will take care to profit by it, so as to keep her cub of a brother in order. He will be terrified to death if she now and then threaten him with the little bit of brimstone that I

mentioned. Ha! ha! ha! Who says now that I don't do some good?"

"Not I!" said a loud voice.

Macheath started, and turning in the direction from whence the sound proceeded he saw right on the hedge by the roadside a man on horseback, on a rising ground in a meadow.

"Well," said Captain Macheath, "who are you, my friend?"

"I think, my man," the stranger said, "you will soon find that out. Your time has come at last. Macheath, your race is run, and you may as well—as all those have done who have gone before you, and had their career upon the road—give in with a good grace."

"Really," said Captain Macheath, "you speak in riddles. You seem to know me, so if you have anything about you worth the taking you may consider that, in the exercise of my vocation, it belongs to me."

"Certainly," the man said. "The only thing I have about me that will fit you are a pair of as well-made handcuffs as ever held the wrists of a highwayman together, and they will be yours shortly."

"Indeed! are you quite sure of that?"

"Yes. You are a prisoner now."

"Well, that is news," said Captain Macheath. "And pray what name do you go by when you are at home?"

"Brand."

"Ho!—ho! In good truth I have heard of you, Mr. Brand," laughed the captain. "You are an officer of the police, and as report says, you are a bold one. And so you have laid your plans so that you have encompassed me at last?"

"I rather think so," Brand replied. "It is my business to take you if I can. I don't believe that you have quite made up your mind to die by a bullet upon the road, so your best plan is to take the thing easy, and give up, in which case I promise you good treatment."

"You are very kind," Captain Macheath said. "I suppose you will take care, you mean, that I am hanged with all due ceremony?"

"With the hanging part of the business I have nothing to do," said the officer. "My work is to lodge you in Newgate, and then they may do what they like with you; so give up at once, and save the unpleasant consequences of a resistance."

"Upon my word," said Captain Macheath, "you are the most jocular person that I have come across for a very long time. What if I decline to give myself up, eh, Mr. Brand?"

"In that case," Brand replied, "instead of your living carcass I shall carry your dead one to London!"

"Indeed!" said Captain Macheath, laughing. "Well, now, Mr. Brand, allow me to give you a word or two of advice, since you have favoured me with so many. I am fond of a joke, and can give and take one. But there is such a thing as carrying a joke a little too far, and my temper is just a little hasty. Now, Mr. Brand, you are safe just now, but I won't take upon myself to say how long you will be so, and my advice to you is that the best thing you can do is to go while you can."

"I would under any other circumstances," the officer said, sullenly.

"And why not now?"

"Because, Captain Macheath, I am quite aware you are speaking under the most serious misapprehension. You are now in rather a narrow country road."

"Granted.'

"Well," Brand continued, smiling grimly, "you have behind you six men hidden in ambush, whom you have passed. Before you there are six more likewise, and well armed. The hedge is too high for you to jump or to scramble over, and here I am with a pistol in my hand, and you are in a trap, my gallant captain."

"Thank you for your information," said Captain Macheath, doffing his hat with a great show of politeness.

"Any attempt to escape will prove useless," said Mr. Brand. "There is a trunk of a tree down across the road about a hundred yards in front of you, so that you cannot get on, and by this time those behind you have barricaded the road in your rear."

"Really, Mr. Brand," said the captain, "you are a clever fellow, and it's a pity you were not brought up to some business in which your abilities would have met with a better reward than they will in the ticklish one you have chosen."

"I am quite content," said the officer, "with my business, and the reward for the apprehension of Captain Macheath, you will grant, may not be a bad windfall."

"Take it, then," said Captain Macheath. "There it is in full, and much good may it do you, Mr. Brand."

As he spoke Captain Macheath drew a long-barrelled pistol from a secret pocket in his saddle, and, levelling it at the officer, pulled the trigger. There was a sharp report, a shriek, and the officer fell from his saddle to the grass, where he lay dead.

The bullet passed right through the centre of the unfortunate officer's forehead and lodged in his brain.

"Now," cried Captain Macheath, as he replaced the pistol in its secret receptacle and armed himself with another loaded one, "let those stop me who dare. Their deaths be upon their own heads."

He touched his horse with the spur, and the creature at once bounded forward as though she were mad.

The short distance of a hundred feet or so were passed in a few moments, and then, sure enough, as Mr. Brand had predicted, there was the immense stump of a tree, with many branches sticking from it in all directions, thrown across the roadway, and behind it half-a-dozen well-armed men.

Macheath felt now that to hesitate would be to be lost, for they could make a target of him from their leafy barricade.

He trusted, therefore, to that good fortune which had so many times, in the most desperate state of his fortunes, befriended him, and giving his horse another touch of the spur, on he dashed.

The horse had courage enough for anything, and at once was among the branches of the tree.

It was next to impossible that the animal could keep its feet under such circumstances, and it stumbled to its knees over one of the long loose branches.

This stumbling, however, had the effect of saving Captain Macheath's life, for the whole six men at the moment fired at him, and the shots all went over his head.

Infuriated at the attack upon him by so many, the captain, without waiting for his horse to move, shot one of them down.

Then a strong man grappled with him; but one ringing blow upon his forehead with the barrel of the discharged pistol sent him reeling to the ground.

Captain Macheath had flung himself from the saddle a t the moment that the horse fell, and now he held it by the bridle close to the head and assisted it to rise.

He thought the best thing he could do was to lead it through the branches of the fallen tree.

"You are dead men if you resist me!" Macheath cried. "I fight for my life! Cowards, make way!"

It so happened that at this moment the men in the rear of Macheath hearing the contest going on in front, rose up from amid the brushwood and ran on to lend what aid they could.

They were not aware of the death of Brand; and in the hurry and excitement of the moment, they, with the heedlessness of people not accustomed to having fire-arms in their hands, discharged a volley at Captain Macheath without reflecting that such bullets as missed him were likely to find their way among the party on the other side of the fallen tree.

One bullet knocked off Captain Macheath's hat.

Another caught him just on the top of the shoulder, making an ugly kind of furrow in the flesh.

He felt nothing but a sudden stunning sensation; and then two of the four men who remained to dispute his passage across the trees fell wounded and uttering the most dismal cries.

The two who remained did not seem to think themselves at all a match for Macheath, although he was encumbered with the care of his horse.

If they had flung themselves upon him they might have brought him down; but, on the contrary, they began scrambling up the hedge, heedless of thorns and blackberry twigs, only intent upon getting quickly out of the way of further danger.

CHAPTER XXXIII.

CAPTAIN MACHEATH LOSES AN OLD FRIEND.

IT was not likely that Captain Macheath would trouble himself much with those of his foes who chose to leave him the field of battle.

He turned all his attention to the extrication of his horse from among the branches of the tree, and that being effected he sprung to the saddle, and giving the creature both spur and rein, off he went at a tearing gallop.

"Hurrah!" he cried. "Hurrah! Safe at last. Mr. Brand, you are not the first clever person who has laid a trap for another and been caught in it himself. Hurrah!"

The exultation of Captain Macheath at finding he had escaped from such a really serious danger was so great that he did not for some time notice that his horse went on very unsteadily; but just as he plunged into a narrow lane he fancied that the gallant creature staggered.

"What ho!" he cried. "Steady, lad—steady! The words had scarcely escaped his lips when the horse fell, and Macheath was precipitated over its head.

It was well for him that his pace was not then great, or from such an accident the Prince of the Highway might most likely have brought his course to a close.

As it was he was rather shaken; but feeling satisfied that he had broken no bones, he was very quickly on his feet.

The horse lay panting upon his side.

Macheath rushed up to the creature and knelt by its head.

It was then that for the first time he saw it had received one of the pistol shots in its neck, and that all its progress from the scene of the conflict was marked by a track of blood.

The faithful creature had no doubt fallen at length from pure exhaustion.

Macheath would rather have encountered any amount of danger himself—aye! and he would have suffered great personal danger—rather than he would have looked upon his horse dying before his face.

That such was the fact there could be very little doubt from the aspect of the creature.

Its eyes were but dimly turned upon Captain Macheath, and it drew its breath by short, fitful inspirations.

The shot in the neck had wounded some blood-vessel of importance and the warm life-blood was now issuing forth in a stream.

"Alas!" said Captain Macheath, as he rose, "my poor steed, my gallant and courageous companion, with whom I have gone through so many adventures, and who has carried me through so many dangers in safety, must we indeed part at last? Alas—alas!"

He stood with his hands clasped before him, gazing upon the horse, which each moment was surely dying.

At length a sharp convulsive shudder pervaded the limbs of the creature, and the mouth opened twice as though gasping for breath.

Then all was still.

Captain Macheath's gallant steed had breathed its last.

For a moment Macheath covered his face with both hands, and he trembled as though some convulsion in imitation of that which had announced the death of the horse had come over him.

Then he took his hands away and said calmly—"That is over."

Even as he spoke he bent forward and inclined his ear to listen.

In the distance he heard loud shouts and the tramp of the feet of men and horses.

It seemed as though a multitude of people were not far from him.

He climbed up the hedgerow, and, grasping the branch of a dwarf oak-tree for support, shaded his eyes with his hands.

He gazed in the direction whence the noise came.

To his surprise he saw forty or fifty country people, some armed with pitchforks, some with flails, and with them about eight or ten men on horseback, who seemed to be directing the others how to proceed.

By their pointing out different parts of the ground to each other as they proceeded Macheath could not entertain a doubt but that they were his implacable enemies.

"They trace me by the horse's blood," he said, "and, perhaps, by some of my own; but I am not yet conquered."

Springing down from the top of the hedgerow, he commenced reloading all his pistols.

Taking those from the saddle of the dead horse that were always kept there, he bestowed them handily about his person, and there he stood considering for a few moments what he should do.

While he so stood he heard the hubbub of the pursuit approaching him closer and closer.

He could almost distinguish what the people said, and more than once he was certain that he heard the word "Murder!"

"Aye!" he said, "murder is the word. They have murdered you, my poor horse; but it will yet go hard with me if I do not avenge you sooner or later. Oh! that I knew the precise hand that fired the shot that has laid you low."

"This way—this way!" he heard a loud voice say. "He is in the lane. Come on!"

"Is he in the lane?" cried Captain Macheath, as he glanced round him.

Then, with amazing speed, he took to his heels and ran until he came to a stile leading into a plantation or preserve. He thought that it would be safer to get into this woody retreat than to remain in the open lane.

Vaulting over the stile he dived at once among the trees.

It was quite a relief to Captain Macheath to get into this retreat after so sharp a run.

He plunged on, now and then torn by the briars, but feeling a sense of security as each moment took him further and further into the intricacies of the preserve.

Twice he started a pheasant, which flew up above his head with a sudden whirr, and once a hare rushed almost past his very feet.

"I shall baffle them for a time," he muttered. "If they even discover that I have taken such a place of retreat as this, they will find it difficult to attack me here; and if they are disposed for a species of warfare in which I can use my pistols with advantage upon them, they may have it and take the consequences."

There can be no doubt but that in the then embittered state of Captain Macheath's feelings he would not have scrupled at the taking of life.

Every few minutes he would now pause, and inclining his ear close to the earth, listen for the distinct shouts of his pursuers.

Upon one of these occasions he heard a loud and continuous cheering.

"That shout of poor triumph is over the remains of the horse," muttered the captain, biting his lips with vexation. "Well—well, let them shout. It certainly is a great thing for fifty people to be so elated over a dead horse; but if I don't change the character of their shouts for some of them shortly I am not Macheath."

With these words he hurried on.

At length, thinking that he had placed a sufficient distance between himself and his pursuers, he paused to rest himself and sat down upon the gnarled roots of an old elm tree.

"So," he said, "here I am on foot at last; and when shall I get such another horse as I have lost? I may look long indeed for one; but still, one I must and will have. Well, it is something that he has only fallen dead into the hands of the enemy. After the many escapes that he and I have had together I would not have had them take the gallant creature alive. Let them now make the most of him. Ah! what is that?"

A loud shout now sounded close to him, and he sprang to his feet.

As he did so he felt a sudden twinge of pain from the wound in his shoulder.

Putting his hand up and glancing at it he found that the blood had trickled right down his arm to his elbow, from whence it was falling drop by drop upon the ground.

"It is so," he said, after a moment's thought. "They traced the horse by the spots of its blood,

"FOOL!" MACHEATH CRIED, "THROW THAT WEAPON AT MY FEET OR YOU DIE."

and now they are tracing me by mine; I should have thought of that. They have found quite sufficient evidence that I have crossed the stile into the plantation, and like bloodhounds they are upon my track again."

He took his cravat and made it into a bandage for his wounded arm, tying it sufficiently tight to prevent the bleeding from being at all excessive.

Then, feeling satisfied that he should no longer leave such a palpable trail behind him, he clambered on through the trees and underwood.

He did not intend, unless absolutely compelled, to leave the shelter of the preserve.

In the open country he would have no chance; but he hoped where he was to succeed in keeping his enemies at bay until night, and then, under cover of its friendly shadows, he might escape.

He paused again to listen.

His enemies were certainly nearer than they had been.

"Let them come," he said. "Some, at least, of them come to death. If I have not the lives of half-a-dozen men in my hands, it will cease to be a matter of regret to me, for I shall myself have gone from this world. Alas! my poor Polly."

He saw close to him a large tree, and the thought occurred to him that if he climbed it and hid among its branches, those who were pursuing him might possibly pass.

"Amid all these trees," he said, "although they may fancy I may be hidden, they cannot pitch upon the right one. Yes, the tree will be the thing, and if it does come to a fight, I think they will be more happy to get out of the range of my fire than I out of that of theirs."

Active as Captain Macheath was, it did not take him many minutes to climb up into the tree.

When there he was surprised to find a smell of smoke pervading its branches, as if from recently burnt wood.

He was just asking himself what this could be when he heard voices close at hand, and peeping down from his leafy covert he saw a man and a lad come cautiously near to the spot.

The man was a large, coarse-looking fellow, with a hideous squint, and the lad was a loutish individual.

Both were dressed in a costume something between gamekeepers and poachers.

Captain Macheath set them down at once for the latter.

"What's all the row in the croft?" said the man. "Eh, Peter—what's it all about?"

"Don't know," said the boy.

"You ought to know, then," cried the man, dealing him a box on the ears. "Take that and find out. You never know anything."

"Do that again," said the boy, "and I'll put my knife in thee."

"Ha—ha!" laughed the man. "Try it, Peter—try it, my boy; only try it, that's all."

"Then don't hit me."

"Only now and then, Peter, my boy, just to bring you up in a quiet way loike. Now, what's the row in the croft?"

"They're hunting a highwayman."

"Oh! is that it? Humph! well, I only wish they may not get him, the wretches. I hope he'll give 'em as many turns and doubles as an old fox. The idea, now, of a-going and a-hunting a feller cretur just for saying 'Stand and deliver' on the highway. You daren't do nothing as is pleasant. If you knock over a brace of partridges or throttles

a hare they has you up, so we oughtn't to wonder at society, Peter."

"Shouldn't I like to take it out of old Squire Adams," said Peter.

This, to the perception of the big man, was such a happy conceit, that he was compelled to hold his sides while he laughed.

Then, shaking his hand at Peter, he said—

"Ah! my boy, you will get into gaol, of course; but you'll do some funny things afore that comes to pass, I do think. We are best under ground though while this hunt is going on. Let's get into the Old Cave, my boy."

CHAPTER XXXIV.

OUT OF THE FRYING-PAN INTO THE FIRE.

THE words, " Old Cave," struck upon the ear of Captain Macheath as being a little remarkable.

After a moment's consideration he made up his mind that they referred to some public-house in the vicinity, for he well knew what odd, fantastic names were given at times to these establishments.

"Ah!" said Peter, "I does like the Old Cave."

"And so does I," said the man, "and if it wasn't for that, I don't think at times there would be a place for a poor fellow to hide his head in."

Macheath began to think that there was something more in the Old Cave remark than he had at first supposed, for if it had merely referred to some public-house, it was natural enough that Peter and his not very respectable-looking friend would have gone off to it at once, instead of lingering near the tree.

All Macheath's doubts and cogitations upon the subject were, however, soon at an end, for he saw enough in a very few minutes more to convince him that the words Old Cave for once must be taken in their literal sense, and by no means figuratively applied to any public-house.

The man, after listening for a few moments, and apparently satisfying himself that no one was within hearing, said—

"Very good. It's all right, Peter. Now for it, old fellow, and if we don't light a good fire and enjoy ourselves a little before the others come home it won't be our faults."

"Not a bit of it," said Peter.

With this the man went to an old broken down trunk of a tree near at hand, and having stooped over it, he pulled out a kind of plug of wood made from the roots of another tree.

"Now, Peter," he said, "you go down."

"Here you goes," said Peter.

The boy, with great dexterity, swung himself up to the top of the old decayed trunk of the tree and let himself right down, disappearing entirely from before Captain Macheath's eyes.

"All right?" asked the man.

"Yes," said Peter. "All's right. Nobody at home, though."

Macheath was a little curious to see how the man would get down and replace the wooden plug in the tree, seeing that it was of rather a bulky appearance and must have been weighty.

But that was done with considerable tact.

He balanced it at the side of the hollow trunk against a projecting branch, and then, having gone down the hollow, he put up one hand and pulled it slightly and it fell into its place.

"Well," thought Captain Macheath, "the place is worth knowing, at any rate, if one should be hard pressed by the Philistines at any time, and certainly I should not feel any scruples in the world in making use of it under such circumstances."

Macheath's reflections concerning the old cavern, however, were soon put an end to by the appearance of his enemies in the immediate vicinity of the tree in which he was hiding.

Half-a-dozen well-armed men came just under the tree.

"I feel quite sure that he is in the preserve somewhere," said one.

"Well," said another, "if so he is as good as taken, for it is not very large, and somebody is placed at every possible outlet, and within sight of each other, too, to give the alarm."

"Then we shall starve him out ?"

"Not a doubt of it ; and in the meantime I shall amuse myself by going through the wood and sending a good charge of shot into a few of the trees upon the chance of his hiding in some of them, for that is not the most unlikely thing in all the world."

"Far from it."

Captain Macheath set his teeth with anger at the idea of being thus baited by a parcel of men whom he had not injured.

The man who so kindly proposed to fire into the tree was a kind of under-gamekeeper.

More men kept straggling in as the others spoke, and Macheath had the satisfaction, if it were any, of hearing the most complete arrangements made for watching the preserve night and day in order to entrap him, while there was a talk of getting more officers from London for the purpose of hunting him out of his place of concealment.

"This wood," he thought, "will be too hot for me probably in a short time, but it will be bad for some of you if you attempt to prevent me escaping from it."

Macheath had not quite made up his mind what he should do ; but as he did not feel any pangs of either hunger or thirst, he felt that he could afford to wait in the tree a considerable time, and perhaps wear out the vigilance of his foes.

The man who had so coolly announced his intention of firing into the tree was very deliberately now loading a double-barrelled fowling-piece, and when he had done so he pointed it at a chestnut-tree, some dozen yards or so from the one in which Captain Macheath was hiding, and fired.

"Have you caught him ?" said one, as a few leaves and short branches came whirling to the ground.

"Never mind," said the man. "It was a scattering shot, and if he should chance to get one of them in his eye he won't see his way quite so plain on the highway, if he should ever take to it again."

Macheath had sought the butt of one of his pistols, but he immediately relinquished his hold again.

He felt how imprudent it would be to shoot that man, although the temptation was very great and the provocation for doing so immense.

"Well," said the fellow, "I will take it for granted that he isn't in the chestnut-tree."

"No," said another ; "and for all I have heard of Captain Macheath, if you were to riddle him with shot, and he had made up his mind to stay in the tree, stay he would in spite of you."

"Yes, that he might, but I don't think he'd feel comfortable ; so here goes for the other tree."

The fellow now levelled his gun at the tree in which Macheath was ensconced, and

caution the captain took was to cover up his face with the lappel of his coat.

Bang ! went the second barrel of the gun.

As good fortune would have it, not one of the shots touched Captain Macheath, although some half-dozen of them lodged in a limb of the tree not twelve inches from his head.

"Hit him now, Sam ?" said one of the men.

"No, I don't suppose I have, and I didn't say I should ; but I could hit such a goose as you at three times the distance."

"Could you indeed, Sam ? Why, you are quite a wonderful character. Do you think Squire Adams will like to supply you with powder and shot to spoil the trees with, stupid ?"

"You mind your own business."

Sam walked sulkily off, reloading his gun as he went.

"Well, my fine fellow," thought Captain Macheath, "it is possible that I may have to leave this preserve without paying you the little debt that I feel I owe you, but I won't do so if I can help it. Sam, they call you ; I shall not forget that."

"Now, my men," said a person, suddenly arriving, "any news of the person we are in search of ?"

"No, sir. Sam has gone blazing away into the trees, but we can't see any traces of the fellow."

"Sam's an idiot !"

"Well, sir, we did tell him not to do it, but he said he would, and now he's gone off to spoil all the fine old wood in the plantation, besides frightening the game out of their nests, and making them clear out of the preserve, sir, for a month to come."

"Dear—dear ! that anybody should be so pested with an idiot. Which way did he go ?"

"Right on, sir, by those sycamores."

Upon this the person, who appeared to be in great authority from the respect he was treated with by the others, went off at a quick pace after Sam.

Captain Macheath was not a little pleased at the idea that something like retributive justice might overtake the man, who, because he had a gun in his hand, could not refrain from doing or attempting to do injury.

After this they left the vicinity of the tree, and Macheath had the satisfaction of knowing that sentinels were placed all round the wood at such intervals that they could see each other, and so spread a general alarm should he make any attempt to leave it.

Once again, and only once, Macheath heard one of Sam's barrels go off; but after that all was still enough, as no doubt he had been stopped from carrying his project of firing into the trees any further.

Macheath now began to reflect seriously what he should do in his emergency.

If he should leave the tree or attempt by a rush to get away, he felt that he would be only making his situation a great deal worse than it was.

He was now under cover, whereas he would be at the mercy of his enemies, to be chased through the open country.

And without his horse what could he do?

"No," he said ; "if I do anything it must be by strategy, under cover of the night. But it is by no means a pleasant idea to sit in a tree till then."

It was rather a grave question when he came

to consider in what way he could better his condition.

Then, after a time, his thoughts reverted to the Old Cave, and scarcely had he turned his eyes in the direction of the singular place when he heard a noise, and the plug of wood that filled up the strip of the aged tree was raised from within and the man made his appearance.

"Humph!" he said, "it's all right. Come on, Peter, my boy—come on."

It was evident that he was well accustomed to lodging the loose piece of aged root upon the projecting branch of the hollow trunk, for it was done in a moment.

And then he scrambled out, being followed by Peter, who was on the ground with the agility of a monkey in a moment.

"Come on, Peter, my boy," he said. "Let's go to Mill-hill, and see what's doing. Who knows but there may be something for honest folks to pick up? Come on, you wiper, will you, and mind you keep your eyes open, and is down upon everything like a shot if you think it is worth the taking."

"I hear you."

"Well, Peter, it is a good thing that you does. Take that."

"Oh! murder, what did you kick me for?" cried the youth.

"Why, Peter, you said you heard me, and I thought you might as well feel me too, you is such a forward, nice boy; so now come on, and whatever you do, Peter, always be civil to everybody as is bigger than yourself."

CHAPTER XXXV.

A TEMPORARY REFUGE.

CAPTAIN MACHEATH, if his circumstances could have permitted him, would no doubt have enjoyed quite a hearty laugh at Peter and the man with whom he had appeared to be very closely associated; but the fact was that the captain's whole attention was too much engrossed in his own affairs just then to smile at the peculiarities of others.

When the man and Peter had got fairly away, and Captain Macheath could no longer hear their footsteps upon the decayed leaves of the preserve, he began to ask himself whether or not it would be prudent to go himself into the cave they had just vacated.

"What can they be," he thought, "but poachers? and from the advice of the man to Peter, it appears that they are not very particular about what they do, so long as they are doing something. I might surely be safe enough with such people, and, besides, I can pay them well, which is rather an important element in the transaction."

There was now only one consideration that caused Macheath to pause before venturing to the cave, and that arose from the man's words to the effect that there was nobody at home, which would lead to the supposition that others besides himself and the boy Peter were in the habit of visiting the cave, in which case there might be rather too many to trust himself and his liberty to.

After about ten minutes spent in arguing the matter pro. and con. with himself, Macheath at length made up his mind to explore the interior of the cave.

When the captain made a resolution he was not long in carrying it out.

He began to make his preparations for the expedition.

Cautiously he descended from the tree, for although no one was at hand, he felt that it would be highly desirable to make as little noise as possible.

He trod lightly upon the ground, and reached the old decayed stump of tree which served as the portal of the cave, concerning which the man and Peter had spoken.

To Macheath it was not a matter of any difficulty to remove the plug of wood, and as he had tolerable tact, he quickly balanced it as he had seen the man do.

All below seemed to be as dark as night, and yet if Peter and his friend had gone down in safety, there was no reason upon earth why Captain Macheath should not.

While he paused for a moment, he heard, or fancied he heard, footsteps approaching.

That at once determined him, and drawing up his feet as he had seen the men do by the aid of a couple of branches of the old stump overhead, he at once let them down into a cavity, and felt that he stood upon something firm.

Then he pulled the plug of wood into its place, and narrowly escaped a severe blow upon the head with it as it came down.

The sensation Captain Macheath felt now was anything but an agreeable one.

He was in a place that he could not move in in any direction but downwards or upwards, and he was in total darkness.

There was no hold for his hands, so he was forced to trust to chance.

Cautiously Macheath put down one foot off the ledge that he stood upon, and then he felt another such a one below, at a distance of about six inches, and from that moment he felt quite easy as to the mode of descent, for that he was on the top stairs of a little flight of steps was sufficiently apparent.

He descended very carefully, for he was rather afraid of hitting his head.

But after getting down no less a number than eighteen of the steps, he found that they ceased, and that he stood upon a flat surface.

Yet he was in the most profound darkness, and he felt all round him without being able to find any mode of outlet.

Under these circumstances, he proceeded right on for about six steps, and then, as he kept his hands stretched out before him, he felt something move to the touch.

At first he started back.

He thought he had touched some person.

But it was only for a moment that such an idea took possession of him, and he immediately advanced and found that what he had touched was a blanket.

After a moment's reflection, Macheath decided not to tear the blanket down; but he moved his hands along until he reached the edge of it, and then he drew it aside, and in a moment he saw where he was.

The blanket covered the entrance to the cave, which was about thirty feet in length and as many nearly in breadth.

The roof was rather low; but by the light of the turf fire, which was faintly burning in one corner, Captain Macheath was able to look well about him.

The walls were composed of hammered earth, and projecting from them in some places were the gnarled roots of old trees which flourished in the wood overhead.

The floor was earth likewise, but hammered quite hard; and from the state of the atmosphere, it was quite evident that there was some mode of ventilation and some sort of chimney by which the smoke from the fire made its escape.

Of furniture there was nothing in the place but a very rough wood table and some stools, apparently got up by the same hand.

An old chair stood in one corner, and upon some shelves fastened by some screws to the walls there were many little odd articles, and a quantity of cooked and uncooked meat as well as some bread.

A large pitcher was in another corner, with a piece of thick board over it, and upon peeping in Macheath found that it contained ale.

"Well," said Captain Macheath, "one might live here a little while in preference to a gaol above ground. It is rather dark, though."

Upon one of these shelves he found a candle stuck in a little square piece of clay by way of a candlestick.

He speedily ignited it at the fire, which spread an agreeable warmth in the place.

What most surprised Captain Macheath was that he could perceive no dampness in the cave.

From this circumstance he came to the conclusion that it was very old indeed, and that from the constant presence of the fire, which no doubt was never permitted to go out, it had got in time so warmed, and the walls and floors so baked, that the damp vapours of the earth could not penetrate into the place.

"Very good," said Captain Macheath. "I am certainly an uninvited guest, but I will make myself as welcome as I can for all that."

With this Captain Macheath placed some of the cooked meat upon the table, and pouring out a portion of the ale into a brown jug, he sat down, quite determined to enjoy himself as well as he could.

In the midst of all this, though, Macheath was not unmindful of his safety.

He looked carefully to his pistols, and ascertained that they were in excellent order, and he kept his ears open to the lightest sound that might warn him of the approach of anyone.

Half an hour thus passed away, and Macheath had, by an ample meal of venison and ham, fortified himself against the pangs of hunger, at all events for the rest of the day.

He now rose to his feet, and taking the candle in his hand, determined to make what discoveries he could in the cavern.

At first sight there seemed nothing to see but what one might take in at a glance.

But Macheath soon found that such was not the case.

He found in one corner another old dingy blanket hanging up, which, by the action of time, and the smoke and heat, partook of the colour of the wall.

"Oh!" said Captain Macheath, "my friends have got an inner apartment, which I will take the liberty of examining."

With the candle in his left hand, he, with his right, moved the old blanket aside, and found on the other side of it a cave about half the size of the outer one.

In this inner cavern it was quite evident that people were in the habit of sleeping, for the floor was covered in many places with old clothing

and rushes, and such other substitutes for bed as the neighbourhood might afford to those who were not very particular.

It was while Macheath was looking round him that he thought he heard a slight noise just overhead.

After listening attentively, he was convinced that footsteps passed over the roof of that part of the cave.

"Someone comes," he said. "I will take my seat by the fire and take the affair easy."

With this view, Macheath sat down by the turf fire again, and kept his eyes fixed upon the blanket.

Each moment he felt more and more convinced that someone was coming, and he could see that the blanket was slightly agitated by a current of cold air that came from the preserve above.

Another moment and Macheath heard the lump of wood pulled back into the hollow of the tree, and then footsteps sounded on the narrow stairs.

The blanket was pulled aside and a man came into the cavern.

"Good day, my friend," cried Captain Macheath.

At the moment the man was so terrified that he stood as still as though he had been turned to stone.

Then, with a shout of dismay, during which the words—

"I didn't do it!" came from his lips, he turned and tried to escape from the place.

But that was just the thing that Macheath did not mean that he should do.

Springing from the chair Macheath caught him by the back of the neck and dragged him into the cave again.

The man's dismay suddenly turned to rage.

He struggled violently and drew a knife.

"Fool!" Macheath cried, in a voice of thunder, "Throw down that weapon at my feet, or you die!"

Then again the fellow, who seemed to think he had been seized by some officer of justice, began to tremble and whine.

"Oh! no—no," he cried; "it wasn't me. Murder—murder! They did it among 'em, they did, and buried the body under Smythe's bed. Oh! I didn't do it, and they wouldn't give me my share. Oh! good sir, let me go, do. Oh! dear —oh! dear."

"Don't be a fool!" said Macheath.

"No, sir. Oh! dear sir, no. Would you like a nice young hare, sir?"

With this the man held up a hare.

"Anything, sir, you like," the man continued; "only don't have me up about it. I am as innocent as a lamb, sir, indeed I am, and, you see, I'm quite a boy."

CHAPTER XXXVI.

STARTLING ADVENTURES WITHIN THE CAVE.

MACHEATH found it quite in vain to attempt to say anything while the fears of the man overcame him in such a way; but he took care to keep between him and the opening of the cavern, so that he should not have the opportunity of making another bolt to escape him.

Captain Macheath could see that, notwithstanding he was a long, hulking sort of fellow, he was very young, and he calmly waited until he had said all that his troubled conscience dictated,

"Have you done?" Captain Macheath demanded, when from sheer want of breath the other paused.

"Oh! dear, yes, sir. Anything you like."

"Very well," said the Prince of the road. "Listen to me. In the first place you must know that I am not only well armed, but that I am accustomed to defend myself, so any attempt at mischief on your part will fall on yourself. Do you understand me?"

"Oh! dear, yes, sir."

"Very good. Now who are you?"

"Why, sir, you'd hardly believe it, but they will try to make out that I am a poacher."

"Indeed," said Macheath, smiling. "Well, how many of you belong to this cavern, or know of it, and make a practice of coming to it?"

"There are six of us, sir, besides Peter; but Peter is only a boy, you see, sir, and I don't count him."

"Very well," Captain Macheath returned. "Now I will calm your feelings by telling you that I am a highwayman, and that I came into this place only to save myself from those who chased me into the wood."

"Why, then, you are the great Captain Macheath?"

"I am."

"Oh! lor'," said the other. "What a treat—oh! dear. I heard 'em all on the road looking for you. Oh! how comfortable I feel to be sure. I thought you were some officer from London, and that you had no end of others all ready to pounce upon a fellow. I feel quite another thing now. My name, do you know, is Luke. They call me Lanky Luke; but Luke without the lanky is my name."

"Am I welcome here?" Macheath asked.

"To be sure. Yes. Oh! of course, you are. They won't find you in this out-of-the-way place You are as welcome as flowers in May. And yet—yet—now I come to think—"

"What do you think?"

"Ned is a thorough bad one, and so is Bill, and they lead the others. No; you had not better stay here, captain. There are some of the fellows and Peter, the boy, too, who cannot be trusted. Be off with you before they come. I know 'em—I know 'em."

There was such an air of sincerity about the manner in which Luke uttered these words that Captain Macheath believed him implicitly.

"I am much obliged to you, Luke, for your friendly caution," he said; "but my danger in the wood while daylight lasts is so great that I feel myself compelled to risk something here, and to try to make some terms with your companions. I can pay them well."

"There's something in that," said Luke.

"When do you expect them?"

"They may come at any time, or not at all to-day, for all I know," Luke replied. "But now I am here I'll stay if you make up your mind to do so, and I'll say all I can to make things pleasant. How came you to know of our old cavern, though? We thought we had the secret all to ourselves?"

"It was a mere accident made me acquainted with it," Captain Macheath replied. "I will pay liberally for shelter until dark, and then I will leave, and the secret shall remain with me as safely as if you had it only in your own bosoms."

"Hush!" said the poacher, and he put his hand up to his ear in an attitude of listening.

"What do you hear?"

"Some of our lot coming. They may take your being here amiss, or they may not. It's just as it happens. But, mind you, I will be your friend, and if anything really goes amiss I'll let you know."

"Thank you," said Captain Macheath, as he held out his hand to Luke, who gave it a friendly pressure—"thank you. It is a strange thing that in the worst extremity of my fortunes I never failed to pick up a friend; and it is equally true as strange that that friend never repented of holding out the hand of kindness to me."

Captain Macheath now heard the sound of footsteps descending the stairs.

The blanket was drawn aside, and two men of repulsive aspect made their appearance in the cavern.

It happened that the first person they cast their eyes upon was their companion, Luke.

They did not see Captain Macheath, who was close to the turf fire and rather in the shade.

If they did observe the figure of a man, they, of course, concluded that it was one of their own comrades.

"There's no end of a row in the preserve," said one of them. "They say that Macheath, the highwayman, is there, and that they are determined to have him out somehow."

"He was there," said the captain, stepping forward, "but he is here now."

The two men started back, and one of them pulled from under his smock-frock the barrel and the butt of a gun, so made that they could be fitted together in a moment.

"What is all this?" the poacher cried. "Are we sold at last? Keep off, will you!"

"We ain't quite done yet, Ned," said the other, "while I have got my little single barrel here."

"I don't know," said the captain, "what you are both putting yourselves out of the way for. My name is Macheath, and I found out your cave by mere accident; and being hard pressed by my enemies in the preserve above, I came to it as a temporary refuge. What you can have to say against that, or how it will serve you to pick a quarrel with me, I don't know?"

"But how are we to know who you are?"

"Stand out of the way!" said the man with the gun—"stand out of the way; Ned and I'll put an end to the matter by shooting him at once. That will be the best plan of all. Stand out of the way!"

"Hark ye," said Captain Macheath, sternly; "if you don't this minute put down that gun, I will compel you."

"You compel me?"

The last three words were scarcely out of the fellow's mouth, when Macheath made such a dash at him, that the poacher could not discharge the piece as he had fully intended to do.

Captain Macheath wrested the weapon from his hands, and swinging it round, dealt him such a blow upon the head with the butt-end of it, that down he went insensible.

"Take that!" said Captain Macheath. "If you think that I am going to stand here and let an idiot like you present a gun at me, you are very much mistaken indeed. Now, Mr. Ned—if that's your name—I have had no quarrel with you. You are poachers, and I am a highwayman. What in the name of all that is rediculous should set us by the ears together?"

"I don't know," said the fellow. "I don't want to quarrel with anybody, not I; only Lu...

CAPTAIN MACHEATH

THE
PRINCE OF THE HIGHWAY.

AT A HEADLONG PACE CAPTAIN MACHEATH RODE TO MEET THE ST. ALBAN'S COACH.

NO. 13.

had no business to bring a stranger into the old cave."

" No," said Luke, " nor did I."

" That is true," said Macheath. " I can tell you that Luke, far from bringing me here, found me here, and was as much surprised as you were. I found out your cave by an accident ; and to save your comrade Luke, here, from any suspicion of having brought me here, I will tell you how I found it out. I was hiding in a tree not far from here, and saw a man and a boy open the trap. The boy was called Peter."

" It must be so," muttered Ned.

" It is so."

" Well, Captain Macheath," Ned grumbled, " we do not wish to do the thing that's unhandsome. We are poachers, and if the secret of our cave is known we may as well go and give ourselves up and get transported at once, for our living has gone likewise. If you keep our secret, and be off soon, there's no harm done, except to George's head, which you needn't have given such a crack."

" There I differ from you, friend," said Captain Mac heath, with a smile. " It was evident from George's conduct that his head was very hard, and I felt, therefore, that it required a very good crack to produce any effect upon it. I will keep the secret of your cave to my dying day, and beyond that if you wish it ; so don't be putting yourself and your comrades out of the way on that score. Deal fairly with me, and I go at dark : but I tell you I am not afraid of you nor all who may come here, and that I will make such a racket about your heads if you play any pranks with me as shall make you remember to-day as long as you live. I don't say that as a threat, but as a warning," continued Macheath, quietly.

" Oh ! well—well, there's no occasion," said Ned, who was evidently cowed, as all bullies are, by Macheath's manner. " There's no occasion to make any disturbance. It's all right now. The others will drop in soon, and then you can make yourself quite comfortable, you know."

" I intend to do so," Captain Macheath replied ; " and if I mistake not, some of them are coming now."

The captain was right.

In the course of a moment or two Peter and the man with whom he seemed to have so close an alliance, offensive and defensive, made their appearance, accompanied by a coarse, brutal-looking man, with violently red hair.

At the sight of Captain Macheath there was a general consternation ; but Ned took upon himself to explain and to smooth over every difficulty, although to Macheath's apprehension his manner of doing so was anything but pleasant, as to him it just translated itself into—" Don't say anything just now, as it may be dangerous, but wait a little until I give you a hint to speak, and then we will do something."

In the course of five minutes more another man made his appearance, and he was the most repulsive-looking of the whole lot.

He was short and thick set, having a kind of roll in his walk, as though very unsteady on his feet.

His features were thick and coarse.

His hair was nearly black, and he had the peculiarity of never looking anyone in the face.

It was evident that obstinacy was the fellow's prevailing characteristic, and that he was decidedly one of the most strong-headed brutes that ever walked the earth.

This man evidently was looked upon by the others as the leader, and his opinion was eagerly listened to.

In a clamouring sort of way it was explained to this newcomer who and what Captain Macheath was, and he regarded him in silence for some few moments beneath his knitted brows.

" How now !" he at length cried. " Are we to be turned out of house and home by highwaymen ? Eh—eh ?"

Captain Macheath made him no answer.

" What do you mean by this ?" he cried. " Are you dumb ?"

" He's rather a dangerous fellow," said one of the men. " Don't go near him, there's no knowing what he may do all of a minute."

" Oh ! ain't there, indeed ?"

With this the fellow waddled up to Macheath — for all he could accomplish in the way of walking was something in the shape of a waddle—and set his arms akimbo.

" Look, Mister Prince of the Highway," he cried, " we don't let lodgings here, and I should advise you in a friendly way to take yourself off about as quickly as you conveniently can. Do you hear ?"

" I hear," said Captain Macheath, calmly.

" Well, and hearing, do you understand ?"

" Perfectly ; but I don't intend to go."

" You don't intend to go ? Come, that's a good one. I'll soon see whether you intend to go or not. Oh ! I am used to such customers as you are, as my friends here know well enough. Are you a bruiser or a wrestler ? Speak the truth."

" A little of both," the captain replied, with a placid smile.

" Oh ! you are—are you ? Then here goes for a tumble. Don't you interfere, my lads. These long slabs of fellows are easily upset, and you'll soon see how he will lower his tone after taking the measure of our floor on his back. Now, old chap, just look to yourself, for I am not at all particular, when I get a chap in a hug, where I pitch him to."

" Then I must not be particular, I suppose ?" said Captain Macheath.

" Not a bit."

The man made a rush at Captain Macheath, and caught him round the loins ; but notwithstanding the exertions he made, and which brought up almost all the blood in his body to his face, he could not move him, and then he was forced to let his pent-up breath go.

This was just the moment that Captain Macheath was waiting for, and taking instant advantage of it, he fairly lifted the ruffian off his feet and hurled him into a far corner of the cavern.

" Will that do ?" the captain demanded.

The fellow lay without breath or motion.

" You have killed him," said one of the others.

" Not at all," said Macheath, " such a fall as that may break a bone perhaps, but it don't kill. Throw a pailful of water over him if you have got one, but you will soon find him get up again."

" Murder !" said the discomfited fellow, in a low voice.

" There, you see," said Macheath, " I told you so."

Two of the other fellows now helped their leader to his feet.

His face was ashy pale, and he trembled so that he could scarcely manage to stand at all.

After a great effort, however, he managed to put on a sickly kind of grin.

"Well, old fellow," he said, holding out his hand to Captain Macheath, "you wrestle well—very well. I don't mind a few falls. Come, we will make merry now."

"As you please," Macheath replied. "All I can say is, that I came here for shelter, and I have met with nothing but attempted violence from one or another of you. I promise to keep your secret, as, indeed, why should I not? What earthly good could it do me to do otherwise?"

"Oh! well, we understand each other now, old friend. The past need not trouble us; come, we will be merry. Get some of the old wine out, comrades."

"What, have you wine here?" demanded Captain Macheath.

"Oh! yes," said the leader of the poachers. "The fact is, a great lord's mansion in this neighbourhood is shut up, while he is somewhere abroad, and there's a good cellar of wine that we have found the way into, and on drizzling, dark nights, when it's difficult to see your hand before your face, we bring away a few dozen. By the time he comes back he will have an empty cellar."

Macheath looked at his watch.

It wants yet some time to the period when I shall make an attempt to leave this place, so I will take a glass with you, at all events," he said. "At dusk I will try to get away."

"That you will easily manage. There is no moon to-night, and the trees in the preserve cast such shadows, that as long as you make no noise, you may get along famously. Come, master, let us enjoy ourselves while we can; life's short, you know."

As the fellow said these last words he winked at the man who had been first seen by Macheath with the boy, and that worthy burst out laughing.

The wink and the laugh that followed it set Captain Macheath thinking what it could possibly mean.

From that moment he became all but certain that there was some plot on foot regarding himself.

"I will watch these rascals narrowly," he thought, "and woe be to them if they try to play me any trick. They may succeed, since there are so many to one, in killing me, but they shall find I am not to be very easily overcome."

There was now a general kind of a bustle in getting more lights, during which the man named Luke contrived to pass Captain Macheath and slightly pinch his arm to attract his attention.

Then he whispered one word—

"Poison."

Captain Macheath did not make any imprudent start or exclamation.

He heard it as though he heard it not.

By a slight touch of Luke's foot with his own he managed to let him know that he was fully cognisant of the friendly warning.

It had not entered Macheath's mind that even these men could be such desperate villains as to try to take his life by poison; but yet he could not for a moment doubt that such was the case.

Of course he determined to be upon his guard.

The men cleared the table in the middle of the cave, and began to place glasses upon it.

"My shoulder ain't quite so supple as it was, but we will make merry for all that, and live till we die," shouted the leader of the poachers. "It ain't always the strongest that live the longest, is it, Captain Macheath?"

"Certainly not."

"Ha! ha! You never uttered a truer word than that in all your life. Now, comrades, quick, and get all ready. Who knows how many of us may be alive and kicking by cock-crow?"

"Life is an uncertain possession, I admit," said Macheath, "and therefore I am a great advocate for enjoying it while we can."

"And so am I—so am I. I will just pop into a cellar and get the wine, and then we shall be all right"

With these words the fellow went into the inner cavern, and after being absent for about five minutes, he returned with two bottles in his hand, and placed them on the table. Carefully putting his hand upon one of them, he said—

"We don't want more than one light; surely we can see the way to our mouths? One light will be plenty."

Two lights had been lit, but now one of them was extinguished, so that a semi-darkness reigned in the cave.

Even the ferocious countenance of the man who called himself the leader of the gang was but dimly visible; but yet his eyes evidently had about them a fiendish, malicious twinkle, which more and more had the effect of convincing Macheath that Luke was right.

"Come now, sit down, old fellow; all's right," cried the ruffian. "The brave and honourable guest that we have here will take his own bottle all to himself, you see, while we drink together. It looks more like as if we thought something of him, you see; and so we do, and I hope we shall have him with us a long time, that I do."

"Thank you," said Captain Macheath. "I am, then, to drink by myself?"

"If you please, and then you can fill as often as you like, you know, without at all waiting for us."

"Oh! thank you; that will do."

The candle was just about half arm's length from Macheath as he sat by the captain, and the latter, since he had taken his seat, no longer kept his hand upon the bottle that he intended for himself and his comrades.

"Come, come," he said, "we waste time."

"Yes," said Macheath, placing his right hand on the bottle intended for him. "We do. But I hope to be better acquainted with all of you, my friends."

As he said these words he waved his left arm, so as to give emphasis to the words, "all of you," and upset the candle.

Nearly complete state of darkness ensued, for the turf fire was at its lowest ebb now, and, taking advantage of the moment, Macheath changed the bottles, taking the captain's one for himself, and placing his by the captain's hand.

"Halloa," said the ruffian, "all right—light up again. Light up. That will do. We have no stint of matches. There's no harm done."

"I really must apologise," said Captain Macheath.

"Not at all—not at all. There's no occasion. Accidents will, of course, happen at times to the best of us."

The candle was speedily lighted, and when it was placed upon the table again, they found Macheath's right hand still clasped round the neck of the bottle, as it had been before the upset, and they little suspected that it was not the bottle he had clutched before.

The leader of the poachers glanced at him, and was satisfied.

"Upon my life, you are a great orator, Mister

Macheath," he said, laughing; "for you suit the action to the word, you do, and away goes the candle. But it's of no consequence; all I say is—drink."

"With pleasure," said Captain Macheath, as he poured out a glass of the wine.

"Now, my lads," said the leader of the poachers—"now, my lads, push me your glasses, and I'll fill them. "All's right, you know! We shall yet live many a long day, I hope, aye! and a night, too, in our old cave, that has sheltered us so long."

"Not a doubt of it," said Captain Macheath.

The glasses were all filled, and while the leader of the poachers was so busy doing so Macheath caught Luke's eye and shook his head.

Luke nodded, and Macheath then felt certain that he fully understood him, and would not drink the wine.

"Bumper—bumper! all," said the leader of the poachers, as he raised his glass. "Now, Mister Macheath, when we take a glass in this sort of enjoying way, the first thing we drink to is the Old Cave."

"Very good."

"So, my boys, I give you the toast of 'The Old Cave!' and Mister Macheath will drink it, I know, in a bumper at once, and leave nothing in the glass. 'The Old Cave!—the Old Cave!' Are you all ready?"

"Yes—yes! All ready."

"Then here goes, and much good may it do us."

"Amen!" said Captain Macheath, as he drank his glass of wine clean up, while the captain and his companions did the same, with the exception of Luke, who cleverly tossed his glass of wine over his shoulder, and then put down the empty glass as though he had drunk it.

When this was done, and the leader of the poachers saw that Captain Macheath's glass was quite empty—indeed, he had watched him drink it, that there should be no mistake about it—he leaned back and laughed cunningly.

"I wish you would let me know the joke?" said Captain Macheath.

"Oh! it's nothing—it's nothing. Take another glass, that's all. I like to see you enjoy yourself. Don't we, comrades?"

"Oh! dear—yes," they all said.

"I will take another glass," said Captain Macheath; "but you must all fill, and this time I will give you a toast."

"Hurrah! All right. Put your glasses this way, comrades. We will all fill, of course. Glass for glass. And now let us have the toast of the great Macheath. How do you feel, captain?"

"Quite charming!" said Macheath—"quite charming."

At this reply the leader of the poachers roared again with laughter; indeed, his conduct was so indiscreet, that more than one of the rascals winked at him to be cautious.

He was a little more quiet accordingly.

"All right," he said. "All's right as possible. Silence for Macheath's toast. Here we are with our glasses quite full. By-the-bye, Mister Macheath, how do you like this wine?'

"Very well indeed."

"You like its flavour?"

"I do," Captain Macheath replied; "I flatter myself I am a pretty good judge of wine, and this appears to me to be particularly pure and good. I feel tolerably certain that there is nothing in it."

"Oh—oh! That's good. Oh! oh!"

The leader of the poachers laughed so immoderately that he nearly fell from his stool, but Captain Macheath did not make any remark about his conduct, and as the others called loudly now for the toast, the captain rose to propose it.

"Gentlemen," he said, "the toast I have to propose is one that is common as an expression in society at large. I don't pretend that it has any over-particular application to the present company, except so far as we are all a little adverse to the laws, and therefore may be able to fully appreciate the sentiment. Are you all ready, gentlemen?"

"All—all."

"Then I give you 'The cunning fox that outwitted himself!'"

The glasses were all emptied, with the exception of Luke's, and he got rid of his wine as before.

The fellows looked at each other a little uneasily, for they did not at all like the wording of the toast, and their leader looked serious.

But he soon rallied, and then he said—

"Pray, what is the explanation of that?"

"There is no explanation at all," Captain Macheath replied; "only it is well, I think, to drink to the cunning fox who outwitted himself, because there is really no knowing what may happen to him in consequence."

"Well, you are a strange fellow."

"Allow me to return the compliment."

"Come—come! we won't quarrel about nothing."

"I never was further from any desire to quarrel than now," said Macheath. "I must confess that I am perfectly satisfied, and your wine is excellent, let it have come from whose cellar it may. I don't think a whole bottle of this would do a fellow any harm."

"You don't?"

"Certainly not. Why should it?"

"Oh! there is no reason at all why it should. How do you feel now? Pretty well—eh? You don't feel at all queer, do you?"

"Not in the least."

"But I do," said a mournful voice from the lower end of the table; "I do, I can tell you. Oh! what have you been about, you stupid fool? I don't feel all right at all."

"Why, what's the matter with you?"

"That's just what I should like to know. I—I shall go down in a minute or two—I know I shall. Oh! dear—oh! dear."

"Good gracious!" said the leader of the poachers, "what is the meaning of it? Mister Macheath, ain't you ill? Don't you feel queer? Tell me only that you feel queer, rather, and it will be such a satisfaction. You must, you do feel queer!"

"Not at all."

"Then—I—do."

"Well," said Captain Macheath, quite calmly, "I thought you did not look the thing exactly, my worthy friend, several times during the last few minutes; but you ought to know best, of course. I hope there was nothing wrong in your wine?"

"Wrong—wrong! what do you mean? Oh—oh! The old cavern is beginning to go round and round with me."

At this moment two of the gang fell from their stools to the floor of the cavern, where they lay perfectly insensible.

Captain Macheath seized the leader by the arms and bawled in his ear—

"Here's to the fox that outwitted himself.

Ha! ha! my friend. Life is short. I changed the bottles!"

The leader of the poachers upon hearing this fell backwards, stool and all, and Captain Macheath rose to his feet.

"I cannot say what abominable drug was put in the wine that it was intended I should drink," he said. "You know best yourselves, and you must take the consequences of it; and whatever they may be, you will recollect that I have nothing to do with them. I hate poison and poisoners. There cannot be in all the catalogue of crimes for which the worst of the human race have been famous any one that can for enormity come near to poisoning. I now leave you to take the consequences of your own acts."

Not one of the villains was in a condition to answer him, and Macheath prepared to quit the cave.

It was then that Luke stepped up to him.

"Captain Macheath, after what has happened here to-night this is no place for me," he said, overcome with emotion. "Will you let me go with you?"

"Certainly I will, with pleasure."

"And you will trust me?"

"Most assuredly," Captain Macheath replied. "You have already done me too great a service for me to dream for a moment that you would play me false now. Come with me; for I can very well imagine that these rascals were never fit companions for you, and probably after this night they might guess that you had some hand in the business, if they live over this affair, which they know best about."

"Oh! yes," said Luke, "they will live, but they did not at all intend that you should. The poison is only, after all, a very powerful sleeping draught, and while you were under the influence of it they would no doubt have given you up to the officers or murdered you."

"Come, then, Luke," said Macheath, "let us leave this place at once. It is no fit one for either you or I. I do not desire any further revenge upon these rascals than I have had. Let them lie, like drunken swine, where they are, until they recover in the ordinary course. We will leave them."

"Oh! dear, won't you take me?" said a voice.

Macheath turned, and saw the boy.

The captain shook his head.

"No; you are by far too amiable a youth for me to have anything to do with," he said. "It's a good thing for you that they were not liberal enough to give you a glass of wine, so you can stay and nurse all your friends here, who may be in need of your assistance."

Captain Macheath took no further notice of Peter, but proceeded at once, with Luke's assistance, to leave the cave.

In the course of a very few minutes they were in the open air.

It was a most exquisite relief to Macheath to be able to breathe once ngain the cool, pure, fresh air, and for some minutes he could do nothing but stand and inhale it with rapture.

"This is pleasant after being so long in the cave," Luke said.

"It is delightful," Macheath replied. "I only wonder how those late friends of yours could bring their minds to pass much of their time in such a place. I would rather lay my head in the open wood upon a few decayed leaves than sleep upon a bed of down in such a place as that we have just left."

"It is not very inviting, but I hope never to see it again; and I daresay you don't want particularly to do so?"

"Far from it, Luke," Macheath said. "I am to the full as sick of it as you can be. It is a pity that there should be such a place and in such hands; but as it really has afforded me a shelter for a few hours, I will not betray the secret of its existence. How shall we get clear of the wood? Probably you know more of it than I do?"

"Oh! yes; I know every nook and corner of it, and there will be no difficulty in our leaving it."

"Do you think so?" said Macheath. "Are you aware that it is well guarded at every outlet upon my account, and that there are sentinels placed all round it within hail of each other on purpose to intercept me, if I should make an attempt to leave it? For they are pretty sure that I am in it somewhere."

"Oh! yes, I know all that; but if you will follow me I will take you quite clear of it easily."

"Lead on, then."

Upon this, the first thing that Luke did was to lie flat upon the ground for a few moments and listen intently.

"Do you mind wet feet?" he asked, as he rose from the ground.

"Not particularly, if there's any good to be got by wetting them."

"The good will be the escape from the wood," said Luke.

"All right, then, I don't mind wet feet at all, so lead on," said the captain. "If that is the only harm I shall come to, I shall think little of it."

"Don't speak, then, except in a whisper, and keep as close to me as you can. In a little while we will leave this place behind us."

Macheath could not at all conceive how he was to escape from the wood; but he placed the most implicit confidence in his new friend, and followed him closely.

And now, even in the darkness, which was intense, it was quite a wonderful thing to see with what tact Luke made his way through the dense wood.

He never appeared to be at a loss, or deviated to the right or to the left of his even course with any appearance of hesitation.

On he went, until suddenly pausing, he laid his hand upon Captain Macheath's arm.

"There is one of the sentinels," he whispered.

Captain Macheath was a little startled at this intelligence. Looking forward in the darkness, he saw the dim outline and the figure of a man with his arms across his breast leaning against a tree.

"That's the fellow," said Luke, "that went about the wood with a double-barrelled gun firing into the trees."

"Is it?" cried Macheath.

"Yes. He is well-known as a brutal fellow."

"Then, my friend Luke, do you know it will be a very severe trial to me to be forced to leave this place without punishing him for his brutality."

"It will be hazardous."

"Never mind that," said Macheath. "Will it seriously jeopardise our escape? If so, I will give up the idea; but I must confess it will give me great pleasure to be even with the rascal and pay him the debt I owe him."

"It may be done. You do not want to kill him?"
"Oh! no—no."

"Well, immediately in front of him there is a deep, stagnant ditch, full of duckweed and in anything but a savoury condition," Luke said. "Now I may as well tell you that the course by which we are to escape is under a little bridge that will take us clear of the wood and beneath which there is a running stream. No one will think that you have a sufficient knowledge of the place to venture under there in the dark, as it looks bad, and you will not be able to stand upright there."

"Is it close at hand?" Captain Macheath demanded.

"Quite; half-a-dozen steps to the right here would take us to it now, so what you are going to do, do quickly."

"I will only send him into the ditch."

Macheath crept gently forward until he got behind the tree against which the man was leaning, and then he doubled his fist.

Suddenly dashing out he knocked him down; but scarcely had he touched the ground when Macheath stooped over him, and, lifting him up bodily, threw him right into the centre of the ditch with a loud splash.

Of course, this was quite enough to spread an alarm among those who were placed to watch the outskirts of the wood, and the consequence was that they began calling to each other.

Luke seized Captain Macheath's arm.

"Come—come, quick!"

"It's done," said Captain Macheath. "I am ready."

They heard the man splashing about in the ditch as they rapidly left the spot.

Luke led the way into the little stream.

The passage under the bridge looked rather frightful.

Indeed, it was quite a matter of courtesy to call it a bridge at all, for it looked much more like a drain than anything else.

But Captain Macheath followed his guide.

In about two minutes they both emerged from it, never at any time having been above their knees in the water.

"We are safe now," said Luke. "Here is the high-road."

CHAPTER XXXVII.

THE ESCAPE FROM THE WOOD.

By scrambling up a rather steep bank they both reached the high road in safety.

"I owe you much," said Captain Macheath.

"No—no; not at all. But let us push on and get out of this neighbourhood as quickly as we can. Don't you hear the fellows calling to one another to keep a good look-out?"

"I do."

"Well, they will be soon running about everywhere," Luke said. "What direction would you like to take? I know all the roads well enough and can easily take you by any one you like."

"I want to go to the village of Kentish-town; but it is a good distance from here, of course?"

"Yes; but the London-road will take us, and then we shall have to turn off to the left and get round Kentish-town, which will be rather a long stretch; but that won't matter. I only wish we had a couple of good horses—we would soon do it."

"Ah! my friend," said Captain Macheath,

"this morning I had as good a steed as ever man bestrode; but the rascals killed her."

"So I heard. Let me think—"

"Of what?"

"Why, of how to get horses," said Luke. "There's a good horse or two in the parson's stables."

"You are not very particular, my friend."

"Not at all," said Luke, grinning. "The parson is too rich to miss a horse or two."

"Very good."

"Well, I was saying, if we could only get hold of a couple of good horses out of the rector's stables, it would be a capital thing, I think. What do you say to it, Captain Macheath?"

"I say Yes, if it can be done; it is quite clear to me that before I am twenty-four hours older I must have a horse, and it is very immaterial about whose stable it comes out of, provided it is a good one and I can make it attached to me—which there is no great difficulty in doing if you try it."

"That I believe, captain," said Luke—"that I believe fully, and if you give your free consent to the plan, I will take you to the parson's stables at once."

Macheath was rather amused at Luke's coolness, for he talked of stealing a couple of horses from the parson as calmly as though he projected something that was not at all of an out-of-the-way character.

By the time this little conversation regarding the parson's horses was over, they were out of earshot of the men who were keeping guard at the wood.

Luke led the way now from the main road into a lane, and then crossed a stile.

"We have only to get across a couple of meadows and we shall come to the parson's stables," he said to Captain Macheath; "which, I have reason to know, are not very well taken care of."

"One would think, though," said Macheath, "that if the horses are valuable they would be well taken care of."

"Yes; but the parson is not quite aware that the man who is supposed to sleep at the stables goes off to drink at the Crown every night, and that the horses are left to look after themselves."

"That will do," said Captain Macheath; "it would be quite a pity not to take some advantage of so lucky a chance."

They now crossed the two meadows in perfect silence.

Crouching down close to an iron hurdle fence, Luke listened for a short time.

"All is right," he whispered. "There's not a mouse stirring. Come on, this way; creep through the fence, and there's less chance of being seen."

They crossed the fence in this way, and then Luke led Captain Macheath right into a stable yard.

"There are a couple of capital nags in there," he said; "but the door is locked, I daresay, though I have known it to be left open as careless as possible; and so it is now—look."

The stable door was only on the latch, and both Luke and Macheath entered it.

The place was much too dark to make any choice of cattle in, so Macheath made up his mind to be satisfied for the present time with the first horse he could lay his hands upon; and accordingly he led one out into the yard.

Luke in a moment appeared with another.

"Don't mount," he said; "let's lead them to the high road first."

This was good advice, but Macheath said in a whisper—

"Can you find a saddle?"

"Oh! dear yes, to be sure; it would be a poor look out to go away without one. The harness-room is close at hand here. Only wait a few moments and I'll soon bring the requisites."

Luke was quite as good as his word, for he was back in a very short time, well loaded with all the requisites for a couple of horses.

"You seem," said Captain Macheath, "to understand this sort of thing, and to be particularly conversant with these premises likewise."

"Why, yes, I am a little—just a little. You see I was once a groom to the rector, and that's how I came to know the place."

"Oh! indeed. Then you probably know the horses likewise?"

"I know that there isn't a bad one in the stable, though I can't exactly say what ones we have hold of, for the old man has been buying some fresh bits of blood since I was in his employ."

While this little bit of conversation was going on, both Macheath and Luke were busy putting the saddles upon the horses, and as they were both very good adepts at that sort of work, they got done—notwithstanding it was in the dark—pretty well at about the same time, and they gently led the horses away.

It was necessary to pull up one of the iron hurdles to get the horses past that fence, but there was no difficulty in doing so, and then they quickly enough crossed the meadows.

They had to skirt the one next to the lane until they reached a gate, which Luke unfastened, and then they got safely into the lane.

"Now for it," said Luke; "get on, captain, as quick as you like, on the London road; and when you come to the turning to the left, which will lead round by Kentish-town, I will call to you, sir."

"That will do," said Captain Macheath.

He urged the horse on, and he was not a little gratified to find, by the pace of the creature, that it must be one of no ordinary value.

The canter that he put it to was remarkably easy, too, so that he was well satisfied.

The darkness effectually prevented him from seeing the colour or any of the points of his steed, but upon the principle that a good horse cannot be of a bad colour, he made up his mind that his was a beauty.

Several times he glanced behind him to see how Luke was getting on, and seeing that he kept the relative distance between them without breaking at all into a gallop, he was satisfied that his new friend's steed had likewise turned out to be of the right sort, and that they were both superbly mounted.

"To the left," cried Luke, suddenly.

And Captain Macheath at once obeyed the direction, and found that they were among those beautiful green lanes that lie so thickly over that part of the country.

"The first to the left," again cried Luke; "and then the second to the right, if you please."

"Come," said Macheath, "you had much better take the lead in these lanes, for I confess I don't know them sufficiently well to be quite certain about my route; I might succeed in floundering through them somehow and in getting to my des-tination, but not with expedition; so I will follow."

"Very well, captain," said Luke. "I will lead now, if you like. I am not unmindful that I am not a companion for you."

"What do you mean, Luke?"

"Why, sir, as I have told you, I was the parson's groom, that's all; and before that I was a poor country fellow; and since that I have been a poacher, captain."

"And what follows from all that, Luke?"

"Why, just that as I have left the poaching, I must take to some sort of service again, that's all, sir. I understand a little bit of gardening, and I understand a horse, and, in fact, there's few things in and about a country house that I could not turn my hand to."

"Why, Luke, I can find you a master, then."

"Can you, sir? Really! and I without a character, too?"

"No; with a good character. I will take you myself. At Kentish-town I have a house, and a garden, and a wife."

"You don't say so, sir?"

"Indeed, but I do; and when I am away on the road it would give me a good deal of satisfaction to know that there was someone there upon whom I could depend as completely as I can upon you. So, if you like to enter my service and stay at home you may do so, and I can promise you liberal wages, at all events, and a good home."

"Can you doubt, sir, for a moment that I would grasp at the opportunity? It's the very thing I would like above all others."

"Then let it be considered as settled, Luke. And now we will push on for Kentish-town at once, and when you get there you may consider yourself quite at home."

"Well," said Luke, "this is indeed a change in my fortunes that I little expected or calculated upon. It has been a lucky thing for me that you came to the old cave, though those rascals were very near taking your life."

"Which they would have done but for you."

"Well, I am glad indeed that I had it in my power to warn you of your danger in time. Turn to the right, now, sir, and then we can push on for a mile without turning."

They rode on, and in due time drew up at the garden gate of Macheath's house at Kentish-town.

At the sound of the captain's footsteps Polly at once rushed out to meet him, and not observing that anyone was with him she cried—

"Oh! where have you been?"

"In all sorts of places, my dear Polly," he said. "But I am safe, you see, and although I really intended to have been here many hours ago this will be a good lesson to you after all—never expect me until you see me."

"I will think of nothing but the joy of seeing you here."

"That will be sufficient, Polly, and the pleasure of seeing you obliterates all the past from my recollection. Luke, take the horses. I will get a light and come to you, and show you the stables in a few minutes."

"Yes, sir," said Luke.

"Who is that?" whispered Polly. "Who is that?"

"A friend who chooses to serve me in the capacity of a servant. He has saved my life, and I have taken him into my service. He will be here always when I am absent, and he will rear sweet flowers for you, and in fact he will be serviceable in many ways, and I believe truly may be thoroughly trusted."

"If you trust him," said Polly, "I will."

"That is right; and now let us find something for supper, for to tell the truth I am rather hungry, and I promise you, Polly, that I will not leave home again until—"

"Until when?"

"To-morrow night, dear one," Captain Macheath replied; "and then I hope to be back to you before the dawn of another day, for it is not often I meet with such adventures as have fallen to my lot during the last four and twenty hours."

CHAPTER XXXVIII.

MACHEATH STOPS THE ST. ALBAN'S COACH.

MACHEATH passed the whole of the day ensuing at his house at Kentish-town.

He did not anticipate anything in the shape of danger there, for he felt quite confident that he was unknown in that neighbourhood, and that he and Luke had not been traced from the wood in which there had been so much peril.

Polly would fain have persuaded him to remain yet longer; but as the twilight approached, the temptation to take to the road again was too strong for him to resist.

"I will promise you to be cautious," he said, in reply to her entreaties; "and you shall be treasurer, too. There is all the money I have; and if I am successful, I hope to add soon a good round sum to it."

"And then you will leave this mode of life?"

"I will."

"You solemnly promise me that, Macheath?"

"I do, indeed," the captain replied. "As soon as we can call three or four thousand pounds our own, I promise you that I will forsake these perils of the road; but until then, Polly, it is my destiny to go out and take my chances upon the king's highway."

Polly felt that it would be quite useless to attempt to dissuade him from going.

She was fain to content herself by the promises that he would be careful of his safety.

She told him that such a promise gave her much satisfaction; but Captain Macheath replied with a smile—

"I make the promise to you as you ask for it; but my own opinion, Polly, is, that safety is not procured by taking care. Experience has taught me that my success has arisen from no care-taking, and that I have far oftener owed my safety to some piece of recklessness upon my part than to any foresight."

"Oh! no—no; I cannot think that."

"It is natural enough, Polly, that you should not think it," he replied. "I could hardly expect that you would. But I know it as a truth beyond dispute."

"Then I will bind you by no promises," said Polly, "for it is your safety only that I care for; so that that be accomplished, I care not how. But before you engage in any unusually hazardous adventure, I would ask you to bestow one thought upon me."

"A thousand!" said Captain Macheath, with a smile.

"Then I will be content."

The night was now creeping on; and agreeably to the order he had received, Luke brought Macheath the parson's horse, which had turned out to be such a good one.

"Hilloa! Luke, this is not the horse," said Macheath, as he looked at the animal. "It had one white foot and a small light-brown star upon the forehead. I noticed as much this morning."

"Not a doubt of it, sir. The horse had one white foot and a light-coloured star on the forehead, just as you say."

"Where are they now, then?"

"Why, you see, sir, as the horse happens to suit you, it is just as well that nobody should know him but ourselves, so I made bold to alter those little peculiarities. I have dyed the foot and the star."

"Oh! that is it."

"Yes, captain," Luke replied; "I will warrant now that not all the cunning and all the learning in the world could make that foot white again, or reproduce that star. The dye is a secret of my own."

"I am very much obliged to you, Luke, for your forethought," Macheath returned; "and I suppose I might meet the parson himself that owned the horse without the slightest danger?"

"Yes, captain; you might meet him and ask him the time of day, and what he thought of your horse, and yet he could not fancy it had ever been in his stable. It's a glorious creature, and worth a hundred pounds."

Captain Macheath mounted and patted the head of the animal.

"I don't quite think I shall ever make such a pet again of a horse as I did of the last one I had," he said. "But time may do wonders, and I naturally take to an animal after a little time."

"You will like this one, sir. May we expect you at any particular time, captain?"

"Well, no," Captain Macheath replied; "and yet it's time to get home before the first cock crows, so if you are up and stirring about that time, it may be as well to look out for me."

"I will, sir."

Macheath waved his hand to Polly, who was stationed at one of the windows of the cottage to see the most of him as he cantered away.

It was Captain Macheath's custom to wear a large horseman's cloak over his riding-dress when he sallied out, and when he got a mile or two from his starting-place would divest himself of the cloak, and rolling it up after the fashion in practice among soldiers, strap it to the back of his saddle.

He wore the cloak upon this occasion, and moreover, the hat he wore was very capable of acting as a further disguise, for one of the flaps had a loop and a button, which he could either let it down by, or fasten it up with, so that in a moment or two his appearance could be very strangely altered indeed.

These were the only precautions in the way of disguise that Captain Macheath generally took.

He trotted through the district of Crouchend, and taking his way right on to the north-west, reached the neighbourhood of Muswell-hill, and so on to the High North-road running directly through Highgate.

At the inns here situated it was customary for the coaches starting from the City to change horses, so that at that time the North-road was at all times rather an animated one.

"Well," said Macheath, as he trotted through Highgate, "there ought to be some business done between this and Barnet. We shall see—we shall see!"

Just before he reached the Wrestler's Inn a four-horse coach started at a rattling pace down the slope towards Finchley-common.

But Captain Macheath had no idea of interfering with the coach.

Its four horses were about two too many for him to manage, so he let it go on and gently trotted on until he passed the valley close to East-end, Finchley, and commenced the ascent upon the opposite side, which would take him right on to Barnet.

"Now," he said, "there ought to be a chance, and I won't be extremely particular as to the shape in which it presents itself."

He took off his cloak and carefully rolled it up and strapped it to the back of his saddle, and then he looped up his hat so that he had a clear view around him.

Then loosening his pistols in the holster, and setting himself in his seat, he felt that he was ready for any adventure.

Scarcely had Captain Macheath made these brief arrangements than he heard the tramp of a horse, and from the shortness of the step he could tell that a very small horse was approaching.

Drawing off a little to the side of the road he waited its approach, and in a few moments he saw a man mounted on a pony, that ambled along pretty well, though evidently hardly equal to the weight of his rider.

"Stand!" cried Macheath.

"Oh! dear, who's that?" cried the rider, in dismay.

"The deuce! if you like," said Macheath, as he rode up to his side. "Now, sir, who are you?"

"Oh! don't. I am nobody, sir, if you please. Who are you, pray?"

"I am somebody," Macheath replied. "I will trouble you for your cash, sir. You can't complain, as I rob nobody."

"No, sir—that is, yes, sir. But I'm a poor singer at one of the playhouses, and I've only got a matter of fifteen shillings in all the world."

"Whose horse do you ride, then?"

"It's my own, sir, if you please," the man said. "I ride into town and out every night, and I find it good for my health, you see, sir, and as I have not much time to spare, perhaps you will be so good as to let me go at once."

"Well, if you are a singer, let me have a touch of your quality in that line," said Macheath. "I am something of a singer myself, and am very fond of music. Come, sir, strike up. Let me hear the quality of your voice."

"Very good. What do you think of this?—

" ' *Since laws they were made for every degree,*
To curb vice in others as well as in thee,
Some day we will have your company
At Tyburn Tree.' "

This was so well sung that Captain Macheath no longer doubted the fact that the man was a professional singer.

"Hark you, my friend," he said. "You have a very good voice and a very good wit. It is a lucky thing for you that I can appreciate both, and particularly the latter. If I do ever get to Tyburn Tree, you are quite welcome to come and see me there; but now as you ride for your health, give me leave to tell you that you make one great and almost fatal mistake."

"Mistake, sir! Pray what is it?"

"You ride too small a horse," said Macheath

"and to convince you of it, I will trouble you to dismount and walk the rest of the way, while your little pony, who is not at all fit to carry so very good a singer, enjoys a run upon Finchley-common until the morning, and don't let me catch you on its back again, that's all, my worthy friend."

"But really—"

"Come—come! no buts for me," the captain interposed. "What do you take that to be—eh?"

"Oh! dear, I can't exactly pretend to say; but it feels very like the muzzle of a pistol near my ear."

"Very good," said Macheath. "If you have no desire that such an ear-wig should make any further progress into your brains, you will be wise enough to dismount at once."

The singer took the hint.

The moment he was on the road, Macheath turned the head of the pony in the other direction, and started it off at a gallop, leaving its discomfited owner some six miles from London on foot and no time to spare.

"Good night," said Macheath. "You can beguile the tedium of the way by practising a little more of the song you have been so very obliging as to sing to me just one verse of."

Humming the tune which the musician had sung, Captain Macheath went off at a trot.

He had not got a quarter of a mile from that spot when he heard the sound of wheels, and as a man on foot passed, he called out—

"What coach is that coming on the road?"

"The St. Alban's coach," said the man.

"Thank you—thank you!"

The man passed on, and Macheath, after listening for a few moments, discovered by the sound upon the road that it also was a four-horse coach.

"Be it so," said Macheath. "I will stop the St. Alban's coach, and see if there be anything to be got inside or out. It will be a hard case if I cannot make something like a decent night's work out of a whole coach-load of people."

Macheath stopped short on the road side, so as not to be actually in the way of the coach.

He watched it carefully as it came on, with its lamps casting a bright glow like an immense fire of flame on each side of the road, lending a passing lustre to the trees and bushes.

At a headlong pace Macheath dashed forward to meet the coach.

The driver pulled up instantly.

"Stir another foot and you are a dead man!" the captain cried. "Philip, keep a good aim at the coachman's head while I speak to the passengers."

Captain Macheath had upon more than one occasion found it to be a very good ruse at night to affect to speak to some associates.

"Oh! they are highwaymen," cried the coachman, "and there's no end of 'em. I can see their eyes glaring through the hedge like glow-worms. We are all dead men!"

"Peace!" cried Captain Macheath. "Not a hair of anybody's head shall be hurt, if no resistance be offered. Comrades, reserve your fire, and by no means use your pistols unless I give the word."

With this, having fully convinced everybody that the coach was stopped by a whole gang of desperadoes, of whom he was the captain, he rode up to the side of the coach.

"Are there any ladies here?" the captain demanded.

"Oh! yes—yes," said a female voice. "Pray

spare our lives, good Mr. Highway-gentleman! Me and my niece Jemima are the only ladies here. Oh! spare us, do, good sir."

"Be under no apprehension, madam. No violence is intended on any account if none be offered."

Dexterously taking from its socket one of the coach-lamps, Macheath held it close to the upper part of the door, so that it shed a clear light within the vehicle, while the shaded side of it was towards his own face.

The coach contained two ladies and two gentlemen.

One of the gentlemen was a mere youth, and looked very pale—the other was rather a ferocious-looking man, with a countenance expressive of great intemperance; and as the light fell upon him, he cried—

"What, are we to be robbed by vagabonds? I only wish I was armed. I would soon put an end to this affair. Ah! that I would—bother me if I wouldn't. Ah!"

"Sir," said Captain Macheath. "I will attend to you in a few moments. Where is Jemima?"

"Oh! gracious," exclaimed an old lady, who was wrapped up in a wilderness of shawls, "he wants my niece. Oh! sir, she is in the corner, sir. Pray have mercy upon us all!"

"My dear madam, you have no cause for apprehension," Macheath observed; "but I must see Jemima, if she pleases."

Upon this rather a pretty-looking young girl of about fifteen years of age emerged from the corner.

"I am afraid you are frightened, but you need not be," said Captain Macheath. "I will trouble your aunt for her money. I don't intend to ask you if you have any. Now, madam, be quick."

"Oh! dear, yes. There's my purse, and much good may it do you, you vill—no, I mean you nice man."

"I have no money, sir," said Jemima.

"But my father-in-law has," said the pale-faced youth, suddenly. "He has not only got a hundred pounds in gold with him, which he was going to give a madhouse-keeper to keep me, when I am not mad at all, but he has just put his gold watch in one of his boots, for fear you should see it."

"Oh! I'll serve you out for this, Master Harry, or the sun sha'n't rise to-morrow," growled the man with the forbidding face. "You young rascal!"

"What's all this about a madhouse?" Captain Macheath demanded.

"Nothing—nothing at all?" cried the man. "You mind your own business. All you have got to do is to rob us, my fine fellow, and be hanged for it at some other opportunity."

"You are a bold man," said Macheath. "Now, my lad, I ask you again what is all this about that you say concerning a madhouse? Never mind this man. I will protect you from him. Tell me the truth.

"The truth," said the lad, "is that by his ill usage this man killed my poor mother; but as I am still in his way, he is going to put me in a madhouse—and my hands are tied, and there is a man on the roof to help him. Nobody but this young lady here will believe that I am not mad. Oh! sir, if you can but find out a Captain Russel, who lives near to Whitehall, and tell him that the son of his old friend, Mr. Ambrose Hill, is in such a difficulty, he will save me."

The tone of voice in which this speech was spoken, rapid and affecting as it was, savoured nothing of insanity.

Twice or thrice the man of whom the lad so spoke made efforts to interrupt him, but a warning glance from Captain Macheath had the effect of letting him see that a perseverance in such a course might be dangerous.

"Well, sir," said the captain to the father-in-law, "what have you to say to all this?"

"Oh! the boy is mad—mad!"

"You and I differ in opinion," Macheath replied. "Allow me, my lad, to assist you from the coach. What do you think of him, Miss Jemima? Has he shown any symptoms of madness since you have been in the coach with him?"

"Oh! no—no!"

"He is as mad as a March hare, sir," said the man. "A likely thing that if he were not he would find time, in the midst of what I call his affliction, to praise this young lady's eyes in such an extravagant manner that the aunt was quite shocked."

"But the young lady was not," Macheath remarked, "and by saying that of him, you have given me the most convincing proof of his perfect sanity, for even by this light I can take upon myself to say that I have rarely seen such eyes."

"They are very, very beautiful," said the youth.

Macheath smiled as he helped him out of the coach, and released him from a rope that tied his hands behind his back.

"Keep close to me," he whispered to him. "I will protect you from anyone who means ill to you."

"Oh! how can I thank you?"

"Hush, we shall have plenty of time to talk," said Macheath. "Now, sir, I will trouble you for the hundred pounds and the gold watch you have so cleverly hidden in your boot."

"There's the money, and I only hope—well, well, my turn may come some day."

"Help!" cried young Harry; "help—oh! help!"

Captain Macheath turned hastily, and he saw a rough-looking fellow holding the lad by the collar and trying to drag him away.

"I belongs to the 'sylum," said the fellow. "He shall come along o' me. We are paid for taking him, and that's all we cares about. Come on, will you?"

The pistol Captain Macheath held in his hand was a heavy one, and without reversing it, he gave the fellow such a crack on the head with the barrel of it that he danced again.

Then Harry having the use of his hands, ran in upon him, and with more power than one would have expected from him, stripling as he was, knocked him down and left him rolling in the road, from which he very comfortably slipped over a little stone parapet into a drain.

Captain Macheath was sufficiently put out of temper at all this not to be very particular in his treatment of the father-in-law.

As he was not very quick or inclined to get the watch out of his boot, Macheath dismounted, and asked Harry to hold his horse for a moment.

"Now, sir," said the captain, "the watch!"

"You have got quite enough already. Be off with you, while you are in a whole skin," was the reply.

Scarcely were these words past the lips of the father-in-law, when he found out the truth that there is a retribution even in this world; for Macheath caught him by the leg, and in a moment he found himself on his back in the road.

Macheath did not trouble himself further to search for the watch.

Having a horsewhip tucked into a place in the saddle of his steed, he possessed himself of it, and began belabouring the father-in-law at such a rate that he did not know how soon to produce the watch.

"Oh! murder!" he cried—"murder! here's the watch! Stop it—stop it! Oh—oh! help! Stop the whip!"

"Oh! you have had enough of that, have you?"

"Yes. Gracious goodness, yes."

"Then, sir, take this lesson from me, and never show your brutal temper when you find that you have met your master. What is your name, sir?"

"Oh—oh! my name is Watts."

"Very well, Mr. Watts, now you may get up and resume your seat in the coach as soon as you please, for I and my comrades will soon be off now. Hilloa, my gallant Philip, you can draw off your eight men, and you, Stephen, can get out of the way with yours. Don't shoot the coachman, he has behaved very well."

"That's a mercy," groaned the coachman, "for I have been giving of myself up for a dead man any time this last ten minutes—that I have."

Watts gathered himself up from the middle of the road, and with many groans got into the coach again.

Macheath shut the door.

"Coachman, drive on!" he shouted.

"Oh! won't I," said the coachman. "With all the pleasure in life I'll drive on. Good night, gentlemen; you might have behaved much worse than you have; and if ever you stop me again I only hope you'll be just as civil and considerate as you have been to-night. Come up! Cluck—cluck!"

The horses started into a good trot, and the St. Alban's coach quickly disappeared from the scene.

The lad who had been rescued by Macheath from his father-in-law remained close to the horse.

"Well, Master Harry," said the captain, "who do you suppose I am?"

"A kind friend to me."

"That is a good answer, but you have heard of such a person as a highwayman, I suppose?"

"Yes," the lad replied; "and I have heard them spoke badly of, while I have heard such a person as a father-in-law spoken well of; but now I feel that in both cases people are wrong—for the highwayman has been a kind friend to me, and the father-in-law has been the worst of foes. Oh! sir, believe me, I am very grateful to you indeed."

Macheath could not but be very highly pleased indeed with this speech.

"What would you like to do?" he asked. "Have you a home that you could return to if I were to take you there?"

"Oh! no—no. This man Watts is master of what was my home. It is Captain Russel, near to Whitehall, whom I would like to go to. He was an old friend of my father's, and I can at once throw myself upon his protection."

"Are you sure of him?"

"As sure as I am of you."

"Very well, then," said Macheath. "I will charge myself with your safe conduct to Captain Russel. As I do not intend to remain on the road

longer to-night, you shall ride behind me, and I will take you to my home, where you can rest till morning."

The lad seemed hardly able to find utterance for his gratitude to Macheath for this offer, and the latter was so much pleased with the liberality and the frankness of Harry Hill's ideas that he felt as if he could have gone through any danger for him.

"If this Captain Russel be really the friend you believe him, your misfortunes will be at an end, and you will have the satisfaction of defeating your uncle," Macheath remarked. "But how was it that you accuse him of killing your mother? I think you made such an accusation?"

"I did—I did."

"Well—well, Harry, if it distresses you to say any more upon that subject do not do so."

"Oh! no—no. It is not talking about it that can add to my distress. I have gone through so much sorrow that it lies too deeply to be lightly ruffled by mere words."

Macheath was quite charmed by the elegant, yet simple, demeanour of the lad; and as they cantered on towards Kentish-town he felt quite a pleasure in listening to him.

CHAPTER XXXIX.

MACHEATH AND HIS YOUNG FRIEND.

"WHEN I spoke of Mr. Watts murdering my poor mother," continued Harry, "I do not mean that he actually lifted his hand against her and killed her; but she died through remorse and sorrow at having married such a man. My poor father had not been dead long before she began to think that Mr. Watts would be a good husband for her; and despite all my prayers and entreaties she married him."

"Ah!" said Macheath, "when a widow is bent upon marrying again all the world may rise up in arms to prevent her, and produce little effect."

"She soon found, sir, that it was only for what she had in goods and money that he married her; and to get entire possession of both he wearied her with solicitations, and when she was, for my sake, firm against them, he commenced a career of ill-usage which soon brought her to the grave."

"Well, I won't say serve her right, Harry," said Macheath, "because she was your mother, and I respect you; but I will say that if a woman, with a child or children, marries again, she don't fall exactly within the sphere of my sympathies, let what will happen to her."

"She died," added Harry, "leaving me the old house and all its contents. Watts tried to persuade me to let him have everything, on condition of giving me a hundred pounds a-year; and when I refused his offer, he commenced a series rather of annoyances than absolutely ill-usage, and finally spread about a report that I was mad, and yesterday brought a madhouse-keeper to the house, and treated me as you saw."

"Well, Harry, never mind," said Macheath. "I will take you to Captain Russel, you may depend, and all will be well. I only hope that you will not be deceived in him."

"My father saved his life once."

"That ought, indeed, to constitute a bond of union between you and him; but we shall see," said Captain Macheath. "You can make yourself comfortable for the night, and all will be well. In the morning I will lend you a horse, and we will ride to Captain Russel's house together."

"But, my dear friend, can you do that with safety?"

"Yes, certainly," Captain Macheath replied. "I can put on a very different aspect to that in which you now see me, and you will find that I can make my appearance in Whitehall without a tremor."

"I am glad to hear that, for not even to save myself from my mother's bad husband would I have you go into any danger."

"Do not fear for me. And now here we are close to my house, Harry, where I can promise you safety and quiet rest, at all events; and in the young fresh hours of the morning we will mount and go to London."

They had ridden at a good pace, so that now Macheath drew rein opposite the garden gate of his own cottage, and in a moment or two Luke appeared.

"Is that you, sir?"

"Yes, Luke; all is well. I have got a gentleman with me."

"Very well, sir. I will open the gate if you will ride in, sir. It's all clear, right on to the stable, sir. I will get a light directly, if you please."

Luke thought that it was much better, considering who and what Macheath was, not to get a light until the horse was right into the yard and the gate closed and locked.

But in a few moments the lantern was brought, and then Luke was not a little surprised to see a youth with Macheath.

"You need not think anything of the young gentleman's presence," said the captain. "He knows who and what I am, and I am quite sure he may be thoroughly trusted with the secret of my residence here."

"I should," said Harry, "be almost induced to kill myself if I imagined you thought me capable of any baseness towards you."

"Make yourself quite easy upon that head," said Captain Macheath. "I have no such thought, believe me; so now come in. We shall require both the horses to-morrow morning, Luke."

"Very good, sir."

Captain Macheath and his companion went into the house, where he soon introduced him to Polly and Annette; but notwithstanding they rung repeatedly for Luke, he was nowhere to be found, and as Polly had sent the servant to bed, they were obliged to wait upon themselves.

We can account satisfactorily for the absence of Luke.

When he let Macheath and Harry Hill into the premises by the garden gate he had seen, or thought he saw, the figure of a man skulking along the roadway.

Not feeling quite certain that such was the case, although his (Luke's) eyes were pretty well schooled to out-of-door sights, he had said nothing to Macheath upon the subject.

The moment he had put the horse in the stable he left the premises by another gate, and crept cautiously up the road close to the hedge for the purpose of discovering if he were right or wrong in his conjectures.

Luke had not got on far in this way before he ran his head against a man crouched down close to an old chestnut tree.

"Halloa!" said Luke. "Who are you?"

"Who are you?" said the man.

"Only a poor fellow looking for a job, sir."

"Ah! indeed, you are looking for a job, are you? What kind of a fellow are you?"

"Well, sir, I hardly know. The fact is, I am not very particular what I do so that it is honest, and I can earn a shilling or two, for times are very hard, perhaps as you know, sir."

"Do you belong to this place?"

"No, sir, I am on the tramp, and don't know what place it is. But I suppose it is Hampstead."

"Humph! I suppose you are a desperate coward?"

"Coward? No, sir, that I am not. I am afraid of nothing in the world, and my friends won't give me any help, because they will have it that I am as strong as a horse, and they keep on saying, 'Why don't you go for a soldier?' till I'm sick of hearing of them, sir, that I am."

"Well, my good fellow, I can give you a job that will not put shillings but guineas into your pocket. What do you say to that, my friend?"

"Say to it, sir? You have only to tell me what it is, and it is as good as done out of hand, sir."

"Then I can do you a good turn. In that house opposite to us there is a man that I have a warrant to apprehend. Now, he is rather a troublesome fellow, and as I am only single-handed here, of course, I am very glad to get some assistance."

"Yes, sir; who is he?" said Luke.

"Why, his name is Noakes, but that is of no sort of consequence," said the officer, for such the man was. "All you have to do is to help me to secure him, and I will put a pair of handcuffs upon him and take him away, and for the job I will give you a couple of guineas."

"But are you sure, sir, he is the man?"

"Quite. By mere accident I was here some days ago, and I saw him come out. I know his face so well that I cannot be mistaken. He is the man."

"But surely, sir, you can get some of your friends that you have told about him being here to help you?" Luke queried.

"Why, you idiot, do you think I would be fool enough to tell anybody, when I want him all to myself?" the officer rejoined. "Not likely. If you don't like the job, say so, and be off at once. It is quite clear to me that your courage is oozing away, and that you will be of no use to me."

"Then, sir, you are much mistaken," said Luke. "I only like to know as much as possible about what I am to do. If you assure me I shall have the two guineas you may depend upon me flying at him the moment you say 'There he is!' and laying hold of him with a grip that he will find no easy matter to shake off."

"You are a fine fellow, and I will make your reward no less than five guineas. There, what do you say to that?"

"Nothing at all, sir, but that I would lay hold of Old Nick and hold him for the same money."

"Come on, then."

"What! are you going to ring at the gate, sir, or knock at the door?"

"Hardly," said the officer, grinning. "What I am going to do is to make my way into the garden through that hedge, and then we can be guided by circumstances."

"So we can, sir—so we can."

If the officer had not been so full of cupidity that he wanted all the reward for the capture of

CAPTAIN MACHEATH

THE
PRINCE OF THE HIGHWAY.

CAPTAIN MACHEATH AND LUKE BURY THE OFFICER'S BODY.

NO. 14.

Macheath himself there is very little doubt but that the career of our adventurer would have ended on that night, for in a couple of hours, with the certainty that the captain was at home, the officer could have brought to it a sufficient force to have made the success of an attack almost a certainty.

The idea of achieving the affair single-handed, or with such assistance as the sum of five guineas could afford to him, was really too tempting to the officer.

And when we come to consider that the reward for Captain Macheath was near to one thousand five hundred pounds, we can hardly wonder that the imagination of the officer was led astray by the glitter of such a sum.

Little did he imagine the snare he had fallen into in speaking to Luke.

They crossed the roadway, and after some little trouble forced a passage through the hedge.

"Now, my friend," said the officer, "the grand thing will be to get him out of the house, you know, for in the open air we can do much more than anywhere else; and he cannot dodge, as he might, up and down staircases and through rooms that he knows all about, but of which we know nothing at all."

"But is he alone in this house?" said Luke.

"No; there are two women, and a sort of stable fellow or gardener, who, I daresay, is as great a rogue as his master; but that is all, and if we are not a match for them, I think it will be a very odd thing indeed."

"Oh! very—very."

The officer began carefully looking at his pistols.

"Lor', sir, you don't mean for to go to say as you will shoot him?" said Luke.

"I don't know what I may do, my good friend. At all events, it makes no sort of difference to you, you know, whether I shoot him or not."

"Oh! dear no," Luke responded. "As long as I get my money, what can it matter to me whom you shoot?"

"Exactly," the officer assented. "Now I would give something to know where that gardener sort of fellow may happen to be. But there is one good thing in this affair, and that is, that as we are on the side of the law, all the alarm that is given is all the better, you know, for us. What if you were to get up to the house and call out in a loud voice, 'Hilloa—hilloa!' I rather think that the fellow I want would come out to see what was the matter, and then I could pop him down in a minute. I don't want to kill him, but I shouldn't mind wounding him in a way that he was quite helpless; for if I can get him to Newgate with a breath or two of life in him, it would be a great thing for me."

"Then you'd shoot him as he came out of his own house to see what was the matter?"

"Of course I should."

"Very good," said Luke. "I somehow don't fancy calling him out without having a pistol in my hand. Will you lend me one of yours, and then I will do it in a moment?"

"Oh! stuff. You will just make a blunder if you have any fire-arms. I have only one pair of loaded pistols with me. You be off, and call him out while I hide behind this apple-tree, and I'll manage him."

"I don't like the job."

"You don't like the job?" growled the officer. "What on earth do you mean by that? Are you

going to tell me that after coming thus far you are going to draw back? Are you afraid, or do you want more money?"

"Why, perhaps I am a little afraid as I have no pistol," replied Luke, pretending to look frightened. "I should feel like a lion if I had a pistol."

"Well—well, take this, then. It is loaded carefully, so mind what you are about with it, and don't fire unless you see me in a difficulty."

"A difficulty?"

"Yes. If you see me in a decided difficulty blaze away, but not before, mind you. And now let us get on."

"Well," said Luke, "it strikes me that you were never in such a difficulty in your life as you are in now, and you never will be in such another in this world whatever your troubles may happen to be in the next."

"What do you mean? Are you mad?" the officer gasped.

"Not at all; but the Noakes that you want is Captain Macheath, the highwayman, and I am his servant. What do you think of your difficulties now? I think you will be inclined to admit that you are too clever by half."

At these words the officer was so completely staggered that he stepped back and tumbled right on a currant bush.

"Get up," said Luke, "and don't bury yourself. Now I have a proposal to make to you, my friend, which it will be the wisest thing in the world for you to adopt, because it gives you just a chance of getting away."

"Murder!" said the officer; "I'm a dead man!"

"No you ain't, but you may be, you know. There's no saying what may happen in a little time. I am quite resolved that you and I shall fight a duel."

CHAPTER XL.

THE DUEL AND ITS RESULTS.

THE officer succeeded in scrambling to his feet, and as the moon just then peeped out from behind a mass of clouds, he and Luke could see each other remarkably well.

"A duel?" said the officer. "What do you mean by a duel?"

"I mean a fair fight, at about twelve paces; you may fire at me, and I will fire at you. If you hit me, you may go off; but if I hit you, I will bury you in the garden."

The officer trembled from head to foot.

"Let me go," he said. "You may take my word after what has happened, that I won't say one word about this place or who lives here; only let me go in peace."

"Yes, I will trust you just as much as I would trust a famished fox in a poultry-yard," Luke replied. "No, you must fight. Come, you can stand where you are, and I will go back twelve paces, or thereabouts. We will fire together, and when I say 'One, two, three,' it will be the signal, you know."

As he spoke, Luke backed along the gravel-path of the garden, but before he had got to the distance he thought of going the officer rapidly raised his pistol and fired.

"Take that, then," he cried, "if you will have it; and I hope it may do you some good, you scoundrel."

"I'm hit," said Luke.

"A good job, too."

The officer ran towards the gap in the hedge; but although Luke had fallen, he still kept his hold of the pistol, and levelling it at the officer, he pulled the trigger just as he was scrambling through the gap in the hedge.

With a loud cry the officer fell backwards, and rolling twice over, there lay without motion upon the pathway.

In another moment out rushed Captain Macheath with a light in his hand; but the wind blew it out instantly.

He then flung it down upon finding that the moon was shining brightly.

"Luke—Luke, what is all this?" he shouted. "Who fired a pistol just now? Where are you, Luke?"

"Here, sir," said Luke, faintly. "This way, sir. Here I am on the grass-plot."

Macheath went forward in the direction of the sound, and to his astonishment, he saw Luke lying on a small grass-plot close to the gap in the hedge.

"Why, Luke, what's the matter?" demanded Macheath. "Speak to me, I beg of you, and tell me what has happened!"

"He has done for me, I think, sir."

"Who—who?"

"An officer, sir, who has been dogging about the place for I don't know how long. He and I have had a shot at each other; but the treacherous rascal took me by unawares, and hit me."

"Where, Luke, where?"

"Right in my ribs, here, sir, I feel the blow of the bullet; and I'm as sick as a dog. I must be bleeding inwardly, sir, as there's none on my clothes; but a man can't get a pistol bullet in his stomach and live, I know. Good-bye, sir; I have done all I could for you, and now I am going."

"No—no," Captain Macheath cried. "I will carry you into the house and see what can be done for you. There's many a bad wound, Luke, got over when it's least expected. Be still and I will carry you gently into the house, my friend."

With those words the captain lifted Luke from the ground and carried him into the house, right into the room where Polly, and Annette, and himself had been sitting.

Polly was excessively alarmed; but when she saw what she thought the dead body of Luke she almost fainted.

"Get some warm water, Polly," said Captain Macheath, "and some linen; tear up anything so that you are quick. Our friend Luke is badly wounded, I am afraid, by someone who came to take my life; but I hope he may recover yet. I will but dress the hurt the best way I can, and then go for the nearest surgeon."

Polly summoned all her presence of mind, and left the room to get what her husband required.

"How do you feel now, Luke?" said the captain.

"Not any worse. I don't know how it is, but the bullet went in here, and I don't feel much of it."

He pointed to his breast as he spoke, and Macheath at once tore open his waistcoat, in which there was a little jagged sort of hole; but, singular to state, there the bullet had stopped, as if, after perforating the waistcoat, Luke had been shot-proof—for, certainly, wound there was none.

"Why, you are not hurt a bit," said Macheath. "It's all fancy, my good friend. I rejoice to say that you are not hurt in the least. Here, swallow this glass of brandy, and you will be all right again in a minute."

Luke could hardly believe his senses, but he tossed off the glass of brandy.

"But I felt the bullet hit me, sir," he said.

"Well, then, Luke, you are a necromancer, for the bullet, if it did hit you, has flown off you again as it would off a plate of steel, for touched you are not."

"But it knocked me right over, sir. Oh—oh—oh! Here it is! Oh!

"What is the matter, Luke?"

"Only look here, sir. Now I understand it. Here's a five-shilling-piece, sir, that you gave me to get a new pair of bridle-ends with; I put it into my waistcoat pocket, and only see, sir, if the bullet has not dented it right into a cup shape. No wonder it knocked me down. It is this, sir, that has saved me."

As he spoke Luke took from his waistcoat pocket the crown-piece that had saved his life, and sure enough the ball from the pistol had indented it so that it would have held a tea-spoonful of any liquid.

At this moment Polly, still pale with anxiety and fright, returned with warm water and some bandages.

"Our friend is all right again," said Macheath, smiling.

"Right!" cried Polly; "is he not shot?"

"No; this coin in his waistcoat pocket saved him. I fancy he will keep it as long as he lives as a curiosity, for he will never have the opportunity of getting such another. Such a thing does not happen twice in a man's life."

"No, indeed," said Polly.

"But there were two pistol shots," said Annette. "Don't you remember that you started up at the first, and that the second sounded in our ears before we could leave this room?"

"There were indeed," said Macheath. "Who fired the other, Luke?"

"I did."

"You did? And pray with what effect? For now it appears, if the officer is off and away, this will be no home for me another hour. We will pack up and be off, Polly, for he will soon bring force enough to make it a matter of impossibility for us to cope with them. This is no home for me."

"Nor for me," sobbed Annette.

"Stop a bit," said Luke. "I strongly suspect that, unless he had a five-shilling-piece in the middle of his back, you will find him lying in the garden. He had his shot at me first, and it was, as you see, sir, a tolerably good one; and then, as I lay upon the ground, fancying my life not worth the next two minutes' purchase, I had my shot at him."

"He fell?"

"He did; and if I am any judge of these matters, we shall find him there still."

"Oh! this is terrible," said Polly.

"It is to your gentle spirit," said Macheath; "but what would you have me do? This man, for the mere love of money, comes out armed with deadly weapons for the purpose of taking my life. What would you have me do? Am I to sit calmly, and allow these men to come at their good pleasure and drag me to a felon's cell, or, for fear he should not be able to do so with perfect safety to himself, maim me first and convey me wounded to the prison?"

"Oh ! do not speak so."

"And yet it is so, Polly. I take to the highway, but I do not take life. On the contrary, I have allowed many a rich booty to slip through my fingers rather than I would obtain possession of it at the price of blood."

"That I am sure of."

Polly clung to him and wept, for she had not yet seen Macheath look so severe, or heard him speak about his position and the perils that surrounded it so seriously before.

"Say no more," she said—"oh ! say no more ! I will return to my chamber. Settle this unhappy affair yourselves, and I will ask no further questions concerning it. It is better that I should know no more."

"You are right, Polly," said Captain Macheath—"you are right ! Go to your room, and leave Luke and me to settle the affair entirely."

"Come," said Macheath to Luke when Polly and Annette had retired, "we must go and see what amount of mischief has been done to the officer. The moon is yet shining brightly, and we need no other light. Come at once !"

"I will follow you, sir."

Macheath and Luke made their way to the garden where the officer lay, and they observed him lying upon his back.

Macheath, who was walking in advance, took but one glance at his face, and then, turning to Luke, he said—

"Quite dead !"

"I thought as much by the way in which he fell. He went over and over like a rabbit when you hit it by a good shot. Well, I do not feel many compunctions, for his attack upon me was so dastardly ; it was like a murder."

"It was, Luke," said the captain ; "but what are we to do with him ?"

"Bury him, captain !"

"But where, Luke ?"

"Here, in the garden, sir. We can easily find some odd corner in which to place him. It is the only safe and easy thing that can be done. He's dead ; he brought his death upon himself."

"I do not see any other mode of disposing of him than by burying him," Macheath returned ; "so it is better that we should do so at once. Get a couple of spades, and we will both set to work."

"Aye, captain !" said Luke ; "we will soon get a trench big enough to put him in comfortably."

Luke went to a tool-house, and soon returned with the spades.

He then selected a very retired spot, where the ground would not be disturbed again, in which to dig the officer's grave.

"Here, sir," he said, "nothing will grow, and it ain't at all likely that anyone who may have his house after you will dig up this bit of the ground."

"Come on, then," said Macheath. "Let's be as expeditious as possible in getting this rather ugly job over, Luke."

They began working with right good will.

In less than half an hour they had a grave dug for the officer.

"I hope that young gentleman you brought here with you will know nothing of this job," said Luke.

"It is not likely," the captain replied. "You had hardly left us with the horses when I showed him to bed ; for he was thoroughly tired out, and could hardly keep his eyes open. Before, however, I retire myself to get an hour's sleep, I will take care to ascertain what he has heard, and what he thinks of it."

"Do so, sir ; for this is a secret that it will be much more satisfactory to think remains in your and my keeping than in anyone else's. I will fetch the body, sir."

"You have no repugnance, Luke ?"

"Not a great deal, sir. Of the two, I would rather this affair had not happened ; but the fellow firing at me in such a cowardly way first, has put out of my head all feeling for him, and I am quite sure that such a man is a good riddance to society."

With this, Luke went away, and presently came back, dragging the dead body along by the heels.

"I could not make up my mind to lift him," he said ; "so there he goes into the grave. Fill up, sir, as quick as you can."

They both worked away in silence, and trod down the earth over the body until the grave was filled up.

CHAPTER XLI.

MACHEATH AGAIN IN LONDON.

CAPTAIN MACHEATH was anything but well pleased with the whole of this adventure.

It involved the taking of a life and the smuggling up of a dead body in a way that was anything but gratifying to his feelings ; and yet, although he considered the thing in every possible light, he could not see how it could have been otherwise managed.

"Luke," he said, "there is now another bond of union between you and I."

"Ah ! there needed no other than what there was. You have given me a home, and you are very kind and good to me."

"But I owe you much, Luke."

"No, captain, indeed you do not ; and I only hope the death of this man will not give you any uneasiness."

"That I cannot help."

"I feared as much," Luke said, "notwithstanding what you said upon the subject and the manner in which you tried to carry it off ; but the more you think of it, I fancy, sir, the more you will see and feel that nothing else could have been done."

"That I freely admit, Luke. It is not exactly the deed itself that has brought regretful feelings to my mind, but it is the necessity for it."

"Well, sir, it is a pity if you look at it in that way."

"It is ; but now go to your rest, Luke, and I will go to mine, and above all things, keep this affair from the knowledge of your mistress. Her gentle mind would be horrified at it, and the idea that the garden held such a secret would haunt her day and night, to her great detriment and unhappiness."

"I would not, sir, wish that she should know it for worlds."

"That is right, Luke. Let the horses be got ready to-morrow morning at an early hour, for the young gentleman and I are going to town upon his business."

"It shall be done, sir."

Macheath went into the house again, and it required all Polly's powers of persuasion to soothe him into even a partial forgetfulness of the scene in the garden.

When the bright morning came many of the

gloomy feelings that the night's adventure had engendered in his mind were dissipated, and he could almost smile at his own fears.

The lad whom he had rescued from the unjust father-in-law looked as happy again as he had looked over-night; and after partaking of a capital breakfast he and Captain Macheath mounted and set off for London.

Macheath upon this occasion rather astonished the lad; for as the captain was going into a portion of the City where he would probably meet with people of fashion, he had attired himself in conformity with their usages.

Macheath, however, did not wish to be at all known as the count, with the highly fashionable reputation that clung around him during his sojourn in the handsome apartments in Spring-gardens; and accordingly he had with great art disguised himself so that those who had known him most intimately would not have recognised him.

His dress was a very handsome suit of velvet, so that he looked remarkably well.

"Now, my young friend," he said, "you know what I am and who I am, but my secret I know well is safe with you, and if you meet me anywhere after to-day all you have got to do is cut away and affect not to know me."

"Oh! that I could not do."

"Oh! yes, it is by far the best plan."

"But my grateful feelings towards you would not let me do it. If I meet you I must long to shake hands with you."

Macheath was affected at this kind and artless gratitude from the lad, but he spoke to him very severely upon the subject.

"Nay," he said, "it would give me the greatest pleasure perhaps to shake hands with you, but if you chance to see me it is quite impossible for you to tell how I may be situated. Recollect that my life is one of the strangest vicissitudes and most hairbreadth escapes; and by your recognising me at some inopportune moment it is just possible you might be involving me in the greatest danger."

"If I were to do that I should never forgive myself."

"I know it would give you great pain, and therefore it is that I ask you to make me a promise."

"I cannot refuse to make you any promise that you may choose to require of me."

"It is just this—that let you see me where you may you will not recognise me. If I do so you will then feel assured that you will do me no harm by speaking to me. Will you give me your word to that effect?"

"I will—I do."

"Then I am quite satisfied, my young friend, and, believe me, it will be no small gratification to me to see you well and happy in the time to come."

"And I you," the lad responded. "Perhaps I shall be able to assist you in getting clear of this terrible line of life, which will kill you if you do not leave it."

"Perhaps so. But let us talk of your own prospects. I will make such inquiry at Whitehall as shall quickly find out this captain whom you wish to see, and then I will wait to discover if he be the friend you expect or not."

"Of that I have no doubt."

Thus discoursing they made their way to London, and notwithstanding they made anything but speed

the distance was so short that they were soon at Whitehall.

"Now," said Macheath, "my young friend, you will go to this gentleman, but do not say anything of me; I will wait for you here, and if your reception by him be all you wish I should like you to come out to me and say so."

"I will—I will."

The lad, who owed so much to the gallantry and the kindness of Macheath, was not absent above ten minutes when he came back, and stood by the side of Macheath's horse.

"It is all right. I have been received in the kindest manner. Of course, in obedience to your commands, I have said nothing of you; but will you now permit me to ask my friend to see you?"

"If you like."

"I will this moment;" and with these words in his mouth he at once went back to the captain, and then Macheath, as he held the rein of the horse that he had lent to his young friend in his hand, urged both the animals forward.

"It is well that we should part here," he said. "He can but do himself harm by any further connection with me, and an interview with this personage of whom he speaks can do me no good. So farewell."

A sharp trot took Captain Macheath past Westminster Abbey, and then, stopping at the first livery stable he came to, he rode down the gateway, and put up both the horses at once.

On foot he, by a circuitous route, walked through the park, and reached the neighbourhood of St. James's.

That Macheath had a design in all this who shall doubt?

In St. James's-street at that period there was one of the finest establishments resembling the modern club that ever was set going in London.

It was kept tolerably select, and the utmost surveillance was kept up at the door that none but the *elite* of society should enter.

Trusting to his appearance, which was highly favourable, Macheath strolled up to the door of this establishment and walked in.

Far from any opposition being offered to him in so doing, the doors were officiously held open for him by the servants.

He entered what was called a news-room, and there found some gentlemen killing time in the best way they were able.

"Is it time yet?" he heard one of them say.

"Hardly, my lord," said the other. "It will be a bore to be too soon at the affair, and I cannot help thinking it will be a bore when we get there."

"Why, the fact is, the prince is rather too young for this sort of thing just yet."

"That's what I think, my lord; and the mystery of the thing is, that we don't know who is invited and who is not. It appears that the prince has given half-a-dozen tickets to some, to bring with them whom they please, while others have had no end of difficulty in getting one."

"Why, how many will be there?"

"It is limited to thirty, I understand; and all that is on the tickets are the two letters 'P. F.'"

"And what do they mean? For, although I have a ticket, to tell the truth, I did not look at it at all."

"Why, the letters mean 'prince's fête, I believe; but let us be off. It is a sharp enough ride to Kew now, and we cannot be much too soon, I should say."

"Very good. Come along!"

"Gentlemen," said Macheath, with all the cool impertinence in the world, "if you are going to the prince's fête at Kew, I can assure you that you are in good time, for his royal highness told me only two hours ago that he hoped no one would come very early, as he had taken a small quantity of claret last night, and was as even princes may be at times."

The two gentlemen bowed, and one of them said—

"We have not the pleasure of knowing you, sir."

"I am Baron Hoge, a noble of the Roman Empire, a general in the Sicilian service, and a relative of her majesty the queen."

The two gentlemen bowed again.

"But," added Macheath, "I do not trouble the queen much, for my age and my taste, I must confess, incline me more to the amusements of the prince, who, if he were a little older, and not quite so selfish, would be very good company and make plenty of amusement for men of the world."

"You speak freely, sir."

"I do. The fact is, none of the family mind what I say; but you will do me one favour, gentlemen, if we meet, as no doubt we shall, at this fête, and that will be to say nothing to the prince of me, as he and I are going upon a little expedition soon, and he doesn't want anyone to know that I am in the country, as it might get round to the ears of the queen, and there is a certain little blue-eyed cousin of hers whom she is rather irate at for admiring your humble servant."

All this was said with such an air of engaging frankness that, men of the world as these two persons were, they were completely taken in by it, and one said—

"Allow me, then, Baron Hoge, to introduce myself—I am Lord Austincourt and this is Colonel Lane. We are both upon tolerably good terms with the prince, and hope to lead a pleasant life with him for the next dozen years or so, as he certainly seems to be in the vein to emulate his illustrious and much-talked-of antecedent, Prince Henry, afterwards King Henry the Fifth."

"He may wish to imitate him," said Macheath, "but the copy will be more unlike the original than I am unlike Hercules, I fancy. Have we time and inclination for a bottle of Bordeaux before starting?"

"Both, I hope," said Lord Austincourt.

The bottle of wine was brought to them, and after duly discussing it, Macheath sent a message to the livery-stable for his horse, describing the one of the two he wanted, and as he had quite arranged that he was to accompany his two new acquaintances to Kew, he mounted at the door of the club, and their horses having been brought round from a neighbouring stable they did the same.

He saw that they very much admired his steed.

"This is a kind and good creature, and will do almost anything," he said. "I thought it cheap at two hundred pounds."

"And so it is," said Austincourt. "I will give the money for it now at once if you want to part with it."

"No," said Macheath. "It is my favourite horse for common use, although I have some in my stable that cost me more than double the amount."

"Can he leap?" cried the colonel.

"A little. Do you see that cart?"

A cart was creeping lazily along, drawn by a donkey, and carrying evergreens, and as he uttered the last words Macheath put his horse at it, and the leap right over the cart was done in a capital and clean style.

"By George!" said the colonel, "I should like to have him. Will three hundred tempt you, baron?"

Macheath hesitated a moment.

"Well, I don't know but that, upon two conditions, it might," he said.

"Name them—name them!"

"First, you must let me ride him to-day."

"Oh! yes, certainly. By all means."

"Then you must come for him yourself to my place, which I will give you the address of before we part to-day."

"That I will with pleasure."

"Well then, colonel, he is yours at three hundred pounds."

The colonel took out his pocket-book, and at once, in the presence of Austincourt, handed out three notes of one hundred pounds each to Macheath, who put them very coolly into his pocket.

"I envy you your bargain, colonel," said Lord Austincourt, "and if I had been flush of cash just now, I would have bid another fifty; but I am devilish short, so it is no use talking about it. Let us push on now, for it is nearly eleven o'clock, and after all we ought to be in tolerably good time, if we are not early."

Upon this they all increased their speed, and Macheath enjoyed a most delightful ride to Kew.

It is perhaps necessary that we should now say a few words about this fête, or private entertainment, which the Prince of Wales was then giving.

George, Prince of Wales, afterwards George the Fourth, was then but a very young man, and could hardly be said to be out of tutelage.

Already, however, he had begun to give ample evidence of those luxurious habits which stuck to him through life, and which have clung to his memory with no enviable reputation.

He had become the petty tyrant of all around him, and, having just awakened to the fact that there was no ordinary limit to his powers of self-indulgence, he had commenced a course of selfishness and luxury.

The old palace at Kew had been for a short space assigned to him as a residence, where it was supposed that he was completing some portion of his education.

But he soon contrived to convert it into these scene of pleasures, and there were those around him who took good care to encourage the growing foibles and vices of the young prince.

A man in such a position will never want sycophants, and already George had his party in the nation, and was accustomed to pass the night with some of the most worthless characters among the aristocracy that could be got together.

This meeting at Kew was intended to celebrate one of those early orgies for which he afterwards became rather too well known, and which he only abandoned when failing health forced him to do so.

"Have you been to one of these little meetings before, baron?" said Lord Austincourt to Macheath.

"Not here," replied the captain, with a laugh that conveyed the idea that he knew all about them somewhere else, and as the colonel and his lordship had not been to any such parties elsewhere, they set it down in their own minds that

Macheath knew a little more than they even did of the freaks of the young prince.

The aspect of appearances at the gate of the gardens and palace at Kew was not such as would have led anyone to suppose that the heir-apparent to the crown of England was there.

Only one servant was on duty; but then the grand object was that the whole affair should be kept strictly quiet.

There was one little difficulty that Macheath had to contend with, and that arose from the fact that he had no ticket, and for the last mile he was full of thought as to how he should get over this trouble.

Accident furnished him with a good opportunity for accomplishing it.

During the ride Lord Austincourt had produced his ticket and replaced it in the pocket of his overcoat, and it so happened that the horse which his lordship rode limped a little just as they got within sight of the royal abode.

"Hilloa!" said the colonel. "Your horse has fallen lame, Austincourt. That's a pleasant job."

"Is he, though? Do you see it, baron?"

"Yes," said Macheath; "but it's probably of no sort of consequence. He has picked up a stone most likely; you see this bit of road is full of them. I will dismount and look at his foot for you."

"Oh! no—no; I will dismount myself. I could not think of troubling you."

"Don't mention that. It is no trouble I assure you, and I am rather a good hand, they say, at anything of this sort. My horse will stand still, or rather, I should say your horse, colonel. Excuse my saying mine."

As Macheath spoke he dismounted, and so did Lord Austincourt, and as they both stooped to examine the horse's foot, in which was a small stone, it was the easiest thing in the world for Macheath to possess himself of the ticket.

"There, it's gone now," said Macheath.

"Upon my word, I am very much obliged to you, baron. I would not have this horse go lame on any account, for I value it very much, and, as all the world knows, I am in no mood just now to buy another."

They both mounted again, and reached the gate of the gardens, at which it was customary for the private friends of the prince to enter.

Then, as they dismounted, the servant blew a whistle, and in a few minutes three grooms came to take charge of the horses.

"Hilloa!" said Austincourt, "there is De Lohm, the prince's valet. I'll be sworn he has come to take the tickets, and if so, it is a very private affair indeed."

"It is so," assented Captain Macheath, with a nod of the head. "Even I am provided with a pass, which upon any ordinary occasion, would not have been requisite, as you may well suppose."

"Certainly not. He is coming," said the colonel.

"Gentlemen," said the valet, bowing, "may I have the honour of taking your tickets."

"Certainly, good De Lohm," said Austincourt, "certainly. I hope both you and the prince are well to-day?"

"Quite well, my lord—at your lordship's service."

Macheath handed his ticket to the valet, who looked at him so scrutinisingly that Macheath felt just a little uncomfortable.

He, however, was outwardly cool, and folded his arms and returned the glance with compound interest.

But the ticket was a pass that he dared not dispute, for on one side of it were the letters "P. F.," and on the other a "G.," and that "G." was written by the prince himself, with a peculiar flourish at the tail of it that the valet knew perfectly well.

"Pass on, sir, if you please," he said, bowing. "This is perfectly right and regular."

"Anybody here?" said Macheath.

"Almost all invited, sir. Thank you, colonel—all right. Pass on, if you please."

"Confound it," said Lord Austincourt; "where is my card? I had it only half an hour ago. Where the deuce did I put it? I have not so many pockets, either. Hang the thing! Did you not see me with it, colonel?"

"Certainly?"

"Yes," said Captain Macheath, coolly; "you took it out of your pocket to look at to be sure. You had it."

"Certainly I had, and I put it in this—no, it must have been this pocket—no. I have not got it, that's quite clear, De Lohm."

"It is a pity, my lord."

"It is. But here is the colonel, who knows I had it and here is the baron."

"Yes," said the colonel; "we are both witnesses to that effect; you know it, baron, as well as I?"

"It is a pity!" said De Lohm; "but there is another witness to the fact that my Lord Austincourt had a ticket, and that is myself, for I sent it to his lordship at the express command of the prince. Pass on, my lord; it is all right. No doubt it has come out of your pocket upon the road, and that shows what a good thing it is to have nothing on the ticket that the uninitiated can understand."

"You are right, De Lohm," said Austincourt, "and very obliging. I am not the man to forget a little courtesy of this kind."

The valet bowed, and the three visitors passed the gate of the royal demesne.

"Provoking!" said Lord Austincourt, "but it was very obliging of De Lohm. Don't mention it, either of you, to the prince. It is just one of the little things that he will pretend to make a great fuss about."

"Not a word of it," said the colonel.

"And my lips are sealed!" said the mock baron. "I know George quite well enough to be perfectly aware that if you tell him anything he generally gets hold of the wrong version of it."

Both the colonel and Lord Austincourt laughed at this remark, and it tended more and more to confirm them in their belief of his position, for if he had not felt quite upon easy terms with the prince, he would surely, they thought, have never ventured upon talking of him so freely.

Macheath allowed his new friends to take the lead, and they went along the paths in the shrubbery that led to the palace with practical familiarity, and at length emerged upon an exceedingly pretty lawn, in the centre of which was one of the most gorgeous flower-beds that the imagination could conceive.

"That is a beautiful sight!" said the colonel, as he looked at it. "They are all rare greenhouse plants, and are taken in at night, but in the daytime they are so well arranged, that they really have all the appearance of growing and flourishing in the open ground."

"They have, indeed," said Macheath.

A loud roar of laughter at this moment came upon their ears from the palace, and then all was still again, as if by magic.

"Ah!" said the colonel, "they are at it, I hear, already."

"Not a doubt of it," said Austincourt. "But I would always rather be a little later, for if one comes early on these occasions, one is obliged to out with all one's good jokes at once, and then for the rest of the affair look as dull as ditch water. Come on; I wonder where they are?"

"Oh! in the painted room, of course."

Captain Macheath said nothing, but he put on a quiet kind of smile, as if he could have said a great deal if he had so chosen; and no doubt his two companions so translated it.

There is nothing like saying nothing to give a man a reputation for knowing a great deal.

"Let us go in," said Austincourt.

They all three reached a little low-arched door, and Lord Austincourt tapped at it with a ring that was upon his finger.

It was immediately opened by a man elegantly dressed in a court suit, who said not one word, but merely bowing, waved his hand for them to enter.

"Which room, Collins?" said the colonel.

"The Painted Saloon, sir."

"Oh! so I thought. Come on, my lord. Ah! there they are again. I wonder what that is at. Nothing very humorous, I'll be bound. A small joke goes a long way at times in certain places and with certain people."

"It does, indeed!" replied Captain Macheath, to whom this remark appeared to be more particularly applied; "but by the laughter now, one would really suppose it was anything but a small joke."

"Ah! but a great noise is no—"

"Hush — hush!" said Lord Austincourt. "Pray recollect where you are, and bear in mind the old saying, 'that walls have ears sometimes.'"

"Thank you for the caution."

At this moment another person, habited like the man at the little door, stepped up to them and said—

"Allow me, gentlemen, to show you into the prince's presence. This way, gentlemen, if you please."

A door was thrown open, and a blaze of light from a room that was closed against the daylight, but brilliantly lighted up with wax candles, shone upon them.

CHAPTER XLII.

AT THE PRINCE'S FETE.

MACHEATH was certainly not at all prepared for the extraordinary scene that presented itself in the room where Prince George was enjoying himself with his boon companions.

He had thought all along that it was rather an odd thing to hold such a class of entertainment in broad daylight; but it had not struck him that that was a state of things that could be easily remedied.

In the most familiar style imaginable, Macheath took his seat at the prince's side, and began to chat with him in such an enchanting way that the prince was enraptured.

"I must know more of you, baron," the prince said. "Come to-night, and I will show you some fun."

"I thank your royal highness," Macheath replied.

The banquet passed away in splendid fashion, and as soon as Macheath turned his back upon the palace he made up his mind to return home for a short spell.

Captain Macheath's object was to ride to Kentish-town for the purpose of calming any fears that Polly might have at his long protracted absence, which neither he nor she had at all expected.

Knowing, however, as she had known, that he had gone upon an expedition that might possibly be attended with some risk, he felt particularly anxious to assure her of his safety, as well as to prepare her for a more continued absence, in case he should return to Kew.

The carouse at the old palace in Kew-gardens had too many temptations for one like Captain Macheath to resist it.

He felt that, while even he could not help despising the entertainer, that there was yet much in the entertainment to enchain the imagination, and to take the fancy prisoner.

"Yes," he said, as he pursued his way at a rapid pace, "oh! yes; I will return and see what may yet be done. I have a shrewd suspicion that, as the night comes, what is now wild riot will very materially alter its character, and we shall have some rich and rare scenes, which it will be well worth my time and attention to study. Yes, I am decided—I will go back."

It was still daylight when Macheath reached Kentish-town, but Luke was on the watch for him, and at once opened the garden gate.

It was so rare a chance for Macheath to reach his home at such an hour as that, that there was more positive danger of observation in the few moments that it took him to pass from the road into it than in half-a-dozen of his usual exits or entrances from his pretty rural abode.

"All right, Luke?"

"Yes, sir; everything is as quiet as possible, sir."

As he spoke Luke glanced about him rather nervously.

"Why, what's the matter with you, man?"

"I don't know, captain; but the fact is I have been a little nervous all day, and I can't get that man out of my head that lies buried over there."

Luke indicated the grave of the officer in the corner of the grounds.

Captain Macheath could not but see that Luke was in a state of fear that he found difficult to repress.

"Why, Luke," said Macheath, in an encouraging tone, "I should hardly have expected this of you, do you know?"

"No, captain, nor I; and if you were always at home I daresay the case would be very different; but as you are not, you see, it alters it very much, and I get brooding on things that it would be quite as well not to think of if one could possibly help."

"Oh! well, Luke, you must not mind all that; you will shake it off in a little time, man," Macheath rejoined. "If you feel dull in the old house, why, you might come out for a ride with me now and then."

"Ah! sir, I should like that very much."

"You shall, then. I am going out to-night, but it is not on the road, Luke, or you should go with me. It is on a special invitation to supper, where I cannot introduce anyone, I fear; but I will think of it within the next hour or so. How is your mistress, Luke?"

"She is quite well, sir, I believe."

At this instant Polly made her appearance to answer for herself.

The radiant look of joy that spread itself over her face at the appearance of her husband was a sufficient answer in the affirmative as to her being quite well.

"How good of you," she said, as she accompanied him into the house, with her arm linked in his. "How good of you to come home so soon this evening. I feared you had been attracted by some wild adventure, and had gone off to carry it out, and that I might not see you for many a long hour."

"I have been attracted by an adventure, Polly," Macheath replied; "and it is but to tell you that I may not return for the whole of the night that I have ridden some miles even now."

"And are you going again?"

"I must."

"Ah! Macheath, you do not love your home."

"In good truth, if I do not love the home, I love the fair and gentle spirit that gives to it all its beauty; so we will just take a little refreshment, and then I must be off; and as I eat, I will tell you where I am going."

It was not commonly the case that Macheath told Polly of any of his adventures; but upon this occasion he could not help thinking that a slight description of the prince's doings at the Royal Palace at Kew would be amusing to her.

Besides, it would have the effect of setting her mind at ease as to where he was going, and, at all events, of convincing her that it was not upon some expedition of great danger.

"How strange," she said, "that one who might be so great prefers to be so little! How can he find enjoyment in such luxuries?"

"Polly, we all act up to our perceptions and capacities," Macheath replied. "The notions of the prince are no higher than those of enjoyment; and so, having large means of seeking such enjoyment, he follows the bent of his inclination."

"It must be so," said Polly. "But you will be very careful not to excite a suspicion of who you really are?"

"Believe me, Polly, that I will be very careful," Macheath returned, smiling. "I do not think that there is the slightest chance of detection as long as I keep my head clear; and that, I think, I can do, notwithstanding all the rich temptations to the contrary. So now, as the shadows are each moment deepening, I feel inclined to be off again."

"Must you, really?"

"I must."

"Ah! then I will not oppose you. Go, and may Heaven protect you for my sake. I know that you have not a bad heart, and so, although—although—"

"Although what, Polly? Nay, speak freely to me."

"I was only going to say that, although all the world would condemn your course of life, I still thought you deserving of some of Heaven's care."

"Come—come, you are getting quite tearful and sentimental, Polly," he said. "You must not send me away in such a mood as this. Let me see you smile before I do."

"I will smile when you come back," Polly replied. "That will be the better compliment of the two, will it not?"

"Well, perhaps it will," Macheath assented; "and now, for another thing, I am thinking that it will be very much conducive to my safety if I took Luke with me to put up my horse somewhere, so as not to be dependent upon the palace servants to get him for me at any sudden moment."

"Oh! yes—yes."

"You will not mind, then, for a few hours, being left in the house by yourself, Polly? I will get back as soon as possible."

"Oh! no—no. When the question concerns your safety, all others give place to it at once," Polly answered, quickly.

"You are too good to me."

"That is impossible," said Polly. "Take Luke with you, and I will shut myself up in our chamber, and not stir from it until I hear your voice. Go now, go at once, for perhaps then you will be the sooner back to me. The hours will seem very long indeed until I see you again. Will you think of that?"

"In good truth I will; and, perhaps, I shall get home again much sooner than I at present think."

"Ah! now, you shall go at once, that you are in such a good mind," said Polly. "I pray you to go."

Upon this Captain Macheath went to Luke, and told him that he would take him with him.

But Luke, after the first feeling of pleasure at getting out a little from the house, looked rather serious.

"Ah! captain," said he, "you are going to take me out from kindness to me; but your good, kind wife will then be all alone, and she will feel very solitary indeed in the house, and every slight noise will fill her full of fears when she knows that there is no one on the premises that will protect her at all."

"Don't think of that, Luke. I have arranged it all with her; so get the horses ready, and let us be off at once."

In about ten minutes they were both on the road.

Luke was mounted upon a nice horse that Macheath had empowered him to buy, hoping that it would come in usefully for Polly when the days were fine and serene enough for her to take a canter in the neighbourhood.

As they rode along, Macheath told Luke all about the adventure at Kew-gardens, for in case of anything going wrong, Luke would be much more likely to be of efficient assistance to him by knowing the whole of the circumstances, than as if he was in ignorance.

Macheath felt certain that he might safely depend upon Luke's discretion, as well as upon his courage.

"What I want you to do, Luke," he said, "is to put up with the horses somewhere as near the gate of the palace garden as you can find a place of entertainment; and thus, if I am forced to leave in a hurry, which may be just possible, I can come to you direct, and mount and be off. About four o'clock in the morning I should like you to keep the horses saddled for any emergency."

"I will, sir. It will be much the safest plan."

"Very good; then we will push on, Luke, for now we perfectly understand each other upon this point."

With this, they put their steeds to a steady canter, by which they got over the ground in capital style; and in a much less space of time than we would have thought it possible to go such a distance across the country as from Kentish-town to Kew, the deep shadows of the old trees in the gardens appeared in view.

"Here we are, Luke," said Captain Macheath.

"So soon, sir?"

"Why, yes, I confess that we have done it rather well, considering the distance; but here we are, Luke, and now the only thing is to find out where to put up the horses. A little place will be the best, as the people are not so likely to be so importunate about your saddling the horses early in the morning."

"Very good, sir. I think I see a swinging sign a little further on. Look, sir, is there not something of the sort?"

"I think so, too; but it seems to be a waif or a stray upon the road-side, for there is certainly no house near it."

"Let us go and see, sir."

They rode up to the sign, which was creaking to and fro, making a melancholy, monotonous tune of its own.

"There is a direction on it," said Luke. "Are your eyes very sharp, sir? Mine won't read it."

"I will try, Luke."

Macheath raised himself in his saddle so as to get very near to the sign, and immediately beneath he found a wooden hand, with a preternaturally long finger pointing down a lane, and on it was written, "The way to the White Lion."

"All right," said Macheath. "That is the White Lion; so at the White Lion we will leave our steeds. It is not two minutes' walk, or one minute's run, from the gate of the palace garden."

Macheath did not intend to go to the White Lion; but he rode down the lane to look at the situation of the house, so as to be sure to know it again, and then he dismounted, and gave his horse to Luke's care.

"Don't expect me till you see me," he said; "but I think I shall not wait until sunrise. However, I must be guided by circumstances, so that, perhaps, I ought not even to say that much; so now good-evening, Luke. Have you money?"

"Oh! yes, sir."

"Very good. Never omit to ask me for whatever you want in that way, as my exchequer is easily filled again if it does sometimes get a little empty."

"Oh! sir, you are very good, but I want for nothing."

Macheath turned out of the lane again, and on foot made his way to the gate of the royal gardens.

He advanced boldly, and seeing a sentinel, he cried—

"Open the gate—open the gate!"

"Sir, I—I—"

"It's all right, Jack," said another, coming up at that moment. "I recollect this gentleman."

The gate was opened, and Macheath, taking a couple of guineas from his waistcoat pocket, gave one to each of the sentinels, who bowed to the very ground upon receiving so unexpected a gratuity.

"I'd give more than this by a good deal," said Captain Macheath to himself, "as the price of my admission to this place."

"Now, Jack," said one of the sentinels to the other, "that's what I call a real out-and-out gentleman."

"I believe you," said the other. "Mind you, I don't mean to say what we shall get as the company goes away, but I always think a good deal of the first guinea."

"So do I."

"Do you know who he is?"

"Not I; but he's somebody, I can tell you, for I heard say as the prince was a little within bounds when he was a-looking at him. We shall find out before the night's over, I daresay, no doubt. The fun hasn't half-begun yet."

"No; but it will soon."

"I believe you, my boy. Mrs. Lee has come, and brought some of the young ladies with her, I take it."

"Not a doubt of that. All those young gentlemen as come in with a special order were girls."

"I knowed it—I knowed it! Ah! me, there is goings on here that would make some folks open their eyes a bit, I rather think. But we makes a good thing of it, so the least we say is the best, I take it."

While this delectable little bit of discourse was going on at the gate of the palace garden, Macheath, with as good a resolution as he could suddenly bring to bear upon the matter, was making his way through the rather intricate garden paths to the palace.

The night had set in by this time, and the garden bore such a very different and mysterious aspect in the deep shadows, that he might well, as he did, pause more than once to ask himself if he could possibly be right in the course that he was taking.

After he had thus stopped for the third time, he found no difficulty in pursuing his way, for a loud, ringing peal of laughter from one particular direction warned him that there was the palace, or, if not, that he should quickly enough fall in with some of the madly-joyous guests of the prince.

"Ah!" he said, "that is the direction. I shall have no longer any difficulty in finding my way now."

He took, as nearly as he could now guess, the route that would bring him to the spot where the sounds were made; but he found that some plants in a large flower-bed obstructed him.

Captain Macheath was not very particular, so he strode through the flower-bed at once, heedless of the mischief that he was doing; and then he heard someone say, in a low voice—

"Who are you, pray? Answer me at once, sir!"

The voice was decidedly a feminine one.

"Oh!" said Macheath, "I am your very humble servant."

"Go away directly."

"How very cruel it is to say go away directly," said Macheath, as darting forward he caught by the arm a figure that he could only just contrive to catch a faint glimpse of in the dim light among the old trees.

There was a summer-house near at hand, and the figure by a sudden wrench got out of Macheath's grasp and rushed towards it.

"That was well done," said Captain Macheath; "but I am after you, for all that, my fair one, for a fair one you are, or you would not be here, I feel quite assured. Why need you be so very particular?"

At that moment the figure turned and discharged a pistol full at Macheath.

As the bullet whistled harmlessly over his head the figure darted into the summer-house and banged the door.

Macheath tried the door, but it was fast.

He tapped gently enough at it, but that produced no effect.

"My dear," said Macheath, who rightly guessed that he was addressing a girl in male attire, "I have made up my mind to speak to you, and to have a look at your face as well as I can see it by the light; and I shall be under the disagreeable necessity of breaking down the door, if you don't ——."

"—— gone!" said the voice from within the summer-house.

Macheath laughed, as, placing his shoulder against the little frail door, he at once forced it off its hinges. The moment that he did so there was a sharp crack, and another small pistol-bullet crashed through one of the panels, escaping the captain only by a hair's breadth.

"Take the reward of your folly!" said the voice. "You have brought this upon yourself, and it but serves you right."

CHAPTER XLIII.

THE ADVENTURES AT KEW CONTINUED.

MACHEATH was on the point of saying something, but he checked himself.

Willing to have some sport with the young lady who could be bold enough to carry fire-arms about with her, and use them upon so small amount of provocation, he thought that if he affected to be hit by the bullet he should probably have a chance of seeing her more readily.

Full of this idea, he uttered a low groan, and then was profoundly still.

"I have killed him," said the voice again, and immediately from the summer-house came the figure. "I have killed him. I am sorry—more than sorry that it is so, but I have killed him. Where are you? Why don't you speak, unhappy man? If you have breath to do so, tell me where you are."

"I am here!" said Captain Macheath, faintly.

"Where—where? Oh! I can see you now. Why did you persevere so madly, and bring such a fate upon yourself? Are you very badly hurt?"

"Not that I know of!" said Captain Macheath, in a sprightly manner, and suddenly seizing the figure in his arms. "Now, tell me who you are, or you won't get away from me again so cleverly as you did before. I forgive you the pistol shots with all my heart. I can stand any fire but that from your displeasure."

"You are a singularly bold man."

"I always was."

"And are you a friend of the prince?"

"My being here ought to answer that question."

"Tell me who you are?"

"The Baron Hoge."

"Very well. Now I ask of you a favour, and make to you a promise at the same time that, if you grant it to me, I will truly keep."

"Name the favour, and without the promise, I will at once grant it. If you really wish to get rid of me at once, I will go; and I much regret that, in the impulse of the moment, I have intruded upon you so much as I have."

"Go, then. That is the favour. The promise is that you shall hear of me again. Does that satisfy you?"

"It does. Good-night!"

In a moment Captain Macheath left the spot.

That this young lady—for that she was young,

her voice was sufficient testimony—was one of those damsels who had been invited to the palace, he could not doubt, and yet there was a style and manner about her that created a feeling in Captain Macheath's mind that there was some mystery connected with her.

He did not expect to hear anything further of her, notwithstanding her promise.

But he now made the best of his way towards the palace.

A loud, ringing peal of laughter now broke upon the night air again.

Captain Macheath was guided in the direction he had to go, and he suddenly came from out of a small, trim path of the garden in front of the palace.

The blinds and shutters of the windows were so well arranged that scarcely a ray of light got out into the night air to show what rooms were occupied and what were not.

But yet there was a kind of halo of brightness about the building which led him to the belief that in many parts of it lights were burning.

Macheath looked about anxiously for the little door at which he had before entered the banquet-hall, where the prince and his companions had held their carouse; but he was puzzled for a time between several doors, and hardly knew which to choose.

At length, in impatience rather than in any certainty of being right, he pushed at one and found it yield to the pressure of his hand.

"This will do, and shall do," he said.

He hardly stepped within the door-way when he heard the wild laughter of some of the guests, and guided by the sound, he went until he came to a large velvet curtain that impeded his progress.

He drew it slightly aside, and found that it opened upon the same room that he had before sat in. But the company was rather altered.

Some strange faces were there that he had not seen upon the former occasion, and about a dozen ladies were present attired in the most extravagant style of fashion.

The whole party were hand-in-hand in performing a wild kind of dance round the table in the middle of the room, to the dim light of only three or four of the wax candles that still remained in the chandelier, which had suffered much from the wine that had been from time to time cast at it.

Macheath looked for the prince, and presently he saw him come round along with the dancers.

He passed quite close to Macheath, so that by merely stretching out his hand he could have touched him; but he let him pass.

The dance, which resembles a revelry, such as one sees in the old mythological pictures of the Italian masters, continued; and the love of frolic entered Macheath's spirit.

When the prince got round again, Macheath put out his foot, and the prince at once tumbled over it, dragging with him the two ladies whom he had by the hands. The others who were following could not stop themselves, and the consequence was that, like a pack of cards that had been set up on end, the whole of the party were sprawling upon the floor.

The prince, being the first to fall, had a tolerable weight to bear, and he roared out for help in such a comical voice of distress that it was with difficulty that Captain Macheath kept himself from shouting with laughter.

If he had done so, however, it would have exposed him to the suspicion of being the author of the trick, so he wisely kept silence as far as laughter was concerned, and stepping into the room, he sat down upon a luxurious sofa in a distant corner.

A table was close to him, upon which was some very elegantly got up confectionery, and while the disordered company was still floundering about upon the floor Macheath amused himself by throwing mince pies and raspberry tarts at the few lights that remained in the chandelier, by which process he succeeded in extinguishing them, and producing intense darkness in the saloon.

"Murder!" cried the prince—"Murder!"

"Lights—bring lights!" shouted some twenty voices.

No one paid the slightest attention to their cries. Whether the attendants were not within hearing, or really thought it was only part of the fun, it is hard to say.

But certainly no one put in an appearance with a light, and Macheath, whose mischief was now fairly awakened, crept to the side of the table, and by giving it a powerful lurch, at once scattered the whole of its contents on to the floor.

Suddenly a bell rung.

It would appear as if the servants had been waiting for this signal, for the door at once opened, and a stream of light came into the saloon.

"Lights—lights!" cried the prince. "I am half killed. Lights here, I say."

Several branches, containing six or eight wax candles, were now brought into the saloon, and the scene of disorder that they made apparent astonished even those domestics, who were not astonished at mere trifles during their time of service with the heir-apparent.

Amid the wreck of the contents of the table lay one-half at least of the guests still upon the floor.

The wine was running about in perfect streams hither and thither, and some of the ladies who had looked so very elegant only a short quarter of an hour before, were in the most woeful plight indeed, with their dresses torn and soaked in different coloured wines that had rolled over them from the table.

The prince sat in the midst of the wreck, looking the very picture of distress and dismay.

His eyes were goggling out of their orbits, and his cheeks seemed swelled out considerably.

"Murder—murder!" was the only word he kept at intervals, as he could collect just sufficient breath to do so, gasping out.

Macheath thought it would be prudent to keep as much as he could out of the way, so he assumed a horizontal position upon the couch, and drawing one of the pillows, with which it was richly and plentifully furnished, partially over his face, he watched the uproar.

As the lights enabled them to see what they were about, some of the guests began slowly to gather themselves to their feet and look about them with dismayed aspects.

They then lifted the prince to his feet.

"Oh! dear," he said. "Oh—oh! what's it all about? Murder! I didn't tell anybody to do all this. How dared anybody? Oh! let me sit down, I am half dead, I declare. I am—I am a dying man."

They helped him to a seat, upon which he sat with many groans, and the ridiculous appearance he cut, with his face and head all streaming with wine, was enough to have provoked laughter in anyone but a court parasite.

The ladies wept plentifully over their spoilt finery, and such a scene of ludicrous woe was never before exhibited in that place.

It was with difficulty Macheath kept from roaring again with laughter; but by dint of cramming a corner of the pillow of the couch into his mouth he contrived to keep quiet.

"You fell down," said a young lady.

"Go to the deuce!" said the prince.

The young lady wiped her eyes, and retired rather a little discomfited at the failure of her attempt to pour consolation into the royal ear; and then, after looking rather wildly about him for a few moments, the prince said—

"Where's Lane? Where's Colonel Lane?"

"Here," said Colonel Lane. "I hope your highness is not hurt?"

"Well, Lane, I hardly know; but how did it all happen? That is what puzzles me."

"It is easily enough explained, your highness. Somebody fell, and we all fell upon him."

"Good gracious, that somebody was me, for I felt as if the whole palace lay upon me, and my stomach was crushed quite flat. Oh! dear me."

CHAPTER XLIV.

CAPTAIN MACHEATH HAS A NARROW ESCAPE.

"NEVER mind, your highness. A good glass of claret will set you all to rights again. The only mysterious thing is, to me, how the table got upset in the midst of it all."

"But it is not upset," said another.

"And yet every bottle and every glass that was upon it is now upon the floor. How is that to be accounted for?"

"Let's go into the Yellow-room," said the prince. "Oh! dear, I feel a little better. Let's go into the Yellow-room. We shall do very well there, and we intended to go there, you know, soon."

"Oh! yes—yes," said all the ladies.

The prince was getting better, although when he rose from the chair upon which he had been seated he staggered a little.

The wine that Colonel Lane had persuaded him to drink had warmed his blood a little, and as he had in reality received no very serious injury, he was rapidly getting the better of his fall and his fright.

"I am afraid there is someone amongst us bent upon mischief to-night, colonel," said the prince.

"Oh! baron, are you here? I missed you. I thought you had left us somehow rather early."

"No; I wish I had, for I am afraid I am cut in the arm with a bit of broken glass. I distinctly saw someone upset the table sufficiently to throw everything off it on to the floor. It was quite a cruel thing to do."

"Can you indentify who did it?" asked the colonel, eagerly.

"Not I. And between you and I, colonel, I think it would not be the province of a gentleman to do so, even if I could."

"You are right, baron; I like your nice sense of honour in this affair. You are quite right. It would not be the thing, as we are all amusing ourselves, although that was, in my opinion, decidedly carrying the joke too far."

"So I think."

"You know it might have been attended with serious consequences to many of us."

"Exactly so, and, as I tell you, I am hurt."

"Now—now!" said the prince. "Let us make our way to the Yellow-room, my friends.

CAPTAIN MACHEATH

THE
PRINCE OF THE HIGHWAY.

THE LEAP RIGHT OVER THE CART WAS DONE IN A CAPITAL AND CLEAN STYLE.

NO. 15.

We have had, I do think, quite enough of this one, surely. Come along—come along. This way. I begin to feel very much better again, but it's a nasty joke for all that."

"It was, your highness," said Lord Austincourt; "and I don't at all envy the feelings of the person who could perpetrate it."

"Nor I," said several.

"I only wish," said one of the ladies, "that I knew who upset the table. Look at my beautiful cherry satin! It is completely destroyed. Only look!"

"Well—well, I'll give you another."

"Oh! how very kind," the ladies cried, and immediately surrounded the prince, who said—

"Oh! be off with you. Do you want to smother me? Protect me, Lane, from these ladies! Recollect who I am. It's high treason to smother a prince! But come along to the Yellow-room; it is all ready lighted, I have no doubt; and there we will have some rare fun. Come on—come on; this way. Don't you look so serious, Celia. Take my arm, if you must— only do look a little pleasant."

These last words were addressed to the young lady who had been requested only a short time before, by the prince, to go to the deuce, and she gladly accepted the peace-offering in the shape of the prince's arm to the Yellow-room.

This Yellow-room, was, in the first place, the largest in the whole palace.

It was called the Yellow-room because the walls were covered with yellow drapery of the richest and most exquisite character.

The roof was very richly painted in some mythological subject, and the floor was covered with a Persian carpet with most brilliant yellow flowers upon it.

Take that room for all in all, it certainly was one of the most beautiful in the palace.

Macheath was rather too intent upon what the human occupants of the Yellow-room were about to pay a great deal of attention to its decorations, although on entering it he was much struck, as no one could fail of being, with its light and beautiful character.

Around the walls of this room there were elegant couches, covered in yellow satin.

In the centre of the apartment there was a rather long, narrow table, upon which was a collection of the rarest fruit that could be procured for money.

Wine was laid upon a buffet in a deep recess, over which hung a small chandelier.

The general lighting of the room was a whole galaxy of wax candles—there must have been forty at the very least in one chandelier that depended from the centre of the ceiling.

Captain Macheath noticed that that chandelier hung very high up, and that it seemed to be too much condensed for beauty.

"Now," said the prince, "all we have got to do is to make as merry as possible, and quite forget the mishaps of the other room. I don't feel any the worse, I assure you all, now; therefore, it is all right."

He did not feel any the worse—therefore it was all right.

It mattered nothing at all what anybody else might chance to feel upon the occasion.

Several of the ladies began waltzing, and the prince cried out—

"Bravo—bravo! That is capital. Suppose we all have a dance now? It will be good fun."

"Take your partners, gentlemen," cried Colonel Lane, in rather a significant tone of voice.

It was evident that two or three ladies were contending with each other for the honour of the prince's attentions, and one said to him in a coaxing tone of voice—

"How well you look! Ah! if you were not a prince, I should love you very much indeed. You have got the most charming colour, too, to-night that can be conceived."

"Have I, Louisa?"

"Perhaps," said another lady, as she dealt Louisa a box on the ear that nearly felled her to the floor—"perhaps you would like a little more colour, and if I mistake not that will go some way towards giving it to you."

For a moment or two Louisa was staggered and stunned by the blow; but quickly recovering, she snatched up a large pine-apple that was upon the table, and attacked her assailant with it with such vigour, that in a few moments she left nothing in her hand but the little bit of stalk, while the face of her foe was completely covered with the smashed fragments of the pine-apple, and presented truly a most ludicrous spectacle to the whole room.

The prince was so highly amused and delighted at this little affair that he was compelled to lie down upon one of the couches to have his laugh out.

The enraged ladies were separated by some of the guests, and made to promise good behaviour upon pain of expulsion; and the prince chose someone else for his partner, so that they were both disappointed.

Macheath offered his arm to rather a pretty young girl.

"Are you better engaged?" he added.

"Oh! no," she said; and then looking at him, she added—"You are not one of the regular guests here."

"No; but I shall be."

"Very good."

She placed her arm within his without any further ceremony.

Someone then clapped his hands together, and a wild kind of galop began right round the room.

It so happened in the midst of this royal revel that one of the dancers overturned a candelabra, and Macheath, taking advantage of the confusion that ensued, extinguished the rest of the lights and proceeded to help himself liberally of the jewels and other valuables worn by the guests at this extraordinary orgie.

Captain Macheath then rushed to the door, and opened it so suddenly that a servant fell upon his hands and knees into the room.

Macheath seized the man by the collar and flung him heels over head into a corner.

The captain closed the door and locked it on the outside.

He put the key in his pocket, and then hurried down the stairs.

Captain Macheath's great object was now to leave the palace.

He had been quite long enough in it to see all that his curiosity had prompted, and as regarded the profit of the adventure, he had certainly been long enough in Kew to make that tolerably complete.

Upon reaching the foot of the stairs, he was at the moment rather confused to find his way out of the palace, and really whether to turn to the right or to the left he could not take upon himself to decide.

While he was in this state of uncertainty a bell rang very violently indeed, and Captain Macheath asked himself if it boded danger to himself or not.

He laid his hand upon his double-barrelled pistol, upon which he knew he could depend, and listened.

The bell rung again, and that it was a peal of alarm there could not be a shadow of a doubt.

"Ah!" thought Captain Macheath, "that comes, I'll be bound, now, from the Yellow-room. The prince thinks that he will capture me; but he will find it a more difficult matter than he perhaps imagines to lay hands upon me with ease."

Then feeling the necessity of coming to some decision with regard to getting clear of the palace, he turned to the right; not with any particular idea that that was the route that would lead him to the garden, but with the notion that it would take less time to try it and come back again if it were the wrong route than to hesitate about it.

"Confound that bell!" he said, as a third time he heard it pealing through the palace.

In a few moments Macheath came to a door, which he pushed open, and found that it led into a room with another door on the opposite side communicating with a passage.

Macheath crossed the room and ran down the passage until he came to a flight of stairs, which ascended again to the upper floor.

But it was no part of his wish to get up again, so he glanced round here for some door by which to leave the passage.

As he did so he heard a scuffling noise, and a man came rushing down the stairs, crying as he came—

"Help—help! Thieves and highwaymen are in the house. Help—help! Murder!"

"You don't say so?" cried Macheath, stepping up to him.

"Oh! yes. Help—help!"

Captain Macheath seized him by the throat.

"Another word, my friend, in such a tone as that," said he, hissing out each word, "and it is the last that you will be troubled to utter in this world. Do you understand me? I am very serious."

The man's knees knocked together with fright.

"Where does yonder door lead to?"

"To—to—that door? That one?"

"Do not trifle with me," said Macheath. "Most folks find that a rather dangerous pastime. Where does yonder door lead to?"

"To—to the library."

"And the library?"

"Op—opens on to the south lawn."

"That's enough," Captain Macheath returned. "Recollect now that there are six of us, and while I go the other five have their eyes upon you. Sit down upon the bottom stair of this flight, and as long as you sit still you are safe; but the moment you move you will have your brains blown out."

Down flopped the man on to the stair, and there he sat trembling in every limb.

"Oh! yes, I'll sit still. For how long would you like me to sit, sir? Only mention the time."

"Half an hour."

The door to which Captain Macheath had pointed was fast; but one rush at it burst it open, and he passed through it into the library.

It was a magnificent room, with five long French windows opening on to one of the lawns.

The captain opened one of the windows in a moment, and out he dashed.

"Thanks to my good fortune," he said, "I am in the open air once more, and all is well. What did that frightened fool say this was? Oh! the south lawn. South—ah! yes. Then my way is to the left if I would reach the lodge gate, and I shall not be exceedingly particular about how I reach there. The beds and the flowers must suffer for my being rather in a hurry. I hope Luke will be at hand with the horse."

Macheath dashed on in the direction that he knew must lead him towards the gates.

But he had not gone far before he came to one of those little kiosk-like buildings which were sufficiently numerous in the grounds, and a female voice cried out—

"Is it you?"

"Of course it is," said Macheath; "but I am rather busy."

"Ah! that is so like you," said the voice. "I will speak to your grace, if it be only for a moment."

"Good night," said the captain.

He dashed on; but he found his course suddenly impeded by a complete maze of flowering shrubs, some of which met him at nearly every turn.

He cleared the bush in front of him, and alighted upon a path, which he pursued rapidly with a well-founded idea that it would lead him to the lodge-gate.

As he reached the gate, and a servant stepped up to open it with the most respectful movement, Macheath heard the clatter of feet.

"Keep the gates shut, Wood!" shouted a voice; "keep them shut! Let no one leave this place. There has been a robbery committed in the palace."

"Yes," said Captain Macheath, blandly; "keep the gates close shut, Wood, whatever you do, until you see me again. I am going for the officers. Be very vigilant, Wood, mind that."

Wood, which was the name of the man who was on duty at the gate, was rather confused, and Macheath was not the man to fail to profit by that confusion.

He swung the gate open and left the garden.

The excuse he had made, too, warranted him in going fast, so that he disappeared in the darkness of the night before the man at the gate or the persons who were rapidly approaching it by another path from the garden could make up their minds whether he was to be stopped or not.

Macheath now desired to meet with Luke and the horses, so he ran to the top of the lane, and taking from his waistcoat pocket a silver whistle, he blew it with a long, faint sound

It was immediately answered, and the sound of horses' feet came sharply upon his ears.

Macheath ran forward to meet the sound, and he then called out—

"Luke—Luke!"

"Here, sir," said Luke.

"That will do. Ah! I see you now. How dark the night has got all of a sudden."

"It has, sir. A regular bank of clouds has covered the sky. Is there any particular hurry, sir?"

"Well, I think there is rather, Luke. But you see I am here for all that, and all safe, too."

"I'm glad to hear it, sir. We will show them a light pair of heels, if need be; and if they will come too close upon us, and get into danger, well and good. They must take the rough with the smooth. This way, sir, for home."

"But I am for London, Luke."

"Oh! then that's quite another thing. We must go to the right."

"Yes, Luke; to the right it is. The fact is, that I have about me some little articles of value that I would rather at once dispose of before I go home. I know a Jew who will deal with me. We will take a trot to his house and turn the trifles into cash, and then we will go home.'

"Would it not be better, sir, to defer going to the Jew until the hue-and-cry is over."

"Why, no, Luke," said Macheath. "The fact is, I daresay some very heavy reward will be offered for me, and I want to be out of the way before the fact is known to my old acquaintance, Moses Monti, or he might be tempted too much, as, after all, you know, Luke, he is but human."

"And a Jew, sir."

"Well, well, it is very seldom that a Jew will betray you; but still, I never like to rely too strongly upon any man, so I will go to him at once, before he has any opportunity of reflecting how much he might make by concocting some plan for my arrest."

."There is good reason, sir, in what you say. Do you hear anybody after us, sir?"

Macheath listened.

"By all that's uncomfortable, yes!" he said. "I hear the dash of horses' feet. You have your arms ready, Luke? We shall have to give them a taste of our quality."

"We will, sir."

They drew up in the middle of the road and awaited the approach of the horsemen.

When they were tolerably near, Captain Macheath cried out, in a loud voice—

"Hold! What do you want on the road at such a pace?"

"That's the man!" cried a voice. "Fire at him! He is far better dead than alive. Fire away."

Bang—bang! went a couple of pistols, and then a couple more, and still the voice cried out—

"Fire away! Kill him, my men; I will hold you harmless."

"Now, Luke," said Macheath. "Fire!"

Luke and the captain fired together.

"Keep at it," said Macheath, and he discharged two more pistols.

"Down with the villain!" cried the voice again. "Fire away, my lads—fire away!"

Only two more dropping shots were fired, and Captain Macheath then discharged the only pistol he had reloaded.

"Now, gentlemen," he said, "if you are disposed for a race. I am ready; and if you can load again as you gallop, I can do the same, and we will stop again at the most convenient open spot we come to, and have another little blaze away. Come on. Hurrah for the road! Ha! ha!"

Away he went, and Luke by his side.

In the space of a few minutes they placed a mile between them and their foes, not one of whom felt disposed to follow them.

Macheath, however, with the bridle of his horse freely clutched in his teeth, kept both his hands at liberty, with which he succeeded in loading his pistols again; but when he found that his opponents had evidently had enough of the affair, he relaxed his speed, and allowed his horse to go at an easy trot.

"That's over, Luke, I think," he said.

"Oh! yes, sir. It was something like a little battle, while it lasted. One bullet went right through my hat, sir, and another has had the kindness just to touch one of my knuckles, but it did it very gently."

"They were all chance shots, Luke. Nine folks out of ten fire half-a-mile over your head with a pistol. They level at you, and then give the trigger a pull which elevates the muzzle an inch or so, and away flies the bullet as harmless as thistledown."

They increased their speed a little, and in a short time reached Gray's Inn-lane, which was then a long, straggling thoroughfare, with fields upon the east side of it, and a great many lonely places between Holborn and King's-cross.

CHAPTER XLV.
THE BETRAYER IS CAUGHT IN HIS OWN SNARE.

"This is not the liveliest spot in the world," said Macheath as they reached Gray's Inn-lane; "but if we find our friend, the Jew, stirring, it will do very well for us."

"It is an early hour," said Luke.

"Yes; but see how the morning is stealing upon us now rapidly, and it will be rather lighter than I should wish, I fear, before we see the old house at Kentish-town again."

"It will, indeed, sir. Is this the place?"

Macheath had stopped opposite to what seemed to be nothing in the world but a dead wall.

Nevertheless, there was a little, low, dingy-looking door in it.

But there did not seem to be any means of opening it, or of conversing with the inmates of the place, if there were any.

"Look about you, Luke," said Macheath, as he dismounted; "and let me know if anyone is watching us."

"Not a soul, sir," said Luke, after he had cast a cautious and searching glance around him. "Not a soul, sir."

"Very good. Then it may be useful for you to know, Luke, that under the step here, which you see is of wood, and not above six inches from the ground, having a hollow space under it, there is the handle of a bell."

"It is ingeniously placed, sir."

"It is, indeed. If you listen sharply you will hear it ring. I have not been here often, but each time that I have come I have heard its tinkle."

Luke did listen, and the moment the captain gave the bell a jerk a clear but distant sound of a bell came upon his ears.

"I heard it, sir."

"And so did I. We shall soon be answered."

In the course of about a minute the upper part of the little dirty door was opened upon a separate pair of hinges to those which belonged to the whole structure, and a form appeared.

"Who is it?" asked the Jew, shading his eyes with his hand, and peering out into the darkness.

"Look again, Moses. Don't you know—"

"It is Captain Macheath."

"It is; and I have some little trinkets and other matters for you to look at which I don't choose to carry home with me."

"Oh! you nice young man. You shall come in directly. I will go and fetch the key. I only now do the best of business, you beauty."

The Jew shut the little wicket, and hurried off for the key.

"You can wait in the lane, Luke," said the

captain. "I will be as short a time arranging matters with the Jew as possible. You know how the bell works; if anything should occur which makes it necessary for you to communicate with me, you can ring it, and I will come at once to the wicket."

"I will keep a sharp look-out, sir."

"Do so. It will not be for long—a quarter of an hour at most."

The Jew at this moment made his appearance again, and opened the door for Captain Macheath to enter.

He poked his old face right out into the lane and saw Luke.

"Ha! my dear Macheath," he said, "you have got a friend? Do you think he has any silver spoons about him! There's a good market for silver spoons."

"I'm sure he has not, Moses."

"Oh! what a pity."

The Jew closed the door, and hobbled before Macheath through a little dim-looking court-yard, about twenty feet square, which led to a dirty little house.

"Does your friend wait for you, my dear Macheath?"

"No; he goes home at once."

"Oh! dear—bless you."

"Why, Moses, how polite you are this morning!"

"It's because it's so early. I like to get up early. I always like a long day, as the gentlemen say at the Old Bailey when they are sentenced to be hanged! Ha—ha! That's a good joke! A long day—ha!"

"Very good indeed," said Macheath, "considering who it came from. But I hope you have plenty of money in this old den, for I have those things to show you that must not go for a trifle."

"Money? Did you say money, my dear? Oh! it never was so scarce. Money is hard to get!"

"I never heard of it being otherwise, Moses."

The Jew coughed, and led Macheath into a small room upon the ground floor of the house.

Upon a table in the middle of the room was a pair of scales for weighing articles of gold and silver and various other articles useful for testing the quantity.

In the centre of the table was a hole that seemed to be partially closed by a conical bag of green cloth, the narrowest part of which hung downwards.

It was into this orifice that Moses slipped the articles that he purchased, and below there was a confederate to receive them and lay them away at once in a place of safety.

"Ah! well, my dear," said Moses, "what is it you have to sell? I half made up my mind to buy no more, it is so difficult to get rid of anything nowadays. I seldom get above fifteen shillings back again, as I'm a sinner, for what I give a pound."

"Gammon, Moses!"

"Gammon, do you call it, my dear Macheath?"

"Yes, and you know it, you old rascal. What you mean is that you get about five pounds for every one pound. That is nearer the mark. But what do I care if you get twenty. It is all the same to me, so that you give me what satisfies me. What do you think of that?"

As he spoke Macheath laid before the Jew a quantity of jewellery.

"Ah! dear me," said the Jew as he looked at the superb articles, and his eyes sparkled again. "What a capital imitation, and what really good gilding!"

"Now, Moses," said Macheath, "I don't wish to be kept here an hour or two trafficking and bargaining with you. I am tired and want to get home. I have set the price of two hundred upon these things, and if you like to have them, there they are. If you will not, say so at once, and I am off, for I will not haggle about them.

"Two hundred — two—two—two hundred! Oh—oh—oh! Two—"

"Very good; I am off, then. I regret having given you and myself so much trouble. They don't suit you, and that's enough."

Macheath began pocketing the trinkets with great speed, and the terrified Jew caught hold of his arm.

"Hold, my dear! One hundred I will give!"

"No—no!"

"A hundred and fifty? Well, well—oh! gracious, I shall be ruined I know, but I will give it—two hundred. Mother of Moses! what will become of me? I feel that I am ruined, and yet I will give the money rather than you should be vexed. Lewin—Lewin, my dear son, come here."

"Who the deuce is Lewin?" said Macheath.

"It is my little boy, and here he comes."

A Jew lad, with the strongly-marked features of his race, crept silently into the room.

"My dear Lewin," said Moses, "you will run to our friend, Shadrach, in Field-lane, and tell him to give you two hundred pounds on my writing till to-morrow; and you will be quick, Lewin."

"Yes," said the boy.

The Jew wrote about two lines of Hebrew character upon a slip of paper, and then gave it to Lewin, who just glanced at it, and a flush came over his face for a moment, which Macheath thought rather singular considering the little moment of the affair.

"Report much belies you, Moses," said Macheath, "if you have any real occasion to send to a friend for two hundred pounds."

"I am poor—I am poor!"

"Pooh! How long will this boy of yours be gone? I am not disposed for any delays."

"You know Field-lane, my dear Macheath? It is only just down the hill, you know. He will be back in a few minutes. Will you have anything to drink?"

"No—no; I have had quite enough already during the night, and might have drowned myself in choice wines, if I had cared to do so. You have got a bargain, Moses, for I believe the things are worth double the money you are about to give for the whole lot."

"Oh! no—no. Oh! dear, no," said Moses. "You are very much mistaken, Macheath. Jewels are down now, very much down, indeed."

"Well—well, I am satisfied, if you— Hilloa! That's rather a sharp ring at your bell."

The bell tinkled furiously.

"Oh! dear—dear," said the Jew, "that's the way with them. If they have such a thing as a two-ounce old snuff-box to part with, they come and ring the bell as if they had all the diamonds in the world in their pockets, and are willing to take half-price for the lot."

The Jew hobbled off to the door, and Macheath followed him across the courtyard.

The wicket was opened, and in a sharp voice, for Moses had not wished to be interrupted until he had quite concluded the little business.

"Who is it? Who is it?" he demanded.

"Captain Macheath!" cried Luke. "Are you there?"

"Yes, Luke."

"Open the door—open the door!"

"No—no!" said the Jew, placing his back against it. "No, you shall not. Help! Murder!"

"Open the door!" cried Luke, again. "You are betrayed, captain. The Jew has betrayed you, I say."

"Ah!" cried Macheath, as he clutched the Jew by the throat, and sent him spinning across the court-yard. "What say you?"

"A Jew boy is bringing at least a dozen officers up Holborn-hill, and they are well-armed."

The door was secured by a bolt on the inside, and Captain Macheath in a moment undid it, and admitted Luke.

"The horses, Luke!" he said. "The horses!"

"All safe. I have put them out of sight, that's all."

"Is there time to mount and be off?"

"No—no. Oh! no."

"Very good. Then this shall be our fortress for a little time, at all events."

As he spoke, Captain Macheath bolted the door again firmly, and turning round, he caught the Jew by the arm.

"You old rascal, so you would give me up, would you?" he cried.

"Mercy—mercy!"

"You don't deserve as much as one would give to a mad dog, you old villain; for I trusted you, as well you know. Come along; I will not let you out of my clutch again."

The Jew seemed to be half dead with terror as Macheath dragged him back into the little parlour again.

They had hardly reached it, when a heavy shower of blows sounded upon the door; and then there came a sharp ring at the bell.

No doubt some of the officers had reached the house a few moments before the boy, and had not known how to ring for admission.

"What is to be done?" said Luke.

"I'll be hanged if I know," said Macheath. "It's rather awkward. Suppose we knock Moses on the head, and then see if there is a back way out of the house?"

The Jew fell upon his knees when he heard this, and in the most abject manner begged for his life.

The knocking continued, and the noise was sufficient to convince both Captain Macheath and Luke that the doors would not stand such an assault for long.

"Oh! spare me—spare me!" cried the Jew. "Rachel—Rachel, where are you?—my little grandchild, where are you?"

The door of the room opened, and one of the most beautiful children that Captain Macheath had ever seen appeared.

She was dressed in the richest costume, and when she saw her grandfather upon his knees, and Macheath in a threatening attitude standing over him, she raised a shriek of alarm, and springing forward, clung to Captain Macheath's arm in an agony of terror.

"Oh! kill me—kill me!" she said, "but spare him. He is old—very old. You will not kill him?"

"For your sake I will not," Macheath replied. "Do not not cry so, my dear. Your grandfather has done us a grievous injury; but for your sake I will spare him."

"Blessings on you!" said the young girl.

The old Jew trembled like an aspen leaf, as he kept on mumbling—

"It's false—it's false, I say! I have done nothing—nothing at all, I say. It is not true."

Bang—bang! went the blows upon the door, and the bell rang furiously.

Much less time had elapsed in all these circumstances taking place than we have taken to tell of them; but yet the danger was imminent.

CHAPTER XLVI.
THE ESCAPE FROM THE JEW'S HOUSE.

"I HAVE it," said Luke. "I have it, sir."

"What?" cried Captain Macheath. "What do you mean?"

"The little girl will not refuse to assist us so long as she feels certain that no harm will come to her?"

"Oh! no—I will not refuse," she cried. "Bid me do anything, and I will do it. You have spared his life. I begin now to understand what he has done to excite your anger. Oh! it was not well done, grandfather—it was not, indeed. He would have betrayed you to your enemies?"

"That's just what he would have done," said Captain Macheath.

"Then, if you will yet spare him, I will do all I can to assist you."

"Your plan, Luke!" exclaimed Captain Macheath. "Your plan——"

"It's just this," Luke replied. "I think that by putting on your coat and hat over the Jew, and wrapping his face up with a handkerchief, you may pass him off for yourself. The lady can have no objection to such a scheme, I am sure. Shall it be tried?"

"Yes," said the girl. "I feel bound to do anything for your good. It shall be done at once, and I will get your friend a long dressing-gown of grandfather's to put on, so that he shall not be known."

"And me, too," said Luke. "Let me have something."

"You shall."

"The plan will do very well," said Captain Macheath.

"Oh! no—no," said the Jew, as he cast a reproachful glance at the girl. "Are you, too, against me? Does my own flesh and blood turn against me? My curse will fall upon your head!"

"No, grandfather," said the girl. "When you are calmer, and feel that your life has been spared, you will be thankful."

She left the room as she spoke, and Captain Macheath seized the Jew.

"Come, Moses," he said; "for once in a way we will do you the honour of making you look like a highwayman."

In the hands of Captain Macheath resistance would have been worse than madness, so the Jew gave in with as good a grace as he could, and only uttered deep groans.

Stripping off his coat Macheath enveloped the Jew in it, and then he tied a handkerchief so round his mouth that while it did not stop his breath it effectually gagged him.

Cutting down a thick bell rope the captain bound Moses with it so that his arms were confined to his sides.

CAPTAIN MACHEATH RETURNED THE GLANCE WITH COMPOUND INTEREST.

The girl returned with two long Jewish coats that buttoned all the way down from the neck to the toes, and both Macheath and Luke were in a moment or two enveloped in them.

The change in their appearance was most remarkable.

"Hark! there goes the door," said Luke.

A sudden crash proclaimed that the outer door was burst open by the officers.

Captain Macheath immediately threw the Jew on the floor, and held him there.

"Help—help!" the captain cried. "This way —this way! We have him all right. Officers, this way."

Luke flung the house-door open, and the officers at once rushed into the room.

"It's all right," Macheath cried. "We have him here a prisoner. Take him with you—you had better get a coach and take him off in it, for he is desperate fellow. I will hold him to the floor."

The principal danger was that the Jew boy would let the cat out of the bag.

But Luke got over that by the moment he saw the boy rushing to him, and catching him in his arms and crying, as he fairly carried him out into the yard —

"Oh! my dear nephew, I am so glad you have come back in safety with these gentlemen. Come along with me now, my dear."

"But—but—" cried the boy.

"Ah! yes—it's all right."

They reached the yard, and then Luke put his mouth close to the boy's ear.

"Hark you!" he hissed. "You are a very clever fellow, I daresay, but I have a pistol here with which I will blow out your brains if you say another word, good, bad, or indifferent, unless I bid you. Now look to it."

The Jew boy fell upon his knees in a moment.

There was a door in the yard that seemed to lead to some out-house, and holding the hopeful young gentleman by the hair of his head, Luke peeped into the place that the door concealed.

It was a coal ———.

"Now, my lad," said Luke, "I will give you a chance for your life."

"Oh! dear sir, how good of you."

"Well, perhaps it is. But you will oblige me by going into that cellar and waiting there until I come and fetch you out, and if you attempt to stir or make the least disturbance while you are there, as sure as you are now a living boy I will rid the world of you, and put an end to your career in this life."

"Oh! mercy—mercy!"

"Go into the cellar."

"I will, sir—indeed, I will," and the boy crawled on his hands and knees to the cellar-door, and then vanished as if heartily glad of finding so good a hiding-place.

"He is safe, at all events," said Luke. "Confound him! he would have spoilt all our plans. Hilloa! here they come."

What attracted Luke now was the curious manner in which the officers were bringing out the person whom they supposed to be Captain Macheath.

They wrapped round the unfortunate Jew a large, rough, great-coat belonging to one of themselves, and as that held his feet together, they had no resource but to bring him out something after the fashion of an Egyptian mummy, one of them holding his feet, and another holding his head.

"A coach—a coach!" cried one. "Has Jones got a coach?"

"Yes—yes!" cried Jones, running into the yard from Gray's Inn-lane. "Here's one at the door. It's all right. The man would not come without double fare, as it was a Newgate job, and I agreed to give it to him."

"Oh! that's all right. It ain't a shilling or two, or a pound or two, that will matter in the affair. Hilloa! Mr. Jew. How much do you expect now for giving us the affair?"

"That, my dears," said Captain Macheath, imitating the Jewish accent. "I shall leave to you."

"You will?"

"Yes, my dears; just what you think proper I will take."

"Will fifty pounds do?"

"Yes, my dears, very well indeed. I don't want to make a large profit by it, my dears, for you see this Captain Macheath didn't behave well to me, at all; so I will take the fifty pounds, and the satisfaction of knowing he will be hung up to dry, my dears, will be worth as much again."

"Well, I take you all to witness," said the principal officer, "that he says he is satisfied with fifty pounds, and that after that Captain Macheath is to be considered our capture."

"Yes. Oh! yes."

"Oh! yes, my dear," added Macheath. "It's all right. I don't want to go back from my word."

"Then," said the officer, taking out a black pocket-book, "there, Moses, is your fifty pounds, and that settles the business. Take it; it's a good note. You needn't look at it, and your liberality in the affair won't be the worse for you, if ever your little establishment here should be routed out, which, you know, may be some day."

"I know it," said Macheath. "Have you got him safe in the coach, my dears?"

"Oh! yes—yes. All's right."

"Then be off with you. Rachel, my little love, you will shut the door after the gentlemans."

"Yes, grandfather, I will."

The officers had no doubt but that all was right, and the confident manner in which the beautiful young girl spoke would have dispelled any if it had existed.

They had put the old Jew in the coach, and were perfectly well satisfied with their bargain, as they now expected all the reward for taking Macheath.

They ordered the coachman to drive them as fast as he could to Newgate Prison. Two of the officers went inside, two got on the coachbox with the coachman, and the rest held on behind or scrambled on to the roof, for they were resolved that Captain Macheath should not escape.

"They will not hurt him?" said the little girl to Macheath.

"Not at all; they dare not. What made him betray me, I wonder?" said Macheath.

"Ah! sir," Rachel returned, sorrowfully, "he is getting old now, and the love of gold is now day by day, and hour by hour, growing upon him. He wishes to amass a large sum that he may leave England."

"Oh! that is it," said Macheath. "He is going out of business. That accounts for the whole affair in a moment. I must now bid you a good-day, for every moment that I linger here is full of danger."

Captain Macheath had again carefully secured about him the rich property that he had brought with him to dispose of to the Jew, and then shaking hands cordially with the girl, he hurried from the house.

In the yard, waiting rather impatiently for him, he met Luke.

"Come, sir—oh! come," said Luke. "Recollect how short the distance from here to Newgate is, and how, at any moment, even before getting there, for all we know to the contrary, the deceit may be discovered."

"You are right, Luke. I am off directly. Where are the horses?"

"This way—this way!"

Luke led the way into the lane, and under cover of an archway both the horses were quietly standing.

To mount was the work of a moment, and off they set at a hard gallop down the Gray's Inn-lane northward, for that was then the nearest way to Kentish-town.

They had hardly reached Battle-bridge, when they heard a great shouting noise behind them.

Upon turning to look in that direction they saw two mounted men in hot pursuit of them.

"Ah!" said Macheath. "They have found out their mistake at last."

"But there are only two of them, sir."

"So I see, and we will give them a little race into the country. There is a lane just by here called Maiden-lane, which is our best way, as it escapes the hill. We will take that, Luke, and if these fellows choose to come after us, which I don't think very likely, they will find it to be the worst for them."

It was clear, from the manner in which those two officers rode, that there was no shrinking upon their part, and that they had quite made up their minds to do the job upon which they had come, or to see some much more substantial reason than danger for leaving it alone.

"Ah!" said Macheath, as he listened to the loud tramp of their horses' hoofs, "those men will not be deterred by a trifle. I deeply regret that they have come upon such an errand."

"But you do not think for a moment, sir," said Luke, "that they can get the better of us, surely?"

"No, Luke," said Macheath, "that is not the reason why I regret their coming; but I do not like to take life, and I am much afraid that these men are of that order, that unless I do, they will not be easily disposed of. But it must be so, I suppose."

"You should not forget, sir, that it is to death they would drag you, and that all their seeming courage is merely because a large reward is offered for you. Self defence is a better motive than that."

Macheath was rather surprised to hear Luke argue the matter so well as he did, for what he said was really very much to the question.

"Luke," he said, "you remove many of my scruples. I know and feel the truth of what you say; it is nothing but the love of gold brings these men after us, and makes them seem so bold and so full of daring, and I will defend myself to the last against them."

"Do so, sir. They come well armed against us, and they deserve all they may get."

"They do—they do!"

"Shall we stop, then, sir, and meet them? There is a nice little hillock close a-head of us, where we can conveniently come to a pause, I think."

"I see the hillock, Luke; but let me advise you never, if you are going to exchange pistol shots with anyone, to take the high ground. Your chances of being hit, if you do, will be ten to one in comparison to what they would be if you occupy a low position. When you are upon an elevation, the bullets that would otherwise go over your head, will hit you almost to a certainty."

"I see, sir, I see—I understand. Then we will wait in the hollow, sir. It strikes me that the moment we come to a stand they will do so likewise."

"It is more than probable, Luke; especially if they see us with arms in our hands."

"Our best plan, sir, will be to take one of them a-piece. There's the fellow with the red coat—I will pay all the attention I can to him, sir, if you will tackle the other; and by that means I don't think we need waste a shot."

"Upon my work, Luke," said Macheath, "you take the thing coolly. Let it be as you say. You attend to the one in the red coat, and I will keep my eye on the one with the blue."

"Do so, captain; and between you and me, I would not give a dump for their lives. But that's their look out, not ours. They will have it, so we can't possibly help it."

The manner in which Luke reconciled himself to the necessity of tackling the two officers, would at any other time have been quite amusing to Macheath; but at that period their circumstances were of rather too serious a nature to permit of mirth.

"Halt!" he said. "This, I think, is the lowest part of the road, my friend."

"It is, sir; and there they come, thundering on. Ah! no, they are already pulling up. They don't like the look of us, after all, and are rather afraid to come to close quarters. It is as I all along suspected, sir. They don't want to come to a fair fight, but they relied upon running us down in course of time, and getting all sorts of help to be upon us."

"Likely enough."

"I am sure of it, captain," Luke replied; "and it's a nasty, spy-like mode of doing business. I'm glad enough that we have put a stop to it by halting. Why, what are they about now, sir—what the deuce is the meaning of this, I wonder?"

One of the officers had taken out a white handkerchief, and fastened it at the end of his riding-whip, and with that fluttering in the morning air as a flag of truce, for such he intended it, he gently walked his horse forward to where Macheath and Luke were standing.

"He wants to talk us over, Luke."

"Talk us over?"

"Yes. That white handkerchief shows that he has got a something or another to say, and that while it flies, he will not attempt any violence, and hopes that he will receive none. I will go forward and hear the fellow."

"Don't, sir—oh! don't."

"Nay; but, Luke, you see it is a regular flag of truce—and it would look bad, indeed, not to go."

"I would not trust him, sir."

"You would not?"

"No," said Luke; "I would not trust one of those fellows upon their oaths, much less upon the strength of a white pocket-handkerchief. Don't you go, sir. Take my word for it, it is only a *ruse*. They can't fight you by fair means, and they want to try to do so by foul. That's the long and short of it, captain."

" If I could but think so for a moment—"

" Do think so, sir," said, Luke, interrupting him. " I don't like the talking part of the affair at all ; but if it must be, you stay where you are, and let me go. You will then see if they mean fair or not."

" No—no ! If there be danger, let me face it."

" I implore you not, sir."

" Nay, Luke, I find that you don't know me yet," Captain Macheath returned. " I have always found the greatest safety by meeting danger half-way ; and, besides, if yonder fellow means treachery, it does not follow that he is to succeed in it. I will keep such a wary eye upon him that he shall find it a difficult matter to wink without my cognizance of the act. Be under no apprehension, all will be right, Luke. Wait for me where you are."

When Luke saw that Macheath would not be persuaded, he made no further opposition, but only took care to place himself in a good position, with a pistol in his hand ready for immediate use.

Macheath rode forward until within earshot of the officer.

" My friend," said the captain, " I think you and I are quite near enough to each other. What have you to say ?"

" Listen to me, Macheath," said the officer. " I have no desire to intrude further upon you than you think proper, and I hope you will listen to me calmly."

" Oh ! I am quite calm ; only I think the sooner you manage to come to the point the better it will be."

" I will come to it at once—a-hem !"

" Very well, go on."

" I was going to say that you played a capital trick with those idiots who brought the Jew to Newgate," the officer rejoined ; " but with that I personally have nothing to do, although my friend yonder has."

" Oh ! he is one of the idiots, is he ?"

" Yes," the officer replied ; " but I beg to state, Macheath, that it will be quite impossible for you to escape, and you had much better take your chances of a comfortable trial at the Old Bailey, than be shot down like a dog on the highway."

" Is that all you have got to say ?"

" Why, to a reasonable man, that ought to be enough, and I trust you will see the propriety of coming back to London with me."

" Upon my word," laughed Captain Macheath, " you are the most impudent fellow I have met for some time."

" Impudent ?"

" Yes, to be sure. Is it not the very height of impudence to make such a proposal to me while a breath of life is in me ? I am amazed at your assurance."

" You are ?"

" I really am."

" Then you refuse the excellent advice I offer you ?"

" Rather !" said Captain Macheath.

" Then perhaps you will have the kindness to take that."

As he spoke, the officer fired a short, holster-pistol direct at Captain Macheath's head.

The contents blew off his hat and singed his hair, but owing to the fact of his horse causing him to stoop at the moment, the villainous attempt did not do him any further injury.

In the confusion of the moment, Macheath could not take upon himself to say whether he was hit or not ; but of the two, he rather thought he was.

The moment the officer had fired this dastardly shot, he turned round and tried to get away to his companion, but Luke came on at a pace that seemed as though he were flying, and then suddenly brought his horse to a dead stop.

" A fair shot for a foul one !" he cried.

Levelling a pistol at the officer, he fired, and the bullet hit him exactly between the shoulders.

With a loud cry of agony the officer fell forward on his horse's neck.

" If that has not yet done for you," said Luke, " there is no virtue in a couple of ounce bullets."

The officer's horse made a mad plunge forwards and half fell, flinging its rider to the earth.

The other officer, seeing that he was now left alone, at once turned, and went off as fast as his horse could take him.

" Oh ! sir—sir," cried Luke, " he has killed you ! I expected it would end in this way, and it is but a poor satisfaction to me, that I have been able to avenge your murderer—for it was a murder."

" Wait a bit !" said Macheath.

" What, captain, are you not mortally wounded ?"

" Not that I know of, Luke," replied the captain, shaking his head. " I don't feel quite so clear-headed as I did, but I don't think there's much more harm done. I fancy if there were a bullet or two in my brains, I should feel rather more confused than I do now, and that's going away fast."

" Oh ! captain, how pleased I am, to be sure," said Luke, joyfully. " I made up my mind that you were done for."

" Did you ?"

" Yes. When I saw the rascal fire straight at your head, sir, what else could I possibly think of it ? I really thought he had blown your head almost off, and I felt as if I were going mad."

" It was my hat, Luke," said Captain Macheath. " I am all right again now. By Jove ! it was as foul and dastardly a shot as I ever heard of one man firing at another. What has become of the rascal ?"

" What, sir, did you not see me settle him ?"

" Settle him, Luke ? Is that a delicate way of saying that you have killed him ?"

" If a couple of bullets through his back will do it I have, and did he not deserve it, sir ?"

" He did," said the captain. " He was an assassin, and all such deserve death from any hand that has the power to inflict it upon them. This is the closest touch that I think I have had yet for my life. If he had but fired another at me he must have hit me, for I was too confused to resist him."

" Thank goodness, captain, the rascal did not fire again !" Luke rejoined ; " but the fact was he thought the first charge had done the trick, and was willing to get away then as quickly as he could."

" Where is he, Luke ?"

" There ! lying on his back in the road."

Captain Macheath shook his head again, for he still felt confused.

Luke thought it was with disapprobation of the death of the officer.

" Surely, sir, you think he deserved it ?" he queried.

" You mistake me, Luke," Macheath replied. " I am not shaking my head at that, but to settle my own brains a little. They seem to have given quite a jump; but that feeling will soon pass away. I think our best plan is to get home as quickly as we may."

"It is, sir."

"Come on, then," said the captain. "We will leave the field of battle to the enemy, if they think proper to come and claim it. It is quite sufficiently satisfactory to us to have obtained the victory."

They went off at a canter, leaving the dead officer lying where he had fallen.

His treachery had been of so glaring a nature that Macheath did not repent what had taken place, as he could not entertain an atom of pity for a man who could behave so treacherously towards him.

"I feel, Luke," he said, "that I am deeply indebted to you for the part you have taken in this affair. I was really at the time unable to defend myself, and the probability is that if you had not come to my rescue the other officer would have finished me."

"It is very well, captain, as it is," Luke replied; "and here we are in the high road of Holloway. We shall soon be at home."

"Precisely," said Captain Macheath; "and I don't know how you feel, Luke, but I will say for myself that I never felt more inclined for a rest than I do now. I am thoroughly weary."

"Ah! captain, if you had not been so you would not have been so easily taken in by that rascal of an officer. I thought you had not quite your usual judgment and sharpness about you."

Macheath smiled at this observation, and in the course of a few minutes they were at the garden gate of the captain's house.

CHAPTER XLVII.

THE COURT JEWELLER—THE ARREST.

"HOME again," said Macheath, "and I am not sorry for it, Luke, for, to tell the truth, I am for once fairly fagged out."

"And no wonder, captain. I think that eight or ten hours' sleep will do no one no harm, and I am quite sure that you want it."

"I really think I do. But neither you nor I must give way to such a long repose as that."

"Not both of us at a time, captain," Luke remarked. "You go to rest, and I will manage to keep my eyes open for a few hours."

"No, Luke," said Macheath. "Bolt and bar the place up—make the doors and windows secure, and then I think we may both repose in safety."

"Then I will sleep in the stable," said Luke. "There's nothing to me so capital and luxurious as a bundle of dry straw. If anything should happen I shall be sure to be on the alert. So you may rest, captain, quite at your ease."

Macheath laughed at Luke's notion of a comfortable bed.

Then, surrendering the horses to him, the captain went into the house where, as a matter of course, he was warmly welcomed by his wife.

Captain Macheath took care, however, before he indulged himself with any repose, to hide, in a secure place, the booty he had brought with him from Kew, and which he had made so unsuccessful an attempt already to dispose of. That the articles he had got possession of were of great value there could be no sort of doubt, and the greatest difficulty was to realise their value.

Nothing occurred for the whole of the day to give the remotest alarm to Macheath; and as he had made up his mind to remain at home for some time, until the affair at the palace had quite blown over, he amused himself about his house and garden.

"Ah!" said Polly, "if you could only always lead this life how happy we might be."

"Do you think so?"

"I am sure of it. Here this day is passing away quite delightfully, and I am sure that nothing can be more pleasing to you than walking in your garden."

"Well," said Macheath, "I admit that I am fond of a country life, but how long that fondness would last I cannot at all pretend to say. It is possible enough that after a time I should weary of it."

"Oh! no," Polly returned. "The country has a thousand charms that you could never weary of."

"Well, perhaps I might be happy enough in it."

At this moment Luke came up where Macheath and Polly were standing to ask something concerning the horses.

"I wish, Luke, that you would mount one of them," the captain said, "and go and try to purchase a newspaper. It is just possible that we might find something about our recent adventures."

"Yes, sir; I shall be able to get one at Islington"

Luke made good speed to Islington and back, and brought Macheath a newspaper.

There was an expression on Luke's face that convinced the captain at once that there was something in the paper interesting to him.

"There is a paragraph for us, Luke."

"Yes, sir; and an advertisement."

"Indeed! That is a rarity. Let me see it."

Luke pointed out a particular part of the paper, and Captain Macheath read as follows—

"To the Baron Hoge.—If the individual calling himself the Baron Hoge will return to Mr. James Sanderson, St. James'-street, the various little articles taken from K., he will receive a five hundred pound note, and no questions will be asked or inquiries made concerning him."

"This does, indeed, concern me; and yet I don't know what to do exactly," Macheath said. "If I thought I could rely upon this promise in the advertisement I would not hesitate a moment to part with the things. I know that their intrinsic value is much more than five hundred pounds; and yet it is a much larger sum than I ever expected to realise for them."

"Why, sir," said Luke, "the fact is that I daresay there are certain parties who are quite as anxious as we can be to keep the secret of the affair at Kew; so that perhaps it really is true that they would gladly enough give the five hundred pounds to hush it up."

"That is likely enough, Luke. You would then counsel me to venture to St. James'-street?"

"No, no, captain," said Luke. "Let me go. If treachery should be intended it won't be so bad as if they got hold of you."

"No, Luke; that would not be fair."

"Oh! yes, captain, it would," the faithful fellow rejoined. "And I feel quite assured that my mistress will consider that it is the best plan."

"No; I would have neither of you go," said Polly, "I would forego the money, and wait until some favourable opportunity should arise of making one-half the amount by the jewels."

"Ah!" said Macheath, "do not forget that you are the banker, and that my object is to make enough to prevent me from being under the necessity of pursuing this line of life. Did we not agree fully upon that? Recollect what a lift the sum of five hundred pounds is towards that object. I think I will go."

"But the frightful risk!"

"The more I think of it, the more I am inclined to think that the advertisement is quite genuine," mused Captain Macheath.

"Oh! captain, do let me go?" said Luke.

"No," Macheath replied, resolutely. "Saddle me a horse, and I will go at once, Luke. The whole affair will be over in a couple of hours. I do not think there is any real danger. I will dress myself as quaintly as I can, and take the things with me. Do not be under any apprehension; I suspect that I know too much of the proceedings at Kew to make it safe to apprehend me."

Po ly burst into tears, for she had a presentiment that this affair would turn out to be most disastrous to Macheath, but she well knew that when he made a determination to try to turn him from it by speaking of its dangers was utterly futile.

"For my sake you will be as careful as is possible," she only said; "you will promise me that?"

"I will, indeed," the captain replied; "but there is one thing I beg of you to remember, and that is, that let what will happen to me, you can do me no good; let you hear what you may, I beg and implore that you will remain here at home, and take no step in the mistaken idea that you can do me a service."

"But—but—"

"Nay, I must get you to promise me that much."

"I will, then. I do. I rely upon your judgment wholly; and if you are of that opinion, I will promise to follow the course you point out."

"Here's the horse, sir," said Luke.

Macheath went into the house, and made some slight change in his apparel.

He likewise carefully secreted about him all the articles that he had brought away from Kew, so that there should be no cavil about his keeping his part of the agreement; and then, with a cheerful air, he started on his perilous expedition.

One circumstance induced Captain Macheath to think that upon this occasion he was going upon a safe errand.

The value of the articles was much over the sum offered, so it was evident that sum was considered to be a compromise of the affair.

"No," said the captain, as he rode along. "The sum of five hundred pounds is but a small one in such a quarter, and I quite understand that it is given to hush up the transaction."

So far Macheath was right.

At the pace at which Captain Macheath rode he soon reached London; and then suffering his horse to subside into a quiet trot, so that no appearance of undue hurry should be about him when he should reach St. James'-street, he quietly entered that aristocratic thoroughfare.

To be sure, there was nothing in the appearance of Macheath to lead in the least to the idea that he was a highwayman; and when he entered Mr. Sanderson's shop, he was received with the greatest possible civility.

"Is Mr. Sanderson within?" he said.

"Yes, sir. Certainly, sir. Pray step this way."

Macheath followed the shopman to a private counting-house, built under an archway leading to a yard, and there he was introduced to the jeweller. When the door was closed, and the shopman out of hearing, Captain Macheath said, in soft and bland accents—

"Sir, I came here in consequence of an advertisement addressed to the Baron Hoge."

Mr. Sanderson started.

"You—you have some little articles for the prince then, I presume, sir?" said the jeweller, trembling, and looking as nervous as possible.

"I have, sir," said Macheath. "I have placed the most implicit confidence in the advertisement, and have come here relying upon the prince's honour to accept the terms offered. I hope that I have not misplaced the confidence that I have so promptly shown?"

"You have not, Mr. a—a Baron Hoge. The prince is extremely desirous that the whole affair should be forgotten. He is quite willing to pass it off as a joke merely. And, therefore, he will freely give five hundred pounds and let the matter drop."

"Very good," said Macheath, as he laid the articles before the jeweller. "There they are and you have nothing to do but to give me the money, and I will be off at once, Mr. Sanderson."

The jeweller rapidly glanced over the articles, and then compared them with a written paper that he had close at hand.

"Quite right, sir," he said; "quite right. I will hand you the money directly."

With these words he proceeded to an iron safe let into the wall, and speedily abstracted from it a note for five hundred pounds, which he handed to Macheath.

"Now, sir," said he, "I only hope that you will make good use of this money. You are a young man—quite a young man—and I am an old one, so you will excuse me for offering you friendly advice. With that sum of money you can surely find some honest and reputable means of getting a living."

"Sir," said Macheath, "far from feeling any offence at what you say, I thank you for having so much kindly interest in me as to say it. I will bid you good morning, well pleased that I trusted to your word and that of the prince, and came here."

"Yes; but really now consider, Mr. What's-your-name, you will not bring yourself to a bad end?"

"It is very kind of you, sir, to speak to me in such a way. I will consider."

"That's right—that's right," said Mr. Sanderson. "You have something in your face, and voice, and manner, that convinces me that you are not a bad—not a very bad young man. I was not prepared to see a person like you; indeed, I was not; and I feel a degree of kindly pity for you. Remember, now, that if you really feel an inclination to change your mode of life you will find a friend in me."

"I will not forget it, sir. Friends are too scarce nowadays for me to hold lightly so kind and generous a one as yourself."

Macheath shook hands with the old gentleman, and walked out of the counting-house with his five hundred pounds in his pocket.

He thought that the shopman cast a very odd look at him, and then through the window into

CAPTAIN MACHEATH

THE
PRINCE OF THE HIGHWAY.

CAPTAIN MACHEATH HEARD THE BULLET WHISTLE OVER HIS HEAD.

NO. 16.

the street, and a suspicion entered Macheath's mind for the first time that all was not exactly right.

His horse was at the door, and no one offered to interrupt him.

Suspicion vanished again, and he gave the boy who held his horse a shilling, and placed his foot in the stirrup to mount.

At that moment he felt himself clasped round the body by a powerful pair of arms, and a voice cried in his ear—

"You are my prisoner, Captain Macheath!"

So unexpected an arrest as this must have confounded Captain Macheath, unless he had really been something more than human.

No other mode than that which had been adopted could have so effectually secured him, and from the moment that the arms were cast around him, the captain felt that he was in experienced hands.

All he could do was to kick vigorously.

"You are my prisoner," said the voice again, "and you may remain so without injury or with it, as you think proper."

"Not yet," said Macheath.

By an effort such as few men could have made, he succeeded in facing his assailant.

But he had scarcely done so, when four men rushed upon him, and he found that they had arranged how to set to work with him, for one took possession of an arm, another of a leg, and so on, until, if he had had the strength of a lion, he would have been overpowered.

"Very good," said Captain Macheath. "I'm taken, that's all."

From that moment he abandoned resistance, for he felt that it would be quite futile against his foes, while in its result it might inflict some injury upon himself that might incapacitate him for any future efforts for his escape.

"Do you give in?" demanded the officer who had first laid hold of him—"do you give in?"

"Yes, rather," said Macheath, coolly. "It's long odds, one to five, don't you think, old fellow? Of course, I'm like the bit of iron that bends when it can't help it, if you call that giving in?"

"All right. Now for the darbies."

"Oh! anything you like in a quiet way."

Macheath had a knack of sticking out the bones of his wrists to enlarge their apparent circumference.

The first pair of handcuffs the officers tried to put upon him were, consequently, found to be too small.

Another pair was fitted on which Macheath knew well he could get his hands out of when he chose.

They then let him rise, or rather they lifted him up, for in the first brief struggle he and the four officers had gone to the ground together.

"Where's the coach?" said the principal officer.

"Coming," said one of the others. "There it is."

A hackney coach lumbered up to the goldsmith's door, and one of the officers tied Macheath's ankles together with a silk handkerchief.

"He is a slippery customer," the officer observed, "and you cannot make too sure of him."

"Wait a bit," said Macheath; "you are not quite sure of me yet."

"Ain't we, though? It strikes me you will dangle for this affair."

"What affair?"

"Oh! you are as innocent as a baby, of course. Now help him in, Joe. You get up behind, Bill. We will get inside along with him."

At this moment Macheath cast his eyes towards the jeweller's window, and he saw the shopman standing close to the door rubbing his hands together as though he thought what was going on quite a capital piece of work.

"Ah! my friend," said Captain Macheath, "I shall recollect you."

The shopman immediately disappeared.

By this time a crowd of persons began to collect, and the questions of "What is it?" "Who is it?" were asked eagerly.

It was the officer who got up behind the coach that, in the pride of his heart at assisting at such a capture, cried out—

"It's that villain, Macheath, the highwayman."

The news spread like wildfire among the crowd, and a wild kind of shout rent the air.

People ran up to the spot from all directions, and "Macheath! Macheath! Macheath, the highwayman is taken!" was shouted by many.

The captain looked quite calm and unconcerned as he heard all this, and he was observed to smile slightly as the coachman began to fret and fume upon finding that his progress was impeded by the people, who would crowd round the vehicle with the hope of catching a glimpse of the prisoner.

"You should have kept your own secret," said Macheath, "and then the people would not have known that it took five of you to overpower me."

"Never you mind about that," said the officer.

"Mind you keep me."

"That we don't care about," the officer replied. "We will lodge you in Newgate. That will be enough for us. If they let you go, it don't matter a brass farthing to us. It's not my business."

"Perhaps it may be, though."

"Drive on, will you, coachman. Drive on!"

The coachman proceeded with difficulty, amid a yelling and shouting crowd.

The officer who had taken his station behind, in resisting the intrusion of some of the more clamorous and curious of the mob, kicked at several of them, and the consequence was that he was pulled down and severely maltreated by the people.

The officer upon the box with the driver presented a pistol at some that would stop the horses, and threatened to fire, and by the time the coach got to the neighbourhood of Charing-cross in its route to Newgate, it was compelled to come to a dead stop, being hemmed in by a mob of about a thousand of the roughest of the London population.

The officers who were with Macheath looked pale and anxious.

"Pull them out!" cried a loud voice.

And then there was a yell of execration at the officers.

The man that was upon the box was afraid to use his pistols, and gave them up to the crowd.

If he had used them, there can be no doubt but that his own life would have been instantly sacrificed.

"A rescue—a rescue!" cried a loud voice. "Let's set him free, for Macheath always gave to the poor what he took from the rich."

"Hurrah—hurrah!" shouted a thousand voices.

"We shall all be murdered," said one of the officers.

Macheath began to think that there was a chance of escape, and so there would have been, but a tradesman upon the spot, who was a constable in his own right, suddenly rushed out with a staff from his shop, and in a little squeaking voice, he cried—

"Disperse, you wretches—disperse! Look at me and tremble! Disperse! Here I am!"

This produced such a roar of laughter, that for the moment all the vigorous intentions of the mob regarding the rescue of Macheath were forgotten.

The valorous constable was seized upon in a moment, and a voice cried—

"Hang him—hang him!"

"No—no," shouted another; "here's a parish pump; give him a good ducking."

"Hurrah!" shouted the multitude, and in the course of half a minute the constable in his own right was under a large pump, while the handle jerked up and down with a vigour that threatened to work it off.

The coach moved on a little.

"Stop the coach," said somebody. "We will rescue Macheath; and as our hands are in, we will pump upon the officers."

This suggestion was received with uproarious delight; but at the moment that both Macheath and the officers thought it would be acted upon, there arose a screaming yell from the mob, and its members began to fly in all directions. The principal officer thrust his head out of the window of the coach, and cried—

"A troop of cavalry, by all that's good! We are saved!"

In less than a minute the mob had evaporated, and Macheath could see the red coats and flashing weapons of the soldiers through the coach windows as they surrounded it.

Twelve dragoons had been sufficient to disperse the mob and leave a perfectly clear space for the coach.

'So much for popular support," thought Macheath. "Well, I am not disappointed, at any rate."

The two officers on the seat opposite to him were whispering together.

"Yes, it's the colonel who has managed that for us," one of them said.

The moment Macheath heard the colonel mentioned he began to think, and the idea that Colonel Lane was somehow connected with his arrest flashed into his brain.

A sergeant in command of the little party of dragoons now came quite close to the coach window.

"Have you got your prisoner all safe, officers?" he said.

"Oh! yes, yes."

"Very well; our orders are to see you safe to Newgate."

"Thank you. I believe you have saved our lives, sergeant."

"Who sent you?" said Macheath.

And the sergeant, thinking at the moment from the tone that it was one of the officers, promptly replied—

"Colonel Lane."

"And how is he?"

"Pretty well, thank you."

"Remember the Baron Hoge to him when you see him."

"The who?"

The sergeant looked closely into the coach, and was mortified enough to find that he had been conversing with the prisoner instead of one of the officers.

With an oath, he turned his horse's head from the coach, and trotted on in advance of his men.

"You are a cool fellow, Macheath," said the officer.

"Why not?"

"Well, of course, there's no reason why you should not," said the officer; "but it is a fact for all that. I don't wish you any harm; but you know, in the way of business, when we had information of where you were likely to be, it was not a very probable thing that we should neglect it and keep out of the way."

"Certainly not," Macheath replied. "I don't blame you. If you can tell me one thing I should be much obliged to you."

"What is it?"

"It's just this. Did Sanderson, the jeweller, give you information that I was to visit his place, or that I was likely at all to be there? I should like to know that. Yes or no."

"Well, it's no harm telling you that he did not."

"But his shopman did?"

The officer nodded, and added—

"He is well paid for it, too, I rather think. Colonel Lane, I fancy, has some particular charge against you, or else he would not be quite so angry."

"Oh!" said Macheath. "I think I understand it all now."

"How do you mean?"

"It's of no consequence," Macheath rejoined. "I am obliged to you for the information you have given me. It can do no one any harm, and it prevents me from being angry at an innocent person. I had reason to suspect Mr. Sanderson of acting treacherously by me, and it is a great relief to me to find that he has not done so."

"You may make up your mind to that," added the officer. "It is very doubtful if the old gentleman knows of the matter yet. But here we are at Newgate."

It was not in human nature for Captain Macheath to feel nothing of a gloomy tendency as he was helped out of the coach into the lobby of Newgate.

There came a bright flush to his cheek as he heard the principal one of the officers who was with him cry out—

"Captain Macheath!"

At the sound of the well-known name there at once ensued quite a commotion in the vestibule of Newgate.

The name was repeated from mouth to mouth, until every officer of the prison who was not upon actual duty in some of its gloomy passages came to the hall to have a look at him, and in the course of a few moments the governor himself reached the spot.

"What is all this?" he said.

"Captain Macheath, sir."

"Is it indeed so? Are you Macheath?"

"I am."

"Then you are as welcome here as you possibly can be. Get No. 27 ready for the prisoner directly. So your career is at end, is it?"

"Who says so?" said Macheath.

"I do, and all the country will say so."

"Indeed! Then you and all the country are very much mistaken, I can tell you. There's something at my heart and brain that tells me I shall yet weather through this storm."

"If you do," said the governor, "I'll make you a present of this, my fine fellow."

As he spoke he pointed to his head, but the captain, with a laugh, said—

"It is not worth the having, or I should certainly claim it."

"Load him with the heaviest irons," said the governor, "and visit him every hour. I will see the Lord Chief Justice about you, Macheath, and he shall direct what course is to be taken concerning you. Come into my office, Mr. Edwards, and I will give you a receipt for the body of this most notorious reprobate."

The governor was lashing himself into a passion, for he was quite provoked at Captain Macheath's coolness

The officers and turnkeys smiled at each other, and one put his tongue in his cheek.

"The old one is quite sour to-day," he said; "but come on, Macheath, we must obey orders, you know; we will make you as comfortable as we can, for all that."

"Your wish to do so is quite enough," said Macheath. "Don't get yourselves into any trouble on my account; I am used to roughing it rather. All I want just now is leave to write a letter."

"To whom?"

"To Mr. Sanderson, the jeweller, of St. James's-street. You won't, I suppose, suspect him of being a friend of mine, will you?"

"Hardly," the officer replied. "You shall have the means of writing your letter; but you must know that in Newgate there is such a thing as paying your footing."

"I know it, and a good thing it is, too, when you have got it to give. There are twenty pounds among you, and if I can get the letter delivered by some of you, I will make it as much again."

Macheath's liberality to the gaolers of the old prison of Newgate was not thrown away.

The cell into which he was conducted by those who had a kindly feeling towards him could not be changed, inasmuch as it was specified by the order of the governor, but in every other respect he had it all his own way.

When writing materials were brought to him he wrote the following letter to Mr. Sanderson, the jeweller in St. James's-street—

"Newgate.

"Sir,—You were kind enough to say that if I wanted a friend you would like to hear from me. I have now something to complain of which I think would be put to rights if represented in the proper quarter.

"I trusted to your word, Mr. Sanderson, and came to your house in perfect confidence. I was arrested almost upon your doorstep, and certainly in consequence of someone giving information to the officers that I was likely to be there.

"The one who gave that information, Mr. Sanderson, was not you. If you can do anything for me I ask it of you. If you cannot I thank you for the kind things you said to me, and still remain your debtor for them, and am—Yours ever,   "CAPTAIN CHARLES MACHEATH."

It was a rule of the prison that all letters written by any of the prisoners to any of their friends in the world outside were to be submitted to the governor.

But Macheath's liberality to the turnkeys got over that difficulty, and his letter which, no doubt, would have been suppressed, never found its way to the governor, but was taken direct to St. James's-street.

"Now," said Macheath, as he flung himself upon the straw mattress in his cell, "now for a rest. There's no very great likelihood of any calls so I shall try to get a sleep; after that I will just turn over in my mind what had best be done if Mr. Sanderson fails me."

With that happy constitutional indifference to surrounding circumstances which carried him through so many difficulties and dangers that would have appalled ordinary men, the captain threw himself on the mattress and closed his eyes.

The cell was very dark and he was very soon fast asleep.

How long he slept he had no means of knowing, but he was suddenly startled by someone crying out—

"Hilloa, there!"

"What now?" demanded Macheath, looking up.

"Get up. You must come before the magistrate."

"Indeed!" said the captain. "Is there any letter for me?"

"Why, yes," replied the voice; "Bill Lee, who is on the outer lock, has got one that he will slip into your pocket as you go out. It appears they want to get you committed to-day, as the sessions are on, so that they may hang you comfortably out of hand in the course of the next half-dozen days."

"Very much obliged," said Macheath, as he gave himself a shake. "I'm all ready."

The governor now appeared at the cell door with a couple of sturdy officers.

"Macheath," said the governor, "you must come to Bow-street now, and then you will hear the charge against you."

"I am quite willing," Captain Macheath returned. "Indeed, I am not a little anxious to hear it, for feeling that I am as innocent as any lamb, it surprises me what charge human impudence can bring against me."

The two officers laughed at this, and the governor called out in an angry voice—

"Silence! Don't let us have any laughing here. Bring him along—bring him along!"

It was quite evident, from the manner in which Captain Macheath was hurried from the cell to a hackney-coach at the door of Newgate, that there was a hope of getting him to Bow-street and committing him for trial before its transpiring that a criminal of such celebrity was there at all.

Just as he passed the man who was at the outer gate, Macheath felt something like a twitch at one of his skirts, and he said—

"Thank you."

"For what?" said the governor.

"Why, for amazing kindness, of course," said the captain. "What in the name of all that's wonderful could I otherwise thank you for—eh?"

"I suspect— Well, it does not much matter."

The governor looked enquiringly about him.

But the face of the man who was at the outer door was so stolid, and, indeed, so stupid-looking, that it was quite impossible to fix him as having done anything to call forth the captain's thanks.

The prisoner now was very anxious to read the note which he felt quite sure was in his pocket, only he feared that if he took it out while he was in the coach he should implicate some of the turnkeys.

He thought he had better wait until he had come into contact with other persons, one of whom might be as well suspected of giving it to him as the man who really had.

With this idea, then, Captain Macheath controlled his impatience until he got to Bow-street.

The coach rattled along with unusual speed to the police-office.

It was quite clear from the two or three ordinary loungers hanging about the door that there was no idea so notable a character as Macheath was to be brought before the magistrate at such a time.

The captain was taken into the court by a private door, and kept in a little room while some communication was made to the magistrate; after which he was at once hurried into the public court, in which there was not above twenty people, but there was a strong muster of officers about its doors.

"What is this?" said the magistrate, affecting an ignorance which certainly was not the case, as it had been all pre-arranged that Captain Macheath should be brought up and committed for trial.

"This man, your worship," said the governor of Newgate, "is charged with highway robbery."

"Oh! indeed. Who is he?"

"Captain Macheath."

"Really? Well, we have heard of you, Macheath, before to-day," said the magistrate. "What evidence have you, Mr. Governor, against him?"

"Here is a witness, your worship."

Macheath was rather amused as well as surprised at the manner in which the business was being conducted.

When a man stepped forward, whom he did not recollect to have ever seen in his life before, and was sworn, he could not make out what it was all about.

"Well, sir," said the magistrate to the witness, "what have you got to say in this matter?"

"My name is Philip Jarvis," said the man, "I am a commercial traveller, and was crossing Ealing-common on the evening of the twenty-fourth of October last, when I was stopped by a highwayman, and robbed of eighty-seven pounds ten shillings and eightpence, all done up in a canvas bag."

"Should you know the robber?"

"Yes."

"Well, look round the court, and point him out if he be here."

"That is the man," said Mr. Jarvis, pointing to Captain Macheath. "I will swear to him."

"Very good. Are there any other witnesses?"

"Yes," said the clerk. "Call Thomas Singleton."

Upon this, another man stepped forward, and upon being sworn, he said—

"I am an agent, and was crossing Ealing-common on the night in question, when I heard a kind of altercation going on, and having been warned that Captain Macheath the highwayman was in the neighbourhood, I hid in a hedge, and saw the prisoner at the bar rob Mr. Jarvis of a canvas bag which seemed to be very heavy."

"Can you swear to the prisoner at the bar?"

"Yes; clearly and distinctly."

"Well," said the magistrate, "what have you to say to this, prisoner? You can say anything you like, but what you do say will be used in evidence against you."

Captain Macheath put his hand into his pocket, and felt that there was a letter there.

He took it very calmly out of his pocket, and while the magistrate looked at him in some amaze-

ment, and the governor and the officers wondered how he got it, he opened it, and read the following words—

"Ask if your counsel, Mr. Charles Braithwaite, is in the court, and trust all to him. This is from the friend to whom you have very judiciously written, and who has not betrayed you."

Macheath crumpled up the little note in his hand.

"I will leave this most unfounded and infamous charge in the hands of my counsel, Mr. Charles Braithwaite, who I believe is in court," he replied, in a calm, cool voice.

"Counsel!" said the magistrate. "Do you mean to tell me that the eminent Mr. Braithwaite is your counsel, prisoner?"

"I do."

"And I am here," said a gentlemanly-looking man, advancing towards the bench. "I am here to look after my client's interests in this matter. Your worship, I presume, will do nothing hastily. We deny that there is the slightest foundation for the charge, and shall be prepared to prove an alibi of the most satisfactory nature by this day week, to which time I have to request that the prisoner may be remanded."

The magistrate and his clerk, and the governor, and the chaplain, all looked at each other in evident perplexity.

They were perfectly startled at the idea of Captain Macheath having counsel ready; they thought that he could not be aware, until he was actually brought to Bow-street, of what was going on against him.

The object was to commit him upon the charge brought against him and then leave his character to hang him upon it.

That Colonel Lane was at the bottom of the proceedings, there could be no sort of doubt whatever.

The magistrate, after two or three preparatory "Hems," said—

"Really, Mr. Braithwaite, you see the sessions are on, and it is an object to society to—to try this man as soon as possible."

"But, sir," said the counsel, "it is a far greater object to society that an innocent man should not suffer. I believe I have a right to demand this week's remand; and if you will not grant it, the judges will postpone the trial until next sessions, upon my application."

"Well I—a—I—that is, I suppose I may as well remand the prisoner until this day week," the magistrate said.

"I think so," said the counsel.

"Very well, then let it be so. Prisoner, you are remanded until this day week at twelve of the clock, when I think it will be my duty to commit you for trial."

CHAPTER XLVIII.

MACHEATH MAKES SOME FRIENDS IN PRISON.

MACHEATH did not think it incumbent upon him to say another word to the magistrate.

He felt that someone was interesting himself strongly in his fate, and he did not for a moment doubt in his own mind but that that someone was Mr. Sanderson, the jeweller, of St. James's-street.

The governor of Newgate, however, did not feel inclined to let the affair blow over quite so easily.

"If your worship pleases," he said, "we can bring another case against the prisoner at the bar, upon which your worship will be able to commit him at once."

"This is monstrous," exclaimed Mr. Braithwaite, with warmth, before the magistrate could reply. "This is truly a most monstrous proceeding. One would be half inclined to think that the great object of those who had brought the prisoner to this court, was to get him hastily committed for trial, so that before he could scarcely know what he was accused of, he might be convicted and hanged! If the jury at the sessions were only one-half as eager to convict as certain parties are commit, there would be an end to justice."

"Well—well," said the magistrate, "let the affair stand over until this day week."

"But—" interposed the governor.

"Sir," cried the counsel, "do you not hear that one of the most upright, and vigorous, and intellectual magistrates of the city has said that the affair shall stand over until this day week? Do you want, sir, to insult the bench by endeavouring to make it eat its own words, and stultify its own decisions?"

This adroit appeal to the vanity of the magistrate settled the affair.

Shaking his head with great pomposity, he said—

"I have decided upon this case, and I particularly desire that no one will interrupt further. Officer, you will immediately remove the prisoner and call the next case."

"Very good," said Mr. Braithwaite, with a scarcely perceptible smile, "I shall call upon my client, to whom, of course, I have free access, in the course of the day."

"I shall be glad to see you, sir," said Captain Macheath.

In the course of a few minutes, Macheath was removed from the court and placed in the hackney-coach again, and rapidly drove towards Newgate.

That the malevolence of Colonel Lane, concerning the horse-selling affair, was at the bottom of the whole transaction, Macheath did not question, and he felt that if he had been committed at that time, while the trials at the Old Bailey were proceeding, there would not be the slightest chance of his living another week.

"Well, Macheath," said the governor, "you manage your affairs pretty well, I rather think."

"Just so," said the captain.

"Here you are, apprehended in the morning, and you are taken before a magistrate in the afternoon, and yet you contrive to have engaged counsel who knows all about your case."

"Just so," said Macheath.

"And," added the governor, getting warm as he went on, "and who defies the ends of justice by getting a whole week's postponement, by which time the sessions will be over, as he and you both know perfectly well."

"Just so."

"What the deuce do you mean by only saying 'Just so' to me?" the governor cried, fuming. "What do you mean by it, I say? It's infamous —it's most infamous and unjustifiable conduct from first to last."

"Just so."

The governor looked at Captain Macheath as though he would very gladly have taken his life; but in the presence of others he dreaded to give utterance to his passion.

The two officers who were likewise in the coach were half-suffocated in the attempts they made to keep themselves from laughing outright.

The discomfited governor was fain to crush himself up into a corner of the coach in silence, where he tried to comfort himself by reflecting upon how uncomfortable he could possibly make Captain Macheath in Newgate.

As for the chaplain, he was too much confounded at what had taken place before the magistrate to be able to say a word. His wits, at the best of times, were none of the clearest; and the extraordinary way in which Macheath had managed to get counsel to meet the charge that was professed against him puzzled him completely.

Upon the arrival of the coach at Newgate, the governor appeared to recover a little of his equanimity.

Perhaps finding himself in his own territory, as it might be called, had the effect of restoring him to something like a reasonable condition.

He did not, however, forget that he had such a grudge against Captain Macheath, and he would do his very best to pay it off.

"Where's Foxton?" he cried, as soon as they were fairly in the vestibule.

"Here, sir," said an individual, whose cunning, leering expression of countenance showed that he was well adapted to be the tool of anyone's bad passions; "I am here, sir, if you please. Happy to wait upon you, sir."

"Oh! I think, Foxton, you said you had the keys of those cells—where are they?"

"Water comes in there, sir?" said Foxton.

"Well—well," said the governor, impatiently, "I daresay it has gone out again. Put this prisoner into one of them. He is as sly as a fox, and as slippery as an eel. As I must keep him for a week, I am determined that he shall be kept in safety."

At that moment there came a loud knocking at the outer gate.

"Who is that?" demanded the governor, angrily. "Who is that knocking? This is not the time for visitors. What the deuce do you want?"

A man's head appeared above the half-door, and a hand presented a slip of paper, which the governor took with a jerk.

As he read it in silence, an expression of astonishment stole over his face.

"Bless me!" he said, "this is an order from the Lord Chief Justice, permitting the bearer to have a private interview with Captain Macheath."

The turnkey hearing these words deemed it his duty to open the gate, and a plainly-dressed gentleman stepped into Newgate.

"I am the bearer of the order," said he, turning to the governor, "and I suppose that you will not throw any difficulty in the way of the interview?"

"Why, no—no!—of course not," the governor gasped. "Who thought for a moment that there would be any difficulty? Of course, the Lord Chief Justice's order is all-powerful here; but it is a mystery to me how you became possessed of it."

"Probably," observed the stranger, as he took a pinch of snuff from a diamond-mounted box. "It strikes me that this is not the only little matter that is beyond the comprehension of the governor of Newgate."

"Sir!" shrieked the governor, almost beside himself with fury, "do you come here to insult me?"

"Oh! dear me," said the gentleman, smiling. "I came here with the view of conversing with Captain Macheath; but it does not seem to me that the signature of the Lord Chief Justice is held in much reverence here, and I shall make it my

THE FIGHT WAS AN EQUAL ONE—SHOT FOR SHOT BEING GIVEN.

duty to state as much to his lordship when I dine with him this evening."

The governor saw at once that he had met more than his match, and at once caved in.

"Sir," he said, "I hope you will accept my apology. Every possible respect will be paid to his lordship's order. Pray excuse me. I have had much to try me. I assure you, sir, the governor of a prison has much to put up with."

The gentleman took another pinch of snuff and bowed.

"Here, Foxton," said the governor, "show this gentleman into the private consulting-room, and let Captain Macheath go with him. Pray, sir," he added, turning to the visitor, "be so good as to follow the warder, and you will find the best accommodation that Newgate can afford."

The stranger followed Foxton, and Captain Macheath was conducted after him.

The private consulting-room was one devoted to interviews between the prisoners and their counsel.

It was dingy enough, and yet comfortable when compared with the portion of the grim old prison devoted to criminals.

The apartment was furnished with chairs and a table supplied with writing materials.

The stranger sat down, and leaning forward, criticised Macheath's appearance.

"Well, sir," said the captain, "I am Macheath, whom you have honoured with your presence. Pray what have you to say to me?"

The gentleman took another pinch of snuff, smiled knowingly, but said never a word.

"You have not been seized with a fit of dumbness, I hope?" said Captain Macheath.

"Come—come!" the gentleman rejoined, "this is neither the time nor the place for joking."

"That is exactly my idea," Macheath replied; "but by the way you have been staring and smiling at me, it seems that you wish to make fun of me."

"Oh! dear no," said the gentleman, in haste. "Pray get that idea entirely out of your mind. I will now explain the object of my visit. Certain circumstances have come to my knowledge which convinces me that you were one of the company at a little entertainment at Kew."

"Indeed," said Captain Macheath, who was much amused at receiving this information; "you don't say so?"

"Yes," responded the visitor. "I happen to know it for a fact, and my present visit is connected with that circumstance."

"Very well, sir," said Captain Macheath. "Go on."

"Of course," the gentleman resumed, and out came the snuff-box again, "you are in a very unpleasant predicament here?"

"That goes without the telling," said Macheath.

"And," the gentlemanly visitor resumed, "the authorities will have no difficulty in bringing such charges against you as will ensure your conviction. Your execution"—another pinch of snuff taken with evident relish—"I may say the execution of so notorious a criminal as yourself, will promptly follow as a matter of course."

"Do you really think so?" demanded Captain Macheath, folding his arms.

"Your own judgment must tell you that, as well, if not better, than anything I can say on the subject, my dear sir."

Captain Macheath merely inclined his head in answer to this.

"But," added the stranger, "if certain persons in a very high position in life chose to interest themselves in your favour you would, at least upon this occasion, be allowed to go free. It would then depend entirely upon yourself whether you erred, or led the life of an honest citizen."

"Very good, sir," said Captain Macheath. "I am listening to you most attentively."

"But," returned the visitor, "you are aware that there is never effect without a cause, and, therefore, if the people I have hinted at hold out their hands to save you, it must be on account of some act on your part which will please them."

"Your language is perfectly clear," said Macheath; "but pray, sir, what is the act I am required to perform?"

"It is simply that you will give me a full and detailed account of all that you saw and heard at Kew," the gentleman replied.

"Is that all?"

"Yes, that is all," said the stranger. "The information is required by certain people of influence, and I hope, considering the position in which you now find yourself, you will not hesitate to tell me all."

"At the price of my life and liberty?" queried Captain Macheath.

"Exactly so," said the stranger. "You are a most attentive listener, and if I read your face aright, I—"

"You read nothing but disgust and refusal," Captain Macheath interposed. "Go back to those you came from, and say that I am no informer."

"You refuse?"

"I do most emphatically," Captain Macheath replied, bringing his hand down heavily on the table. "You may also tell your friends that they are mistaken in their man. I will not intrude upon any man's privacy and then blazen forth all I chance to see and hear. I was taken in a sneaking way, and if I am to die, I will suffer death without feeling at the last moment that I have played the part of a poltroon and a spy."

"Then," said the stranger, "I take it that you are determined to keep to yourself all you saw and heard at Kew?"

"I do, sir, and will."

The visitor took as much snuff as his thumb and fore-finger would encompass, and fell into a train of thought.

"Sir," said Captain Macheath, breaking the silence, "have you had your say? If there is anything more, please make me acquainted with it and go."

"You are too hasty, Macheath," the stranger remarked. "A great deal too hasty."

"In what respect, sir?"

"Ask yourself the question?" the visitor rejoined. "You now have a chance of escape which any other man in your predicament would not hesitate a moment to embrace. Think again. Do not let your temper get the better of your discretion. I offer you most excellent terms, and I think you ought to accept them."

"That may be your honest opinion, but it is not mine."

"Well, then," said the gentleman, "in plain language, I tell you that if you choose to tell me what took place at Kew, you shall not only be free within four and twenty hours, but walk out of Newgate prison a much richer man than you were when you entered it."

"And I, sir," responded Captain Macheath, "tell you in just as clear language that I reject your terms."

"Well," the stranger observed, "I suppose I must consider our interview at an end. It is new to me to find a man of your age and capabilities in love with punishment and death."

"I have no love for death," Macheath replied; "but I am not entirely lost to all feeling of honour. Perhaps you think it strange for me to say so, but, sir, I hold that there is more principle in putting a pistol to the head of a man who is as strong and well-armed as myself than turning spy and traitor for the sake of saving my neck."

"I will leave you to your fate, Macheath," said the gentleman. "My mission is at an end."

"It is," Macheath responded. "You can go at once. I have not the slightest wish to detain you."

The stranger moved towards the door.

"You may take charge of the prisoner again," he said, addressing the warders. "My interview is over. Please show me the way out of this horrible place. Bah! it is almost impossible to breathe here."

"There!' said Macheath, when he was taken back to his cell. "That bother is over, and now I suppose they will let me go to sleep."

And asleep he was in a few minutes.

How long he slept he did not know.

He was roused to consciousness by the light of a lantern flashing before his eyes, and starting up saw two warders were in his cell.

The governor of Newgate stood with his back against the cell door.

"He is awake now," said one of the warders.

"Do your duty then," replied the governor, smiling maliciously.

"What on earth are you after now?" demanded Captain Macheath, as he started up. "You don't hang a man before putting him on his trial, I suppose?"

"Oh! dear no," said one of the warders. "We have only come to fit you up with a few pretty steel ornaments. Out of compliment to you they are of extra strength, so you see it took some little time to get them ready, and here we are to put them on."

"Please yourself," said Macheath. "It is some satisfaction to think that you are afraid of me, and of that I am quite convinced."

"Oh! dear no," exclaimed the governor, in a pompous tone of voice, "we are not afraid of you; but, as I told you, that having got you I intend to take precious good care that you don't give me the slip. If you get out of Newgate I will consent to eat those irons first and you afterwards"

"Rail on," said Macheath. "You can't place iron on a man's hopes or spirits. I intend to laugh and make merry in spite of you. Ha! ha! ha! Why, to look at us one might think that I was the head gaoler and you the prisoner. You look as gloomy as if you had been doomed to dance from Newgate to Tyburn at the cart's-tail, with the hangman's whip to keep you lively."

"Have your joke," the governor growled. "The laugh will be on my side soon. I am used to the bravado of such rascals as yourself, but I think that the air of Newgate will bring you down a few pegs."

"It will fail for once," said Captain Macheath.

The two men now set to work to fix a very heavy set of fetters upon the captain's limbs.

A portable anvil and a basket full of blacksmith's tools had been brought into the cell.

"Now, Macheath," said one of the men, "be so good as to stand still, and I shall not hit your shins with the hammer."

"If you do," Macheath responded, "it will be the worse for you, my fine fellow. I like a joke as well as most people, but I can give and take, so just bear it in mind."

The man did not seem inclined to despise the warning, and he set about his work with the greatest of care.

The hammer had not descended many times when the governor was sent for, and at once he left the cell, but not before having left instructions that Macheath was to be double ironed, if the warders thought necessary.

"The governor is a nice, pleasant man to live with, I should think," said Macheath.

"Don't blame us," observed he with the hammer. "It ain't our fault that you are to wear the heaviest irons that were ever put on a man who found his way into Newgate, but we must obey orders, you know."

"Oh! of course not. I don't blame you in the least," said Captain Macheath. "You are only doing your duty, and for that matter so is the governor. He has every right to do his best to keep me here, but he might look a little more pleasant over the job."

"So he might," the man remarked.

"Go on," said Macheath; "you may rivet the rivets as tight as you like."

"I say, Bill," said one of the men, "I think I hear someone in the passage. I shouldn't wonder if it is old Bennett, the governor, again. He is always sneaking about to see whether we do our duty. Just run out and pretend to tumble over him, and if you can, kick him in the shins accidentally—for the purpose, you know, so much the better."

Bill ran out of the cell, and the moment he was gone the other man closed the door with one hand and gave Macheath a file.

The captain concealed it instantly in the breast of his coat.

"Thanks, my friend," he whispered. "If ever I get my freedom again, I will find you out and reward you well."

"Hush! Bill is coming back again."

"Why, there's nobody about," said Bill, as he returned to the cell. "Why did you send me on such a fool's errand?"

"Well," replied the other, "there's somebody coming in earnest now."

"And a woman, too," said Bill, "if I am any judge of footsteps."

CHAPTER XLIX.
THE GOVERNOR'S DAUGHTER—INSIDE AND OUTSIDE THE PRISON.

FOR a moment Captain Macheath thought that Polly had heard of his capture and had found her way into the prison.

His heart beat fast, but he soon discovered his mistake.

It was a woman who peeped into the cell, but not Polly.

An oval face, with laughing blue eyes, and lips like twin cherries, met the captain's gaze.

Macheath smiled, wondering how so fair a flower could bloom within the grim walls of Newgate, when one of the men explained that the young lady was Bertha, the governor's daughter.

"Well, miss," said the captain, "I hope you have not come to mock at my capture?"

"Oh! no," Bertha replied, advancing timidly into the cell. "I heard that—that—"

" Captain Macheath was taken?"

" Yes."

" And so you thought you would see what he was like?"

" I cannot deny it," Bertha said. " I hope you will pardon my curiosity."

" Don't mention it," Macheath returned, gallantly. " I suppose you were told that I was a beetle-browed ruffian, with bloodshot eyes, and dog-like teeth?"

" I must confess that the description I received of you was not very flattering," Bertha said; " but—but—"

" Come, come," interrupted Macheath, gaily. " I am not fishing for compliments. Whatever I may be like, I am not seen at my best here."

" I pity you from my heart," Bertha said— " indeed I do ! Experience here has taught me to read faces, and judging by yours I am sure that you deserve a better fate than—"

" A sharp ride to Tyburn and death at the hangman's hands," said Captain Macheath, interrupting her.

Bertha shuddered, her eyes grew dim, and she was visibly affected.

" What I meant to say," she remarked, after a pause, " is that I think you might have employed your talents in such a way as never to have come here at all."

Macheath bowed.

" I appreciate the kindly sentiments you have for me," he returned. " Necessity has turned many honest men dishonest, and bad laws make bad men."

" Beg pardon, Miss Bertha," said one of the warders, " your father will be here presently, and he will go on nicely if he catches you here."

" For goodness' sake ! don't run any risk on my account," said Macheath.

Bertha tripped out of the cell, but before she did so she gave the captain a look plainly indicating that he had not seen the last of her.

As soon as the meeting was over the warders departed, and when the sound of their retreating footsteps had died away Captain Macheath took the file from its hiding-place, and touched it lightly with his lips.

" Cold as you are, you are warmer than the hearts of most men," he said. " Hail ! herald of liberty, I will try your sharp but friendly teeth upon these fetters before many hours have passed away."

Then he began to think of Bertha.

" How charmingly pretty she is," he mused ; " and how odd that she should visit me here. It may have been out of curiosity, as she said ; but let me see how I can profit by it. No—no ; I'll think of her no more. How shall I amuse myself ? Hah ! a good thought. I will leave a memento of my visit here on the walls."

Macheath took the file, and using the sharp end of it, inscribed the following verses on a flat stone—

" Captain Macheath was in Newgate thrown
For a crime that wasn't a bit of his own ;
And his enemies declared that decreed it should
be
Macheath should swing on the gallows tree.

" But the captain he knew a gay thing or two,
And of tricks of escape he was up to a few.
He laughed as he sat in the old stone cell,
And he thought a fresh gallop were just as
well.

" ' The time hangs heavy,' said Captain Macheath.
" 'Tis better to ride on the wild breezy heath
Than wait for the warders with the darbies
ringing,
Which isn't the very best sort of singing.' "

" Plague take it ! I am not in the verse-making mood to-day," said Macheath as he put the file away, " so I sha'n't do any more ; and what I have done I don't much like. So there's an end to it. And now for a slumber."

The captain threw himself upon the floor of the cell ; but he had not been there above a moment or two when, as if the fates had determined to keep him from any repose, the door was opened, and in walked the governor, with his clerk a few paces behind him.

" What the deuce now ?" cried Macheath. " I tell you what it is, I shall leave these lodgings without any notice if you don't leave me alone and let me have a little quiet."

" Macheath," said the governor, " I come to you as a friend to you. Of course you can easily conceive that I pity very much the melancholy situation you are in at this juncture."

" No I can't," said Macheath.

" But I assure you—"

" Oh ! then I agree with you. I have not the smallest doubt of your assurance."

The governor looked angry.

" Give me leave to say, Macheath,' he observed, " that this is not only a foolish, but it is an ungrateful reception to one who comes to do you a kindness."

" It would be," said Captain Macheath.

" And it is."

" I shall be better able to say yes or no to that proposition, Mr. Governor, when I know what it is that you call a kindness."

" Very well. Be it so. In the first place, then, I may remark that I am very much afraid that I am outstepping the lines of duty in coming to you at all just now, and that I ought not to do it."

" Well, it is quite optional, you know," replied the captain. " There's the door, and you can but go again. There's one thing, too, you may make sure of, and that is that I shall not come to you."

" Well, well ! we will let that pass."

" Go on, then."

" I have had a conversation with a gentleman upon your case who feels that it would be a sad thing if a young man of your talents and general acquirements were to go out of the world in such a dreadful way, as by the hands of the hangman !"

" What," cried Macheath, " another gentleman interested in my case ? Give my compliments to him, and tell him that I quite agree with him."

" I will ; but he and I have arranged that such an appeal is to be made in your favour to high quarters that we are fully sure that at the last moment you will be saved."

" Thank you !"

" You don't seem to be much elated at it," said the governor. " I was called away just now to have an interview with the gentleman."

" Oh ! yes, I am elated," said Macheath ; " but I never make much account of things before they happen. So, you see, I am never greatly depressed at misfortunes nor over-elated at the idea that anything extraordinary is likely to occur in the way of good fortune. It is much the best to take everything in an easy way."

"Perhaps it is; but, of course, if we are able to do anything for you in the way we wish, it must be upon the plea that you are very contrite for the past. In fact, we can urge nothing else."

"Oh!"

"And so you quite comprehend that—that—in fact—"

"I'll be hanged if I do," said Captain Macheath; "and I suppose you will tell me I shall be hanged if I don't."

"Ha—ha!" laughed the governor, in a forced manner. "Ha—ha! A very good joke, but not, just now, very seasonable, I think. Were I you I should be rather too seriously inclined to joke as you do."

"Were you me, governor," Macheath said, "you would do as I do; but, as you say truly, all that is to no purpose. What more have you to say as a consequence of this new-born sympathy with me?"

"Why, I have now to point out to you the course which the gentleman and I have decided upon as the best for you to pursue, in order that you may aid our exertions as much as possible."

"Oh! very good. What is the course?"

"It is, when you are put on your trial, to plead at once guilty to the indictment."

The clerk, who was about three paces behind the governor, immediately held up a piece of paper above his head, so that Captain Macheath should see it.

Upon the paper, in large characters, was the word—

"No!"

Macheath nodded, and the clerk immediately put the paper into his pocket again.

The governor had a suspicion that Captain Macheath was looking at something over his head, and he faced about suddenly to the clerk, who, however, put on such a meek and stupid look that he disarmed all suspicion.

"You need not wait for me, Mr. Brown," said the governor.

"Thank you, sir."

The clerk left the cell, and then the governor put on as pleasant a look as possible.

"Of course," said he, "this is a private interview, and on the whole I rather approve of your being reserved before the clerk. Now we can talk freely. You will, then, plead, as I say, guilty at the sessions?"

"Oh! no."

"No?"

"Certainly not. I couldn't think of such a thing."

"But really consider now, while I convince you that—"

"It's of no use your talking," said Macheath. "Unless you can convince me that I did the special robbery they charge me with, which I am convinced I had nothing to do with, I will not plead guilty; and as I know you cannot convince me of that, inasmuch as the robbery never was committed at all, and it is a mere made-up case, you may spare your arguments on the subject, and me the trouble of listening to them."

"Do you really mean to tell me," said the governor, "that for a little peccadillo of this sort you will refuse to save your life?"

"Yes."

"Oh! nonsense, nonsense," said the governor, sharply. "Now, Macheath, you are joking with me; but I find I must be more explicit with you. I am empowered by certain parties, whom I must not name, to make you a certain promise, which is, that if you prove guilty, you will be reprieved on the scaffold."

"Ah! that will be too late."

"Too late?"

"Yes, to be sure. If once you get me on to the scaffold, I'd just as soon be hanged as not."

"Impossible."

"Oh! not at all; and besides, do you know," added Macheath, "if it got as far as that through me pleading guilty, I'm afraid something might happen to the messenger with the reprieve, and he would arrive too late by a few minutes, so that I don't mean to run the risk, if it's all the same to you, Mr. Governor."

"Then do you mean to tell me that you are so pig-headed as to refuse an actual offer of your life from an illustrious person when it is made to you, just because it is done in the illustrious person's way, and not in yours?"

"That's just it."

"Very good—very good," the governor responded. "Oh! you will repent of this, sure enough. Very good, sir; I have done my duty, and made the offer, and there's the end of it. It does not matter to me one straw one way or the other, so I bid you good-day, and leave you to your own folly and obstinacy."

"Thank you."

The governor strode to the door, and then turned suddenly.

"Macheath," he said, "do not send me away with a refusal to the illustrious person. Think again. It is for your own good I speak, and to save you from an ignominious death."

"How affecting!" Macheath said, sneeringly, "if the gammon did not so much predominate over everything else I do believe that you would draw tears from my fetters."

The governor said no more, but bounced from the cell, mightily chagrined at the discomfiture.

"That's over," said Macheath, and once more he laid himself down to rest.

But this visit of the governor had had the effect of disturbing his mind if it had failed in the object it was intended to promote, merely to betray him into going quietly to death, for there cannot be a doubt that the object was to get Captain Macheath lulled into fancied security up to the very moment when the fatal cord would be about his neck, and then nothing would be easier than to destroy him.

"It is a hard thing," Macheath muttered, "that my life should be hunted. It is true enough that I have done many an act that makes me amenable to the law, but, strange to say, it is not for one of those acts that I am to be persecuted, but for something that I never did at all."

The captain thought over the matter, until, full of weariness, and amid the silence of his cell, he fell fast asleep, and was only roused by the door suddenly opening, and a voice uttering his name.

"Hi lo! who calls?" exclaimed Macheath, as he sprang to his feet and rubbed his eyes to thoroughly awaken himself.

The flash of light dazzled him, but presently he made out the form of the friendly warder.

"Oh! is it you?"

"It is. I bring you a note."

Macheath held the letter to the light and he saw, written in a straggling hand in pencil, the following words—

"You were quite right in keeping your own counsel. Traps are set for your destruction.

They say that they will hang you like a dog; but I think they will be mistaken. I will save you. B."

"Who on earth is ' B. ?'" Captain Macheath ejaculated. "If the name commenced with ' P' I could understand the meaning of it very well."

"I am sworn to secrecy. The note was written by a lady."

"That I can see by the style," said Macheath. "But what lady."

"Can't you guess?"

"I'll be hanged if I can !" Captain Macheath replied. "I know of one woman only who is really interested in me now, and, poor girl, she little dreams that I am here."

At this moment there was a slight noise outside the cell.

The warder started and matched up the lantern.

"You'll get nothing more to-night, prisoner," he said, in a gruff tone of voice, "and so I can tell you. As to the extra bottle of wine you say you will require to-morrow, you had better speak to the governor about it."

Macheath took the hint.

"Well,' he replied, "you need not be so ill-tempered. I asked you a civil question, and I think you might have given me a civil answer. Well, good-night, and I hope your repose will be as easy as mine."

The warder left the cell hastily, and in doing so nearly fell over the governor.

"What do you mean by being in Macheath's cell at this time?" the head official demanded, sharply.

"The prisoner called out that he wanted to see somebody."

"Let him call until he is hoarse," the governor said. "What was that I heard about a bottle of wine?"

"He wants two instead of one to-morrow."

"Does he?" said the governor, laughing "If Macheath isn't careful he will find that I consider the usual prison diet good enough for him."

The warder shuffled away without saying another word, and the governor, having made sure that the cell door was secure, went to his apartments.

The time for closing Newgate came.

This was announced by a clanking of chains, the shooting of bolts, and the tramp of heavily-booted warders as they changed ground.

Bang !

The great door had closed, and not a soul could leave or enter the hideous old prison until nine o'clock the next morning.

It was almost as dark without as it was within.

The stars were hidden by heavy louring clouds, showers of cold, searching rain fell occasionally, and the wind moaned and sighed dismally above and about the grimy walls as if bewailing the fate of the hapless beings shut out from the world.

Now and then a rumbling of wheels broke the stillness of the night as a carriage or hackney coach whirled by, and occasionally the flash of a watchman's lantern bade prowlers of the night hide themselves.

It was just a quarter past twelve when a man and a woman wended their way from the direction of Smithfield and stood before Newgate.

The man wore a cloak that reached from his shoulders to his heels, and the features of the woman were entirely hidden by a thick veil.

"But," she was saying, "there may be some mistake. Many men have taken the name of Macheath, and they may have got the wrong one after all."

"I wish I could think so," the man rejoined. "You see, my good mistress, all the circumstances point to the capture of the captain, for the capture was made outside Mr. Sanderson's shop, and we know who went there, and for what purpose."

"Oh! Luke—Luke," cried Polly, for she it was; "why did he not listen to me? There is no hope—no hope. If I could only see him for a moment it would be some comfort."

"Well," said Luke, gloomily, "I think that can be managed without much difficulty. But let us keep on walking, or we may attract the attention of some prying eyes if we remain standing here."

Poor Polly, heart-broken, and downcast to the very depths of despair, leaned heavily upon the arm of Macheath's faithful servant.

They walked on until they reached Ludgate-hill, then as quiet as if the thoroughfare belonged to a city of the dead.

"I should like to ask you a question, madam," Luke continued.

"As many as you like, my good fellow."

"Did your friends ever know that you were married to Captain Macheath?"

Polly started.

"Friends ! I have none," she said; "but those whom I called so in days gone by have, to the best of my belief, no knowledge that I am married."

"Then, to put it plainly, they have never cared what became of you?"

"I fear not," said Polly, sobbing.

"As far as they are concerned I don't see that there is anything to cry about," Luke remarked, bluntly. "Dry your eyes, good mistress, and listen to me."

"Yes," Polly replied, "I will try to be calm. I will listen to you, as I know you will give me the best of advice."

"I thank you for that," Luke replied. "Now, mistress, I must be plain with you. Your father is a thief-taker, and he knows Macheath."

"Alas ! yes."

"I think it is a good job that he does know the captain," Luke rejoined, "because if you play the part I am going to put before you well I think you will be able to see your husband before this time to-morrow night."

"I am all attention, Luke," said Polly, brightening up—"proceed."

"You must go home—"

"Go home !" interrupted Polly. "Oh ! no, I could never think of doing that."

"You must indeed," Luke urged; "and after the first surprise is over you must say that you have been living in retirement on the little money you had in your purse when you went away."

"Well ?"

"Having broken the ice so far," Luke continued, "you will then begin to talk of Macheath. You must say that he half-confided in you with regard to an enormous treasure which he had buried, and if your father uses his influence for you to see him in Newgate, that you think you can come to the bottom of the secret."

"That sounds feasible enough," Polly said. "I am compelled to admit that my father is an avaricious man; but Luke, what will happen if he takes it into his head to go to Newgate and see my husband himself?"

CAPTAIN MACHEATH

THE
PRINCE OF THE HIGHWAY.

"THANKS, FRIEND," SAID MACHEATH.   "IF I GET MY FREEDOM I WILL REWARD YOU WELL."

"You must guard him against that, mistress," Luke responded, "by saying that Macheath is an obstinate man when questioned by men, but in the hands of a woman he is mere clay to be moulded according to her will."

"I will go," Polly said, "and I could not go at a better time than this, for it is just at this hour that my father is busy with his associates. Where will you wait for me, Luke?"

"Not a dozen yards from your father's house," Luke replied. "Take this," he added, taking a whistle from his pocket, "and should there be too much bother for your liking, sound a call, and I will be with you in one second."

"Good, faithful Luke!" said Polly, holding out her hand. "What I should do without your services in this extremity I do not know. Come, let us be going."

CHAPTER L.

MACHEATH FINDS A FRIEND IN BERTHA, THE GOVERNOR'S DAUGHTER — THE CAPTAIN PLAYS A PART THAT SUITS HIM BADLY.

WHILE the conversation recorded in the foregoing chapter was going on, an odd thing happened within the walls of Newgate.

Macheath was still abroad as to who "B.," the author of the kindly but mysterious note, could be, when he heard a sound resembling the creaking of a heavy door.

The cell was so pitch dark that the prisoner could make out nothing an inch from his nose, and he was still more bewildered when he heard a soft, sweet voice utter his name.

"A woman, as I am no sinner!" thought Captain Macheath. "Am I asleep or dreaming, or is this a visitation from the other world? Who calls?" he demanded, now speaking loud enough to be heard at the other end of the cell, but with extreme caution.

"A friend," the voice replied.

"An angel, I should think," murmured Captain Macheath.

At that moment the cell-door closed, and the key grated in the ponderous lock.

In spite of Macheath's boldness, and he was as brave as a lion, there was something so inexplicable in this visit that he felt his heart flutter and the blood mount into his cheeks, for the thought flashed into his brain that some kind of deceit or treachery was intended, for, after being badgered by the emissaries of illustrious personages, it struck him that they might plot to put him out of the way and save the trouble of a trial.

False as this notion was, as it presently turned out to be, Macheath braced himself up, and springing to his feet, stood with his arms stretched out ready to ward off any blow.

To his great astonishment a lantern was turned full on his face, and as soon as his eyes became accustomed to the light he saw that the visitor to the cell was Bertha, the governor's daughter.

On one arm she carried a basket covered with a snow-white cloth, and as she placed it gently on the floor she raised her face to the prisoner and smiled pleasantly.

"You did not expect me," she said.

"Expect you?" replied Captain Macheath. "Of all people in the world you are the very last I thought of seeing here."

"That shows that a brave man should never despair," Bertha rejoined. "I have brought you some supper prepared by my own hands, and a bottle of good old Madeira from my father's cellar."

"You are very kind," Macheath said.

"Oh! no," Bertha said. "Do not call it kind. I sympathise with you in your distress just as much as if you were my—"

"Brother?" suggested Captain Macheath.

"Well, yes; if you will have it so," said Bertha. "I bribed the warders to let me come here; and, see! here I have the keys of the cell and the door at the end of the passage."

"The deuce you have," thought Captain Macheath. "If, instead of sleeping, I had made good use of the file I might have stood a good chance of being home at Kentish Town before daybreak."

Bertha seemed to divine what was passing in his brain.

"Yes," she said; "I have the keys, and I also know that you have a file concealed about your person."

Captain Macheath started and bit his lip.

"Fear nothing from me," Bertha said. "I am your true friend, and will prove myself so at the first opportunity, but you must not make any attempt to escape at present. It is useless—it would be madness to even think of it. When the time is ripe I will let you know, and render you my aid."

As Bertha spoke she laid her hand on her heart and sighed.

It was then that Captain Macheath made an awkward discovery. Bertha was in love with him.

He watched her as she unpacked the well-filled basket, and placed before him a feast which might have pleased a king.

The action of the kind-hearted, impulsive girl set Macheath thinking deeply.

What should he say to her?

Should he tell her the whole truth—tell her about Polly, who was no doubt crying her eyes out for him at home—or should he keep his domestic affairs locked up in his own breast?

Though he had refused freedom from others, life and liberty were dear to him.

He was wondering what course he should pursue when Bertha spoke.

"Let me see you eat and drink," she said. "In the earlier part of the day you looked almost happy; but now your face wears a sad expression. The wine is of the best and will do you good," and she filled a glass and handed it to him.

"To the bravest of the sex!" he said, touching it with his lips. "Bertha!—may I call you Bertha?"

"Oh! yes," she replied, blushing. "I wish you to call me by that name always," and Bertha hung her head to hide the tears that had melted into her eyes.

Macheath pretended not to notice the girl's emotion.

He drank the wine with apparent relish and then turned his attention to the more solid refreshments.

"So I have found a friend at last," he said.

"A friend at last!" Bertha said. "But you have friends outside these walls?"

Captain Macheath hesitated before replying.

Whatever his faults may have been, deceit and heartlessness were not among the number.

But by an odd chance, by the appearance of this romantic girl, who had evidently fallen in love with him at first sight, life, liberty, and return to the wife he loved dearer than his own existence, were all his for the asking.

Why should he not take advantage of such an opportunity?

Bertha would learn to forget him in time, if, indeed, she did not despise him.

"Such a man as I make no friends," he said, casting down his eyes. "Think of what I have been and what I am now. But a few hours back I was a highwayman—hunted, a price set upon my head, and now I am here in chains, awaiting the doom of a malefactor—a thread snaps, and I pass away from the world for ever."

"And yet there must be some maiden, or perhaps a wife, who is pining for you at this moment."

Macheath went pale to the lips as he thought of Polly. Instead of replying he sighed and shook his head.

Bertha smiled and her eyes brightened.

"To-morrow," she said, "my father goes away from London on business. I will come to you again, if you will let me."

Macheath caught her in his arms and kissed her.

"My darling—my better angel!" he whispered.

He let her go, and as Bertha softly withdrew from the cell Macheath threw himself down and groaned.

"What have I done?" he thought. "Foul villain that I am to tamper with the affections of this noble-hearted girl! Have I changed? Has the courage I arrogate to myself that I posssssessed oozed out at my finger ends? Am I so degraded, so lost to the dictates of my heart, so false to my wife, that I have allowed myself to play the part of a mean, contemptible wretch?"

That night Captain Macheath was a miserable man, and as he tossed from side to side on his hard bed, little did he dream of the part Polly had been playing.

CHAPTER LI.

POLLY STARTLES A SELECT COMPANY AT HER FATHER'S HOUSE — THE RESULT OF HER VISIT.

MR. PEACHUM was entertaining company.

Blear-eyed men of the lowest type of humanity drank and ate of the best, and pledged their host in brimming bumpers of sparkling wine.

Mrs. Peachum busied herself in making her husband's company welcome, and the feast was at its height when a mere youth in age, but whose face was that of a cunning old man, burst into the room.

"News—news!" he cried. "Captain Macheath is taken!"

All eyes were at once turned upon Peachum.

The man who combined the business of a fence (receiver of stolen goods) and police agent did not quail.

"Gentlemen," he said, placing his hand on his snuff-coloured waistcoat, "I assure you this is not my work. Upon my honour I have had nothing to do with the business."

"Your honour, indeed!" observed a drunken ruffian, sneeringly. "Ha! ha! ha! Why, Peachum, don't we know that it is your business to put us all away when we have served your purpose? Well, what matters? Give me a short life and a merry one. No man was born in this world to starve, so let us laugh while we may!"

"Bravely spoken, Bolter," said Peachum, as he knocked the ashes out of his pipe, and inserted a fresh supply of tobacco. "What is life but a rough and tumble after all?"

"And yet, Mr. Peachum," growled another ruffian, who squinted horribly, "no man cares to end his life at the end of a rope, though you seem to make so light of it. Suppose you try the experiment?"

Peachum's face turned a dirty hue, and almost matched with his snuff-coloured garments.

"Ha! ha! ha!" he laughed, as soon as he recovered his self-control. "That's a rare joke—the best joke I have heard for a long time. Well, there is no knowing what may happen."

"I see a stranger on the wick of the candle!" cried Mrs. Peachum. "Upon my life there is another—one—two—a lady and gentleman!"

Peachum stared, drank a glass of hot liquor at a draught, and then glared angrily at his wife.

"Peace, you superstitious fool!" he said. "What the devil has a candle to do with strangers?"

"You wait and see," Mrs. Peachum returned. "Hark! what is that?"

"What's what?" Peachum gasped, as he clutched the arm of a chair.

"What's which?" demanded Bolter, drawing a pistol from his pocket, and weighing it in his hand. "I say, Peachum, I hope for your own sake you have not invited a few officers to join the company. You are a good actor, and for all I know you may be putting this on. If you are playing the traitor you may as well say Good-bye to this world, for I'll blow your brains out."

"Gentlemen," groaned Peachum, appealingly, "I assure you I am as innocent of thinking or doing you harm as a lamb. Had you not better retire? You know the secret room."

"Somebody is trying the door!" Mrs. Peachum screamed. "Away, all of you!"

Peachum rushed across the room, and touched a spring cunningly concealed in a wall.

A panel turned on a pivot, and the men, taking the hint, disappeared one by one.

Mrs. Peachum then took up some needle-work, while her husband, seizing in his trembling hands a tattered and well-thumbed newspaper about a month old, began to read aloud.

Tap—tap—tap at the front door.

"Who on earth can it be?" said Peachum, whose face was now perfectly livid. "Don't you think we had better put out the lights?"

"A nice thing that would be certainly," his better-half returned, sneeringly. "Bah! When trouble is at hand, a woman is worth half-a-dozen men."

"So she is," asserted Peachum, humbly. "So she is, my dear."

"So she is, my dear!" his wife repeated, as she tilted her nose in the air. "You are not of the same opinion. You can rave, and bawl, and swear, and threaten when in your cups, but you are a coward at heart."

"Only a little nervous, my love," Peachum stammered. "Tell me what you think I ought to do, and I'll do it."

"Go and see who is knocking. When trouble comes it is better to face it out."

Peachum's legs almost gave way under him as he shuffled across the room and down the dark passage.

"Who is there?" he demanded, when he had reached the door.

There was no reply, but the tapping went on at regular intervals.

Streams of perspiration were now pouring down Peachum's face.

"Who is there?" he cried again, in a louder key.

Still no answer; but the tapping went on as before.

"It must be some drunken fool who has made a mistake," Peachum thought. "At all events, I suppose I had better open the door, or I shall have my wife here."

His strength seemed to have almost left him, and it was with much difficulty that he pulled back the bolts and turned the key in the creaking and complaining lock.

On opening the door he was agreeably surprised at seeing nobody more terrible than a veiled woman before him.

"How now?" he cried. "What do you mean by knocking honest people up at this time of night?"

"I have something of importance to say to you," the veiled lady replied. "May I come in?"

Peachum thought he knew the voice, but his mind was in such a confused state that he could not have sworn whether he was on his head or his heels.

"No, you can't come in," he replied, gruffly. "You've made a mistake. The man you are looking for does not live here."

"I think he does," the lady said, quietly. "Does not Mr. Peachum reside in this house?"

"No."

The lie trembled on his lips, but the word was uttered, and he could not recall it.

"Then I do not know my own father!" said the lady.

"Mercy on me!" cried Peachum, as he staggered back as far as the opposite wall. "Why, it is Polly!"

"Yes, it is I," she said, lifting her veil; "and I don't suppose you are very glad to see me. Fear not, I have not come to trouble you for long—"

"It's no trouble," Peachum interposed, with a hypocritical whine. "Your poor mother has been crying her eyes out about you for ever so long. She has had three doctors, and ever so much brandy to keep her up. Oh! Polly, why did you leave us for—"

"Hush!" said Polly, interrupting him, and holding up her finger. "Not a word. I know of whom you would speak, and his misfortunes have brought me here."

"His misfortunes, indeed," Peachum growled under his breath. "Serve him right. If he had put himself under my wing he would have had years of life before him. But come in, Polly," he added aloud. "Oh! how glad your mother will be to see you, to be sure."

Polly required no further invitation, but walked down the passage and into the room in which her mother was sitting, stitching away as demurely as if she had never in her life dealt with anything more harmful than an old tattered waistcoat.

The garment with the needle and cotton adhering to it fell to the ground when she saw who the visitor was.

"Wench! Minion!" she screamed. "How dare you show yourself under this roof? How fares it with your gallant lover, Captain Macheath, who had me maltreated and hustled about by a crowd in the open street? Does he sing merrily like bird in a cage? Forsooth, minx! You ought to be in the next cell to the one that holds him."

"And so this is the welcome you promised me," said Polly, turning to her father who had crept into the room after her.

"Welcome!" Mrs. Peachum shrieked. "Welcome to you! Welcome to a highwayman's mistress!"

A deep red flush mounted into Polly's cheeks.

"It is not true," she said, "and were it so, it would ill become a mother to insult a daughter."

"You are no longer a child of mine," Mrs. Peachum hectored. "I renounce you! Go hence. Go back to the place you came from. Away! before these hands that nursed you when a babe strike you down at my feet."

"Come—come, wife," said Peachum. "We haven't heard what Polly has to say. We mustn't be so hard on her as to condemn her without a trial. The worst of criminals sometimes get the benefit of a doubt, and mind you, whatever may have happened, Polly is our own child—our once-beloved daughter."

As Peachum finished speaking he took from his pocket a yellow handkerchief fully a yard square, and while he wiped his eyes, hid his face and head entirely.

His wife bounced up and down the room some half dozen times and then threw herself into a chair.

"Well," she said, turning her eyes upon Polly, "what have you to say for yourself?"

"Nothing."

"Oh! she has nothing to say for herself," sniggered Mrs. Peachum, hysterically, as she beat her hands together. "Hear her! Do you mark what she tells us? She has nothing to say for herself. Had I dared to speak to my mother in that fashion she would have broken my head with the first thing that came handy."

"If she had done that before I married you," Peachum thought, "what a happy man I should have been."

"I repeat," said Polly, turning again to her father, "that for myself I have nothing to say, besides that since the hour I left this roof my life has been beyond reproof. I have been living with friends, who discovered me in dire distress, and who have been as true as steel to me."

"Nice friends, I should say," muttered Mrs. Peachum, keeping up a drumming with her feet upon the floor. "Well?"

Still looking at her father, Polly went on speaking—

"Macheath is in prison," she said. "He told me that he loved me, and promised to make me his wife. We were parted because he had to fly before the officers of justice; but he also made me another promise."

"What was that, Polly dear?" demanded Peachum, who by this time had resumed his seat in the arm-chair. "Wife, don't look so cross. It is our own Polly after all, and I am sure she has brought us some good news."

"That all depends on what use you make of it," Polly returned. "Well, Macheath's promise to me was that if he ever fell into such trouble as to ensure his death, he would, if I gained admittance to the prison under the pretence of being his wife, tell me where he had hidden all his treasure."

"Ha!" cried Peachum, squeezing his hands together, "I knew our Polly would never play us false. She is the same dear amiable girl that she ever was."

Even Mrs. Peachum beamed upon her daughter, and tried to squeeze a few penitent tears out of her eyes; but the effort was a failure.

"Now," continued Polly, "Macheath is in Newgate, and knowing, father, that you have considerable influence with the officials, I come to you to get me an order to see my—the prisoner."

"Oh! that s as easy as kissing your hand," said Peachum. "Bennet knows me well enough. He and I oblige each other at times. We understand each other, and he knows that it would be bad policy to quarrel with me. I'll write you out an order at once, Polly; but I suppose the morning will do. Of course you will sleep in your own room to-night?"

"No," Polly replied. "I must go back to my friends. They are waiting up for me."

"Who are your friends?"

"I have promised to keep that a secret for the present."

"Well—well!" said Peachum, as he spread a sheet of paper before him and took up a pen, "just as you like, Polly. Here is the order; but you will not be able to see Macheath until Wednesday week, as I hear that Bennet is going out of town, and then not until after four o'clock."

"Why not?" Polly faltered.

"Because the chances are that he will be committed to-morrow, and brought up on the day following," Peachum replied; "but, of course, his trial will take several days, so you will have ample opportunity of seeing him before he takes his final ride to Tyburn."

Polly shuddered and trembled as she took the order.

In another minute she had left the house, and was on her way back to Kentish-town with the ever-faithful Luke.

CHAPTER LII.

MACHEATH IS BROUGHT UP TO ANSWER FOR HIS SINS.

MACHEATH was committed for trial.

One night his slumbers were disturbed by strange dreams.

He fancied that after he had been condemned, and the judge had solemnly pronounced his sentence, two large cats came into the court, and one of them twitched off the black cap from the judge's head, while the other got on the front of the dock, and said—

"Captain Macheath, catch hold of my tail and fear nothing."

He then thought that he laid hold of the cat's tail, and that she immediately, after spitting and foaming at everybody, swelled up to the size of an elephant, and then flew out of the top windows of the court with him.

The other cat then, he thought, cried out—

"This is the way we prevent a *cat*-astrophe."

Macheath laughed so in his sleep at this that it awoke him.

He found himself cold and shivering in his gloomy cell.

"How ridiculous!" he said, as he turned over.

In a few minutes he went to sleep again.

This second sleep was a profound and dreamless one, and it was not disturbed until a rough voice cried—

"Six o'clock, Macheath, and here's an artist wants to take your portrait."

"Take my portrait?" cried the captain.

"Yes; he says it will sell capitally, so he begs that you will sit still for half an hour while he does it. Here he is. The sheriff has given him a pass into Newgate."

"Yes, Captain Macheath," said a fellow, sidling into the cell. "I will make a sketch of you in your fetters, and after your sentence it will sell well, and I will get you, if you please, likewise to write your name at the corner, of which I will have a facsimile taken, so you see it will be all in proper business-like order, won't it, eh? Ha—ha!"

Macheath made but two strides towards the unhappy artist, and seizing him by the nose he held that organ as though it had been in a vice.

"Oh—oh! Murder—murder!"

"What's the row now?" said the turnkey, as he lazily returned to the cell.

"Nothing particular," said Macheath. "I am only quietly advising this gentleman to take himself off, instead of me, that's all."

"Murder!—my nose! Help!—oh! Death! Murder!"

Macheath let him go, and then as he turned to leave the cell he aided his retreat by giving him an impetus behind that sent him right into the arms of the turnkey.

"Hullo! Where are you a-coming to?"

"Oh! let me go—let me leave the ruffian who has no taste for the fine arts! Where's the door? Oh! he has ruined my nose."

"Be off with you, will you?"

The discomfited artist rushed along the narrow passages, and made the best of his way out of Newgate.

"Rather cool that," said Macheath. "What next, I wonder? I suppose I shall have someone coming to ask for my last dying speech and confession, and telling me very composedly that it will be worth something as a business fetch after my execution."

"No," said the turnkey, as he came back; "they will get up that without troubling you, and I would lay a wager of a hundred guineas to one that they are getting all that up in the Dials now."

"I shouldn't wonder."

"Bless you! they set to work upon such matters in good time."

"They must, or they would not get them out in the way they do; but I suppose it is one of the things one must put up with as the price of celebrity. And now I don't care how soon I have some breakfast."

Captain Macheath's liberality had not been thrown away in Newgate.

The turnkeys provided him with a nice breakfast, which he took good care to do justice to; and by the time he had finished it, he was told that his solicitor would be glad to see him.

Macheath was full of impatience to see him, and at once requested that he might be brought to his cell.

The moment the solicitor appeared Macheath said, eagerly—

"Any news from the—"

"Hush!"

"Yes—yes. I understand; but you know who I mean?"

"I do. He has sent someone to me who says there will be distinctly proved an alibi."

The tone and manner of the solicitor as he gave this information to Macheath was quite sufficient to show that he felt confident as to the result of the trial.

Perhaps the advocate had information that Macheath did not possess, and so from that deduced a confidence that the prisoner could not feel.

"You don't seem over pleased," said the lawyer.

"No," replied Captain Macheath. "I must confess I expected something better than the production of people who would indulge in a little hard swearing at the trial."

"Never mind what they indulge in," said the solicitor, "so long as they save you."

"Granted; but do you think really that so stale a device as the attempt to prove an alibi would have any effect upon the court and the jury?"

"I do."

"Well, sir, I defer to your better judgment, then."

"Understand me, Macheath," said the lawyer. "You or I could easily have produced parties who would have deliberately sworn you were anywhere at the time that the alleged robbery was committed. But would the court believe them?"

"Hardly."

"Upon that, then, I ground my hopes. If Prince George should produce anyone to make such a statement, the probability is that it will be someone that the court must believe."

"There is something in that."

"There is everything in it. And now let me advise you to say nothing, with the one exception of a general denial of the charge, for a certainty that you did not commit it, although you are unable to say where you were on the night in question."

"I see."

"You understand that if you were to make any statement you might be severely committing those who come forward, and—"

"Hush!" said Macheath. "I hear footsteps."

The attorney was prudently silent in a moment, and then the cell door was opened, and a couple of officers made their appearance, accompanied by the governor of Newgate.

"Your time has come, Macheath," said the governor.

"What do you mean?" said Macheath. "Do you want to hang me offhand without judge or jury?"

"No; but you must come into court to plead. You are wanted, and I hope, if things should go wrong with you, you will, at least, admit that you met with civil treatment here from me."

"I think my best plan," said Macheath, "is to admit nothing, but leave all that to my legal adviser."

"As you please," said the governor. "You will please to follow me, though, in the meantime, for the judge won't be kept waiting if he can help it."

"Who is sitting to-day?" Captain Macheath demanded.

The governor turned to him with a smile and mentioned the name of a judge who had acquired a notoriety for his severity and his liking to condemn poor wretches to the gallows when he could possibly find a pretext to do so.

"Oh!" said Macheath, "it's he, is it?"

"Yes. A very humane man he is."

"Very likely. He is called the hanging judge, I have heard; but not he, nor all the judges, and all the princes in the land, can hang a man unless he is proved to be guilty in this country, that's one comfort."

"Oh! a great comfort," said the governor. "A very great comfort indeed; and we all suspect very much that you are as innocent as one of the Babes in the Wood."

The chaplain was hovering round the door of the cell.

There could be no means of doubt but that all the officials of Newgate looked upon Captain Macheath as a condemned man.

It was generally understood that when a man of his notoriety got fairly into the clutches of the law that there was an end to his career.

"I will wait for you when the trial is over," said the chaplain.

"Thank you," said Macheath; "but I shall go home when I am acquitted."

"Acquitted?" said the governor. "Ha—ha!"

"Alas!" said the chaplain, "he is very obdurate."

"Yes," said Macheath; "and with all deference to you he will continue to be so. Lead on—I'll follow, Mr. Governor."

The governor seemed, as in truth he was, anything but pleased at the easy and confident air and manner of his prisoner.

He could not believe it possible that he would escape the sentence of death that was virtually passed upon him by the judge and jury already.

The route from the cell to the court was then a much more intricate one than it is now, and it took about seven or eight minutes' walking to reach the dock.

The moment Captain Macheath appeared there was a buzz and conversation in the court, which was crowded to excess.

The prisoner was surprised to see before him and on both sides of him nothing but a sea of faces.

But the fact was that the news of Macheath's arrest and committal for trial had soon spread over London, and everybody believing, as indeed they might well do, that the captain's career was at an end, the greatest exertions had been made by thousands to be present at his trial.

Of course, only those who succeeded in getting into the court were such as liberally feed the door-keepers.

It was calculated that there was a crowd without that, at a moderate computation, could not comprise less than three thousand persons, all eager for admission.

Upon the bench sat almost the whole of the high civic authorities who had a right to be there, including the Lord Mayor.

There were among the barristers at the table several Members of Parliament, and others who had been attracted by curiosity to see Captain Macheath, concerning whom the most strange and extravagant stories had been circulated.

In his anxiety concerning his own affairs, Macheath had quite forgotten that he was such a public character as he now found himself, and he rather shrank from the amount of observation that he found he now caused.

His appearance was strikingly in his favour; and so far does appearance go that many of the spectators thought it would be a pity to hang so very handsome a man.

Perhaps those who thought so were principally the ladies, for an unusual number of the fair sex had pushed their way into the court to hear the trial.

It was asserted by the door-keeper that since the court had been built there had not been so many ladies in it at one time.

The judge was evidently in no very good humour.

The evident interest that the prisoner excited from his youthful and handsome appearance, seemed to gall him wonderfully.

Surely it could not be that his own ugliness looked the more hideous in consequence of the contrast with the manly beauty of the man who tame before him to be tried upon a charge affecting his life.

Certainly there was not a person present in the court who did not observe, when he turned his eyes again upon the judge, that there was a scowl upon his face that had not been there before.

It is not often that the Old Bailey practioners of the law take a great interest in a prisoner; but upon this occasion there never had been known such an attendance of gentlemen of the wig and gown.

When in court all their eyes were turned upon Captain Macheath.

The attorney-general, who was in court, bent a long and earnest gaze upon the prisoner; and then turned to his notes, which he diligently examined, for he was to conduct the case against Macheath on behalf of the crown.

"Officers," said the judge, when he found that the buzz of conversation and the hum of many whispers anything but subsided—"officers, take into custody anyone who you may observe disturbing the quiet of the court!"

This was a threat that had its effect, although no one was taken in custody; but the officers made a show of great activity, and pushed some of the most quiet and inoffensive of the spectators out of the place, to show that they meant business.

With his eyes half shut, the captain leant back in his chair, and calmly waited the course of events.

"Prisoner at the bar," said the clerk of the arraigns, "do you answer to the name of Captain Macheath?"

All eyes were turned upon the captain, who in a clear, musical voice, that was strangely in contrast with the rapid nasal twang of the clerk, said—

"I do."

The clerk then read the indictment in the way that indictments are usually read at the Old Bailey—that is to say, in such a style that if they were written in Sanscrit there would be almost as much chance of learning what it was all about.

Everybody there knew that this was, after all, but a mere form, and they only just heard towards the end of it that Captain Macheath had done something against the peace of our Sovereign Lord, the King.

"Prisoner at the bar," then said the clerk, "do you plead Guilty or Not Guilty to the charge that is entered in the indictment now read?"

The governor fully expected that he would plead Guilty, and he had almost got ready to take him from the court again, when, to his indignation, Macheath said in a firm voice—

"Not guilty!"

"Hurrah!" cried a voice in the crowd.

The judge sprang from his seat; but immediately resumed it again, and while his lips turned white with passion, he said, in a low tone—

"Officers, bring that person before me, if you please!"

This was easier said than done.

The officers had all the will in the world to bring "that person" before the court; but either no one could find out who it was or really no one would do so, and after the most anxious enquiries, no one, with any semblance of justice, could be laid hold of as the guilty party.

While the search for the indecorous interrupter of the court was going on, the eyes of the judge, with a flashing expression, were here, there, and everywhere, and at length they settled upon Mac-

heath's face, which wore a very quiet kind of smile.

"Officers," said the judge again. "Where is the man who interrupted this court?"

"We can't find him, my lord," said an officer.

"You must find him."

Again the officers pushed everybody about, and the Lord Mayor offered a reward of five pounds; but it was of no avail. The man could not be found.

"You cannot discover the author of the outrage upon the decency and solemnity of the court?" said the judge.

"No, my lord," replied the principal officer.

The judge turned to one of the sheriffs.

"It is quite clear, Mr. Sheriff," he said, "that the officers of the court are entirely unfit for their duty."

The sheriff bowed.

"Therefore, I hope they will at the end of the sessions be all discharged, Mr. Sheriff."

The sheriff bowed again, and the judge, although he strongly suspected that the sheriff would see him further before he discharged the officers of the court, was compelled to be satisfied with the bow of acquiescence.

"Let the trial proceed," he said. "Who conducts the prosecution in this case?"

The attorney-general rose and said—

"I have the honour to appear, my lord, on behalf of the crown in this case."

"Very well, Mr. Attorney-General. Pray let us get at the facts as soon as possible."

Again the judge leaned back in his seat and half-closed his eyes, which was with him a regular habit, and the attorney-general began his speech for the prosecution.

"My lord, and gentlemen of the jury—

"The facts which I have to lay before you regarding the criminality of the prisoner at the bar, and concerning which it will be your duty, in conformity with the oaths you have this day taken in this court, to come to a judgment, lies in an exceedingly small compass.

"Gentlemen, it is a fortunate thing for society that miscreants like the one who is now at the bar of this court are at length most certainly stopped in their career of crime by some clear case like the present, concerning which there can be no sort of cavil or doubt whatever.

"It appears then, gentlemen of the jury, the prosecutor in the case, who will appear before you, was passing along a rather unfrequented road near to Ealing common, and that he was then and there robbed by the prisoner at the bar of certain monies. Not only will this be deposed to by the person who was so robbed, but another witness, worthy of implicit credit, will give corroborative testimony.

"Under these circumstances, it is quite needless for me to take up the time of the court by any declaration of facts that will best come from the lips of the witnesses; and, therefore, I will call the person who was robbed into the witness-box who will clearly depose to that circumstance, and identify the prisoner at the bar as the robber."

The judge mildly nodded his head, as much as to say—"That's quite enough—it's all settled."

The same shabby-genteel looking person who accused Macheath at the police office was placed in the witness-box, and he told his story in as nearly as possible the same words that he had used when at Bow-street. The other shabby person then was called, and in the same cool manner corroborated the statement.

Macheath was asked at the end of each of their examinations if he had any questions to ask, and he replied—

"No. What is the use of asking men questions who do not come here to speak the truth, but to get up a case?"

"Have you any more witnesses, Mr. Attorney," said the judge, "to call in this case?"

"No, my lord; I think that the case is clear."

"Oh! quite. Well, prisoner, what have you to say in answer to the clear and conclusive charge against you?"

"I must protest," said a counsel, rising and settling his wig upon his head, "I must protest against such language from a judge to a prisoner accused of an offence, and standing at the bar of this court."

"Protest, sir!" said the judge. "What do you mean?"

"I mean, my lord, with all due respect for the office you fill, purely what I say, and I again say it, that it is disgraceful for a judge to prejudge a case to the jury in the way that this case is attempted to be prejudged."

"Sit down, sir!" roared the judge; "your speaking at all is a gross impropriety, and an intrusion, and an insult to the court."

"Indeed!" said the counsel, "that is a new doctrine in an English court of justice, that for a prisoner's counsel to speak at all is an insult to the court, and an intrusion! I appear here for the prisoner at the bar, to answer the charge now brought against him, and I will answer in spite of any judge."

The judge had just discretion enough left to see that he could not with any profit to himself contend with the counsel, who was only asserting a right, concerning which there could be no dispute.

The fact was, though, that neither the judge nor anyone else had had the smallest idea from the mode in which the case had been conducted that Macheath had any counsel to speak for him.

The crowd in the court was evidently quite delighted at the firm stand that the counsel made against the judge; and it was only the full and complete knowledge of the fact that the officers were keeping a wary watch, and were quite anxious to pounce upon and apprehend somebody, that kept a demonstration of satisfaction from taking place in the court.

"My learned friend," said the attorney-general, "appears for the prisoner. It would have been but usual upon the part of my learned friend and courteous to the court and to the prosecution to have let us known that."

"The fact is," said the captain's counsel, "the case has been brought forward in so vindictive and unusual a spirit, that I thought I might as well be in the fashion, although contending for the right against all that was wrong, and all the power that authority could bring to bear against my client."

"Pray attend to the case, sir," said the judge; "we don't want any extraneous remarks."

"Oh! they are galling, are they?"

"Silence, sir!"

"I will not keep silence. I stand here as much upon my right as you sit there. I do not like, I do not invite collisions between the bench and the bar; but I have a duty to perform here to-day, my lord, which is a higher duty than your duty, and I will do it."

"Go on—go on," whispered the attorney-general, who was very solicitous to put an end to the contention with the judge. "Do go on. This will do no good, you know."

"Not a bit; but we find upon—"

"Well, well. Go on."

The counsel smiled, for he was upon private terms of great intimacy with the attorney-general, and then addressing himself to the jury, he spoke to the case—

"Gentlemen of the jury,—Probably, appearing here as I do for the prisoner at the bar, it may appear to you surprising that up to this moment I have said nothing, nor in any way or manner interfered with the progress of the case. It might have been supposed that I would have cross-examined the two very glib and capitally-spoken persons who came into court to give their evidence against the prisoner at the bar; but I felt, gentlemen of the jury, that by saying one word to either of those witnesses I should only be throwing away the valuable time of the court, and not at all advancing the interests of my client, who, I shall be able to prove to you, is as innocent as you or I of the charge this day brought against him, and distinctly sworn to by the two witnesses."

The confident tone in which the counsel pronounced this last sentence evidently had its effect both upon jury and spectators.

The judge did not betray by the movement of a single muscle that he even heard what the counsel said, but the attorney-general looked inquiringly curious.

"If, gentlemen of the jury," continued the counsel, "I had questioned those witnesses I should have got nothing from them but an obstinate reiteration of what they had already sworn to. That swearing consists, gentlemen of the jury, of two points. The first is that a robbery was committed in a particular place; and the second is that the prisoner at the bar was the person who committed the robbery. Now, gentlemen, with regard to the first half of the swearing, I have nothing to say. I do not know, and, as far as regards my case and my duty to my client, I do not care whether or not a robbery such as has been described by the witnesses was really committed."

The judge made a note upon the paper that lay before him.

"But," continued the counsel, "as regards the other moiety of the swearing, I can say much, and it does materially matter to my client whether that he lives or not. Gentlemen of the jury, it is, to say the very mildest of it, a very great mistake indeed."

The two witnesses upon this looked very indignant, and whispered to each other.

"Gentlemen," continued the counsel, "I am in a position to prove to you that when the robbery was said to be committed the prisoner at the bar was some ten or eleven miles from the place mentioned; and if such were the case he must have had a very long arm indeed in order to rob the person who this day has deliberately sworn to his identity."

"You intend to attempt to prove an alibi?" said the attorney-general.

"No; it is no attempt. It is positive and undoubted."

"Oh! very well. It is nothing to me."

"Yes, it is much to you. Gentlemen of the jury, my learned friend says it is nothing to him; but I say it is much to him, for I know my learned friend well, and I am perfectly aware that nothing will give him such genuine satisfaction as to see the prisoner at the bar walk from this court a free man this day after being acquitted by you of the crime so unjustly laid to his charge."

The attorney-general smiled slightly, and the brows of the judge came down so low over his eyes that they were completely hidden, with the exception of a small twinkling spot at the corner of each.

"This robbery," continued the counsel, "was committed on the night of the 14th of October last, between the hours of ten and twelve."

"Or thereabouts," said the attorney-general.

"Oh! we are not particular to an hour or two," said the counsel for Macheath. "Only let us know your time and we are satisfied."

"A witness may certainly make a mistake as to an hour or two. Perhaps the prosecutor had no watch with him?"

"Let us have him up again, then."

"With all my heart."

The prosecutor was recalled, and it was evident to all the court that he was in a state of great agitation.

"Calm yourself," said the counsel. "Unless I am obliged to do so I will not set about proving where you were on the night in question. It will be sufficient for me to prove to the jury that the prisoner at the bar was not upon the spot you mention at the time you name. Now, sir, at what hour did this robbery happen?"

"I may be mistaken as to the hour."

"Nothing more probable; and as to the identity of the prisoner likewise."

"Oh! no."

"Oh! no. You are quite sure of that?"

"I am."

"And will you deliberately swear that you are not mistaken as to the robbery altogether, or that is the most likely mistake of all?"

"No; I'm not mistaken as to that I was robbed."

"Very well; you were robbed. We will admit that fact, as we are in law forced to admit a great many fictions. When were you robbed, sir?"

"Well, I cannot swear to the hour."

"Will you swear to the place?"

"Yes, of course, I will."

"Yes, of course, you will. Why, the only wonder to me is, that you don't mend your evidence, and swear that it was in the county of Middlesex, or some adjoining county, at some time unknown!"

Even the jury smiled at this, and the spectators would have indulged in a roar if they had only dared to do so, but the judge looked too dangerous.

"I don't know what you mean," said the witness. "It is a hard thing to be robbed and then bullied."

"Oh! very hard, indeed; but, for all that, let us come to the point again. Where were you robbed?"

"Close to Ealing-common. In a road leading from the common."

"Was it dark?"

"Oh! yes; very dark indeed. That I will swear."

"And it was not midnight?"

"No—no."

"Very well, then. It is quite clear that you depose to the robbery taking place somewhere close to Ealing-common, and at some time between sunset and the hour of twelve at night, and that

the prisoner at the bar was the man? Are we to take that as your evidence?"

"Why, yes."

"Very good. You may go down, and I can only say you are a very capital witness, in my opinion, whatever my learned friend who is for the prosecution may think of you."

The man looked confused and anxious as he descended from the witness-box, and the counsel, turning to the jury, said, in a solemn tone of voice—

"Gentlemen of the jury, it is not for me to say lightly that the gentleman who has just left the box has committed perjury. It is far more pleasing to my feelings, and I am sure it will be far more pleasing to yours to believe that he is mistaken, and that in deposing to what he has in the court this day, he has deposed to what he believes to be the truth, however far from it it may be in reality.

"It is not at all necessary that I should go out of my way to fix upon that witness the stigma of perjury.

"It will be sufficient if I show you, as I have done, that he is a witness who is very likely to be very much mistaken, and then prove to you upon other evidence that the prisoner at the bar was not from the hour of sunset until midnight anywhere near the spot where the robbery was alleged to have been committed.

"That, gentlemen of the jury, it will be my task to prove to you by such witnesses as I think you will feel induced to place every credit in, and whose statements will be so clear and precise that they will not admit of the shadow of a doubt."

"Then you really intend to call witnesses in support of the alibi plea?" said the attorney-general.

"I do."

"Well, I give you fair warning that I shall cross-examine them. We all know how easily witnesses to prove an alibi can be procured in London."

The judge smiled slightly.

"Yes," said Macheath's counsel; "and, unhappily, our experience in this court is sufficient to let us all know how easily witnesses may be brought forward to swear away a life upon the most broad and tangible assumptions."

"Call your witnesses," said the judge.

"I will, my lord. I now call the Countess of Downbourne."

"The who?" said the attorney-general.

"The Countess of Downbourne."

"Oh!"

The judge almost shut his eyes completely as through the throng an elegantly-dressed lady was conducted to the witness-box.

She was duly sworn, and then the counsel said to her—

"Are you the Countess of Downbourne, madam?"

"I am."

"Do you recollect anything remarkable occurring on the fourteenth of October last?"

"I do. I went in my own carriage, accompanied by Lady Harriet Scrope, as far as Hadley, to visit the Earl of Bute. It was a very dark night indeed, and after getting some distance up the northern side of Finchley, the postillion let the two right-hand wheels of the carriage slip into a ditch, and it was all but upset. We were in the greatest alarm, and as there was but one postillion, he was afraid to leave his horses. Our footman was thrown from behind the vehicle and severely hurt. Our cries for assistance for some time were quite unavailing, but at length a horseman dashed up to the spot, and with great strength and gallantry rescued us from our perilous situation."

"Unhurt ?"

"Quite so, for the carriage had not really upset, although if he had not arrived at the moment he did it is highly probable that it would have done so."

"What happened next, madam ?"

"We were profuse in our thanks, and as the footman was much hurt, he was left at the next inn, and we both requested the gentleman who had done us such good service to accompany us the remainder of the way to Hadley, which he consented to do."

"In the carriage ?"

"No; he rode his own horse by the side of it, now and then exchanging a few words with us as we proceeded, and we both thought him a very great protection indeed upon the road."

"Did you part with him at Hadley ?"

"No. He wished to bid us there good-night; but we prevailed upon him to enter the earl's house, and he supped with us, and passed the night there; for a heavy rain came on, and the earl positively would not let him go. In the morning we saw him again, and thanked him for the service he had rendered us, and then he left the earl's mansion."

"Did you know who he was ?"

"No; but we all concluded that he was some cavalry officer."

"Did he mention that was his profession or station ?"

"Oh! no. We never, of course, asked him who he was, and he did not volunteer the information. It was a sufficient introduction to us that he had done us very great service; and the Earl of Bute considered that likewise to be a sufficient introduction to him; so no questions were asked of him."

"Now, your ladyship will, I am sure, excuse me for what I am about to say; but as this is rather a grave and solemn judicial inquiry, we are compelled to be, consequently, very precise in what we do."

"Oh! I am quite willing to answer any necessary questions, and shall not feel in any way offended at them."

"That is the answer I fully expected from your ladyship; and, therefore, I ask you if, upon your solemn oath you can aver that the circumstance you have narrated to the court, took place on the evening of the 14th of October last ?"

"I can aver it upon my solemn oath. I have with me now a memorandum that I made upon the subject in a pocket-book, and I know likewise, from other circumstances, that I am right in the date."

"Very well—that is all I have to say to your ladyship upon that point; and now I have to ask one important question."

There was a death-like stillness in the court, for anyone could very well guess that that important question related to the identity between the gallant stranger, who, on that night of the 14th of October, had rescued the ladies, and supped with Lord Bute, with Captain Macheath, the prisoner at the bar.

The judge looked stern and cold, and the attorney-general was evidently very much interested; for he knew the countess perfectly well, and was perfectly taken by surprise at her appearance and her testimony in court.

"Have you, madam," said the counsel, "seen the chivalrous stranger, who did you such a service, since that night ?"

"Yes."

"Upon what occasion ?"

"To-day in this court, arraigned for his life. That is the man !"

She turned, and pointed to Captain Macheath, who bowed low in the dock; and, in defiance of the judge and the officers, a cheer burst from the crowd that was so simultaneous and so sudden that the officers stared at each other in a state of bewilderment to know how to interfere with such an universal expression of opinion.

It is quite surprising how some trifle will turn the tide of popular feeling.

Even the attorney-general began to look staggered, as he saw that the countess, without any hesitation, pointed out Captain Macheath as the gentleman who had behaved so gallantly upon the occasion referred to.

Macheath's counsel saw that he had procured in evidence from the lady all that he required.

"Madam," he said to her, with great courtesy, "I have only now very much to regret that public justice required your presence here upon this occasion, and now to state that I will not further trouble you."

The countess was about to leave the witness-box, but the attorney-general rose, and in a bland tone, said—

"One moment, if your ladyship pleases."

"Certainly, sir."

"Did you miss anything after the departure of the prisoner at the bar from the Earl of Bute's house ?"

"Miss anything, sir ?"

"Yes; I ask if you missed any property."

"Certainly not."

"Then you may depend upon it, madam, that you are mistaken in the identity of the prisoner at the bar, with the person who was so gallant to you upon the road. Allow me to beg that you will look at him again, madam, and in all seriousness again ask yourself if he is the man."

"I have sworn that he is the man."

"And to that you still adhere ?"

"I do, sir."

"Very well, madam. I hope without offence I may entertain an opinion, in which I have no doubt the jury will coincide with me, that you are most grievously mistaken. I will not trouble you further."

The countess withdrew from the witness-box at once, and then Macheath's counsel resumed speaking—

"The next witness I shall call for the substantiation of this alibi is the Lady Harriet Scrope, who was with the Countess of Downbourne upon the occasion in question."

The appearance of the young lady who now stepped into the witness-box was very much in her favour.

She was not above nineteen years of age and of the most charming aspect.

There was not one person in the court, the ladies of course excepted, who did not feel that it was quite a treat to get a sight of so much beauty.

"Allow me, Lady Harriet Scrope," said Duval's counsel, "to ask you if you have heard the evidence of the Countess of Downbourne ?"

"I have, sir."

"Upon your oath do you corroborate that evidence?"

"I do, in every particular."

"Then pray look at the prisoner at the bar, and to the best of your knowledge and belief, say if he is or is not the person who rescued you and the countess from your unpleasant position upon the night in question."

"He is that person. I have no doubt whatever upon the subject."

"You swear to his identity quite distinctly, then?"

"I do."

"Very well, Lady Harriet; I shall not trouble you further. My learned friend who is for the prosecution, may or may not have something to say to you."

"Nothing whatever," said the attorney-general, as he gave his brief a push across the table, which his professional brother quite understood to mean that he had had enough of it.

"Then, gentlemen of the jury," said Macheath's counsel, "I have no more to say or to do, but to submit to you the evidence now brought forward in favour of the prisoner, as one of the clearest and most conclusive alibis that was ever proved in a court of justice; and I feel quite sure that you will coincide with me in that view. As I have called witnesses for the defence my learned friend prosecuting for the Crown has a right to reply."

"No," said the attorney-general, "I have no no reply to make."

"In that case," observed the judge, "I shall postpone the summing-up of this remarkable case until to-morrow. Let the prisoner be removed."

CHAPTER LIII.

"HOW HAPPY COULD I BE WITH EITHER!"— WHY THE JUDGE DID NOT SUM-UP.

IT was just four o'clock when Captain Macheath was taken to his cell.

"Take particular care of him," said the governor, who brought up the rear. "Take good care of him, warders. Notwithstanding his alibi the law won't allow him to slip through its fingers."

Macheath smiled but made no reply.

Bertha, who had seen him every day from the date of his incarceration, promised to visit him as soon as possible after the rising of the court, and from this Macheath rightly conjectured that the girl had heard from her father that the trial under any circumstances would be adjourned.

Guilty or not guilty it would not do to hurry over the trial of such a man as Macheath, else the fashionable sightseers—the ladies who quizzed and laughed and smiled when a man's life was hanging on a thread—would be sorely disappointed.

As soon as the captain was safely locked up, the governor left Newgate to dine with some friends and to tell them how nicely Macheath would be tricked in spite of the evidence for the defence.

The governor knew that the judge would sum up dead against the prisoner, and that the jury—some of whom had an inborn horror of highwaymen—would hesitate before giving Macheath his liberty.

As a matter of fact "the benefit of a doubt" was a rare thing in those days, and many an innocent man went to an ignominious death through the ignorance and bias of twelve men, who, not being in many instances able to write their own names, set at naught the oath taken in the jury box, and altogether failed to understand it.

The governor had not left Newgate many minutes when the door of Macheath's cell opened, and a warder with his forefinger upon his lips appeared.

"What now?" the captain demanded.

"Don't be alarmed," said a silvery voice; "it is only I!"

And in walked Bertha, smiling and tossing her head jauntily.

"See here, Bertha," said Macheath, when they were alone, "I am beginning to grow tired of this sort of thing. To-morrow, for all I know, my doom may be pronounced in spite of what has been said on my behalf, and then my enemies will take care to put me out of the way as quickly as possible."

"They will never put you out of the way," Bertha returned. "Do you not trust me?"

"Have I not trusted you?" Macheath rejoined. "But it seems to me that I am as far off escape as ever. I wish," he added, with pretended petulance, "that I had relied upon myself. The warder gave me a file, but you made me give that up to you."

"Yes, I did," said Bertha, "and why did I beg of you to give up the file? I was fearful that my father might take it into his head to have you searched, and besides—besides I want to feel that you owe your escape to me, and to me alone."

"Well," said Macheath, as he placed his arm round her slender waist, "and pray when am I to have the honour of being set at liberty by your pretty self?"

"To-night," Bertha replied. "See, here is a duplicate key of your cell. At midnight the warders will assemble in the great hall to change guard. Make the best of your time then. Keep to the left until you see a door open. Do you follow me?"

"Perfectly," said Macheath. "If ever a drowning man caught at straws my ears are drinking in your words."

"The door," Bertha resumed, "will be left open by me, but I shall be nowhere to be seen. You will enter the room before you, raise a window leading to the leads, and there, in the left-hand corner, you will find a rope by which you can lower yourself into the street."

"My preserver—my better angel!" cried Macheath, "how can I repay your kindness but by everlasting gratitude and the sacrifice of my life to one so dear to me."

"Am I so dear to you?" Bertha demanded, as her eyes flashed with a joyous light.

"Of course you are," Macheath replied. "Confound it!" he thought, "shouldn't I catch it if Polly heard me."

"When you are free," Bertha resumed, "you will write to me, and address your letter to the Cross Keys, in Cheapside, will you not?"

"I have told you so a hundred times," Macheath said, lowering his eyes. "I am to write in the name of John Saunders, is that not so?"

"Yes."

At this moment there was a commotion in the passage leading to the cell.

"I tell you I will see him, and at once," cried a voice. "Refuse me admittance at your peril. They did not dare to challenge me at the gate, and I dare you to do anything but your duty. Out of my path, fellow, and lead me to the cell in which Captain Macheath is imprisoned."

The captain's heart sank within him.

He knew that the voice was his wife's, and that voice had been music to his ears a thousand times, but now it thrilled him with horror.

"All right, lady," replied the warder. "Macheath has a visitor with him. I think it is his—his solicitor. You shall see him in less than half an hour, if you are patient."

Bertha ran across the cell, and laid her hand upon the door.

"Stop!" Macheath cried. "If you—if you have any love for me stay where you are."

"Why?" Bertha demanded, as the colour mounted into her cheeks, and her eyes flashed fire.

"Oh! I don't know," Macheath replied, with a groan.

"There is a woman talking outside, and I'll know who she is," Bertha said.

As he spoke she unlocked the cell door, threw it open, and stood face to face with Polly, who immediately recoiled as if she had been stabbed to the heart.

Recovering her self-control she walked into the cell, and, seeing Macheath, she uttered a loud cry of mingled grief and joy, and, extending her arms, rushed forward to embrace him.

But Macheath, feeling that for once he was a coward at heart, had rehearsed his part.

"Woman," he said, regarding Polly coldly, "who are you, and why are you here?"

For a moment Polly was dumb with amazement.

The floor of the cell seemed to glide under her feet, and a film gathered before her eyes.

She lost sight of the fact that Bertha was standing near and gazing at her sneeringly, and in such a manner as only a woman in love knows how to look at a rival.

"Who am I? Why am I here?" Polly repeated, clutching at her fast beating heart. "Cease this funning, Macheath. Am I not your own true, loving wife?"

"Wife!" screamed Bertha. "Wife! Do I hear aright, or is this woman mad?"

"This woman is not mad," Polly said, turning upon Bertha. "This man is my husband, and consequently I am his wife."

Bertha walked backwards until her tottering feet were stayed by the wall.

"His wife—his wife!" was all she could gasp out from her pale and bloodless lips.

"Yes, his wife—wife—wife!" ejaculated Polly. "My husband asked me what I did here. He is not himself; this fearful place has played havoc with his senses. Minion, it is for me to ask who you are, and what is your business here."

"Oh! murder," thought Macheath. "I must put a stop to this."

"Madam," he said, bowing to Polly, "there is some mistake. Your husband may have taken my name, and perchance is in some other prison, but I—"

"Oh! Heaven," cried Polly, aghast, "is it possible that this man whom I have trusted with my safe keeping through life, and for whom I have suffered so much, denies me?"

"Yes, he denies you," Bertha said, springing forward. "Woman, if you are not bereft of your senses you are a disgrace to your sex."

"You lie!" Polly exclaimed. "Hussy, I give you the lie in your teeth!"

Macheath now thought it time to interpose himself between the two infuriated ladies.

"How happy could I be with either, t'other fair charmer away!" he said. "Come—come! your pretty pink nails were never made to scratch each other. Have done with this farce!"

"Farce!" panted Polly. "Am I not your wife?"

"Wife—forsooth!" replied Macheath; "sorry a wife have I."

"Farce!" cried Bertha. "Am I not your accepted lover?"

"I love nobody but myself," said the captain.

"Oh! how I have been deceived," Polly sobbed.

"And I too," moaned Bertha.

"Ladies," said Macheath, "this is a strange coincidence. You are both dreaming or, I fear, suffering from hysteria. Permit me, at all events," here he pointed to Polly, "to wish you a very good day and to wish you well."

He would have given worlds, had they been in his power to bestow, to be able to whisper a few comforting words in Polly's ear, to make a clean breast of everything, and tell her that his love was as steadfast as ever.

Polly, pale and trembling, fell back, and was caught by the warder, who carried her in his arms to the gate.

"Let me out," she groaned; "let me breathe the fresh air. They said I was mad! Oh! that I could lose my senses and blot out all memory of the cruel scene which has robbed me of my love—robbed me of my life! Let me out!"

Luke was waiting for her in the street, but it was a long time before the faithful fellow could get from his mistress what had happened.

"Humph! It is curious, to say the least," Luke said, when he knew all; "but I will not believe that the captain is so base. There is something more in this than meets the eyes. Depend upon it, Captain Macheath has some method in behaving as he did."

"Method!" Polly cried. "Pray what kind of method but a disgraceful one could he have in denying me? And then that brazen-faced baggage—"

"There's the mystery," interposed Luke, scratching his head. "Well, my good mistress, cheer up. Most things are open to explanation, and I have got it into my head that the captain will give Newgate the slip to-night, and I shall make it my duty to keep close watch, in case that I have made a right guess."

"You only say this to comfort me," Polly said, between her sobs. "Oh! Luke—Luke, that I should have lived to hear such words from his lips. Whatever he may have been to other people, he seemed good and true to me."

"And is," insisted Luke. "Mark my words, mistress, Macheath can never change towards you. There is something which is at present a mystery to us; but I'd stake my life that everything will come right."

"Did I not see that woman with my own eyes?" Polly urged. "Did I not hear her demand of him—my husband—whether he was not her accepted lover?"

"And what said Captain Macheath?" Luke asked.

"He said—'No.'"

"Just so," said Luke.

"But he denied me, too," Polly returned—"his wife!"

"That's where the mystery comes in again, and where it will now stop until we shall get an explanation," Luke remarked. "My good mistress, I was disguised to-day and was in court. The judge then said he would sum up the case

CAPTAIN MACHEATH

THE
PRINCE OF THE HIGHWAY.

"HOW HAPPY COULD I BE WITH EITHER—T'OTHER FAIR CHARMER AWAY," SAID MACHEATH.

some time to-morrow. If he does sum up, I shall be wonderfully mistaken if Captain Macheath is seen standing in the dock to listen to what his lordship has to say."

Polly only shook her head and then sobbed all the more.

Luke deeply sympathised with his heart-broken mistress, but he did not attempt any consolation, for he knew that it was far better that such an acute sufferer should give free vent to her feelings.

"Take me away from the sight of these horrible walls, will you?" Polly asked, turning to Luke.

"That I will, ma'am, and gladly, too," Luke replied, "but I'll feast my eyes on them to-night from dark to dawn."

"I fear it will be a futile task, and one difficult to accomplish."

"No, it will not. Never mind about that," said Luke. "I will not lose sight of Newgate one moment longer than I can possibly help."

Meanwhile a strange scene was being enacted in Newgate.

Captain Macheath and Bertha stood looking at each other with no great pleasure.

Neither of the two had spoken for more than a minute.

The contrast between Captain Macheath and Bertha was very great.

Macheath's face was pale, whereas Bertha's was crimson, and each moment the colour rose higher and higher.

"Captain Macheath," said Bertha, "you have deceived me."

Another pause ensued, Bertha looking the while straight into Captain Macheath's eyes. Suddenly she exclaimed—

"You are a coward!"

"I plead guilty to that impeachment," Macheath replied, "and I also confess that I am a fool into the bargain."

"And I have a confession to make," Bertha rejoined. "I had often heard you spoken of as a man who, although taking to the road for a livelihood, gave help to the helpless, succoured the weak, and ever ready to crush the oppressor."

. . . . on

. . . . at your mercy, but do not think for a moment that I ask you to extend it to one so lowly fallen as myself."

"Hear me out," Bertha returned, passionately. "I pitied and I loved you, Macheath. I would have risked all to save you—aye, given up all —home, my father, my life. You speak of having fallen—"

A sob checked her utterance, and with her hands clasped upon her heart, poor Bertha rocked herself to and fro in a paroxysm of uncontrollable grief.

"You speak of having fallen," she resumed. "How fallen am I! The law of old says, 'Thou shalt do no murder,' and you have murdered me —killed my heart. Macheath, that woman who was here just now is your wife."

"Yes, she is," replied Captain Macheath, scarcely above a whisper. "She is my wife."

"And so," said Bertha, "you have played a double part—"

"I'll hear no more," Macheath cried. "I love my wife. It was for her sake, for the hope of returning to her, that I deceived you. I beg your pardon. I am ashamed of myself. I care not

how soon the end comes now. The hangman must do his work. Leave me, I beg."

"Not yet," Bertha said. "Tell me, Macheath, what will become of your wife when you are—gone?"

"I know not," Macheath replied, bitterly. "I can only hope that she will live to forget me, and in time to come find a husband worthier than I have ever been."

Bertha strode forward, and then sank on her knees at his feet.

Macheath was astonished at this proceeding, but as Bertha drew a bright keen file from her bodice he was fairly bewildered.

"What now?" he exclaimed.

"I am going to set you free," Bertha said, quietly.

"No—no," he said, hoarsely; "leave me to my fate."

"You shall have your liberty," Bertha returned, "if not for your own sake, it shall be for your sorrowing wife's."

"Great Heavens!" Macheath ejaculated, lifting his manacled hands, "how many women are there like this one in the world?"

"Thousands—millions," Bertha replied, as she worked away with the file. "Men talk lightly of women without knowing what sacrifices they are capable of making. What you have done for your wife's sake, that would I have done for my lover. Go to your wife and tell her that you found a sister in me. Tell her that though the warmth of a lover's love has died away for ever in my breast, I am your friend and hers."

Captain Macheath was so overcome that he shed tears. He had never been more deeply moved.

"You unman me," he said, brokenly. "Your words stab me sharper than a dagger of the finest steel."

Bertha made no reply, but went on with her work as if she had been used to it all her life.

"There!" she said at last, "your fetters are nearly cut through, and you can easily snap them asunder. You will find all as previously arranged. And now, adieu! Should we never meet again, bestow a kindly thought upon me at times."

"One word!" Macheath cried, in a broken voice.

"No," Bertha said, as she approached the cell . . . . time is at hand when you must make the attempt to escape. Make the best of that time, for it will be short. The warders assemble in the hall to change guard for a quarter of an hour only. Adieu!"

In another moment she was gone, and Macheath sinking down upon the bench, placed his hands before his face and sobbed like a broken hearted child.

"Better that I had died," he moaned, "for it would have been a far, far better fate than have all the low cunning my nature could summon to deceive her. Worm that I am! I feel I could dash my dastardly head against these walls. This will be a lesson for life."

The time passed away slowly, and as the hours went by Macheath grew calmer.

The sound of a clock reached his ears through the grating of the cell door.

He had often listened to the chiming, and mused upon the fact that even a man with youth and health has but a short time to live.

Half-past eleven o'clock.

Another chime!

In a few minutes the warders would be changing guard.

Macheath looked down at the file Bertha had left on the floor, and then began to pace the cell, as had been his custom night after night before lying down to sleep.

A ray of light flashed through the grating.

"Macheath !" said the gruff voice of a warder.

"I am here."

"Do you require anything more to-night ?"

"No."

"Then may you sleep well. Good-night."

"Same to you, old fellow," said Macheath. "You might get a barber to come over in the morning. I want shaving, and my hair dressed, so as to look presentable in court."

"I'll see to it," the warder replied.

"Thank you," Macheath said. "Any news from the outside ?"

"They say you will be hanged."

"What !—in the face of such an alibi as was established in my behalf ?"

"Oh ! that goes for nothing when judge and jury have made up their minds," the warder said, with a chuckle. "Hallo ! there goes twelve o'clock, and I must be off. Keep your spirits up."

"I will," Macheath said, "if only to spite my merciful judge and jury. Bertha, angel in a woman's form !"

When the sound of the warder's heavy footsteps had died away, Macheath wrenched off his irons.

It cost him no great effort to do so ; for so cunningly had the governor's daughter filed them that they snapped and fell away like brittle glass.

It was with a fast-beating heart that he inserted the duplicate key in the lock and turned it.

The grating of the lock had never attracted his attention before, but now it seemed to echo down the corridor.

He was outside at last, and slipping off his boots he carried them under one arm, and commenced to glide swiftly between the dark and gloomy walls.

He remembered that Bertha conjured him to keep to the left.

He did so, and presently he saw a broad band of light flooding the stone pavement.

No guiding star could have been more welcome to him.

Before him was an open door.

Quick as thought he passed through it, closed and locked the door, and then made his way to a window.

He pushed it open, and it made no more noise than if the hinges had been purposely oiled to assist in his escape.

The fresh night air blew strangely upon Macheath's face and he thought that he had never smelt anything so sweet in his life.

He was now on the leads, and as he crossed them quickly he could not help smiling at the warders changing guard, and who might be under his feet at that moment.

The rope—where was the rope ?

After groping about in the darkness for a few moments he found it, and prepared for the descent.

Looking over the parapet he saw that the street was clear.

Ding dong ! St. Sepulchre's Church clock chimed the quarter after midnight.

Captain Macheath threw the rope over the wall, clutched it firmly in his hands, and went down.

He stood in the street.

He was free—free to return to Polly and tell her the real truth.

Captain Macheath was about to make off at the top of his speed when he heard a low whistle, and a man darted from a doorway in Newgate-street.

"Ha !" said the captain, as he braced himself up for a struggle, "it seems that I am no sooner out of the frying-pan than into the fire."

"Hush !" said the man. "Not a word. Don't you know me, captain ?"

"Why, it's Luke !" Macheath gasped.

"Yes, it's Luke sure enough," said that individual. "Here's a hat, sir, and here's your sword."

"Luke, my faithful—"

"Not another word, captain. I might as well stand here and ask you how you got rid of that beautiful Newgate jewellery. Your horse is on Holborn-hill."

"Where, Luke ?"

"At the old Angel Inn, at the corner of the market."

"That's right," said Macheath, "and if I live for the next ten minutes I will be upon his back." Macheath and Luke went on side by side until they reached the corner of the Fleet-market, which has been long swept away, when a murmur of voices disturbed the night air.

Luke, drawing a pistol, went on a little way in advance.

"Quick, captain—quick !" he said, hoarsely. "The hawks have missed you and are on the wing."

At that moment two officers, hidden by the shadow of a house, darted out.

One of the men threw his arms round Macheath's waist and held him tight.

Macheath caught the other by the throat.

"All right," he said, cheerfully. "You've got me ; but I've got the other."

The officer's face turned blue under the pressure of Macheath's fingers, and the captain, suddenly dashing him down, turned upon the other, and lifting him clean from his feet, hurled him on top of his half-stifled companion.

It is a marvel where a crowd springs from, no matter what the time of night it may be.

Little time as this adventure took, a number of men had appeared as if by magic.

The cry "Macheath has escaped !" rang through the air.

"This way," Luke shouted ; "this way for your life, captain."

"Aye, see to him," shouted the mob. "Hurrah ! for Macheath."

With a yell and a shout the throng trampled over the fallen officers, and in less than a minute Macheath and Luke passed under the gateway of the old Angel Inn.

"This way—this way," cried Luke, as he dragged the captain through the mob that pressed closely upon him.

A man was waiting with two horses ready harnessed and saddled.

In less time than it takes to record the fact Macheath and his faithful servant were mounted.

"My friends," said Macheath, addressing the crowd, "if you wish me and my friend to escape, you will make room. I thank you for your kindness, but it is a kindness that will deliver me into the hands of my enemies."

"Which way, Macheath ?" shouted a man.

"Up Holborn !" replied the captain.

The mob swerved as if actuated by a common

impulse, and Macheath and Luke dashed through a lane of human beings.

The horses were slightly terrified at the noisy demeanour of the crowd, and inclined to be restive, but this satisfied Macheath that they were fresh and fit for the work before them.

"Farewell!" cried the captain, lifting his hat.

"Hurrah!" roared the mob. "Good luck to you, Macheath."

"Now for it," said the captain. "The sooner we bid good-bye to these streets the better, but we must not tire our steeds. I think a sharp trot will serve our purpose, as it will puzzle the warders, even if they can ride, to find horses at this early hour."

"A sharp trot be it," Luke replied. "Our horses can gallop when called upon, and that's a comfort."

"On, then!"

Off they went on steeds that thought nothing of trotting eight miles an hour, or even ten when put to it.

Holborn-hill was soon left behind, and in a very short time horses and riders turned into Tottenham-court-road.

"This will do," said Captain Macheath, as he drew rein.

"Yes, sir," Luke returned. "And now allow me to congratulate you upon your escape. Was there a woman in the case?"

"As I believe that you are true and faithful to me, do not ask that question," Macheath said.

"I beg your pardon, captain."

"No need for that," Macheath said, hastily. "The question was a natural one, after all, for I daresay you have heard what took place when Polly came to see me?"

"Yes," Luke thought; "and I have no doubt but that you will hear of it again."

But, like a wise man, Luke kept his thoughts to himself and held his tongue.

"Well, captain," he said, after a slight pause, "I must say that matters looked as if they were going to take an ugly turn. To tell you the truth, I began to despair, and little dreamed that you and I would be riding together on the high-road so soon."

"My time has not come round yet, Luke," Macheath said, with a thoughtful expression. "It might have come but for— Well, well, you will hear all about it soon enough."

"Hark!" said Luke. "If I am not mistaken we are pursued after all."

Macheath brought his horse to a standstill and listened.

"Yes," he said; "or at all events I hear horses' hoofs. Let us get out of the highroad, Luke. But you have not told me how she is at home."

"As well as can be expected," Luke replied, with a furtive glance out of the corner of his eyes at his master. "You couldn't expect to hear that she was merry, could you?"

"Luke," Macheath said, "I have been much to blame, and though I love my wife dearly, as you know, I feel that I would rather face a regiment of soldiers than her just now."

"Well, captain," Luke returned, "if you love your wife, it is very plain to me that she loves you. She'll be glad enough to see you, never fear. I daresay," he added, slily, "that she will ask you a few questions about—"

"Speak of her as the woman who saved me," Macheath said.

"I'll think of her as such," Luke said. "Captain, the horses are drawing nearer. Here is a turning to the right which will take us into a neighbourhood that looks as if it had been laid out in market-gardens."

Tottenham-court-road, so familiar to London and its visitors, is now one of the busiest and most bustling thoroughfares of London, but in Captain Macheath's time it could boast of only a few private houses of quite a rural aspect.

It was no false alarm.

Horses, mounted by determined men, were approaching.

Macheath and Luke, turning their own steeds into a lane, seemed to have the effect of throwing the pursuers completely off the scent.

More than once, during the next few minutes, Luke dismounted, and stretching himself out flat, laid his ear upon the ground to listen.

Each time that he did so he reported to Captain Macheath, who sat with swords and pistols ready for any emergency, that the tread of the horses' hoofs became fainter and fainter.

"We have outwitted them, captain, I think," said Luke.

"Let us hope so," Macheath returned; "and now as you seem to have a good knowledge of this locality, can you name a likely house where we can refresh ourselves? For my own part I am half dead with hunger and thirst."

"Yes, I can, captain," Luke replied. "Your words remind me of a house where I think we can stay until all danger is past."

"That's the style," said Macheath. "The atmosphere of Newgate still hangs about me, and come what may I shall be none the worse for a good meal and a few hours' rest."

Luke now led the way, and presently he pointed to a house lying back from the road, and almost invisible in consequence of being sheltered by a number of trees.

"That's the Blue Boar," he said, "and Tom Adams isn't the man to turn away a guinea or two."

Luke and Macheath dismounted and led their horses up a narrow path by which the inn was approached.

Luke turned out to be a true prophet.

Tom Adams, the landlord of the Blue Boar, did not seem to relish the idea of turning out of bed at such an hour; but when he discovered that his customers were men willing to pay handsomely for such accommodation as his house afforded, he grinned affably and bowed low over his capacious waistcoat.

A substantial meal was soon put on the table, and while Tom Adams went to see the horses stabled, assuring the captain with a knowing wink that this was not the first time he had been called upon to do such work, Macheath and Luke made good play with their knives and forks.

Macheath then stretched himself out upon a couple of chairs, and slept as easily as if he were upon a bed of down; but Luke, who could not have closed his eyes for ten thousand pounds, sat near the door watching and listening.

Nothing occurred until daylight came, and then Luke deemed it wise to waken the captain.

"Ha!" said Macheath, as he started up. "What! I am not in Newgate? And you here, too, Luke?"

"Yes, captain; and may the day be a distant one when I shall be compelled to part with you again."

"I dreamt that I was in that confounded cell, and that the jury had given their verdict against me, without troubling to see me in the dock."

"Ha—ha—ha!" laughed Luke. "You see it isn't as bad as that, captain. If you are ready I am. The sun is rising and people are getting about."

"Quite ready," said Macheath. "What about the horses?"

"I'll go and see about them at once," Luke replied. "The stables are close at hand."

In a few minutes all was ready for the departure, and Tom Adams having been recompensed even beyond his hopes or dreams, Macheath and his faithful attendant set out once more.

Luke, in his wanderings previous to knowing Macheath, had made himself so well acquainted with the north of London that he could have drawn a fairly accurate map of the locality had it been necessary.

Leaving the Blue Boar the adventurers travelled on until they came to a cluster of small cottages.

To the surprise of Captain Macheath Luke turned his horse's head into a yard, to the great danger of a brood of chickens just let loose.

"Surely," said Macheath, "this is not the way?"

"Yes, it is, captain," Luke replied. "Follow me, and all will be well."

"Hallo!" demanded a woman, appearing at one of the cottage doors, "what do you want here, you old vagabond?"

"To go through your garden into the meadows beyond," said Luke. "There's a broken fence we can easily get through. It was in that state years ago, I know. Here it is."

The woman stared as hard at Luke as if he had been a wizard.

"How did you know that the gap was here?" she asked.

"That's my business," said Luke; "and it ought to have been your husband's to keep his premises in repair."

"He is too fond of the ale-house to do anything but drink and smoke," the woman returned.

"And you are too fond of gossiping, or you would have done it yourself," Luke added.

The woman stared again, but made no reply, and Macheath and Luke passed into the meadows.

"You see that group of chestnuts, captain?" said Luke.

"Yes."

"That's the point we must leave the meadows," Luke added. "Close to the trees runs a lane inclining to the right, which will bring us out upon the homeward road."

"All right, Luke," said Macheath. "I will leave everything to you. Heyday! here comes the fattest man on the smallest pony that ever carried such a weight."

Luke shaded his eyes with his hand for a moment.

"It's the farmer, by all that's unlucky!" he said.

"What farmer?"

"Farmer Hobbs, the owner of the meadows."

"Oh! hang Farmer Hobbs," said Captain Macheath, contemptuously.

"Halloa! there," roared the fat farmer on the small pony. "Halloa! there."

"Halloa away, ye mountain of flesh!" said Macheath. "If I were not in such a hurry I would have some fun with you."

Notwithstanding that the pony was so heavily weighted, it came up at a clumsy gallop.

The farmer was puffing and blowing, and looked as savage as if he had been robbed of a thousand guineas.

"What do you mean by trespassing on my land?" he said, as soon as he could speak.

"Is this really your land?" Luke asked.

"Yes, it is."

"Then," said Luke, "I'll just give you a piece of good advice. Cut up your land into squares and take it home. We don't want it."

"Of all the cheek!" Mr. Hobbs gasped.

"No, you've got all the cheek," Luke retorted, "and it strikes me, sir, that you were in the way when mouths were served out. Did you happen to hit your head on a door-scraper when you were young?"

This question made the farmer more furious.

"I'm not going to stand here listening to your impudence," he cried. "Just you go back again."

"What!—all the way back?" Macheath demanded, with a smile.

"Yes, all the way back, to be sure—every inch of it," said Farmer Hobbs.

"Why, my friend," Macheath returned, "we have only just arrived in this pleasant place, and it would look foolish to go back again. Our way lies in the direction of those chestnut-trees."

"But you are trespassing on my land!" Hobbs bellowed. "Didn't you see the board with 'Any person found trespassing on it will be prosecuted according to law' painted on it?"

"What law? Your law, I suspect."

"No—the law of the country," Hobbs almost shrieked; "the law that lays scamps and scoundrels by the heels."

"I saw no board," replied Macheath, quietly; "and if I had I should not have paid the slightest attention to it."

"You defy the law then?"

"Most certainly."

The farmer blew himself out like a balloon, and trembled all over like an unsteady jelly.

"Good day," said Macheath.

"Hold!" cried the farmer. "I am not to be done like this. You shall go back, I say."

"So shall you," Macheath retorted. "Get out of my way, unless you desire a back-fall off your pony."

"But I say you shall go back," Farmer Hobbs insisted.

"Listen to me, my friend," said Macheath. "You are keeping us waiting. Shall is not a word that I understand unless I use it myself. You had better be civil, or I will give you such a thrashing as will not leave a whole bone in your body."

"Oh! that's the game, is it?" cried Farmer Hobbs. "We'll soon see how we can manage a fellow like you. I'm not without help I can tell you; and if I put this whistle to my lips I shall have a dozen of my men here in no time."

"If you put that whistle to your lips I'll make you swallow it as sure as you are a living man," said Macheath.

"You will?"

"Most certainly," said Macheath. "I am a man who keeps his word. I will not only make you swallow it, but choke you into the bargain."

"You will?"

"Upon my word I will."

"You had better put that toy away," Luke chimed in; "my friend never says anything without meaning it."

"And in this instance," added Captain Macheath, "I shall keep it to the letter. Be off before you discover that you have paid too dear for your whistle."

Farmer Hobbs looked dubious.

He took off his hat and ran his fingers through his shock head of hair.

"Well," he said, sheepishly, "I don't mind whether I get my men here by whistling or going to them, so I'll just trot off. Hang me if I don't believe that you are a pair of highwaymen."

"You have come to a very prudent resolution," said Macheath. "Now, Luke, my good fellow, we will be off. We have wasted more time with this man than would have taken us to the high road that leads to Kentish-town."

"I fear we have, captain," Luke replied.

The farmer, who now saw that the trespassers were not exactly the sort of men to be trifled with, made off in one direction, while Macheath and Luke, giving rein to their horses, rode away at full gallop.

They made such good speed that the meadows were soon cleared.

An obstacle suddenly presented itself.

This was a hedge, a terrific leap in itself, but all the more dangerous because the road below was fully six feet lower than the meadow land.

"I am out of my reckoning for once," Luke said. "What do you think, captain—shall we try this break-neck jump?"

"Try it—yes," Macheath replied. "I feel sure that neither of our horses will fail us."

"All right. Here goes."

Both now put spurs to their horses, Macheath waving his hat in triumph, and Luke half turned in his saddle with a pistol in his hand ready to quiet any of the farmer's men should they put in a too sudden appearance.

The leap was a fearful one, but the splendid steeds never faltered for an instant.

Over they went, and then down.

Crash came their hoofs upon the hard ground, but all was well.

"Bravo!" cried Macheath, exultantly. "I suppose you know the way now, Luke?"

"Every inch of it," said Luke. "To the right. Hush! someone comes. Do you not hear a horse at full gallop, captain?"

"There is no mistaking the sound," Macheath replied. "Let us turn our horses under the shadow of the trees and see who it is."

The halt was made at a bend of the road and until horse and rider had turned the corner neither could be seen.

Suddenly the stranger appeared in sight, and turned out to be a youth, who, though seemingly of slender build, was a thorough master of the splendid horse he rode.

"Why, he is quite a boy," said Luke.

"A boy he may be, but he is a magnificent horseman," Macheath returned, abstractedly.

"Why, what is the matter with you, captain?" Luke demanded. "You have turned pale all of a sudden. You don't look yourself at all."

"I am well enough," Macheath replied; "but if it did not seem too improbable I should take it upon myself to say that that silver-laced hat was mine."

"Yours, captain?"

"Yes," said Macheath, "it is mine or an exact copy of it; but if mine it is a puzzle how it came on yonder youth's head. I will question him."

"Don't, captain."

"Oh! nonsense; I must."

Captain Macheath rode forward, but suddenly he checked his horse with such violence that the animal fell back upon his haunches.

Under the hat were the features of his wife, Polly.

She looked up, recognised him, and with a loud cry and an upward motion of her arms, reeled in the saddle.

Macheath leaped from his horse and caught her in his arms.

"Luke!" he cried, in dismay. "This is my wife. She has fainted, or is dead. The shock of seeing me has proved too much for her."

"She has only swooned," Luke said. "Hold her, sir, while I run to a spring hard by here and fill my hat with water. Steady, captain, steady. Give my poor mistress as much air as possible."

Captain Macheath was kissing Polly's cold, pale lips, but he took Luke's hint and desisted.

In a few minutes Luke returned with his hat brimful of water, and commenced sprinkling his mistress' face with it.

"Courage, captain," said the faithful fellow. "See, she is coming round."

Polly opened her eyes slowly.

"My wife, listen to me," said Macheath. "All is well. I am free again. Calm yourself. You shall know all in good time. Whatever I may have done I have not been false to the oath I took at the altar."

"Your voice comes to me as in a dream," Polly replied, faintly. "I am better now. Then you are free?"

"Yes; free as the air," said Macheath. "Are you strong enough to walk by my side while I tell you all?"

"Yes—yes!"

Macheath concealed nothing from Polly, nor did he excuse himself in any way.

"I played the part that I might come back to you," he said, in conclusion; "and, Polly, you cannot find it in your heart to say that you do not forgive me?"

"I forgive you freely," Polly returned; "but, oh! this seems too good to be real. Tell me again that you are safe and well."

"I am quite well, dear wife," Macheath said. "And now let me thank Luke in your presence."

"Yes; we are both very much indebted to him."

"Nobody can feel that more truly than I do," Macheath said; "and Luke knows that if I do not say much to him, that it is because I cannot thank him sufficiently."

"You will both oblige me by saying no more about it," Luke observed.

"Very well," Macheath replied, smiling, "we will spare your blushes, my friend. Services such as you have rendered me and my good wife can never be repaid with words, so you are quite right in stopping me saying too much against them."

"I only did my duty," Luke said, turning his head away as a film gathered before his eyes.

"Well, well," added Polly, "you are our friend, Luke, and as such you must allow us to praise you a little now and then."

"Now, wife," said Macheath, "you must tell me how it is that, after hearing from Luke that he left you at Kentish-town, I now find you on the highroad disguised in male attire. Have you, too, turned highwayman?"

"Alas! no."

"TUG AWAY!" SAID CAPTAIN MACHEATH. "YOU'VE GOT ME—I'VE GOT THE OTHER."

"Oh! you mean to be one, though?" said Macheath.

"No—no," Polly replied, shuddering, "and Heaven knows how happy I should be to take you from this most fearful and dangerous course of life."

"Ah! that is a hope that we will talk of another time; but now tell me how it is that you are from home, Polly?"

"I will; but we must not remain here."

"Not remain here?" cried Captain Macheath and Luke in a breath, as they glanced around them with the expectation of some approaching danger.

"No," said Polly. "Let us proceed, and place as large a space as possible between us and the house which was once our home at Kentish-town."

"Ah! there is danger, then?" exclaimed Macheath.

"There is," Polly replied. "It is true that Luke left me full of hope and expectation of speedily seeing you again; but scarcely had he gone an hour from the house when it was broken into by six men, who roughly demanded of me who I was, and required me to admit that it was your house. I steadily refused, but they only laughed at my refusal, saying that they had come to search the house, and had no doubt but that they would light upon some hidden treasure."

"The rascals!"

"I was terrified," Polly resumed, "and yet I preserved my presence of mind wonderfully, considering all things. I would have left the house, but they, divining my intention to do so, locked me up in my own bedroom, and being quite satisfied that they had me securely, they left me to myself."

"And you escaped?"

"I did. You know that this sort of clothing was in one of the wardrobes, and this hat hung upon a nail close to it. I hastily attired myself as you see me, and opening the window carefully, I made a safe and easy descent into the garden by the aid of the old vine."

"Yet it was perilous, Polly," said Macheath.

"Not at all. I had but to clutch firmly to the vigorous shoots of the vine and to find a foothold, of which there were hundreds, and so I got in perfect safety to the ground."

"But you are mounted. There was no horse in the stable?"

"True," Polly replied; "but I did not leave the bed-chamber without taking care to secure about me all the money that from time to time you have given into my keeping; so the moment I got free of the garden, which I happily did without observation, I ran to the livery stables that are not far from the church, and boldly walked into the yard and asked if they had a horse to sell."

"It was bold indeed."

"Perhaps imprudently so, but they were all civility, and did not seem to have the least suspicion, but that I was some extravagant young gentleman who had more money than wit. I gave them fifty guineas for this nag."

"And not dear," said Luke.

"Do you think not?"

"I am sure of it. It is only fit for a light weight, but it is as neat a little animal, to all appearance, as I have seen."

"Then I have not thrown away the money?"

"A plague take the money!" said Captain Macheath. "That is of the very least possible consequence. It is your safety that is everything."

Polly looked at him with a smile.

"You see, then, that I am safe," she said. "They gave me a saddle and a bridle into the bargain, and here I am."

"But where were you going?"

"To London," Polly replied; "but it was pure chance that brought me this way."

"A lucky chance, dear Polly," said Macheath. "They may stay as long as they like at the old house waiting for me, and they may do what they like with it. You have brought from it the most valuable of its contents, Polly."

"Yes; all the money."

"Nay, do not fancy for one moment that it was the money I alluded to," Macheath returned. "Indeed and in truth, I had forgotten that again. It was yourself, dear Polly, that I called the most valuable of the contents of the house, and, since you are here with me again, and we are all unhurt, if you were as poor as Job himself it would not concern me much."

"Nor me," said Polly.

"Nor me," said Luke.

While this little conversation was going on, Captain Macheath, Polly, and Luke pursued the contrary route to that which led to Kentish-town.

They had made some progress in placing a large space of country between them and that place.

After what Polly had related it was quite clear that his old home was now no place for Captain Macheath, and as far as Luke was concerned, the reader is aware that he had his own reasons for wishing to inhabit any other place but that house, in the garden of which was a recollection that always distressed him.

The question, however, of where they should go was one that very shortly arose in the course of their talk, and Macheath was just upon the point of turning to Luke to say something upon that point when a faint "Halloa!" from a distance came upon his ears.

"What is that?" Polly demanded.

"I hardly know yet," Macheath replied; "but it is worth our attending to. Such outcasts of society, as I suppose we may consider ourselves to be, are interested in every unusual sound that may arise."

Luke was listening attentively.

"Suppose, sir," he said, "I ride back a little, and try and find out what it is about. I won't go far."

"I don't like you to rush into danger, Luke," said Macheath. "You may be known, for all I can say to the contrary; and our enemies may pounce upon you for having been seen in my bad company."

"I am not afraid of that," said Luke, "if you will only let me go."

"Hush!" whispered Polly. "There may be no occasion; for, if my ears don't deceive me, I hear someone coming on horseback."

Both Macheath and Luke listened now attentively for a few moments, and were soon enabled to confirm what Polly had said; but as only a single horse was approaching, they resolved to go on at a quick walk, and let whoever it may be overtake them.

It did not require many minutes for that to ensue, and a young man, mounted upon a very good-looking hack, was about to ride past, when Macheath called out to him—

"Halloa! my friend, is anything amiss?"

The young man paused and turned to the friends.

"No, gentlemen, nothing amiss ; but it appears that Captain Macheath, the highwayman, has escaped from Newgate, and I'm sent to Highgate to give a letter there to the justices about a lot of mounted men on the different roads."

"Oh ! I understand," said Macheath. "We thank you for your news. You had better ride on now."

"Thank you, sir, I will," replied the man, immediately putting spurs to his horse.

CHAPTER LIV.

A MEETING WITH THE PRINCE.

IT was now necessary that Macheath and his friends should decide on some more definite plan of placing themselves in security.

After some little discussion it was decided that they should ride some fifty or sixty miles into the country south of London.

But it was no easy matter to get southward, as all the principal roads led to London.

Of course, Captain Macheath had no idea of going through the metropolis ; but he thought that if he could get by cross-roads and lanes to the banks of the Thames, near Richmond, he would cross the river, and then shape his course up one of the great roads that ran down to the south coast.

Whether or not Captain Macheath intended to transact a little professional business as he went along or not, we shall soon see.

If he had any scruples about doing so, we must take them as entirely arising from the fact of his having Polly with him, and of the dread he felt of getting her into any danger.

For the next hour they rode on without exchanging much conversation with each other.

The fact is, that they were too anxious to talk.

As for Luke, he would have thrown himself in the way of meeting death rather than any injury should have come to Macheath.

There can be but little doubt regarding the wisdom of the course which Captain Macheath now adopted, and he was glad that Polly fully coincided with him in it.

By taking a considerable round they managed to get into the neighbourhood of Fulham, and finally crossed the river by the aid of the old wooden bridge that connected that district with Putney.

"Now, Luke," said Macheath, "our course is tolerably easy, I suppose ?"

"Yes, captain, it is," Luke replied. "Let us get towards the south-east, and we shall soon place a sufficient space of ground between ourselves and our foes as to make it not very likely that they will interfere with us."

"But if we go on in such a direction," said Polly, "we shall reach the sea-coast."

"That is a fact," said Captain Macheath ; "and I think I shall not at all be disinclined to do so. What say you to a trip to Hastings? I have been told that there we may find some amusement and possibly some profit."

"Amusement there is plenty," said Polly ; "but when you talk of profit, Macheath, I have a fear that you contemplate engaging in your dreadful pursuit."

"Oh ! Polly, call it not dreadful, for who knows what it may not enable us to do? The object I now have in view is to leave as soon as I can this precarious mode of life, and retire with you to the country, and in a few years Captain Macheath will be forgotten."

"Never !" said Luke.

"Never what, Luke ?" demanded Polly. "Do you mean to say that such a happy state of things can never be accomplished ?"

"Oh ! no, you misunderstand me. I mean that Captain Macheath will never be forgotten while the world stands."

"It may be so," said the captain, laughing.

"Alas !" sighed Polly, "I would have wished it were otherwise."

They had made good speed while they spoke, and where rapidly traversing a road in the direction they wished to go, when from a side thoroughfare there suddenly dashed out a lady upon horseback.

It was quite evident that the horse was running away with her, and that she was fast losing control over the movements of the animal.

Without a moment's hesitation, Macheath rushed forward and caught the horse by the rein, and in a few moments succeeded in calming it.

"You are only alarmed, I trust ?" said Captain Macheath to the lady.

"Oh ! that is all," she replied ; "but you must tell me to whom I am indebted for my safety."

"It is sufficient, madam," replied Macheath, "that I have had the happiness of rescuing you. I have the honour to bid you good-day."

"Not so. Here comes one who will be as grateful to you as you can wish, for he has the power to be so."

As the lady spoke, Macheath heard the clatter of a horse's feet in the lane, and to his great surprise, no other than the Prince George emerged from it into the high road.

"Hilloa ! Emma," he cried. "I thought you were gone. How did you stop that mad-headed horse, that you will ride in spite of all I can say to you to the contrary ?"

"I did not stop it," the lady replied, "but here is a gentleman who has left his friends, and who has kindly done so. If he had not, I don't know what might have been the result ; but I will not ride the horse again."

"I'm sure," said the prince, "I am very much obliged to the gentleman, and beg him to accept my thanks."

"Your royal highness is too good," said Macheath, as he took off his hat and bowed.

"The deuce take it—he knows me," said the prince.

"Ha—ha !" laughed the lady ; "you are not so easily forgotten, George, if anyone has once seen you. Your beauty makes an impression."

The prince looked rather annoyed at having been so easily recognised, but after looking at Macheath for a few seconds in silence he said—

"It is the very man."

"What very man ?" asked the lady.

"I trust your royal highness," interposed Macheath, "will be so good as to keep my secret."

"I will, and you be as good as to forget that you met Prince George."

The lady looked from one to the other of them during this little mysterious dialogue.

"But I must and will know who he is," she said. "Come, sir, who and what are you ? I see by your appearance that you are a gentleman, but I want to know your name."

Captain Macheath remained silent.

"No, this must not be," said the prince ; "it really must not be. The gentleman has a good reason, of which I am well aware, to conceal his name, and I cannot have him pressed upon the subject. Who are these people watching us?"

"Friends of mine, your royal highness," said Macheath; "but they neither of them know you personally."

The lady had been looking keenly at Polly for the last few moments, and now she said, abruptly—

"What is that girl dressed in men's clothes for?"

"Girl in men's clothes?" cried the prince, with sudden emotion. "Is she pretty? Where is she? Oh! there. By Jove! she is an angel."

"I should not like to make that remark concerning a lady who was under your protection," said Macheath.

The pointed way in which the captain uttered those words was quite sufficient to let the prince see the admiration he evinced for Polly was not very pleasing to him (Macheath), and the prince quite understood him.

The lady did so likewise, and gave a slight toss of the head, as much as to say—"Pho! I don't care a straw about it."

Prince George was about to say something, when suddenly both Polly and Luke rode up.

"We are lost, captain," Luke cried. "There is a party approaching that we cannot contend with. We are hemmed in upon both sides."

"Oh! fly," said Polly—"fly! We will remain here and detain your foes until you are far away."

Captain Macheath was annoyed that they should both come up to him and the prince, and so freely proclaim their fears.

"What is the meaning of all this?" he said. "I see no one but friends, and hear no one but friends."

Macheath was not in a position to see or hear anything upon the high road, for he was some ten or twelve paces down the lane, whither the prince had slowly backed his horse; but now that the captain rode out into the open road he saw that to his right there was a troop of cavalry riding towards him.

"Hemmed in indeed," he said, "but not lost, Polly."

He at once trotted to the prince.

"Your royal highness has already shown me such great favour that I feel I am asking too much to request one more boon at your hand," he said.

"What is it? Say on."

"It is that you will let this lady, who is my wife, and this young man, who is my attached and faithful friend, remain for a few minutes under your protection, for there is great danger to me and to them."

"But yourself, man," said the prince. "What are you to do?"

"I will take my chance, and fight my way through them if possible, and if I cannot, why I can but fall; and my last words will be thanks to you for protecting the only living beings that I feel anxious about, on account of their attachment to me."

"No," said the prince, "that must not be."

"You will not?"

"Don't misunderstand me," said the prince. "I will do more than you ask of me, but you must remain here likewise. If I have the power to protect them I have also the power to protect you, sir."

Both Luke and Polly were quite amazed to hear

Macheath use the words "royal highness," and they could not look enough at the person who bore that title.

As for the lady who was with the prince, she seemed each moment to be getting more confused and more angry at the mystery in which the whole affair was wrapped.

"This is folly," she said. "There is no time for you now to engage in foolish adventures on the road. Come away."

"Not yet," the prince replied; and approaching Polly he said, in as engaging a tone as he could assume, "Be assured that I will not only protect you, but I will protect him, in whose fortune you are interested."

"My heart thanks you," said Polly.

"Oh! nonsense," cried the other lady. "I wonder you are not ashamed of yourself to appear in the public thoroughfares in male apparel. It is disgraceful."

"Oh! madam," said Macheath, "there are more disgraceful things than that, as no doubt you are well aware."

"What do you dare to mean to insinuate, sir? I am the Marchioness of Morton."

"I thank you for the information, madam. It may be interesting in case I should meet with the marquis."

"There, now," said the prince, "a pretty affair you have made of it; but that is always the way with you. The moment you lose temper you lose discretion. Now, if it were not that I know I can depend upon the honour of this gentleman, your imprudent declaration of who you are might be productive to you of many disastrous consequences."

The lady bit her lips with chagrin.

"Rely upon me," said Captain Macheath. "The words uttered in an incautious moment shall never pass my lips again, and if you even suspect that I could play you so treacherous a game you shall have it in your power to do me a still worse turn should you see reason, by declaring that I am—"

"Oh! no—no," cried Polly—"do not."

"Nay, surely I may trust this lady with my name—may I not, madam?"

"You may," said the marchioness. "I confess I am dying with anxiety to know who and what you are. If it be a secret, I will keep it."

"Then, madam, I am known as Captain Macheath."

"What! Macheath the highwayman?"

"The same. But, although I may at times cry 'Stand!' to a true man on the king's highway or give a temporary fright to a lady, I yet never broke my word or played a treacherous part to one who trusted me."

"That is true," said the prince; "so now, let there be no ill-blood in the matter. I for one feel that I am under great obligations to Captain Macheath, and I will alone face the soldiers, who are close at hand."

"Do so," said the lady. "I am quite satisfied. I have been longing to have a good look at Captain Macheath, the celebrated highwayman; but nothing was further from my thoughts than meeting him to-day."

It was quite evident from the conduct of the troop of soldiers that they recognised Macheath.

"Halt!" cried the prince, riding forward.

The soldiers at once mechanically pulled up, and the officer in command cried out—

"This is the coolest piece of insolence on the

part of a highwayman that ever I heard of. Pray, sir, who are you?"

"A superior officer to you, sir, and I desire that you consider yourself as under my orders. I am a general in the service."

"A what?"

"A general."

"A general rogue, I suppose."

The prince's face flushed with passion.

"Lay hold of that man," the officer said. "He is an associate of Captain Macheath's. Clap a pair of handcuffs upon him. He is a very dangerous character."

"You had better beware, sir, what you do," said the prince. "It is a pity, captain, that you do not know me. I shall have to place you under arrest, I fear, for this breach of discipline. I announce myself to you as a general in the army, and order you to place yourself and men under my orders. Do you still refuse?"

"There is but one general in the army of your age," said the captain; "and he has still a greater title."

"Well?"

"Why, you don't mean to have the impudence to say that you are the Prince of Wales, do you?"

"Precisely."

"Oh! indeed. Well, of all the pieces of impudence that ever I came near this is the worst. But there happens to be a brother officer of mine at the rear guard who is personally well known to the Prince of Wales. Give my compliments to Lieutenant Fane, and ask him to ride up this way."

A sergeant at once trotted off upon the errand.

"A fine day, captain," said the prince.

"I don't care whether it is a fine day or not. Don't speak to me, sir. You are our prisoner."

"Very well. I merely remarked that it was a fine day. I thought that even a prisoner might take that great liberty."

"Well, of all the confounded impertinence," said the officer, "that ever I heard of this is the worst. Oh! here comes Lieutenant Fane. It is a good thing to proceed regularly in these cases."

"Did you send for me, captain?" said a young officer, riding up from the rearguard.

"Yes, Fane. Just look at that person on the chestnut horse, and tell me if you know him."

"Oh! How should I know him?" said Fane, as he turned a supercilious glance upon the "person."

In a moment his whole manner changed, and he instantly saluted with his sword.

"It is the prince," he exclaimed. "I hope your royal highness is well?"

"Pretty well, Fane," said the prince, quietly.

The captain drew back a pace or two, thoroughly bewildered.

"I want you, Fane," added the prince, "to be so good as to assure your captain that I am a superior in the service; and as a field-marshal, I am, I think, authorised to give him orders."

"Good Heavens! your highness, who doubts it?" said Fane. "There is surely no one who would not be anxious to obey your orders."

"I don't know that, Fane."

The captain advanced, looking as pale as death. He held his sword by the blade, as he said—

"To whom am I to surrender my sword, your royal highness, as I presume I am now under arrest?"

The manner of the officer was so extremely crest-fallen that no one could help pitying him.

"Deliver your sword to no one but to me, sir,"

the prince said, "and I shall then have the satisfaction of returning it to you. You could not know that I was the Prince of Wales; but I did hope that I should not have been mistaken for anything but a gentleman."

"Pardon me, your highness. I—I—"

"No more, sir. Let the past be forgotten."

The officer bowed, and took his sword again, and stepped back a pace or two with a look of intense chagrin.

"To business now," said the prince. "What do you want with me? Speak at once, sir."

"Oh! nothing—nothing, your royal highness," the crestfallen officer said. "I am searching for the notorious highwayman, Captain Macheath, that is all."

"Very well, sir, you do not suspect that I am that individual, do you, nor that any of my friends, who are some little distance behind me in the lane, answer such a description."

"Oh! dear, no. I—that is—"

"Then proceed, sir, about your business. Good evening, sir."

"I have the honour to wish your royal highness good evening."

"Would your royal highness desire us to escort you?" demanded the captain, turning back.

"Oh! no—no; you go on as you were, and let this little affair rest quietly.

"Good-day, Fane."

The lieutenant bowed, and the prince then, with a salute to the captain and the troop, turned his horse's head down the lane.

As may be well supposed, Macheath and his friends had been anxious spectators and listeners to what had passed between the prince and the officers, and while they could not but feel gratified for the firm stand which the prince had made for them.

"You are safe at present," whispered Polly, "but it will not last."

"I fear not."

"It cannot. We must take immediate advantage of the lull in the tempest of danger that has surrounded us, and fly."

"Hush—hush! the prince approaches."

"Macheath," said the prince, "a word with you."

The captain rode forward.

"I think you can be useful to me," the prince said, "in a little affair that I have on hand that requires courage and address."

"I shall be happy to be of any service to your highness."

"Do you really mean that?"

"I do, indeed. I owe you my life, and I owe to you the safety of one who is dearer to me than life."

"Oh! well, never mind that. It was not at all likely I was going to let them take you; but I can't explain further to you just now what I want of you. You must meet me in London."

"As your highness pleases."

"Of course, you know St. James'-park well?"

"Perfectly."

"Very good; then you know the wall of Carlton House - the wall enclosing the garden?"

"I do, your highness."

"That will do. You must be at that wall this evening, if possible, at ten o'clock. A man will come up to you and say—'One, two, three,' to which you will be so good as to reply—'Four, five, six,' and then you will submit yourself to his guidance. Are you willing to do this for me?"

"Quite so."

"And I may depend upon you as regards punctuality and all that sort of thing?"

"Your highness may."

"Very well then—that is all I need say to you just now. Take care of yourself, Macheath; you know that you are in rather a ticklish position. Good-day."

Without taking another glance at Macheath or his companions, the prince turned towards the lady, and said, gaily—

"Now shall we be off?"

"It is almost time," said the marchioness, with an air of vexation.

The prince trotted away, and after hesitating for a few moments, and no doubt during that short period having something of a conflict with her temper, she went after him at full speed, and they both disappeared round a turn in the lane, apparently rather on the wrangle.

"Well," said Macheath, "this is rather a nice state of things."

"What do you mean?" Polly demanded.

Luke, too, looked inquiringly, and the captain, who had made no promise of secresy, so far as they were concerned, told them exactly what the prince had said to him, to which they listened with alarm and surprise.

"What can it mean?" said Polly. "You do not suspect treachery?"

"Oh! no—no."

"It is an odd thing," said Luke; "and yet it will be quite out of the question to attempt to dispute the commands of the prince. It would be as foolish to do so as it would be unfair."

"But the danger, the great danger?" urged Polly.

"That must be encountered," Macheath remarked; "and recollect that whatever danger I may now fall into, I have a powerful protector in Prince George."

"Yes, his will may be good to protect you, but his power may fail to do so. There cannot be a doubt but that if he could he would, but even he dare not interfere too openly with the law."

"There is no human enterprise without some risk," said Captain Macheath. "I have promised the prince to meet him. I will keep my word and my appointment at any risk. You are of that opinion, Luke?"

"I am, captain."

"And you, too, Polly, upon reflection, will be of the same mind?"

"I am already," Polly replied; "and while I tremble at the risks you must run in going to London just now, I yet could not conscientiously advise that you should break faith with the prince after the generous manner in which he has befriended you."

"That is spoken like yourself, my wife."

"Ah! how could I feel otherwise? But I will rely upon you, for my sake, to be careful as you possibly can of your safety."

"That I will."

"Then I am content that you should go."

"Polly, and you too, Luke," said the captain after a pause, "I cannot come to a conclusion in my own mind whether or not it would be better for us all three to go to town or not."

"That I must leave to you, sir," said Luke.

"But you have an opinion?"

"I have, sir; and it is that we should all go. I think that there is greater safety by us all going. A lodging can easily be got for us; and if anything should go amiss, we shall be at hand to aid you."

"And what is more," added Polly, "I shall be at ease in my mind, comparatively speaking, instead of being a prey to the frightful suspense if I were some miles from you and could not see you frequently."

"It is decided, then," said Macheath. "Let us go to London. It often happens, and to none has it oftener happened than to me, that by going, to all appearances, into the very jaws of danger, I have escaped, while by taking a course that looked like almost the assurance of safety, I have dropped into great peril."

They at once put their horses to the trot, and went down the lane at a good pace.

It seemed most singular to Macheath that a short half-hour should so completely alter his course of action.

But a little while since and he had been intent upon getting as far from London as possible, and now he was actually thinking on what would be the most direct route to the metropolis.

They went right on over the Surrey side of the river till they came to old Battersea-bridge, which they crossed, and then made their way into the West-end of London. Macheath decided on putting up at Pimlico, so as to be near to the prince.

Notwithstanding Pimlico was then anything but a choice or fashionable locality, there were some old, large, rambling houses in it; and without meeting with any adventure worth the recording, Macheath and his two friends found themselves near the back of old Buckingham House, upon the site of which some portion of the present palace now stands.

"Captain," said Luke, "if I might advise, I should say, let us put up our horses somewhere first, and then seek a lodging on foot. It will be necessary, too, that you think of some name to call yourself."

"You are right, Luke. What shall I name myself, Polly?"

"Call yourself Colonel Park," Polly replied, "and we shall none of us forget the name as we are so near the park."

"Be it so, then; I will be Colonel Park, and you had better be my brother John, and you, Luke, what will you be?"

"Oh!" said Luke, "I will be a confidential servant, supposed to be sent with you both by old General Park to look after you."

Luke took the horses to a stable hard by, where he left orders that either Colonel Park, or his brother John, or himself should have access to them at any time; for he did know, of course, what emergency might arise.

"It's all right," said Luke, when he returned. "The horses are very well housed now indeed."

"That will do," said Macheath; "and it was much better that you should take them, and that we should not be seen, as the ostler now cannot give any description of us to anybody who may be curious enough to inquire to whom the cattle belong."

"That is a great point," said Polly; "and now for a house."

After walking a little distance they saw a large, old-fashioned looking house with an immense chestnut-tree before the door, and in the window of which there was a bill announcing that the lodgings were to let

Macheath knocked at the door, and it was answered by a woman whose rather fiery-looking visage seemed to proclaim that she was rather intimate with the brandy-bottle; but, after all, a

CAPTAIN MACHEATH

THE
PRINCE OF THE HIGHWAY.

BOTH NOW PUT SPURS TO THEIR HORSES—MACHEATH WAVING HIS HAT IN TRIUMPH.

red face is not always an infallible sign of a hard drinker.

"We have come to look at the lodgings," said Macheath.

"Yes, sir. How many does the party consist of?"

"Myself, my brother here, and my servant."

"Very good, sir; pray walk in. I only take in and do for gentlemen. I don't want lady lodgers. They are no end of trouble, and so mighty particular, and such a plague with their hooks-and-eyes and all that sort of thing, that I have made up my mind only to let to gentlemen."

"A very wise resolution," said Polly; "you will find us very little trouble. My brother, the colonel, is very much out, and as for me, I am one of the quietest people in the world."

At the title of colonel, which Polly took care to bestow upon Macheath, the woman was evidently mightily pleased, and, taking them up a rather crazy flight of stairs, she showed them a suite of ancient, dingy-looking apartments.

There were no less than five rooms all opening one into the other, and some of them having doors on to the staircase.

"This is the very place for us," whispered Macheath to Polly. "It is cut out for us—we must have it."

"What is the rent?" Polly asked.

"Did you ever see such nice rooms in all your lives, gentlemen?" said the landlady, who was determined to expatiate upon the accommodation of her apartments. "Large and airy they are, and as quiet as if you were at the bottom of a well, and as cheerful, too, as sunshine in May. The last gentleman that had them died, poor man."

"Of the cheerfulness," queried Macheath, "or that well-liked feeling you describe?"

"No, sir, of the gout."

"Oh! that is quite another thing; and now will you have the goodness to name to us the rent of the suite of rooms?"

"And only look out," said the landlady, throwing open a window. "There's a prospect of the park."

It was quite clear that the landlady was determined Macheath should not know the rate of her rooms until she had explained all their perfections.

"In this small room," she said, "the last of the lot, there's a turn-up bedstead, that you see, in the day time stands up against the wall quite easily, and when you want it down—"

Bang came the bedstead down with a good sweep through the air, for the landlady had unconsciously touched a little button that held it up, and in an instant she was hidden from sight beneath it, being knocked flat by it in its downward progress.

"Ah!" said Macheath, "when you want it down, down it comes."

"Murder!" shrieked the landlady.

Polly was compelled to put her head out at the window to laugh while Luke released the landlady, who rose in a very great fluster indeed, declaring that the bedstead had never done such a thing before, and she had had it seven years.

As it was only the sacking that had struck her, she had not sustained any serious injury.

"I think it would be a capital thing if one had any troublesome visitor to place him just under this bedstead, and then release it, when it would quite extinguish him," said Macheath, with a smile.

"Oh! dear, yes, sir—it would. I wonder if the tax-gatherer would like it when he comes bothering?"

"He would not like it, madam; but I don't think he would venture upstairs again. And now, perhaps, you will be so good as to tell us what the rent really is?"

"The rent, sir, for yourself and your little brother, and your servant, sir, of the whole five rooms, with all convenience and attendance?"

"Yes—yes."

"Well, it will be two guineas a-week."

"Very good—that will do. We will take them."

"Without extras?"

"What do you mean by extras?"

The landlady, by the readiness with which Macheath had agreed to give the two guineas a-week, was in an agony at the idea that she might have got more for the asking, so she immediately replied that she would make a little bill of the extras at the end of every week, and let him have it.

"All right," said Macheath.

"Yes, sir," said Luke, "and I daresay if the general comes to town that he will be quite pleased to see you so comfortably situated."

"The general, I presume," said the landlady, "is your worthy father?"

"Yes," said Macheath, "that is the old pump."

"The old who, sir?"

"The governor," said Polly. "The old pump we generally call him, out of affection, you know."

"Oh! dear me, really. Well, I suppose you can oblige me with a reference, gentlemen, of course?"

"Yes," Macheath replied, as he laid two guineas upon the table. "There are two references, and if his majesty's head stamped in gold will not do, I am quite sure that nothing will."

"It's quite right," said the landlady, as she pocketed the guineas; "I am quite delighted to let my rooms to such highly respectable gentlemen, I assure you, only you will easily imagine that it's right of me as a lone widow, though I have left off my caps, to be particular."

"Quite; and now, madam, you will consider that we hold possession of this suite of rooms. When we want anything, we will ring the bell, and you can get it for us, and put it down in the bill."

This was precisely the arrangement that suited the landlady.

With a profound curtsey she left the rooms.

CHAPTER LV.

WHAT HAPPENED IN THE OLD HOUSE.

"SHALL we be comfortable here for a little while think you?" said Macheath to Polly.

"Oh! yes, husband."

"Hush! do not call me by that name. Landladys, in addition to having keys that will open all your locks, have frequently places from which they can overhear what you say."

"I will call you brother."

"Do so, and I will call you John. Of course, our stay here will depend entirely upon what the prince requires of me; and that I shall, no doubt, know all about to-night."

"I only hope," said Polly, "that he does not want you to take the dangerous part of some enterprise that he himself shrinks from."

"Oh! I do not anticipate that, Polly," said he,

"you are forgetting, and doing the very thing you blamed me for. Can you not call me John?"

"Oh! dear, yes. John you shall be, and dear John, too. But we will now put our landlady's powers of entertainment to the test by ordering something to eat of her."

Macheath rang the bell, and the landlady herself answered it so promptly that one could hardly, with all the charity in the world towards her, imagine that she could have been very far off.

To be sure, the kitchen might be near at hand, but the promptitude of the landlady was such that in order to account for it consistently it ought to have been at the top of the stairs.

"Did you ring, sir?"

"Yes," said Macheath. "You will be so good as to get us something to eat as quickly as convenient, and go to the nearest wine merchant's and procure a bottle of Madeira."

"Certainly, sir. Oh! dear, yes. Perhaps chops, as being the sort of thing that can be got amazingly quick, will suit for to-day, gentlemen?"

"Very good; chops be it."

The landlady bustled off to execute the order.

"Ah! I am afraid she was listening to our conversation," Polly said.

"And so am I," replied Macheath; "but she cannot have overheard much of it, I think, after all, and we really said so little, and that must have been so completely incomprehensible to anyone who did not understand what we were talking about, that I have no apprehension."

"They are very curious old rooms," said Luke, suddenly coming into the apartment where Polly and her husband were sitting.

"I think they are, Luke."

"I like them on that account," Polly added.

"I have made a survey of them," Luke said. "There's no end of odd old hiding-places and cupboards, and all sorts of secret-looking nooks. I should not at all wonder if there were secret panels in the walls, and winding staircases, and all that sort of thing, in the old place."

"You don't mean that, Luke?"

"Yes, captain, I do; and I think it would be a capital thing if we could find out some of the odd hiding-places."

"So it might, and to-morrow, Luke, we will have a good look about us," Macheath replied. "It is too late to-day to do so, and I confess to being somewhat wearied; and, indeed, I feel as if I wanted sleep."

"There is quite time enough," Polly said, "for you to take an hour or two's repose before your hour of appointment with the prince," Polly said. "Your eyes look languid; and, indeed, I am full of astonishment at the little sleep that suffices for you."

"The fact is," said Macheath, "I feel desperately sleepy, so I will just partake of the landlady's chops and a glass or two of the wine, and then I will have a sleep until nearly ten o'clock; but I must rely upon you, brother John, to awaken me."

"Oh! yes," said Polly, "that brother John will do, you may depend upon it. How capitally we are getting into the habit of calling each other as we have agreed."

"Yes," remarked Luke; "and, for my part, I almost feel as if there really were an old General Park, who has deputed me to look after you, captain."

Both Macheath and Polly laughed at this speech of Luke's.

The door opened in the midst of their mirth, and the landlady entered with a large tray in her arms, containing the repast.

"I hope, gentlemen," she said, "that I have not kept you at all waiting, if you please. I made all the haste I could."

"Not at all," said Macheath. "I think you have been wonderfully quick about it indeed, and very nice the chops look, too. If the wine only is as good, we shall be very well off."

"I hope it is, sir. I asked for the very best, and told them that it was for real gentlemen, that I did."

"Thank you, madam."

The table was laid with considerable activity by the landlady.

"Perhaps your luggage will soon come," she said.

"There will be no more luggage than the two little valises that you see," replied Macheath.

"Oh! certainly, sir; that is all right."

With this she left the room, and Polly, looking at Macheath, said—

"What did she mean?"

"Only that she looked forward to having the rummaging of a lot of trunks and boxes, that is all. These kind of people like you to bring in a quantity of miscellaneous property, and then they think there is a chance of laying hold of some of it."

"I do not like that woman's manners," Polly remarked, with a slight shudder.

"Never mind her manners," laughed Macheath, "as long as her chops and wine are good; so let us set-to at once. Sit down, Luke. Come—do not hesitate; sit down and let us begin."

The chops and the wine both turned out to be excellent, and even Polly, although she had taken a dislike to the landlady, could not help owning that it might be by possibility a mere prejudice.

"We must not judge of people by their looks," she said, "for if we did, I am quite certain we should never have come to live in this place at all."

"Certainly," said Captain Macheath, "our hostess is not dangerous on account of her beauty, I must say. You will have no cause for jealousy, Polly, upon her account."

"Not the least."

"She will very likely be communicative enough to me," said Luke. "I will take an opportunity of getting into conversation with the servants; and no doubt, in her great anxiety to ascertain from me all the particulars about General Park and the family, she will be very confidential herself."

"There is no servant here, that is quite clear," said Polly.

"No; nor, to all appearance, anyone in the house but herself," added Captain Macheath; "although I do not see that such a state of things, as long as we are properly attended to, ought to make any difference to us."

In such like discourse the dinner was dispatched, and then Macheath, who felt that it would be quite impossible for him much longer to resist the feeling for sleep that had crept over him, went into one of the bedrooms, and flung himself upon a bed.

In a short time he was in profound repose.

When Polly ascertained that her husband was in sound repose, she returned to the room in which Luke was waiting.

"Luke, I do not like this house that we have got into," she said, in an anxious tone of voice,

"Oh! now, brother," said Polly, with a smile, "Tell me truly what you think of it, and of the woman who seems to be the sole inhabitant of it."

"I don't know what to think," Luke replied. "I know so little of the habits and of the people of London, that I am hardly able to come to a judgment."

"But you do not like the woman?"

"Certainly I do not, and yet I cannot say why; but, if you will permit me, I will go downstairs and try to get into conversation with her, when I shall be better able to come to some opinion concerning her."

"Do so, good Luke—do so at once," said Polly. "There need be no hurry, for I will find some amusement while my husband sleeps in looking over the books that are here."

"I shall not be long gone," said Luke. "People either will not talk at all on their own affairs, or they will tell you a great deal in a short space of time."

With these words Luke left the room, and Polly began to look over a quantity of books that were in one corner of the large and gloomy apartment.

Some of these books were upon a table, and some were upon the floor; but what attracted Polly's attention was that the names seemed to have been erased from nearly every one of them.

There was a profound stillness in the house.

The evening was visibly creeping on, Polly felt that she would have to procure lights soon; but while she could possibly see she read on.

The door of communication to the adjoining chamber where Macheath lay sleeping was open, so that she could hear his regular breathing as he slumbered, and as the darkness increased she became more and more absorbed in the interest of the book she had picked up.

If Polly had been asked to define why it was that she felt very odd and uncomfortable, she would have been puzzled to find a reply; but if she had been required to say with perfect truth how she did feel, she must have replied, decidedly frightened!

Yes, as Polly sat in that large, solitary room, a strange feeling of terror came over her.

What was there to be frightened at?

There she was, in apparently a secure enough temporary home close to many persons and other houses.

There was nothing particularly solitary in the aspect of the house, and, more than all, she was so close to Captain Macheath, that, as we have said, she could hear him breathing in the adjoining chamber; and she knew that she had to raise her voice to awaken him.

And yet Polly felt her heart beat rapidly, and her breath come and go in such strange spasmodic gaspings, that she began to be very much alarmed indeed at her condition.

"What is the meaning of all this?" she said, in a whisper. "Is this illness, or what is it? What does it mean? What does it portend? Oh! when shall we be free from danger?"

Such questions were easily asked, but by no means so easily answered.

"This will not do," she said. "It is a foolish, weak superstition. I must shake it off. Why, I never felt this at Kentish-town, where I have spent nights alone, and when the wind has been whistling and roaring in the chimneys!"

She trembled, for she plainly heard something like a deep-drawn sigh from the apartment occupied by Captain Macheath.

She turned her head towards the door and distinctly saw a sight that served to freeze her blood.

With a slow and stately movement there came from the inner room a female figure, clothed in white drapery.

It did not seem to walk, and, indeed, Polly felt that walk it did not, but it glided along, just touching the floor.

The face of the figure had a strange, misty look about it, and the eyes appeared to be fixed upon Polly.

Oh! what a horror it was to look upon those eyes.

The figure did not attempt to approach Polly.

If it had done so she felt that there would have been some danger of it driving her distracted, but it moved along the room diagonally towards the door that led out on to the stair-landing.

Almost petrified with terror Polly continued gazing at it as it went along, and when it reached as near as might be the centre of the room it paused, and seemed to be regarding her with a look of intense grief.

The pause lasted only a moment or two, and then it glided on again with the same strange and noiseless movement as before.

The door leading from the apartment on to the staircase had been carefully closed by Luke when he had left the room, and even in the midst of her fright poor Polly wondered if the figure would open it, or, finding it closed, go back again to the chamber from whence it had come.

The figure did neither.

As soon as the apparition reached the door of the room it hesitated for a moment and then passed through the solid door and melted away.

It was gone!

Polly sprang to her feet and uttered a cry of terror.

It seemed as if the departure of the apparition had had the effect of at once releasing her faculties from the bondage in which they had been so intensely bound up.

As she uttered the terror-stricken cry Polly rushed into the adjoining chamber and was caught in the arms of Macheath, who had sprung from the bed in an instant.

"What is the matter?" cried Captain Macheath. "What is it, Polly?"

"Help—help!" she shrieked in accents of terror.

"Yes—yes, Polly; I am here. Do you not see me? What is the matter with you? What has happened?"

"Oh! my husband—my husband!"

"Yes, Polly. That is right. Speak to me. What has produced this condition in you? Are you terrified?"

"I am—I am!"

She would have fallen to the floor had not Macheath supported her.

There was a large, old-fashioned arm-chair in the room, and he placed her in it, entreating her to tell him what had caused her to cry out in such a way.

"Polly—Polly!" he said, "I implore you to take me off the rack of dread that I am on, and tell me what has happened to terrify you in this way. Is it anything connected with Luke?"

"Oh! no—no—"

"Then what is it? You are not hurt?"

"Oh! no—no. Not hurt; but I'm horror-stricken."

"Horror-stricken?"

"Yes—yes. Heaven preserve us, it is a warning of something, I feel assured. There is danger somewhere. I shall never recover this day—this hour!"

She burst into a flood of tears.

"Good," said Macheath, "now she will be much better. Weep on, Polly. These tears will save you, poor girl, from further suffering. Do not attempt to check them."

Poor Polly could not have stopped her tears if she had been ever so much inclined to do so, for they came in spite of her.

It was nature relieving herself of the super-abundance of excitement that had ensued upon the appearance of the spectre.

For more than ten minutes Polly sobbed; but then she was quieter, and she felt wonderfully better, and was able to look up into Macheath's face and speak.

"Oh! husband," she said, "how weak you will think me, and how wicked, too."

"Weak and wicked?" he said, with a smile. "Why, Polly, you are quite resolved to bring accusations enough against yourself, I think."

"Yes; but I am indeed weak and wicked."

"Pray explain, and if you convince me that you are weak, you shall not convince me that you are wicked."

"I will tell you. You naturally wonder to have seen me in such a state of suffering; but I tell you that I have seen an apparition."

"A what?"

"An apparition. Nay, do not laugh at me, for if this were the last moment I had to live, or if my life depended entirely upon my stating the truth to you, I could say nothing but what I have said."

"Polly, I do not laugh at you. Do not fancy for a moment that I do. From my heart I believe that you believe you have seen an apparition."

"But you do not believe it?"

He shook his head.

"It would be very difficult indeed," Macheath said, "to induce me to believe it."

"I shall doubt no more," said Polly.

She spoke with such a shudder, and in such a tone of voice, that showed her thorough and deep-seated conviction of the fact that she had seen an apparition, that Macheath became not a little curious to hear what account she had to give of an appearance that had terrified her so much.

"Well, Polly," he said, "since you will have it that you have seen this apparition, let me know all about it."

"You shall," Polly replied; "but we will go into the other room, and then I shall be able to show you how it was that I saw it, and where it come from, and whither it went. Come, come."

Macheath, to humour her, accompanied her.

She led him to the chair upon which she had sat when she saw the figure, and then drawing a little footstool close to him, she sat down at his feet, and held by one of his hands, to give herself a greater sense of security.

"Why, you tremble yet," he said.

"Oh! yes, I cannot but tremble. I do not wonder at that, the marvel would be if I did not."

"Well, now for the story."

"Yes, yes, you shall hear it," said Polly. "Oh! husband, are you certain that we are alone in this room, even now? Do you feel assured that there are no beings of another world hovering around us, and watching us with eyes that we cannot see, and listening to us with ears that are not mortal? Are you certain of that?"

"How can I be certain of any such thing,

Polly? Come, shake off these dreamy terrors, and by this time to-morrow you will be the first to laugh at this story of an apparition."

"No—no! Oh! no!"

"Well, then, go on and tell me all."

Polly began in a faltering tone of voice her narrative, and Macheath listened in all seriousness to what she had to say, nor did he even interrupt her till she got to the end of the story. He could not doubt that Polly was firmly convinced of the truth of what she asserted.

Her manner was quite sufficient to force him to that conclusion.

"Well, Polly," he said, "now that I have heard your ghost story—"

"You do not believe it, Macheath!"

"Nay, there you are too quick. I do believe it, But—"

"Ah, I knew an exception was coming."

Macheath smiled as he added—

"But, Polly, I likewise fully believe that, over-come by fatigue, which you well might be, you went to sleep in that chair, and that then this vision appeared to you, or seemed to appear to you."

"Oh, no—no!"

"Yes, Polly," he insisted, "it must indeed have been so. Nothing else could by any possibility have produced such an effect. Half a minute's sleep would have been quite sufficient to set you free from the control of imagination, and then who shall say what strange visions it may not produce?"

"It is impossible for me to take upon myself to say to a moral certainty that it is not so," Polly returned, "but this much I can say, that if I was sleeping then, I am now."

Macheath was silent for a few moments.

"Polly, you will freely admit, I presume, that if there be any truth in the appearance of supernatural beings, that it is not a common phenomenon?" he said at last.

"Certainly not."

"Then when it does come, we ought to expect that it is for some object."

"Yes, we ought, indeed."

"Then, pray, Polly," demanded Macheath, "what object can be obtained by a figure in white crossing a room, apparently merely for the purpose of giving you a fright? If this apparition had had anything to communicate, why did it not do so? If it came to give you a warning of any description, it failed to give it."

"I know," Polly replied, mildly, and in a low voice, "I know well, that all the argument is upon the side of those who deny the existence of the supernatural, but nothing will shake my belief in what I have seen in this room."

"Then we will say no more about it, Polly, and you should, as forcibly as you can possibly do so, adopt another line of argument to the effect, that if everything you ever heard of—"

"Or saw."

"Well, or saw—be strictly true as regards apparitions, there is no reason why you should be frightened at them."

"There is more in that argument than in a thousand against a belief in such things, and that is the feeling that I should like to cling to in the matter. But here is Luke."

Luke at this moment made his appearance in the room.

"Well, Luke, have you made any discoveries regarding our singular hostess?"

Luke shook his head.

"No," he said, "and I don't think that there is any great deal of chance of doing so. She seemed very well pleased to get me to talk to, and made all sorts of inquiry about General Park, which I answered in the best way I was able, without saying too much : but when I strove to induce her to be communicative in return, I found that she was not at all inclined to be so. I don't like the place."

"Nor I," said Polly.

"But why don't you like it, Luke ?" Macheath asked.

"I will tell you, captain," Luke replied. "The landlady had occasion to go to the door while I was talking with her, and seeing a large cupboard in the room, I thought I would open it to see what she had in it, when I saw a large sack."

"A sack? What sort of a sack, Luke ?"

"Nothing of a sack merely, but this sack had something in it that looked, by the odd shape that it made the sack assume, so like a human body—"

"A human body !" cried Polly.

"Oh ! no, no !" said Macheath. "Impossible. You found that it was no such thing, Luke ?"

"I had no opportunity of coming to a conclusion upon the subject, for while I was making some efforts to untie the knot into which a piece of stout cord was drawn that fastened up the neck of the sack, I heard the woman coming back, and I had no resource but to hastily close the cupboard again."

"It is strange," said Macheath, as he paced the room in thought.

CHAPTER LVI.

MYSTERIES OF THE OLD HOUSE.

THE state of alarm into which Polly had been thrown, combined to the mysteries below stairs, contributed largely to her fears. The apparition that she had seen had prepared her mind for any that might succeed it ; and, indeed, she felt as though it would be quite impossible that something of a fearful character should not come after such a circumstance.

It was some few minutes before Macheath spoke again, and then advancing towards Polly, he said, with a smile—

"Why, you are allowing yourself to be more frightened each moment. Surely you ought to arouse from your terror rather than improve upon it in this way."

"Yes, I should, but—"

"But what ? Come now—let me see you smile away those fears," said Macheath. "What were you going to say ?"

"Just that every circumstance seems to add to the fears that you think so idle, or that you would fain, for my peace of mind, affect that you think idle. I cannot smile."

"Well, then, I must smile for both of us," observed Macheath, gaily. "In the first place, you sit half asleep in a chair waiting for me, while I am wholly asleep, and some shadow from without passes across the wall of the room, and you take it at once for an apparition. Is it not so?"

"I wish I thought it so."

"Oh ! you must," he said. "And then up comes Luke with a cock and bull story about something in a sack."

Luke shook his head.

"Oh ! no, captain, it is no cock and bull story —that is to say, not to my thinking. Of course, sir, it might have been a dead body in the sack."

"Well, that is candid," laughed Macheath.

"But then it might," said Polly.

"Or perhaps it was a sack of potatoes—or of lumber of any kind, or perchance a pig."

"It might have been a pig," said Luke.

"This is trifling with me," said Polly, "although I know and feel that it is done with the best motives of silencing my fears, ; but I tell you, that if I were to live for a hundred years I should never get rid of the impression and of the firm opinion that it was an apparition that I saw cross the room."

A short pause followed these words. Macheath was upon the point of saying something, when three distinct taps came upon the wainscotting of the room.

Luke turned as pale as death, and Polly looked as though she were ready to faint.

Even Captain Macheath could not help feeling at the moment some degree of surprise.

"Who heard that ?" he said. "Did you both hear it ?"

"Yes—yes."

"What was it like ?"

"A tap on the wainscotting," said Luke.

"Yes," Polly gasped, "that was it."

"Then it is no ghost," cried Macheath, "for how can that which in itself is immaterial make a material noise ? This is some trickery, and I can only warn those who are practising it that they will find it anything but a joke to encounter me."

"Oh ! no—no," cried Polly, "it is no trick."

"It must be, and it is," said Captain Macheath.

"Ghosts only come to one person at a time," said Luke, timidly.

"Oh ! is that it ?" laughed the captain. "Are they afraid of their appearance being substantiated by witnesses ?"

"It is said so," Luke replied.

"Very good," said Macheath. "You, Polly and Luke, go into the next room, and shut yourselves in, and leave me and the ghost to settle our affairs as best we may together."

"No," said Polly ; "could you suppose that we would leave you to the chances of such an encounter ?"

"Don't think of it," said Luke.

"But I will think of it, and if you won't both of you go into the next room and leave me here for the apparition to come to me if it likes, I will go in there, and leave you both here."

He made a movement to leave the apartment, but Polly ran up to him, and clasped her arms round him.

"No—no," she cried, "I implore you not to go. Let me beg of you not. For my sake do not."

"It is for your sake, Polly, that I would do so. Let me ask of you, as a favour, that you will let me go."

Macheath uttered these words so seriously that Polly felt that it was not possible to prevent him. She released him from the hold she had taken of him.

"Go," she said, "but call to me if you see anything or hear anything, and if there is nothing, do not be gone long. Oh ! do not keep me above a moment or two in suspense."

"I will not."

With a firm step Macheath went into the bedroom in which he had enjoyed the short repose that he had been so much in want of.

He closed the door with great care, and finding

"YES," SAID MACHEATH, "WE ARE HEMMED IN—BUT ALL IS NOT LOST."

the key on the inside, turned it in the lock, so that neither Polly nor Luke could come suddenly into the room and take him by surprise, for they might startle him by doing so without intending it.

The feeling that came over Captain Macheath, when he found himself now alone after what had happened, could not be defined as fear, but was rather the excitement of expectation.

The only thing that he seemed to be very sensitive about, even to the verge of what perhaps looked like fear, was that anything should be behind him; so, with great alacrity, he placed his back against the door, and then, in a low but by no sort of means a tremulous voice, he said—

"Come."

This word had hardly escaped his lips, when a sort of current of air seemed to come through the room, and directly opposite him he saw the spectre of a man wrapped in a shroud.

It was a horrible, ghastly figure.

Macheath drew his breath shortly and thickly as he gazed.

To him it looked liked a figure, and for the moment he forgot the idea of Luke's that such appearances must be spoken to before they can give any utterance to a sound.

With amazing difficulty then he uttered the one word—

"Speak!"

Macheath had expected that some sound would meet his ears, but he was not prepared for the one that did do so.

It was one of the most unearthly laughs that he had ever heard in all his life.

It seemed to stop the very current of his blood to hear it, and to freeze his heart.

In a moment the figure was gone.

Captain Macheath turned and unlocked the door, and stood upon the threshold, looking into the next room more like a spectre himself than a living, breathing man.

"Oh! husband," said Polly; "thank Heaven you are here again."

"All's right, captain, of course?" said Luke; "there was nothing?"

"Nothing!" gasped Macheath.

He could not understand how after that horrid laugh they could both be sitting there so calmly, and could speak to him in such ordinary and common-place accents.

That they could avoid hearing such a sound did not lie within the compass of rational belief; and that, hearing it, they should think nothing or so little of it, was staggering.

Yet such seemed to be the fact.

"What did you hear?" he said.

"Nothing!" Polly replied.

"Nothing!" said Luke, and then they both looked at him as though they would add—"What was there to hear?"

Macheath sat down upon the nearest chair and drew a long breath.

"To be sure, what was there to hear? Nothing—nothing!" he said, hoarsely,

The manner in which Macheath uttered these last words, was of itself in every way calculated to arouse Polly's suspicions.

Luke, after a glance at his master's face, felt quite convinced that he had seen or heard something in the inner room.

Macheath could not help seeing what they both felt, and he spoke as calmly and firmly as he could to them.

"Let me beg of you both," he said, "to shake off these fears. Pray remember that I have an appointment that I must not break. It would be the height of ingratitude for me to break it. You know to whom I allude?"

"The prince?" replied Polly.

"Yes, the prince expects me, and I must attend to the appointment I have made with him, or for ever forfeit his friendship by breaking it. Now, while I am gone, do not allow yourself to be overcome by vain fears. I put my trust in your natural courage to resist superstitious impressions; and as for you, Luke, in leaving my wife to your care, I leave you all that I hold most dear upon earth."

"You shall not put your trust in me in vain," said Luke. "I will protect my mistress with my life."

"Of that I feel assured," Macheath responded. "You are well armed, and, if you like, I will leave you one of my double-barrelled pistols besides. And now, as you both see, that night has come indeed, and it is time for me to go."

"Yes, Macheath," said Polly, as the tears gushed to her eyes, "go—go, at once, and banish me from your thoughts."

"Polly, is that a kind speech?"

She burst in tears.

"Nay, do not weep," said Macheath. "You will soon get the better of this fear. Believe me, I do not think there is anything to dread. My advice is for you to go and lie down and rest, for you must be in need of it, and Luke will remain in this room and keep a good guard, I am certain."

"That I will," said Luke; "and when you are gone, captain, I shall feel free from superstitious fears, for I shall know that I have a duty to perform, and I will fight out against them."

Macheath was very well pleased to hear Luke say this, for he knew that he was speaking his real sentiments upon the occasion, and that he might thoroughly depend upon him.

"Now, Polly," he said, "you hear what Luke says, and let me hope that you will feel more serene, and quite understand that in Luke you will have an efficient friend and protector. Are you content that I should go?"

"I am—I am, indeed."

"Then farewell for a brief space. Of course, I cannot take upon myself to say how long the prince may require my services; but if that time should extend beyond the night, I will adopt some mode of letting you know."

"I will go and lie down, for I am not fit to remain up," said Polly. "I am fatigued as well as terrified."

"Well, it is the best thing you can do. Let me escort you to the further room, and you will, perhaps, sleep the greater part of the time away that I am absent from you."

"I hope so. Indeed, I hope I shall."

"Be assured you will, if you keep yourself quiet."

Leaning upon Macheath's arm, she went into the room where he had so firm an impression that he had seen the apparition between the windows.

He could not help casting a glance in that direction as he entered the apartment, but there was nothing unusual.

Macheath then returned to Luke and spoke seriously to him.

"Luke," he said, "I confess to you that I do not like this house—I confess to you that I have my suspicions that it is not one in which we would like to remain for long; but I think that I can manage so that you will be free from any attack to-night."

"How can you manage that, sir?"

"By speaking to the landlady of some unexpected luggage," Macheath replied. "Of course, if this be a house in which there is anything in the shape of plunder going on, it will be then put off until there is more to be got; but if anything should occur to induce you to think that it is decidedly unsafe to remain here any longer, take your mistress by one hand, and with a loaded pistol in the other, march out of the house at once."

"I will, sir—I will."

"Pass right through the park, then, and go out of it by the narrow gateway at Spring-gardens. Then go into the first inn on the right-hand side that you come to, and wait for me."

"What is the name of the hotel, sir?"

"Ah! that I don't know, Luke," Macheath said. "All that I am aware of is, that there are hotels in that neighbourhood in plenty, and that you will be sure to come to one, and I tell you to take the first one on the right-hand in order that I may know where to come to you."

"I quite understand, sir."

"Very good. Then remember, Luke, that I leave my wife in your care, and that I look to you to defend her."

"That I will, sir. You may be quite assured that I will not stir from this room, and so I shall be within call on the moment, should anything occur to require my services."

"Be it so; and now good-bye, Luke."

"Oh! captain, do not say Good-bye—it has such a woeful sound with it," Luke said. "Only say Good-evening. That will be much better, because that sounds as if we were quite sure to meet again, sir."

"Very well; let it be Good-evening, then, if you please."

Macheath shook hands with Luke, and then he at once left the room in order to keep his appointment with Prince George.

The captain was not unmindful, though, of what he wanted to say to the landlady as he went out, and pausing in the passage of the house, he tapped at the door that happened to be the nearest to him.

"Oh! sir, is that you?"

"Yes," said Macheath. "I merely wished to speak to you for a minute; but if you are busy, it don't matter."

"Oh! dear, no. Pray walk in, sir. Walk in—hem!"

"I am going to make some purchases in London to a very considerable amount," said Macheath, "and I hope that everything I buy will be quite safe in your house, as I am informed that in London there are some of the most daring thieves that can be imagined."

"Oh! sir, you might place sacks of gold in this house, and be quite sure that no thieves could get at them," simpered the landlady.

"Well, I am glad to hear that, very glad," said Macheath. "The plan I am going to adopt is to have the tradesmen come here with their goods for my inspection, and then I can choose what I like, and they can take away the remainder of them, you understand?"

"Perfectly, sir; and I can only say that all property will be quite safe. When do you intend bringing it here, sir?"

"To-morrow, I hope," the captain replied.

"I am now going to call upon some silversmiths to make an appointment with them to come here at particular times, and bring some of their goods to show. I have not the money here to pay them, but my uncle has given me leave to give written orders upon his bankers for the amount of whatever I may purchase in this place."

"Oh! that is very convenient indeed."

Captain Macheath politely took leave of his landlady, having, without a doubt, impressed her with the idea that he would bring a quantity of valuable property into the place in the course of the next day or two.

"Now," said Macheath, "for the prince."

The night had now got to be almost as dark as it would be.

A heavy bank of clouds had risen from the south west, and had stilled every breath of air, and obscured every particle of twilight that else would have remained.

Macheath could hardly see the trees in the park.

"How dark it is," he said. "This may be against or in favour of the enterprise the prince wants to send me upon for aught I know; but let it be what it may I feel myself bound by the tie of gratitude to go upon it."

When Macheath came to the wall of old St. James's Palace gardens he walked along for some time in the deep gloom of its shadow.

Suddenly a man, wearing a slouched hat and a cloak that completely enveloped his form, crossed his path.

Captain Macheath paused, and instantly laid his hand upon one of his pistols.

"I should not wonder," said the man, "if you are a friend."

"To whom?" said Macheath.

The man approached close to him, and then said, in a whisper—

"To a prince."

"I am. And you?"

"Am the same. Pray follow me."

"I suppose it is all right; but I had hoped to meet his royal highness himself about this spot."

"You shall shortly," said the man. "Come on, if you are not afraid to do so."

"Afraid? That is an expression that, as regards my own feelings, I do not understand. Lead the way, and I will follow you, sir, be you whom you may."

"You will not regret it. When I said afraid I did not mean to impute the feeling of fear to you—I only meant that you might be apprehensive you were making a mistake, and following the wrong person. One, two, three, four."

"Five, six, seven," answered Captain Macheath.

"Right."

The man led the way for some little distance along the wall, and then he suddenly paused, and although the night was now much too dark for Macheath to see that there was a door yet, from the rattle of a key in a lock he could deduce the fact that there was one in the wall.

"Come in," said the man. "The door is open."

If Macheath had had any suspicions before regarding the man being the right person for him to follow they were dissipated now upon his finding that he had such easy access to the garden of the palace, and Macheath, therefore, followed his guide through a narrow doorway without the least hesitation.

"This is the palace garden?" said Macheath.

"Yes; but allow me to beg the favour of your being silent. We have a sentinel to pass, and it is as well that he should hear nothing but the pass-word, which will enable us to clear his post."

"Certainly—certainly."

The man walked on now with the rapidity of one well accustomed to the place, and took a short cut over a little plot of grass to reach the path he wanted.

"Who goes there?" said a voice, and at the same time there was the rattle of a firelock, as it was brought to the breast of the sentinel.

Macheath's conductor immediately replied—

"The prince at home!"

"Pass on," said the sentinel, and the butt of the musket rang upon the ground again. "Pass on!"

"I will recollect that pass-word for to-night," said Macheath to himself, "for there is no knowing but it may be useful to me. 'The prince at home.' That is it. I shall certainly not forget it."

The man hurried on now faster than before, but in Macheath he had one who could have followed him at any speed.

At length they reached the palace, and the man paused at a window that seemed to open right to the ground, close to a thick clump of brambles of some sort, which the captain could only see the black outline of against the house.

"Be still, now, for a few minutes, if you please," said the man in the cloak.

He tapped very cautiously.

Macheath would have had the greatest difficulty in seeing that it was a window at all that his unknown friend knocked at, if a lamp some distance off had not cast a ray direct upon it.

Tap—tap! the man went with his nails against the glass.

For a few moments there was no reply, and the man had just muttered something in a tone of surprise, when the window was hastily opened, and a voice said—

"Is it you, Chalton?"

"Yes, your royal highness."

"Oh, has he come?"

"I am here, your royal highness," said Macheath, "if you allude to me. I am here according to my orders. Nothing but death should have kept me from you, after receiving your commands."

"Oh, that is all right, then," said the prince. "Come on both of you. You know how to manage the window, Chalton?"

"I do, your highness. Come on, Macheath."

"Come on is very easily said," thought the captain, "but I wonder if it is all level within the window, otherwise one may have an ugly fall. Mr. Chalton," he said aloud, "is there any step or descent here?"

"No—no; walk right on."

"That will do."

In another moment Macheath was through the open window, and by the tread he felt that he was on a very soft carpet.

It was like snow to his feet.

The room, however, continued to be in total darkness.

The man named Chalton closed the window, and Captain Macheath heard it made fast, and then the prince spoke again.

"You are nearly to your time, Macheath," he said.

"I was in hopes, your highness, that I was punctual," said Macheath.

"Yes—yes, perhaps I am wrong; but as the night was so particularly dark, I thought perhaps you would have been a little earlier, that is all. But there is time enough — quite time enough. Hem! Oh, quite."

It was evident that the prince had something to say that he did not very well like to say, but yet that he felt must be said.

"I trust," he said, "that as a man of gallantry, you think nothing of a little intrigue—eh?"

"Nothing whatever, your royal highness, except that it is about one of the pleasantest pastimes going."

"That's right—that's quite right," said the prince, with more vivacity than he usually showed. "I like that. And so now I will tell you at once that I must get you to carry off a young lady."

Captain Macheath was silent.

"She is quite willing herself," said Chalton, in a low tone, "only she prefers being taken to coming away herself, you see."

"That's it, Chalton, that's it," said the prince. "The fact is, Macheath, that the girl, to save appearances and to give herself an opportunity of saying she could not help it afterwards, wants to be run away with, and to pretend all the time that it is against her will. Do you understand?"

"Perfectly."

"Very well. Of course, I don't wish to show in the matter at all. The fact is, the stupid people she belongs to have a sort of suspicion, you see, that someone of rank is after her."

"But they have not the remotest idea that it is his royal highness," said Mr. Chalton.

"Oh! no," added the prince, "not the least, nor would I have them think that for a thousand pounds."

"I will be careful upon that head," said Macheath.

"Very good. Of course, I tell you all this in perfect confidence; but the stupid people suspecting that someone was after her, packed her off to a school very quickly at a place called Hanger Hill."

"It is near Ealing?" said Captain Macheath.

"Precisely. I was by the merest accident in the world that I found it out, for the affair was managed very well indeed; but there she is. It is not much of a school, is it, Chalton?"

"A finishing academy, your royal highness, for young ladies."

"Just so; and you understand that what I want you to do is to get her away and to take her to Kew. Will you do it?"

"If I can."

"That is enough. Of course you can. I don't see what great difficulty there can be in the matter. Of course, I shall leave all the main details of the affair to you. By Jove, she is the most beautiful creature I ever saw, or thought that there was in the world to see!"

"Is she so very beautiful?"

"She is beyond beautiful a long way. It is quite impossible that I can give you any idea of her. You couldn't describe her. Nobody could. And yet her friends are nobody."

"They are some low people in business somewhere," said Chalton, "but of no account; so you see nobody's feelings will be hurt."

"Certainly not," remarked Captain Macheath. "Of course such people cannot have any feelings to hurt,"

The tone of sarcasm in which Macheath uttered these words were too fine for the prince's apprehension, and he said—

"No—certainly. That is all right enough as you say. They have no feelings to hurt; and as for the girl, sweet little creature as she is, by Jove she is worth a million of money down upon the nail, that she is! I would give every race-horse and every diamond I ever saw to make her my wife without grudging them."

"I have no doubt," said Macheath, "but that she does credit to your royal highness's taste. She must be beautiful."

"She is—indeed she is. Her name is Rosa—"

"Hem!" said Chalton.

"Oh, I think Macheath ought to know her name," said the prince. "It is Rosa Bell."

"Rosa Bell!" repeated the captain.

"Yes; that is her name, bless her!" said the prince. "And now, Macheath, I don't know anyone who is more fitting than you are to conduct this enterprise. Of course, you will have every assistance, and if you perform the matter to my satisfaction, you may count upon me rewarding you well."

"I owe already a heavy debt of gratitude to your royal highness," said the captain. "I am only too happy that I am able to be of any service to you. I understand, then, that the young lady is quite willing?"

"Oh! yes," said Chalton and the prince too; and then Chalton added—

"I humbly beg your royal highness's pardon."

"Oh! no matter," said the prince. "You see, Macheath, that for us to run away with her is just what she wants, although she thinks we are noblemen connected with the court merely; and in order that the schoolmistress shall not make bad report of her, she will pretend not to like leaving the school at all; but you must look upon that as all show, and bring her away as if it were really by force."

Macheath felt a little uneasy about the truth of the statement.

"I shall obey your royal highness in all things," he said, after a pause. "I shall require more minute information regarding the school, though."

"Oh! yes; you shall have every information. Chalton will be good enough to see to all that, and you will have him with you, and others to any number you think proper. A carriage will be at your disposal, and all I require of you is, to take the conduct of the expedition, and to plan it."

"Then, in fact," said Macheath, "I am to find the means of taking a young girl by force or by fraud from a boarding-school."

"Well, that's about it."

"And the only thing is, that as it is by her own consent, the transaction is not one of such iniquity as it otherwise would be?"

"Exactly so; but I warn you that she will resist you, or affect to resist you, and as all females from four years old to a hundred can command tears at pleasure, I am told she may cry, and all that sort of thing, at a great rate."

"So long as the young lady is only acting," said Macheath, "I shall not object to her playing her part as well as she likes."

"Very good! then that is all settled. I hope and expect that you will be successful, and I will, with such hope and expectation, be at Kew in the course of an hour or so at the outside. This will be a very good time to set about the business, and I leave it to you to execute."

"Your highness must have some tolerable amount of confidence in what I can do in an hour," said Captain Macheath.

"Oh, yes. I have—I have. An hour is a long time."

"How many persons am I to have with me?"

"As many as you like."

"If," said Chalton, "myself and two others will be sufficient, it would be safest to confine it to them. Will that do?"

"Certainly. The fewer the better. I am quite ready to go at once upon the expedition; but I beg to warn you that it may take a much longer time to carry out than I think, or than you may think; and if you go to Kew in an hour's time, do not be impatient if I should not arrive with the young lady quite so soon."

"That will do," said the prince, "I leave it quite to you. You do the best you can."

"If you will follow me, Captain Macheath," said Chalton, "I will take you to those who will go with us, and to the carriage. This way if you please."

"Good evening for the present," said the prince.

"I have the honour," said Macheath, "of bidding your royal highness good evening, and the hope that I shall soon be able to report to you the certain success."

Chalton laid his hand upon Macheath's arm to lead him from the room.

The captain expected to be taken through the open window again; but such was not the case.

Chalton opened a door in the wall opposite to the window, and led Macheath into the interior of the palace.

This curious interview with the prince had taken place in the dark, so that Captain Macheath had not had the slightest opportunity of noticing the expression of his face.

Perhaps his royal highness was not particularly anxious that the captain should notice the expression he wore upon the occasion; or there might be other and sufficient substantial reasons for conducting the interview in the dark.

After passing out of the room in the charge of Mr. Chalton, the darkness was quite as great, until, after traversing a long passage, a room door was opened, and Captain Macheath was ushered into it.

A table lamp was burning and shedding a soft and pleasant light about the apartment.

For the first time Captain Macheath got a good look at Mr. Chalton.

That individual was tall and of good figure.

After they both entered the room they looked with mutual curiosity at each other for some few minutes.

"I think we shall know each other again, Captain Macheath," said Chalton.

"I shall certainly know you again," was the captain's reply. "Pray what appointment are you supposed to fill about the palace?"

"None."

"Humph! You are then in the private service of his royal highness?"

"Perhaps," said Chalton, "the best way is to ask no questions, and then you will not run the risk of having false statements made to you. I do not mean to speak offensively—nothing can be further from my intention; but, if I do not very much mistake you, you are a man who likes plain dealing."

"I do."

"So I thought, and, therefore, I speak to you in such a style. Now, here are plenty of refreshments of all kinds on the side table. Help yourself, and, as soon as you conveniently can, make up your mind as to what course you will adopt to carry out the wishes of the prince."

"My mind is already made up."

"Indeed?"

"Yes; I will go with you and the two persons you alluded to, and carry the young lady off at once, despite of all opposition. I will ask to see her, and if once I do see her, she is booked for Kew Palace within the next hour."

"Well, you almost take my breath away."

"Why so?"

"Just because the affair would be an endless job to the people who before were in the confidence of his royal highness in these little matters. They would have planned, and plotted, and 'counterplotted, and gone such a round-about way to work, that there would have been no end to their complications in the matter."

"The shortest way is the most direct to all objects."

CHAPTER LVII.

MACHEATH FINDS SOME DIFFICULTIES IN HIS WAY.

"Not a doubt of it. But come, let us have a glass of wine to the success of our little expedition."

"One, and only one, then."

"As you please about that. You will find it of the right sort."

Chalton poured himself out a glass of wine, and then presented the decanter to Macheath, who likewise helped himself.

"To the success of our enterprise!" said Chalton.

"Agreed," said Macheath. "If you are ready to start, I am."

Mr. Chalton led the way, and Captain Macheath followed him from the room.

Mr. Chalton led the captain to one of the smaller courtyards of the palace, and after giving some whispered directions to a man who was there, he turned to Macheath.

"Our carriage and two assistants will meet us in St. James's-street in the course of a few minutes from now."

"Where you please," said Macheath. "It does not matter to me. You know the way to the school, I suppose?"

"Oh! yes, I ought to know it, for I have already made two attempts to get speech of the young lady and failed. I don't mind telling you as much, for the authorities of the establishment, I assure you, are not a little vigilant."

"I thank you for the information."

They left the palace by the old gate opening on St. James's-street, and sauntered up one side of that highly fashionable thoroughfare.

"Here is our vehicle," said Chalton.

A carriage and pair of horses in charge of a postillion stood there.

Two men were seated in the carriage, and they respectfully touched their hats to Chalton and the captain.

"They know nothing of me, of course?" whispered Macheath.

"Nothing whatever, but they will expect you are some court favourite, and they will be as obedient and respectful to you as though you were the prince himself."

"You have already possessed them with that idea?"

"Well, perhaps I have."

"That will do," said Captain Macheath. "Then drive to Hanger-hill immediately and we will see if we can't get this little adventure over at once."

"You are a wonderful man, Macheath."

During the journey to Hanger-hill, Macheath's thoughts more than once wandered to the lonely lodging in which he had left Polly and Luke, and he would have given anything to know what was going on there.

The heroic manner in which his wife Polly had clung to him in all changes of his fortunes had had a sensible effect upon him.

When the carriage stopped he awoke with a start from the reverie into which he had fallen.

"Here we are," said Chalton.

"That will do then. Let us alight."

"How silent you have been, Macheath! I would not interrupt you, for I thought you were probably devising some plan of operations at the school."

"In good truth," Macheath replied, "I forgot that there was such a place. My thoughts were in another direction entirely; but now I will give them entirely to the prince's affair."

"I beg of you to do so. If I had thought your mind had been otherwise engaged I should have taken the liberty of rousing you. But there is Hanger-hill, and a wild and desolate spot it is, too. What a mad riot the wind is making among the trees, to be sure."

"Do you call that a riot?"

"Indeed, I do."

"Well, then, my good sir, it is quite clear that you are town-bred, and have seen very little o' the country and its phenomena. Why, I have known the wind tear up an oak by the roots, and play with it as though it were a rush."

"Hem!" said Chalton.

Macheath smiled to himself at Chalton's incredulity.

He ran up a bank of earth and glanced around him.

He had a general knowledge of that part of the country, and he wanted to try and see if he could recognise the exact spot where he was.

"All right," he said. "Now I know where I am."

"Do you?"

"Yes; I have been all over these meadows many a time. What establishment, by-the-bye, is that yonder? I have often seen it, but never knew whose it was."

"That is the school."

"Indeed, are we so near?" demanded the captain.

"We are, and it behoves us to be cautious," Chalton replied. "And now, if it's a fair question, what do you mean to do?"

"It is a fair question, and I will answer it frankly," Macheath said. "I intend to go up to the mistress of the house and to demand admission in the usual way. The first person who comes to the door I will seize and hand over to your keeping, and then I will walk into the house and find Rosa Bell and carry her out of it. I should say, rather, that our two friends can keep the door, and you and I had better go in together."

"Very well, they can but scratch us."

"Scratch us? What do you mean by that?"

"Why, I believe there is nobody in the house

CAPTAIN MACHEATH

THE
PRINCE OF THE HIGHWAY.

"SPEAK!" CRIED MACHEATH.   THE ONLY REPLY HE RECEIVED WAS A HOLLOW LAUGH.

of a male description, and, therefore, the ladies may try to use their nails upon us. But we shall soon see; I sincerely hope the attempt will be successful. The carriage had better stay here with the driver, I suppose?"

"Certainly. Now come on, if you please, Mr. Chalton."

Chalton beckoned to the two men to follow them, and the whole party strolled very leisurely down a narrow lane that led to the front gate of the school.

The lane terminated in a broader road, and at the juncture of the two was an iron gate. A massive bell hung in the centre at the top of the gates, and a very slight examination convinced Macheath that they were fast locked.

"Well, now," said Chalton, "here we are at a stand still."

"Not quite," the captain returned. "We see the bell here, or what looks very like one, although, perhaps, it is an ornament merely."

"What shall we do, then?"

"You will see. All we have to do is, by hook or by crook, to get hold of Rosa Bell and take her to Kew. I suppose the captivation of so young a girl was no difficult matter?"

"Captivation?" said Chalton. "What do you mean by captivation?"

"Why, has not the prince captivated her—that is to say, made her fall in love with him?"

"Oh—ah—hem!"

"Why do you say 'Hem?'"

"'Twas nothing at all, believe me. I was at the moment thinking of something that by no means concerned this affair at all. But pray ring the bell."

"I will."

Macheath laid hold of the massive old iron bell-wire, and gave it such a pull that the bell set to tolling at a rate that was enough to alarm the whole neighbourhood; but probably the tone of the school-bell was pretty well known to all within ear-shot of it.

"That ought to bring somebody," Macheath observed.

"It will, too," said Chalton.

"Then let me request that you will keep out of sight while I speak to whoever may come to answer the bell."

Upon this, Chalton and the two men retired on one side, and hid themselves in the shade of a tree.

Macheath could hear footsteps approaching the gate, and presently a figure, carrying a lantern.

In a few minutes this figure halted opposite to the gate, only that it took care to keep some yards from it.

"Who's there?" said a sharp female voice, that betrayed that it had contracted much of the asperity of age.

"A visitor, if you please, madam," said Macheath, in as soft and insinuating a tone as he could possibly assume.

"To whom?" said the voice again.

"To the respected proprietress of this establishment, madam," Macheath replied.

"Oh! then, you can come again to-morrow."

"Dear me," the captain said, "that will be very inconvenient indeed for me, for I have come some distance to speak to the respected mistress of this school about placing a young lady under her care."

"Pray, what is your name, sir?"

"Smith, madam. Olianthus Probeck Olwerthy Smith, is my humble name, madam."

"Oh!" she said, and turned to walk away.

"This is very extraordinary conduct, permit me to say," added Macheath. "I thought, of course, that one of the first objects of a scholastic establishment was to get pupils, but here it seems not to be the case."

"Certainly not," said the lady, and she walked away.

Mr. Chalton, who had listened to the conversation, now stepped forward.

"Ah! that's how they served me," he said. "They wouldn't let me within the gates. You may depend upon it, my good sir, that the people in this house are as jealous as dragoons, and are thoroughly upon their guard against any intruders."

"That is just what I wanted to find out," said Macheath. "Our course is now quite clear and easy."

"Clear and easy?"

"Yes; to be sure," the captain responded. "Now I know exactly the kind of humour the people of the house are in, and I can adopt a course which will, of course, succeed. It would have been a pity, though, to throw away a decided chance of doing the job at once."

"And pray, then, what can you do now?"

"Get in without their leave."

"Oh! that is it, is it?"

"To be sure it is," said Captain Macheath. "I am at a loss to conceive how any other course can be adopted. If you must enter a house, and the people won't let you in, you must get in by some means without their leave, and that is the course I propose adopting, if you see no objection to it, Mr. Chalton. If you do, I shall listen with all the respect in the world to your suggestions. Pray go on."

"Oh!" said Chalton, as he made a mock bow of great apparent respect, "it is not for me to raise any objection. The conduct of this enterprise is certainly in your own hands, and for my own part, I feel that I have only to obey you, which, believe me, I shall do willingly, aiding you as effectually as it is in my power to do."

"That I believe you will," Captain Macheath, returned, "and therefore I tell you that we must make our way into the grounds of this house, and into the house itself. I do not think that we shall encounter much opposition. The very audacity of the affair will paralyse them with astonishment."

"There is something in that," Chalton said, musingly, "and I am perfectly willing that the plan should be tried, at all events. No doubt we shall be able to effect a retreat by the same way that we get into the premises, if we should see that it is absolutely necessary for us to do so."

"Not a doubt of that. But if I retreat it will be in the company, I hope, of Miss Rosa Bell."

"I hope so, too; but before we go, allow me to hope that you will not persevere against all hope."

"That I will not!"

The only thing that Macheath was anxious about, was to find out the hour at which the whole establishment, scholars included, retired to rest for the night, as he did not wish to make the attempt to invade the premises until that event had taken place.

It was only, however, by conjecturing upon the subject that any conclusion could be arrived at, as no positive information was to be had.

Captain Macheath thought that if he waited until it was half-past eleven o'clock, he ought to be able to conclude with perfect truth and safety that no one would be up in the school.

Mr. Chalton was of the same opinion.

"We have three quarters of an hour to wait," said Macheath, "for now it wants but a quarter to eleven. The time will hang rather heavily upon our hands, but that cannot be helped."

"And it will be cold, too," said Chalton, as he stamped upon the ground.

"That we can remedy by exercise," the captain replied. "I prefer a sharp walk up and down the lane."

Chalton assented to this, and during the period they had to exist in each other's company they entered freely into conversation.

Chalton was very guarded, though, as to what he said about the prince, and Macheath did not think the less of him for being so, as he being in the confidence and employment of the prince, was bound above all others to keep his secrets.

At length the three quarters of an hour passed away, and Macheath declared his intention of immediately commencing the enterprise.

Chalton seemed to be a little nervous about it now that the time had come.

During the walk down the lane they had discovered a part of the high brick wall enclosing the grounds of the school.

In order to afford greater facilities of descent, Captain Macheath procured from the man in charge of the carriage a spare trace and a rope that they had with them.

"I daresay, Chalton," he said, "that you are not quite so good a climber as I am, so, if you please, I will go first, and fasten the trace to the bough of yon fig-tree that grows near the wall, and you will find it of material assistance to you as you climb up."

"I am more obliged to you than I can express," said Chalton, "for I must confess, as you surmise, that my climbing days are pretty nearly over, although that is a fact owing more to the inactive life I lead in a palace and a prince's service than to age."

Macheath smiled at Chalton's confession.

With great care he ascended the corner of the wall with the trace on his neck, so as to have it ready to fasten to the branch.

There did not appear to be anyone moving in the garden.

Macheath listened most attentively to catch the slightest sound that might arise from it, and heard nothing.

He fastened the trace, by the aid of its buckle, to the tree, and found it of immense assistance to himself in getting over the wall.

"Is it all right?" whispered Chalton, from the .ane.

"Hush! Don't speak so loud," said Macheath. "There is no one here. Let the men come up before or after you, as you think proper."

"Oh! I will come. They will follow. I suppose the trace is quite tight?"

"Yes—yes; it can't possibly give way. You may fully rely upon it. Have you got a good hold of it now?"

"Capital!"

Macheath stood upon the top of the wall, balancing himself by the branch of the tree, while Chalton ascended by the aid of the trace.

Macheath then secured one end of a stout piece of rope firmly to the wall, and lightly swung himself down by it, and alighted upon the ground as softly and as comfortably as it was possible to do.

Dark as the night was, and rainy, there was yet the dim kind of perception of objects which anyone whose eyes have got accustomed to the night air is sure to have after a time.

Captain Macheath steadied the rope with his foot as Chalton descended.

The other two men then followed.

"Let one of them stay here," Macheath said, "and show a light if he hears any alarm."

"I will do that, sir," said one of the men. "I will remain, if your honour chooses."

"Very well, do so; and recollect that you are not to move from the spot. You are to consider it as your post, to keep it until I come to you again."

"I understand, sir. All right."

"Very good—then we will go now."

It would have been impossible for anyone to see the three dark figures now moving along the garden with stealthy steps.

Their forms were so mingled with the foliage of the tall trees and the deep shadows that they were completely hidden.

On they went, more like three spectres than three living men, bent upon an errand concerning which Macheath had his very serious doubts indeed.

By keeping a course of right angles with the inner face of the garden wall, Macheath calculated upon soon coming upon some traces of the house.

He was right, for after passing through a complete belt of tall trees shading it from observation from the road, he saw the building quite plainly against the night sky.

For some minutes the captain took a long and steady look at the house, and then Chalton, who was close to him, spoke in a whisper, saying—

"Well, what do you think of it?"

"Think of what?"

"The school-house. It was formerly the abode of one of the richest Catholic noblemen of England, and they say that before it came into his hands as a secular residence, that it had been a nunnery of great repute and size."

"Size enough," Macheath remarked, "there is, in all conscience. Do you see any light in any window?"

"Not the ghost of one."

"That's awkward; but, perhaps, we are on the wrong side of the house to see. We will go round it."

"It will be as well to keep as far off it as possible while we do so. I would advise that we keep in the shadow of the trees."

"Be it so. It is good advice."

Slinking along as though they had come to rob the premises—and so they had in one sense—they all three now got round some straggling outbuildings to another face of the house, and then upon the upper floor Macheath counted no less than five windows in a row, the whole of which were faintly illuminated.

"What does the light mean?" Chalton demanded.

"If I am not very much mistaken," Macheath replied, "I should pronounce those five windows to belong to the dormitory of the school."

"Oh! of course—of course. Not a doubt of it."

"Well, then, friend Chalton, it seems to me that there is where we must go with as little delay as possible, and find, among all the others, the young lady who is to go to Kew with us. I suppose she will declare herself."

"Oh! yes, yes—that is, I don't know though."

"You don't?"

"No; for there is nothing that she is so anxious about as to preserve the idea that she goes without her own consent. You will know her by her hair, which is of a beautiful golden tint—not yellow, nor the least touch of red—in fact, I don't know how to describe her hair, it is so very beautiful."

"I'll find her, then," said Macheath, laughing, "if I have to pull the nightcaps off all the young ladies in the school."

"Well, now, the only difficulty is, I suppose, how to get into the house."

"It is."

Macheath remained for some minutes in silence, looking up at the windows.

There was a light balcony outside running along the whole length of that side of the house, and the height from the level of the garden was somewhere about twenty feet—rather a formidable height to get up without any aid.

"Oh! for a ladder," said Macheath.

"A ladder, sir?" said the man who was with them. "I saw one lying along by the stumps of the trees yonder, and nearly broke my shins over it as I came after you just now."

"Did you, indeed? That is the very thing we want. Go and get it at once, for a more fortunate discovery could not be. It will be everything for us to get at that room without the trouble, the toil, and the risk of going through the house."

"I'll soon bring it, your honour," said the man.

"Ah!" whispered Chalton, as he rubbed his hands together nervously, "that ladder being seen by Jennings is quite lucky—oh! quite. What a mercy it is that no one has interrupted us as yet?"

"It is a piece of good luck," Macheath assented.

"Good gracious! what's that?" said Chalton.

"Hush—hush!"

A strange noise came upon their ears, and deepened into the unmistakable sounds of a battle between two cats, who fought and spat and swore at each other in a most diabolical manner, and finished by scampering over Chalton's feet.

He fell down upon the grass and uttered a cry of alarm.

"Peace," said Macheath, "do you want to ruin all? How can you be such a idiot! One might surely have expected something like common discretion from you."

"Oh, dear!—oh, dear!"

"Silence!" hissed Macheath.

"Yes, I am—I will—that is to say, what two fiends they were, to be sure!"

"Oh! stuff. You are a pretty fellow to come here upon such an enterprise as this, and allow yourself to be frightened by a couple of cats."

"Were they cats?"

"To the best of my belief, they were," laughed Macheath. "What did you take them to be if they were not cats?"

"Fiends, sir—fiends?"

"Oh, nonsense! Come now, get up. Here comes our friend with the ladder, and I look forward to the speedy termination of our adventure now. Ah! that's the very thing."

"It's a deuce of a weight, your honour," said Jennings.

"Never mind that," Macheath returned. "I only hope your reward will be as heavy, in good current coin, too. Place it carefully up against the balcony. Now—now—I have a hold of it. Gently, that will do."

The ladder answered as well as if it had been made for the express purpose.

When it was fairly raised to the balcony, the passage to the upper floor of the house was as well established to anyone as active as Captain Macheath as if it had been a well-trodden high way.

"You are actually going to venture?" said Chalton.

"Yes, rather."

"Oh! well, don't suppose that I hang back in any way—quite the reverse; only it is a risk."

"Very well, then, Mr. Chalton," said the captain, "if you have the slightest objection to running that risk, my advice to you is to go home as quickly as you possibly can."

"Don't say that. I was only joking."

Chalton's teeth chattered as he spoke; but Macheath was charitable enough to suppose that the cold might have something to do with that.

"Now, Jennings," he said, "you will recollect that your post is at the foot of the ladder, from which you are not to stir until you see me. If anyone should interfere with you, of course you will adopt some mode of giving the alarm, and I shall be be quite near at hand enough to hear you."

"Very well, sir."

"Do so. That will answer the purpose very well indeed."

"And what do you want me to do?" said Chalton.

"Nothing; but just come up to the balcony, and wait for me. You may assist me if there should arise any occasion for help."

"Very well. Oh! dear, yes. I will help you, and, of course, I fully expect that you will be so good as to inform the prince that I was as active and as eager and efficient as possible in the whole affair from first to last."

"It would be a very strange thing," said Captain Macheath, with a laugh, "if we did not praise each other to the very echo. Come on!"

The captain ascended the ladder lightly, and soon stood on the balcony.

Chalton followed him.

"Stay here," whispered Macheath. "Keep a hold of the ladder, and then I shall be quite sure of where to find you."

"Yes—yes; I will."

The fact was that the captain, discovering that Chalton was in a state of terror, decided to get rid of him.

He now silently and cautiously approached one of the windows opening to the balcony.

A glance through a little crevice by the side of the blind showed him that his supposition regarding the room being the dormitory of the school was perfectly well founded.

The room into which Macheath peeped was a very extensive one indeed, being lofty as well as spacious, and down each side of it he saw a row of little bedsteads with dazzlingly-white dimity curtains to each of them.

Upon a bracket high upon the wall was an oil lamp.

The profound stillness in the apartment was good evidence that the young ladies were asleep.

"It's a thousand pities," thought Macheath, "to disturb all these young creatures now upon an errand of this sort; but what can I do? I am quite pledged to the prince to carry out this affair for him to the very utmost of my ability, and I must not now shrink from it, let the consequences be what they may."

The mode of getting into the room did not present itself as a very easy proposition.

Indeed, there was only a hope regarding that point in Captain Macheath's mind, and that was that, as the room was on the upper floor of the mansion, and so apparently inaccessible, it was just possible the windows might not be made fast in any way.

"I can but try," the captain thought, "so here goes!"

It was quite a ticklish affair that trying if the window that he was close to would open, for he knew that some windows would not open without creaking, which would be quite enough to awaken the young ladies.

He could only hope that that one went upon the silent system.

The framework of the window stuck a little, which at first made Macheath think that it was really fast.

But it suddenly gave way, and the window gave a slight kind of squeak.

"The deuce take it!" said Macheath, "they will be all up now."

He listened attentively to hear what effect the noise would have upon the young ladies in the dormitory.

He was not kept very long in doubt.

"Oh! what's that?" demanded a voice from one end of the room.

Macheath felt very much tempted indeed at that instant to reply "Nothing;" but he restrained the impulse, and then another voice in the dormitory said—

"I am quite sure it was something."

"The horrid cats!" said a third.

"Oh! you needn't say horrid cats," cried another; "for if there's anything in all the world prettier than another now, ain't it a nice little kitten?"

"Oh! yes," cried some half-dozen of the young ladies all at once; "but it is quite a shocking thing that they will grow to be cats in such a little time."

"You had better all be quiet and go to sleep," said one, from a remote corner of the room, "or you will wake Miss Garret, and then we shall all catch it."

"So we shall," said several.

"Oh! but we shall all say it is you," cried one, "and then, if we all stand by each other and declare it's true, you will be punished and we shall all escape, and that will be such fun."

"Oh! be quiet, do."

Some of the young ladies laughed, but in a few moments silence reigned again in the school dormitory.

There was something about the whole affair that jarred upon Macheath's feelings.

"I will do nothing hastily," he thought; "I will keep my eyes about me, and my ears open, and if I find that I am being deceived in this business, I will adopt such a course as may be consistent with my feelings."

The silence in the dormitory did not continue for very long.

How could it be expected to do so, with such a number of young ladies in it?

In the course of the next few minutes one of them called out—

"I say—I say!"

"Oh! what?" said another.

"What! suppose it's thieves?" cried one, in evident alarm.

"Oh! stuff," said a third.

"Silks and satins!" said a fourth.

There was a slight laugh at this, for it was one of the little stock jokes of the school to cry out when anybody said stuff, "Silks and satins," and being quite a comprehensive little joke, it was always successful.

"I declare now," said another, "that I will call out to Miss Garret, and tell of you all, if you don't be quiet."

"Oh! do," said several others in mocking tones.

"Of course, if there's any tale-telling in the school, it's sure to come from Miss Robinson."

"No—no," said a calm, sweet voice. "Pray rest all of you, and don't tell any tales of each other."

Chalton pinched Macheath's arm slightly.

"That's her," he said.

"Oh!" said Macheath. "Then she is in the far corner by the fireplace."

"Is she?"

"Yes. I saw her head as she spoke even now. How delighted she will be when she finds us here, won't she?"

"Oh! very—very, indeed. Her name is Rosa."

"Yes; I know that. But, as I was saying, how impatient she must be for us to take her away from school?"

The secretary made a kind of humming noise, which almost degenerated into a cough, and no doubt would have done so, only that he felt the danger that would attend any such demonstrative sound.

If Macheath had any doubts before of the character of the enterprise, the conduct of this man would have dispelled them.

From that moment he felt convinced that the whole affair was the genuine abduction of a girl from a boarding-school.

But still he felt that until he had such an assurance from the lips of the young lady herself he had no right to assume positively such a state of things, and, therefore, he would not give up the enterprise.

It was with such a feeling as this that Captain Macheath persevered with his design.

Chalton had not the least suspicion that anyone could have any kind of scruple at doing that which they were well paid for.

Chalton thought from the first that it was quite a needless piece of delicacy upon the part of the prince to deceive Macheath.

What his royal master had done, however, the secretary did not feel himself authorised to undo, so he kept up the delusion to a certain extent, although not so far as to prevent anyone of an ordinary penetration from seeing through it.

Under such circumstances, Captain Macheath, with all his tact and experience of the world and its affairs, was not likely to be deceived.

CHAPTER LVIII.

HOW MACHEATH KEPT HIS WORD.

THE good-tempered appeal that had been made by the girl seemed to have had its effect upon the rest of the inhabitants of the dormitory, for there was a general cry of—"Good-night—Good-night!" and then all was still again.

It seemed as if they all settled themselves for the night.

"What do you think of it now?" interposed Chalton. "Is it time yet, think you?"

"It will be soon. In a few more minutes I think we may venture to make a bold attempt."

"Which you will make?"

"If you please; but I thought that you would probably like to take the credit of having made it with the prince."

"Oh! dear, no."

"Very good; I promised to carry off the girl, and I will do it; but you must aid me by clearing the way for my retreat when I have once got her. That is all I require from you."

"That is just what I can do nicely," Chalton replied; "and, I think, by the measures we have taken, there can be no difficulty in the way. We shall all come off with flying colours."

"Not a doubt of it."

The stillness in the dormitory had now continued long enough to convince Macheath that the young ladies must be all asleep.

But even he—with all his courage and coolness in enterprises of all kinds and descriptions—felt a little daunted at the idea of showing himself, lest someone might be awake and raise an alarm.

Captain Macheath waited five minutes, and then, as Chalton was getting very impatient, and hinted that Macheath did not like the affair, the captain slowly opened the window of the room.

No one moved or made any sound, so that he was quite confirmed in his idea that they all slept soundly.

He got into the room with such extreme caution that he made no noise whatever.

As he stood upon the floor of the sleeping-chamber the flush of shame was upon his cheek at the seeming unworthy part he was acting.

To stop a man upon the highway and boldly demand his money looked almost like a piece of rare courage in comparison with what he was about now; but he calmed himself with the reflection that he had better motives in the affair than circumstances would seem to warrant.

"I come to save, not to destroy," he whispered to himself.

And then he softly stole along the floor towards the bed on which lay the young girl who was the object of the expedition.

The mode in which Captain Macheath intended to proceed, was to fold her in a wrapper and carry her off at once to the window, and so down into the garden and off the premises.

He had reached to within three or four paces of the bed, when one of the young ladies suddenly cried out—

"Oh! who is that?"

Macheath felt that any further secrecy was quite out of the question, and that the activity of his movements would alone be of any use in bringing the affair to a successful conclusion.

With one bound he was by the bedside of the young girl, and before she could open her eyes even, he had rolled a heavy wrapper twice round her, lifted her in his arms as though she were a mere doll, and was making his way towards the window with her.

This was done so quickly that it was all but accomplished before the others in the dormitory could gather breath to scream; but when they did the uproar was prodigious.

"Murder—help! Oh! murder—murder!"

Such were the shouts, mingled with shrieks, indicating nothing but the very extremity of alarm, that came from some dozen or so throats at once.

Captain Macheath felt staggered and alarmed at the noise.

He was out of the window in a moment, nevertheless, and still holding the young girl in his arms, and got into the garden he hardly knew how, and ran along more by instinct than with any fixed purpose until he reached the wall.

The sound of screaming was now mingled with that of some immense bell ringing, and it was quite evident that if they did not get off the premises as quickly as possible, a general alarm would be given to the neighbourhood.

How he got actually into the road, Captain Macheath could hardly have told; but he did so, and then in a loud voice he cried—

"The carriage—the carriage!"

"Here, sir, this way," said one of the men. "This way, if you please, sir. Here is the carriage."

"Drive on—drive on!"

"But Mr. Chalton, sir?" said one of the men.

"Hang Mr. Chalton!" cried Captain Macheath. "Drive on at once, will you?"

"Yes, sir."

In another moment the horses were lashed to a perilous speed, and off they went towards town.

Captain Macheath had the young girl upon his lap, and what amazed him most was, that she neither spoke nor moved.

"Is it possible," he said, "that I am, after all, deceived, and that she is quite willing for the departure?"

The carriage dashed on fiercely.

Sometimes it met with rather a bad piece of road, and then the jolting was terrific.

Still the girl neither spoke nor moved, and in the intense darkness of the night—for the suburbs of London were then rather worse lighted than they are now—he had no chance of seeing her face.

"I hope," he said, at length, "that the abduction from school is really with your own consent—that is to say, I do not exactly hope it, but I should like to hear you say that it is so."

She made no reply.

"Let me beg that you will tell me," he added, "as your assurance, one way or the other, will guide me very much what to do."

Still no reply.

Captain Macheath began to get a little alarmed, and for the first time it now struck him that it was just possible the young creature, through fear and amazement, had fallen into a swoon.

This notion, when once it took possession of him, gathered strength each minute, and gave him much concern, for it entirely interfered with the course of action he had laid down for himself, inasmuch as it prevented him from discovering from her own lips whether or not she was a willing party to the intrigue.

The horses still tore on at a kind of half-gallop, and it was quite evident that they were very rapidly approaching London.

Captain Macheath felt that he ought to moderate the speed, and he tapped upon the front glasses of the carriage until he arrested the attention of the postillion, who, therefore, with some difficulty, pulled up.

"Not so fast," said Captain Macheath.

"Any pace you please, sir."

"Go at a moderate one, then. There is no occasion for such speed now whatever."

"I am glad of it, sir; for it is not doing the cattle any good to set them to such a pace."

"Very well—that will do."

"WHO GOES THERE?" CRIED THE SENTINEL, BRINGING HIS FIRELOCK TO THE PRESENT.

The coach now proceeded with quiet moderation, so that Macheath had time to think; but the more he thought the more thoroughly perplexing did he find his situation become.

If he took the young girl to the palace at once he might be betraying her; and if he took her elsewhere he would be placing himself in a great difficulty.

While he was in this state of conflicting thought the young creature uttered a deep sigh.

"Thank goodness!" said the captain, "she is recovering, and now there is a chance of my hearing from her own lips what she really thinks of this affair."

"Oh! what has happened?" she said, faintly; "where am I now?"

"Be assured," said Captain Macheath, in the gentlest tone of voice he could assume, and in a low one, too, for he wished by all means that it should escape the attention of the postillion, "be assured that you are with one who will befriend you to any extent that you wish him. I am not your enemy, although circumstances may have made me appear so."

"Oh! Heaven."

This ejaculation, and the tone in which it was uttered, was all but convincing to Macheath that his first suspicion was perfectly right, and that the young girl had no hand whatever in the atrocious plot that had been too successful.

"Speak to me now, I implore you," he said, "and let it be the truth that you speak, for upon what you say will hang your future fate. Did you, or did you not, wish and expect to be carried off?"

"Oh! now I recollect," she said. "Oh! Heaven, have mercy upon me."

"Answer my question. Was this abduction with your own connivance or not?"

"Oh! save me. Save me, if you have one spark of feeling in your heart!"

All Macheath's doubts, if he could be said to have really had any up to this moment, now completely vanished.

"Don't speak so loud," he said, "and listen to me."

"Oh! yes—yes. Heaven give you the heart to aid me!"

"Hush! I had it from the first. Now, attend to me. In the first place, I make you a positive promise that I will save you."

"You will, indeed?"

"As I live, and if I live I will," said Macheath.

"Who are you?" the girl demanded.

"That I cannot at present tell you; but let it suffice that I would not have taken you from the school, and so seemed to play the part of the vile agent of he whom you have most need to dread, if I had not known that, if I did not do so, someone else, who would have too truly discharged his duty to him instead of to you, would have taken my place."

"Yes—yes; I understand."

"But still further, let me tell you that even I was to the last moment deceived into the belief that you impatiently awaited to be taken away."

"Oh! no—no. How shall I assure you of the falsehood of that?"

"You need not say one word upon that head," the captain replied. "I am quite convinced already of it, so we will look upon that as settled. The only thing I am now anxious about is that you should feel equally convinced of my wish to behave to you with good faith."

"I am. I do not—I will not doubt you."

"That is well, but—"

"Why do you hesitate?"

"No—no; I don't hesitate. I will not hesitate for a moment. I tell you that the prince has it in his power to be to me a good friend or a bitter enemy. When he finds that I have played him false in this case, although it is in the cause of virtue, I shall experience his hatred."

"The prince, said you?"

"I did."

"Alas! then, the suspicions of my poor parents were but too true."

"Does it make any difference to your feelings that you now know, without a doubt, the rank of your admirer?" said Macheath.

"None—none."

"I am glad to hear you say that; and now, let the consequences to myself be what they may, tell me where I shall take you to, and I will do it."

"Home—home! To my father's house!"

"Where is that?" the captain demanded.

"In the Strand," the girl replied. "I will show you the house; and, oh! sir, if you will indeed take me home, I shall pray for you always as the best and truest friend I ever had, or can ever have in all the world."

"I will do it. Hilloa! postillion."

"Yes, sir?" said the man.

"You will go direct to the Strand with us."

"The Strand, sir?"

"You rascal, do you hesitate?"

"Why, sir, I was to wait at Hyde Park Corner for Mr. Chalton," said the postillion, "that is all, sir; but if you insist upon my going to the Strand, of course, I shall obey you, sir, as you are the only one left of the party to give me any orders at all."

"Very well. Do as I bid you, then. Go to the Strand."

"All right, sir."

As the vehicle went on towards the Strand, he tried to think of some plan of operation by which he might deceive him as to what was actually about to be done.

Unfortunately nothing occurred to Captain Macheath which would help him out of the dilemma, and he therefore resolved to trust to circumstances turning out right; but he would not allow the man to see where the young girl alighted, but ordered the coach to be stopped at a very dark corner by Northumberland House.

"Is this," he whispered to the girl, "near your house?"

"Yes—oh! yes."

"Very well, I will carry you to your father's door, for you cannot walk in the condition you are in, and then I must leave you to make your own explanation to him of what has occurred, and of the escape you have had."

"You will come in and listen to his gratitude?" the girl pleaded.

"Another time, perhaps, but not now," said Macheath. "You need not get off your horse," he shouted to the postillion, "I can manage without you."

Macheath opened the coach door and sprang out.

He took the young girl in his arms, still enveloped as she was in the wrapper, and ran along the Strand with her, until she stopped him at a hosier's shop, saying—

"Here is my home."

"Very well," he replied. "The place is all shut up, but I will soon knock them up. I see a light in one of the upper rooms."

"It is my mother's bed-room," sobbed the young girl, who seemed now upon the point of losing all her self-possession.

"Be calm. Hold up only for a little longer, and you will be in your mother's arms."

Macheath knocked loudly at the door, and he soon had the satisfaction of seeing the reflection of a light through the fanlight over the door.

Another moment and the door was opened.

"Dear me," said a female voice, "who is this that's knocking so loud at this time of night?"

"Mother! Mother!" cried the girl, as she left Macheath, and rushed into the passage.

"Good-night!" cried Macheath.

Without a word from mother or daughter he ran along the Strand to where his carriage was waiting.

"Now to Hyde Park Corner," said Captain Macheath to the postillion.

Off went the horses again, and the journey was soon accomplished.

Leaping from the carriage Captain Macheath found himself face to face with Chalton.

"I managed to procure a horse," said the latter. "What a time you have been! Where is the girl?"

Macheath's rapier flashed from its sheath.

"Dog!" he cried. "Draw, and defend your life!"

"What?" Chalton yelled.

"You have mistaken your man," Macheath hissed. "I know all. Draw, I say, for by the sky above one of us must die to-night."

Chalton backed a few steps as he drew his sword, and then made a sudden rush at Macheath; but the captain was too quick for him.

"Take that!" Macheath cried, as he plunged his sword through Chalton's body. "You will do no more mischief on this side of the grave."

Chalton dropped his sword, and, uttering a yell, fell dead.

Macheath turned and fled, leaving the postillion petrified with terror, and as motionless as if he had been glued to the saddle.

CHAPTER LIX.

WHAT HAPPENED AT THE LODGING WHILE MACHEATH WAS AWAY.

IT is hardly to be supposed that after the very strange and suspicious circumstances that had occurred in the mysterious lodging before Captain Macheath left, everything should be quiet and in good order.

We will, therefore, present to the reader now what took place after Macheath's departure.

It seemed to Polly, when the door closed upon her husband, as though she was completely abandoned to some dreadful fate, the perplexity and misery of which were only slowly developing.

By Captain Macheath's advice she had gone into the bed-chamber, with the hope that she would be able to sleep away the greater part of the time that he was absent, but nothing could be very well more utterly fallacious than that hope.

The state of dread and agitation that she was in effectually got the better of fatigue, and she could only lie upon the bed and conjure up to herself all the frightful surmises which an active imagination in such a state of undue excitement is ever apt to do.

Luke remained in the outer room, resolved not to give way to sleep, but to keep a watch upon the safety of his mistress, who had been so particularly committed to his charge.

Luke acted with great judgment, for he considered that the special duty he had to perform was to protect Polly.

He fastened the door of the outer room as firmly as he could, and having looked to his pistols, he made up his mind to sit up and wait until Macheath's return.

From the quietude Luke had every reason in the world to believe that Polly slept, and much pleased he was at the idea that she did so, for it made him think that the period of Macheath's absence would seem light to her.

There could not have been a greater mistake, for Polly was perfectly wide awake.

She had a light in the room, and to all appearance it was one that ought to go on burning for some hours; but from the moment that she lay down upon the bed the light appeared to grow more and more dim, and to show evident symptoms of going out.

Why it should do so defied all conjecture, as there was really plenty of candle left, and it was quite incredulous that the light should deliberately expire of its own accord, which it seemed to be intent upon doing.

This was the first singular circumstance that alarmed Polly, and she could do nothing but fix her eyes upon the light in surprise as the flame of it dwindled and dwindled each moment, until it got to be a mere little blue flicker.

"What can this mean?" said Polly to herself, in a whisper. "Is this house full of horrors that are not of this world?"

It seemed to be that such was, indeed, the case, if one might judge from the singularity of the events that had already taken place within its walls.

After the light had got to such a miserable pass as that, and after it had ceased to give anything like illumination to the apartment, it went no lower; but, contrary to Polly's expectations, who, to be sure, thought it was going completely out, it still preserved the little blue flame.

"What will happen next?" she said, in a ton of alarm, although it was not above a whisper.

A strange sound, something like a deep sigh came upon her ears at that moment.

As she heard it she thought that the whole current of her blood stopped in its accustomed channels with terror for a moment; and yet she knew not why she should be so alarmed at a sigh.

After the sigh everything was so profoundly still that in a few moments the idea that it must have been merely a thing of imagination instantly suggested itself to Polly, and she recovered a little from the state of strange alarm into which she had been thrown.

One glance at the mysterious candle, however, threw her back again into the same condition.

And yet she tried hard to reason with herself and to rise superior to the many terrors with which she was surrounded.

"What have I to fear from the supernatural world?" she said. "I am guilty of no injury that should in any degree make me specially obnoxious to such beings; so why should I allow myself to be thus terrified?"

All this was very well.

Thousands of people before Polly's time, and thousands after, have reasoned in precisely the same way.

But yet they have found it impossible to shake

off the terrors connected with a subject that had nothing at all to do with reason, and which was all vague conjecture, appealing to the fancy rather than to the judgment.

We do not pretend here to give any opinion with regard to the long-disputed question of whether apparitions can exist as a part of the great scheme of creation ; but it is a strange thing that all men fear the supernatural, even if they deny it with their judgment.

The candle now looked just like some little blue star in the darkness of the chamber ; and certainly, if it gave any light at all, the rays were swallowed up in the darkness.

Every object in the apartment was in a state of gloom.

Polly's terror was fading away a little, but only a little, when the deep sigh came again.

"It does mean something," she said, "and something will come of it. Oh! Heaven, what is that? What do I see?"

Her eyes were fixed upon the blue light to which the flame of the candle had been reduced ; and then, just within the dim halo that it cast around, she saw the outline of a face.

There was nothing in that face of a particularly terrifying character.

It was rather intense sorrow and anguish ; but still it was terrible from the fact that no one who had looked upon it could for a moment believe that it belonged to this world.

It was this that gave the horror to what otherwise would have courted no other feeling than sympathy.

Polly tried to speak.

She tried to scream, but it was all in vain.

It seemed as if the sight of that face had wrought a spell over all her faculties, and prevented her from the exercise of any of them but such as were merely necessary to enable her to see and to appreciate the terror with which she was overwhelmed.

She could not have turned her eyes away from that face if the wealth of worlds had been offered her for doing so.

She continued to gaze at it with a fascination that would not be resisted ; and then, without movement, it seemed just within the faint sphere of the light.

What object could the apparition have?

How long a time elapsed, during which she could do nothing but gaze upon that face, Polly had no means of really knowing.

To her it appeared an age, although in reality it was only a few minutes ; and then it slowly faded away, and twice as it did so she heard the same deep sigh that had before disturbed her.

The candle burnt up again slowly to its usual yellow flame.

What with surprise and terror, Polly was unable to make any movement for some time, even now that she had so far recovered as to be free from the frightful fascination of that face ; but at length she did manage, in a faint voice, to say—

"Luke !—Luke !"

Amid the silence of the night generally, and the still more wrapped stillness of that room, Luke heard the voice calling to him.

To rise and rush into the chamber was the work of a moment.

"Did you call?" he cried. "What is it?"

"Oh, help—help !"

Luke looked about him in astonishment.

He could see no foe to contend against, and

Polly was sitting up in bed, looking very much scared.

"What has alarmed you?" he said. "I see no one."

"No, not now—not now !"

"Was there anyone here?"

"Alas ! I know not, but I have been frightfully alarmed, Luke. Did you hear nothing?"

"Nothing but your voice when you called me. You said, 'Luke, Luke !' did you not?"

"I did ; but it was as much as I could say. Oh ! Luke, believe me, this place is haunted. Do not start—it is indeed. But whether it is so haunted by good or by evil spirits, I cannot tell. A further stay in it, though, would drive me mad."

"Alas ! you must have been dreaming."

"No—no—no !"

"But what have you seen?" added Luke, who, now that his first surprise was over, felt quite convinced that Polly must have gone to sleep, and allowed her imagination picture to her what was not real. "What was it that you suppose you saw?"

"Do not say suppose, for I actually saw it," Polly rejoined.

"Tell me what it was and where it was," said Luke.

"Oh ! Luke," Polly cried, "you are a good and faithful friend of my husband's, and I beg of you for his sake to take me away from this dreadful place at once. I cannot stay here ; I have seen the face of a being who is not of this world glaring at me in this room."

Luke felt very uneasy, and kept glancing around him as though he fancied that Polly's words might excite the reappearance of the spirit she was talking of.

"It is gone," she said, "but I saw it as plainly as I can see you, and we must leave this place at once."

"Oh ! reflect a little," said Luke, "before you come to that conclusion. How will Captain Macheath know where to find us if we go from here?"

That was a point of the question that had not occurred to Polly, and it rather stopped her in her desire to leave.

"But what can I do?" she said. "These rooms are full of horrors, and such appearances only come for two purposes—"

"Two purposes !" said Luke ; "and pray what are they?" He was glad to get her into any conversation which was likely in any manner to divert her from her fears. "What two purposes are they that such beings make themselves visible to us for?"

"The one is to threaten, and the other is to warn."

Luke was silent.

"We have done nothing that we should be threatened for," Polly added, "and, therefore, I cannot believe that it is for anything but to warn us that these appearances take place here. Oh ! Luke, there is danger in this place. Danger to life. What shall we do?"

"In the first place," said Luke, composedly, "we will be quite calm and collected, otherwise, if there be danger, we shall fall an easy enough prey to it."

These words, spoken with calmness and courage, had a great effect upon Polly.

"Oh ! yes," she said. "I agree with you there. We must be calm and collected, of course, Luke. That is evident."

"I am glad it is so evident to you," Luke

replied; "for now it will enable you to reason upon what has occurred to you. In the first place, you see, I am here, and well armed; and, in the second, if you go from here, we miss Captain Macheath; and in the third—"

Luke paused.

"Well, in the third—come, Luke, what then?"

"You will forgive me for saying that it is just possible, although I do not assert that such is the case, that you have dreamt all that you fancy you have seen."

"Oh! no—no."

"Of course," added Luke, "I do not mean to say for one moment but that to you it appeared a reality; but it is always as well to mistrust one's own senses in affairs of this kind."

"Think you so?"

"I am sure of it," Luke continued. "Your mind was prepossessed by superstitious feelings. You are very much overcome by fatigue. Your fears are all awakened for the safety of Captain Macheath; and in the midst of all that you lie down to rest, and a slight sleep comes over you, which steeps the judgment in repose and in action, but which leaves the imagination wide awake and master of the brain."

"Well, Luke, perhaps you are right, after all," said Polly. "But I shall be very glad when we leave this mysterious house."

To say that Polly was at all convinced by what Luke said in the matter of the appearance that she had seen, would be to say too much; but his words had the effect of soothing her with a doubt of the reality of the spectre.

"I hope," said Luke, "that you are now convinced there was no reality in what you thought you saw, and that you feel now at peace?"

"I can't gainsay your reasoning," Polly said. "Of course, it may be as you say, but I do not think it. Are all the doors fast?"

"They are."

"Have you examined the walls to see if there are any traces of secret modes of entering the rooms?"

"I have, and all seems to be quite secure."

"I will strive to be content."

She shuddered as she spoke, and looked around her in such a terrified manner that it was quite evident it would be in vain trying to convince herself that what she had heard and saw was not real.

"You will watch over my safety, Luke?" she added.

"With my life."

"I am satisfied. You will be within call?"

"The slightest sound shall bring me to you," Luke replied. "When I have a duty to do, I am not one to shrink from it. I promised Captain Macheath, who, from being his servant, now permits me to think myself his friend, that I would watch over your safety, and I will keep my word."

"Then leave me, Luke," said Polly. "I will not call to you if I can help it unless there be occasion. But if I should do so, you will forgive me."

"Let me beg of you," said Luke, "to grant me one favour."

"What is it?"

"It is that you will give an alarm at once, whether you are certain that there is any real danger or not."

"You are very good and kind to me, Luke," Polly replied, "and I will call to you should anything occur."

Luke left the room and half-closed the door, as it had been before; but when he reached the outer apartment his countenance changed wonderfully.

"Oh! would that we were out of this place," he muttered. "Oh! would that Macheath were back. I dread the next few hours. What may they not bring forth of terror to us?"

It was only wonderful that Luke had been able to put so bold a face upon the matter to Polly as he had done; for if there were any species of fear to which he was particularly obnoxious, they were those which had superstition for their basis.

Luke sat down in the same chair that he had previously occupied.

But now he shifted it along until he got the back of it right against the wall, so that he felt tolerably sure nothing could come behind him, and he was likewise in such a position that he could command a good view of the entire apartment.

"I shall be cold," he said; "but that is better than terrified out of my life, and, perhaps, exposed to all sorts of danger. I will keep my eyes wide open, at all events."

With this resolve, Luke sat glaring into vacancy, letting the fire go out for want of attention.

How still the house was, and how still the whole neighbourhood seemed to be!

It was only now and then that, from afar off, Luke could hear the faint rumble of some hackney-coach or other vehicle as it passed the neighbourhood; and then all was still again as the very grave.

"Oh! Macheath—Macheath!" he whispered to himself, "where are you now? Why do I not hear your welcome tap at the door—why do I not see your face, and feel that all is well?"

Scarcely had Luke got to the end of this reflection, than he heard a faint noise as of someone moving their hands over the wall in one part of the room.

He glanced in that direction; but he could see nothing.

A terrible fear began to take possession of Luke.

Still the strange noise against the wall continued.

If Luke had not been so prepossessed with an idea that there were no supernatural sights and sounds to be met with in that house, he would probably have come to the conclusion that it was just possible the sound he heard might come from the other side of the wall.

But such an idea did not just then strike Luke.

He was prepared for a phantom, and he could not just then turn his attention to what people of real flesh and blood and wickedness might be about to do in that old house.

The odd noise continued.

Luke began to fancy that the light was burning blue.

But that was only fancy, and shows what the imagination can do when it is allowed full scope and power over the judgment and the senses.

Perhaps if Luke had not, more by instinct than reflection, riveted his gaze upon that part of the wall from which the singular sounds proceeded, he would have been in too great a state of alarm to pitch upon it after a little time; but as it was, he never removed his eyes from it.

It was well that he did not.

We must premise, now, that the walls of all the rooms upon that floor were of old wainscot-panelling, as yellow as possible with age, and with abundance of dust collecting upon every available spot upon the mouldings where it could lodge itself, so that a hand passed over the woodwork might be expected to produce just the sort of sound that Luke heard.

It did not take long now to alter the state of affairs in those gloomy old rooms, and the alteration was rather astounding.

At first, when Luke saw that a portion of the old wainscot wall was moving aside, he thought that surely he was dreaming.

But when he saw a flash of light, he took quite a different view of the case.

From where he sat he could observe well all that took place, and now it was strange what a complete revulsion of feeling took place in Luke.

All his ideas that he was about to be subjected to the horrors of some supernatural appearance vanished on the moment, and he became possessed of the idea that it was a mortal and strictly human danger that was now at hand.

"Ghosts do not move panels in walls, nor carry lights," thought Luke ; "and such being the case, I am armed against whatever may now happen."

It was quite evident now that some persons, who were a great deal better acquainted with the old house than either Luke or Macheath was, were now coming into the room through a secret door in the old panelled wall.

Wider and wider opened the tall, narrow slit, until it was about two feet from side to side, and then Luke saw an arm with a small lamp and then a head.

The head was not of the most prepossessing appearance in the world.

"Thieves," thought Luke, "and in all probability murderers, have made this place the scene of their operations. We shall see what they will be at now."

The hand and the head remained for about half a minute at the opening in the wall and retired abruptly, and in a manner that betrayed fright.

Luke was quite at a loss to conceive what could have created the alarm.

But after a little thought he decided in his own mind that it must be the light which was burning in the room, and which, no doubt, gave the depredators the idea that someone was sitting up.

It was quite a good thing that this sudden alarm had been given to the thieves, for it had the effect of giving Luke time to thoroughly recover himself and make such arrangements as would best suffice to meet the danger.

Luke now dodged behind the chair upon which he had been sitting.

He knew well that he could depend upon his pistols, and that they were loaded with care.

He took them both from his pockets and prepared for action.

The feeling of superstitious fear entirely faded away before the real danger that now beset him, and he did not feel the tremor of a single nerve as he waited the reappearance of the man who had taken so stealthy a look into the room.

The only great dread that Luke had was that they should make noise enough to awaken Polly, and that she, perchance, in her fright rushing out, should create more danger than he, Luke, could save her from.

But that, after all, was only a remote possibility.

It was a full minute before the head appeared again at the opening in the wall, and this time it was not accompanied by the hand nor by the light.

The latter, no doubt, was considered to be superfluous, since a candle was burning in the room.

Luke strained his ears to catch the slightest sound that might be made, and he heard a low, rough, harsh voice say—

"I think it's all right enough."

"Hush !" said another voice—"hush !"

"Oh ! there's nobody here," said the first speaker. "I tell you it is all right enough. The room is empty. Come on, will you ?"

Luke kept his eyes fixed upon the opening in the wall, and he saw a man attired in a dark coat step into the room.

Immediately after him came a woman, carrying a light, and the first glance at this woman was sufficient to assure Luke that she was no other than the landlady of the house.

All that had been before only suspicious was now fully confirmed in a moment, and Luke felt convinced that he and his friends had taken up their abode in one of those houses of murder which abounded at that time.

CHAPTER LX.

LUKE AND POLLY ARE BESIEGED IN THE OLD HOUSE.

LUKE kept his eyes firmly fixed upon the pair of worthies who had by such secret means entered the room.

He had a fear that they might yet have further force at hand ; but that was soon dissipated, as no one else made an appearance in the apartment.

Even then Luke could have taken both their lives ; but until he had further proofs of their murderous resolves, he could not bring himself to act violently against them in any way.

In fair and open fight he would not even scruple to use his pistols ; but to shoot anyone from behind the chair looked so much like an assassination, that he dreaded to execute such justice even upon those persons who, let their intentions be what they might, could not come to the room for good.

"Well," said the man to the woman, "you see it's all right enough—don't you now—eh ?"

"Hush ! I say."

"Oh ! I ain't speaking at all loud. Nobody will hear me, I'll be bound."

"But you don't know that."

"Yes, I do," said the man. "Hold your row, will you ? I don't want to be bothered. I don't feel quite well. I'm delicate."

"You always are."

"Well, I know I am," growled the fellow. "I ain't one of the strongest people in the world, you know. You ought to have let me have a drop more brandy."

"But you had a great quantity."

"No, I didn't. Do you call half-a-pint a quantity ? Oh ! dear, I feel rather queer already."

"Come—come, you are all right enough," said the woman. "You know you have done many an odd piece of work in these rooms before tonight."

"Yes, I have ; but somehow I feels rather queerish on this 'ere occasion. But I suppose I must do it. Have you got the brandy-bottle ?"

"I have it with me !" responded the woman, hastily. "There it is ; but don't take too much, for you know you are not very strong, and that if once you get drunk you will be good for nothing at all."

"Oh ! it's all right."

The landlady handed this delightful-looking

CAPTAIN MACHEATH

THE
PRINCE OF THE HIGHWAY.

CAPTAIN MACHEATH STEADIED THE ROPE WITH HIS FOOT AS CHALTON DESCENDED.

gentleman a small flask bottle, and he placed it to his lips, and evidently did not take it away again while anything remained in it.

"Ah!" he said, as he drew a long breath, "there wasn't much after all—not much, by any manner of means."

"Quite enough. And now set to work, for although they may be asleep in the next room we don't know a moment when they may wake up, and in that case I know what you would do."

"What?"

"Run away, to be sure, for you are a coward at heart, you know you are. Oh! you needn't look at me in such a blustering style. I know what you are well enough, and as you get your good and full share of the booty I don't see that I need mind what I say to you."

"Now," said the fellow, "by all that's desperate, if a man had only said one half as much to me, I should have eaten him."

"Peace—peace; set about your work at once. You must make short work of them, I tell you, or there will be no good done."

"Very good."

"It will never do to leave one alive to tell the tale of what has happened in this house."

"I know that. But do you think there's enough booty for the trouble."

"I do," the woman replied. "My opinion of the people is, that they are fugitives, and under such circumstances, they are sure to have brought away with them property of value, which we may as well have as they."

"A great deal better."

"Very good—I quite agree with you there. Now set to work about the business. Come on; I will assist you, as usual. This way—this way. You see there is no one here, so we will make our way to the sleeping room."

"But stop; didn't you say there were three of them?"

"Yes; but I told you one had gone out, and surely you and I can manage the others."

"I should think we could," said the ruffian. "If they are both fast asleep, I don't mind trying what I can do in the matter, and I shouldn't at all wonder if I succeeded. Hem! come on. I'll stab the man while you hold the girl in disguise, you know."

"Yes—yes."

"And then I'll stab her!"

"Will you, indeed!" thought Luke.

The murderous pair proceeded now at a very slow pace, and trod stealthily towards the sleeping chamber.

Before they reached half-way to the door of it Luke rose up from behind the chair.

"Hold!" he cried.

This exclamation, as might be expected, had a startling effect upon the wretches.

The woman uttered a scream and fell to the floor, while the cowardly ruffian of a man, making a rush to leave the room, stumbled over her and fell sprawling.

It was not possible but that all this noise should have the effect of awakening Polly.

She had dropped into an uneasy slumber, and hearing the racket in the outer apartment, she at once sprang from the bed and listened intently.

Luke made a rush towards the prostrate foes with the intent of taking them both prisoners, and then leaving the house; but, as bad luck would have it, he ran against the table and upset the candle.

In a moment the apartment was in complete darkness.

Luke had every reason in the world to expect that some mischief would be attempted; but what most interested him was to protect Polly.

He knew the direction in which he had fallen, and rising rapidly, he ran in the direction of the bed-room, and luckily finding the door he made his way into it at once and closed it.

"Mercy! oh, help!" cried Polly.

"Hush. It is only I," said Luke. "Where is your light?"

"Gone out, Luke. Is there danger?"

"There is."

Luke placed his back against the door, lest the murderers should enter in the dark.

"We are beset in this place," said Luke, "by those whose object it is to take our lives. Has there happened anything to alarm you since you have been in this room?"

"Oh! yes—much—much. Where is my husband?"

"Not yet returned, but we may expect him every minute. Let us listen, and perhaps we may be able to conjecture what these wretches are about."

They listened intently.

All was still, and Luke was lost in wonder as to what had become of the woman and her associate in crime.

He recollected that he had about him the means of getting a light, and he hastily availed himself of this, and shed a bright glow over the room.

"Did your candle burn out?" said Luke.

"No—no; it is here. I can't tell you how it went out, for it died away without apparent cause. Oh! Luke, this place is full of horrors and mysteries."

"It is; but don't be alarmed."

"I cannot help it, Luke," said Polly. "I am truly terrified. I have seen a sight here that the boldest might shrink from."

"Indeed!"

"A being not of this world, Luke, has been in this chamber."

"You do not mean that?"

"In good truth I do. I saw it as plainly as I now see you. I was lying upon the bed between sleeping and waking, and I saw it, Luke."

"You were, perhaps, more sleeping than waking."

"No—no. I know what you would say; you would try to persuade me that it is all a dream; but in truth and indeed it was not so, Luke. But hark! I think I hear something."

"And so do I. Hush!"

They both listened again.

Luke felt convinced that someone was upon the other side of the door, making a strong effort to open it.

He had contrived to shoot a bolt into its socket, so that the door was secure enough against anything but actual violence; but the manner in which the bolt was strained showed that the pressure against it was very great.

"Light the candle," whispered Luke, "and then place it out of the way of the door. I will question the intruder."

Polly took the expiring match from Luke's hand and lit the candle with it, while he called out—

"Who is there?—who is there?"

There was no answer for a minute or two, and Luke thought that he heard a whispered conference going on.

"Who's there ?" he said again.

"Oh ! it's all right," replied a voice. "I am your friend."

"What friend ?"

"Oh ! your friend who left you a little while ago, to be sure. Don't you know me ? Open the door."

"Confound your impudence !" thought Luke. "I should like to get a pop at you, if I could, but I suppose that is quite impossible. Preserve us from such friends, say I."

Luke was standing quite close to the side of the door where the hinges were situated, and owing to the wood being shaken a good deal there was a crevice between the door and the wall.

Luke found, to his cost, that something besides a current of cold air could get through that crevice.

The long blade of a knife was suddenly thrust through, and gave him a slight wound in his side.

"This is a friend's trick, is it ?" said Luke.

A volley of the most terrible oaths was the only reply to this.

Luke did not hesitate a moment in what to do.

He drew one of his pistols from his breast-pocket, and pointing it fairly at the middle panel of the door, he pulled the trigger.

With a crash the bullet sped on its way through the panel.

The report of the pistol in the room was terrific, but still it was not so loud as completely to drown every other noise, and Luke felt quite certain that along with its echoes he heard a cry of pain.

"The rascal is hit," he said.

"Come away, Luke—come away," said Polly. "They will fire again."

"Well thought of," said Luke.

He dropped to the floor in a moment, but yet not a moment too soon, for a bullet went directly over his head.

Luke got out of the line of fire, and also placed Polly out of danger.

She trembled very much, and was evidently in a great state of terror.

"Cheer up," said Luke. "I don't think we shall come to such an end as those wretches outside intend for us. Let us believe that we are born for something better than to be murdered by them."

"Heaven help us !"

Bang—crash ! came another shot into the room.

This one was fired within six inches of the floor, for it was, no doubt, shrewdly suspected that the other had gone too high to do any mischief.

"We are lost," said Polly.

"Not a bit of it," replied Luke ; "let them fire away. They have sent two shots at us and done no mischief, and I am quite sure that my first bullet did its duty. I will give them another on the chance of it."

Luke waited a few seconds before he fired again.

He thought it very likely that whoever had fired the last shot into the bed-room would immediately get out of the way, and he intended to give that individual time to gather confidence to come back again.

After about half a minute Luke fired through the middle panel of the door.

The yell that immediately rose was truly terrifying and Polly placed her hands over her ears so that she might shut out the awful sound.

"This is indeed a dreadful night !" she exclaimed.

"I think I had him there," said Luke.

"Oh, this is too terrible !" cried Polly. "When will my husband come home to us ?"

"Fear nothing," said Luke. "The probability is that our foes will leave us. I am certain I have hit one of them now. That cry could not be mistaken. It was a death-cry."

"But how still they are now, Luke !"

"The stillness of death."

"Alas ! alas ! It is very dreadful to have to do such things."

"Yes," said Luke; "but you will recollect that it is in self-defence. We have the choice of defending ourselves as best we may, or of being murdered in this villainous place."

"I feel, I know how much I am indebted to you. But for you, in all probability, I should now be dead."

"Do not speak in that strain, I beg of you. I am only doing my duty to you and to Captain Macheath ; and, at the same time, you should recollect than I am defending myself."

They were now silent.

Both listened most intently, but strange to say, after the terrific yell all was still.

This silence was perplexing to Luke and Polly.

It left their imagination in full play, and prevented them from taking any steps to rescue themselves from the awkward position in which they were placed.

Indeed, after about five or six minutes, it became scarcely endurable, and Luke felt half inclined to open the door.

Polly, as she looked in his face by the dim light of the candle, which was now getting a long wick, seemed to discern what was passing in his mind, and she said—

"Do not run useless risks, Luke. We are in comparative security at present. Let us remain so."

"As you please," he said ; "but I begin to feel assured that our enemies have left the next room."

"But we do not know that, Luke."

"Certainly not, and, therefore, I will be very careful. Yes, I should like to ascertain the fact, and I think it may be done. In the first place, I can't imagine that we had more to contend with than the man and the woman."

"Think you not ?"

"That is my opinion," Luke replied, "and such being the case, you know, if I have shot the man, there is nothing particular to hinder me from going out of the room. Yet I will try a plan that will let me know if they are in ambush for me."

Polly was terrified at the idea of the door being opened at all ; but she did not like positively to stop Luke from doing what he was about.

She watched him with interest.

Luke took off his coat and hat, and putting the latter on top of a stick that he had in the room, and wrapping his coat round it, he held them both up to about the same height of himself.

He then opened the door cautiously, and thrust out the dummy.

No doubt if the enemy had been there, so likely an opportunity of sending a bullet into his head would not have been allowed to pass ; but nothing occurred, and Luke felt that the siege of the room was raised, and that he and Polly might sally forth in comparative safety.

"Do you see anyone ?" Polly demanded.

"Not a soul," Luke replied. "You may depend we have routed them, and that we have the place to ourselves. Come out of the room. I can't help thinking that we shall be safer here; the windows look to the street. We can call for assistance easily."

"Yes," Polly observed, "and when my husband comes here, we can warn him of the dangers that may await him below."

"We can bring the light, for I have a pistol ready charged in each hand. Hold it as high as you can."

Polly did so, but she and Luke had not advanced half-a-dozen paces into the room when she uttered a cry of horror and tottered into a seat.

She had stepped into a pool of blood.

Lying on his face upon the floor was the ruffian who had accompanied the woman into the room upon their infamous expedition, which had been so signally defeated by Luke's bravery and alertness.

"Dead," said Luke, as he turned the body over with his foot. "Quite dead. That was my last shot."

"This is terrible," cried Polly. "I pray you take me away from this place at once. I can't remain here. The dreadful appearance of that body, and the awful scent of blood in the air, will drive me mad. Oh! take me away at once. We will wait in the street for my husband. I implore you, Luke, to take me away!"

"I will," said Luke. "But pray be calm. You forget that others may be in the house, as well as the woman. Be calm, I pray you, and we'll leave presently."

The tone of voice in which Luke spoke reassured Polly.

She was silent and still, although her feelings were deeply affected by the proximity of the dead body.

Her reason might tell her over and over again that the villain weltering in blood amply deserved his fate; but reason has an up-hill fight ever with the feelings and the imagination, and Polly could not reconcile herself to remain in the same apartment with that dreadful witness of the result of crime before her.

"If I were alone," said Luke, "I would march down to the street door with my pistols in my hands, but I dread to go with you."

"Why do you dread to go with me, Luke?"

"Because I know not what mischief might be done to you in the event of an attack upon us. It looks cowardly to stay here, when, for all we know, there may be nobody but an old woman to interfere with us; but she might rush upon you with a knife, or fire a pistol at you; and what, then, would be the use of my mastery over her if you were hurt or killed?"

"You speak the truth, Luke."

"How could I face Captain Macheath?"

"How indeed!" said Polly. "Say no more, Luke. I will abide by whatever decision you may arrive at."

"Very well," Luke returned. "Then let us remain where we are until Captain Macheath comes home. I will throw up the window and watch for him; or if I should see anyone in the street who looks likely to be able to assist us shall I call to him?"

"Oh! yes, yes."

"But, remember," Luke continued, "it is an important object with the captain to remain hidden in London. You are well aware upon what a thread, so to speak, his life hangs."

"Alas! alas! in the midst of my own trials and dangers I had grown selfish, and, as you say,

Luke, I had forgotten the danger he is in. We will wait for him."

"You have come to a right decision," said Luke, "I feel assured, and one that Captain Macheath will approve of when he comes back. I will now open the window and watch for him, for it is necessary that he should be put upon his guard before he enters the house."

"I will watch for him, too," said Polly, "because I think that will be the better arrangement, seeing that you can keep an eye upon the door of the room in case of a surprise, and so doing will relieve me from looking at that dreadful body."

"As you please; but I will remove the body, for I like the look of it no more than you do."

As he spoke, Luke laid hold of the dead bravo by his feet, and dragging the body into the inner room, closed the door upon it.

Suddenly Polly clapped her hands together with delight.

"He is here! He is here!" she cried.

"Hurrah!" cried Luke. "Call to him."

"I will," she cried. "My husband—my husband!"

Captain Macheath had just come in sight of the house, when he heard Polly calling to him from the window in this way.

CHAPTER LXI.

ON THE ROAD AGAIN.

WE know that the captain had been exceedingly anxious to get back to the mysterious lodging-house, but that he had got so bewildered amid the intricacies of the West-end as quite to lose his way, or he would have been there half an hour earlier than he was.

When, however, he got within sight of the house and saw Polly at the window, he guessed that something was amiss, although it took off more than one half his anxiety to see that she was well and able to call him.

In a moment he was beneath the window.

"Polly—Polly! what would you say to me?" he said. "I have come home as soon as it was possible for me to do so, I assure you."

"Oh! yes, I know that well," Polly cried; "but I am here to warn you. There is murder in this house. Luke and I are prisoners in this room and I am here to warn you."

"Prisoners?"

"Yes. Come to us, but be careful how you come, for there are foes in the shape of assassins in the lower part of the house. We had a narrow escape from them."

"We will soon see that," said the captain.

With one bound he flew at the street door, which, not being fast, opened against his weight.

Not a soul opposed his progress as he proceeded towards the staircase.

If such had been the case, there is very little doubt that, after what Polly had said, it would have fared but badly with the interposer.

He bounded up the stairs and reached the door of the room, which he flung open in a moment, and to Polly's joy held her in his arms the next instant.

"Good Heaven! Luke," he cried, "what is the meaning of all this?"

"The meaning," said Luke, "is, that I am quite delighted to see you. Did you meet no one below?"

"Not a soul,"

"That is strange," said Luke, "for we dreaded to leave the room lest we should be exposed to an attack from someone whom it would be impossible to guard against. They must have forsaken the house."

"Oh! husband—husband!" Polly cried, "what a joy it is to find you returned and quite safe. You have gone through all the prince wanted you to do, and are unhurt?"

"Completely so; and you?"

"Oh! Luke protected me, or I do not think that I should have lived to look upon your face again."

"My heart misgave me when I left you," said Captain Macheath, "that all was not well, and I have endured great anguish of spirit in thinking of you. But let us leave this place at once We can easily get our horses and be off. London is not the sort of place for us. I hate it; and this house is a most ill-omened one. You have been threatened, I suppose?"

"A little more than threatened," said Luke. "I have been compelled to shoot one rascal. His body is in the adjoining room."

"Ah, indeed! Has it come to that?"

"Yes," said Polly, "it has indeed. I thought that we were both lost, and that you and I would never meet again. But come away. There is a weight upon my heart. I cannot breathe in this house. Oh! take me away at once."

"Come, then, we will not remain another minute," said Macheath. "It is sufficient for me that you are both of you unhurt, and that you, Luke, have retaliated on one of the enemy, so we will be off at once. This way. Come—come. Fear nothing, Polly, for, upon my word, I do not think there is a soul in the house besides ourselves now."

"It is no doubt deserted by that hag of a woman," Luke remarked, "and, after all, there were no more than herself and the man whom I shot to oppose me. The midnight murderer does not want many accomplices to do his work."

Polly leant upon Macheath's arm.

He held a pistol ready for immediate service, and Luke followed them closely, likewise with a pistol in his hand, and keeping a wary eye about him, lest suddenly, when they least expected it, they should be attacked.

In this way they reached the street-door, and as they passed out of it without any interruption they were only the more confirmed in their opinion that the woman had but that one man to assist her, and that she had fled from the house.

A sleepy-looking watchman was at the corner of the street, and for a moment Macheath thought of sending him to the house.

He, however, abandoned the idea, as he considered it might get him into an altercation with the guardian of the night as to the propriety of going with him or not.

"I won't trouble the watch," said the captain to Luke; "but I will write to the magistrates about it as soon as convenient, so that it may not be supposed that a murder has been committed in this house, which the appearance of the dead body might otherwise lead the police to think."

"They would be sure to think so," said Luke.

"Not a doubt of it. And now for our horses."

It was not above ten minutes' work to get the horses in readiness.

When they were mounted Captain Macheath considered for a moment or two, and then he uttered the one word—

"Hounslow."

Polly had often heard that that neighbourhood was one in which Macheath had committed some of his most daring exploits, and her heart sank when he thought of going there.

"Oh! husband," she said, "will you be safe in such a neighbourhood?"

"As safe as I am anywhere, Polly."

"Do you think so, Luke?"

Luke did not say anything.

His glance at Macheath showed that he wished to entirely defer to him in the matter.

"I tell you what, Luke," said the captain; "we will go to the old inn at the verge of the heath called the Reindeer, and there we shall be safe enough, I promise you. But I have an idea in my head which, after all, may take us to London again."

"What is that?"

"Why, you know that I have been always most successful with the aristocracy, and I think if I can come out again at the west end of the town that there is still an opening for me. The season for all the principal entertainments of the nobility is close at hand. Vauxhall-gardens will be open, and there will be some half-dozen masquerades at the Opera-house."

"Alas!—alas!" said Polly.

"Why do you cry 'alas?'"

"Because I foresee much danger in all these."

"Oh! no; you are really much mistaken, Polly," said Macheath. "These are the kind of scenes, I assure you, in which I am best able to succeed."

"You do not like the life on the road?" said Luke.

"Yes, I do at times. It is a delightful relief to me to be on a good horse on a cloudy night on the road. The freshness of the country brings a charm to my spirits after a little experience of the saloons of London, and then I tire again, and long to get back again to a London life."

"But you said you hated London," said Polly.

"Ah! I was vexed when I said so," Macheath replied. "This adventure that the prince sent me on, and the danger that I found you had passed through, combined to vex me. But come, here we are fairly on the road to Hounslow. How beautiful and fresh the country is. See how the mist is rising out of the little valley there by Acton."

"It is beautiful," said Polly.

"Very beautiful indeed," added Luke. "Why, when the morning sun shines through it, it looks like a tissue of gold."

"It does. And now it rolls off over the tops of the trees, and you can see the pale blue wreaths of smoke from the chimney-tops, where early fires are being lighted. Ah! I think the country beats the town hollow."

"Yes," said Polly, "the dear country for me. You will both laugh when I tell you that the extent of my desire gets no higher than some pretty little cottage, with its flower garden, and its fruit trees, and perchance a little rivulet bubbling by it, and singing sweet, murmuring sounds the whole day long—"

"Somebody is coming," Macheath interposed, "so we will hear all about love in a cottage another day. Hark! do you hear anything, Luke?"

"Yes, the sound of a horse's hoofs."

"Let us proceed slowly."

"Oh! for my sake—" Polly began.

"Well, dear one, what can I do for your sake?" said the captain, interrupting her.

"Nothing, dear. It is that you should not do something that I pray you, and you understand me."

"I do; you are afraid that I should stop this person?"

"I am," said Macheath.

"Then I promise you that I will not," said Macheath, "and that, if I am not interfered with, I will let him pass me as if I were the sheriff of the county, and he an attorney. Will that satisfy you?"

"It will, Macheath, and I thank you."

By the time this conversation was over a horseman riding at a dashing pace was close at hand. Glancing at him, Macheath perceived that he was some half-pay officer.

"Hilloa!" cried the man as he reached the party. "Hilloa! Halt! I say, halt!"

Captain Macheath drew up, and so did Polly and Luke.

There was a slight—a very slight flush—of colour on the captain's cheek, which both Polly and Luke knew brooded mischief; but the man who had promoted it was too stupid to notice it.

"Come, sir," added the man. "Do you not see that my horse is lame?"

"If you please, sir," said Macheath with an air of affected humility, "I do. It is in the near fore-leg."

"Very well. I don't care which of you dismount, for you seem all pretty well mounted; but I must trouble one of you to lend me your horse, and take mine, till I get to Guildford, where, probably, I shall leave it for you. So be sharp dismounting, one of you, as I am in a great hurry."

Luke looked at Polly, and Polly looked at Luke in amazement.

"Is there anything else, sir," said the captain, "in a small way, that you would be pleased to order, now that you are about it!"

"Come, come—no insolence! Dismount at once, one of you. You are in no hurry, I daresay, and I am; and if you are, that makes no difference to me. Quick—quick!"

"We will consider, sir, just a little, if it is all the same to you," said Macheath. "We hope you won't be violent, sir, if you please, as we are very simple, honest folk."

"Oh! no," said the fellow, stroking his whiskers. "There is no occasion for any violence, I daresay."

"We humbly thank you, sir."

"But perhaps—ah—you—ah—don't know who I am?"

It was clear that the fool was quite gratified with the respect and humility displayed by Captain Macheath.

"Oh! yes, sir, we do."

"Ah! indeed. Who am I?"

Captain Macheath looked him right plainly in the face, as he said, in a clear tone of voice, and with the greatest deliberation—

"The greatest idiot I ever met with in all my life without the shadow of a doubt."

If a thunderbolt had suddenly fallen at his feet the man could not have been more amazed than he was at this speech.

He could do nothing but glare at Captain Macheath for some moments in silence, and so they continued looking at each other.

"Sir," said the stranger, "I begin to think you are a ruffian."

"Sir, I know you are an ass," Macheath retorted.

"A what?" cried the messenger.

"An ass!" replied Macheath, coolly.

"Oh! indeed. Very good, sir. Then allow me to tell you that I am a king's messenger, and that, by virtue of my office, I am empowered to seize any man's horse for the service of the State. This, sir, is my badge of office—the silver hound. Perhaps you have heard of such a thing?"

"It ought to have been a silver donkey!" said Macheath, "and then it might have been mistaken for your portrait."

With a bound of his horse, which sprang forward under the impulse given to it by Macheath, he was close to the messenger, and dashing the muzzle of a pistol right into his mouth, to the detriment of his front teeth, the captain cried—

"Your money or your life, sir! I am a highwayman!"

The messenger fell off his horse, and lay at full length on the road, as if the very fright had killed him.

"Oh! that is enough," cried Polly. "Let us ride on now. That is enough. Come on, I pray you."

"The rascal," said Macheath, "to come with such insolence to me, upon the highway, too. Hold my horse a moment, Luke."

"Oh! you will not kill him?"

"I kill him, Polly?" said the captain, laughing. "Oh! dear, no. Why, what put that idea into your little head, eh?"

"You are not angry then now?"

"Not a whit."

Luke held the captain's horse while he rapidly dismounted and approached the prostrate king's messenger, who, when he saw him coming, managed to get up to his knees.

"Oh! dear sir, spare my life," he whined.

"Confound your life!" said Macheath; "if I were to take it, it is the most worthless article you are possessed of, I daresay. Where were you going?"

"To Guildford, sir, if you please. To the high-sheriff of the county, with a note from the Secretary of State."

"Give it to me."

"Oh—oh! then I shall be cashiered, I shall indeed."

"Give it to me."

With reluctance the messenger handed the letter to Macheath, who put it in his pocket.

"Now give me the silver jackass—I mean the hound—that you have round your neck."

"Oh! dear sir, spare me that; I can assure you that I—"

Captain Macheath took out his pistol again, and at the sight of it the terror of the messenger was so great that he gave up the badge of his office, and a gold watch, and a well-filled purse, all in a moment.

"Now, what's your name, sir?" said Macheath.

"Captain Smith."

"A captain! Indeed! you are a pretty captain. Pray what were you before you became a captain?"

"I was confidential valet to Lord Nhoodel, sir."

"Indeed! That is the way public offices are filled in this country, and the army is disgraced. Farewell, captain. Your horse, I see, has comfortably bolted away through a gap in the hedge into the meadow, and if you value your neck I advise you to take any road but the one you see us pursue. Do you hear?"

MACHEATH HEARD THE SHOUTS OF THE PURSUERS AS HE REACHED THE CARRIAGE.

"Yes—yes!"

The gallant captain fell flat on his back again.

He was afraid that at the last moment Captain Macheath might think it safer to blow his brains out than to leave him to tell the story of how he had been robbed; and then the captain left him and mounted his horse again.

"You have not hurt him?" said Polly.

"Hurt him? Certainly not," Macheath replied. "He is not worth the hurting. He is only frightened a little, and if you were to see him to-morrow by the time he has completely recovered, I have no doubt you would find he was as great a man as ever, and in all probability he will tell how he was attacked upon the highway by a desperate gang of highwaymen, and his property and his despatch to the high-sheriff of the county taken from him."

"There is no doubt of that," said Luke. "But will you not see what the despatch is about?"

"Yes; but it is rather prudent to have a gallop first. Our horses are quite fresh, as they have had a long rest, and a gallop of a couple or three miles will do them more good than harm."

"It will," said Luke.

Upon this they all three started off, and at capital speed passed a couple of milestones, and were close on to a third before Macheath drew rein.

"I do not think that our friend, the king's messenger, will catch us now," he said, smilingly. "Shall we go on to the Reindeer? Here is a lane to the right that leads to it."

"Why, if I might be so bold as to suggest such a thing," said Luke, "I should say that breakfast would not be the most disagreeable sight in the world just now."

"Ah! to be sure. A thousand thanks, Luke. Why, Polly, you must be half famished by this time."

"I must own," Polly replied, "that I am not so romantic but that I can look with pleasure upon my breakfast."

"Come on, then, to the Reindeer; it is only a mile down this lane, and we shall soon be there."

The ground was soon passed over.

Captain Macheath pulled up at the door of the Reindeer, which was a well-known inn upon the border of Hounslow, the landlord looked at him from an upper window, and cried out—

"Why it's Mac— Oh! I mean it's the colonel."

"That's right," said the captain, "caution is the word. When gentlemen travel they don't choose that their name should be blazed about, even to the morning air."

"To be sure not, colonel," cried the landlord. "To be sure, and there are few men who could draw rein at the door of the old Reindeer who would be one-half so welcome as yourself."

"And my friends, I hope too," said Macheath.

"Aye! and a hundred of them if you like."

"Very good. All I want, then, is that you forthwith place your friendship into the shape of a good breakfast."

"That I will do. Wait a minute."

The landlord was soon outside.

"I hope nothing serious is amiss?" he whispered.

"Oh! no," Macheath replied; "only I should like our cattle put into a safe place."

"Yes, I know—where you can lay your hand on your horse's mane at any moment you please?"

"Exactly so. I don't know that there will be

anyone here inquiring for me or anybody like me; but we will take possession of your most private apartment, if you please."

"So you shall."

"Is you daughter, Bessy, at home?"

"To be sure she is."

"Well, you see that young gentleman on the bay horse? Perhaps you will allow Bessy to attend to his comforts."

"Eh—what?"

Captain Macheath laughed.

"Pooh! man, Bessy will not object, particularly when you tell her that it is my wife dressed *en cavalier* for the convenience of travelling."

"Ah! I see; that will do. And now for the breakfast."

CHAPTER LXII.
THE JOURNEY TO GUILDFORD.

THE little adventure with the king's messenger seemed but to have added zest to the capital breakfast which mine host of the Reindeer placed before Captain Macheath, his wife, and Luke.

They enjoyed a hearty laugh over it.

"But, captain," said Luke, "you have not looked at the despatch that the fellow had to carry to the sheriff at Guildford."

"By Jove! no; but I will do so now," Macheath replied. "What can it be all about, I wonder? We shall soon see! I am not very particular about the confidence of State officials."

"Considering," said Luke, "that State officials are not very particular about other folks' confidence, I don't see why you should be."

"Certainly not, Luke. This is the despatch—

"'SIR,—By this you will please to consider it a foremost duty to make every possible exertion for the apprehension of Captain Macheath, the highwayman, and some associates he has with him. His Majesty's Government desire that you spare no expense in the matter, and state that the Treasury will defray all such charges with great willingness. Let this note be a sufficient authority upon your part to call upon the military power to aid you in any emergency connected with the object herein mentioned.—I am, sir, yours very truly,

"'SAMUEL SOUTH, P.S.'"

"What the deuce does he mean by 'P.S.' at the end of his note?" Luke demanded. "It is rather strange."

"Oh! that is easily understood," replied Macheath. "Sir Samuel South is the private secretary for the Home Department, and this is what the 'P.S.' means. The letter has a more significant meaning. It means danger."

"Yes, husband," said Polly. "They hunt you still."

"That is true," the captain replied, "and it is a chase that I don't think they will ever tire of. Well—well, we must meet the exigencies of the moment as best we may. What do you advise, Luke?"

"I hardly know what to say."

"And you, Polly?"

"Ah! you know that I have but one wish, and that is for your safety, and that the only advice I could give you is to keep out of danger."

"That is quite impossible," Macheath rejoined. "Danger is the very air I breathe, and the only way I can get out of it is by going into my grave, so that is not to be thought of any longer. What say you to going on to Guildford at once—or at night, suppose we say? You look fatigued, Polly, so I would like you to rest till nightfall."

"But why to Guildford?"

Captain Macheath laughed.

"It would be a very unhandsome thing not to deliver the letter to the sheriff, don't you think?" said Captain Macheath. "When so great a man as a State official writes to so great a man as a sheriff of a county he likes him to get the epistle. Now what is to hinder us from going to Guildford and seeing what we can do there in the way of business?"

"Oh! husband—husband," exclaimed Polly.

"Oh! what do you fear, my wife?"

"Everything. You are so fond of running into the lion's mouth. I should have thought that Guildford would be the last place you would have thought of going to."

Luke shook his head.

"There, you see," said Macheath, with a smile, "Luke knows much better than you do, Polly. But in all sober seriousness, let me assure you that I do not think that there is any danger in going to Guildford. In the first place, I am confident Captain Smith will not go there. It will take him some days to recover from the fright, and we shall be safe enough."

"But why go at all?"

"I owe this same sheriff a grudge, although he never saw me," Macheath replied. "Once when it could have done him no harm to let me go, he, on the contrary, took a delight in hunting me. I foiled him; but I made a resolve that he should hear of it."

"The captain will go," Luke observed.

"Then he will not go alone," said Polly. "If it must be so we will all go—and yet, pardon me, Luke, for speaking so hastily for you."

"Luke is quite at liberty to go or stay," said Macheath, "a fact concerning which Luke is perfectly well aware, I rather think."

Luke looked hurt.

"Where you go I go," he said. "I thought that was quite sufficiently understood long ago."

"So it was, Luke—so it was," cried Macheath, as he shook him by the hand. "So that is all settled, and we will go to Guildford as soon as the sun has set."

Polly felt that it would be as useless as it would be ungracious to attempt to dissuade Macheath from his project.

She abstained from further persuading him, and quietly retired to enjoy the repose she so greatly needed after the great fatigues she had undergone.

The day soon slipped away, and once more the travellers were in the saddle.

Macheath made some alterations in his appearance, but Polly still retained her masculine attire, and Luke put on a very sober-looking cravat, intending to pass for a clerk.

"If we don't get anything else," said Macheath, "we shall have some amusement; so come on. Good-evening, landlord, and good fortune attend you always, and your fair daughter, Bessy."

"The same to you," cried the landlord; "you are a trump, I must say."

In another moment they were off, and making good speed on the shady side of the lane till they got into the highway.

Then at a more moderate pace they went towards Guildford.

"Now," said Macheath, "I have no doubt but that we shall get an invitation to the sheriff's house; and if so, I am determined to give him

such a lesson as will, I hope, prevent him for the future joining in the hue-and-cry against any unfortunate individual who may become obnoxious to his authority. There is a wide difference between a man doing his duty and going out of his way to be a partisan in the matter."

The air was exceedingly grateful and refreshing to the senses, and even Polly got rid of most of her fears as she rode on by the side of her husband.

The distance they had to travel was by no means great, and they soon came to the outskirts of the town.

Several persons on horseback and on foot passed them.

At length a servant in livery, who was going in the same direction as themselves, was about to pass them at a canter, when Captain Macheath called to him and he drew up.

"Don't let me interrupt you if you are at all hurried," said Captain Macheath, "but can you tell me if the sheriff of the county is at Guildford at the present time?"

"Oh! yes, sir. I am one of his servants. He is staying at his house in Guildford, sir, till Miss Forsyth is married."

"And who is she?"

"His youngest daughter, sir. She is to be married this morning, and then there is going to be a grand ball and a supper, sir, in honour of the event, and at midnight the bride and the bridegroom are going to Paris for a time."

"Oh! indeed," said the captain. "I suppose the bridegroom is some young and handsome man?"

"Young and handsome, sir? Lor' bless you! did you never hear of old Hunkers, the lawyer at Guildford?"

"Never."

"Why, then, sir, that is the man. They do say, but I don't know how true that may be, so I shouldn't like to swear to it, that he is worth some half-a-million of money."

"A good round sum, if he be worth half of it," Macheath observed. "He is older than the lady, then?"

"Just a little, sir," the servant replied. "Miss Annie Forsyth is just seventeen, and old Hunkers is about sixty-eight. That's all the difference, sir. And he is as ugly as a demon, while she is as beautiful as an angel. Why, if she were a child of mine, though I am a poor fellow, she shouldn't be sold to old Hunkers—no! not if I had to beg bread from door to door."

"You are an honest fellow," said Captain Macheath.

"Oh! sir," the man continued, "when I think of the whole affair it turns my blood hot and cold. I know I shall lose my place, for I can't help looking what I think, and I should not be at all surprised if I suddenly break out and say something that may astonish them all. But perhaps I have as good as done it now, for you may be friends of old Hunkers."

"Certainly not."

"Well, I'm glad that he hasn't a friend that looks so much like a gentleman. But it's the sheriff you know there, and that will settle my business all the quicker, I take it?"

"No, my good fellow, we know none of the parties," said Macheath. "My only business with the sheriff is to bring him a letter, and I never saw him in my life, and from what you say of the manner in which he is capable of sacrificing his own child for money I don't want to cultivate his acquaintance. But still, you are an imprudent man."

"I imprudent, sir ?"

"Yes, to be sure. Here you open your heart to the first stranger you meet with upon the road, not knowing at all who he is."

"Ah ! sir, when one's heart is full it will run over, sir. I and Mary, the under-housemaid, you see, sir, are going to make a match of it. We have made up our minds, as soon as we can call fifty golden guineas all our own, to take a country inn. So, you see, sir, after all, I don't care much for the sheriff, nor for old Hunkers, either."

"You are a frank, free-spirited fellow, and I hope we shall meet again," said the captain. "What is your name, my friend ?"

"They call me Robert, sir, but my name is Robert Brown. Nobody thinks of calling me Brown, though. Good-day to you, gentlemen."

Captain Macheath and his friends looked at each other for some few moments in silence after Robert the groom had left them.

"This is but too common a case, I fear," said Polly, at last.

"Common ! It is common. But I hope that it will likewise be common enough for those who hear of such a piece of villainy to do their best to thwart it. It is really and truly too bad."

"It is monstrous," said Luke.

"What kind of idea can this sheriff have of the feelings of his child ?" said Polly.

"None at all," cried Captain Macheath. "You may depend that he is one of those common-place, vulgar souls who fancy that money is everything."

"Calm yourself," said Polly. "I know you feel strongly upon this question. But let me ask you one thing—what can you do in the affair ?"

"Yes," said Luke, "that is the question."

"It is indeed, and in truth it is," replied Captain Macheath. "I feel that I can but make one reply, and that is that I can do absolutely nothing in the matter."

"It is so."

"Well, well, let us go on to Guildford," the captain said, "as quickly as we can, and banish from our minds the melancholy thought, for, in good truth, it is a melancholy one, that there are fathers in the world who will sell their daughters to the highest bidder. It is monstrous."

They had now reached a portion of the road which was bounded by tall banks.

A sound suddenly came to their ears.

It consisted of sobs from someone whose heart seemed bursting with the intensity of grief.

"Who can that be ?" said Macheath, drawing up.

"Hush !" said Polly. "There it is again. I never heard utterance given to so much sorrow before."

The sound of their horses' hoofs did not seem to have had any effect upon the mourner, who was evidently in that extremity of woe that he—for it seemed to be a male voice—had thrown off all regard for the world, its thoughts and opinions, and given himself up wholly and entirely to the expression of his deep affliction.

"Oh ! speak to him," said Polly, "speak to him. It is terrible to hear one so suffering—speak to him."

"It is horrible—I will," the captain replied. "Hold my horse for a moment, Luke. I will get up the bank and see, if I can, who it is."

Macheath sprang from his saddle in a moment and ran up the bank.

When he could look into the meadow beyond, he saw some dark object lying down ; but the sobs and the moaning immediately ceased.

"Hilloa !" said Macheath. "What is the matter ?"

"Nothing," said a faint voice—"nothing."

"Yes ; but it is something."

"No—no ! Go your way in peace and leave me. That is all I ask of you. It is not much of a favour surely ?"

"None at all, and it sounds very reasonable indeed," said Macheath ; "only as you are in great affliction and seem to be a very young man, I offer you frankly and freely such assistance as I can give you. If it be poverty that afflicts you in this way, here is gold."

"No —no—no !"

"If it be sickness you shall mount my horse, and I will take you on to Guildford and see that you are properly attended to," the captain continued. "If it be sorrow, let me tell you that, at one time or another, such is the lot of all, and that it is a poor philosophy that falls down by the roadside to bewail it. You do not answer me. Well, perhaps this is, after all, a very impertinent intrusion upon my part, and I apologise to you for it."

"Oh ! no—no. Kindness can never be impertinent, sir. I thank you with all my heart and soul."

"That is well. Come, now, get up."

"Oh ! no—no. Let me lie here and die."

"Die, did you say ?"

"Yes ; it is my only hope now. What has life to give me in exchange for what I have lost ? I see nothing but despair in the future."

"Indeed !"

"It is so, sir. Farewell !"

"Shall I tell you why you see nothing but despair in the future ?" said the captain.

"How can you possibly know ?"

"Yes, I do know," Macheath replied. "It is just because you cannot see far enough, that is all, my young friend. The future has too many changing hues to be all like despair. Pray, how far into futurity do you think you can see ?"

"The reasoning is all upon your side, sir," said the young man, in a calmer tone, "I am prone to admit that ; but the feeling is all on mine."

"Come, now, rouse yourself up," said Macheath, "and speak to me like a man. I have two friends with me who will likewise advise with you. Despair, indeed ! That is a word that no young man ought to use, except to wonder what it means. It is merely another term for cowardice."

"Do you think so ?"

"I am sure of it. There, now you are upon your feet, and you feel better already. Now, what is the matter ? Tell me at once, and frankly, like a man."

"Sir, I do not know what it is that induces to tell you ; but it seems as if something whisper to me to do so, and I will obey the admonitio In a word, sir, I am a clerk in the service of th sheriff of the county. My name is Harry Lucas, and from the moment I caught a glance of Annie Forsyth, his youngest daughter, I loved her with all my heart."

"Really ?" said the captain, smiling. "Go on."

"Yes, sir ; and once I met her when she was alone—"

"And you told her as much ?"

"Well, I hinted at it," the young man continued ; "but she burst into tears and told me never to think of her, for her father had forced her into acquiescence with a projected marriage with one whom she could never love."

"The cowardly rascal!"

"It was cowardly, sir; and so when I heard that it was all arranged, and that this night my Annie, as I have been in the habit of fondly styling her, was about to be sacrificed, I felt maddened, and came here with a determination to put an end to my existence."

"Pooh—stuff!" said Captain Macheath, contemptuously.

"Stuff, sir, do you say? Do you treat my sorrow with so much cold indifference?"

"Certainly not. I treat only your despair in that way. Why, have you no spirit? Have you no bravery about your love? Were I you I would snatch Annie Forsyth from old Hunkers and her father, even if she stood upon the very steps of the altar."

"Hunkers! Gracious Heavens! then you know—"

"All about it," interposed Macheath. "I know that the sheriff is about to sell his daughter to old Hunkers, and that the ceremony is to take place to-night at twelve."

"Yes—yes."

"And after that they are going to Paris."

"Oh! yes. It is so."

"And I know of a coward, who comes to a field and lies down under a hedge to cry, instead of acting like a man."

"A man!—I will act like a man. By Heaven! I'll blow up the whole of Guildford rather than Hunkers shall have her! I'll throttle Hunkers first. I'll take her away before them all, and woe be to him who stays me!"

CHAPTER LXIII.

THE SHERIFF IS INTERVIEWED.

WHEN young Harry Lucas spoke in this way Macheath burst into a peal of laughter, and then took him by the hand.

"That is the right spirit," he said. "Why didn't you think of all that before—eh?"

"I am ashamed of my folly."

"Nay, it was not folly. No natural feeling ought to be named folly. Chance has made my two friends acquainted with the facts of the case, and as we sincerely sympathise with you and the young girl we will do all we possibly can to aid you."

"I cannot thank you as I ought."

"Don't attempt it. Come this way at once," said the captain.

The young clerk followed Captain Macheath to the road, but there was no occasion to tell Polly and Luke what had taken place, for they had both ridden close to the hedge, and overheard every word.

"In the first place let me ask you a question," said Macheath, "which you ought to have asked yourself some time ago."

"What is it, sir? I will fairly and truly answer it, I assure you, be it what it may."

"Then have you the means—provided you were to marry her—of supporting the sheriff's daughter?"

"Yes."

"That is boldly and well answered," said Macheath. "Now, what are those means?"

"Simply these," Harry Lucas replied. "My mother is in independent circumstances; she resides on a pretty little farm of her own not very far from here, and has a life investment in two thousand pounds, which at her death will come to me."

"Very good," said Macheath. "That is quite sufficient. However, you will easily imagine that if you run off with her the sheriff is not likely to draw his purse-strings in your favour."

"The sheriff, sir, has not a farthing in his purse that he can call his own. He is a hopelessly ruined man, and it is with old Hunkers' money that he hopes to be able to hold up his head in the world."

"That makes his conduct all the worse," Macheath returned, "for if he were well to do himself he might plead that it was his anxiety for his daughter's happiness that makes him act as he does."

"You put the case fairly, sir."

"Well—well, Master Harry Lucas, never mind that. We will do the best we can for you. Do you really think that Annie loves you?"

"Ah! yes. She whispered to me as much one day."

"Oh! that is quite enough," said the captain. Why, you rascal, and yet spoke of dying in yonder meadow after you had won the heart of a young girl? Stuff! Don't let me ever hear of such nonsense again. And now let me tell you that I am bound to the house of the sheriff with a letter addressed to him, urging him to take immediate and active measures for the apprehension of Captain Macheath."

"Indeed, sir?"

"Yes, and you shall go with me."

"But I shall be known in a moment."

"Not so," Macheath said. "We have the means of altering your appearance a little. Luke, I fancy that in the valise you have ample means for transforming our young friend here into something rather different to what he is?"

"Oh! yes," Luke replied "if we could only get a light, and I don't see why we should not arrange all that at the first cottage we come to. The people won't be able to tell but what it is merely some jest that we have on foot."

"Surely not. Let us push on at once. Jump up behind me, Mr. Lucas. My horse will carry double for a short distance without inconveniencing himself in the least."

"For Annie I will do anything," said the young man, as he sprang upon the horse's back. "You have given me a hope which, I trust, will only be crushed along with my existence. But will you pardon me for asking who you are?"

"Permit me to keep that a secret for the present."

"Pardon me for asking you the question. I had no right to do so. All I ought to think of doing is to thank you for your great kindness to me."

"I see a light," said Luke. "We are close upon some house."

"I know it well," said young Lucas. "It is the first of a few detached cottages, occupied by laundresses, at the commencement of the town. A little further on you will see the lamps burning in High-street."

"That will do," said Macheath.

He dismounted and rapped at the cottage door. The summons was answered by a woman.

"We want you to permit us the use of your fire-side for a few moments, and for which we will pay you what you please," said Macheath. "We are intent upon a little frolic, that is all. It is one that has no harm in it,"

"Oh ! certainly. Walk in, gentlemen."

"I will hold the horses," said Polly.

"Nay, bring them into the garden, and tie them by their bridles," Macheath returned. "They will not stray then."

This was done, and the whole party entered the laundress' cottage.

Luke brought with him the valise, and to the astonishment of the woman, and also to the surprise of Harry Lucas, he took from it a complete change of gentlemanly attire, and a pair of false moustachios, which, when put on, so completely altered the young man, that the most intimate associates would not have known him.

In fact, when he was completely disguised by Luke, and took a glance at himself in the little glass on the laundress' chimney-piece, he started back, as he exclaimed—

"This is truly wonderful !"

"I hope, gentlemen," said the laundress, "that you are after no mischief."

"None in the least," Macheath replied, "I assure you again that it is a harmless frolic, and contemplates doing good instead of evil."

As he spoke he placed a guinea in her hand, which acted like a charm, for it banished all her scruples at once, and she did not stand upright again while they remained in the cottage, but kept up such a profusion of curtseys, that it was a relief to them all to get away.

Macheath enjoined her to secrecy, and they left her calling down upon herself most exemplary vengeance and all judgments if she ever said a word about the affair.

"Confound that woman !" said Macheath; "what a tongue she has, to be sure."

"She has indeed," laughed Polly. "I can hear her yet."

They found the horses all right, and then as the distance to the town was very short, Harry Lucas said he would rather walk it, and he was rather solicitous to know what plan of operation Macheath had concocted with regard to Annie Forsyth.

"Upon my word," said the captain, "you ask me a question that I confess puzzles me. We must be entirely guided by circumstances. All we know just now is that it wants good four hours to midnight, and, therefore, Annie is not married; and all I can see my way in is, that no doubt the sheriff will ask us to stay to the wedding, and that circumstances must be our guide as to what further proceedings we are to adopt."

"One thing," said Polly—"one thing will be very essential, and that is, that Mr. Lucas should, as soon as possible, procure an interview with Annie, so as to prepare her with the idea that something will be done."

"Oh ! yes—yes," said Harry Lucas. "I am sure that, by this time, her positive horror at the match must overcome every other feeling."

"This way for the sheriff's house," said the young lover. "It is the largest one in the town. This way, gentlemen, if you please, round this corner."

They turned rather abruptly, and came to the High-street, when there could not be any doubt as to which was the sheriff's house, for it was illuminated from the basement to attic.

A band of music in the roadway immediately facing the house was executing most horribly, out of all time and tune, some of what were called popular airs, and the whole town seemed to be quite in an uproar upon the occasion of the wedding.

"What a strange hour for the ceremony twelve at night is ?" said Polly.

"It is," replied Lucas; "but I was given to understand that such was the wish of the bride. What could have been her motives, except that she might avoid observation, I do not know."

"She should never have consented at all," added Polly; "she must be a very weak-minded girl."

"I beg your pardon," said Lucas—"I beg your pardon, young sir. She is not a weak-minded girl. She is as admirable in her mind, as she is beautiful in her person. Pardon me for contradicting you, but to my heart she is all goodness and all perfection."

"Believe me," Polly returned, "I do not think the worse of you for this genuine and noble confidence in her whom you love. It is my prayer that you may ever feel towards her as you do now."

"Oh ! I can know no change."

"You are a real lover, and deserve to be happy."

Harry Lucas was raised in Polly's estimation by the manner in which he had defended Annie Forsyth from even the shadow of blame, and she was now as willing as Macheath could be to do all that was possible to save the young girl from the agony of an union with one so unsuited to her as old Hunkers.

"Hush !" said Lucas, as he tremblingly laid his hand upon Captain Macheath's arm. "Here we are at the door of the house. Dare I enter it ?"

"To be sure. Follow me, and put a bold face upon the matter."

CHAPTER LXIV.

CAPTAIN MACHEATH ASTONISHES THE OLD BRIDEGROOM.

A THRONG of servants filled the hall of the sheriff's house.

Everything in and about the place had the appearance of wealth, and no wonder, for rich old Hunkers paid for all, and he had more money than even the exaggerated reports gave him credit for.

The entire house was handsomely fitted up, and a number of guests had arrived.

They were for the greater part the sheriff's creditors, who, now that they fancied he was selling his child for gold to pay them, decided that he was a very nice man, and that they always thought so.

There were some even who went so far as to launch out in praise of old Hunkers himself.

Alas ! what will people not do when there is plenty of money to gild over the follies and offences of others.

One of the servants, seeing that four strangers entered the hall, at once advanced to them, and said, politely—

"Will you favour me with your names, gentlemen ? You are the guests of the sheriff, I presume ?"

"No," Macheath replied. "I am come upon business."

"Business, sir ?"

The servant looked aghast at the idea of anybody coming on business at such a time.

"Yes," added Macheath; "you will be so good as to tell the sheriff that a gentleman from the Secretary of State wishes to see him."

CAPTAIN MACHEATH

THE
PRINCE OF THE HIGHWAY.

LUKE SAW AN ARM WITH A LAMP AND THEN A HEAD.

NO. 22.

The servant made a very low bow.

"Please, gentlemen, to step this way," he said.

They were now led into a reception-room that was blazing with wax-lights and fitted up with great taste and luxury.

The bow windows were filled with choice plants, and, take the room for all in all, did great credit to the upholsterer.

"I will tell my master, sir, that you are here," said the servant.

He then retired; but before the friends could make a single observation to each other, the door of the room opened, and there came an old man attired in a style that made his age look positively repulsive: he had on such a dress as some youth might have worn on his wedding day.

He stooped very much, and his form looked like an old parchment bag half stuffed out with rags.

His teeth projected from his lips, and his eyes were half hidden beneath his shaggy brows.

He looked more like a hideous old ape than a man, and the gaudy apparel that he wore was certainly, upon his part, a singular exhibition of bad taste and folly.

Tottering on his spindle-shanks into the middle of the room, this old being cried, or rather mumbled—

"Where is the sheriff—where is the sheriff? I want the sheriff! I—I want him! Where is he?"

"Hunkers," whispered Harry Lucas in Macheath's ear.

"I thought as much," said the captain.

"Eh—eh? What do you say?" cried old Hunkers. "Have you seen the sheriff?"

"Worthy sir, no," said Macheath; "but allow me to congratulate you upon this happy occasion."

"Eh? Who are you—who are you?"

"A gentleman from London, sir. Nobody, I declare, would guess now, Mr. Hunkers, to look at you, that you were fifty years of age."

"Fifty—eh? Did you say fifty?"

"I did, sir."

Old Hunkers was quite delighted to have no less than eighteen years at once taken off his age, and then to be told that he looked younger even than that showed him to be.

He grinned and mashed his old jaws together, and perked himself up, and strove to put on a gay air.

"Why, a—a—yes, eh? I rather think that I carry my age well," he said.

"No one better, sir?"

"Ah!—you think so?—eh? Well, now, just looking at me with the advantages of dress, now, how old—eh?—how old should you say that I was if you saw me for the first time, eh—eh?"

"Come a little more into the light, sir."

"Yes—yes—eh? Well, now?"

"Just turn round, sir, and let me get a good look at you. Round again, sir. That will do."

"Well—eh?—well, now, what do you think?"

"I should say at once, then, that you were about five or six-and-forty," said Macheath.

"Do you mean it?"

"I do indeed, Mr. Hunkers. I have seen all conditions of men, and am generally considered, I assure you, to be rather a fair judge. But we will hear what my friends say. What do you think?"

"I differ from you a little," said Polly. "I think the gentleman scarcely looks forty-two at the utmost."

"And," said Luke, "when you look at his back he don't look that. A fine figure never really looks old."

The old man was so delighted that he laughed until he brought on a great fit of coughing.

He was compelled to sink into a chair while Macheath patted him on the back.

"I—I am better now!" he gasped. "It was a—a—something flew down my throat. Thank you—very gentlemanly people indeed—creditors of the sheriff, no doubt, but very gentlemanly men. Oh —oh, dear, I am afraid the day will be too much for me. Oh, dear!"

At this moment a portly-looking personage entered the room.

He had a great fat face, and indulgence and self were the obvious characteristics of his mind. This was the sheriff.

This was the man who wanted to sell his daughter to old Hunkers.

"Some gentleman wished to speak to me," said the sheriff, in a pompous tone.

"I am that gentleman," said Captain Macheath, advancing. "I am charged with a letter to you, sir, from the Secretary of State."

"Oh! very good, sir, very good," observed the sheriff. "Pray take a seat, sir, if you please. It gives me great pleasure to hear from my friend the Secretary of State. Oh! Mr. Hunkers, pray pardon me, my dear sir, I did not see you. None of my lazy fellows told me you had come, my dear sir. I hope I see you well?"

"Pretty well, Mr. Sheriff, pretty well. I wonder my servants in the hall did not tell you their master was here—eh?—ah!"

It was quite clear from this little bit of badinage that old Hunkers felt a gratification in humbling the sheriff, whose great fat face took a different colour as the old man spoke.

"Ha—ha!" he laughed, "you are facetious, sir."

"Oh! dear no, not at all—not at all," said old Hunkers. "Never—never, I assure you. Only this affair costs me a trifle you know—eh?"

"Yes, my dear sir, yes—certainly, as you say," said the sheriff, uneasily. "A good joke, truly. Will you permit me to read this letter, Mr. Hunkers?"

"Yes, oh! yes; you may sit down, too, upon one of my chairs, Mr. Sheriff, while I reach some wine for these gentlemen."

The sheriff looked as if it would have given him the greatest satisfaction to have crushed Hunkers; but he bottled up his wrath and smiled as he read the letter.

"Why, Mr. Hunkers," said the sheriff, "this letter, from my friend the Secretary of State, begs me to be so good as to do what I can to apprehend Captain Macheath."

"Indeed!"

"Yes, sir; and, of course, I shall write my friend a suitable reply."

"Oh! pooh—stuff. Don't call him your friend. He is no such thing," said Hunkers. "You know as well as I do that he don't know you from Adam, and that it is only an official letter, that's all, and if he thought you were so poor as you are, he would remove you from the commission of the peace —ha!"

"How facetious you are to-night," said the sheriff, biting his lips.

Then turning to Macheath, he said—

"Gentlemen, I am very much obliged, and need not detain you. I will send one of my servants with a reply to the Secretary of State."

"One of mine you mean," said Hunkers.

"As you please, sir. Hang it!" said the sheriff.

"Eh? What does he say?" cried Hunkers, "I didn't hear it."

"Cursed old thief!" muttered the sheriff, as he walked to one of the windows to try and recover his temper.

After a few minutes he returned with a bland smile.

"Good evening, gentlemen," he said.

"Stop," said old Hunkers. "I know a gentleman when I see one, and it's quite a treat to have good comj a iy at one's wedding instead of a parcel of people who will come because somebody owes them money. Gentlemen, will you do me the favour of staying to the ball and supper?"

"With pleasure," Macheath replied.

"Well—but—" interposed the sheriff, "I—I—"

"Yes, you are quite right," interrupted Hunkers. "You have nothing in the world to do with it. I pay for all."

The sheriff bowed.

"And so," continued Hunkers, "I rather think I may be allowed the little privilege of inviting who I like. Pray step upstairs, gentlemen. You will find refreshments there in abundance, and my servants will attend upon you. The sheriff is my guest likewise, and a very nice man he is when you come to know him so well as I do, and how to manage him. Ah—eh?"

The sheriff could not speak for anger, and Macheath and his friends, highly amused, went upstairs to a handsome drawing-room on the first floor.

The moment the sheriff was alone with old Hunkers, he turned to him, and, half in anger half in entreaty, he said to him—

"Oh! Mr. Hunkers, how is it that you take a pleasure in the presence of others in talking of this matter, which, between you and me, ought to be kept perfectly private."

"Private—private! What do you mean, Mr. Sheriff?"

"I allude to our little money arrangements, Mr. Hunkers, and I cannot help saying that I think it is too bad—much too bad of you always to be teasing and twitting me with the fact that you are the richer man of the two."

"Richer? Oh—oh—oh!"

"What do you mean, sir?"

"Why, that anybody may be richer than you, and yet have nothing at all, Mr. Sheriff," Hunkers replied. "You are five thousand pounds in debt, and that makes you, you know, five thousand pounds more than a beggar. Eh—don't it?"

"Sir, this is conduct—these are expressions—that—that—"

"You won't put up with. Very good, Mr. Sheriff. I can keep my money, and you can keep your daughter."

"But, Mr. Hunkers—"

"Good evening, Mr. Sheriff," the old man spluttered. "If you are not pleased with my way and my money I can carry them elsewhere."

"Stop—stop, my dear sir. You misunderstand me—indeed you do. I beg of you only to be a little considerate. That is all, my good friend, Mr. Hunkers, and before strangers, too. That is all I ask of you."

"Yes; but ain't it true that you are a beggar?"

"Well—well!"

"Oh! indeed. Why, what a humbug you are, Mr. Sheriff."

"Sir!"

Old Hunkers made no further remark but tottered upstairs, and as he went he rubbed his old hands gleefully.

The cogitations of the sheriff, when he was alone, were of much the same character as regarded their gross selfishness.

"Curse that old rascal!" he said. "If it wasn't that he is as rich as I don't know what, I would have kicked him out of the house at once; but what can I do? Let him have Annie? It's quite a necessary sacrifice, for what would become of my comforts, I should like to know, if he didn't lend or give me money?"

This was the way the worthy sheriff reasoned; and then, putting on as smiling a face as he could, he followed old Hunkers upstairs to the drawing-room, where our four friends were already arrived.

Poor Harry Lucas was in such a state of agitation for fear Annie should be in the drawing-room, that Macheath was afraid he would betray himself.

"Remember, Mr. Lucas," he whispered, "that you have our incognito to see to as well as your own, and that if you are so imprudent as to let it be known who you are, we shall be under the necessity of leaving the house at once."

"I will be careful—indeed I will."

"Be calm. Come in now."

Luckily for Harry Lucas, Annie was not in the room.

The fact is, the poor young thing was at that moment lying upon her bed in an agony of tears, and wishing herself dead rather than the bride of old Hunkers.

There were twelve or fourteen guests in the drawing-room, so that the entrance of Macheath and his friends did not excite much attention.

This was a state of things which gave the confederates an opportunity of saying a few words to each other.

"Now, you must take the first opportunity you can of getting a few minutes' private conversation with Annie," Macheath said to Lucas.

"Oh! would that I could."

"You can and must," urged the captain. "If you determine upon doing so, you will find no great difficulty. It is quite essential you should ascertain her feelings with regard to the present arrangements, and whether she will aid us in anything we may attempt."

"Yes—oh! yes. I understand. I will try."

"Very good. You must follow her from the room boldly when she leaves. In the crowd and confusion it will not be noticed whether you are going downstairs to the reception-room or not."

"Hush!" said Polly. "Here is Hunkers."

Rubbing his old withered hands together, Hunkers entered the room, and glanced about to see if the bride were there.

A darker shade came over the old man's face when he found that she was absent.

"Pray, ma'am, have you seen Miss Forsyth?" he asked.

"No, Mr. Hunkers, she has not come downstairs yet; but she will be here directly."

Presently the door opened, and the bride entered the room.

Annie Forsyth was truly a beautiful girl.

She had the sweetest blue eyes in all the world, and a mass of dark glossy hair; her complexion was delicately fair, and her mouth was beautifully shaped.

"Oh! my Annie," whispered Lucas.

"Hush," said Macheath—"hush!"

Old Hunkers hobbled up to the girl.

He seemed as though he would devour her with his greedy eyes.

"Well, my dear—eh?" he said. "How are you? Quite well?"

Annie shuddered; but what reply she made was uttered in too low a tone to reach the ears of Captain Macheath.

"Ah!" said the sheriff, rubbing his great fat hands together. "There is nothing like love in this world, is there now?"

"And gold?" said Hunkers—"and gold, eh?"

"Why, a—yes, that is to say—and gold."

Harry Lucas was in such a rage that he asked Captain Macheath if he did not think the best plan would be for him to throw old Hunkers out of the window and so make an end of him.

"No," said Macheath. "Come over to where they are, and let us hear, if we can, what they say. You see that they are generally avoided. Luke, you engage that Miss White in conversation, that she may not interrupt us."

"I will," Luke replied, readily.

Macheath, Polly, and Lucas contrived, without exciting attention, to place themselves so close to old Hunkers and Annie that they with ease overheard all they said.

Poor Annie was all but broken-hearted at the dismal prospect before her.

"Well, my dear, ain't you delighted to think that we shall soon be man and wife?"

"No, sir."

"Dear me—eh?—you surprise me? Most girls are pleased to get married, and I don't see why you should be an exception."

"Mr. Hunkers," Annie replied, "I love another, and if you marry me it will be at your own risk, I warn you. Will not that move you?"

"Not a whit."

"Oh! horror—horror. I cannot and will not make this frightful sacrifice."

"Then you destroy your father."

"Mr. Hunkers," Annie pleaded, "you are rich —very rich; no one knows, as I have heard you say yourself, the extent of your wealth. Oh! sir, could you not save the father and spare the child?"

"Yes, I could."

"And you will—you relent? Oh! tell me that you will."

"Certainly not."

Annie shuddered and said no more.

"I tell you, girl, you shall be mine," old Hunkers continued. "I have made up my mind to it, or your father shall sleep even this night in prison. To provide against any emergency, I have a baliff in the house even now, who, at a word from me, will arrest him, and then if he likes to cut his throat, he shall have every chance of so doing."

CHAPTER LXV.

ANNIE PERPLEXES THE DESIGN OF THE CONFEDERATES.

ANNIE FORSYTH was making her way as rapidly as she could to her boudoir after the painful interview she had had with old Hunkers, and it was fortunate that Harry Lucas was just in time to see which way she went.

Luckily, there was no one in the way, so, with a bounding step, and taking three stairs at a time, Harry ascended to the second floor; but before he could reach the landing, Annie, little suspecting who was in the house, had reached her own room and closed the door.

"Which is her room?" said Lucas to himself.

"Ah! yes, I recollect. This must be the door, according to the plan of the house, of the room through the window of which I used to throw bouquets of flowers that it cost me no little trouble to get."

He approached the door and listened.

The sound of someone audibly sobbing within confirmed him.

"It is her room," he said, "and that is her voice. My Annie, I come to save you. I am here—I am here."

He placed his hand upon the door as he spoke and turned it.

The girl was kneeling on the floor, with her face resting upon her hands upon the seat of an easy-chair, and she was sobbing bitterly.

"Annie!—my Annie!" cried Lucas.

With a cry of surprise and terror she sprang to her feet.

"Annie!—dear, dear Annie!"

Poor Lucas quite forgot at that moment that he was disguised.

"Oh! Heavens!" she cried, "what is the meaning of this? Help!"

"Hush—Annie, hush! Do you not know me?"

"Know you? Oh! no—no."

"Not know Harry Lucas?"

"Harry Lucas?"

"Yes. Oh! look at me, and satisfy yourself that I am indeed the Harry Lucas who loves you so well, and who, at least, thought he would live in your remembrance."

He smiled, and tore off the false moustachois.

With a cry of joy she flung herself into his arms.

"Harry—Harry, you have come to save me?"

"I have."

"I thought that you had forsaken me, indeed I did. They said you had left Guildford. Oh! what a world of agony I have suffered since last we met. Harry—Harry, you will not believe what I have suffered."

"My darling," he said, "I have indeed come to save you. You shall not be made the victim of this detestable marriage."

"No—no, I cannot wed that vile man, I cannot—I cannot."

"You shall not."

"Hush! What is that? I hear footsteps."

"So do I."

"Someone comes, Harry—hide. No; I will make the door fast. It may be someone coming here."

She flew to the door and fastened it just as someone tapped at it.

It was then with great difficulty that she could muster composure sufficient to speak.

"Who is there?"

"It is only I, my dear," said Miss White.

"Well?"

"Open the door, love. I want to speak to you."

"I will soon return to the drawing-room, Miss White—very soon, and then I will seek you."

"But it is only I, my love—it is Cousin White; don't you hear, Annie?—Miss White, my dear. Open the door."

"Not now, cousin. What is it you have to say?"

"Why, it is, that if I were you, I would die before I married that old ape. There now! I have said my say, and I feel all the easier."

With these words the spinster bustled away from

the door, and descended to the drawing-room to give the sheriff a second edition of her opinion.

Annie turned her pale, tearful face towards Harry Lucas, and he stepped up to her.

"You see," he said, "what everyone who dares to think at all thinks of this dreadful union."

"Harry—Harry, what would you have me do?"

"Fly with me at once from this house. I will take you to my home, and we shall be happy,"

"But—but—"

"Nay," Harry cried, "do not begin to doubt now, my darling Annie. You know that I love you with all my heart, and if you only think you love me a little while we shall be happy. I happened, while below, to overhear all that passed between you and old Hunkers a little while ago."

"Then, Harry, you heard his threats against my father," Annie said; "you heard how he had, with a diabolical ingenuity, arranged, that in the event of my refusing him my hand, he would this very night cast my father into gaol."

"Yes. I heard all that, Annie."

"Well, what can I do? What can you say to it?"

"Simply that I do not see that it constitutes a sufficient reason for you to commit worse than suicide."

"I commit suicide?"

"Yes; is it not a thousand times worse to go into church and vow that you love and honour Hunkers?"

"Oh! Heaven direct me—Heaven direct me!" Annie cried. "What shall I do?—what shall I do?"

"Come away with me at once. I have friends here who are firm and true to me, and who will aid us. Only say the word, and, in open defiance of them all, we will fly from this place."

"I dare not. About the power of Hunkers to throw my father into gaol there can be no mistake. Such things are done every day."

"Yes; and how much less cruel, by a million times, would that circumstance be than your sacrifice to Hunkers? Oh! Annie, what do you think of the man who would purchase his own ease and security at such a sacrifice? Answer me that, dearest?"

"Leave me—leave me, Harry! I say leave me. You will drive me mad! I must save my father! Say no more to me if ever you loved me."

Terrified at her manner Harry Lucas hastily left the room.

Quite shocked and bewildered at the manner in which Annie had dismissed him from her presence poor Harry Lucas marched down the staircase to seek the advice of his friends in the drawing-room.

Luckily Captain Macheath was near the door, and saw the state of agitation he was in.

"Why, you are out of your mind, my friend," said Macheath. "Come out into the street if you have anything to tell us. The servants will know us again when we return."

"It is no use to return. I had better die at once. I will take poison to-night, and there will be an end to all my sorrows at once."

"No, you must come downstairs, I tell you. Where are our hats, I wonder?"

"In the reception-room below," said Luke. "This way. Be calm, Mr. Lucas, whatever you do, for already some of the servants are looking at us with rather suspicious eyes."

They all four sallied out into the street then,

and after they had got some distance from the sheriff's house, they paused in rather a dark spot close to a garden wall.

"Now, Lucas," said Macheath, when he knew all, "just you listen to me. If old Hunkers weds Annie to-night, blame me for it."

"He will not wed her," said Luke.

"He will not?" cried Lucas.

"No," added Luke, as he pointed to Captain Macheath. "He has said that he will not, and I will take his word in preference to the whole of the arrangements of the sheriff, and all the determinations of old Hunkers."

"You amaze me," said Harry Lucas. "Are you a conjuror, sir? or what occult powers have you that enable you, in defiance of the intentions, apparently as fixed as fate, of other people, to say what shall be and what shall not?"

"No," observed Captain Macheath, with a smile; "I am not a conjuror, but I have an indomitable will which nothing can subdue. I hold it as a principle that there are very few things indeed in the world that a man may not do, if he has the pluck."

"You amaze me!" said Harry Lucas again.

"Well, I hope you will be pleased as well as amazed. What is the time?"

"Half-past ten," said Luke.

"Very good, and the wedding is not to take place till twelve. We have plenty of time to manage matters in. Where does Hunkers reside, Mr. Lucas? Is his dwelling in Guildford?"

"Oh! yes. He occupies a detached house near the outskirts of the town, where he carries on his money-lending by which he has made such a fortune."

"Good—that will do," said Macheath. "Now let us got to Hunkers' house at once, for it is from there we will begin our operations."

Harry Lucas looked thoroughly bewildered.

He could not imagine what they were to do at Hunkers' house; but the manner in which Captain Macheath had spoken gave him a gleam of hope.

"I will obey your directions implicitly," he said; "and of one thing I feel assured, which is, if you cannot help me out of this difficulty and distress, no one can."

"Come on then at once," added Captain Macheath. "It is well to lose no time."

Of course, the town of Guildford was well known to Harry Lucas.

He had no difficulty whatever in leading the friends to the money-lender's house.

It was a gloomy looking place, enclosed by a brick wall.

"Now tell me," said Captain Macheath. "Does he keep many servants?"

"Many servants?—not he. An old woman and a boy are all his household, and he nearly starves them to death. "No—no. Hunkers is not the sort of man to allow himself to be eaten up by servants."

"Well, so I should suppose," Macheath remarked. "And now we will see who is at home."

With this, he, finding that the great gates were fastened, rang the bell.

After about two or three minutes waiting, there came an old woman, carrying a lantern, and hobbling along in such a manner that she seemed almost more ancient than her old master.

"What is it?" she cried, stopping short six paces from the gate as though she suspected someone might put his hand through the bars and catch hold of her. "What is it—eh?"

Captain Macheath thought that with this "eh?" she had very much the manner of old Hunkers himself.

Probably she was a relation, or had caught his style of speaking by long residence with him.

"Mr. Hunkers, ma'am—I want to see Mr. Hunkers," said the captain in a hurried tone of voice.

"Then he ain't at home."

"Well, but—"

"Oh! it's no use bothering," said the old woman. "I tell you he ain't at home, so you may as well go away at once, for you won't be let in here. A likely thing, indeed, that I am going to open the gate to every jackanapes that comes and says he wants to see Hunkers."

"But, my good woman—"

"Go away, I say. You have got your answer, I hope."

"Come—come, don't be foolish," said Macheath. "I daresay Mr. Hunkers, as he is not quite a youth, has gone to bed by this time, for it is close on to eleven; but if you will tell him that I have come to pay him the three hundred pounds due to him, he will see me, without a doubt."

"Three hundred pounds, do you say?" said the woman.

"Yes, that is the amount; and if he don't take it to-night, there is a great probability that he will never have the chance again to do so."

"You don't mean that? Stop!" cried the hag.

"Oh! I can't stop to dispute with you about it. If you like to take the consequences of refusing to let me see him, why there's an end of it."

"No. But don't go. Three hundred pounds—what a sum of money! Stop! I assure you he is not here. The fact is, sir, the old fool has gone to get married to a little bit of a girl that might be his grandchild."

"You don't mean that, surely?" Macheath rejoined.

"Yes; but I do, though," the old woman replied. "I'll lead her a pretty life, though, when she comes here; I'll be bound she sha'n't be able to say her soul is her own. But come in, sir; I will send Dick for Hunkers, and if he were in the middle of the marriage ceremony he would come to the money, I know, the old villain!"

With this the old woman opened the gate, but she was rather alarmed when so large a number of people as four marched in.

"Don't be alarmed," said Macheath. "It's all right; these are friends of mine."

CHAPTER LXVI.

HUNKERS DOES NOT GET HIS THREE HUNDRED POUNDS.

THE old dame was anything but pleased.

The fact was that Captain Macheath only had stood forward and conversed with her at the gate, and she had no idea that there were three other persons besides.

She trembled so much with anger and alarm that she could hardly hold the lantern.

"You are distressing yourself for nothing, my good madam," said the captain. "In this gentleman with the mustachios you see the young officer who borrowed the money. In me you see an attorney, who feels that it ought to be paid. In this young man," turning to Polly, "you see my clerk, and in this gentleman," turning to Luke, "you see a friend of the young officer's; so it is all right, I assure you."

"I hope it is," grumbled the old woman; "but I can tell you that if you were all the housebreakers and highwaymen in the world, you would get nothing here, for beyond two dozen red herrings and the dregs of a cask of small beer, there's nothing in the house; and as for his money, Hunkers is too good a judge to leave that at home."

"We neither want his herrings, nor his beer, nor his money," Macheath said. "We came to pay him what is due to him, and then we will be off at once, for we have no desire to stay here."

"Very well, I'll send Dick to the sheriff's house. You must know the old idiot is going to be married to little Miss Annie, the sheriff's daughter. Nothing would serve him but her dainty ladyship. Bah! I hate such folly."

"So do we."

"And the little slut is not above seventeen—a mere child that ought to be kept in a nursery."

"So she ought," assented Captain Macheath. "Highly proper. That is precisely our opinion of the matter, madam. And now, if you will be so good as to send the Dick that you speak of, madam, to Mr. Hunkers, we shall be very much obliged to you indeed."

By this time the old woman had led them to the house, and introduced them into one of the most miserable of all miserable parlours conceivable.

It was quite clear that the grate had not had a fire in it for years, and the few articles of furniture that were in the room were of the commonest and most wretched description.

The total value of everything in the apartment could not possibly exceed the sum of five shillings.

"This is the best parlour," said the old woman, "and, I suppose, this is where the bride thinks she will sit when she comes home; but she sha'n't. The things cost a deal of money."

"So I should think," said Macheath.

"Ah! you may say that. Don't put your foot on the rail of the chair, young man. What do you mean by it?"

"I won't," Polly replied, demurely. "I forgot, at the moment, that I was in such a gorgeous place, I assure you, madam."

"Forget, indeed! I am astonished at you!" croaked the old woman. "Why, that chair, only sixteen years ago, cost a matter of eightpence, and I do believe it was worth twopence more. But I will send that rascal of a boy to Hunkers. Oh! gentlemen, you don't know what a hand I have with that boy. It's nothing with him but eat—eat—eat from morning till night, and he makes no more of a penny loaf than as if it cost nothing at all. Dick—Dick—Dick, I say!"

"Here I am!" said a voice.

"Come here, you vile, gormandizing wretch, you, and take the gentleman's message."

"Well, here I am," said the boy; "precious hungry, as usual. You haven't got such a thing as a pound of rumpsteak and ingins about you, have you, Mrs. Cottle, and something for to wash it down with?"

"Oh! you vile wretch. Gentlemen, I do believe he would eat what he says just now if he could only get it."

"Oh! wouldn't I," said the boy. "I often wish, Mrs. Cottle, that you was a nice fat young duck—wouldn't I make up a rousing fire, and do you brown in no time, and have a good feast for once in a way."

"THE VILLAIN IS DEAD," LUKE SAID. "HE DESERVED HIS FATE."

"You wretch—you cannibal!" cried the old woman.

"Well, Dick," said Captain Macheath, who could hardly restrain his laughter, "here is half-a-crown for yourself, and we want you to go to the sheriff's house and to tell your master, Mr. Hunkers, that a gentleman is waiting for him at home to pay him three hundred pounds."

"Oh! won't I."

"Half-a-crown!" shrieked Mrs. Cottle —"half-a— Oh! give it to me, you vile boy. Give it to me to keep for you this moment."

"Don't you wish you may get it, old 'un?" retorted Dick. "Do you see anything particklar green in my eyes? No, rather not, I think."

"Oh—oh—oh!" murmured the old woman, as Dick scampered off with the half-crown in his possession. "Oh! dear—oh! dear. Half-a-crown!"

"Madam," said Macheath, "I feel that we have given you much trouble, so, if you will accept of half-a-guinea, we shall be happy to hand it you; but we don't want to offend you by the offer in the least, if you take it as such."

"Offend me? Oh! gracious, no," cried the hag, with a shriek of delight. "Me offended? Oh! gentlemen, I assure you I am the humblest person as is. Give me the money this moment, if you please."

Captain Macheath gave Mrs. Cottle the half-guinea, which she received with a profusion of expressions of gratitude, saying—

"Thank you, gentlemen. I only hope you will come here again, that's all. It's good, I suppose —hem! Thank you kindly, gentlemen. If it ain't good, I can pass it off on old Hunkers. I am very much obliged to you, sir, indeed, and shall be always glad to see you. It's quite a comfort to find real gentlemen coming to the old house at times. Of course, it's a sad trial to me to think that that little hussy of a sheriff's daughter is coming here, with her airs and graces, to eat us out of house and home; but I'll be even with her—I'll let her know what's what, I'll warrant—the odious little wretch! To think of marrying at her age, too!"

Captain Macheath and his friends were very much amused at the violence of Mrs. Cottle's indignation at poor Annie, and they encouraged her to say such extraordinary things about her that Polly interposed and changed the subject.

While all this was going on at old Hunker's house the boy Dick, highly stimulated by the half-crown, went at once to the sheriff's house, and much disturbed the mind of old Hunkers by delivering the message about the three hundred pounds.

"But what are the men?" said Hunkers.

"Don't know," said the boy; "but they have got lots of money."

"How do you know that?"

"Why, they gave me ever so much."

"They did? Then allow me, Dick, to take care of it for you."

"Oh! no, thank you, master," said the boy; "I can do that myself easy. What shall I say to the gentlemen? That you won't come, sir?"

"Oh! no—no," Hunkers gasped, "don't say that. Run back and say that I am coming as fast as I can. Dear me, what's o'clock? Oh! just upon eleven. That will do; I have plenty of time —plenty of time. I will just tell the sheriff that I shall be back in half an hour at the outside. No —the best way will be to say nothing at all. So that I am back in time to go to church it will be all right enough, of course."

With this old Hunkers, with a mortal dread of losing the three hundred pounds, set off at a trot for his house.

Now, the old usurer was engaged in so many monetary transactions that there was nothing at all out of the way in anybody coming to pay him such a sum as three hundred pounds, only he could not call to mind who it was that owed him such a sum at that precise time.

But he had no doubt he should know the parties when he got home.

"It is not a sum to let go by one," he muttered, as he tried to run in the street, but was forced to stop owing to its bringing on his cough. "Dear me, the more haste the worse speed, as the proverb says, so I had better go slow and easy, after all. I wonder who it can possibly be?"

The distance was so short, however, that, notwithstanding all his trouble to get along, and his cough, and a stitch in the side, too, that he gave himself by his exertions, he soon stood at his own gate, and rang a lusty peal at the bell.

Old Mrs. Cottle answered him.

The first question he asked of her was—

"Who is it?—who is it?"

"Don't know," was the short reply.

"You don't know? What do you mean by that, you old jade? Did they not leave their names?"

"No, stupid!"

"Confound you! what do you mean by this insolence?" Hunkers roared. "It would serve you right if I were to discharge you at once. I have put up with you and your impertinence too long—eh?"

"Oh! indeed, have you?" yelled the old woman. "My impertinence, indeed! I only wonder who you expect would live with you but me, you ruffian? Perhaps you think that because you are going to bring home a young wife you can do without me; but I'll soon let you know—"

"Hold your tongue, will you?"

"No!"

"Then I'll kill you, you hag!"

"Hag! Do you call me a hag, you elderly vampire? How dare you call me a hag, I should like to know, you dreadful old wretch?"

How long this violent contention between old Hunkers and the amiable Mrs. Cottle would have lasted it is hard to say; but the old man was in too great a state of anxiety to see the stranger who had to pay him the three hundred pounds to remain any longer contending with her.

With a howl of passion, he rushed into the house and left her victorious.

A miserable rush-light was burning in the parlour, which had been placed by Mrs. Cottle for the convenience of the visitors, and by its feeble beams they had the pleasure of seeing old Hunkers make his appearance in the room.

Luke immediately went past him, and placed his back against the door, and Captain Macheath advanced towards him, and looked him in the face.

"Well, sir," said Hunkers, "my money— money! Upon whose account do you come to pay me three hundred pounds? I beg that you will be quick, as I have some important business waiting for me to transact shortly."

"Oh! there is no hurry, Mr. Hunkers."

"But there is, sir."

"But I say there is not. Really, it's very uncivil to contradict a person in this kind of way, Mr. Hunkers."

"Pay me at once, sir. Whose bills are they you want to take up?"

"Oh! stuff, nobody's."

"Nobody's?"

"Certainly not," said Captain Macheath. "I only wonder how a man of your tact and experience could have been taken in by so flimsy a pretext. All we wanted was to get you here, that was all, Mr. Hunkers; and as a bit of cheese tempts a rat, we thought that the mere mention of money would tempt you, and the event has quite justified our idea."

At these words uttered by Captain Macheath, rage and fear struggled for mastery in the heart of old Hunkers, and he trembled so fearfully that they all thought that moment of passion and alarm would be his last.

He recovered after a few moments.

With his very lips deathly pale, he gasped out—

"What is the meaning of this? Who are you—what are you—what do you want? If it be robbery, there is not a sixpence in the house."

"It is not robbery."

"What then—what then? What do you want with me?"

"To be quite plain with you, Mr. Hunkers," said Macheath, "we do not intend to allow you to marry Annie Forsyth."

"Ah!"

"Oh! you may start and stamp your foot," cried the captain, laughing; "but, recollect, you have not before you one who owes you anything. Such people as you are only powerful where you have lent your money, and the unhappy wretch to whom you have lent it cannot pay you. To such you may play the braggart, and the great man. To such, your wild, hideous passions may be terrible."

"You wretch! how dare you speak to me in such a way?" Hunkers bellowed.

"Hark you, Mr. Hunkers," said Captain Macheath, sternly, "if you were not a very old man you should not wag your tongue so insolently at us with impunity. We should ask you if you were tired of your life."

As he spoke, he took a pistol from his pocket, and place the muzzle of it against the miser's cheek.

Turning deadly pale, Hunkers sank into a chair.

"Now, sir, you see we are in earnest with you," said Macheath.

"Oh!—oh!—oh! spare my life!" Hunkers moaned.

"Your life!" returned the captain, scornfully. "You ought to be thankful to anyone who will take it. What is life to an old trembling wretch like you, that you set such store by it? Your life, indeed! Which, now, do you value most?—your money or your life, Mr. Hunkers?"

"Oh! my money—no, I mean my life—that is, my money. Oh! spare me," the miserable wretch stammered.

"You don't know which."

"Alas!—alas!"

"You may very well say 'alas,' for you had dared to dream of plunging that young creature, Annie Forsyth, into misery for life. Out upon you! That was truly a most rascally transaction."

"What is that to you?" demanded Hunkers, trying to speak fiercely.

"Oh! you are not subdued yet, Mr. Hunkers?" said Macheath.

"No, I am not. But, of course, if four men attack one, what can the one do, eh?"

"Well, Mr. Hunkers," the captain observed, "you have more boldness than I gave you credit for; but, after all, that may be more affected than real. The probability is that you are cunning enough to see that we are not the likely sort of persons to do you any serious injury and that if we accomplish our purpose of hindering you from marrying Annie Forsyth that we shall be tolerably satisfied."

"I don't care."

"Oh! you don't care? Well, we shall see. Now, if you are anything of a judge of faces, Mr. Hunkers, and will look at mine, you will come to the conclusion that I am one of those persons who are exceedingly likely to keep their word."

"Well, what of that?" gasped the miser.

"Just this," said Macheath, "that you shall write a letter to the sheriff declining the hand of his daughter Annie, and suggesting that she should marry a young man, named Harry Lucas, who, being young, and one whom she can really love, is a much more suitable match. Do you understand that?"

"Yes, but I won't do it," Hunkers yelled.

"You won't?"

"No, I won't."

"Very well," said Captain Macheath, with all the coolness imaginable. "Then, Mr. Hunkers, we will hang you forthwith. Look round the room, my friends, and see if there be any nail strong enough to bear this old man's weight, and we will hang him out of hand in a moment, so that, at all events, the marriage will be effectually put a stop to at once and for ever."

"Here is one," said Luke, "and here is a strong piece of cord at the window which will carry double his weight."

"Be quick about it, then," said Macheath.

Luke made a noose in the cord and put it round old Hunkers' neck, and then placed the table under the nail in the wall, to which he fastened the other end of the cord.

"He will hang capitally," said Luke; "as soon as we jerk the table away from under him I'll give him a good pull by the legs, which will finish the business for him."

Up to this point the old man had preserved silence; but now, when he saw that one kick to the rickety table would leave him suspended, he quailed before the prospect of death, and roared out—

"My life—my life! Oh! spare my life! I will write the letter. Anything, so that you leave me my life."

"Very good," said Macheath.

"Shall we let him down?" said Luke.

"Yes, it will be as well; but keep the noose round his neck."

"If you are going to take my life at any rate," said old Hunkers, "I don't see any good in doing your bidding."

"We are not going to take your life at any rate," Macheath replied. "What is your life to us? It is much easier for us to leave it to you than to take it. But you may take another obstinate determination which may make it necessary for us to string you up, and I swear that if you give us any more trouble we will do so, despite all you can say to the contrary."

Hunkers was silent.

He began to find that those with whom he had to deal were not exactly the sort of people to trifle with, and that if he really had any respect for his life the best thing for him would be to do their bidding without further hesitation.

Old Mrs. Cottle by this time became very curious to know what the rather long interview between Hunkers and the strangers in the parlour portended.

She hobbled from the kitchen and tried to listen, but her senses were not quite so acute as they had been forty years before, so that that good lady only heard a very indistinct murmur of voices, and feeling cold, she shrunk back again to consult Dick, who, notwithstanding his appetite and his aggravating ways, was a great oracle to Mrs. Cottle, who found that his knowledge of the world was something prodigious.

"Now, Mr. Hunkers," said Captain Macheath, "be quick, and write what we shall dictate to you."

"Well, well—what you like, now."

"Where are your writing materials?" Macheath demanded. "What you have to do must be done properly, and without any appearance of hurry or compulsion, or it will defeat our intentions."

"I will get them," said Hunkers, doggedly.

"Do so and be quick about it."

The old man shuffled along to a cupboard in one corner of the room. He opened the door and seemed to be looking about in it.

Little did Captain Macheath or his friends think that old Hunkers would have courage to attempt anything of a hostile character; but the fact was, that the old man had money in the house, and he could not divest himself of the idea that it was after that the strangers had come.

Now, we know that a hen in defence of its chicks will turn upon a dog, and so a miser, in defence of his money, gets desperate, and has a false show of valour in defence of it.

Such was the case with Hunkers.

Suddenly turning, he cried out in a croaking voice—

"Now, you wretches, I will soon clear the house of you!"

As he spoke he presented a blunderbuss at the confederates, and to their surprise they found themselves confronted by a huge bell-mouthed brass barrel.

"Confound him!" said Macheath, as he dashed forward to seize the weapon.

Click went the lock, but, fortunately, the blunderbuss missed fire.

In another moment Captain Macheath seized the weapon, and turned the muzzle up to the ceiling. Quick as thought Hunkers put the blunderbuss upon full-cock again, and pulled the trigger.

The second attempt sufficed.

Off it went with a roar that shook the house; but the contents lodged in the ceiling, and by the recoil of the fire-arm, old Hunkers was hurled into the cupboard.

The candle went out by the concussion of the air, and one half the panes of glass in the windows were broken at once.

If Mrs. Cottle had been ten times more deaf than she was such a noise as this could not possibly have failed to rouse her, and, accordingly, both she and Dick made a rush into the room.

Dick carried the rushlight with him that they had been sitting by in the kitchen.

"Murder!" shouted Mrs. Cottle.

"Oh! what a lark," said Dick.

Old Hunkers now rolled out of the cupboard, and looked as if he were at his last gasp.

"Silence!" cried Captain Macheath, "nobody is hurt. It is of no consequence. Mr. Hunkers was only showing us the blunderbuss, when it went off accidentally."

"Oh, lor!" cried Dick, "and ain't bits of the old ceiling coming down."

"Dear me," said Mrs. Cottle, "what an old fool he must be to get up to such tricks."

"Woman!" cried Hunkers, "you are a beast! Fetch the police!"

"Beast, in your teeth, Mr. Hunkers," shouted Mrs. Cottle, whose ire was so kindled at the epithet that she paid no attention at all to the conclusion of the sentence, and then she flounced out of the room.

"Dick," said Captain Macheath, "it is pen, ink, and paper that your master means. Do you know where to get them?"

"Oh! yes; in the kitchen. You know he don't sit here. It's in the kitchen he does all his writing, and that sort of thing."

"Very well. Bring him the means of writing a letter, and there will be another half-crown in your pocket."

"Oh! won't I!"

The moment Dick was gone from the room, Macheath turned round to old Hunkers and said—

"Now, sir, for this delicate attempt upon all our lives we might, and most people in our situation would, take a bitter revenge; but considering that you were but defending yourself, we will regard the matter in that light and pass it over. Do our bidding, and you will not find the consequences near so great as you might expect."

Hunkers expected nothing but death for the act he had attempted; but Captain Macheath's words reassured him a little.

"You intend to spare my life?"

"Your life is in your own hands."

"How is that! How can that be, when here I am quite helpless and surrounded by men, any one of whom might kill me?"

"Write what I shall dictate, and you live."

"I will; only let it be quickly over now, and go your way. I am weary of this dreadful evening."

"Here you are," said Dick, coming back with an old desk, and placing it upon the table. "Here you are, old Hunkers!"

"You rascal, how dare you speak to me in that way?" growled the miser. "Hold your vile tongue! Be off with you! I'm glad he is gone."

"Now Mr. Hunkers," said Macheath, "write, if you please."

"Yes—yes, I will. Tell me what to write."

"To Mr. Forsyth.

"Sir,—I hereby beg to inform you that I renounce all idea or intention of marrying your daughter Annie; and I think that Mr. Harry Lucas would be the best person you could bestow her upon.

"I am, sir, yours obediently,

"JEREMIAH HUNKERS."

The old man groaned as he wrote the above; but he did not make any opposition to so doing.

All idea of resisting the commands of his persecutors was now past, and he duly folded up and addressed the letter to the sheriff.

"You may depend that Hunkers will not be quiet after we leave him," Luke whispered to Captain Macheath.

"I am thinking of that."

"He will try to baulk us. That old man has a spirit in spite of his craven looks."

"You are right, Luke," said the captain. "I will take measures. Mr Hunkers?"

"Well, what now?"

"Has the chimney in this room been swept lately?"

"What do you want to know that for, eh?"

"For a special reason," replied Macheath.

"Well, then, it hasn't been touched since I have been in this house, and it won't be either, I can tell you," said the miser. "I'm not going to the expense of sweeps."

"Very good, Mr. Hunkers. Now, we will trouble you to get up that chimney as quickly as you can."

"What?"

"I have spoken in plain language," said Macheath. "We will trouble you to get up that chimney. Surely you understand that?"

"But I won't get up the chimney—I'll be hanged if I do."

"You will be hanged if you don't."

"Oh, stuff!"

"What's that by the side of the fire-place, Luke?" Macheath demanded.

"A toasting fork."

"The very thing," said the captain. "Give it to me. Now, Mr. Hunkers, will you get up the chimney or will you not?"

"Murder! Don't be poking me with the prongs Murder! Oh, don t! Oh!—I will—don't—help! I'm going—oh, oh! Murder! I'm getting up the chimney. Do you wish to kill me! Oh, don't—don't—mercy! Have mercy upon me!"

Captain Macheath continued poking old Hunkers with the toasting-fork with all the deliberation in the world, and the old miser sprang to the fire-place as though he had been the youngest and most active sweep that ever was, and began scrambling up the chimney with quite an alarming alacrity.

The soot fell down in great lumps, and in blinding showers, and the old rascal's voice was still heard calling "Murder!" in the chimney, only that it sounded very faint and smothery, as Macheath kept pegging away with the fork at his legs.

At last they too disappeared, old Hunkers was fairly in the chimney, and out of sight.

"Are you nice and comfortable up there?" Macheath demanded.

A volley of smothered curses was the only reply.

"Ah, very good," said the captain. "Now, old Hunkers, as your wedding dress will be rather the worse for the little adventure, you had better hold on as well as you can, and hang the consequences."

More curses and soot came down the chimney.

"Now, Hunkers," cried Macheath, "I am fixing a pistol so that we shall have the satisfaction of leaving your life entirely in your own hands, you know, and you can do just as you please."

Hunkers groaned, and Macheath made a rattling about the bars of the grate to convey to him the notion that he was really carrying the design of fixing the pistol in so dangerous a position, although in reality he never brought any of his fire-arms near the grate, and had no intention of doing so.

Whether or not old Hunkers felt sure that there was such an amount of danger in descending, the mere doubt would be sufficient to keep him where he was long enough for Macheath's purpose; so there he left him, and turning to his friends, he said—

'Now let us go to the sheriff's house at once."

"Hark!" said Luke.

"What is it? Is there any alarm?"

"No, but I hear a clock striking."

"Then it is twelve!" cried Harry Lucas, "and they will take Annie to the church."

"Well, my friend, you know that the bridegroom is not there, so you need not despair. It is twelve, and we have no time to lose. Let us, instead of going to the sheriff's house, go at once to the church. Come on—let us lose no time."

"It will be better, will it not," said Harry Lucas, "that I assume my own appearance?"

"That you can easily do. Take off the moustache and you are yourself again. Come on—come on!"

"Good night, Hunkers," said Luke.

"Yes, good night," said Macheath."

"And, Hunkers," called out Harry Lucas up the chimney, "don't you know me?"

"Go to the deuce!"roared Hunkers.

CHAPTER LXVII.

SHOWS HOW A LITTLE CONFUSION TOOK PLACE.

LEAVING the house they soon came within sight of the church, and they saw at once that it was lighted up, and that there were several carriages at the door of it.

"She is there!" said Harry Lucas, in tones of emotion.

"Be calm, my friend, be calm," cried Captain Macheath. "Everything must be done now with judgment."

"Yes—oh! yes. I will leave all to you, and what you direct shall be my law. I owe everything to you. Every hope of happiness that I have in the world now you know that I owe to you."

"Say no more on that head, but come on at once."

With hasty steps they approached the portal of the church, which was quite blocked up by the carriages and servants.

A portly beadle, with his wand of office, was there, but he did not think proper to obstruct Macheath and his friends, although he made a movement as if he meant to do so.

In another moment they entered the church.

The singular hour at which—in accordance with the wish of the bride—the ceremony had been appointed to take place had occasioned a great deal of surmise and anxiety in Guildford.

There are few persons who would not have felt some little degree of hesitation at walking into a church upon such an errand as Macheath was upon; but we have had amply sufficient opportunities of knowing that his nerves were tolerably steady.

As for poor Harry Lucas, Polly could see, even by the faint light in the church, that he was as pale as death itself.

"Courage—courage," she whispered to him.

"Yes—yes, I will nerve myself for anything."

"Recollect that it is for Annie's sake all this is done."

"I will! Her name is a spell that shall not leave me. I thank you for naming her to me."

Macheath quickened his pace and reached the wedding guests; and as he did so he heard the sheriff say, in a voice of vexation, not unmingled with dread, that something was amiss.

"Dear me, what can keep our friend, Mr. Hunkers? It is past his time now, nearly twenty minutes."

"And he so very punctual a man of business usually, too," said one of the guests in tones of busy.

"Father, I will not remain here longer," said Annie. "Let us go."

"Ah!" said the sheriff, as he heard the footsteps of Macheath and his friends speedily advancing up the aisle. "It's all right. Here he is at last. Come, come, my friends, we won't say anything to vex the bridegroom now that he has come; for nothing but some very important business could have detained him."

Annie began to sob bitterly.

"Mr. Sheriff Forsyth!" said Captain Macheath, in a clear voice.

"Sir,' cried the sheriff, "I—I—am in the church, and an arrest is not legal."

"I do not come to arrest you, sir, but bring a message from Mr. Hunkers, if you please," said Macheath.

Annie, upon finding that it was not Hunkers himself, dried her sweet eyes, and looked up with some degree of interest and hope.

"A message, sir?" added the sheriff, looking very red in the face. "A message, did you say, from Mr. Hunkers? Sir, we would rather see that gentleman himself than hear any message from him at such a time as this."

"Is the old man ill?" said one.

"Silence!" cried the sheriff. "I wonder at the indelicacy of anybody saying is the old man ill?"

"Is he dead?" said another

"Oh!" cried the sheriff. "What indelicacy, upon the very moment of a man's marriage! I am shocked—I am quite shocked, and could hardly have thought it possible that anyone could behave in such a way, in a church too. I suppose, sir,"—addressing Captain Macheath—"you come to tell me that the bridegroom will very soon be here to go through with the interesting ceremony?"

"No, sir."

"No, did you say? Do my ears hear aright?" cried the sheriff.

"Your ears do you justice, Mr. Sheriff," said Captain Macheath. "Here is a letter from Mr. Hunkers, to explain why it is he positively declines marrying Miss Annie Forsyth."

A cry of joy burst from the lips of Annie as the ladies gathered round her to console her; but she burst through the throng and made her way to Captain Macheath.

"Oh! sir, do not trifle with my feelings," she said, "but tell me truly. Is the purport of the letter you bring a renunciation of my hand upon the part of Mr. Hunkers?"

"It is."

"Never mind, my dear," said all the ladies in chorus. "Never mind, my love!"

"The men are all wretches!" said one old maid. "I was served in this way twenty-two years ago."

"Don't faint, my love, if you can help it," another said to Annie.

"Faint!" she cried. "Faint because I am not to be made such a sacrifice that death in any shape would have been infinitely preferable? Oh! no—no. What a happy release is this! I am happy once again."

"Good gracious!" gasped the sheriff.

"My dear sir," said one of the guests, "allow me to look at the letter."

"Is it really true, though?" cried everybody now. "Is it true, Mr. Forsyth, that Mr. Hunkers won't be married?"

"Quite true—that is—I think—I don't know."

"You can bring an action," said an attorney, shuffling up to the sheriff. "An action, my dear sir, and heavy damages. Breach of promise, you know."

"Be quiet."

"Yes, certainly. Mum is the word, my dear sir—mum is the word. We will trounce him. But advise the bride to be deeply affected. If she goes on in the way she is, we shall not win, my dear sir."

"Annie," the sheriff groaned.

"Yes, father, I am here."

"Wretched girl."

"Oh! don't say that, father! I am not a wretched girl at all. I never was so delighted in all my life. It is like a reprieve from death."

"She is light-headed," said the sheriff, alarmed.

"Stick to that," whispered the attorney, "it's a good idea. Stick to it."

"I will. My poor, my unhappy child! What must be a father's feelings to see the effect of the deep disappointment upon you! Alas—alas—alas! that bright and—and beautiful intellect has received a shock, and is no more what it was. Oh—oh! Ah me, I am an unhappy father."

"Good," said the attorney, "that will do it."

"Father," said Annie, with a smile, and quite a provokingly sane look, "you are quite mistaken. It is the marriage that might have driven me mad, but not the breaking off of it."

"She will ruin all," whispered the attorney. "You will never recover a farthing if she goes on in that way, my dear sir."

Macheath saw that the sheriff had put the letter into his pocket, and had no intention to let its precise contents ooze out, so he thought that it was rather time to interfere in the matter, and he said—

"But, Mr. Sheriff, I was present when that letter was written, and Mr. Hunkers intended, most probably, that it should be read to the bride."

"Indeed, sir?"

"Yes, Mr. Sheriff; and if you doubt the fact, here are other gentlemen who were present likewise, and who can confirm it."

"Yes, I can," said Polly, and Luke, and Harry Lucas, all in a breath.

The sheriff looked provoked.

"When one gentleman," he said, "addresses another, he has no right to dictate to whom he should show it."

"Oh! very well," said Captain Macheath; "then it will be my duty to state what was in it to all concerned; and if the sheriff does not show the letter itself to dispute the accuracy of my version of it, everybody will be able to take that as pretty good proof of my correctness."

"Hear him—hear him!" cried several. "What was in the letter, sir?"

"I will tell you."

"My dear sir," said the attorney, who had sidled round to the captain's elbow, "allow me to suggest that—"

"No, sir, I don't want any suggestions; so, for the good of all, I will state that in the first part of the letter Mr. Hunkers stated that upon reflection he felt convinced that the disparity in the ages of himself and Miss Annie Forsyth was such that no happiness could be looked for from the union."

"How true," said several.

"I thank him at last," said Annie. "I did not think that he would take so just a thought, but I did him great injustice."

"There—there; very good, sir," said the sheriff, "we don't want to know more; that is all that can be of any importance, my dear sir. That will do.

CAPTAIN MACHEATH

THE
PRINCE OF THE HIGHWAY.

"HALLOA THERE!" CRIED MACHEATH. "WHAT IS THE MATTER, MY FRIEND?"

Come home, Annie, my bereaved, heart-broken child; you are still most welcome to your father's arms."

"But I should like to hear what further was in the letter, sir," said Annie.

"You shall," added Macheath. "It stated that as he knew a young and worthy man was sincerely attached to you, he hoped that you, with him, would know what real happiness was, and that his name was—"

"That will do—that will do," cried the sheriff.

"His name?" said Annie.

"Is Harry Lucas!" cried Lucas, springing forward and catching her in his arms, and kissing her twenty times,

"Stop!" roared the sheriff.

"It is true," said Macheath, speaking about an octave higher. "It is quite true, Mr. Sheriff. That was the name mentioned in Mr. Hunkers' note."

"It's false, and, besides, I don't approve of it, and so it is of no consequence whether it is true or not."

"But your daughter highly approves of it."

"She does not, sir. She is light-headed."

"Captain!" whispered Luke in Macheath's ear, "captain, I say!"

"What is it, Luke?"

"Danger!"

"Ah!"

"Captain Smith, the king's messenger, is at the door of the church with half-a-dozen constables; what is to be done?"

CHAPTER LXVIII.

AFFAIRS GET RATHER SERIOUS FOR MACHEATH AND HIS FRIENDS.

THE intelligence which Luke brought to Captain Macheath was indeed of a serious character.

"Luke, we must escape by some means," he said. "Leave it all to me, and I will pull everybody through this bother."

Annie still clung to her lover.

"I will put an end to this," said the sheriff. "I command you to come home at once."

"Farewell!" said Annie to Lucas. "Farewell!"

"Oh! no—no," whispered Lucas. "This is an opportunity that will not occur again. Let me take you at once to my mother's."

"Oh! if I dared."

"There is no one to prevent you, Annie. You have heard sufficient of her to know you will be safe with her. This is a crisis both in your fate and mine, dear one, and if you will not now act with energy and be happy, the chance may never come again."

"But my father—"

"He will make up matters to-morrow morning with old Hunkers, and another day will be fixed for your wedding."

Annie shuddered.

"Oh! Harry, if, indeed, I thought that—"

"It is certain."

"I am yours, then—I am yours. Take me away."

"Oh! joy—joy."

Away they went down the aisle and were outside in a moment.

Luke turned the key and locked the sheriff and his party in.

"They are safe enough now," he said,

"Quick!" cried the captain. "I hear the sound of horses' hoofs. Our enemies draw near indeed."

"The vaults!" said Harry Lucas.

"What do you mean?" demanded Captain Macheath.

"I can conduct you to the vaults," returned Lucas. "Follow me quickly."

"Anywhere," said Macheath, "for we cannot fight a troop of soldiers."

The fugitives now, led by Lucas, entered a side door.

"Descend at once," Lucas said. "There is, indeed, no time to lose. Descend, I pray you at once."

Luke began the descent, and Annie and Polly followed him closely.

"Where are you all?" said Macheath.

"Here," replied Lucas. "Here, and all safe. Listen, I can hear people moving above. The officers must have broken the church door down."

"Yes," said Macheath, "and they are just beginning to search. How many steps are there here? I have come down six."

"Oh! there are three times that number. Come on; it is all fair ground at the foot of the stairs."

"Luke!"

"I am here. I think I know what you want; it is a light."

"It is."

"Ah! but," said Harry Lucas, "I fear that will be impossible to procure here."

"Not so," Luke replied; "we always carry about us the means of getting a light. We often owe our safety to such a wise provision."

Luke lit a match, and succeeded by its aid in igniting a wax-taper, and as it burnt slowly up into rather a sickly flame, they were able to see something of the gloomy region into which they had penetrated.

"Hold the light higher, Luke."

Luke did so, and then they had all a good view of the place. They had all got to the foot of the stairs, and they were standing upon a considerable thickness of sawdust, with which the ground was literally strewed. The space in which they were was about twelve feet square, and several passages branched off from it.

"This is a strange place," said Captain Macheath.

"It is," said Lucas. "I have heard that in olden times there were strange doings in these vaults, and that in the dark days of persecution for religion's sake they were often converted into dungeons."

"Not a doubt of it. Were you ever here yourself before, Lucas?"

"Only once, and that was upon the occasion of a law suit regarding an estate in the immediate neighbourhood, when a search was made in these vaults to see if any coffin had a plate upon it bearing the name of one of the litigants. Then I and some others had a slight view of the place."

"Hush!"

"They are looking for us inside the church as well as out of it," said Luke.

"But they will not find us," said Captain Macheath. "I think no one is likely to imagine but that we have found some mode of outlet from the church before now. This will not be a likely place to search."

"Far from it."

"Come on, then, as we are here, and let us sesome of the wonders of these receptacles of the dead."

"You should say the terrors," remarked Annie Forsyth, with a shudder.

"Pardon me," added Macheath. "I see that I was wrong now in asking you to advance beyond this spot. It is well to keep young minds free from the terrors that otherwise, in happier moments, might haunt them."

"Oh, listen !" said Polly, suddenly.

They were all as silent as the grave, and then they heard distinctly some blows given to the iron door at the top of the staircase.

"We are lost !" said Annie.

"Say, rather, found," whispered Lucas. "But yet there is a hope."

"Hush—hush !" said Macheath. "They are coming now. Hush !"

The door leading to the vaults was opened, and at the same moment Luke extinguished his light, and all was darkness again.

"Yes, gentlemen," said the beadle, "yes, gentlemen, these are the vaults; but, I assure you all, as they hasn't been opened no how for I don't know when ; so it don't seem likely that they should have found out such a place."

"Indeed, it does not," said another.

"Well, but," cried a man in a cracked disputative voice, "we are hired to search everywhere, and you know upon that principle we should look here as well. If it comes to giving up looking in one place, because It ain't probable they are there, we may just as well give up the search altogether, for I contend that people always do get into improbable places."

"Well—well, you go down," said another.

"Nay, why should I go alone? They might pop a bullet into me in a moment or two, and nice I should look then."

"Well—well, let's go down a little way, at all events."

"Come on, then. Hold the light, one of you. Bring two lights. That will do. Now look to your pistols, and come down. We won't have anyone say that we did not look everywhere."

Upon this Harry Lucas laid hold of Macheath by the arm, and said in a whisper—

"Follow me, all of you. It is our only chance."

They none of them knew very well where Harry Lucas proposed to lead them, but they followed him.

He took a passage to the left which was also covered with sawdust, so that the sound of their footsteps was completely lost

The roof and walls of this passage reeked with an unwholesome moisture, and they could all feel how very bad the air was to breathe by a feeling of oppression at the lungs, such as it would scarcely have been possible to endure for any length o time.

"Oh, husband," Polly whispered, "this is some dreadful home of the dead."

"Courage—courage," said Captain Macheath.

"Yes, but where are we going ? A thousand unknown fears oppress me, and I feel ready to sink to the earth."

"Let me support you, Polly. You will not sink I am sure, while my arm is around you.'

"No—no, I shall not."

"Come now ; courage, Where are we, Mr. Lucas ?"

"Stop," said Lucas. "Let us listen if our enemies are near at hand or not. Do you hear anything ?"

"Yes, the murmur of voices I hear," said Macheath, "and that is all ; but whether they come from the church above, or from persons in these vaults, I can't say."

"I will go on a little way towards the path we have trodden," said Luke, "and ascertain."

"Do so—do so. We will await your return, good Luke."

Before Luke had gone many paces the sudden flash of a light came upon their eyes, and they could no longer doubt that the officers were determined upon making such an examination of the vaults as would thoroughly satisfy them.

Luke was back again in a moment.

"They come !'

"What are we   do now ?" said Macheath, as he took his pistols from his pocket, and began to adjust them for use.

"Resistance will be madness," said Luke. "If we cannot hide from them we are lost. Recollect, captain, that if we fire upon them they will return the shots, and in that case my good mistress or Miss Forsyth might come to injury."

"That is true," said Captain Macheath, as he coolly replaced his pistols in his pockets. "Let them come now."

"It is all over," said Polly.

"No," exclaimed Harry Lucas, suddenly. "I opened the door of one of the vaults. Come in, all of you. We may yet elude them. They are only walking through the passages as we have done. Recollect, they have not yet opened any of the chambers of the dead."

"True—true," said Macheath.

"A light for one moment," whispered Harry Lucas. "One of the matches that you have got will do. Your enemies will not see it, having a light themselves, and I want to know where we are."

Luke produced a light, and before it expired they all saw the open door.

It was of iron, and led to a vaulted room.

Above the door was rudely sculptured the arms of the family to whom the vault had originally belonged.

There was no choice now but to remain in the passage, and be seen and captured by the officers, or to go into this open vault.

They embraced the latter alternative, and at once crossed its threshold.

Harry Lucas closed the door on the inside, and all was still.

"It is very strange," said Captain Macheath, "that the air is purer in this place than in the long passages outside."

"It is much purer," said Polly. "I can breath here without difficulty."

"And so can I," said Annie.

"That is a circumstance I cannot account for," said Lucas. "I should like to see the place, though. Will you light another match, Mr. Luke, and let us look about us for a few brief seconds ?"

"Willingly."

The match was lighted, and as Luke held it up they saw around them, and a fearful sight it was.

Upon shelves all round the vault were coffins, and human bones lay scattered on the floor.

"Oh ! this is dreadful," said Annie.

Out went the match and all was darkness again, and before they could say another word they heard the voices of their pursuers just outside the door ; but Lucas was doing something to the door which puzzled Macheath.

"What are you about, Lucas?" he whispered. "Are you trying to fasten the door?"

"I am not only trying, but I am fully succeeding in doing so."

"How do you mean? How is that possible?"

"Why, it seems odd to have fastenings on the inside of the door of a vault, but while the match was alight I saw that there was a couple of good strong bolts."

"You did?"

"In good faith I did. One at the top and another at the bottom, and they are now in their sockets, so that I think our friends outside have no orce sufficient to break in here."

"This is most extraordinary," said Macheath. "What possible motive could there be for putting fastenings upon the inner side of the door of a vault?"

"It is inexplicable," said Lucas.

"Not so," whispered Luke. "I have an idea upon the subject which I will let you all know by-and-bye; but at first let us consider that we have enough to do to listen to what our enemies are about."

This was too self-evident a proposition to be denied, and they were all as silent as the mouldering remains of the dead inhabitants of that apartment.

They could not detect any ray of light from the passage, which led them to think that the door fitted into its framework so well that they might if they chose have a light without incurring any danger.

Still, they abstained from such an indulgence, for it was better to err upon the safe side.

"There is no one here," said a voice from the passage; "it is no use making ourselves sick with the pestiferous atmosphere of this place. There is no one in the passage."

"But the vaults themselves—the actual vaults, you know, we have not been in any of them."

"No, nor are we going," said the first speaker. "Here is a door."

"Yes, gentlemen," said the beadle, ' that there door leads to the family vault of the Fritles—a very great family in Guildford many years a-gone by, I assure you, and that's their coats of arms over the door."

"And what's become of the family of the Fritles now, Mr. Beadle?"

"Dead and defunct, sir."

"What! all of them?"

"Yes."

"Well, it can't offend them, then, if we take a look into their vault. Open the door, Mr. Beadle. What! is it fast?"

"So it seems, sir, for it won't move. Now, sir, they tells funny stories about these Fritles."

"When they were alive, I suppose?"

"Oh! dear, no, sir. The funniness was all when they was dead, gentlemen. They do say that whenever a Fritle was buried, or, rather, put on the shelf in the family vault, and the door left just close, the dead Fritles got up and bolted it on the inside till another of the family went dead."

"The deuce they did!"

"Yes, gentlemen; and, would you believe it, once the Fritles gave leave to a gentleman of the name of Podgers to put his wife in the vault, but when they came with the coffin to this door it wasn't open!"

"You don't mean that?"

"Yes, I do. The dead Fritles in the inside wouldn't undo it to let in a Podgers."

"Oh! I say, it's no use staying here. Why, this vault is enough to make one's hair stand on end. Suppose all the dead Fritles were to take it amiss our coming here now, and suddenly pounce out upon us? I wouldn't be here if such a thing was to happen for a thousand pounds."

"Nor I," said another.

"Nor I," cried the beadle; "because, you see, gentlemen, I being the beadle of the church they would be sure to be down upon me."

Every word of this legend concerning the Fritles and their family vault was heard distinctly by Captain Macheath and his friends, and he thought it too good an opportunity of alarming his pursuers to let slip.

Watching his opportunity when there was a lull in the conversation, and when it might be supposed that they were all looking at each other with terrified aspects, Macheath tapped with his knuckles on the inside of the door, and made a strange moaning noise at the same time.

For a moment or two the men in the passage immediately outside the door of the Fritles' last home were too much petrified by fright to move or speak; but presently, with one accord, they turned and fled.

It was truly ludicrous to hear their cries of alarm and shouts for succour as they ran along the passage towards the staircase that would lead them into the open air.

Some fell down and were run over by the others, and the beadle was the most afraid of the whole lot, and roared for mercy as if all the Fritles, each with a good cudgel, were at his heels.

"I think that has settled them," said Macheath.

"Yes, for the time," said Luke; "but it is doubtful if those who wait in the church the report of their exploring party will take the same superstitious view of the matter."

"Well, Luke, you were saying that you had an idea connected with the bolts on the inner side of this door."

"I have, and that idea is, that the bolts would never have been there if there had not been some other mode of exit from the vault, and, what is more, the freshness of the air convinces me that such must be the case."

"A light, Luke," said Macheath. "You are right."

Luke now lit one of the tapers, and it soon gave sufficient light to enable them to take a thorough look all round the vault.

It was then that, in the roof, at that part of the wall which seemed to have been built up, they found a narrow opening, about half the width of a brick, through which there came a current of cold air.

"We must pull down this bit of wall," said Luke, "and the sooner we set about it the better, for I am quite convinced that it will lead us to freedom by some route that will not be suspected. Come, captain, you have a pistol with a spring bayonet to it, and that will work capitally. For myself, I will be content with my knife."

CHAPTER LXIX.

THE ESCAPE.

LUKE placed the light upon the corner of a coffin, and then both began to work upon the wall.

It did not take many moments to convince them that they would find no difficulty in getting a portion of it down.

The bricks were but badly cemented together,

or else the damp air had had the effect of preventing the mortar from thoroughly hardening.

Harry Lucas searched through the vault with the hope of finding something by the aid of which he could help his friends; but he was disappointed.

"Come, Master Lucas," said Macheath, "you can do quite as much good by moving the bricks as we loosen them."

Harry Lucas set about the task with a good will, so that the united exertions of the three very soon succeeded in moving a portion of the wall quite large enough for a moderate-sized person to pass through.

While this was going on, Polly and Annie were conversing together, and avowing to each other an eternal friendship, and Annie was bitterly lamenting the course of life that Captain Macheath pursued.

The reader is well aware that she could not possibly lament that course of life more than Polly herself did, and the tears coursed down the cheeks of the latter as Annie hinted at what might be the dreadful termination of such a career as Captain Macheath's.

"I know it all," she said. "I dream of it, and awaken to shudder at the awful visions of the night. Alas—alas! I am very wretched."

"Ah! now," said Annie, "I regret that I touched upon such a theme, since it is one upon which you feel so deeply."

"Could I feel otherwise than deeply?"

"But there are those who would not. Pardon me, though, for making such a subject one of discussion between us."

"There needs no pardon. It is so natural a thought that those who feel kindly disposed towards me or him cannot but speak of it."

"Now we shall get out of the vault," cried Lucas. "What is it that engages your joint attentions so deeply?"

"Nothing—nothing!" said Annie.

"Are you successful?" demanded Polly.

"Yes—behold. There is a passage beyond this vault."

"And it leads to freedom," said Captain Macheath, "for I can quite plainly feel the fresh air coming upon my face, and in that case we shall soon be out of this gloomy region entirely. Come along."

Macheath took charge of Polly, and Lucas of Annie while Luke carried the light, and so they all got through the opening in the wall.

The passage into which they emerged from the vault was very narrow, and they had not proceeded half-a-dozen paces along it, when a current of cold air blew out the light.

"Hilloa!" said Luke, "how is this? I can feel the open air raising the very hair upon my head. Where are we?"

"Here is the solution of the mystery," said Captain Macheath. "There is a grating over our heads."

He pointed it out, and they could see the sky and the stars were shining.

The grating was not above four feet above their heads, so that Macheath could very easily reach it, and by Luke's aid he did so, and one vigorous push opened it.

"We are saved!" cried Captain Macheath. "I will get up, and then help you all out. That will do. Thank you, Luke."

Macheath drew himself through the opening, and in another moment stood in the churchyard.

What a feeling of exquisite relief it was now to find that he was in the pure open air again.

The wind was sighing amid the branches of the old yew-trees; but the sky was clear, and thousands of bright stars were shining.

"This is truly beautiful," said Macheath.

As he spoke, he heard a trampling sound outside the wall of the burial ground.

The wall was not above five feet high, so that there was no difficulty in his seeing over it.

He shrank behind a grave-stone and then he saw the whole troop of men ride past within six feet of him and take the London road.

It was quite evident that the hunt for the fugitives was given up as unsuccessful. It took some three or four minutes for them to pass, and not one cast a look to the old churchyard.

No doubt all of them were glad to be released from a duty which never comes with a pleasant idea to the military.

"Gone," said Macheath, as he made his way back to the grating, and then, stooping over it, he added—"Did you all think I had forgotten you?"

"No, captain," said Luke. "We heard the sound of horses' feet."

"Yes, it was that sound that detained me. The officers have all gone by."

"Then we are saved."

"I hope so. Polly, where are you?"

"Here, husband, here!"

Polly held up her arms to him, and Captain Macheath had no difficulty in drawing her up through the grating.

He then did the same to Annie, and when they were both safe and seated upon an old tomb, he assisted Lucas and Luke to emerge from the region of the vaults, and then closed the grating.

"Rest in peace, mouldering remains of the Fritles," he said. "It has not been with any wish to disturb you that we have this night trespassed upon your last resting-place, and can only hope never to have the necessity of cultivating your acquaintance again."

A feeling of joy came over them all now that they stood in the open air.

Polly clung to Macheath, and looked tenderly up into his face; and Annie, as she was clasped to the heart of her lover, seemed to feel that all her trials were over, and that there was nothing now to come but a long, sunny period of pure happiness.

"Well," said Luke, "I am glad to see you all so comfortable."

"My dear Luke," said Macheath, with a smile, "you must fall in love and marry."

"Not I, captain. I don't mean my words as any reproach to you, because if such another loving heart as you can call your own were to be offered to me, I should be only too happy to accept of it; but I don't think our life is exactly the sort of one to bring a young and tender girl to share."

Macheath made no reply to this.

Perhaps, notwithstanding the highly complimentary kind of accompaniment that Luke had given to the remark, it touched him a little too narrowly.

Harry Lucas advanced towards Macheath.

"What shall I say in the way of fervent thanks to you all," he said, and his voice trembled as he spoke. "How is it possible that I shall ever be able to assure you of the deep sense of gratitude that pervades my heart?"

"And mine likewise," said Annie.

"By your silence," Macheath replied. "Believe me, it is so sincere a pleasure to me that I am at times able to do such little kindnesses as I have done to you repays me for all trouble and danger. But, now, let us quit such a subject, and let me advise you, Lucas, to proceed to your mother's house as quickly as possible."

"I will. There you will remain, my Annie, in safety and in honour beneath her roof."

"I know I shall, Harry."

"And it is better, too," added Macheath, "that we should part as soon as possible, for your further association with us can do you no good. We will see you a little on your way, and then you can forget that you ever encountered Captain Macheath."

"Can you think so meanly of us?" said Harry.

"Enough—enough!" said the captain, with emotion. "Let us get on now. Oh! my friends, you do not know what sensations of bitterness and regret you awaken in my heart when I see that you are happy and virtuous, and at peace with society."

CHAPTER LXX.

ON THE ROAD AGAIN.

POLLY was sobbing bitterly while this dialogue was proceeding, for it deeply affected her, inasmuch as it bore so directly upon that subject which was ever dear and present to her heart, namely, the possibility of Macheath leaving his pursuits and taking up some honest calling.

"Come," said Macheath, suddenly. "This is the way."

With these words, he walked rapidly towards the gate, so that further conversation with him was then out of the question.

The little party followed him in silence, but the thoughts of all were engaged on the possible means of rescuing Macheath from the consequences of a course of life which sooner or later was sure to be fatal to him.

The route which Harry Lucas wished to take with Annie led past the house of old Hunkers, and they naturally enough rather hesitated about going that way.

"Never fear," said Macheath. "I'll warrant he is still in the chimney."

"The chimney!" repeated Annie, with surprise."

"Yes, my dear," said Lucas. "We thought that such would be the most appropriate place for old Hunkers to pass his wedding night in."

Harry then gave her a brief history of all that had taken place at old Hunkers' house, at which she could not help laughing, although she thought, she said, that they had been a little too severe upon the old man.

"Are you not going to let him down from his uncomfortable place of punishment?" Annie questioned.

"Not I."

"Nor I," Macheath added; "if he should remain there till doomsday it will not matter to me. A more thoroughly selfish old rascal I think I never came across. But I wonder where our friends, the officers, are?"

"Don't speak of them," said Polly. "They may make an appearance when we least want them. Let us get out of the town as quickly as we can. I shall have a lively recollection of Guildford as long as I live."

"I shall always love the old town for Annie's sake," said Lucas. "It will, in my mind, ever be associated with her, and, therefore, it will have a

claim upon me which it otherwise would want, no doubt."

"You are right," said Polly, "and I give you great credit for speaking so freely the true sentiments of your heart. You will be very happy, Annie Forsyth, as you deserve to be."

"I thank you," said Annie; "but—"

"Stop, all of you," said Captain Macheath. "Step into this gateway, and stoop low. There are some men coming. Do you not hear them?"

"Yes—yes."

"Then it will be just as well to escape a collision if they are foes, and also observation if they are indifferent to us. They might recognise you, Annie."

"They might."

"And me, likewise," said Harry Lucas, "for I am pretty well known in Guildford; and now that I am not disguised, there are few persons who would not be able to name me in the town."

"Capital reasons for caution," Macheath remarked. "Let us keep out of the way."

The gateway which the captain had alluded to seemed to lead into the yard of a builder; but it afforded them a good shelter, and they waited till the danger was past, for it was a danger.

About six or eight men, in a disorderly kind of throng, came on, and as they neared the spot, it was quite easy to hear what they were saying.

A very few words of their conversation was sufficient to announce that it related to the fugitives, and before they had quite passed, Macheath felt quite clear that they were the officers.

"I tell you," said one, "it's of no use now staying another moment in Guildford. He is off, and if once he has got fairly mounted and out of the town, he is out of our clutches by this time, you may be sure."

"Ah! and twenty miles away," said another: "though I don't know how the deuce we came to miss him. He was in the church."

The men passed on and the sound of their voices died away.

"A close touch that," said Luke.

"Very," returned Macheath; "but then, you know, Luke, a miss in these matters is as good as a mile, and as they have passed us, it is all the same to us as though they were at Jericho."

"So it is."

The friends thought it prudent, however, to wait a little time in the builder's yard, so that the officers should get some distance from the spot before they emerged on to the road again.

At length Macheath intimated that he thought they might venture with safety, and, accordingly, they sallied out.

Their route to where their horses had been left took them exactly past old Hunkers' house, and they were not a little curious to discover whether or not he had had the courage to release himself from his rather painful situation in the chimney.

Captain Macheath could hardly think it possible that old Hunkers would remain in such a situation, but Luke would have it that there he was still, and argued that he was quite incapable of a sufficient amount of calm and cool reflection to enable him to leave the place.

"Well, we shall soon see," said Lucas.

In the course of the next three minutes they were on the opposite side of the road, which was flanked by a thickset hedge.

A strange noise from the top of the house came upon their ears, and after looking up for a few moments, Macheath said—

CAPTAIN MACHEATH SEIZED THE BLUNDERBUSS AND TURNED THE MUZZLE TOWARDS THE CEILING.

"Do you see anything particular about that stack of chimneys, Luke?"

"Yes, I do. I am tolerably long-sighted, and one of the particular things that I see is a dark object clinging to one of the chimney pots."

"Then that dark object must be our old and rather dark friend, Hunkers, I should say?"

"Not a doubt of it."

The odd noise continued, and it was quite evident that old Hunkers was mingling his groans with the night wind, but had not the courage to call out loudly for help, lest the threat that Captain Macheath had held out to him of someone being on the watch to shoot him should turn out to be true.

"Surely," said Annie, "he is sufficiently punished now?"

"Do you think so?" said Lucas. "The old rascal! I should never think he was sufficiently punished for the cruel suffering he has made you endure."

"But the result of all that is that I am yours, and so, you see, Lucas, how out of evil springeth good."

"Yes, I see that; and if I thought that old Hunkers repented of his rascalities, which I am tolerably sure he does not, I, too, could pity him."

"Let him down," said Polly. "Oh! do let him down."

"You forget," said Macheath, "that I can have but very little control over a man who is on the top of a house."

"But you can call to him that his charge is past."

"Yes," said Luke, "and alarm the neighbourhood."

"It must not be done," said the captain. "It does not want more than half an hour to daylight, and when that comes Hunkers will see that there is no one in his way, and that he can descend in safety. Let us go."

They passed the old money-lender's house, and made the best of their way to the quiet inn where they had left their horses.

Everybody was in bed and asleep, but Captain Macheath rang the ostler's bell several times loudly, and then a night-capped head popped out at one of the windows, and the voice belonging to the head called out—

"Hilloa! what's the matter? Is Guildford on fire?"

"No," said Macheath. "I am sorry to disturb the house, but we want our horses that we left here early in the evening."

"Oh! it's all right—all right. Jem is getting up; I can hear him moving about, so he will soon attend to you."

"Thank you."

"Good-night, or, rather, good-morning, and a pleasant ride to you, gentlemen."

The landlord then popped in his head from the casement and closed it again, and in the course of a few minutes the ostler appeared, and let them into the stable yard.

He did not seem very well pleased at being disturbed at such an hour.

"My friend," said Macheath, "when I give anyone extra trouble I give them extra pay, so take that guinea, and get us out our horses as quickly as you can."

"Lor, sir! don't mention the trouble. I don't mind what I do for a real guinea—I mean a real gentleman, your honour. I'll get up any hour of the night to serve you, sir."

The ostler, who had seemed to be half-asleep before, now became as wide awake and active, and in a short space of time the horses were at the door of the inn.

"Now, Lucas," said Macheath, "which is your route?"

"Straight on for half a mile or so, and then down the road to the right, which will take us to my mother's farm."

"Very well. Then we will bid you good-bye at the corner of the road you speak of, and til then we can easily accommodate the pace of our horses to your own, unless you don't mind Annie riding behind me for a little way, while I give Polly into your charge."

"If it will not be a trouble to you, I shall thank you."

"All right. It's no trouble."

The road which Harry Lucas was to take was soon gained, but Macheath would not leave them there, but cantered down it until they came to a stile which would lead them across a couple of meadows to Mrs. Lucas' farm, and then he paused.

"Now, indeed, we part," he said, "and all I have to do is to bid you good morning, and to wish you all manner of happiness."

"That happiness," said Harry Lucas, as he grasped the captain's hands, "is entirely of your own making, and your name will be always remembered by us both with affection."

"It will, indeed," said Annie, who could not control her tears.

"Enough," said Macheath. "Do not let us part with even the look of sorrow upon our faces. Farewell!"

Polly and Annie embraced each other tenderly, and they parted. Captain Macheath put his horse to a gallop, and the others followed him, till turning round to Luke, he cried—

"Here we are on the road again."

Luke glanced at him, as he said—

"Would it not be well first to find a home for—"

The significant inclination of Luke's head towards Polly filled up the sentence.

"No, Luke! oh! no," Polly said. "But when I say no, believe me that I appreciate your motives, and thank you for your good kindness to me. But it may not be. I have made up my mind now, that where he goes there will I go. His dangers shall be my dangers."

"And can you bring me into so much peril?" said Macheath.

"I bring you into peril?"

"Yes. Do you think that while you are with me I could attend to anything in all the world but to you? In seeing that you were not hurt, and in protecting you, I should come to destruction myself. Who is there in all the world that I have to love or to think of but you?"

"Husband," said Polly, "your last words put me in mind of a question that I have often thought to ask you. Have you no relations in the world?"

"Yes, Polly, I have; but they forget me and I forget them. And yet there is one whom I should like to see. My father had a sister who was kind to me in my childhood. I know not where she is, but I should like to see her and shake her by the hand once again."

"And where is she?"

"That I know not, or before this I should have made some attempt to see her. I don't mean to say, though, that I have been very active in trying to find her out, feeling that my acquaintance is not a good credit to anyone."

"Hush!" said Luke; "a horseman comes."

"Get aside, then," said Captain Macheath, "for he belongs to me."

"Oh! you will not—" Polly began.

"Will not what?"

"Stop this traveller who is approaching?"

"It is my business so to do. You had better ride on, you two, and then it will not be supposed that you are in any way connected with me."

Captain Macheath's manner was quite sufficient for Polly to see that any remonstrance with him would be quite fruitless. She and Luke then trotted on, and Macheath, turning his horse's head in the direction from whence the traveller was coming, met him at a walk.

The person whose destiny it was to be stopped upon that eventful occasion was a big, burly-looking man, on a powerful black horse, and, indeed, take him altogether, he was a sort of person to look at that few persons would have felt inclined to stop on the highway alone.

"Stand!" cried Macheath. "Your money or your life!"

The man pulled up and looked amazed.

"Why, you impudent rascal," he said, "do you think I am going to let myself be robbed on the highway by one man?"

"Yes."

"Well, then, you are mistaken. I am armed."

"So am I. What are your arms?"

"Fire-arms."

"Then, in the name of all that is abominable, why don't you produce them, and have it out? If you will have bloodshed over the fate of a few paltry guineas, begin it, and get it over as quickly as you can."

With these words Captain Macheath produced a bright-barrelled pistol, and held it to the head of the horseman.

"Well, you are right," the man said, turning deadly pale. "I don't want to take the life of a fellow-creature for the sake of a little money. There is my purse."

"How much is there?"

"About ten pounds."

"Go on, then. I believe you have more about you, but I never do things in such a shabby way as to search a gentleman. Go on, and think yourself well off that you listened to me in time. What good on earth would it have done you to have had your brains blown out?"

"Oh! none—none," said the stranger, shuddering at the very idea. "None at all. Have you any objection to tell me who you are?"

"They call me Captain Macheath," he said.

The stranger did not wait to hear any more, but galloped off as hard as he could.

As he passed Luke and Polly he called out to them—

"I say, look after your pockets. Captain Macheath, the highwayman, is on the road. You had better look sharp, or he will be down upon you before you know where you are."

"Thank you," said Luke.

The man rode on at full speed, and presently Luke saw two officers approaching.

Bidding Polly to canter her horse to the shelter of some trees, and to take charge of his own steed, Luke dismounted, and advanced on foot to meet the constables.

One was exceedingly fat and ferocious looking, the other lean and nervous.

"Hi! my fine young fellow," cried the corpulent one. "You see who we are, so don't try to trifle with us. What are you doing here?"

"Minding my own business," Luke replied; "and you will do well to look closely to yours."

"No impudence," thundered the constable.

"Certainly not," Luke returned, drawing a pistol and presenting it full at the man's head. "Perhaps you wish to be made acquainted with this little article? For all I know you may be highwaymen in disguise."

The lean constable skipped behind the fat one, and backed him up most manfully.

"Put that nasty thing away," the corpulent officer yelled. "My good fellow, my kind friend, we are not highwaymen, but officers of the law, and in search of Captain Macheath."

"There he goes, then," said Luke, pointing to the fugitive horseman. "He was riding towards me when he suddenly turned aside. Perhaps the sight of you scared him."

"That's it," said the rotund constable. "Come along, Jem."

Off they went running like mad, but with as much idea of catching the horseman as stopping a mountain torrent with a fork.

Luke burst out laughing as soon as they were out of hearing, and returning to Polly, vaulted into the saddle.

"We will join the captain now," he said.

They were in the act of doing so when they heard the sound of wheels.

Two gentlemen in a gig approached, and it was evident that they had been warned by the flying horseman, but keeping to the road had missed speaking to the constables.

"Have you seen anything of a highwayman upon the road?" one asked.

"No," said Luke.

"Well, there's a man on horseback just passed us who called out to us to look out for Captain Macheath."

"It's not likely," said Luke, "But if you do meet him, the best way is to give in quiet, for he is a desperate fellow."

"Catch us at it! We are going out shooting and have plenty of arms with us. Are you riding our way?"

"No, gentlemen. I wish we were, because, of course, in union there is strength. We are going in this direction. Good-bye!"

"They will kill him," said Polly.

"Not a bit of it. He will stop them both."

"But this is terrible. If he goes on stopping everyone on the road that he meets, the result must be certain destruction at last."

"Oh! no—no. Not at all. Pray, be composed. We shall have him galloping after us all right in a little while."

The two men in the gig now drove on very carefully, and with rather scared looks.

They had a couple of guns slung in front of the vehicle, and in the lower part of it there was a kind of box for the reception of a pointer, who was snugly reposing upon some straw.

Macheath saw them coming, and suddenly emerged from a lane.

"By Jove! there he is," said one of the gentlemen.

"Oh! no," said the other; "that's no highwayman."

"Don't you think so? Oh! it's him. Get out the guns."

"Yes—oh! dear—yes. You shoot him."

"Not for the world. I wouldn't have his death at my door, poor fellow! Let's pity him, and give him a few pounds, and tell him to repent."

"But he won't, I'm afraid."

"Won't what?"

"Repent, or take the few pounds, either. Here's the gun; you hold the barrel of it towards him, and I'll pull the trigger. Now for it. Here he comes. Oh! if it should miss him. Now! Are you ready?"

"Yes."

Bang!

"Where is he?

"All right, gentlemen," said Captain Macheath; "try the other barrel. It's my turn, though, now."

Bang went one of Macheath's pistols, but he purposely fired over their hends.

Crack went another, a little nearer, and the two sportsmen fell flat to the bottom of the gig.

Laughing gaily, Captain Macheath rode up.

Polly had heard the shots fired, and in spite of all that Luke could do to persuade her of the impolicy of the step, she rode back, calling aloud to her husband.

"All is right," Macheath shouted back. "Away with you. There is no harm done, and the battle is fought and won. Away with you at once, for someone may come up."

Luke quite understood that what the captain intended was, that whatever happened upon the road he and Polly should not in any way seem to be connected with it, so he took the bridle of Polly's horse and turned it again.

"Now, gentlemen," said Captain Macheath, "my time is valuable if yours is not, and you will be so good as to hand me your money as quickly as you can."

"I'm a dead man," said one.

"So am I," said the other.

"Get up, will you?" cried Macheath, "or I shall be forced to make you."

"We are no more among the living," said the first one who had spoken. "We are now as those who have been."

"Quite so," groaned the other.

Macheath saw that their fright was such that nothing but force would have any effect upon them; so he stooped from his horse, and seizing one of them by the collar, made him sit up, and thrust a pistol against his face.

"Your money!"

"Money! Cash, do you mean?"

"Yes."

"Oh! here it is! Take it all. There it is. It's all I have."

A glance at the pocket book assured Captain Macheath that there were notes in it, and that satisfied him.

"He put it in his pocket at once, and releasing the man, dragged up the other, and went through the same process with him; but he was gone too far in fright to know what was wanted of him, yet he took his purse from his pocket, and handed it to Macheath.

"Now drive on," said the captain. "I would advise you both to be very careful, though, how you proceed, and if you meet anyone upon the road who stops you, your answer will be 'Twenty-two.'"

"Twenty-two?"

"That is a watchword, or signal, that will protect you, for I have quite taken possession of this road, and some of my men are in all sorts of disguises, so if you meet any of them, and, fancying

they are strangers to me, say anything about being robbed, some hasty and heedless one may shoot you."

"Oh! dear—oh! dear. And ain't we shot, sir?"

"You ought to know that! I fired twice at you, and purposely missed you. If I had fired again, your brains would have been scattered over this road. Farewell!"

Macheath turned from the gig, but he had scarcely done so, when he heard quite a rush of wheels, and the cry of—

"Clear the way! Hoi—hoi!"

He saw a postchaise, with four horses, coming along at a dashing pace.

He had just time to get to the side of the road as it whirled past, but one of the wheels caught the gig, and upset it and its occupants into a ditch.

This occurrence caused a slight detention of the postchaise, and a man with a pistol in his hand thrust his head out of the window nearest to Macheath.

"What the deuce is the matter?" he demanded.

Macheath laughed, to which the passionate man replied by at once discharging the pistol at his head.

"Take that to stop your grinning. Drive on, postillion—drive on!"

The bullet passed so close to Macheath's face that for the moment he thought he was struck, and so staggered was he at this piece of brutal and reckless mischief, that the postchaise had got into motion before he could make up his mind what to do.

He drew a pistol from the saddle in a moment and took aim, but a footman who was in a rumble behind, as he saw the movement, ducked his head—

"Oh! don't—don't fire," he cried. "Mind the girl—you may hit the young girl."

These words caused Macheath to pause.

He held the pistol in his hand while he advanced at a gallop after the coach.

"What girl? What girl do you mean?" he cried. "I'll fire if you don't tell me."

CHAPTER LXXI.

FURTHER ADVENTURES ON THE ROAD.

THE affrighted footman looked fearfully around and pointed to the interior of the carriage to signify that there was a girl there, and then out came the head of the furious and irascible man again.

"What! ain't you dead?" he roared. "I thought I had shot you—you vagabond."

"Stop!" cried Captain Macheath. "Stop, I say."

The head had popped in again, but it was only for a moment, and then out it came again, accompanied by a hand and a pistol.

Macheath was waiting for this, and he fired at the head directly, which disappeared the moment the report of Macheath's pistol was heard.

The footman in the rumble was so alarmed that he scrambled up to the top of the coach, and from thence fell into the road.

Captain Macheath was going at full speed, but the sudden appearance of the footman in the road bewildered and frightened the horse, so that it shied and stumbled. Macheath was nearly unmounted, and as it was he thought that if he secured the footman it would be the best thing he could do, as he would assure him who the carriage belonged to and who the bully that had fired at him was.

Polly and Luke now came up, and Macheath, while he soothed his horse, called out to Luke—

"Seize that man, Luke; don't let him go on any account, I shall have something to say to him."

"All right," said Luke. "I have him."

Macheath's horse was so disturbed by the firing and by the unexpected appearance of the footman in the middle of the road, that it was with the greatest difficulty his rider could pacify him.

When the footman found himself in Luke's custody he gave up his life for lost, and getting upon his knees he howled in such a manner that Luke was compelled to threaten him before he would be quiet and attend to what the captain wanted to say to him.

"Oh! yes," he exclaimed at length. "Oh! dear, yes, I will answer anything you like—indeed I will, if you will only spare my life. Oh! dear, what good would it do you to kill a poor fellow like me? I assure you it would do you no good at all."

"Silence!" said Captain Macheath; "you are going the very way to make us think of knocking you on the head for the purpose of stopping that abominable clattering of yours. Silence, until you hear what I have to ask of you, and then make your replies short and distinct."

"Oh dear! yes, I will. I am a poor—"

Luke gave him an admonishing tap on the top of his head with the butt end of a pistol.

"Whose carriage was that?"

"Major Brook's, gentlemen, and he—"

"Silence! What young lady was that you mentioned?"

"Why, I'll tell you all, upon my life," the footman replied. "We have been looking after her for a long time; but at last the major has got her, you see. He had been on the watch; and having the carriage all ready, she was caught up and popped into it before she knew where she was, and there she is, with a silk pocket handkerchief over her mouth."

"Who is she?"

"Why her name is Thornton, sir."

"Thornton?" said Macheath. "Where does she live? Tell me that at once. Where did she come from?"

"Finchley, sir; but I don't know the exact house. They say, that is, the major's valet says—and he carried on all the affair—that she lived with her mother, a widow, and he says she is just eighteen years of age."

"But—but—"

Captain Macheath paused.

"What am I to think," he then added, and for a moment or two he looked to the ground and seemed absorbed in reflection. Then looking up, he added—

"Where is this Major Brook going with the girl?"

"To Dover, sir. I don't mind telling all, for I shall not go back to his service again."

"I thank you for your information," said Macheath. "If you have anything else to tell, tell it now."

"Nothing, sir," the footman replied. "But here's the letter that caused the young girl to meet the major on the high road, you see. I picked it up as it fell from her pocket in the struggle to put her into the coach."

Macheath took the letter.

"This may enlighten me," he said.

He opened it, and cast his eyes over it. As he did so he turned white with passion; but he folded up the letter again and put it carefully in his pocket.

"My good fellow, I thank you," he said, handing the footman a few guineas. "Take this as an earnest of my good feeling towards you. Farewell."

"You didn't happen to want a fellow as footman?"

"No—no, I can't take you. I am much beholden to you, my good man, and wish I could do you any service."

"Thank you, sir. If you had only seen that young creature's face as I saw it, you would feel all the blood in your body boiling."

"Silence!" cried Macheath, in a voice that made them all start. "Silence, I say. My blood does boil. Let him injure her? No, by all that is sacred I will not. Come on, Luke. Polly, follow me."

Captain Macheath put his horse to full speed, and set off at a pace that it was rather difficult to follow, so that Polly had to call to him.

"Finchley — Finchley!" shouted Macheath. "The nearest way to Finchley is what I want. Do you know it, Polly, or you, Luke?"

"I do," said Luke, "and can show you."

"That is well; let us ride hard."

"Oh! husband!" cried Polly, "what is the true meaning of all this? You terrify me. There is more in the affair than meets the eye, I feel assured. Oh! tell me what it is and what it all means before you go further. You know well that I am with you heart and soul, and that I will aid you in every possible way in what is right. All I ask of you is, that you should trust me."

"I will—I will. Luke, don't go away. I want you to know what I am about to explain."

Luke would have left Macheath and his wife to themselves, but now he rode up to them.

"Listen to me, both of you," he said. "I feel that there are such things as foretokens in this world. You both heard me, and recollect, I daresay, that not an hour ago I was talking of my aunt?"

"Yes," said Polly.

"Well, her name is Thornton."

"Ah! now I see."

"Yes, you see some of it, but not all," said the captain. "I have reason to believe that this young girl who is in the coach is Lucy Thornton, my cousin, the youngest and the fairest of my aunt's family. My design is to go to Finchley first, and see my aunt, and then to start for Dover. What say you, Polly? Will you go with me?"

"With all my heart."

"And you, Luke?"

"To the end of the world, if you like."

"Be it so then. This young creature must and shall be rescued."

"But are you quite sure that a similarity of names merely does not lead you to this belief?" said Polly. "Only think if that should not be your cousin Lucy—if the tale you have heard from the footman should not be true. I do not say that it is false; but you know there is room for doubt."

"No, there is none."

As Macheath made this remark he took from his pocket the letter given him by the footman.

"Read that," he said, "and read it aloud, so that Luke may hear it, and when you have done so, I think you will see that there is no room to doubt the fact of the young girl being my cousin."

Polly took the letter, and read from it as follows:—

"MY COUSIN LUCY,—You are but a young girl, but Heaven has by a strange chance given to you the power to serve me. It is true that since we were children you and I have never met; but yet you may remember your young playmate, who, by being some seven years or so older than yourself, was the partaker of your sports.

"Dear cousin Lucy, you know the life that I have led; report has come to your ears full of my deeds; but now I yearn towards a better life, and I will, if you will see me, explain to you how it is that you can aid me. If you will be at the place mentioned in the enclosed slip of paper, which you should take with you as your guide, as a rough plan is drawn upon it, at the time there mentioned, I will meet you; but if you tell anyone of this, all is lost.

"Oh! Lucy, will you come and save me from death and despair?

"This is from your old playmate and loving cousin, "CHARLES MACHEATH."

"Charles Macheath?" cried Polly.

"Yes, you see that this letter purports to have come from me. By some means or another, those who would betray the girl found out her relationship to me, and have practised upon her gentle, loving nature in my name to deceive her; but, oh! they shall rue the day they thought of such a plan."

"Alas!" said Polly, "I see it all, and I admit that there is no room for doubt."

"It is most villainous," said Luke.

"And it shall be avenged," cried Captain Macheath. "No doubt this letter had all its effect upon her, and so she fell into the snare that was laid for her. Poor—poor Lucy! I remember you well, a little smiling, blue-eyed child. But this will drive me mad! I must be doing something. Let us be off now at once. Oh! what fiend in human shape could have written that letter? Forward!"

The day was now near to its close, and they all drew up at a little alehouse and inn called the Heifer. Polly looked very much fatigued, and as Macheath lifted her from her horse he said—

"You and Luke will stay here, dear Polly, while I go and look for my aunt. I will not be long."

CHAPTER LXXII.

THE WIDOW'S HOUSE ON FINCHLEY COMMON.

POLLY would fain have persuaded Captain Macheath to take some refreshment before he left the inn, but one glass of wine and a crust of bread was all he would eat or drink.

There was every accommodation at the little roadside inn, and Polly was fain to wait until the return of her husband.

There was one thing, however, that enabled her to wait with some degree of patience, and that was, that she knew he was not going on any enterprise of danger, but one of mercy.

For a variety of reasons Polly was well-pleased at the idea of leaving England. She hoped that Captain Macheath would never return to it, but that he might be persuaded upon the Continent to turn his abilities to some better account than on the highway.

The ideas of Captain Macheath himself flowed in a very different direction.

He had but one thought now, and that was the rescue of his pretty little cousin, Lucy Thornton, from the hands of a villain.

He considered that he was bound by every tie to rescue her, and, moreover, it appeared to him as if by such an act he would seem to be making up to her family in some manner for the disgrace he brought upon them.

The old common at Finchley was at this period but thinly inhabited.

A cottage here and there only appeared peeping from the thick foliage of its orchard and garden, while a large estate or two occupied the greater portion of the landscape.

It was with strange sensations that Captain Macheath, on foot, for he had left his horse at the inn, approached his aunt's cottage.

"What will be the end of this career that I have shaped out for myself?" said Macheath, as he came in sight of the cottage. "Well, it has been half my choice, and half necessity, so I must pursue my destiny."

He rang the bell.

For about five minutes he waited, but no one came near the gate, and Macheath began to feel rather anxious about his aunt, and he rang again.

Then a woman came and looked at him through the lattice-work of the door.

"What do you want?" she said.

Before Macheath answered this woman he took a good look at her, and certainly a more unprepossessing looking personage it would have been impossible to conceive.

She was above the ordinary height of women, and of a sharp, dark, frowning aspect.

"Is this Mrs. Thornton's cottage?" Macheath demanded.

"Well, what if it is?" said the woman.

"I asked a plain question," Captain Macheath said, "and I want a plain answer. Who are you that you thus domineer at the gate of a lady's house?"

"Hoity-toity!" cried the tall female, giving her head a toss enough to jerk it off; "and who are you that come here with your impudence?"

Macheath controlled his rising anger.

"I want to see Mrs. Thornton," he said.

"Well, then, you can't."

"And why not, madam?"

"Because she is indisposed, and can only see her most intimate friends, so you had better go away at once."

Before the captain could reply to this insolent speech a man's voice, to his surprise, called to the woman from the garden—

"Flora, my love, who is that?"

"Oh! I don't know, but he sha'n't come in. It's some man wishing to see Mrs. Thornton."

"Oh! well, of course he can't come in. Mistress Thornton is very unwell, and we are at her request taking care of her, that's all."

The man advanced, and presented a portly, bloated appearance, and such a villainous expression upon his face, that Captain Macheath at once took a dislike to him.

"So," he added, in a pompous way, "any business that you may have with Mrs. Thornton you will be so good as to communicate to me at once, and I will answer it. My wife and I are taking care of her. My name is Jilky, sir."

"Oh! that's your name, is it? Well, I have particular business with Mrs. Thornton, and I request you to allow me to speak to her. Go and tell her that a gentleman is here who has particular business with her."

"We decline," said Mr. Jilky, giving his head a slight shake. "We decline, my good sir."

CAPTAIN MACHEATH

THE
PRINCE OF THE HIGHWAY.

"QUICK !" CRIED MACHEATH. "I HEAR THE SOUND OF HORSES' HOOFS."

"Go away," said Mrs. Jilky. "Go away, sir."

"Oh! very well," said Macheath.

Retreating a pace or two he lifted his foot, and made such a dash at the garden gate that the lock of it flew off and hit Mr. Jilky so sharp a rap on the side of the head that he tottered and fell into a gooseberry bush, and the door flying wide open, Captain Macheath walked deliberately into the garden.

Mrs. Jilky uttered a scream.

"Oh! scream away, ma'am, it don't make the least difference to me, I assure you," said the captain. "You can scream as much as you like."

"My dear!" cried Mr. Jilky. "Oh! murder. I cannot get out of the bush. Yes, I have. Oh! dear—oh! dear. My love, don't scream, it's of no use. The neighbours do not like us, and they will not come. It is our painful lot to be doubted and persecuted all over the neighbourhood."

"Hold your tongue! You are a fool," said Mrs. Jilky. "I tell you you're a fool to go on in that way. Now, sir, who are you?"

"I decline telling you," said Captain Macheath.

"Then out you go, sir. I am a weak woman, but I won't have you here. Out you go, sir, at once."

With this the weak woman flew at Macheath like a tigress; but he saw her coming, and stooped so as to make a back for her, and over she went with such a certainty that if they had planned it it could not have been done better.

"Now, madam," said the captain, "try it again."

Mrs. Jilky, however, had had quite enough of it, and she sat in one of the beds of the garden looking the picture of discomfited rage.

"Now, I don't know what right either of you have here," said Captain Macheath. "If Mrs. Thornton, however, chooses to have you, that is her business and not mine; but you have surely exceeded your position by denying her to anyone who may call at the cottage. I told you I had business of importance with her."

"Oh! dear," said Mr. Jilky again. "What shall we do?"

"Kill him if you be a man," said Mrs. Jilky.

"A good idea that, madam," said Captain Macheath. "I am quite qualified to take care of myself, I assure you."

With this Macheath, paying no more attention to the Jilkys than as if they had been a couple of plants in the garden, walked towards the cottage.

As he reached the door he saw a young girl, of about fourteen or fifteen years of age, sitting on the step, crying.

"Who are you pray?" he demanded.

"Oh! sir, I'm Mrs. Thornton's servant, sir, if you please."

"Well, what's the matter with you? You needn't shrink and tremble in such a way as that. What ails you?"

"They have been ill-using me, sir," the girl replied. "Mrs. Jilky beats me so that I shall die if I stay here, and I don't like to leave Mrs. Thornton, for she is very good to me, and she is ill now. Oh! sir, what shall I do? Mr. Jilky, too, beats me, and they want to kill me between them, I think."

Captain Macheath felt a flush of anger rising to his cheek.

"Tell me, girl, who are these people, Jilky?" he said. "What right have they here?"

"That I don't know, sir. They live in the neighbourhood, and as soon as they heard that Mrs. Thornton was ill and laid up they came and took possession of the house."

"Indeed! Now, of all the unparalleled pieces of insolence that ever I heard of, this beats them. Does Mrs. Thornton like their company?"

"Oh! dear no, sir, she never could bear them. She never did like them at all, and nobody else in the neighbourhood does, sir; and if Mrs. Thornton had been well, they would never have got into the place, sir."

"Upon my word," said Captain Macheath, "this is about the coolest thing I have heard of for a long time. And where is Mrs. Thornton?"

"Upstairs in her own room, sir. It's the loss of Miss Lucy, if you please, sir, that has all but killed her."

"Oh! no doubt—no doubt. I will go to her at once."

Macheath entered the cottage, and ascended the staircase that led to the rooms above. He opened the door of one chamber, but no one was there, and then he heard from the adjoining room a faint voice say—

"Oh! who is there—who is there? Because I am helpless am I to be the prey of anyone who chooses to come into the house? Speak, who are you?"

Macheath opened the door and walked into the room.

His aunt, looking much older than he thought to have found her, was partially dressed, and sitting in an easy chair by her bedside.

Her eyes were red and swollen with weeping, and she looked at Macheath with alarm, for she did not know him, and he for a few moments was too much affected to speak.

"Aunt," he said, at length, "I have come to see you."

The old lady uttered a cry of joy, and was nearly fainting.

But Macheath ran forward and supported her in his arms.

"Come, now, don't be cast down. I have come to help you to recover Lucy, and I will do so."

"Oh! Charles—Charles," was all she could say. "And so you are really my nephew?"

"I am indeed, aunt. Don't you feel sure that I am?"

"Let me look better at you. Draw up the blind, Charles, and let me look well at your face and eyes."

Macheath did so, and then, with a deep sigh, she said—

"Ah! yes, I know you now, and I should know you among a thousand, Charles, you are so like your poor dear mother."

"Am I so?"

Macheath felt a choking sensation as he spoke.

"Yes, you are; and she was so good, and so beautiful, and so true. But, oh! can it be really true that—that—"

"Go on, aunt."

"That you are the highwayman who they say terrifies everybody, and who will come to a bad end? Can this be possible?"

"Aunt, you need not listen to one-half of what you hear in this world," said Macheath. "Chance has brought me acquainted with the fact of the abduction of my cousin Lucy, and I have set for myself the task of saving her; so you may be certain that she is not entirely left to her fate. I want you to tell me all you know of the affair."

At these words Mrs. Thornton's tears flowed, and for some time she was unable to speak; but again she recovered, and then she told him all she knew of the affair.

It was that a man, having the appearance of a gentleman, had haunted the place for some days, and finally called and asked if a couple of rooms in the cottage were to be let at any price, and upon being answered in the negative, he had politely gone away, and that on the next day she had observed that Lucy was frequently in tears, and that upon her disappearance Mrs. Thornton had been so much affected that she had to take to her bed.

It was evident that Mrs. Thornton had no idea of the name of the villain who had thus invaded her peaceful home, and Macheath did not think fit just then to inform her, lest she might mention it imprudently, and it should have the effect of paralysing his efforts to recover Lucy.

CHAPTER LXXIII.

MACHEATH TAKES A HASTY RIDE TO DOVER.

No doubt Captain Macheath would gladly enough, under other circumstances, have lived for a short time beneath the roof of his aunt, but he only stayed long enough to drive the Jilkys off the premises.

Well he knew that each moment was precious, and by the time he got back to the inn at Finchley where he had left Luke and Polly, he was fretting at the delay that had already taken place in the pursuit of Major Brook and Lucy Thornton.

Polly was eagerly looking for him, and Luke had taken care that the horses were thoroughly refreshed, and ready again for the road. The slight rest and rub down that Luke had taken care that they had contributed not a little to freshen them.

"Is all right?" said Macheath, as he entered the inn.

"Quite," replied Luke; "there has not been a soul here since you left a short time ago."

"No, sir," said the landlord, who was close at hand, "the more's the pity; but somehow we don't get the custom that we once did. Ah! times are not what they were."

After liberally paying for what had been had, Macheath sprang upon his horse, and Polly and Luke were soon by his side. The landlord was sorry to lose so liberal a customer, and stood looking after them as they went.

A man was coolly smoking his pipe by the stable door; and taking it from his mouth, he pointed with the stem of it at the captain, and said, with all the deliberation in life—

"Do you know who that was, landlord?"

"Dear me, no. How should I?"

"Well, I do."

"Who was it then?"

"Lor' bless me, I thought, to be sure, you knew by the way you looked at him. Come now, you do know."

"Upon my word, I don't."

"Oh! well, I'm bound to believe you."

"Do you know?"

"Certainly! it's Captain Macheath, the highwayman."

The landlord was so astonished at this information that, after staggering back a pace or two, he actually sat down upon his own door step, just in time for his wife to very nearly fall over him as she came to the door.

"Dear me," she said. "What's the matter?"

"Oh—oh—oh!" was all the landlord could say.

"Why, drat the man, what does he mean? What is the matter with him now? Have you been to the old ale butt, John?"

"Oh! dear no, wife; but what do you think? Oh! dear me, I have had such a chance!"

"A chance of what, idiot?"

"Why, do you know, that tall fellow with the black hair, and the little moustache on his lip, was no other than Captain Macheath the highwayman."

"Goodness gracious!"

"Yes, and if we had only laid hold of him, there would have been at least five hundred pounds reward. Think of that."

"Yes," said the man with the pipe, "that's about it; but as for laying hold of Captain Macheath, that is quite another affair."

"Yes," said the landlady; "and if we had done so, and could have done it, I should have expected every guinea of the money to bring us nothing but bad luck. No, John, let us go on as well as we can, and if we are poor we can't help it; but never let it be said that we got money by selling the life of anyone."

The man with the pipe walked slowly up to the landlady, and took her hand and gave it a shake.

"Bless you! missus," he said; "Captain Macheath saved my life once. Bless you! marm. You will do more good by saying what you have said than as if you had all the rewards that were offered for all the highwaymen that ever were."

"But, dear me!" cried the landlord, "do only consider—five hundred pounds! Why, we shall not make half as much as that in a whole year, I assure you."

"Hold your tongue," said the landlady, "and don't make a fool of yourself. Come in doors at once—do."

The man with the pipe strolled leisurely off, and the landlord, with deep regret that the five hundred pounds had escaped him after it had seemed to be thus, as it were, quite in his grasp, followed his wife into the house as an obedient husband should do.

Before this scene at the door of the inn had come to an end, Captain Macheath had got a couple of miles off, and there he and Polly and Luke had paused to consider what would be the most direct route to Dover, whither they did not entertain a doubt but that the major, with Lucy Thornton, had gone.

After some little pro and con. upon the subject, Luke undertook to be their guide to Dover, as he happened to be tolerably well acquainted with the greater part of the way, so he rode on about twenty paces in advance.

The pace they now went at was not one that well suited conversation, and nothing very important transpired in the first stage, which they made a twenty-five miles' one.

The horses, without showing positive distress, were in need of a pause, and a halt was made.

All along the road Macheath had made inquiries regarding the appearance of such a carriage as that occupied by the major and Lucy, and he obtained frequent assurances that such a vehicle had passed on only a few miles ahead of him, and yet, by some extraordinary means, he could not overtake it.

Of course, being mounted upon good horses, they might easily enough have come up with a vehicle of any description, and it was not till they reached the inn at which they now stopped that they came to anything like a fair understanding of how it was that they missed the major's carriage.

There they heard that there was what was called a lower road as well as the high one which they had traversed, and that at once settled the difficulty, as, no doubt, the major had diverged to the lower road, thinking it better for his purpose, as it was less frequented than the other.

And now, were it not for the absolute necessity of resting the horses a little time, Macheath, in his impatience, would have been off again at once ; but any arrangement that was based upon humanity to animals always met with a ready acquiescence from him, and he determined that he would not abridge the hour that the animals absolutely required for rest and refreshment.

At the expiration of that time they were all upon the road again, and to all appearance the horses seemed as though they were quite capable of doing another stage of twenty-five miles without any trouble to themselves.

We need not pursue the journey to Dover in all its little incidents. Suffice it to say that after one other rest for the horses, and then a sharp trot, Macheath and his friends reached their destination, and drawing up at one of the principal hotels, Macheath flung himself from his horse.

"I want to know if you have seen a gentleman who is wounded, and a young lady with him ?" he said. "They came in a travelling-carriage !"

"What, the mad young lady, sir?" was the reply.

"Mad?" said the captain. "Oh, no ; she is not mad. Quite a young lady, I mean. But not a mad person."

"Oh, dear, yes, sir ; she is mad. The gentleman said she was."

"The villain !" exclaimed Macheath, for now it struck him at once that that was the excuse the major had made for the state of terror that Lucy would be sure to be in, and for the purpose of putting an end to all speculation concerning what she might say or do at the inn.

"Well," the captain remarked, smothering his feelings as best he could, "they are the people concerning whom I inquire, I believe. Are they here ?"

"Oh, dear, no, sir."

"I am too late, then ?"

"If you want to see them, sir, you are, indeed. The fact is, sir, they have gone off to Calais in the mail packet about two hours ago, sir. The young lady—poor thing !—had to be carried on board, for she took it into her head that her uncle was not her uncle."

"Well, can you tell me when I can cross the channel ?"

"To-morrow."

"To-morrow ? Not before to-morrow ?"

"No, sir, you can't. There's the mail packet as comes from Calais to-night will be going back again and you can go back again with her."

Macheath turned rather abruptly from the waiter, and spoke to Polly and Luke in a low tone of voice.

"We cannot do better," he said, "than put up here for the present. Do you two stay at this house while I go down to the water-side and see what can be done in the way of procuring means to cross the channel. It is ridiculous to stay here till to-morrow, with only some twenty miles of water to cross."

Captain Macheath then left the house and proceeded on foot to the water-side, where he eagerly inquired if by any means a boat or vessel of any kind could be got to enable him to cross the water to Calais.

"Why, yes, it's smooth water enough," said a rough-looking fellow, "and there's a nice little consarn riding at anchor there that would do it in a couple of hours in a lively fashion, if so be as the job paid her."

"What do you want ?"

"Well, perhaps a matter of five guineas."

"That will do," said Macheath, "I have a lady and gentleman at one of the inns to fetch, that is all. There is no luggage, and we shall be here within the time you have just mentioned to me. Be sure that you are ready."

Macheath hurried back to the hotel, and he, his wife, and the faithful Luke lost no time in returning to the water-side.

They were in the boat which was ready to convey them to the vessel, and a boy went with them to take the wherry to shore again.

The little vessel, which resembled a pilot boat more than anything else, was soon reached, and the whole party stood upon her deck, and never left it until they did so to step upon the Calais shore.

CHAPTER LXXIV.

CONCLUSION.

FURNISHED with plenty of money, Captain Macheath was not long in obtaining information of the man he was in search of.

Major Brook rented an old chateau a few miles from Calais, and Macheath, procuring a horse, determined to ride thither alone.

His object was to make an inspection of the exterior of the building, and to decide upon some plan of entering it before returning to Polly and Luke.

Though upon fresh ground the captain seemed perfectly at home, but so quiet was the country that he began to wish for some adventure just to take the edge off the dulness.

He had not long to wait.

Suddenly a puff of smoke came from behind a tree. A ringing report followed and Macheath felt a bullet whistle past his ear.

"Bravo !" cried the captain as he rode in hot haste to the tree. "An inch nearer and I should have been an ear short."

A villainous looking rascal wearing a patch over one eye scampered away, but Macheath called upon him to stop or die.

The ruffian, uttering a howl of terror, threw himself flat on his back and begged for mercy.

"Mercy," cried Macheath, as he dismounted and held a pistol to the miscreant's head. "This is the sort of mercy I will show you. Who are you ?"

"Major Brook's servant."

"Oh ! So he suspects that I am coming."

"Yes, and I was told to stop you."

"You very nearly accomplished your object," Macheath said, laughing. "Listen to me, I will spare your life on one condition."

"I will do anything," the man gasped.

"Then you will return with me to my friends, and after that show me the best way to enter Major Brook's chateau."

"That I will do," the man replied.

And Macheath conducted him back to Polly and Luke in triumph.

That same night all four stood before the major's chateau.

"Now guide us," said Macheath "and beware of playing me tricks."

"I will guide you," the man said, "into the kitchen; but the woman you will find there is devoted to the major, so it won't do to trust to her any more than to Miss Devaux."

"And who is Miss Devaux?" demanded Captain Macheath.

"Oh! she calls herself the housekeeper."

"I understand; and who else shall we have to encounter?"

"I daresay there will be the secretary. He is a mere lad of about eighteen years old, but as wicked and vicious as it is possible to suppose any human being to be. But I must assure you that the major, by bribing the French authorities, is protected by them."

The man whom Captain Macheath had so fortunately encountered now led the way round the front of that building, and across a marble courtyard. After they had proceeded for some distance they saw light shining from two windows, and the man pausing said, in a cautious tone—

"That is the great kitchen."

"Oh! very well," said Captain Macheath. "I will soon be in it."

"Oh! monsieur, be careful of Suzanne—she is one of the most violent of women, and would think no more of running you through with a spit than of performing the same operation with a fowl."

"I will take care of myself you may depend. Indeed, I rather rejoice at the opportunity of letting this Madame Suzanne know that she has found one who can and who will master her."

The man who had given the description of Suzanne, the servant at the chateau, was evidently in great fear of her, for he took good care to get as far in the rear as possible.

"Follow me, Luke," said Macheath. "Of course all we can do with this Suzanne is to tie her up in the kitchen, and prevent her from being mischievous or noisy, and it will entirely depend upon herself whether that operation is performed with ease and comfort to her or the reverse."

"Precisely so," said Luke.

Macheath then wispered to Polly to keep back, and by no means to allow the woman to make any attack upon her, as it would be impossible for her to resist it.

"I will take care of myself, you may depend," Polly replied.

The light from the windows of the old kitchen was quite sufficient to enable Macheath and his friends to see an old-fashioned doorway with an overhanging portico, which, no doubt, led into that portion of the establishment.

Macheath begged them all to pause on the door-step while he went in alone and confronted Suzanne. Luke was, however, close at hand in case he should be wanted.

Quite boldly, and without making any effort at concealment, Captain Macheath opened the door of the kitchen and walked in. There was no passage, so that he was in the large apartment at once without any trouble.

A good fire of immense billets of wood was burning upon the hearth. From the ceiling hung by an iron chain a lamp, in which was burning some lumps of grease.

Sitting on a low wicker chair by the fire was a woman of about fifty years of age, with an enormous red face, and a Norman cap upon her head. She seemed to be nearly asleep, and Macheath had no difficulty in seeing that she was rather a large specimen of the fair sex.

Opposite to the door at which the captain had entered the kitchen he saw another, and as he, rightly enough, conjectured that it led to the other part of the chateau, he wisely took care to place himself between it and Madame Suzanne.

"Hilloa!" cried Macheath, as he saw that no notice was taken of him. "Hilloa there!"

Suzanne sprang to her feet as though she were under the influence of an electric shock.

"Who is that?" she cried.

"Only I," Macheath replied,

"You—you? And who, pray, are you?"

"Well, that don't much matter, I suppose, so long as I am somebody. The fact is, I have come to see the major."

"Oh! have you?"

"Yes," said Macheath, "and I will trouble you to tell me what part of the chateau he is in, as well as what part of it I shall find a young English girl in, who was brought here yesterday only. Come, be quick."

"Oh, yes, I will be quick," cried Suzanne; and turning to a corner of the kitchen she caught up a long roasting-spit, and made such a sudden attack at the captain with it, that he had some difficulty in darting out of the way.

"So Madame Suzanne," he said, "that is the kind of reception you are inclined to give me, is it? Well, we shall soon see who will get the best of that matter."

With these words Macheath dexterously passed the infuriated cook and caught her by the back of the neck.

"Well," said Macheath, as she dropped to her knees, "are you tired of this?"

"Wretch! I will have your life."

"Oh, very good—go on."

She now fought with desperation, but the captain kept his hold, until she was fairly exhausted, and then he said—

"Luke, my boy—where are you?"

"Here," said Luke, who had been holding the door ajar.

"Come on, then. We must tie this young lady's wrists together, Luke, for I don't think she will be quiet long, and if you can find a cord, Luke, give it me."

"Yes. All right. Here is plenty of cord hanging from a nail here in a corner."

In a few minutes, though, Suzanne was fairly conquered and tied hand and foot, and a cork put between her teeth, so that he could not even make a noise to warn the other inhabitants of the chateau of danger.

"Come in both of you," said Macheath to Polly and the men who were outside. "We have arranged matters with Suzanne, you perceive."

After some few seconds given to deliberation as to the best plan to pursue now, Macheath walked slowly on, followed by all the party, until he came to a door covered with red cloth, which, no doubt, had been established where it was for the purpose of shutting out all noise from the domestic portion of the house from reaching the other part of the building.

The captain pushed open this door, and found himself at once in the hall of the chateau, just within the principal entrance.

"LISTEN," SAID MACHEATH. "I WILL SPARE YOUR LIFE ON ONE CONDITION."

"Here we are," said Macheath, in a low tone, "but I no longer hear the voices that a few moments ago were so apparent to us all."

"Permit me to suggest," said the major's man, "that Miss Devaux and the major have gone up stairs to the round tower where the young English girl is imprisoned."

"Ah ! think you so ?"

"Yes ; but—"

"Silence ! I hear a footstep. Let us hide in this room."

From the hall there ascended a flight of very handsome stairs, the balustrades of which were richly gilt, and the walls painted in allegorical subjects of great beauty.

It was down the staircase that Macheath heard the sound of feet coming, and he and his friends had just time to take refuge in an apartment close at hand, when, through the narrow opening that he left in the door, he saw a tall, thin female coming down the stairs rather quickly. There was a very handsome lamp hanging in the hall, suspended by a gilt chain, which, although very much the worse for wear of some twenty years, still at places reflected the light, and had a rich and costly appearance.

The major's man touched Macheath on the arm and whispered in his ear—

"That is Miss Devaux, and I do think, if anything, she is more violent than Suzanne the cook."

The tone of terror in which the major's servant had spoken to the captain of this Miss Devaux amused him ; but he made no remark about it, for he was too intent upon watching the proceedings of that individual.

She seemed to be a woman of about forty-five years of age, and her face was evidently inflamed by drinking. A frown of severity was upon her brow, and a more forbidding countenance Macheath had never seen.

To his mind she looked worse than Suzanne.

She had got about half-way down the stairs, when a voice from a man above called out to her—

"Devaux — Devaux !"

"Well, what now ?" she said, pausing and looking up.

"You had better tell Suzanne to fasten the kitchen door."

"Oh ! nonsense. There is no one to interfere. I will bring up the wine, and if this little piece of English obstinacy don't like to drink it, we will resort to other means, that is all."

"Yes—oh ! yes ; of course we will."

"Will you go and speak to her at once ? I will soon be with you. Perhaps you may frighten her before I come. Try it."

"I will—I will ; don't be long."

"Oh, no—no. Go along, do."

The sharpness with which she spoke showed sufficiently that she had not much respect for the major, for it was he who spoke to her.

Miss Devaux came down the stairs very deliberately, and crossed the hall. It was quite evident that she was about to open the door ; the reflection of a light from the apartment shone out into the passage.

Miss Devaux disappeared.

"Stay where you are," said the captain. "I think, after settling the cook, I can surely manage this woman."

Stepping to the door of the apartment, which had lazily swung shut, Captain Macheath at once opened it, and entered the room.

"Good evening, Miss Devaux," he said.

The person thus addressed uttered a cry of surprise, and then turned and faced him, with rage depicted upon her countenance.

"Who are you, sir ?" she demanded, haughtily.

"No friend to you."

"But who are you, and what do you want here ?"

"That you shall soon know."

"I suppose one word will suffice to describe you. You are a robber ?"

"I have not come to rob, whatever I may be," Macheath replied, "and my advice to you, madam, or miss, is to be quiet and civil."

"Let me pass."

"Oh, no."

"Then take the reward of your folly in intruding into this house."

As she spoke, she suddenly drew from the folds of her clothing a small, triangular-shaped dagger and made a rush at Captain Macheath ; but she deceived herself very much if she thought that he was the sort of person to be taken by surprise by anyone.

He caught her by the wrist, and held her with a grasp of iron.

"Hold, madam," he said. "You are in the hands of one who is well able to take care of himself."

At the sound of the struggle, Luke made his appearance, and catching the lady round the waist, he dragged her back.

"Tie her as we did the cook," he said. "I don't know really but that this one is the most vicious of the two."

"Tie me ?" cried Miss Devaux. "If you do that, you are stronger, both of you, than I think you."

With this she commenced a struggle with Luke of the most desperate character, and it was with great difficulty that Macheath could get hold of her, and seat her upon what looked like a small ottoman in the middle of the room. He held her fast round the waist.

"Luke," he said, "have you any cord ?"

"Yes—yes."

"Then tie her feet and wrists, for she is still fighting like a demon."

"Murder !" said Miss Devaux. "Oh, murder !"

"Stop her mouth, Luke."

"All right. I have quite a nice little gag that I have made on purpose for her. There you are, ma'am. Now you may kick as long as you please."

Captain Macheath still held her tightly round the waist from behind on to the ottoman, while Luke tied her ankles together, and then her wrists. But she still made all the exertion she possibly could to get away, and seemed to be half frantic.

"Can't you be quiet ?" said Luke. "It is of no use knocking yourself about in that way."

Then, addressing Macheath, Luke continued—

"I don't see anything of the lad they mentioned who was here, and my impression is that now there is no one in the house but the major to contend with. Let me, therefore, beg that you will remain here and allow Luke and me to finish this adventure "

Luke was quite as desirous as the captain could possibly be to bring the affair to a speedy decision and they both ascended the grand staircase with speed, and found themselves in a long corridor, hung with many paintings in richly gilt frames. At the farther end of the corridor they saw a door half open, and upon proceeding towards it they found that it connected with a flight of narrow stairs.

"This leads to the tower, you may depend," said Luke.

"Let us ascend then. Ah! did you hear that?"

"Yes—a girl's voice."

"Oh! have mercy upon me," said a low wailing voice. "What have I ever done to you that you should drag me from my home?"

"Come on," whispered Macheath, and with a bound or two he was up the narrow staircase.

"To be deceived in so cruel a way, too, by my cousin!" added the girl.

"Well," said a voice, "I have no objection to tell you, if it is any consolation to you to know it, that your cousin, Captain Macheath, had no more to do with the letter you received and brought you into my power than the man in the moon."

"Is that possible?"

"It is true."

"Alas!—alas!" sobbed Lucy; "and I have blamed my cousin, while he was innocent! Oh! sir, if he did but guess my situation, it is not the sea that would keep him from coming to my rescue."

"Indeed! Well, I can tell you that no doubt he is hanged by this time in England for some of his highway robberies."

"Oh, no—no!"

"But, I say, oh, yes. Where, in the name of all that's diabolical can that woman, Devaux, be all this time. Drinking as usual, I suppose."

"Mercy!" cried Lucy. "Oh, Macheath—Macheath, my much injured cousin! where are you now?"

"Here!" shouted Macheath as he dashed the door of the turret open, and strode into it.

"Oh!" cried Lucy, "it is—yes, it is—my cousin, Charles! Oh, thank Heaven! The joy—the joy!"

She burst into tears, and rushed into Macheath's arms.

The major's countenance assumed a perfectly purple tint with rage, and he bellowed out—

"Rascal, what do you do here? How came you here?"

"Oh, sir, I will explain all that."

"Explain be hanged, sir! Help—help! Where are you, Peter? Help here. Suzanne—Devaux—curses on you, where are you all? Andrew—Andrew!"

He would have rushed from the room, but Luke stood in the doorway, and gently stopped him, saying—

"Not yet, sir, if you please."

"Villain! I will knock you from top to bottom of the staircase."

"Try it," said Luke.

The major retreated, and caught up an iron bar, but at the moment that he did so Luke closed upon him and wrested it from him.

"Don't hit him, Luke—don't hit him," Macheath cried out. "I want him in as whole a condition as possible shortly."

"Very good," said Luke.

"Lucy, calm yourself," added the captain; "you are saved now. I and my friends have possession of the chateau, and you have nothing more to fear. I will not lose sight of you now until I place you in your mother's arms again."

"Oh, cousin—this seems like a dream. How came you to find out this dreadful place?"

"That, together with all other particulars, we shall have ample time to talk about; my business

now is with this gentleman. Major Brook, I suppose you call yourself a gentleman?"

"Go to the deuce, sir!"

"I should be very sorry to go anywhere with such a certainty of meeting with you," Macheath returned; "but, as it is, I demand of you the satisfaction of a gentleman for the insult you have been guilty of towards this young lady. I have considered the matter, and although I should be quite justified in shooting you as one would a mad dog, I will prefer the milder and more gentlemanly course, and I tell you plainly that you must fight me."

When the major saw how resolved his enemy, was, he trembled as though all his vaunted courage were about to desert him.

Poor Lucy, too, was scarcely less terrified than he, for now she began to comprehend that her cousin was not satisfied with rescuing her from the horrors of her situation, but that he intended, with so chivalrous a spirit, to give the major, perhaps, a chance of killing him. This was a state of things which, to the unsophisticated sense of the young girl, was most unreasonable.

"Cousin," she said, "do you think that I could see you endanger your life against that of such a man?"

"Let me take my own course, Lucy."

"No—no, indeed, and in truth you must not. Come away with me at once from this dreadful house, the very air of which seems terrible to me to breathe. Oh, come, come."

"Soon, I hope and expect, Lucy; but I must and will settle affairs with this man first. Now, sir, your answer to what I have proposed."

The major made a desperate effort to recover his usual bullying tone and manner—

"Who are you, then, sir? It is, I suppose, not a very unreasonable thing for me to ask who it is who breaks into my house at this time of night, and coolly asks me to fight him on equal terms?"

"Let it suffice, sir, that I am this young lady's nearest male relation, and that gives me a title to be her defender. Lucy, oblige me by going down stairs, if you please. You will soon find kind friends who will welcome you."

"But, Macheath—"

"Nay, will you not do so little for me after all the trouble that I have taken in your behalf?"

"Anything in the world, cousin; but I cannot—I dare not leave you to the villainy—the treachery of this man."

"My faithful friend, Luke, will stay with me."

"Must I go?"

"Yes, Lucy, and go quickly."

"Let the girl stay," said the major, his lips quivering with rage and fear. "Why do you send away a witness to your violence, sir? Let the girl stay."

"No, coward, the girl shall not stay. Go, Lucy."

Lucy reluctantly left the room; and Captain Macheath made a sign to Luke to fasten the door.

"Now, major," he said, "I might, as I said before, shoot you like a mad dog, but you shall have the chance for your life that I do not believe you would give to anyone else."

"Do you wish to murder me?"

"Oh, dear, no."

"Then be off with you, and take the girl with you, and I only hope I may never look upon her or you again."

"No, sir; you shall fight."

"Then, in a word, sir, I will not fight."

"You cannot mean that? Are you really an officer in the army?"

"Go to the deuce, sir. I won't be bullied and cross-questioned by you, or by any man breathing.'

"That's right, Major Brook; and so you will fight?"

"I am wounded."

"That is no bar to the pulling the trigger of a pistol, major. Here are an excellent pair of weapons. This room is just about long enough for the purpose. Take one, and place yourself where you will, and my friend will give the word to us both to fire."

"I will," said Luke.

"I will meet you in England, sir. The laws of France are severe, and if either of us should fall, the survivor would be involved in much trouble. I say, sir, that I will meet you in England, where and when you will; but I will not fight a duel here, with no friend by me, and between four walls."

"Is that your determination, major?"

"It is."

"Luke," said the captain, "open the window."

Luke flung open a small latticed window, and looked out for a moment.

"Is it far down, Luke?"

"Well, I should say it is about sixty feet.'

"That will do. Now, major, as you will not fight, it becomes my painful duty to throw you out at this window, and leave you to take your chance of the result of that escapade."

"Out at this window? Why, it is certain death and a horrible death too."

"Then you will prefer fighting?"

"Give me a pistol; anything is better than that. If I must fight with a savage, why, the sooner it is over the better."

"Perfectly my idea, major."

"Are they both charged?"

"Yes, with ball, and primed carefully."

"Very well, sir," said the major. "You force the duel upon me, recollect."

The major took one of the pistols from Macheath and strode to the farther end of the room, pulling, as if accidentally, a table between him and his foe as he went; and then he turned sharply, and raising his pistol, cried—

"Take it, then, if you will have it!"

The sharp report of the pistol rang through the room, but, from the look of the major's eyes, Macheath had had his suspicions that some such a course might suggest itself to him and he was ready to avoid the shot.

"Villain!" shouted Luke.

"Oh!" added the major, who, through the smoke, could not tell what had been the effect of his shot, but who, hearing nothing, thought it was mortal to Macheath. "Oh! I have a pistol of my own for you, my fine fellow, and so I will get rid of you both."

As he spoke, he fired at Luke, and hit him on the outside of the arm, only tearing his coat and making a gush of blood by the passage of the bullet just under the skin.

"Try it again, major," said Macheath, coolly. "Have you any more shots to oblige us with?"

"Confusion, I have missed him!"

"To be sure you have."

"You won't kill a man in cold blood? You are surely a gentleman, and not a murderer?"

"Cold blood do you call it, major?" said the captain. "Murder do you call it! Oh, very good, sir; you miscall things strangely. Who here would think of murdering you, I should like to know?"

"Then you will spare me?"

"Hark you, major. We are fighting a duel; you have had your shot—a little too soon, to be sure, but still you have had it—and, according to all rules, it is now my turn."

"No, no!"

"But I say, yes—yes. Stand firm now, major; you are an officer and a gentleman, and know what fair play is in these matters, of course."

The major shuddered up against the wall of the room as though by some means he could reduce himself to such a small space that it would be impossible to hit him.

"Are you indeed a coward?" asked Macheath, contemptuously.

"No, confound you!"

"Take that, then."

Bang! went the pistol, and with a loud cry Major Brook fell to the ground. The report echoed through the mansion, and a volume of blue smoke whirled round the heads of the party.

"It is done," said Macheath, "and yet—"

"And yet what? said Luke.

"I wish I had spared him."

"Well, captain, it is too late for regrets now. Come away at once. I presume that your journey to France has now accomplished its object, and that you have no desire to stay here any longer?"

"Not here, truly," Macheath replied, "nor will I return to England. Luke, I am tired of this life. I will see Lucy safe on her passage home, and then we will make our way to Spain. I made up my mind to begin a new life in a new country when we were crossing the channel."

"Did you, captain?" Luke returned; "this will be joyful news to my good mistress."

. . . . .

Captain Macheath was as good as his word. With Luke, he and Polly made all haste to Spain, and lived there in comfort and happiness. If Macheath ever returned to England, he did so under an assumed name; but there were those who declared that they had seen the well-known figure, not clad in scarlet coat, but in the sober attire of a country gentleman.

These rumours were scoffed at, and passed away from minds of men like a tale that is ...

THE END.